Sasha Wagstaff

Recipe for Love

headline
review

First published in 2012 by HEADLINE REVIEW
An imprint of HEADLINE PUBLISHING GROUP

First published in paperback in 2012 by HEADLINE REVIEW
An imprint of HEADLINE PUBLISHING GROUP

1

Cataloguing in Publication Data is available from the British Library

ISBN 978 0 7553 7819 7

Typeset in Garamond by Avon DataSet Ltd,
Bidford-on-Avon, Warwickshire

Printed and bound in Great Britain by
Clays Ltd, St Ives plc

Headline's policy is to use papers that are natural, renewable and
recyclable products and made from wood grown in sustainable forests.
The logging and manufacturing processes are expected to conform
to the environmental regulations of the country of origin.

HEADLINE PUBLISHING GROUP
An Hachette UK Company
338 Euston Road
London NW1 3BH

www.headline.co.uk
www.hachette.co.uk

For Daisy, the best little sister.
And for all other sisters out there who are
hopefully friends for life.

Prologue

'What a catastrophe, sir.' The young police officer looked ashen. 'I've . . . I've never seen anything like this before.'

Umberto nodded gravely in agreement. 'It is indeed terrible. The whole family, gone.' Feeling a shiver, he crossed himself. He had seen a landslide once before, but the damage it had caused hadn't been nearly as devastating as this. 'It will take a long time to clear this up; we're going to need to call in officers from nearby towns, maybe even from Naples. We'll have to secure the area too.' He swiftly mapped out a list of tasks for his colleague who, glad of something practical to do, raced off to gather teams of staff together.

Umberto picked his way through the debris and grimly shook his head. The landslide had destroyed some good agricultural land as well as a vast lemon grove, but the most tragic outcome was that an entire family had been wiped out. Their house, a humble abode at most, had been destroyed beneath the avalanche of rocks and mud that had tumbled down the hillside without warning.

Perhaps it was for the best in some ways, Umberto thought to himself. He paused and listened, frowning. No, he must have been mistaken. He stepped over a boulder and stopped. There it was again. A pitiful whining sound, like a small animal. Umberto leapt into action. He knew he should wait for his back-up team, especially since the area wasn't secure, but he didn't stop to think. Not caring about his own safety, he tore through the piles of rubble, his fingers bleeding as he frenziedly searched. His muscles ached and sweat poured down his face as he made his way through roof tiles, stones and wood. Then he saw him, a small boy, his face pale, streaked with dust and tears.

Umberto reached in and pulled the boy free, letting out a howl of pain as he tore the ligaments in his shoulder. The boy couldn't have been more than four or five years old and his dark eyes were full of terror. Scooping him up, Umberto staggered to the edge of the rubble and, as his team arrived, he collapsed, clutching the boy. Handing him over to a colleague, he issued strict instructions about his welfare, before succumbing to the attention of the medics.

As his shoulder was treated, Umberto made a decision. The boy should be whisked away before news of his survival spread, to another region . . . another country even. What kind of life could he have here in Sorrento, with no family and a name synonymous with scandal, with revenge? No, the best thing for the boy would be a new life, away from here and away from everything his family were known for. And then maybe he could start anew, never knowing anything about his former life.

Wincing with pain as he glanced at what was now the Disanti estate, Umberto hoped to God he was doing the right thing.

Chapter One

'*Torta alla noce e cioccolato,*' Cassia Marini typed, deep in thought as she relived the moment the luscious cake had touched her lips. Her eyes flickered towards the window, but finding herself in something resembling a post-orgasmic haze, she barely noticed the crowds of commuters. She returned to her column.

'Torta alla noce e cioccolato *is a deliciously rich Sicilian cake with nuts and chocolate,*' Cassia typed, letting out a slow, satisfied breath. '*It has a luscious buttery pastry base that melts in the mouth and a fluffy, vanilla-drenched sponge layer that oozes flavour. But the real surprise is the . . .*'

Oblivious to the early April sunshine dappling the keys of her laptop, Cassia paused and, forgetting how hideously late she was, she recalled, with indescribable pleasure, the heavenly dessert she'd sampled at a new Italian restaurant in Soho the night before. The sumptuous Sicilian cake had been a triumph, a magnificently self-indulgent crescendo to what had already been an exquisitely satisfying build-up. The restaurant had taken the unusual step of allowing her to reproduce the cake recipe for her column and the heady memory of the glorious dessert created the perfect description in Cassia's mind.

'*The real surprise is the unctuous, wickedly indulgent chocolate sauce layer sandwiched cheekily between the cake and the pie shell . . . the rich sauce simply oozes decadence and its scrummy, bitter-sweet taste combination is utterly, utterly sinful. Trust me, readers; this is a sensual experience not to be missed.'*

Firing the piece off to her editor, Gena, Cassia wondered where her boss was. Gena had been missing in action all day. Sweeping from meeting to meeting, barking into her phone and appearing only once that afternoon to grab half a biscotti and a slug of double espresso in place of lunch, Gena had sailed by, dropping mysterious hints about a 'sensationally exciting' prospect. Cassia was mildly intrigued but she didn't have time to hang around and wait for Gena to emerge from another marathon meeting, so she started to pack up.

'You're working later than normal tonight.'

Cassia looked up. Pete, the colleague who had been after her job since he'd arrived at *Scrumptious* magazine six months ago, was throwing his jacket on with ill-disguised hostility.

'I wanted to finish this piece about that new restaurant,' Cassia said shortly, standing up. She knew Pete didn't like her; he made jibes about her family background and he was wary of the friendship she had struck up with Gena.

'Doesn't your boyfriend mind you constantly putting work before him?' Pete asked, his smile not reaching his eyes.

'Finn works pretty long hours himself,' Cassia snapped, tired of feeling as though she was on a field of combat. 'He's working on a particularly complex case at the moment,' she added, knowing she sounded vague. Finn worked in a City law firm and he'd been plugging away to secure a major promotion for the last few years, but Cassia was never entirely sure exactly what he did, mostly because he didn't discuss his work much.

'Yes, but you're a girl,' Pete smirked, tossing the chauvinism across the desk with arrogant disregard. 'With famous parents to boot.'

Cassia bristled. There it was again. Sometimes, she wished she'd used her mother's surname at work so that no one could accuse her of hanging on to her father's coat-tails. But then, her mother was even more famous, so Cassia wasn't sure it would have helped.

Tugging a small, red box out of her desk drawer, she ignored Pete and checked the contents. Inside the satin were Cartier cufflinks she'd had engraved with Finn's initials entwined with her own, diamonds nestling in the letters. Not the most thrilling of presents but she knew Finn would adore them and she had saved up for ages to buy them – just like her apartment in Pimlico and everything else she owned.

Pete whistled. 'Fancy,' he commented.

Guessing she'd probably lowered his opinion of her even further, Cassia grabbed a dress bag from the filing cabinet and headed to the Ladies, not noticing she'd knocked her notepad to the floor. She had worked extremely hard to get where she was, taking various low-level magazine jobs over the years, keeping the identity of her parents hidden and clawing her way up the career ladder. It was only when she moved to *Scrumptious* magazine a year ago that Gena had made reference to her background, proudly telling the rest of the staff that their new food editor was the daughter of Marco Marini, the well-known food writer and restaurateur. The fact that Cassia's mother was the famous TV actress Diana Marini-Blake had caused more gasps around the room and an embarrassed Cassia couldn't help wishing Gena had kept quiet, particularly when it caused the odd staff member to make jealous remarks. *Scrumptious* was a relatively new publication, jostling for position with the glossily popular *Delicious* and *Olive*, but with stunningly vibrant photography, appetising recipes and a fine line in erotically charged food descriptions, it was the food magazine of the moment – largely thanks to Cassia's sensual writing style. Described as 'the sexiest food writer in history', one smitten interviewer who had picked up on Cassia's marketability had claimed that she made Nigella Lawson sound 'prudish and prissy'.

Putting Pete out of her mind as she got changed, Cassia threw on a figure-hugging cream dress that had a demure, scooped neckline and a knee-length pencil skirt. Leaving her long, dark hair coiled up on top of her head but pulling a few tendrils down to soften the look, she outlined her eyes with smoky pencil and added three coats of chocolatey mascara. Surveying her reflection in the mirror, Cassia frowned.

Too curvy, she decided critically, smoothing her hands over her ample hips. And the dress a little . . . conservative, perhaps? Whilst chic, it was feminine and safe, rather than wildly exciting. But then, Cassia thought, hoping the train to Kent was running late as usual, Finn loved her look. Before she'd met him at university eight years or so ago, Cassia had a vague idea she might have been more adventurous in her dress sense and pretty much everything else. *I was wild and impulsive once,* she thought with a flicker of surprise. *What had put a stop to that?* Jules's abrupt change from loving sister to out-of-control teen for one, she supposed, which had put the brakes on her own crazy behaviour. Just occasionally, Cassia harped back to her exhilaratingly crazy youth longingly but she knew Finn would heartily disapprove. And as for his mother . . .

About to immerse herself in a cloud of spicy Habanita perfume, Cassia paused, remembering that Finn wasn't keen on the exotic scent. Opting for a more conservative floral, she hurried out of the toilets and bumped into a smirking Pete. Noticing he was holding her notebook aloft, Cassia's heart sank.

' ". . . the luscious sauce simply oozes decadence," ' he quoted sarcastically, ' "and its scrummy, bitter-sweet taste sensation is an erotic experience not to be missed." It's practically pornographic, Cassia! You do know the magazine is about food, not sex, don't you?'

Annoyed to find tears pricking at her eyelids, Cassia tried to snatch her notebook out of his hands. 'I didn't realise you got your kicks from jerking off over my private notes, Pete.' She was on edge about seeing Finn's family but Cassia knew she couldn't allow someone like Pete to see how much his bullying got to her. 'You should have said, I'd have written some sexy food speak especially for you. And for your information, most people can see a connection between sex and food.'

Pete turned scarlet. Noticing how sexy she looked in the classy dress, he was appalled to find his groin bulging. Thrusting Cassia's notebook in front of it, he tried, with some difficulty, to look unconcerned.

'Enjoy your weekend, Pete,' Cassia sighed, stepping into the lift. As the doors closed, she sent Finn a quick text to tell him she was on her way and hurried to the station. The text she received back was from Gena, not Finn. It was marked 'URGENT', so she called Gena back immediately, only to get her voicemail. She left a message and stepped on to her train. It was Finn's thirtieth birthday and Pete's words about putting her job before her boyfriend had struck home. She intended to give Finn her full attention at the party tonight so if Gena called back, she'd answer the call but just quickly, to find out what was going on. Tonight, it was all about Finn, Cassia decided resolutely.

Wiping her hair away from her sweating brow, Jules wondered if she was ever going to be able to get away from the tedious party. The events company she worked for had organised the glittering ball in aid of a well-known, commercially driven animal charity and its rich, snobby patrons were in full attendance. Headed up by the mayor and his wife, the men wore handmade tuxes accessorised by silk paisley handkerchiefs, and the women sported stiffly coiffed hair and frilly pastel frocks. They wore their dusty heirloom diamonds without any sense of irony whatsoever and they clearly had high expectations for the event.

Jules had hopelessly messed up two events that year and she knew she was on borrowed time but she was guiltily aware that her pathetic love life had been preoccupying her of late. Wearing a sedate black dress and with her shoulder-length blond hair tied back in a neat ponytail, Jules couldn't wait to get away and drown her sorrows. However, she knew she had to pull out all the stops this time so she carefully checked the handwritten notes the mayor's wife had given her. So far, so good, Jules thought, looking around. She had followed the request for 'absolutely no balloons, but plenty of fresh-cut flowers, ribbons and chair swathes in the charity's signature yellows and greens' to the letter. The food was 'top notch', as Finn and Louisa's father Henry would say. A starter of poached asparagus with quail's egg Hollandaise and a trendy micro salad – one of Jules's personal recipes – had been a triumph and it was shortly to be followed by a rare beef Wellington and a splendid baked Alaska studded with sparklers. Jules glanced at a nearby raffle table. Instead of the usual naff microwave ovens and unwanted bottles of sherry, this lot were offering gorgeous Barbados apartments, pretty platinum bracelets and cases of vintage champagne bearing exclusive labels and absurd price tags.

Jules checked her phone again, irritated to discover that the cheating gym instructor hadn't contacted her, not even with an apologetic crawling text. Feeling sorry for herself, Jules chewed her fingernails, wondering why she had such a talent for picking unscrupulous, unreliable men. She felt a familiar stab of envy for Cassia, who seemed to lead a charmed life. A fantastic job, an incredible apartment in a sought-after part of London (plus a part-share in the apartment she and Finn lived in), and, of course, Finn Sunderland himself. Not Jules's type remotely, but Finn, handsome in a russet-blond-with-lovely-blue-eyes kind of a way and clearly a devoted, trustworthy guy, was practically the perfect boyfriend.

Watching a stream of waitresses wearing black pinafores over crisp white shirts spiralling out of a nearby doorway bearing steaming plates, Jules sighed and wished she could find a career that made her heart sing the way that Cassia's clearly did. She frowned as she noticed several guests recoiling as they eyed their plates.

'Eeeugh!' shrieked a lady with hair like a bird's nest. Her hand fluttered to her chest. 'How could this have happened?'

Another pushed her chair away from the table in disgust. 'I'm not eating that!' she cried indignantly.

The mayor's wife, a regal and rather scary-looking lady in her late sixties, stood up. 'Who is responsible for this?' she demanded in a querulous voice.

'F-for what?' Jules asked nervously, stepping forward with a sinking stomach.

The mayor's wife stabbed a finger at the steaming plate in front of her. 'This. Beef Wellington. *Rare* beef Wellington,' she added, turning her nose up. Noticing Jules's blank expression, she shot her a withering glance. 'You're clearly not the person in charge,' she huffed, 'but for your information, this was supposed to be a vegetarian dinner. We are an animal charity, after all.'

Jules turned pale. She hadn't been told it was a vegetarian dinner; she was absolutely certain . . . she faltered as she spotted a note in the stack on her clipboard. As clear as day was the word '*VEGETARIAN*', in capitals, underlined for emphasis. Jules swallowed. How on earth could she have missed that?

'I'm . . . I'm just going to find out who might have made such a *terrible* mistake,' she stammered, backing out of the room in a panic. She didn't have a clue what to do; rather like event organising, damage limitation wasn't her forte. Cringing at her cowardice, Jules tore off her black dress to reveal the tiny pink shift dress covered in sequins she was wearing beneath. Hastily handing her notes to a colleague, she explained the mishap and apologised for her early departure.

'Family duties,' Jules cited, half honestly. Grabbing her handbag, she swapped her flats for some killer silver heels and headed outside, pleased to find Louisa sitting on a bench. Louisa was Finn's younger sister; Jules had met her years ago at a family party that Cassia had dragged her along to and they had become such good friends, they now shared a flat.

'What's happened?' Louisa asked, instantly cutting off a phone call. 'Have you been fired again?'

'Not yet,' Jules said edgily. 'Vegetarian dinner, rare beef Wellington,' she added by way of explanation.

Louisa suppressed a sigh and hailed a taxi. She knew Jules hated messing up all the time however blasé she might appear on the surface. 'Come on, let's get going. My brother is turning thirty and I'm sure Mother has laid on the party of the century for her favourite child.' She pulled a face.

Jules climbed into the taxi, showing an awful lot of tanned thigh which had the taxi driver craning for a better look. 'I expect so. Your mother doesn't exactly hide her favouritism, does she?' She glanced at her watch. 'We'll probably still beat Cassia there. She works later than anyone I know.'

'She loves her job.' Louisa shrugged, checking her blond, elfin hair in her compact mirror. 'You'd do the same if only you could find something you enjoyed doing. I do the odd late night at the gym now too because they want me to head up more classes.'

Jules fell into a glum silence for a moment. Why did she seem to be the only one who couldn't figure out what to do with herself? She rolled her shoulders, determined not to be a party pooper.

'So. Who's going tonight?'

Louisa re-applied her lipstick. 'Oh, you know. The usual bunch of chinless wonders Finn mixes with at work. And I do believe my unreliable shit of a younger brother is going to be there too, back from a glorious tournament in America, I think.

10

I expect we'll have to listen to a blow-by-blow account of each racket swipe.' She arched a brow. 'But on the plus side, some hot totty in the shape of some hunky tennis pros?'

Jules pulled herself together and prepared to dazzle. Hunky tennis pros sounded like the perfect antidote to her horrible day and she had always had a bit of a crush on Louisa's brother Dom, even if he was something of a Lothario. Unreliable shits were her speciality, after all, she thought ruefully.

Finn Sunderland straightened his ice-blue tie in bemusement. His mother had gone totally overboard with the party arrangements; in fact, she had surpassed herself, even by her own scarily high standards. Granted, it was his thirtieth birthday, but he certainly hadn't anticipated the vast marquee bedecked with fairy lights, the live band playing Pachelbel's Canon at a discreet volume and no less than three caterers attending to the needs of the guests bunched in groups across the lawn. His parents' enormous garden was studded with dozens of lit torches to throw light across the various winding pathways. The late evening sunshine was still holding out, allowing some warmth in addition to the patio heaters dotted across the neatly clipped grass. The grass tennis courts he and his brother Dom had spent their childhood pounding were tastefully lit up too; new floodlights streamed brightly across the faded grass and crusty white court markings.

Still, Finn thought as he sipped a glass of Veuve Clicquot with a small, ripe strawberry bobbing in it, the unexpectedly dazzling opulence of the party suited his plans perfectly. Not that his mother had any inkling what he had up his sleeve, but really, her timing was perfect. Finn wasn't quite sure what her reaction would be but he hoped she'd be pleased. And on reflection, why shouldn't she be?

Smoothing down his russet-blond hair and quickly checking his watch, he wondered what time Cassia might arrive. This was one night he'd prefer her not to be late. Her job at *Scrumptious* magazine could be very demanding, which wasn't ideal since his own role at Lovetts & Rose seemed to be taking up more and more of his time.

Maybe things will change in the future, he thought hopefully. Cassia might be devoted to her career right now, but who knew what impact upcoming events might have?

Finn watched his mother, Grace, circulating amongst the guests, ever the polite host. Having abandoned her usual daytime uniform of tweed skirt and silk blouse, she wore a conservative cocktail dress in pale blue with a frilly collar and a flared skirt. Trim and fit with a helmet of silver-blond hair that wouldn't move in a force nine gale, Finn couldn't help feeling a rush of affection for his rather severe-looking mother. A keen gardener who belonged to various charitable committees, Grace could appear shrewish and acerbic at times and although she had never openly admitted it, she clearly didn't think any woman was good enough for her beloved son.

Finn raised his glass to her as she glanced in his direction, making sure she knew how impressed he was by all her efforts with his birthday party. For all her faults, his mother was unquestionably loyal to her family and soft-hearted if one dug deep enough. Clutching Billy, her beloved Jack Russell to her chest, Grace smiled back happily at Finn, bringing to mind the old adage that people were like the dogs they owned. Like Grace, Billy had a tendency to snap at anyone in the vicinity, whereas his father's golden retriever Fred was amiably happy with an easy-going temperament, just like his owner.

'Bit over the top, isn't it?' said a voice behind Finn. 'I mean, I know you're ancient and all that, but I wasn't expecting all this glitz and glamour.'

Finn turned and shook his brother Dom's hand warmly. 'Me neither.' He grinned. 'But I guess there have to be some perks to getting old, right?'

Knocked out in an early round at the US Men's Clay Court Championship in Houston and sporting an enviable tan that his open-necked, white shirt complemented perfectly, Dom was feeling pleased with himself. Not expected to even be noticed at the high-profile tournament, he had managed to impress some important officials with his showy, courageous play. And despite his early exit, he had conducted himself well, especially for a newcomer, Dom thought with some satisfaction.

A professional tennis player with a rather lacklustre CV to date, he had recently found his stride, especially on grass, and he was expected to do well at Wimbledon in a few months' time. He had clocked up some notable statistics on the junior circuit, as well as earning himself a few wild cards to big events such as Queens and Wimbledon in the past, and had secured himself a new coach; he was all set for the big time on the full, adult circuit. He loved the attention he was receiving from the media, the tennis circuit and most especially from all the beautiful girls who followed the game with slavish devotion, and he was milking his moment for all he was worth.

'Happy thirtieth, bro.' Dom raised his drink to Finn and realised both their glasses were empty. He grabbed two more from a passing waitress, who eyed Dom appreciatively.

'Gosh, she's pretty,' Dom murmured absently. 'Must get her number later.'

Finn smiled. The baby of the family at twenty-two, Dom emanated charisma, was ferociously ambitious and notoriously badly behaved – the total opposite of himself, in fact. Nonetheless, they were incredibly fond of one another. Knowing Dom was not so much spoilt as neglected, Finn tended to cut him some slack. It was hardly Dom's fault their mother was so besotted with her firstborn that no one else, including Louisa, got a look in.

Dom handed Finn a present he'd hastily bought in the airport, and drained his champagne like a man who had been trapped in a desert for a month. 'My coach frowns on drinking,' he explained with a pained expression. 'I haven't been able to convince him it improves my game, but I'm absolutely sure it does.'

Finn tugged a silk tie in a shocking shade of pink out of the wrapping paper. It was more Dom's style than his own but he dutifully removed his traditional-looking blue tie and replaced it with the pink one.

'Suits you.' Dom nodded approvingly, wiggling the tie into place. 'Wow, I really must congratulate Mother on hiring such gorgeous girls this evening,' he commented, catching sight of another extremely pretty waitress.

Finn eyed his brother affectionately. He didn't know whether to admire Dom or give him a kick up the backside for his champagne lifestyle and wayward attitude, but as long as his brother was happy and doing well for himself, he wasn't going to criticise him. Their mother could do that very well without his help, Finn realised.

Buoyed up by his recent success, Dom was about to launch into a speech about his new coach's expectations for him at Wimbledon but remembering that it was Finn's birthday, he made an effort to talk about something else. 'How are things going with Cassia?'

Finn smiled. 'Very well, actually. We've been together for a long time but I think I've finally realised how serious I am about her.' His blue eyes gazed into the distance for a moment. 'I reckon she's the one.'

Dom almost laughed out loud. His brother, known for being cautious in the extreme, had being seeing Cassia for what? Eight years? Only Finn could take nearly a decade to decide his girlfriend was 'the one'.

Not noticing his brother's amusement, Finn became earnest. 'I can see a future with Cassia . . . marriage, children . . . the works.'

Dom recoiled comically. 'Stop it; you'll mention the dreaded word "commitment" in a minute.' Noticing his brother's vexed expression, he added hastily, 'Oh, don't get me wrong, Cassia is beautiful. And intelligent too. If anything, I don't understand why it's taken you so long to see how great she is.'

Dom meant it; Cassia was drop-dead gorgeous and one of the classiest women he'd ever met. The only downside with Cassia, in his opinion, was that she was far too sensible. Once or twice he thought he might have spotted something unpredictable behind her nut-brown eyes but it always disappeared so quickly, Dom had come to the conclusion that he must have simply imagined it. Still, if she made his brother happy, Dom didn't care how sensible Cassia was, and if he was honest, Finn was pretty uptight himself, so they were probably a perfect match.

'Ignore me, Finn; I'm pleased for you,' Dom said, clapping him on the shoulder. 'It's just that any mention of commitment brings me out in a rash.' He gave a mock shudder.

Catching sight of Cassia's dark head moving among the crowd, Finn smiled at Dom. 'Maybe you'll meet the right girl one day, Dom, and then you won't run a mile when she stays for more than one night.' He paused and an odd expression crossed his face. 'Excuse me, Dom; I have something to do . . . join me in the marquee?'

Marching up to Cassia, Finn wrapped his arms around her neck and kissed her. 'Finally! Where have you been?' She smelt gorgeous; she was wearing the understated flowery perfume he liked. Finn smoothed a tendril of dark hair out of her face, thinking again how lucky he was.

Cassia smiled, pleased to see him. 'Sorry, work stuff as usual.' She was glad Finn wasn't holding her lateness against her – unlike Grace who had made her disapproval plain by shooting daggers at her from the marquee as soon as she arrived. 'Happy birthday, by the way,' she added, grabbing Finn's lapels. 'I'll give you your present later. Not *that* kind of present.' She laughed, seeing him raise his eyebrows. 'Well, maybe, but I have a proper gift as well.' She stood back and gave him an approving once-over. 'Great suit . . . and is that a new tie?'

Finn toyed with it. 'Dom bought it. It's a bit flashy, I know, but he's my baby brother so I put it on.' Feeling nervous, he cleared his throat. 'Listen, I have something to say to you . . .' Clutching her hand, he ducked inside the marquee with her, making for the stage. Stopping by the microphone, he tapped it self-consciously. 'Excuse me, everyone, can I have your attention, please?'

Looking out, Finn saw his mother frowning faintly at him, her cool blue eyes questioning. His father, Henry, a jovial man with a rounded stomach and reddish hair that set off his freckles perfectly, raised his glass of red wine in salute. Dom sidled in with one of the waitresses and his sister Louisa arrived arm in arm with Cassia's younger sister Jules. Finn took a deep breath; there was no time like the present. Then he realised Cassia's mother, Diana, might not have arrived yet, but now that he was up on the stage, he was caught up in the moment.

'Ahem . . . now that I have you all here, I would like to propose a toast. That is . . . I'd like to propose.'

There was a collective gasp from the watching crowds, the most audible one emanating from Grace. Oblivious, Finn turned and took Cassia's hand, not even noticing her gaping at him in disbelief. He had thought long and hard about this and he wasn't about to be deterred from his carefully thought-out plan. Kneeling down, he drew a small, black ring box out of his pocket.

'You'd make me the happiest man alive if you would agree to marry me,' Finn said solemnly, looking up at Cassia. He struggled to remember the lines he had written out laboriously over the past few months and he flipped open the ring box to buy himself some time.

'We've been together a long time, Cassia. We've supported each other through ... er ... through thick and thin and I can't think of anything more wonderful than settling down with you and, ummm, creating a home ... with some children ... you know, one day.' Drawing a mid-sized, round diamond set on top of a slim, platinum band out of the ring box, Finn held it up.

Jules's mouth fell open and she shot a shocked glance at Louisa. Louisa was staring at Finn and Cassia, but she didn't look upset about her brother's proposal. Jules turned back to the stage, trying to get a look at the ring. She felt certain that the diamond Finn had chosen would be classic rather than ostentatiously large and that the band probably had a perfectly worded inscription inside. Jules experienced an unpleasant stab of envy. Bloody Cassia, why did she always, always land on her feet? She seemed to be followed around by aggravating fairies that sprinkled magical glitter wherever she trod.

Louisa frowned at Jules, not entirely sure why she looked so deflated. Finn and Cassia had been dating for donkey's years; their engagement was hardly a big shock. Louisa stole a glance at her mother, realising she looked even more stunned than Jules, her cheeks red and her mouth twisting as though she had swallowed a wasp.

Up on stage and aware that Grace looked thoroughly appalled by the turn of events, Cassia swallowed. Realising she hadn't said yes to Finn, she turned to him, squeezing his hand as she speedily got her thoughts together. Despite the amount of time she and Finn had been together, she hadn't seen this coming but knowing Finn as she did, Cassia was sure he had probably spent months, years even, planning the event, from the carat, cut and clarity of the diamond he was holding up to the sweet and, most likely, scripted speech. Spontaneity wasn't his thing, even if the moment Finn had chosen had seemed like an impulsive one, but that was one of the things

Cassia loved about him. Her decision was made in an instant.

'The answer is . . . yes,' she said. Her heart thumped briefly at the enormity of the moment, but she knew she was doing the right thing.

Finn jumped up and clumsily pushed the diamond on to her finger. 'Does it fit? It does? That's amazing . . . I'm so pleased.' Whispering in her ear, he asked if she fancied getting married that summer. Having thought about proposing for nearly two years now, Finn couldn't see the point in a long engagement.

Cassia blinked in surprise. Guessing his suggestion had, like everything else, been pondered long and hard, she supposed he had probably already looked into it. Half-expecting him to produce a shortlist of venues, cake-makers and florists, Cassia nodded. 'Why not?' She laughed.

Grace stepped forward, pasting a stiff smile on to her face. 'Finn, Cassia . . . what . . . lovely news. I didn't have a clue this was going to happen.' She directed this at Finn who grinned back at her amiably, clearly oblivious of his mother's distress. Henry clambered on to the stage beside Grace and hugged Cassia. 'Congratulations, darling. I couldn't be happier.' Shaking Finn's hand heartily, Henry drew his son close. 'Good boy,' he boomed. 'She's a wonderful girl; you know I have a fearful soft spot for her . . .'

Cassia smiled, wishing Grace was more excited about the news, and then blushed as Dom jumped up next to her and pulled her in for a cheeky kiss.

In the midst of all the cheering and popping champagne corks, someone in an elegant white dress stumbled in tugging a young Hispanic-looking man after her. More than a little tipsy, Diana Marini-Blake, Cassia and Jules's mother, was in high spirits and she made her late entrance with panache. She was used to being stared at after years of being photographed and lusted after and she shimmied confidently through the crowds, greeting people and introducing her new boyfriend, Angelo. Belatedly, she realised something exciting had just happened. Cassia was on stage being twirled around by Finn who looked rather dishy in a daring pink tie. And she spotted Jules watching them with a scowl.

Diana was struck by how much Jules reminded her of herself at the same age; it was like watching a movie of her younger self back then. The sneer hid a vulnerable heart and, Diana suspected, deep insecurity about never meeting a man who would take care of her. Diana had felt the same way before she had met Marco all those years ago and she longed to reassure Jules that she would find someone special one day. She made a mental note to speak to her later.

Pushing her recently chopped blond bob out of her eyes, Diana swept to the stage, dragging Angelo behind her. Hearing the gasps of recognition as bystanders realised who she was, she relished the theatrical moment.

'Darlings,' she cried grandly. 'I'm only a teensy bit late . . . what on *earth* have I missed?'

Chapter Two

Miles away in Sorrento, Italy, Rocco Disanti threw the sheet off his naked body and stood up. Pulling on a pair of tight, black boxer shorts and leaving his tanned chest bare apart from a simple platinum chain with a cross on it, he glanced over his shoulder at Stefania, whose lithe body was stretched out beneath the cream silk bedsheet, her long blond hair spilling artistically across the pillow. Fast asleep, she somehow still managed to look sleek and together, the complete opposite of how she should look after the sexual marathon they'd just enjoyed.

Rocco drank the remains of a glass of champagne he found on his bedside table and winced as he felt his hangover kicking in. The party last night at the family restaurant in Sorrento had been glitzy and drink-fuelled. Held to celebrate more than seventy years in the restaurant business, the party had also been arranged to mark Rocco's achievements since his grandfather, Nico, the backbone of the family, had passed away. Rocco felt a pang in his heart. He and Nico had been close; everything he had learnt about cooking and the restaurant business came from their tight bond, from the days he had spent watching spellbound as his grandfather created magic in the kitchen, to his adult years when he had soaked up knowledge about the restaurant business like the proverbial sponge.

Rocco wished fervently his grandfather was still around to guide him; he missed his gentle decisiveness and his infectious enthusiasm. Even as his health deteriorated and his lungs succumbed to emphysema, Nico had remained upbeat, full of ideas for using the Disanti fortune to turn the business into a glamorous chain. Initially only responsible for running and cooking in the Michelin-starred Sorrento restaurant, Rocco had steadfastly devoted himself to his grandfather's dream, creating glittering sister restaurants in London and Paris, with plans underway for another high-class eaterie in one of the most prominent casino hotels on the Vegas strip. Rocco still wasn't sure about Vegas as a location for a Disanti restaurant, especially when the emphasis had always been on a classy ambience and fine dining, but his parents had insisted.

Running a distracted hand over his short, conker-brown hair, Rocco wondered if he had taken on too much. But even as he did so, he realised it didn't matter either way. What choice did he have? The Disanti cooking gene had bypassed his flamboyant mother, Flavia, and along with Rocco's father Gino, she was far more interested in promoting and developing the Disanti 'brand'. They were true celebrities, frequently seen on TV shows and doing endless book tours for the coffee-table books Rocco created. He knocked back a couple of headache pills with some flat champagne. His grandmother Sofia always joked that he was the Italian Gordon Ramsay but, despite his admiration for the chef, Rocco didn't see it. He was a businessman certainly – he had become the reluctant figurehead of the family because of his cooking skills – but he was also extremely private. He was rarely in the kitchen these days and he hardly ever made appearances on television or conducted interviews, despite constant requests and his grandmother insisting his brooding good looks could boost his already A-list presence. Rocco wasn't interested; he left the celebrity stuff to his polished and ever-ready parents, relying on his professional reputation to carry him rather than courting the media.

He headed into the vast kitchen he'd had built in the converted barn he occupied at the Disanti family home, realising he was starving. The party had started at midday with speeches and an endless flow of vintage champagne. A veritable feast had followed, proudly hosted by his grandmother Sofia, and the table had heaved with wonderful, succulent dishes. As well as a mouth-watering selection of freshly baked breads and colourful, Mediterranean-style salads, there were plates of *ravioli al granchio*, crab ravioli in a creamy sauce with cayenne, Parmesan veal cutlets that melted in the mouth, a buttery risotto with quail that ran out in minutes and some courgettes baked with aubergines, a favourite of Nico's.

After some sweet almond cake, figs drenched in grappa and a warm Milanese trifle that had reduced one guest to tears of awe, more champagne had appeared, along with case after case of good Chianti.

Wishing he hadn't guzzled so much of the fizzy stuff, Rocco grabbed the ingredients for a simple artichoke omelette. Quickly, he sautéed some artichokes in butter, adding cream and seasoning. He beat some fresh eggs with salt and pepper and cooked them in another pan. When the mixture was almost set, he added the artichokes and expertly folded the omelette in half.

Rocco leant up against the kitchen counter and forked the eggs into his mouth as he stared out of the open balcony windows at the view. The Disanti estate sprawled out in front of him, occupying several thousand feet of prime Sorrento land. Strewn with picturesque orange and lemon groves that gave off the most wonderful aroma in season, the estate was dominated by the main house – a veritable castle by Italian standards – and the famous restaurant. Set to one side, the tall, majestic building sat against a backdrop of citrus groves and the creamy terracotta exterior boasted imposing arched windows, a ground-level terrace and a high-level balcony. Bedecked with statues, the balcony allowed diners to enjoy a breathtaking view of the Bay of Naples with Mount Vesuvius in the distance.

Tearing his eyes away, Rocco remembered something and groaned. Earlier in the evening, buoyed up on champagne and success, he had agreed to a favour for the wife of Gianfranco, a close childhood friend who now lived in England. The details were hazy but Rocco vaguely remembered offering an inside glimpse into himself and his business in exchange for invaluable publicity about his new Vegas restaurant. Rocco knew he must have been drunk to agree to such an idea over the phone; the last thing he needed was intrusion into his life when he was so ridiculously busy. Disanti's Sorrento had recently been damaged in a freak storm and it needed repairing, something Rocco simply had to get on top of.

Still, a promise was a promise, he thought ruefully, finishing his omelette and washing it down with some ice-cold water. He just hoped whoever turned up – remembering the phone call the night before, he assumed it would be a woman – didn't get under his feet. Rocco adored women with a passion, he thought of them in the same way he did food, sexually, obsessively and with respect, but he had so many demands in his life at the moment, one more might just tip him over the edge.

He seemed to be surrounded by women who relied on him. His grandmother Sofia was apple-cheeked, motherly and caring but since Nico's death, she had been oddly anxious about some age-old curse she believed had befallen the family and she leant heavily on Rocco for reassurance. Rocco's teenage sister Aurelia was a beautiful and much-in-demand model who was also fearfully spoilt. An Italian princess in the making, she was due to get married to Dino, the only man Rocco believed could successfully handle his sister, in the summer. And as for his on-off girlfriend Stefania, Rocco mused, he wasn't sure he could have found himself a more challenging girlfriend. Slinky, capricious and breathtakingly pretty, she thought nothing of turning up out of the blue from Rome and insisting that he drop everything and focus on her.

'Rocco, are you there?'

Heading to the balcony, Rocco caught sight of his parents, surrounded by designer luggage.

'We're off on our tour,' Flavia trilled, positioning a wide-brimmed straw hat on her dark hair. Wearing a peacock-blue couture dress with high slingbacks, she didn't look as though she could possibly have given birth to one child, let alone three. She also didn't look remotely fazed at being confronted by the sight of her hungover son in nothing but his boxers and she gave him a jaunty wave.

'See you in a few months,' she added vaguely. Flavia didn't want to let on to Rocco just how many dates they had committed to throughout Europe to sign their new cookbook and meet fans, especially since their prolonged absence would mean Rocco dealing with the business single-handedly.

Gino waved a tanned hand as he surrendered a bulging suitcase to a member of the family's press team. 'Call us if you need anything!' he said airily, safe in the knowledge that Rocco wouldn't dream of doing such a thing, even in an emergency.

'Have a good trip,' Rocco replied drily, baffled by their obsession with their celebrity lifestyle. He couldn't think of anything more irritating. As his parents and their entourage of PAs, make-up artists and hairdressers settled inside gleaming black cars, he watched them with a mixture of fondness and exasperation.

'What's going on?' Stefania asked in a silky voice from the balcony doorway. She had clearly just emerged from the bathroom; her make-up was immaculate and she smelt like freshly picked violets, betraying a recent spritz of perfume.

'Waving my parents off . . . eating,' Rocco replied, gesturing to the empty plate on the table. 'Would you like me to make you something?'

She shook her head, her mane of hair falling across her eyes. 'No thanks.'

He nodded, unsurprised. Stefania was slim and toned, she ate healthily and exercised often and while she looked good on it, Rocco wished she would allow him to cook for her once in a while. It was one of the few pleasures he had in life now that the business side of things had taken over.

He looked at her, wondering what it was about her that made him keep coming back for more. She was stunning, but he had been out with plenty of attractive girls in his time, so it couldn't be that. Stefania was bright; despite only being twenty-five, she owned a company in Rome that did PR for various restaurants and bars, but again, Rocco rarely dated airheads. He couldn't put his finger on exactly why he and Stefania had been seeing one another for the past year, just as he couldn't pinpoint what it was that was stopping him from making a serious commitment to her.

'Are you . . . coming back to bed?' she said, raising doe eyes to his. Her gaze drifted over him; she admired Rocco's striking looks, from his olive-green eyes with their sooty lashes and his sexy, brooding mouth to his broad, tanned chest and narrow hips in the exceptionally tight shorts . . .

Rocco hesitated. He really wanted to go and check the storm damage the restaurant had suffered a few days ago, but as Stefania moved from the doorway, her blond hair grazing her pink nipples, he decided he might just have time to tumble her back into bed after all. He scooped her warm, naked body up against his, all thoughts of family commitments and promises to childhood friends forgotten.

*

Jules cycled furiously. It was Saturday, the day after the party, and she was attending one of Louisa's punishing spinning classes at the local gym, the perfect way to let off steam.

'Stand up on the pedals!' Louisa shouted, standing astride her bike like a sergeant major, albeit one in a hot-pink leotard with a matching headband. Heading up the class in front of a video of Eric Prydz's' 'Call on Me', which was both cheesy and strangely motivating, Louisa almost appeared to be getting off on her students' pain as she threw bossy commands at them.

'And now . . . CYCLE! Come on, give it everything you've got, girls! Do you want a fat bum or a firm little peach like hers?' Louisa jerked her head at the video screen behind her and showed them all how it was done, clenching her buttocks tightly.

Gritting her teeth as her calves protested, Jules did as she was told and gave it everything. She didn't want a fat bum. Cassia was the one in danger of developing one of those, Jules thought to herself. She bit her lip, knowing she was being a bitch. It was just that Finn's birthday party had been a real low point, a disappointing end to a day that had almost resulted in her being jobless as well as single and shat on. Jules knew that was ridiculous, but she couldn't help feeling peeved at the way the evening had ended, just because it had made her feel so inadequate.

It had started off well: champagne, delicious canapés and a plethora of male talent in the shape of Finn and Dom's close-knit circle of hunky friends. A mixture of City types and professional tennis players, complete with bulging wallets, biceps or both, they had flirted and danced and promised exotic dates. But just as Jules had been about to choose one of the gorgeous men to wine and dine her after the party, Finn had done the whole down-on-one-knee thing.

Depressed at the injustice of it all, Jules pushed her thighs to screaming point. It was the story of her life, wasn't it? For

Cassia, the universe provided fabulous jobs, to-die-for flats and a romantic late-summer wedding; for Jules, a dead-end career, a flat she rented with Louisa because she couldn't afford to buy a house when she kept getting fired, and a veritable queue of cheating bastards who would faint at the thought of proposing.

How could their lives have turned out so differently? Jules wondered. Was it really down to a cruel twist of fate that Cassia seemed so blessed while she seemed to constantly struggle? Jules caught her breath as her past threatened to wind her. Agonising memories often caught her unawares like this, creeping up like shadowy ghosts and curling cold fingers around her. Jules squeezed her eyes tightly shut for a moment, trying to push them away. Suddenly aware that the thumping music had ceased, she slumped over the bike.

'Wow, good workout!' Barely out of breath, Louisa bounded over. 'Feeling better?'

Jules nodded, gingerly dismounting. She was fit but the spinning class always left her feeling sweaty and out of breath. She didn't need to look in a mirror to know her normally rosy cheeks were probably now unattractively scarlet, but that was the least of her worries.

Louisa could see that Jules was feeling low and she wondered if Jules had lost her job after the vegetarian mix-up at the charity event. 'Did you speak to your boss?'

Jules pushed sweat-stained locks of blond hair out of her eyes. 'Jan wanted to sack me, I could tell, but I played the "I've just been dumped" card and she took pity on me.'

Realising Jules's mood was probably more to do with Cassia's engagement news than anything else, Louisa changed tack. 'I think you need cheering up,' she announced, handing Jules a bright pink gym towel. 'We need to go out on the town and we need to meet some new men. There's this gorgeous guy I've been wanting to—'

'That's exactly what I need,' Jules interrupted, her eyes brightening. 'A distraction, someone to take my mind off things.'

Louisa nodded, digging out her phone. Sometimes she wished Jules wasn't so self-absorbed when things in her life went wrong because she could hardly get a word in edgeways. When she was happy, Jules was the best person to be around, but when a relationship hit the skids, she really couldn't do anything but wallow.

'Right, well, I know any number of eligible men I could hook you up with . . .'

'There is one man I have my eye on, actually,' Jules said, stopping Louisa from speed-dialling every single man in her iPhone. 'You'd really be doing me a favour if you could set me up with your brother Dom.'

Louisa laughed then stopped. Dom? Jules had to be kidding; Dom was the last person she should be hooking up with. He was a serial shagger who dated models, tennis groupies and the more attractive female players on the circuit and Louisa couldn't imagine Dom would be into Jules, who, whilst pretty, was incredibly needy; desperate to settle down and be looked after – hence her unnecessary despair at being single at the tender age of twenty-four. Louisa felt that Jules sent out the wrong vibe with her wild, carefree partying – which was why she tended to end up with losers and cheats.

'Dom is a player,' she warned Jules, wondering if her friend was on self-destruct at the moment. 'And not just when it comes to tennis. He's a bed-hopper with no morals whatsoever. And he's barely in the country,' she added, clutching at anything that might deter Jules. 'Now that his game has finally picked up, his schedule is gruelling.'

Jules looked offended. 'Oh well, if you don't think he'd fancy me in a million years,' she huffed, feeling even more dejected.

Louisa sighed, knowing there was no reasoning with Jules in this mood. 'Fine, leave it with me, but don't blame me when it all goes horribly wrong later on, all right?' Louisa wondered for the umpteenth time what had happened all those years ago to make Jules seem so resentful and down on herself.

Reluctantly sending a text to Dom, Louisa mentally crossed her fingers and hoped Jules might find whatever it was she was searching for soon.

'More tea, Henry?' asked Grace, holding up a teapot shaped like a cottage. Looking the epitome of a 'proper' housewife with her silver-blond hair styled neatly and wearing a conservative outfit, she stared coolly at the back of *The Sunday Times*.

'Don't mind if I do, darling,' Henry replied over the top of his newspaper. 'Is there any cake?'

Grace gave him a withering stare, knowing the newspaper hid a rotund stomach that was just the wrong side of cuddly. 'No, there isn't any cake, Henry,' she commented rather sharply. 'And even if Cook had been baking today, I'd be telling her to keep it in the kitchen because you really don't need any more cake.'

Henry flipped his newspaper over and felt his golden retriever Fred flop down warmly on to his feet. 'No one *needs* cake, Gracie. It's a pleasure, not a necessity.' Reaching down to rub Fred's silky ears, he sipped his tea, resolving to go into the village tea shop later to track down a slice of his favourite iced coffee sponge. Or maybe Jules might bring him something homemade and delicious, Henry thought hopefully. He had always found it odd that Cassia's sister was such a fantastic cook; it didn't fit with her reputation as the consummate party girl.

Grace fiddled with her bone china cup, the jerky movements revealing her inner tension. 'What do you think about Finn's proposal, Henry? I still can't believe he planned it all without telling me. I mean us.'

'Romantic bugger,' Henry returned warmly. His affable grin showed just how delighted he was with the turn of events. 'He's been planning it for a very long time, by all accounts. Marvellous, wasn't it?'

Grace gave him a disdainful glance. Her eldest son's proposal had been far from 'marvellous', in her opinion. Priding herself on always knowing what was going on with her children, Finn's proposal had taken her breath away and Grace detested being caught unawares. She had known he was serious about Cassia; they'd been together for over eight years and that meant something in Finn's world because he wasn't the type to lead a woman on or give them false promises. Grace had always known deep down that her eldest son had chosen his partner for life, even if it had taken him a while to get round to making it formal. But she couldn't help feeling put out that she hadn't even suspected Finn was about to propose.

Dom was the opposite, of course, Grace thought distastefully. She had always detested the casual way her youngest son paraded his one-night stands in front of them. But Finn was different, he was sensible and loyal which meant his proposal to Cassia had been sincere and their loosely discussed wedding date in September would happen, without fail. Grace felt a moment of guilt as she acknowledged how much her heart sank every time the engagement flitted into her head. More than anything, she wanted her firstborn to be happy, but she couldn't shake off the feeling that Cassia wasn't right for Finn.

'What the matter, Gracie?' Henry asked, putting *The Sunday Times* crossword to one side without letting the sigh he felt on the inside show. Having been married for nearly thirty-five years, he had a sixth sense where his wife was concerned. Outwardly, she appeared calm and unruffled in her green tweed skirt and oyster-coloured silk blouse, but Henry knew better. Sensing her disquiet from the opposite side of the table, experience had taught him it was better to give her his attention now, rather than at a later date when she had pondered whatever was bothering her. Henry's existence became far more challenging when Grace was troubled and, frankly, he preferred an easy life.

Grace met his eyes, cross that he could read her so well. 'It's Cassia,' she confessed. 'I just don't think she's the best person for Finn.'

'Really?' Henry's hazel eyes widened. 'I think Cassia's top notch, I really do. She's beautiful, intelligent and independent. What's not to love, darling? I personally think Finn's made an excellent choice.'

'Oh, Henry!' Grace snapped in exasperation. 'It's about more than looks and brains, it's about compatibility.'

Henry nodded in agreement, personally believing Finn and Cassia to be superbly well-matched. He really couldn't understand why Grace seemed to have it in for Cassia, but it had been that way from day one. Secretly, he wondered if his wife resented Cassia's career – Grace seemed to think all women should be housewives. About to defend Cassia again, he remembered that he only ever got tartly scolded for his troubles, but truthfully, he was intensely fond of her. Whenever they were alone, he and Cassia would chat about fine wines and food and he thought she was the most fabulous girl. Henry couldn't help thinking no one would be good enough for Finn in Grace's eyes; historically, she had always given his girlfriends a tough time.

'I think Jules would be a better match for Finn, as it happens,' Grace stated, out of the blue.

'Jules? Cassia's sister, Jules?' Henry stared at his wife incredulously. Jules was sweet and lovely-looking, but surely she was the unreliable type? And she could be a bit catty when the mood took her, he thought, remembering a family party where Jules had been overheard commenting disparagingly on the size of Cassia's hips.

31

Grace slowly nodded. 'Jules is the most amazing cook, isn't she? And she keeps that flat she shares with Louisa as neat as a pin. Louisa is the messy sort, but there are always fresh flowers and clean towels.'

'And she doesn't have a particular career to speak of,' Henry offered, knowing his old-fashioned wife would approve of such a thing. He also noted the unspoken comparison to Cassia; in spite of her foodie background, she was fairly hopeless in the kitchen and she probably didn't have time to buy flowers and arrange them in vases. Still, Henry was sure Cassia was the right girl for Finn; regardless of her dedication to her career, she patently adored Finn and as far as Henry was concerned, that was all that mattered.

'Good point,' Grace said, raising her eyebrows delicately. Knowing that Finn had always thought of Jules as Louisa's irritating, man-mad friend and that he wouldn't think of her as suitable girlfriend material, she let go of the wistful idea of them getting together.

'At least we have a wedding to look forward to,' Henry said brightly, trying to pep Grace up. 'Perhaps Cassia might ask you to help out?'

Making a noise similar to a horse snorting, Grace knocked back her tea as though she was drinking a stiff gin and tonic. 'I think we both know that won't happen,' she said, starting to put the tea things back on to the tray.

Henry flipped his newspaper open again, idly wondering if he could sneak off for a round of golf later on.

On Monday morning before work, Cassia watched Finn emerge from the shower. Grinning at the sight of him bare-chested with nothing but a small, white towel slung around his waist, she began to pin her long, dark hair up in a neat chignon.

Chatting to a contact about a possible wedding venue with his mobile tucked under his chin as he punched his well-muscled arms into a crisp, white shirt, Finn winked at her.

'That's right . . . the end of September. Yes, I'm being serious. Why would I joke about such a thing? Nothing? All right, the cancellations list it is then.' He rolled his eyes at Cassia as he hung up. 'Honestly, am I speaking Japanese?' He grappled with his new Cartier cufflinks, surrendering his wrists to her as she stepped in to help. 'These are amazing, Cass. Thank you.'

She finished fastening them. 'You're welcome. Finn . . . September for the wedding – that's what? Just five months away.'

Finn looked unfazed. 'Tons of people get married with a few weeks' notice, don't they? I just don't see the point in waiting when we've been together for so long.'

He straightened his tie, deciding not to mention that his job at the law firm was always quiet at that time of year; he didn't want to appear unromantic. He had no idea why it was quiet then; he was sure legal issues still needed sorting out after the holiday months, but there it was. He had thought long and hard about when they should get married and he was sure he – they – would be doing the right thing by just getting on with it. Now that they were engaged, Finn honestly couldn't see any reason to drag it out.

Cassia could see his point. They'd spent the weekend together at Finn's London flat after his proposal, going for long walks, talking about the party and the engagement. But Finn was preoccupied with his job, a topic which had eventually overshadowed all talk of weddings. Involved in a high-profile case he hoped would provide him with the perfect platform to impress his bosses, Finn had confided his fears about not moving up the career ladder, especially now that they were getting married.

Cassia listened and sympathised, but she couldn't help thinking Finn might be better off accepting that he wasn't one of life's movers and shakers. He was hard-working and exceptionally bright but he wasn't a high-flyer; promotion would most likely come steadily and precisely, the way everything in Finn's life seemed to materialise.

Fluffing dark pink blusher on to her cheeks, Cassia tried to get her head around the fact that she was getting married soon. If she hadn't been so focused at work, she was sure she might have picked up on the signs that Finn was about to propose; conversations had taken a more serious turn recently, with plenty of references to marriage and children sprinkled throughout.

She glanced at him. It was a cliché, but he was her rock. He was handsome and funny and considerate, but more importantly, he was reliable, a quality Cassia had always craved in a man. Having seen most of her parents' friends divorce and remarry with careless regularity, she had always wanted to be with someone she trusted.

'Do you think your mother is happy about the news?' she asked, transfixed for a moment as her engagement ring caught the April sunshine streaming through the window. She wasn't prone to such girly observations but she had to admit that the ring was extremely pretty. Maybe not quite her taste . . . she preferred antique styles, but it really was lovely.

Finn shrugged his arms into his well-cut, dove-grey suit jacket as he juggled his phone and briefcase. 'Of course she is. Why wouldn't she be?'

Cassia was glad Finn had missed Grace's hostility after his on-stage proposal, but a part of her did wish he wasn't so blind to his mother's obvious dislike of her. Every time she mentioned it, Finn dismissed her comments immediately, reassuring her that his mother adored her. He did the same thing now, dropping a distracted kiss on to her forehead. Pausing, he looked down at her, putting his hands on her shoulders. 'And quite right too; you're perfect for me and she knows that.'

Cassia said nothing, knowing she would sound petty if she went on about Grace's disapproval of her too much, but she knew she was right to be wary of Finn's mother. Her own mother had given her some thoughts on the matter once, telling her that mothers of sons could be perfectly normal and lovely, but that some were a 'type'.

'Trust me, Cass,' Diana had said darkly, 'there are some for whom there will never be a woman good enough for their beloved male offspring.' She had gone on to describe such women as blinkered, possessive matriarchs who would never sufficiently warm to the woman who would replace them in their son's lives. Diana had warned Cassia not to bother trying to impress Grace and that she would be better off accepting that she would never measure up.

Realising her mother was wiser than she had given her credit for, Cassia put her future mother-in-law out of her mind. Her thoughts drifted to Jules. Her sister had looked on enviously when Finn had proposed and Cassia had wanted to reassure her that she would meet someone as great as Finn one day. But it wasn't just about meeting the right man and Cassia knew that.

Years ago, she and Jules had been close – sisters in the truest sense. They had played together happily, laughed at the same things and argued ferociously before making up, hugging and borrowing toys, books, clothes and make-up from one another. Then, around Cassia's twentieth birthday, it had all gone spectacularly wrong. Overnight, Jules – at the time a lovable, sensitive sixteen year old – had turned into an aggressive, scornful girl, so full of hate, she could no longer bond with the sibling who had sung her praises since birth.

Desperately hurt at Jules's sudden rejection of her, Cassia, once a hedonistic party girl who lived to have fun and enjoy life, had adopted a new persona of her own. Looking back, she supposed she became level-headed and cautious in an attempt to provide a contrast to the monster Jules had become as she hurled herself into pleasure-seeking and wreaking havoc. Cassia was as bewildered today as she had been back then by the abrupt personality change.

Cassia followed Finn out of the flat and hurried to the station after him.

'Did you manage to get hold of Gena?' Finn asked, buying a newspaper from a stand in the station and tucking it under his arm. 'I was surprised she didn't make it to the party.'

'No, I didn't, but I left her several messages,' Cassia said with a frown. She'd forgotten about Gena with the whirlwind of the proposal, but Finn was right, she hadn't made it to the party. Cassia briefly wondered what was going on but guessed she would find out once she got to work.

Finn kissed her firmly, clutching her hand. 'We're doing the right thing, aren't we? Getting married, I mean.'

Cassia smiled up at him. 'Of course we are. Doing it in five months' time is a bit crazy, but I agree, what's the point in waiting?' As Finn dashed off to get his train, Cassia paused by a stand full of wedding magazines.

What sort of dress would she wear? What colour flowers would she have? Would Jules agree to be bridesmaid?

She allowed herself a few minutes to indulge in fantasies of towering cakes and romantic venues before heading off to catch her train. She hoped she could juggle her wedding plans with her demanding career, but she couldn't help feeling a warm glow inside every time she caught sight of the ring on her finger. She was getting married! What could be more exciting?

'Oh, darlings, how am I going to find the perfect outfit in such a short space of time?'

Sitting in the middle of the Fifth Floor Café at Harvey Nichols' flagship store in Knightsbridge for maximum exposure, Diana was lunching with her agent, Felicity, and two girlfriends. Shunning the more sumptuous restaurant because she liked the rooftop view and the opportunity to mingle with other thespian types, Diana was regaling her friends with details of her daughter's engagement, leaving out the fact that she had actually missed the vital moment by arriving hideously late with Angelo.

'Honestly, who gets married five months after the announcement these days?' she was saying as their yellow fin tuna niçoise salads arrived. 'I mean, they've been together for yonks, what's the rush? Oooh, there's Nigel Havers . . . cooee, Nigel!'

Felicity sipped her kir royale with an ironic smile. 'Perhaps they're in love,' she commented. 'I remember a couple once who simply couldn't *wait* to dash up the aisle after they got engaged.'

Air-kissing Nigel as he left, Diana waved a dismissive hand but looked sheepish. 'Me and Marco? Oh, that was so long ago, Fliss!'

She paused, lost in memories. Gosh, she'd forgotten how desperate she and Marco had been to get married, but now she thought about it, it had been mere moments after he'd slipped the vintage-style sapphire ring on to her finger that she'd dashed out and bought a gorgeous silk minidress in the palest shade of champagne. They had taken a cancellation at the nearest register office in London a few weeks later and clutching a bunch of faded pink roses wrapped in sopping tissue paper bought from a florist's stall en route, Diana had married Marco, just as the press had got wind of the scoop. They had stepped outside to hundreds of flashbulbs going off and they had kissed, his head as dark as hers was blond; an iconic image that had been splashed across every newspaper in the country, the photos dug out and reprinted every time something relating to either of them became newsworthy.

Heartbreakingly, the photographs now reminded Diana of Marco's death. Since his shock exit from life three years ago, journalists had waxed lyrical about his demise, printing his food columns with plenty of reference to the glamorous actress wife he had left behind.

'Besides that being a veritable lifetime away, we didn't actually invite anyone else,' Diana said abruptly, glossing over how emotional she felt as she thought about Marco. He was dead and even though she still loved him, Diana had resolved to bury her guilt and enjoy herself. It was just that, every so often, thoughts of him almost made her come undone. She grabbed her glass with shaky hands.

'What does *that* have to do with anything?' smiled Rachel Ellis-Jones, Diana's former voice coach.

Diana made a concentrated effort to pull herself together. She had grieved for Marco for a long time – she had grieved for him when he was still alive, if she was honest with herself. But, she reminded herself, she had moved on. She'd had many boyfriends recently, young ones at that. Angelo, her latest, was young enough to be her . . . well, her son, at the very least.

She realised Rachel was still waiting for an answer. 'Well, I think the guest list for Finn and Cassia's wedding will be enormous and that means everyone has to find outfits, doesn't it?' Draining her kir royale in one gulp, she leant forward. 'My daughter is very lucky, you know. Finn is rather hunky, one of those reddish-blonds with the most fabulous blue eyes. A little dull, perhaps . . . but not everyone craves excitement, of course.' She paused, catching sight of the faint, blue veins on the back of her hands. She winced. 'It's lovely news, but it does make one feel rather . . . *old.*'

'You're not old,' scoffed Maggie Silvin, a make-up artist who'd worked on Diana's upmarket TV sitcom five years ago. 'I have to use more make-up on the boys on those dance shows than I do on you – not that I've made you up for a while,' she added pointedly.

Diana sighed. 'No one wants me any more, Mags. I'm at that funny age where I can't quite play a grandmother – thank

God,' she shuddered dramatically, 'but no one believes me as a mother figure either, although I can't imagine why. I *am* a mother, after all, but perhaps I'm a teeny bit more glamorous than the average?'

Felicity almost choked on a piece of perfectly cooked tuna. Diana was a darn sight more glamorous than the average mother and she knew it, mainly because she spent a fortune looking after herself. Besides which, she simply refused to grow old gracefully. Felicity happened to know that Diana had shaved several years off her official age a decade ago.

Hesitantly, Felicity put her fork down, wondering if now was the right time to broach the subject she'd been meaning to discuss for a while.

'So sorry to interrupt, but aren't you Diana Marini-Blake?'

They all looked up as a pleasant-looking man in his forties approached their table.

Diana inclined her head modestly. She knew it was an unusual choice to place her married name before her maiden one, but it worked, so she had kept it that way for years. She smiled up at the man who was staring back at her in awe. 'I am she, but you're far too young to remember me, I'm sure!'

'Not at all,' he stammered, going pink. 'I had the biggest crush on you when you were in *Power to the People*. They used to rerun the show on one of those Sky channels.' He pulled a business card out of his pocket. 'Would it be too much of an imposition to ask for an autograph?'

Scrawling her name artistically across the card, Diana was secretly delighted. She had a lot to thank Sky for – their reruns had relaunched her career a few years back and she had been inundated with offers. Felicity had been dancing a jig for a while but the work had dried up now and Diana couldn't wait to get back to an attention-grabbing acting job. Thankfully, a fortune amassed when she was at her peak, plus an astonishingly large sum of money and property left to her by

Marco, kept Diana in the manner to which she had become more than accustomed. She liked to claim poverty, especially when it suited her, but in truth, she was extremely stable, financially speaking. Diana didn't *need* to work but she desperately wanted to.

As the fan left, gratefully clutching her autograph, Diana let out a sigh of contentment. Being recognised was such a pleasure, especially when she'd been out of the limelight for so long.

'You love it, don't you?' Felicity said softly as Maggie and Rachel left the table for a gossipy restroom visit. 'The attention, the adulation.' She saw that Diana was about to protest defensively and she held up a hand. 'Oh, I don't blame you, Dee, not one bit. But it makes me realise how much you must actually miss acting. I mean, being recognised is one thing but doing what you love, that's priceless, isn't it?'

Diana nodded, her eyes downcast. Felicity was right. She loved being famous and she adored signing autographs but acting was her real love. After Marco, acting had been the one thing that made her heart skip a beat.

And now she had neither, Diana thought unhappily.

Felicity put her hand out and covered Diana's. 'I know, it's hard. And that's why I'm talking to you about this part.' Drawing a script out of the huge handbag she always carried around with her, she placed it carefully on the table. 'Don't say no before you've read it, please. It's a play, not a TV part . . . due to be put on in the West End in a few months' time. It's a character part, a good one. It would be the perfect comeback role for you because it's so challenging, it will show everyone what you're made of – that you're capable of so much more than soft glamour roles.'

'On stage? A character part?' Diana looked horrified. Deeply offended, she demanded to know more. 'Is this all you're being sent for me now, roles where I get to be ugly?'

'You could never be ugly,' Felicity said sincerely. 'It's not that kind of part. Please read it and see what you think. Don't judge it until you've read it.'

Diana stood up, knowing she was on the brink of tears. 'I won't do it, Fliss,' she mumbled, gathering up her shopping bags, bags that were full of the anti-ageing products and expensive make-up she used to make herself feel better. 'I . . . I . . . just can't. I'm sorry . . . charge the lunch to me and say goodbye to the girls for me, would you?'

Diana hurried out of Harvey Nichols, leaving Felicity holding the rejected script. Outside, Diana called Angelo and demanded that he meet her at her flat. She wasn't above making a booty call or whatever the term was; all that mattered was soothing her wounded ego and feeling desirable again.

'Sorry we kept missing each other on the phone, but can you see now why I was so desperate to get hold of you?'

Cassia stared at Gena, unable to believe what she had just heard. The travel part of her role as food editor had always been thin on the ground, much to her consternation – until now. And this . . . this was an opportunity of a lifetime, something that didn't come along twice and a trip she would be mad to turn down. But the timing was terrible. Cassia stared at Gena's head of spirally blond curls.

'Are you absolutely sure we can't move this to another time?' she asked, shell-shocked. Gena had never made an exception for her because they were friends but Cassia hoped to God she might do it this once. It appeared not, however.

Gena shook her head emphatically. 'No way! He's doing this as a favour to me – well, to my darling hubby, actually. Rocco and Gianfranco go back a long way, you see, but Rocco is, as you're probably aware, tediously private. He never agrees to things like this and that's exactly why we need to get in quick and take him up on his offer. It took all weekend to arrange as it was,' Gena added, looking tired. 'Phone calls back and forth, discussions about time spans and God knows what else, which is why we didn't make it to Finn's party.' She refrained from adding that Rocco had agreed to the trip whilst under the influence of vintage champagne and good Chianti.

Cassia bit her lip, feeling anticipation rippling through her stomach. She had to do it; she simply had to. But how could she with a wedding to plan?

Gena frowned as she flipped through several messages on her phone before refocusing her attention on Cassia. 'This whole thing has been worked out around the opening of his Vegas restaurant in September, Cass, so we have to strike now.' She leant forward. 'That's the deal. You get to live and work alongside one of Italy's most famous chefs, Rocco Disanti – I mean, who wouldn't want to do that! He's one of the sexiest chefs around. Arrogant, granted, and most likely a horrendous tyrant in the kitchen, but who cares? And then there's the rest of his glamorous family. Those fame-hungry parents, the model sister – who's a spoilt little princess, by the way, but oddly likeable.' Gena munched distractedly on a biscotti. 'And there's the other one, the genial younger brother who dresses like something out of *The Godfather*. What's not to love?'

Cassia tried to push down a surge of excitement. 'How long would I have to go for?'

'Six to eight weeks max,' Gena informed her. 'The idea is that you would write a roving column about the food, the restaurant and, above all, about Rocco, and you could write lots of articles about the area while you were there too. We have the new online magazine which I think will be a brilliant way for you to provide pieces from Sorrento on a weekly basis and I have some wonderful ideas for some special features . . .'

Cassia listened with half an ear, her mind working overtime. Could she do it? She wanted to, more than anything. She bit her lip, thinking of her father. An orphan who had arrived in

England from southern Italy as a child, he had always wanted to look into his background and find out who his real family were. Cassia felt a pang as she realised he wouldn't be walking her down the aisle.

'Well?' Gena sounded impatient. 'What do you think?'

Cassia forced herself to concentrate. 'I really want to do it,' she admitted, feeling guilty about Finn and about their wedding. 'Not just because the chance to spend time with Rocco Disanti would be incredible, but because I could find out about my father's Italian heritage.' She leant forward. 'Could I do that, do you think? Look into his background, see if I could find out who his family were?'

'I don't see why not. Rocco is exceptionally busy so you're bound to have some free time but with all the work I have planned for you, you might end up being there for a bit longer if you want to go down that route.'

Cassia mulled the idea over. She couldn't imagine Finn being thrilled about her disappearing to Italy when they were planning their wedding, but the chance to feel reconnected to her father was irresistible. And Finn knew how much her father meant to her.

'I'd prefer it if it was only the six or eight weeks and I have no idea if I can get Finn on board . . .' Cassia breathed out jerkily, not sure she could commit. It was madness, surely? She couldn't just jet off to Sorrento like this . . . could she? Cassia wanted to do it so badly, mostly for her father, although she couldn't deny that the chance to get to know Rocco Disanti was an opportunity no food writer worth their salt would turn down.

One of Italy's most successful chefs, Rocco Disanti was as well-known for his moodiness as he was for his exquisite food and high-class restaurants. Notoriously private, Rocco was an enigma, a brooding and, some said, sexy man who rarely conducted interviews with anyone, let alone allowed a journalist to live in his family's home and spend time in his restaurants. Rocco must be a very loyal friend to Gena's husband.

'Nice ice,' Gena commented, nodding at Cassia's engagement ring. 'Very Finn, tasteful and classic.'

Cassia smiled. 'I know. I think he was nervous, you know. He'd planned the whole thing to the letter and then he ended up dragging me on to the stage and blurting out his speech on impulse.' Her face fell. 'I really hope he's going to be all right about me going to Italy.'

'Of course he will be. Finn worships the ground you walk on, so even if he's a bit disappointed at first, I'm sure he'll come round.' Gena eyed her friend fondly. Despite her conservative appearance, Cassia was a passionate character and her sensual writing style proved it. Gena was absolutely certain Cassia was the right person to get close to Rocco and, delighted as she was about the engagement, she hoped it wouldn't stop her from making the trip. The alternative was Pete and besides him not looking as sensational as Cassia did, Gena couldn't imagine his sarcastic style enticing Rocco to open up about his cooking and his restaurants.

'Well, what do you think?' she asked, determined to pin Cassia down. 'This is all about getting to know Rocco the chef and, hey, if you can find out more about your father at the same time, this has to be the best opportunity for you.'

Cassia smiled, knowing Gena would also benefit enormously from her moving to Italy for a few weeks. It would be a serious scoop for *Scrumptious* magazine to get up close and personal to a chef who had, until now, been loath to talk to any English magazines.

'I'll do it,' she said decisively, standing up. 'I don't know how I'll do it, but count me in.'

'Really?' Gena looked ecstatic. 'That's brilliant news! This is going to be great for *Scrumptious* magazine, and for you too, Cassia; I just know it.' She gesticulated wildly, something she had picked up from her Italian husband. 'And you can always discuss weddings with Rocco's sister Aurelia. She's about to marry that gorgeous Aussie model she's been dating for the past few years.'

Cassia arched a brow, not sure Aurelia Disanti would want to discuss her dazzling wedding plans with the likes of her.

'Well, apart from the fact that the trip clashes spectacularly with everything else in my life, this is great,' she said, allowing herself to feel happy about it for a moment. 'Thanks, Gena, I really appreciate the opportunity.'

Leaving the room, Cassia's mind was buzzing. Not only did she have to convince Finn that going to Sorrento for the next few weeks was the 'best thing that could have happened', she had to persuade his family – Grace, in particular – that she could still organise a wedding when she was hundreds of miles away.

Cassia gulped. She couldn't see her prospective mother-in-law supporting this idea, not one little bit. If Grace had thought she was an unsuitable wife for Finn before now, this latest news was bound to tip her over the edge.

Chapter Three

Rocco bent his dark head over the veal dish and inhaled the delicious aromas. *Vitello tonnato* was an unusual but famous Italian dish which combined meat and fish. The veal, usually topside tied into a sausage shape, should be tenderly poached for a few hours in a seasoned white wine liquor, before being sliced then covered in a tart mayonnaise containing tuna, capers and gherkins.

'The veal needs to be sliced more thinly,' Rocco commented, inspecting the meat with a fork. 'And the sauce . . .' He tasted it again, his brow furrowed. He glanced at his watch discreetly; Stefania was heading back to Rome shortly. 'The sauce is almost there, Antonio, but it needs more capers. And . . . a little more fresh parsley, perhaps. We might even add a few anchovies as these capers aren't as salty as our usual ones. But apart from that . . .' He kissed his fingertips. 'Superb, Antonio. That can go on next week's menu.'

'Very good, chef.' Antonio nodded respectfully, withdrawing the dish with obvious relief. Rocco Disanti was a tough boss to work for because his standards were so exacting, but Antonio had never learnt so much in his life. He loved presenting new dishes for the Disanti's Sorrento menu, but he also dreaded it because he hated disappointing Rocco, who contrary to popular assumption did not lose his temper in a spectacular display of waving arms and rapid-fire abuse. He was more likely to become cold and distant when displeased, an icy withdrawal that Antonio, along with the rest of the restaurant staff who hung on Rocco's every word with slavish devotion, tried desperately to avoid. Watching Rocco command his team with an almost sexual power, Antonio sighed and wished he had half Rocco's charisma.

'More fresh porcini . . . remember, the risotto must be meaty, and deliciously earthy,' Rocco said, moving around the kitchen as his olive-green eyes expertly assessed each work station. 'And make sure the Parmesan is added at the last minute, please, with just a touch of black pepper.'

Silvana, a plain, earnest twenty-year-old trainee sous-chef who had relocated from Sicily for the chance to work with Rocco, stared at him as though he was a choice dish she couldn't wait to devour. She blushed and grabbed a handful of porcini and stirred them into the glossy batch of rice.

Rocco, more concerned with the storm damage to the west wing of the main restaurant, didn't even notice Silvana's adoration. Mostly affecting the exterior, the storm had caused roof tiles to come down and there were several patches on the walls needing attention.

'What about the desserts?' he asked Antonio distractedly. He glanced around the seating area, transfixed, as ever, by its beauty. The sumptuous art deco furnishings made for a sophisticated yet relaxing atmosphere and the wide, sweeping archways, topped with the magnificent frescoed ceiling, were a constant talking point. The lighting greatly affected the overall interior, with natural sunlight giving the restaurant a golden, dappled feel, while the blue-black evening light and soft lamps positioned high up near the ceiling created a romantic, almost starry effect. The outside tables and the ones positioned by the windows were the most sought-after, affording diners awe-inspiring views of the distant coastline.

Antonio cleared his throat. 'I was thinking of a blood-orange soufflé,' he said hesitantly, not sure if Rocco would approve of a dessert that was more traditionally associated with France. 'And we've had several requests for *pasticcio agli agrume*, the meringue pie with the citrus custard. Also, I wondered if an almond rice pudding might be . . .'

Listening with one ear to Antonio's descriptions, Rocco wondered where his family were. His grandmother Sofia was in attendance, dressed in black as she had been since her husband Nico died. She was efficiently prepping the evening staff on that night's menus as well as updating them on any high-profile clientele who had tables booked. Rocco thanked God she liked rolling her sleeves up and mucking in. Still, he did think her enthusiasm seemed to be waning of late. It would be almost undetectable to someone who didn't know her as well as he did, but he was sure something was up. Her twinkling green eyes had been lacklustre for the past few months and that wasn't like her.

But where was Raffaelo? Rocco looked round for his younger brother. A big hairy brute of a man with a genial smile and dazzling manners, Raffaelo was in charge of maintenance and security at the restaurant but he often seemed preoccupied, or even absent, despite there being an awful lot to do in order to get the place back to its best. In addition to the outside damage, the storm had also cracked an internal window which needed replacing immediately.

Rocco had offered to train Raffaelo as a chef but his brother had no interest in food, apart from eating it; he preferred to use his hands for manual labour. Rocco often wondered if Raffaelo resented his own success, but he had never detected so much as a hint of jealousy in his brother's demeanour.

'Aurelia!' Rocco yelled, catching sight of his sister skipping through the restaurant with her arms full of glossy magazines. She halted guiltily, realising she couldn't escape, and Rocco turned to Antonio. 'The desserts sound good, but the soufflé . . .' He paused and Antonio's mouth twitched with regret.

'I like it,' Rocco said unexpectedly. 'As long as we use semolina and the Moro blood orange, the one from Sicily. It is both bitter and sweet, which will offset the richness of the soufflé and it will give it an authentic Italian flavour. Very good.' He dismissed his chef with a polite nod and greeted Aurelia curtly.

'Where have you been? You promised to help out with the promotion of the Vegas restaurant but I haven't seen you in here for a fortnight.'

Aurelia's lip curled childishly. 'Oh, don't be mean, Rocco, you know I've been busy with my modelling.'

Rocco scoffed and tweaked the magazines in her arms, noting that they were nearly all wedding-related. 'Your absences have nothing to do with your assignments and we both know that. It's this wedding of yours that's stopping you from fulfilling your promise.' He pulled a face. 'Perhaps you shouldn't have fired your wedding planner.'

'Oh, so now it's the guilt trip?' Aurelia protested, hands on hips. Her stance was cocky but her trembling lip made her look younger than her nineteen years. 'That wedding planner was a disgrace, she couldn't get a thing right and she kept telling me I couldn't have my dream wedding. Outrageous! And for your information, my modelling career is very demanding. My latest shoot is in the grounds of the estate . . . Grandmother agreed to it,' she added hastily, before Rocco could ask. It was partly true; her grandmother had agreed to the idea in principle, provided Rocco was in favour of it, but Aurelia had conveniently forgotten that part of the deal.

Absolutely ravishing with long, dark curls, deceptively innocent-looking green eyes and a mouth the colour of crumpled pink rose petals, Aurelia, being the only girl in the family, was horribly spoilt. Very much used to getting her own way and her mother's daughter to a T, she thought nothing of pouting, cajoling or turning on the tears to get her own way. On cue, she widened her eyes angelically.

'Rocco, my favourite brother, I thought you'd be pleased for me. I'm marrying Dino, the love of my life.' She twirled a dark curl on her finger and gestured to the magazines. 'Don't you understand that I want my wedding in Capri to be the most perfect, beautiful day ever? Don't you realise that the press will be out in full force to take photos and talk about every last detail, from the designers we're wearing to the colour scheme we choose?'

Grudgingly realising this was probably true because the media treated his beautiful sister like Italian royalty, Rocco nonetheless felt exasperated. It was all very well her focusing on her wedding but who was going to take care of the publicity for the new establishment? He had scant time on his hands as it was and short of hiring someone else, which would take up even more of his time, he had no idea who he could rely on. No one in the family, it appeared – apart from his grandmother, that is, and he couldn't very well expect her to do more than she already did at her age.

'I thought you were getting married here, in Sorrento,' Rocco said with a frown.

She flapped a hand. 'Yes, yes, we will marry in the Church of St Francis, with a ceremony in the cloister.' The famous Chiostro Di San Francesco was often used for musical concerts and art exhibitions. 'But then we will all travel to Capri for the reception.'

Rocco shook his head in wonder. Only Aurelia would want to marry in one location and then ferry her no doubt enormous guest list to an island for the reception.

'I have a copy of that English magazine you were talking about the other day,' Aurelia interjected, taking the opportunity to distract Rocco from her unfulfilled promise. '*Scrumptious*, that was the one, wasn't it?' She tugged the magazine out of the collection under her arm and handed it over. 'There's a picture on page ten of that journalist who might be coming here.' Aurelia's expression was openly despairing. 'She's rather frumpy, if you ask me, and a little overweight, too.'

Rolling his eyes at the shallow comment, Rocco flipped the magazine open to page ten. He frowned; far from the dowdy, fat girl Aurelia had just described, Cassia Marini was, in fact, rather gorgeous. Not traditionally pretty or stick-thin like Aurelia, but she was unusual-looking and rather exotic – very Italian, in fact. And far from being fat, she was curvaceous, like a movie star from the fifties.

Rocco shrugged. He didn't care what this journalist looked like; he was more concerned with how on earth he was going to find the time to chat to her and give her 'inside access' or whatever he had drunkenly promised Gianfranco and Gena on the phone.

'Who is that?' Stefania asked, appearing out of nowhere and coiling herself round Rocco. Leaning over his shoulder, she inhaled his aftershave, wishing she didn't have to go back to Rome. She glanced at the magazine without real interest before giving Aurelia a brief smile. The two women had little in common and weren't exactly friends but they were civil to one another, at least.

'It's Cassia Marini,' Rocco informed Stefania. 'She's the food writer I mentioned might be joining us here.'

Stefania assessed the photograph critically, her eyes lingering on Cassia's shapely hips. 'She clearly enjoys her food a little too much. How long will she be here for? And how much of your time is she going to take up?'

Rocco flipped the magazine shut impatiently. He made allowances for bitchiness when it came to Aurelia because she was his sister as well as being rather immature, but he detested it when Stefania behaved that way. Hiding a smile at Stefania's obvious possessiveness, Aurelia took advantage of the moment and slipped away.

'I couldn't be less interested in her looks, Stefania,' Rocco commented with a frown. 'Walk with me to the kitchen,' he instructed in a chilly voice. 'I need to check that all the fresh produce orders have been set up.'

Aware that she had annoyed Rocco in some way, Stefania sulkily hurried to keep up with him. She didn't like the idea of any woman occupying Rocco's time, even if she was a journalist; Rocco was hard enough to pin down as it was and Stefania had high hopes of convincing him to open a restaurant in Rome once the massive Vegas eaterie was completed.

'The journalist will be here for no more than a couple of months,' Rocco said in a more conciliatory tone. 'She's been tasked with getting to know the "real me", whatever that means. Vegas like their chefs to be very visible, very much part of the brand.' Rocco shrugged. 'This is the best way for me to publicise myself as the face of the company. And promote the Vegas restaurant. *Scrumptious* magazine is linked to an American publication and since the online version has been launched, Americans can't get enough of it. The food writer will then be present for the opening in Vegas to report back on it.'

'Why don't you just let her move into your apartment?' Stefania threw back, her hands on her hips. 'You're clearly excited about her arrival.'

Rocco lost patience. 'You're being ridiculous.'

Well-known for her temper, she exploded. '*Ridiculous?* I'm being *ridiculous*? What, because you're going to let some … some fat English food writer move in here to spend time with you?' She grabbed the closest thing and hurled it all over him. There was a shocked gasp around the kitchen as the dish crashed to the floor and broke loudly on the tiled floor. Staff gaped at Rocco, who was now covered in Antonio's veal and tuna dish, mayonnaise and capers sliding greasily down his Armani suit.

Realising she had gone too far, Stefania flounced out of the kitchen before Rocco could react.

His cheek twitching furiously, Rocco took the cloth a dumbfounded Antonio handed him and wiped his suit down. Too professional to show how livid he was in front of his staff, Rocco licked his finger and gave his sous-chef a tight smile.

'Definitely needs more capers,' he asserted, heading towards the door.

Once out of the kitchen, Rocco paused, looking down at his ruined suit angrily. Something really had to be done about Stefania; the question was, what? Did he need to end the relationship before it got any further out of hand? Or was the fact that she was the only woman who had interested him for this long a sign that they had a deep enough bond to last?

Rocco had no idea but he did know Stefania was likely to become even more troublesome once the food writer arrived. Letting out a heavy sigh and wishing he could head off on his motorbike to ease his stress levels, he tore off his sauce-stained suit jacket and ditched it in a nearby bin.

'There you are!'

Finn wrapped his arms round Cassia, struck as ever by how tiny her waist was. Clutching a cake box, she was wearing a sundress in a shade of nondescript beige but the simplicity of the dress couldn't completely hide her curves. He smiled. He liked her in neutral shades; bright colours offended him. Finn realised he often forgot how staggeringly beautiful Cassia was; he had seen her almost every day for the past eight years they had been together so he guessed he might not always voice his thoughts. Noticing she seemed anxious, Finn forgot to say how great she looked.

'Don't worry about my parents,' he murmured, jerking his head in the direction of the sitting room. 'They're thrilled.' He kissed her nose. 'I can't believe we'll be married soon. It's crazy, isn't it? Mother can't wait to discuss all the plans tonight.'

Cassia kissed Finn back, a feeling of trepidation stealing over her. She had barely seen Finn over the past week and he had been so obsessed with a case at work, she hadn't had a chance to discuss the secondment to Italy with him. Wearing a smart suit with a tailored shirt, Finn appeared to be still in work mode now, his phone in his hand and his clear blue eyes focused. Cassia wondered if he ever switched off; he always seemed to be thinking about work. His phone rang day and night and unless they were actually in bed, Finn would invariably answer. She couldn't criticise him for it, however, because she was just as guilty of absorbing herself completely in her career.

Speaking of which . . . Feeling the need to get it over and done with, Cassia grabbed his arm as he headed in the direction of the sitting room. 'Finn, wait. I have some news.'

'Oh?' Finn gazed down at her, a smile tugging at the corners of his mouth. 'You look very serious. Why do I think I'm not going to like whatever it is?'

She looked regretful. 'You probably won't.' Filling him in quickly about the secondment to Italy, she watched his face closely in an attempt to gauge his reaction. Apart from a slight frown furrowing his brow, it was impossible to guess at Finn's inner thoughts, but at least he wasn't exploding. But then, Cassia reflected, when did Finn ever explode?

'I know it's horrendous timing and I really hope your mother doesn't hate me for it, but it's such a wonderful opportunity, not only to spend time with a top chef and write my column from Italy, but also just to . . . be in Italy. You know how much I've always wanted to look into my Italian heritage. My father never got anywhere when he tried to find out more and I promised him I'd try for him at some point. It's . . . it's so important to me.'

Finn stared at her, not sure what to say. He knew Cassia's last comment hadn't been an attempt at emotional blackmail because she wasn't that way inclined but it did make it harder for him to be negative in any way. He was aware Cassia had had a deep bond with her father and his death had hit her hard; this trip would be incredibly significant for her. Still, he wondered if it could be rescheduled and, tentatively, he said so out loud.

'No, the secondment is set in stone because of the opening of the Vegas restaurant. Trust me, that was one of the first things I asked Gena.' Cassia chewed her lips, suffused with guilt, and reached out to touch his hair. 'But I promise I can still give our wedding my full attention, even in Sorrento. Italy's pretty sophisticated, you know, they have fax machines and everything.' She grinned at him endearingly, hoping he knew she was only teasing to lighten the moment.

Finn didn't smile but mostly because he was mulling over the news. Cassia heading off to Italy for six weeks or so wasn't great in itself, and now that their wedding was on the horizon, it was even more disappointing. About to say they were going to need a serious rethink, Finn caught the expression in Cassia's dark eyes and realised how desperately she wanted to go to Italy. He didn't have the heart to tell her it was a bad idea. He had a feeling his mother was going to take a dim view of the situation but she was just going to have to deal with it. Also, privately, he hoped the trip might extinguish once and for all the latent wanderlust he had always suspected Cassia harboured.

'Of course you should go,' he told her breezily. 'I'll miss you like crazy, of course, but I know how much this means to you.'

Cassia reached up and kissed him. 'Oh, Finn, thank you! I know this is the worst possible timing but I'll make it work, I promise.' She nuzzled his neck, inhaling the Boss aftershave he always wore which smelt reassuringly Finn-like. 'I can't believe how well you've taken the news.'

'Don't get me wrong, I'm gutted,' Finn told her honestly. 'But it's only a couple of months, worst case, right? And with my mother's help, I'm sure we can still arrange the wedding for September. If that's what you want, that is?'

Cassia nodded emphatically. 'Of course it is. I can't believe this has come up just as we got engaged, but I truly believe we can work round it.' She had toyed with asking Finn to postpone the wedding but had decided against it. She simply couldn't find it in herself to let Finn down; besides, she really wanted the wedding to go ahead as planned.

Finn felt glum at the thought of barely seeing his fiancée for the next few weeks, but he didn't show it. Greeting his parents, he quickly told them about the trip to Italy.

Cassia, expecting Grace to criticise her judgement, was wholly unprepared for the strength of her reaction.

'You can't be serious!' Grace shot out of her armchair, her chilly blue eyes blazing for once. Bristling in a fern-green twinset and a sensible, flared skirt in off-white, every fibre in her body radiated disapproval.

Henry, wearing a smart blue shirt that complemented his red-blond hair, frowned at the harshness of Grace's tone and put down his paper. Glancing at Cassia, he could see how uncomfortable she felt and he shot her an encouraging smile. Grateful for Henry's support, however silent, Cassia swallowed. 'I know it's not ideal,' she began, but she was unceremoniously cut off before she could finish her sentence.

'Not ideal?' Grace echoed in disbelief. The look of horror on her face suggested Cassia had decided to go on a pilgrimage to Brazil for a year, rather than a work assignment in Europe for six weeks. 'There is a wedding to plan, Cassia! How on earth will you organise that from Italy?'

'They're very sophisticated there now,' Finn offered mildly, winking at Cassia. 'They have fax machines and everything.'

Grace looked unamused. 'Very funny, Finn. Fax machines

aren't the issue here. There are guests to invite, venues to book. It was a tight timeframe to begin with and now we're looking at a very tricky situation indeed. These details need to be taken care of immediately.'

Cassia felt Grace was being overly dramatic. 'I have assured Finn that I am absolutely committed to organising our wedding and that I will devote myself to giving it the attention it deserves.' She looked at Grace pleadingly, wishing she had been able to warm to her more. 'It's my wedding day, Grace. I want it to be utterly perfect, like any bride-to-be, so please believe me when I say that I will do everything in my power to make it incredibly special.'

Grace pursed her lips sourly. Cassia really was the limit. How on earth could she even think of jetting off to Italy at such an inappropriate time? It underlined every concern she had about Cassia and proved without a shadow of a doubt that she was more focused on her work than her personal life. Finn might be a workaholic, but he was allowed to be, Grace thought, gazing at him through absurdly rose-tinted glasses. All he was doing was working hard to provide a stable home life. Besides, weddings weren't a man's concern, were they?

Reading her thoughts and feeling defensive, Finn stepped in. 'Mother, this isn't just a work trip for Cassia; she's going to have a chance to find out more about her father's Italian heritage. You know how disappointed Marco was when he couldn't find out about his parents.' Finn slipped his arm round Cassia's shoulder. 'Staying in Sorrento is going to give her the opportunity to really look into it.'

Grace sat back, pursing her lips. She felt even more antagonistic towards Cassia after Finn's speech. She could hardly be too critical about Cassia's decision to go to Italy if part of the reason was to do with discovering more about her beloved father. She felt momentarily thwarted by the emotional curve ball but she still didn't approve of Cassia's decision – or the timing.

Henry cleared his throat. 'Aren't we all getting a bit over-excited here? It's only Italy, not Outer Mongolia.' Ignoring Grace's frosty glare, he carried on, even though he knew he would be guaranteed a tongue-lashing later on. 'I'm sure Cassia has a good idea of the sort of wedding she'd like, even now. Am I right?' Giving Cassia a convivial nod, he widened his eyes to encourage her to convince Grace she already had some plans underfoot.

Luckily, Cassia was able to do just that. She wasn't one of those girls who had a teenage scrapbook packed full of dress designs and colour schemes but she knew her own mind, so she had a very vivid idea of the kind of wedding day she'd always dreamt of. Also, realising Grace might put her on the spot, Cassia had taken the precaution of buying a shockingly expensive stack of wedding magazines the day after her chat with Gena and she had spent the night reading them from cover to cover with the ferocious focus of someone studying for an exam.

Seeing that Cassia was about to provide her thoughts about the wedding, Grace grabbed a nearby notepad and pen, preparing, with barely disguised disdain, to make notes.

'I think our wedding should be small but stylish,' Cassia started, glancing at Finn for moral support. 'A meaningful ceremony in a beautiful building, nothing stuffy or too old-fashioned, you know? A small wedding with a real sense of romance and style is the way I see it. Sort of *Pride and Prejudice* meets *Sex and the City*.'

Catching Grace's scornful expression, Cassia hurried to explain. 'Carrie and Big, you know? Er . . . that is . . . classic, with a few designer touches. Simple, romantic, but incredibly sophisticated.' Swallowing, she valiantly forged ahead. 'A simple colour scheme, maybe cream and old gold with touches of deep red – or purple, maybe? Not too many flowers but a hand-tied bouquet of something classic . . . roses and peonies, I think.

Not too much pink, it's not really my thing. And I've seen these gorgeous low table pieces with trailing greenery . . . and a vintage, ivory MG to arrive in would be lovely . . .' her voice petered out as Grace's blue eyes turned flinty.

'I had something rather grander in mind,' Grace offered, her tone challenging. 'A traditional church ceremony followed by a large reception with Pimm's or soft drinks would be wonderful. No canapés but some upmarket nibbles – little game pies, tiny cold soups, perhaps.' She nodded, warming to her theme. 'I was thinking along the lines of an old hotel with clean lines and plenty of natural light, something period but newly renovated, perhaps.'

Cassia's heart sank in distress. Grace had just described the wedding from hell. A church? Neither of them were religious. And a newly renovated period hotel? How grotesque. Cassia glanced desperately at Finn. She'd envisaged crisp, fruity champagne cocktails, not Pimm's and some interesting canapés, not something snobby no one wanted to eat. Small details but ones that already seemed to be slipping from her grasp.

Grace started making notes of her own, crossing through Cassia's suggestions one by one. Cream and old gold as a colour scheme? Hardly suitable. No, a more fitting colour scheme would be . . . perhaps green and yellow? And a bouquet of roses with peonies? *Really?* How very . . . middle class. Grace gave a slight shiver and made a mental note to persuade Cassia that the stiffly formal but opulent, overarm bouquet of Calla lilies with steel grass she'd already discussed with a high-class florist in town would be far more appropriate.

As for low table pieces, absolutely not. Tall vases with a single, sparse lily would do nicely. Grace realised she was going to have to take a firm hand with Cassia and suddenly seeing the advantage to her prospective daughter-in-law being out of the country for most of the wedding planning, Grace decided to take another tack.

'We have a large family and I would hate to offend anyone when it comes to the guest list. But I can easily handle that side of things – unless you feel able to sort it all out from Sorrento?'

Cassia hesitated. She didn't want to offend anyone either, least of all Grace, but she didn't want the guest list running into the hundreds. 'Maybe you can let us know who you'd like to invite and we can take it from there?' she suggested, pleased when Finn slid his arm round her waist. At least they were presenting some sort of united front. She had hoped Finn would chip in and back up her ideas but she supposed he hadn't really thought too much about the details yet.

Grace nodded pleasantly, able to be benevolent now that she'd realised how she could work the new situation to her advantage. Once Cassia was safely ensconced in Sorrento, she would take hold of the wedding plans with a steely grip and there would be no more talk of cream roses and small guest lists.

'There, that wasn't too difficult, was it?' Finn smiled, oblivious to the tension in the room. 'I'm so glad we've got that all worked out because I really just want to look forward to the big day and not think about how much I'm going to miss you over the next few weeks.'

Henry got to his feet. 'Hear, hear!' he boomed heartily, giving Cassia a hug. She handed him the cake box, apologising for bringing a shop-bought present. 'Sorry, Henry; you know Jules is the one with the light hand when it comes to cakes.'

Cassia wondered about Grace's abrupt about-turn; she was not at all convinced by her sudden acquiescence. Grace clearly planned to use her absence to impose her own ideas on the wedding. Cassia felt aggrieved but she certainly wasn't going to mention it to Finn who seemed totally blind to his mother's faults. But she couldn't help feeling sidelined already. And what hope did she have once she was away in Sorrento?

*

Jules picked her way through the throng of handsome tennis players. The event had been a triumph so far; everyone had a drink in their hands, some delicious and deliberately down-to-earth food was doing the rounds and the entertainment – a sexy songstress wearing a glittering, crotch-level dress – was wooing the crowds in breathy tones.

Thank God for that, thought Jules, letting out a sigh of relief as she checked that the decorations were in the correct tennis club colours and that no outraged vegetarians were exclaiming over their carnivorous meals. Her boss had advised her that the event at the club, a charity event for top coaches and tennis executives, was absolutely her last chance at holding on to her job, and scared of finding herself unemployed, Jules had for once put an enormous amount of effort into the arrangements, checking every minuscule detail. She was amazed at what she had managed to achieve in a relatively short space of time but she wasn't sure she could pull it off regularly. Organisation wasn't her best quality and she had to work exceptionally hard to remember everything. She sighed, wishing she could find a job that suited her, but since her skills lay mostly in the domestic arena, she couldn't seem to find a good fit for herself. Spinning round, Jules found herself nose to nose with Dom Sunderland.

'Hello, you,' she exclaimed, blushing slightly as his chiselled jaw came into view. 'How lovely to see you again.' Wearing a dark, silk-lined suit that made the most of his well-muscled biceps and thighs, with a hyacinth-blue tie that seemed to make his eyes even more attractive, Finn's younger brother epitomised the image of a fit young sportsman in his prime.

Louisa had told her that Dom had hardly been in the country this year; his tennis schedule, now that he had moved out of junior events and into the adult arena, was apparently insane. He spent his life jetting to exotic locations, playing in tournaments and doing whatever he could to push his world ranking into the top fifty. Jules knew Dom was fast gaining attention as the next big thing in tennis and she couldn't help feeling rather over-awed and flustered in his presence.

'I didn't realise you'd be here tonight,' she added, her eyes taking in his broad shoulders.

Enjoying her not-so-discreet scrutiny, Dom gave a casual shrug and sedately sipped the one glass of champagne he planned to drink that night. Knowing he was under the watchful eye of his coach, as well as being rather out of favour right now, he planned to toe the line – at least until he managed to make his excuses and leave.

'My coach insisted. These charity events are very much part of the lifestyle and one has to do one's bit, don't you think?' Jules looked very pretty tonight with her blond hair clipped up and her cheeks stained with pink, Dom thought, and her slender legs looked good in a black dress that was slightly too short for her role as event organiser.

'Oh, absolutely.' Jules nodded. Truthfully, she was clueless when it came to tennis, or any sport for that matter, but she wasn't about to tell Dom that. 'How have your recent matches gone? Louisa said you've had some important ones this month.'

'Not too badly, actually.' Dom inclined his head, attempting modesty and failing. 'Two quarter-finals and one slightly disappointing performance, but I was playing one of the best seeds in the world, with a recurring ankle injury, so there wasn't much I could do.'

Casually, Dom mentioned a very well-known player who won almost every match he played, enjoying the way Jules's eyes widened at the name-drop. Dom smoothly glossed over the fact that he had arrived late because he'd been with a stripper he'd picked up the night before, as well as playing with a crippling hangover, details he knew wouldn't do him any favours in a public arena. His coach had been furious with him and he'd released a hasty statement blaming a pulled ligament for Dom's shockingly poor match.

'That's brilliant!' Forgetting she was essentially staff, Jules threw her arms round Dom's neck and planted a kiss on his cheek. 'Good for you, you must be thrilled by your quarter-final places.'

Dom squeezed her waist. 'I really am. And of course it proves to all those doubters out there that I actually have some sort of talent.' He raised an eyebrow. 'Including my mother. I don't think she ever thought I'd make something of myself – unlike Finn, of course.' Dom looked down into his empty champagne glass. 'Rather disappointing when your own parents don't believe in you but I suppose the best thing you can do is prove them wrong.'

Hearing a bitter edge to his voice, Jules warmed to him even more. She held on to his shoulder deliberately for a moment. 'I know the feeling, my father never thought I'd amount to much either.' She glanced round at the tennis club, remembering she was working. 'And to be fair, organising these sorts of events isn't really too impressive, is it?'

'Oh, I don't know.' Dom smiled, sensing a kindred spirit in Jules for the first time. 'I think you've done a wonderful job.' Spotting a shapely redhead spilling out of her satin minidress, he took advantage of Jules's downcast eyes to shoot the girl – surely a glamour model – a flirtatious wink.

'Thank you, it's one of my better efforts,' Jules said, not noticing. Absurdly attracted to him, she gave him one of her most alluring smiles. 'I'm glad I'm not the only one who lives in the shadow of a sibling,' she continued. 'I've spent my life listening to my father going on about how amazing Cassia is, so I know how wearing you must find it.'

Dom gave an ambivalent shrug. Truthfully, he wasn't par-ticularly worried about his mother focusing on Finn; her intense pride and admiration for his older brother had always allowed him a great deal of freedom, freedom to chase pretty girls indiscriminately and devote himself to tennis, which basically meant he lived the life of Riley. Besides which, his black sheep status meant his misdemeanours were merely sighed over whilst his more impressive achievements attracted surprised applause. The pressures on Finn to be perfect were immense and Dom couldn't be more relieved that he was able to live his own life without the weight of such gruelling expectation.

'What do you think about Cassia going to Italy?' he asked, changing the subject. He had been surprised when Finn told him about the Sorrento trip but Cassia had always been committed to her job and with the added attraction of discovering more about her father, he could see why she would want to grab the opportunity with both hands. He couldn't help wondering if Finn minded more than he was letting on, but he guessed his brother might be hoping the trip would be a final swansong before Cassia settled down to the business of being a corporate wife.

Jules shook her head. 'I think it's ridiculous! She has a wedding to plan, for God's sake. Why on earth would she want to jet off to the back of beyond and write about some moody chef?'

Dom wasn't sure Sorrento was the back of beyond, exactly, but he could tell by Jules's lifted chin that it would be pointless to correct her. He wondered why Jules took every opportunity to lay into Cassia, especially when her words didn't always ring true. Dom was sure he saw a flicker of guilt in Jules's eyes whenever she criticised her sister but she did a good job of acting as though she couldn't stand the sight of her.

Seeing one of his friends making furtive gestures about a couple of girls who were clearly up for some fun, Dom hesitated. His sister Louisa had been bombarding him with texts hinting that he should ask Jules out but he wasn't sure it was a good idea. Jules was exceptionally pretty and he fancied her, but he couldn't decide if she was a one-night stand kind of a girl or not. She behaved that way, but from what Louisa had told him, Jules was keen to settle down and he wasn't sure he wanted to get involved with anyone right now.

'Oh, I think I need to pitch in with coffee duties,' Jules said crossly, noticing that the waitresses were suddenly rather thin on the ground. She guessed a few of them had sloped off with the players.

'That's a shame,' Dom said, leaning in and brushing a kiss against her ear. 'I was hoping we could spend some more time together.'

Jules beamed, thinking his blue eyes were like Finn's, only brighter. 'That would have been lovely. Another time, perhaps?'

Dom nodded vaguely, his eyes already darting around the room to see if the glamour model had left yet. Tennis wasn't a sport that attracted such women, usually; it tended to appeal to middle-class society girls and their mothers, who were admittedly often up for a party (sometimes together) but Dom fully intended to pursue gorgeous lingerie promoters whenever possible. Jules could wait.

Reluctantly Jules headed into the kitchen. She re-emerged with a pot of hot coffee and proceeded to fill cups with a bright smile in place. Looking up, she paused as she noticed Dom leaving with a curvaceous redhead in a tight, corseted dress that barely covered her g-string. Her spirits plummeting, Jules guessed she'd missed the boat with Dom – at least, as far as tonight was concerned.

'What the hell do you think you're doing?' yelled a red-faced tennis coach as he leapt out of his seat with wet trousers.

Realising she'd tipped scalding hot coffee all over the man's crotch, Jules put her hand over her mouth in horror. Crushed that Dom had chosen a busty airhead over her and certain she now faced unemployment, Jules did what she always did when the shit hit the fan and fled.

Smiling at a text from Finn wishing her good luck for her journey, Cassia couldn't believe she was actually going to Sorrento. Finn had never been keen to visit Italy. He preferred locations with more temperate climates and he wasn't especially into what he called 'cultural European' breaks so Cassia's love affair with Italy had always been a personal thing.

Hearing the doorbell, she stepped past the pile of luggage in her hallway and opened her front door, wondering who might be calling for her when her taxi driver was booked for later on.

'Oh good, I haven't missed you, darling,' Diana said, stepping over the threshold almost regally. Wearing a bright blue body-con dress that made the most of her slender figure, teamed with high heels with distinctive red soles, she looked far younger than her years, from a distance, at least. 'I couldn't remember what time your flight was, but I hoped I might catch you before you left.'

Cassia was puzzled. Her mother, as gushy as she could appear at times, was hardly the sentimental type and she had already phoned to wish her a safe journey.

'My cab will be here soon.' She gestured to her pile of luggage.

Diana chewed her lip. 'Yes, of course. Are you flying directly to Sorrento, darling? Does it have an airport? I can't remember. Or maybe Naples . . .' Her voice trailed away.

'I'm flying to Naples and being picked up there,' Cassia said, sitting on the edge of her sofa. 'Not my favourite thing, flying, but it has to be done. Mother, when you ramble like this,' she added more gently, 'it's because you're trying to find the words to say something. Just . . . say whatever it is and stop worrying about it.'

Diana nodded. Her eldest daughter knew her so well. 'Yes, yes, I must. Well, I wanted to say how happy your father would have been that you're making this trip.' Catching sight of a photograph of him on the wall nearby, she faltered. 'He . . . Marco would be very proud of you right now. As he always was of everything you did.'

Cassia's face lit up. Her beloved father, who had died some three years ago now, would definitely approve of her secondment to Italy. Not only would he see it as a chance for her to become more involved in food and travel writing – his absolute passion – but she knew he would also think of it as a great adventure. And for some reason, Cassia couldn't help thinking it was about time she had an adventure. She had no idea why she suddenly felt so stuck in her ways but this trip made her feel like she had in her late teens before Jules's personality change had knocked a sensible domino in her direction.

'I've arranged it with Gena that I can spend time looking into Dad's side of the family,' Cassia said, vaguely gesturing to the fridge in case her mother fancied her usual glass of chilled Chablis. 'He was told he was born in Sorrento, wasn't he?'

Diana shook her head at the offer of wine and smiled sadly. 'Yes, I think so.' A shadow of guilt crossed her face and she seemed lost in thought for a moment.

Cassia wondered what she was thinking. Her mother often looked remorseful when she talked about her father; it was something that had baffled Cassia for years and she had always been reluctant to press her mother about it, although she wasn't quite sure why. Her brow furrowed as she thought about her childhood. It had been a happy but rather strange existence, peppered with periods of utter bliss that were sometimes – and with increasing regularity as time went on – spoilt by furious arguments and noisy door-slamming.

Cassia could recall the moment when she had worked out that her parents were famous. It was her fourth birthday and she had been opening expensive presents from her parents' friends for almost two hours solid, watched by a heavily pregnant Diana and a doting Marco. Bookcases containing stacks of books written by Marco, as well as hundreds of his well-thumbed cookery books, sat alongside the Shakespeare plays and classic novels Diana would often be found immersed in.

The front doorbell had rung, jauntily signalling yet another delivery of elaborately wrapped gifts and Cassia had gleefully flung the door open, only to find herself almost blinded by flashbulbs as crowds of photographers went crazy. Yanking her back inside and slamming the door, Marco and Diana had exchanged shaky glances, concerned for their child's welfare.

'They probably want to find out when the baby is due,' Marco had said, putting a protective hand over Diana's swollen belly.

Turning away, Diana had looked stricken before bursting into emotional sobs that had seemed rather over the top in the circumstances. As innocuous as the incident had seemed to a four-year-old Cassia, that was when she had officially realised her parents were different from those of her friends, that in the eyes of the world's press and of overzealous fans, Marco and Diana, the glamorous English actress and the handsome Italian travel writer, whose joint offerings to the world beguiled and fascinated in equal measure, were perceived as public property.

Wishing she understood her parents – and their bizarre relationship – better, regardless of the fact that her father was now dead, Cassia glanced at her watch.

'Are you worried about Grace?' Diana asked suddenly, interrupting Cassia's reverie.

'In what way?'

Diana lifted her brows, her forehead remaining bizarrely smooth. 'The wedding plans, darling. I can imagine that woman being rather forceful when it comes to such things, and with you tucked away in Italy for however long, you could find yourself at a terrible disadvantage.'

Cassia pulled a rueful face. 'I'm only going to be there for about two months at the most, but . . . you're not wrong about Grace.' She quickly updated her mother about the recent meeting at the Sunderland household. 'Henry was very supportive as ever, but when it comes down to it, we all know Grace wears the trousers.' She shuddered. 'I think my plans for an intimate, classy wedding will go out of the window once Grace takes over.'

'Then I shall make it my business to keep her in check,' Diana said resolutely, her wide blue eyes utterly convincing. 'Don't look like that, darling,' she admonished, catching Cassia's doubtful expression. 'I can be quite influential when I want to be.'

Cassia peered out of the window and spotted her cab. 'I'm sure you can, but Grace is an absolute pro at this sort of thing. She puts the "F" in formidable, and that's an understatement.' She paused. 'If you're serious about fighting my corner, you might need these.' Cassia drew the notes she had made about her wedding out of her handbag and handed them over. 'I've discussed everything with Grace, but I don't think she was listening.'

Diana took them and decided she would rather like a glass of chilled Chablis, after all. She helped herself and quickly read the notes. 'Don't you worry about a *thing*, darling,' she assured her daughter confidently. 'You leave Grace to me. I totally see where you're coming from with your Carrie and Big-themed nuptials. I'll make sure you get your perfect day.'

Sceptical her capricious mother would be any sort of match for steely Grace, Cassia gathered up her luggage and, taking one last look around her apartment, left to catch her flight to Italy.

Forgetting her heartfelt promise to champion her eldest daughter's wedding preferences almost as soon as the door had closed, Diana settled down on Cassia's comfortable Conran sofa and flicked the TV on. Delighted to find a Sky channel showing reruns of an eighties sitcom she had featured in, Diana was soon lost in memories as she watched herself playing a beautiful femme fatale with bigger shoulder pads than Alexis Colby in *Dynasty*.

Chapter Four

Cassia climbed out of the car. The Amalfi coast, seen through the car window from the airport, was simply beautiful – breathtakingly so. Rising out of a stunning, turquoise sea and craggy cliffs, the villages and towns seemed to merge into one another, almost as if they had naturally evolved with the volcanic rocks they were nestled within. And Sorrento, full of brightly coloured houses, tiny boutiques and lively squares with Italians chatting over espresso, was a revelation. Bathed in sunshine and ruffled by a mild sea breeze that drifted off the clear, calm sea, it had the cool air of a bygone era. Cassia could just imagine Sophia Loren and Dean Martin strolling through the cobbled streets in the 1950s when Sorrento was *the* holiday resort of the moment, their glamour enhanced by their chic surroundings.

She remembered it from holidays with her family but she hadn't visited the area for some years. Turning to take in the view of Disanti's Sorrento, the famous restaurant, Cassia gasped. It was magnificent, and far more striking in real life than it looked in photographs. The creamy terracotta exterior with its surrounding statues, the scented orange and lemon groves that gave the restaurant a colourful, authentic backdrop and the breathtaking terrace . . .

Stunning didn't even begin to describe it, Cassia decided, helping the driver Rocco Disanti had sent to collect her haul her luggage out of the boot. The driver politely rejected her help and carried her luggage up to the main house.

The roof was dappled with late April sunshine, softening the edges and giving it a rosy glow, but it was an imposing building. She realised it must have several bedrooms, in addition to the extensive grounds which were filled with fruit trees. Inside the restaurant she could see staff hurrying around in preparation for the lunchtime service; but there was a precision to their movements, an almost military discipline to the organised speed with which they carried out their duties.

It's a different world, Cassia breathed to herself. The Disanti family were one of the wealthiest in Italy, traditional, influential and hot-blooded, by all accounts. Rocco, renowned as a chef and businessman, was also famous for bedding strings of beautiful women, although it seemed that for the past year he had only been seen with one woman, a stunning blonde. Possessing an icy temper and a keenness for privacy, Rocco apparently detested being gossiped about, which was going to make Cassia's job all the more difficult.

Looking up, she caught sight of a tall, tanned man with cropped, conker-brown hair heading towards her. Wearing sunglasses and an expensive-looking suit despite the warmth of the sun, the man appeared professional but deeply preoccupied. This must be the infamous Rocco Disanti. As he came closer, he removed his sunglasses and Cassia realised how striking he was. Intense, olive-green eyes framed by dark lashes, a sensual mouth and what looked like broad shoulders beneath the well-cut suit. Cassia knew she'd be lying if she said he was anything other than exceptionally good-looking, but he had an arrogant, distant air that was vaguely off-putting. She hoped he wasn't going to be difficult to work with.

'Cassia Marini?' he asked, holding his hand out. He smiled briefly and his eyes creased at the corners but it was fleeting.

'Rocco Disanti. How nice to meet you. I do hope you enjoy your stay here.'

Cassia took Rocco's hand, feeling it grasp her own warmly. He was speaking in rapid Italian and she hoped she was going to be able to keep up because she hadn't spoken a word of it since her father had died.

Catching sight of a man with a camera lurking nearby, Rocco's expression turned apologetic.

'Sorry,' he said in English, realising she was struggling to follow what he was saying. 'It is the press, they would like a photo of us both. I picked one of them and agreed to a photo – it's easier in the long run, otherwise we'll have crowds of them gathering at the door each day. Do you mind?'

Cassia gulped, thinking she probably looked hot and sweaty after her flight. 'I . . . er . . . I don't exactly look my best. But all right, I suppose I don't mind.' Unused to such scrutiny, she raked her fingers through her hair and straightened her dress self-consciously.

Rocco politely put his arm round her and turned on a smile. 'It's big news around here, you see,' he murmured as the photographer took a few shots. 'I don't usually let anyone shadow me and the press want to see who's managed to convince me to change my mind.'

Cassia couldn't help feeling that Rocco's warm hand on her shoulder was a little presumptuous; they had only just met, after all. Perhaps it was the Italian in him, she thought, or more likely he was simply a consummate professional. Rocco abruptly let his arm fall away when the cameraman had taken his shots, and Cassia realised the latter was the case. Realising she hadn't formally thanked him for letting her stay at the villa, she gave him what she hoped was a charming smile.

'I'm . . . er . . . I'm privileged to be here, Mr Disanti,' she attempted in rusty Italian. 'I hope I won't get under your feet too much.'

'It's Rocco and I'm sure you won't.' His expression suggested she'd be crazy to get in his way. Or perhaps he thought her Italian was painful; Cassia wasn't sure. 'Shall I show you around quickly?' Rocco remained pleasant but detached. 'Then you can get settled into your room in the main house.'

'That would be lovely,' she managed, bristling slightly. Clearly, he wasn't happy about her presence, however polite he was trying to be. She sighed. It was hard enough being away from home and from Finn, but if Rocco didn't even want her here, what was the point? She followed him up to the restaurant, noting the brooding hunch of his shoulders.

'I'll give you a quick history of the restaurant,' Rocco said, speaking in slow Italian so she could follow him.

Expecting him to look bored at this point as he had no doubt delivered the speech hundreds of times, Cassia was taken aback when Rocco became more and more impassioned as he talked about his grandfather and the legacy he had left behind. Mentally jotting down the key parts of his summary, Cassia couldn't help being mesmerised by his expressive hands and the bright spark of enthusiasm in his eyes. It was as if he had suddenly come alive. Although he was giving her a factual rundown of events, his creativity and passion for his life and his restaurant in Sorrento came through unapologetically and he possessed a fascinating restless quality that suggested pent-up energy. He paused, watching her.

Cassia realised she should say something. 'That's amazing . . . thank you. Listen, you . . . er . . . must forgive my efforts at speaking Italian,' she added hesitantly, trying to demonstrate that she had, at least, a passable accent. 'I used to chat with my father in Italian all the time, but I'm afraid I'm very much out of practice now . . . since he died. My father lived with various foster families, you see, but they always made an effort to ensure that he had Italian lessons. One family had an Italian grand-mother and she talked to my father constantly.' Cassia stuck to her original plan, even though she now realised it was going to be tough. 'If you don't mind, Mr Dis— er, Rocco, I really would like to stick to speaking Italian while I'm here. I promised myself I'd give it my best shot so I could get back into it, to honour my father, you know.'

Rocco shrugged, refraining from comment. Her Italian was clumsy in places, but he had to admit that her accent was good. He glanced at her discreetly as she took in the stunning vista of the restaurant. The photograph he had seen in *Scrumptious* magazine hadn't done her justice at all, Rocco realised. Her dark hair and slanted, deep brown eyes were far more exotic in person and her body was lusciously curved, giving the impression she had been poured into the conservative beige suit she was wearing. She rather resembled an exquisite figure from history, an empress from Roman times, perhaps, with her dewy skin and flowing, chocolate-hued hair held back with a simple comb.

Rocco shook himself and reminded himself that Cassia was there to infringe upon his time and personal space and that he couldn't care less what she looked like. He wished for the umpteenth time he had withdrawn his offer to Gena and he cursed himself for having such strict integrity when it came to promises.

'Disanti's Sorrento,' he announced, sweeping his hand to encompass the interior. 'As I said before, my grandfather, Nico, created the restaurant some seventy years ago, when he was very young – an incredible achievement, really. Of course, the Disanti family have always had money, but my grandfather was the first person to create a viable business. He was a self-taught chef and this was once a bistro, but it became a renowned restaurant once he had learnt to hone his skills.' Rocco gestured to the countryside. 'He also acquired land many years ago from a local family. After that, it was a case of making the most of the assets he had, and he fixed his sights on becoming one of the best chefs the world had ever seen.'

Cassia wasn't sure if Nico had achieved that, but Rocco certainly had. She looked up and gasped at the incredible frescoed ceiling. She fumbled for the Italian words she needed to describe how moved she was. 'Look at that, it's so beautiful. I can't imagine how people can concentrate on eating when they have something so sensational above their heads.' She realised she might have sounded rather dismissive of Rocco's culinary expertise and hurried to correct herself. 'Well, I'm sure they can if they're eating your amazing food, of course, but still . . .'

Rocco smiled briefly. 'Thank you. I hope you'll dine in the restaurant soon. I'd be very interested to hear your opinion of the service – and the menu, naturally.'

Cassia gulped. She hadn't bargained on having to provide Rocco with feedback on the competence of his staff or the food that was served. She only hoped she could do Disanti's Sorrento justice with her writing and that she didn't offend Rocco in any way. He was aloof and rather irritating, but if they didn't get on, Cassia knew she would never get more than the carefully concoted information about him that magazines had achieved in the past.

'I'll introduce you to my family later,' Rocco informed her, wondering why she looked a little vexed.

'My grandmother is usually to be found in the restaurant somewhere,' he said, more to fill the silence than anything else. 'As is my brother – he's in charge of maintenance and security.'

Maintenance and security? Cassia sensed a story. She had heard Raffaelo Disanti assumed a low-key role in the restaurant business, but she had no idea he did something so menial. Surely he must be jealous of his glamorous older brother? From what she could remember from her internet searches before the visit, Raffaelo was a brute of a man, possessing none of Rocco's good looks or talent. He'd be inhuman if he didn't feel at least slightly put out with his lot, Cassia mused.

Rocco cleared his throat. 'My parents are off doing a book-signing somewhere in Europe,' he added, his tone suggesting he was less than impressed by this. 'I have absolutely no idea when they'll be back so you may or may not get to meet them.'

'What about Aurelia?' Cassia asked. 'Isn't she about to get married? I read on the plane that her nuptials are going to be the celebrity wedding of the year in Italy.'

Rocco grimaced. 'Yes, Aurelia is rather busy with her personal life at the moment.'

'I sympathise,' Cassia said emphatically. 'I'm getting married myself in a few months' time. Well, at the end of September.'

Rocco's dark brows knitted together. 'Really? How will you arrange everything if you're here?' The question had a flat edge, as though Rocco was exasperated by the news.

Cassia flushed, taken aback by the annoyance in his voice. Why was everyone being so negative about her wedding? She had experienced enough of that back home thanks to Grace but Rocco didn't even know her, so he had no right to be judgemental.

'My in-laws are taking care of most things. It's not ideal, believe me, but I don't have much choice,' she said coolly.

Rocco wasn't sure why he had reacted so badly to the news, but he supposed he hadn't thought of Cassia as a breathy bride-to-be. He had assumed she might have a boyfriend back home but that her presence in Sorrento meant that she was career-focused. Rocco wasn't sure he could deal with another gushing bride-to-be going on about flowers and shoes, especially one he didn't have time for in the first place.

His mouth tightened. 'I'll show you the rest of the restaurant now. Do follow me. I'll make sure that photographer sends copies of his pictures to Gena so she can add them to the new issue of *Scrumptious.*'

Cassia caught her breath at how easily he had switched back to professional mode. He wasn't exactly welcoming but at the same time he clearly didn't want anything to interfere with publicising his Vegas eatery.

'I am Stefania,' said a voice behind them in English.

Cassia turned to find an exceptionally pretty blonde behind her. Heavily made up but ravishing nonetheless, the girl was dressed in tight jeans and a low-cut top that made her figure look sensational. Her expression, however, was anything but friendly.

'I am Rocco's girlfriend,' Stefania added pointedly.

'How lovely to meet you,' Cassia said in Italian, holding her hand out and wondering why the atmosphere had suddenly become tense. 'Please don't worry about speaking English on my account. I'm . . . er . . . very keen to improve my Italian while I'm here.'

'I'm not surprised,' Stefania remarked sarcastically, reverting to her mother tongue.

Cassia gaped inwardly at Stefania's rudeness. She might not be able to string a full sentence together, but like most people who had a basic grasp of a language, she understood far more than she could articulate. Stefania had obviously taken exception to her for some reason. Cassia suddenly felt homesick and isolated.

'Stefania owns a PR company in Rome,' Rocco explained, his calm tone at odds with the intense look in his eyes. 'She's visiting for a while.'

'Wonderful,' Cassia returned breezily. 'It's nice that you have some time together. I think I'll get settled in now if you can point me in the right direction?'

Rocco inclined his head, the image of politeness. He looked faintly embarrassed at Stefania's interruption. 'I'll show you there myself.' He led the way, glancing over his shoulder to check that Cassia was following him.

Alone in the room Rocco had taken her to, Cassia sank down on the vast, silk-clad bed. This wasn't what she had expected at all. Rocco might be glamorous and privileged with an enviable lifestyle, but he was also moody and intractable. She wondered what the rest of them were like. And why on earth had Rocco agreed to her making the trip when he so obviously resented the intrusion? She, along with everyone else, knew how private he was, which was his prerogative, of course, but if he really preferred to be left alone, what had possessed him to go ahead with what could effectively be a two-month-long interview?

Her mouth twisted ruefully. Working in journalism made her acutely aware of the benefits of good publicity, but for some reason learning that Rocco was just as focused on promoting the family brand as his celebrity-obsessed parents made him seem shallow and superficial. Behind the brooding charisma was he really just a fame-hungry rich kid who happened to be handy with a kitchen knife? Well, that was what she was here to find out.

Back in England, Louisa was taking a seat in Finn's office.

'Jules is going to pop in before she starts going round all the local job agencies,' she said, settling on the rather masculine chrome and black corduroy sofa that took up one wall of the office Finn was using while a more senior colleague was on holiday. 'Sorry about my tracksuit, I've come straight from work.'

Finn nodded, thinking that her turquoise and pink tracksuit looked brightly incongruous against the modern backdrop of mirrors and glass in the office. It was also giving him a headache, although he did realise that might be down to working sixteen-hour days.

Louisa winced as she realised that she was about to dump extra work on him. 'I said you might be able to give her some words of encouragement because you're such a consummate professional when it comes to all things work-related. I thought you could . . . oh, I don't know, help her with her CV, give her some interview advice, maybe.'

Finn looked up from his pile of legal paperwork and groaned. 'Are you serious, Lou? I simply don't have the time.' He gestured to his towering workload. 'I have to read all of this and cross-reference it before the case goes to trial – tomorrow.'

Louisa looked apologetic. 'Gosh, sorry, Finn. You were the only person I could think of who could help her . . . the best person, in fact. Jules is . . . she's rather lost at the moment, you see. She's been fired again and I don't think she knows what to do with herself.' Louisa sighed. 'I honestly don't think she's cut out for event organising.'

Finn rubbed his eyes tiredly. 'I'm struggling to see exactly what Jules is cut out for, Louisa. She hasn't held down a single job for the past three years or so as far as I can see.'

'That's not fair, Finn,' Louisa protested. 'I know it looks that way, but she's actually very good at certain things.'

'Such as?'

Louisa considered. 'She cooks an amazing soufflé and I don't have to lift a finger in the flat. Jules just works on . . . Jules time, that's the problem. And she loses interest in things when they're not working out very well.'

'She's the same with men from what I recall,' Finn replied, flipping through some papers before tossing them to one side. 'Sorry, that sounded rude. I'm just so ridiculously busy at the moment. What with work, Cassia leaving for Italy and all the wedding plans, I'm pretty much drowning.'

Louisa looked hopeful. 'You need a PA,' she said. 'Maybe Jules could—'

'God, don't even think about it, Lou!' Finn shuddered. The last thing he needed was a party-hard, easily bored PA screwing up all his meetings and turning up late with a daily hangover. He really wished Louisa hadn't suggested he help Jules out;

they were hardly close. Being Louisa's best friend and Cassia's sister, Jules often appeared at family gatherings and parties and while Finn was able to chat politely to her for a while, he had never felt that they had anything much to say to one another. The fact that she could often be inexplicably hostile towards Cassia didn't make him warm to her either.

Catching sight of Jules approaching the office, Louisa stood up. 'What's the deal with your promotion?' she asked Finn.

He looked downcast. 'God knows. I'm beginning to wonder if I'm in the wrong department or something, I can't seem to get a handle on anything.' He let out a short laugh. 'Maybe I'm more like Jules than I thought.'

Guessing that Finn was also missing Cassia, Louisa shot him a sympathetic glance. By far the cleverest in the family, Finn worked his butt off but he had been with the same law firm for years, moving up the ladder at a snail's pace. He'd been passed over for promotion a few times so far, not so much, Louisa suspected, because he wasn't capable of taking on a more senior role, but because he wasn't one of life's dazzlers. He was keen and loyal and steady, but that often meant he was overlooked for the more rousing opportunities in life.

'Do you blame Cassia for going to Italy?' she probed curiously. 'It's just . . . it was all a bit unexpected, especially so soon after your proposal.'

Finn stared past her. 'I suppose I probably would blame her if she didn't have such an emotional reason for wanting to go. Everyone knows how she felt about her father. There's no way I could stop her from going when she had a chance to try to get to grips with his family history.' Deep down, Finn knew he felt a glimmer of resentment towards Cassia for going to Sorrento, but only because it was such terrible timing. Still, if the trip gave her some sort of closure, it couldn't be a bad thing.

'I'm sure it will all be fine,' Louisa reassured him. 'You and Cassia are as solid as a rock.'

'What's happening with your work?' Finn asked, realising the conversation had been somewhat one-sided.

Louisa's eyes lit up. 'Really well, actually. I've been doing lots of extra classes and my boss has asked me to—'

Stopping abruptly as the door opened, Louisa suppressed a sigh. Finn was the only one who showed any interest in her life and she couldn't even get five minutes to talk to him about things.

Ever the gentleman, Finn hid his annoyance at the interruption and let Jules in.

As Louisa left, Jules wafted past wearing too much perfume. Dressed in a tight black suit with a pencil skirt, a belted jacket and some very unsuitable-looking, strappy heels, she seemed flustered. Her hair, though freshly washed, was loose around her shoulders and she was wearing bright red lipstick.

Finn was fairly sure ankle straps and low-cut tops would be inappropriate in most interview situations, but he didn't know how to say such a thing out loud.

'Thanks so much for doing this,' Jules started, perching on the edge of the sofa Louisa had just vacated. She fiddled with the belt of her suit, wondering if the scarlet top she'd chosen to go with it showed too much neat B-cup. 'I . . . er . . . know you're probably terribly busy and everything.' Frankly, Jules thought the whole thing was a bad idea. She knew Louisa was trying to be helpful but Finn, as nice and sweet as he appeared to be, wasn't the sort of person she normally hung out with. How much did he know about CVs and interviews anyway? He'd got his job with the swanky law firm he worked at straight out of uni so he hadn't exactly had to do the rounds.

Jules bit her fingernails, realising that chatting to Finn put her on edge. She had no idea how much he knew about her relationship with Cassia, but she guessed he probably didn't view her favourably.

For his part, good manners prevented Finn from telling her that, yes, he *was* terribly busy, he had back-to-back meetings, a mountain of reading to do, and pep talks really weren't his thing.

'Not at all, not at all,' he said, taking a seat behind the desk again. 'I just hope I can help you.'

Jules grimaced. 'God, the testosterone is practically seeping out of these walls, isn't it? I can practically sense the tang of manly ambition in the air.' She crossed her tanned legs. 'It's like sitting in a great big jock strap.'

Despite himself, Finn laughed out loud, glad Jules had broken the ice. 'So. Show me your CV and let's see if we can tart it up a bit. I'm sure there must be something we can use.'

With a doubtful smile, Jules dug a crumpled copy out and handed it over. Being fired from the events company had been such a low point, even though she knew deep down she couldn't blame her boss after her recent mistakes.

Finn scanned it. Good God, it was horrendous. It wasn't in chronological order, it was badly laid out and it was very obvious that Jules had left a few of the jobs in a less than professional manner. Finn wasn't sure he could make the document look good without telling some serious untruths.

'It's dreadful, isn't it?' Jules flushed. She tried to snatch it back but Finn was too far away. 'I get fired a lot. It's . . . I'm . . .' She gave up and rolled her shoulders. 'Oh, whatever. I'm a crap employee. That's all there is to it.'

Finn glanced at her. Just for a second, Jules had seemed vulnerable and much younger than her heavily made-up face suggested. The moment passed though; within seconds, Jules looked brittle and cocky again.

'I just can't seem to find my niche in life. I wish I could be more like Cassia. She figured out what she wanted to be after hanging on our father's every word.' Jules shrugged.

'I thought Marco taught you a lot too,' Finn responded coolly, disliking Jules's dismissive tone. 'Isn't he the reason you're such a great cook?'

Jules felt unexpectedly flattered at Finn's comment and she wondered if it had been Louisa or Cassia who had told him she was brilliant in the kitchen. Not that it mattered in the scheme of things, she thought to herself. 'I suppose so,' she admitted grudgingly. 'I can't imagine why Cassia struggled so much with that side of things, she's so into her food.' Jules stopped, realising she had sounded bitchy; she had been commenting on Cassia's obsession with food from a writing point of view, not in relation to her weight. About to correct herself, Jules faltered when Finn shot her a look of dislike.

'Let's get to work,' he said briskly, keen to get Jules out of his office. 'Now, about this bank you worked in five years ago . . .'

Sitting on the veranda at the front of the main house, Aurelia frowned and fanned herself with a menu card. Drinking coffee while perusing some sumptuous menu plans for her wedding breakfast, she'd had a prime view of the English food writer as she arrived. Naturally nosy, Aurelia cast aside the mouth-watering choices of lobster-themed appetisers and stared at her brother and their new guest.

Watching Rocco striding quickly through the restaurant as he gave Cassia Marini a guided, if rather hasty tour before being accosted by a hostile-looking Stefania, Aurelia could tell he was already regretting his decision to allow someone to shadow him for the next few weeks. It would undoubtedly be fantastic publicity for his new Vegas establishment, especially since Disanti's wasn't well known in the States, and it would most likely boost revenue in the London branch of the restaurant, which had been lacklustre of late due to some staffing issues or some such thing. With *Scrumptious* magazine's incredible online following in America, Aurelia was sure all the inconvenience was worth it. But she knew her brother and she was sure he would detest having someone following him around.

And what of their new house guest? Good shoes – Prada, if Aurelia wasn't mistaken, but the dress, so unadventurous, and what a dreary shade of beige! And she was positively old, Aurelia thought, in her late twenties, at least. Nineteen years old and unable to imagine leaving her teens, let alone heading down the wrinkled, saggy slope towards thirty, Aurelia shuddered at the mere thought of it.

Feeling a kiss on her neck, she smiled and lifted her face for a proper kiss, her rose-pink mouth inviting. Dino good-naturedly obliged before throwing himself into a chair and helping himself to a black coffee. A chiselled, blond model from Sydney, Dino was laid-back and extremely likeable, the perfect foil for Aurelia's tempestuous, outwardly stroppy persona. He was also half-Italian, which was another reason the Disanti family had taken him into their fold so readily. None of them had questioned Aurelia's desire to marry at such a young age because they all knew Dino was the yin to Aurelia's yang – or rather, he was the only man who would put up with her tantrums and still find her adorable. And Aurelia was so obviously in love, no one had the heart to bring up the issue of their ages.

'What are you up to, gorgeous?' Dino eyed the wedding magazines with a grin. 'Ah, the food. Your family will have a say in that, I'm sure.'

Aurelia twisted a dark curl round her finger, a childhood trait she still adopted when she felt vaguely naughty. 'Well, I was engrossed in lobster appetisers but I have been nosing at our new house guest for the past ten minutes.' They conversed in English, the one language apart from Italian that Aurelia had managed to master, thanks to a long stint modelling in London where she had shared an apartment with three Cockneys who resolutely refused to contemplate a foreign language.

Dino, the son of an Italian entrepreneur who had moved to Australia in his thirties and married an Australian model, could speak Italian perfectly well, but he was more comfortable with English.

'This journalist Rocco's going to be gadding about with?' Dino shaded his eyes against the sun. 'Can't see him having the patience for that somehow, he's far too busy.'

Aurelia wasn't sure what 'gadding' meant but she got the gist. 'He already looks frosty,' she agreed, her eyes sparkling with mischief. 'Frosty, is that right? Anyway, she's very plain, the food writer, unfashionable too.'

Dino raised his sun-bleached eyebrows but said nothing. He, too, had watched the English journalist arrive, and as far as he could see, she was rather gorgeous, like a young Sophia Loren, in fact, all flowing dark hair and hourglass curves, but he knew better than to say such a thing to Aurelia. His fiancée was beautiful but she was also vain and surprisingly insecure when it came to other women.

Seeing Aurelia's grandmother, Sofia, approaching, Dino gave her a broad smile. He liked the old lady immensely; she was sprightly, spirited and very Italian. Some might find her intimidating but Dino knew she was a pussycat beneath her strict exterior. The fact that the adoration was mutual was a bonus.

'Have you seen Rocco?' Sofia asked in rapid Italian. She bent and offered her rosy cheek to Dino who kissed it reverentially. She wore black most days, out of respect for her dead husband, Nico, but with her still-dark hair up in a bun and discreet make-up, she had a certain style.

Sofia was a typical Italian 'nonna' – what she said went, especially when it came to traditional recipes and what sauce, pasta or brand of tomatoes to use. As far as Dino could make out, the only justification for everyone following Sofia's lead was 'that's what Nonna says/uses/buys', but Dino was used to this; his father had said the same about his own, long-departed nonna. 'He was in there with that magazine woman.' Aurelia pulled a face. 'She looks dull.'

Sofia narrowed her eyes. 'Don't be so quick to judge, little one,' she said in English. 'She will be very useful for publicity. Besides, how does her being here affect you?'

Aurelia pouted. 'It doesn't, I suppose. I just hope she doesn't get in the way of my wedding plans. I'm so busy with everything.' She waved an airy hand. 'What with the team arriving soon for the model shoot . . .'

'Rocco agreed to that?' Sofia asked, narrowing her eyes at Aurelia and deciding not to mention how foolhardy her granddaughter was for firing her wedding planner. 'You did ask his permission, I hope?'

'He knows all about it.' Aurelia avoided her gaze and held up a menu card. 'How does lobster ravioli sound as an appetiser?'

'Delicious.' Sofia looked stern. 'I hope Rocco does know, Aurelia, otherwise you could cause him unnecessary stress. And that is something we could all do without, frankly.' She headed back inside, making a mental note to forewarn Rocco of yet another inconvenience.

Dino, not sure what all the fuss was about, leant across to give Aurelia a kiss, his amiable brown eyes meeting hers teasingly.

Aurelia kissed him back and let out a contented smirk. By the time Rocco found out just how huge the photo shoot was that she had organised on the Disanti estate, it would be too late for him to do anything about it. Besides, how annoying would it be from Rocco's point of view? He'd be too caught up with keeping the silly English food writer out of his business to worry about photographers and stylists. Flicking her dark curls over her shoulder as Dino's tanned fingers stroked her neck languidly, she leant into him adoringly and forgot all about Cassia Marini.

Hoping Jules was out looking for another job, Diana was annoyed to find her youngest daughter sunbathing topless in her back garden. The late April sunshine wasn't exactly blisteringly hot but it was good enough tanning weather for a sun-worshipper like Jules. Finding the garden neat and tidy, Diana glanced through the patio doors. The inside of the house was also spotless, as expected, and Diana knew that Jules would be behind the freshly cut flowers and the sparkling worktops. Jules took a surprising pride in her possessions and abode, even when rented.

Diana glanced at her daughter and let out a small, exasperated sigh. Seemingly without a care in the world, Jules was stretched out on a lounger clutching what looked like a homemade mojito, her only adornments pink-edged Ray-Bans and tiny, emerald-green bikini bottoms. Her perky breasts, like the rest of her, were smothered in glistening oil and pointed towards the sun.

'Can't the neighbours see you?' Diana asked, nodding towards the houses that backed on to Jules's.

Jules shrugged. 'Who cares? If they get off watching me go brown, it's not my problem.' She pulled a face, not remotely bothered. 'I leave the uptight stuff to Cassia, remember?'

Diana ducked under an umbrella to protect her skin. Jules might be too young to worry about wrinkles but Diana couldn't afford such luxuries. These days, her golden glow came in a spray can; the leather-skinned look was distinctly passé at her age.

'Day off?' she inquired blithely.

Jules frowned at her mother over the top of her sunglasses. 'Not as such. I'm just . . . chilling out between interviews.'

Diana helped herself to a mojito from the jug on the table. Dunking a thick sprig of mint in her drink, she eyed Jules caustically. 'Darling, the modern woman needs to work. You don't want to end up relying on a man for money, do you?'

Jules pushed her hair out of her eyes, hoping the sun was turning it blonder. She couldn't help thinking it would be rather nice to be taken care of by a man, regardless of how much he earned. Or maybe, looking at it from another angle, it would be nice to take care of a man, Jules thought in surprise. Looking after perennially messy Louisa wasn't exactly fulfilling but it would have to do for now. She glared at her mother. She had been happily whiling away the time fantasising about herself and Dom in all the gossip magazines, him bedecked in preppy Calvin Klein and herself in a tight, Kiri satin dress, and the last thing she needed was criticism and taxing questions about her income. She felt insecure enough about her job situation without her mother swanning in wearing a glamorous outfit that screamed Harvey Nics. 'Why are you looking so bloody pleased with yourself?' she sniped, old resentments rushing to the surface.

Diana wished Jules wasn't so prickly. It made for tense relations between them, with snide accusation a common theme. Diana stirred her drink with her finger. 'I'm thinking of making a comeback,' she said grandly. 'Fliss, my agent, thinks this is the perfect time for me to re-establish myself.'

Draining her mojito noisily, Jules looked bored. All her life, she'd had her mother's amazing acting career shoved down her throat and she couldn't be less interested. Friends thought she was incredibly lucky to have been brought up by a Shakespearean actress turned soap star and a handsome, Italian restaurateur and food writer, but all they saw was the glamour and the money. None of them knew what it was like to live in the shadow of famous parents, especially ones who were nowhere near as perfect as they seemed to the outside world, Jules thought sourly.

'I don't have a part secured just yet,' Diana was saying, ignoring Jules's crushing lack of response. 'Fliss has a few things in mind but I haven't decided what to do yet.' She frowned, thinking about the character part Fliss kept badgering her about. But it was theatre and Diana wasn't remotely interested in that; she was known for her TV roles these days and treading the boards was something she had done when starting out.

Jules sneered and tipped more oil into her hands. 'What sort of parts are you looking at, Mother? Grannies?'

Diana flinched. Jules always knew how to hurt her and she delivered her blows without compunction. 'Not a granny, no. Not unless you have something thrilling to tell me,' she added flippantly, doing her best to hide how bruised she felt.

'As if. You'll have to rely on Cassia for that kind of news,' Jules said, turning away slightly as she briskly rubbed oil into her breasts. 'Although since she's buggered off to Italy, you might have to wait a bit longer for grandchildren because I reckon this secondment could cost Cassia her relationship.'

'Don't say that, darling,' Diana chided, sure that wasn't the case. 'Finn is utterly besotted with Cassia. I honestly can't see him backing out of their engagement just because she's gone to Sorrento for a few weeks. And Cassia is equally devoted.'

Knowing her mother was probably right, Jules seethed. Only Cassia could put her career first and still manage to keep her perfect boyfriend.

'And she's not just going for work reasons; she's going to look into Marco's Italian . . .' Diana's voice petered out when she saw Jules turning away. God, how could she have been so crass?

Jules smacked her hand down on her lounger. 'How utterly perfect for Cassia,' she spat. 'Now I can't even slag her off for buggering off on a jolly for the sake of her career.'

Watching her daughter glowering, Diana felt a rush of regret. She wished she could say something, wished she could make Jules feel better, but the words stuck in her throat. She saw her own flaws starkly mirrored in Jules and she would do anything to prevent her daughter making the same mistakes she had. They both lashed out when they were suffering, usually at people they loved, and both of them had the capacity to retaliate with devastating results. Tentatively saying as much, Diana found herself on the sharp edge of Jules's tongue.

Jules sat up and tore off her sunglasses. 'Well, nobody's perfect, right, Mother?' Her words were loaded with meaning.

'That's enough,' Diana told her, standing up. Her cheeks felt flushed and as much as she'd like to blame the sunshine or the mojito, she knew guilt was very much at the root.

'Is it?' Jules stared back at her.

Diana swallowed. 'We've been through all of this, Jules,' she said in a low voice. 'Is there really any point in prising open old wounds?'

Jules flinched.

'You'd do far better concentrating on getting another job,' Diana said, not unkindly. 'I know it's tough but you need to get yourself out there.'

'I know,' Jules said, tears pricking at her eyelids. She thrust her sunglasses back on to her nose to hide her distress. 'Finn gave me a pep talk the other day and it really helped.'

'Finn?' Diana was surprised. She wasn't aware Jules ever bumped into Finn when Cassia wasn't around and she couldn't imagine they would ever become friends. 'That was kind of him. Well, I hope it works and you have another job soon. I'll see myself out,' she added, realising Jules wasn't going to bother to get up.

About to say sorry as her mother made a quick exit, Jules closed her mouth. Why should she apologise? She hadn't done anything wrong. Settling down again, she arched her back and thrust her breasts towards the sun, doing her best to push all the bad thoughts away.

Chapter Five

The following morning, Cassia awoke from a surprisingly relaxed sleep and headed out on to the veranda attached to her room. She inhaled the heady scent wafting up from the tangle of purple and lavender wisteria that hung over the balcony. May was only days away and the area was blossoming into life.

Glancing back inside the palatial suite she'd been given, she also realised she hadn't done enough research as far as the Disanti family were concerned. She had known they were rich – they were one of the oldest, most influential families in southern Italy – but she really hadn't expected such sophisticated grandeur. Her suite featured an enchanting fresco of cherubim above her bed, while exquisite and no doubt priceless oil paintings adorned the walls.

The red Italian marble bathroom should have been gaudy but somehow it managed to be opulent yet understated. Tasteful furnishings and a sumptuous bedspread of oyster-coloured silk finished the suite off beautifully. The writing desk fitted perfectly too; it had been delivered the night before, an ornate but welcoming piece of furniture in pale wood that had been slotted next to one of the windows.

Surely Finn would love it here, Cassia thought as she headed back inside her suite. Or maybe not. Attracted more by good golf courses than incredible food or views, Cassia realised she needed to show Finn a bit more of the world so he could broaden his horizons. If only she could tear him away from his job, she mused, absent-mindedly helping herself to one of the handmade chocolate truffles that had been left on her bedside table.

Cassia checked her watch and wondered what he was up to. Was he missing her as much as she was missing him? She'd only left yesterday but it felt like a lifetime ago; the Disanti estate was so far removed from her familiar backdrops of London and Kent, she felt as if she'd been dropped into another world.

Cassia closed her eyes as the bitter chocolate ganache in her mouth melted away to a delicious, nutty centre. God, they were divine; she could write an entire article about the sensual experience of the dark, almost savoury chocolate disintegrating with salty richness to reveal a decadent almond paste . . .

Brought up short by visions of Jules mocking her for gorging on chocolate before breakfast and realising she was running late, Cassia closed the box of truffles and checked her appearance. Throwing a thin, cream cardigan on over one of her Jigsaw work dresses in case it was chilly and making sure her dark hair was tied back and professional-looking, she headed downstairs to the sunny room Rocco had mentioned was used for meals. She had no idea what the plan for the day was but she wanted to make sure she looked ready for work and not as if she was on holiday. Judging by the way Rocco had reacted to the news of her impending wedding and his apparent concern that she might be distracted from her professional objective, she could just imagine his lip curling with contempt if anything in her demeanour hinted that she was even remotely off duty.

Not that her mind could ever be off-duty in these surroundings, Cassia thought, staring out at the view. All at once, her writing brain kicked in and she longed to capture thoughts of black olives glossily drenched in drizzles of extra virgin olive oil, of huge, fragrant lemons hanging heavily from their branches and begging to be eaten, and of freshly made pasta, coated in silken sauces topped with fine gratings of white truffle . . .

Suddenly noticing a rounded woman with adorably rosy apple cheeks in a smart, black dress, Cassia smiled at her, not sure if she was staff or a family member. The woman, pouring out cappuccinos, smiled back, gesturing for Cassia to take a chair at a table covered with a pristine white cloth.

'Thank you.' Cassia accepted a cup. 'These pastries look divine,' she added in Italian, enjoying the mouth-watering aroma of freshly baked bread and sweet pastries. She could see piles of *cornetto*, the Italian version of the French croissant, some plain, some filled with cream and others containing fruity jams. There were also *ciambella*, Italian fried doughnuts, and savoury breads and plates of frittata.

'Pastries are my speciality,' the lady said proudly, nodding at Cassia to take one. 'I made them all myself this morning.'

Cassia helped herself to a plain *cornetto* and dunked it in her coffee. She eyed the older woman curiously. She was sure the woman couldn't be part of the small discreet team of staff she had seen darting in and out of bedrooms in the main house in stark black-and-white outfits; her dark hair was artfully coiled up in a bun and her black dress, though simple, had an elegant cut.

'I am Sofia, Rocco's grandmother,' the woman explained as though she'd read Cassia's mind. Gathering up some cards with menu plans scrawled on them, Sofia took a seat next to Cassia, her keen eyes assessing her. 'And you are Cassia Marini. I do hope you have settled into your room.'

Cassia felt embarrassed not to have spotted the resemblance between Rocco and his grandmother. They possessed the same olive-green eyes, although Sofia's were considerably more welcoming than Rocco's.

'It's beautiful here,' Cassia said, feeling Sofia scrutinise her. 'I feel as though I'm staying in a hotel.' She hoped her rusty

Italian didn't grate too much and she resolved to find a way to brush up on her verbs. Whenever she had chatted in Italian with her father, he had always put more focus on her accent and how naturally Italian she sounded; grammar and verbs had never been his strong point.

Cassia was struck by how motherly and affectionate Sofia seemed. Having expected a typical Italian nonna who ruled her family with an iron fist – especially a family of this size and status – Cassia was pleasantly surprised to be greeted by this comforting, twinkly-eyed lady. Granted, she looked as though she would fight like a lion for her family if they were under threat and Cassia was sure what Sofia said was gospel, as it was in most Italian families, but she was by far the friendliest face Cassia had encountered since she set foot in Italy.

Sofia smiled. 'I hope we're not as formal as all that!' she responded, sipping her cappuccino. She watched approvingly as Cassia devoured the *cornetto*, pleased that at last she had found a female who didn't mind the odd indulgence.

Unlike Stefania, Sofia thought with a frown. Stefania was such a health freak, she ate like a hamster. And as for Aurelia, she tended to survive on gallons of good coffee and the smallest portions known to man. And she never touched pastries, not even on her birthday, Sofia thought with regret. Cassia Marini was a stunning woman with a figure most men would lust after. Ripples of chocolate-brown hair and dark eyes like the centre of one of Rocco's handmade truffles, Sofia realised Cassia looked more exotic and more Italian than most Italian women she knew. And what a pretty name. Was it short for Cassiopeia, perhaps, the constellation? Or had the name been chosen because of its connection to the lovely spice cinnamon? She asked Cassia.

'Cinnamon.' Cassia smiled. 'My father chose it.'

'It's beautiful,' Sofia said, idly wondering what Rocco had thought of this ravishing woman when he'd met her the day before. Still, with Stefania around, he had probably been whisked away from Cassia at the first opportunity. Sofia felt briefly troubled as she thought about Stefania. A striking girl, of course, but did she really have Rocco's best interests at heart? The constant demands for attention, the insistence that he set up yet another restaurant in Rome perturbed Sofia. She couldn't help thinking Stefania was desperate to prise him away from his family and keep him all to herself. Surely, if the girl loved Rocco, she would be doing her best to get him to slow down, to take some time off.

Sofia grimaced and turned back to Cassia. 'Have you met the rest of the family?' she asked, making a small mark on one of her menus.

Cassia shook her head. 'Rocco gave me a rundown and some basic family background but I haven't been introduced to Aurelia or Raffaelo yet.' She licked buttery pastry crumbs off her lips and wondered if it would be inappropriate to mention Sofia's dead husband, Nico.

'I assume Rocco told you about Nico setting the restaurant up,' Sofia said, taking the initiative. 'Ah, don't worry, we talk about him constantly around here. He was such a dynamic man and he achieved so much for all of us. The family came from humble beginnings, you know. They didn't always own this land and they didn't have this villa. They lived on a small corner on the edge, working for another family. The land was won after a bitter battle and the family became rivals . . . but oh, I won't bore you with the details. Needless to say, once Nico was old enough and he was responsible for the family, he built the villa and the restaurant. He never wanted the family to go back to the poverty they once knew.' Sofia's eyes misted over fondly as she talked about Nico. Aware that she was speaking to a stranger, she pulled herself together with a roll of her slightly plump shoulders. 'We should celebrate our dead loved ones, don't you think, Cassia? I can never understand why some people refuse to acknowledge someone when they've died.'

'I couldn't agree more.' Cassia nodded, thinking the coffee was the best she'd ever tasted, probably helped by the view. Dazzled, Cassia gazed out across the vast, lush countryside for a moment, savouring the sight of the lemon and orange groves, which were heavily laden with fruit.

'Do you talk about your father?' Sofia asked softly. 'I hope you don't mind me asking, but I am a great fan of his travel diaries.'

Cassia was pleased. 'Of course I don't mind. He died three years ago, but my mother and my sister can't seem to bear to mention him.'

It was a fact that had hurt and baffled Cassia for the past three years but she hadn't ever been able to get to the bottom of it. Whenever she attempted to mention her father, even to comment on how much she missed him, Jules would turn away angrily and her mother would look pained.

Sofia raised her dark eyebrows. 'What a shame. Marco Marini . . . he was also a restaurateur at one time, if I remember rightly?'

'Yes. But only on and off. It was his writing he really lived for. Travelling around, writing about his culinary experiences, that was his real passion. An amazing cook too,' Cassia added, 'although my sister inherited that particular talent rather than me.'

'Nico and I did a fair amount of travelling in our youth and it was wonderful.' Sofia glanced at Cassia, noting the way her fingers curled and uncurled around her coffee cup and the fire in her dark eyes when she talked about her father and his passion for writing and travel.

Sofia narrowed her eyes astutely. She sensed a restlessness in Cassia, something that belied her outwardly calm exterior. She was ambitious, that was for sure, but it was more than that.

Was it hunger, perhaps? A desire to see the world and make the most of it – and of herself? Sofia realised Cassia reminded her of Rocco in that way; behind his rather cool persona, the one he presented to the public, there was a passion and zest for life that surprised those who didn't know him well.

'What do you think of the new venture in Vegas?' Cassia asked, realising she should focus on why she was in Sorrento. 'It's a little different from the more classic locations of the other Disanti restaurants, but I'm looking forward to hearing all about it and promoting it as much as possible.'

Sofia's soft expression clouded over. 'Vegas, that was Flavia and Gino's choice, not Rocco's, and he has come under criticism for it, if I'm honest. Flavia believes the Disanti brand needs to grow, and that we need a face for the brand.' She shuffled the menus jerkily, the gesture betraying an inner frustration. 'Rocco undoubtedly has a good face for it, but that is not the point, is it? We have enough money, and Rocco is successful enough for all of us to live in luxury for the fore-seeable future. And we certainly don't need another restaurant in Rome.'

'Rome?'

'Stefania is desperate for Rocco to open another restaurant there, but I wonder how much that has to do with generating money and kudos for her PR company.' Sofia stopped abruptly. Cassia might be known for her food writing rather than any kind of salacious tittle-tattle, but she was still a journalist.

'Rocco is under so much pressure,' Sofia went on. 'I would love to see him less stressed, more settled, you know? He should be cooking, not drowning under paperwork.' She paused. 'The Disanti family, we have been through so much.' She spat something in Italian that Cassia didn't understand, her green eyes flashing. 'That rival family I mentioned, they caused the Disanti family so many problems.'

'In what way?'

Sofia hesitated, not sure if she should talk about it but she liked Cassia and found herself opening up. 'They believed they owned all of this land but Nico's family looked into it and ancient deeds proved that they were the true owners.'

'Really?' Cassia was fascinated. She hadn't heard anything about a rival family when she'd looked up the Disantis before.

'Oh yes . . . the Giorelli family. We don't speak of it too much now, but it was terrible. I was only, oh, about eighteen at the time. I had been dating Nico for a few years – we had just become engaged, actually.' Sofia leant forward. 'The Giorellis were forced to leave, which as you can imagine caused very bad feeling. They left, but not before they laid a curse on the Disanti family.'

'A curse?'

Sofia's expression became defensive. 'I know it sounds absurd, Rocco is always telling me this. But I was there. The Giorellis tried destroying the property first of all – petty damage, fires, that sort of thing.' The set line of her jaw suggested she was angry rather than scared at this memory. 'It was horrible but nothing major happened. Then Rosita, the great-grandmother, put a curse on us all, me included.'

Cassia felt a shiver.

'People said Rosita was a witch,' Sofia continued. 'She laid a curse on the family and on this land, saying that one day we would suffer, that it would all be taken away from us.' She crossed herself rapidly with her small hands.

'And has anything ever happened?'

Sofia raised an eyebrow. 'Well, Nico had an accident when he was building the villa. He narrowly avoided death when a roof collapsed on him. Also, the restaurant was flooded the first year it opened and no one ever discovered what caused it.' Sofia paused. 'Oh, and Rocco nearly drowned as a child. It was in the swimming pool, he fell in when the cover was on and couldn't get out. Nico saved him but Rocco wasn't sure how he had managed to fall in the pool in the first place, especially when he wasn't supposed to be there. And someone was seen loitering around the property that day, but of course nothing was ever proved.'

Cassia frowned. She wasn't a superstitious person, so she wasn't sure what to make of Sofia's comments. Surely there could be logical explanations for each incident? The villa might not have been secure when Nico entered it during the construction and there could have been any number of reasons why a newly built restaurant flooded. As for the near-drowning incident, Cassia wondered whether Rocco had simply been playing truant and had fallen in the pool by accident, claiming bewilderment by way of an excuse.

'I can see that you are sceptical,' Sofia said shortly, standing up and starting to clear away the breakfast things. 'That's fine, I'm used to it. It happened more than fifty years ago, but I do still worry about that curse. And nothing would stop me protecting my family, Cassia. Nothing.'

Seeing that in spite of her cuddly appearance, Sofia was indeed a strict Italian grandmother, Cassia fervently hoped she hadn't offended her.

'I honestly can't imagine you have too much to worry about now. Are any of the family still alive?'

Sofia shook her head. 'All of them have passed away. The entire family were wiped out when a devastating landslide swallowed their property.' Sofia stared past Cassia. 'There were rumours that a small child, a boy, had survived, but he never materialised. If he was still alive after the landslide, he disappeared without a trace shortly afterwards. Some say to England, that he went there as an orphan and never knew where he came from.'

Cassia went cold momentarily. Hearing about the possibility of a small boy surviving and sent to England made her think of her father. What a strange coincidence. It reminded her that she must start to look into his history, and she resolved to do it immediately, before she became too involved with writing her column.

Sofia was unaware of Cassia's thoughts. Lost in memories as she thought of Nico, she felt a pang of loneliness. They had been so happy, she and Nico. They had suffered losses together, they had enjoyed successes, but they had always been side by side, loyal and in love. It was hard to carry on without him, but as she had done for the past four years or more, Sofia knew she must.

Cassia noticed that Sofia looked oddly deflated, almost wistful, but then she turned back with a determined look in her eyes.

'I have to sign off the lunch menus for the restaurant. It has been lovely talking to you.' Giving Cassia a polite nod, Sofia pushed the plate of pastries towards her. 'Do help yourself and I hope you enjoy your stay with us.' With that, she left the room.

Munching on another pastry, Cassia stared at the view thoughtfully. The talk of curses and near-deaths had unnerved her slightly, but she was sure Sofia was being fanciful. Nothing, not even curses from rival Italian families, could spoil this beautiful, tranquil vista.

Finn glanced round the champagne bar, sure it wasn't his scene. Missing Cassia and out of the office at a reasonable time for once, he'd taken Dom up on his offer to view a nightclub his brother was thinking of investing in. It would make a relaxing change to catch up on some brotherly chit-chat rather than eating alone in the apartment he sometimes shared with Cassia. But finding himself reclining awkwardly on an amethyst-coloured, velvet banquette in the VIP area of a glitzy new club in the heart of south-west London, Finn was beginning to regret his decision. He could see several young rugby players, groups of glamorous, leggy girls wearing designer dresses and heels, plus a good selection of up-and-coming actors and newish pop stars and he most assuredly didn't fit in. His eyes nearly popped out of his head when he spotted a member of the royal family. A distant cousin, admittedly, but one of the sporty kind whose legs looked fantastic in a miniskirt. She was surrounded by a group of posh-looking private school boys in snazzy suits and some girls wearing what looked suspiciously like real fur as they sipped fancy-looking cocktails. Music boomed out across the dance floor, which was a writhing mass of sweaty bodies, some of whom seemed to have recently vacated the Pineapple Dance Studio, judging by the way they were hurling themselves athletically around the club.

Finn sighed. He did hope Dom wasn't expecting him to strut his stuff; Cassia always laughingly told him his dance moves tended towards the 'Dad' variety.

'What do you think?' Dom asked, striding up with two lurid purple cocktails topped with a head of cream. Wearing a sharp, silver-grey suit with a casual white linen shirt, he looked like every girl's dream of a hunky sportsman on his day off. His blond hair had been cropped short and his eyes looked as blue as the Mediterranean on a good day. 'Isn't it amazing here?' He was in his element, mixing with the beautiful people. He'd always thought he should have been upper class rather than middle class and, to be fair, the young hip crowd fitted him like a glove. 'Like Boujis or Whisky Mist, this is the place where the upper-class in-crowd hang out.'

Finn awkwardly accepted the cocktail. 'Er . . . yes. It's . . . impressive.'

'Isn't it just? Here, taste this, bro. It's called a Purple Heart. See, they fashion a heart shape into the cream and it's purple.' Dom laughed.

Thinking that the name was flippant and slightly offensive given the real meaning behind the Purple Heart medal the cocktail was named after, Finn gingerly took a sip. He winced as the vodka, cream and cassis hit the back of his throat. He had no idea what else had gone into the cocktail to make it look so purple, but it was pungent and fruitily alcoholic.

Dom clapped him on the back. 'So, your opinion, please. Do you think I should invest in this place or not? I know the owners and it's the perfect place to party.' He waved an arm around, encompassing the celebrities and mirrored ceilings in one swoop. 'More importantly, there are upper-class legs and tits everywhere and it costs five hundred quid membership a year for each and every one of these rich kids to down their champers in here.'

Finn wiped cream from his lip and wished he'd gone home. Even his empty-feeling apartment would be better than sitting inside this pimped-up garish club. Finn had no idea who owned it but he could only imagine it was a porn king or whatever they were called. But he did not want to burst Dom's bubble of enthusiasm. It couldn't have been fun for his brother to grow up feeling like second best when it came to brains, career success and good decision-making. He had their mother to thank for that but Finn couldn't help wanting to atone for her sins occasionally, just to give Dom a boost.

'Er . . . I don't know, Dom. It's not really my cup of tea, or Purple Heart or whatever.'

'Well, of course it's not!' Dom rolled his eyes and languished against the banquette. 'I know you hate this sort of thing. I meant, what do you think of me investing in it?'

Finn looked vague. He was intelligent but he wasn't exactly business-savvy. Also, he loathed risk-taking and he tended to skim his salary into sensible, safe investments each month which were then managed by a financial adviser and a team of investors. He wouldn't dream of investing in anything that didn't relate to the usual bonds and savings and he certainly wouldn't put his money behind a tacky nightclub.

'Can you afford it?' Finn asked eventually.

Dom waved an impatient hand. 'Yes, of course. Well, I've got most of the money, anyway. And I'm doing well on the circuit at the moment. I'm really starting to earn my place on the court these days.' He pointed to the dance floor. 'That's a member of royalty right there, Finn. Royalty!'

Finn took another sip of the Purple Heart and winced. 'Well, if you can afford it, I guess that's a step in the right direction.' He looked dubious. 'Do Mum and Dad know about this?'

Dom finished his cocktail and started on Finn's. 'Of course not. As if I'd tell them. Mother disapproves heartily of me as it is.' He shook his head. 'No, this is just something I want to do for myself, Finn. I can tell them about it when it makes me loads of cash. The owners are hoping to create more of these clubs across the country, you see, so once that happens, I'll be making my investment back and then some.'

'Well, I guess you must know what you're doing. Have a look at the figures, though. That's what you should do if you're putting large sums of money into something like this.' Finn glanced at his watch discreetly, wondering if it would be rude to make a move. As much as he enjoyed Dom's company, he could hardly hear himself think in the club and he should probably catch up on some case notes.

'Ah, here's Jules.' Dom leapt up and greeted her with deliberate kisses on each cheek. Spinning back round to Finn, he gestured to Jules. 'Louisa was meant to be coming to check the club out but she had something else on so Jules stepped into her place. Wasn't that nice of her?'

'Er . . . yes. Hello, Jules.' Standing up, Finn kissed Jules's cheek quickly and gave her his seat. He hadn't seen her since the day she had turned up at his office clutching her CV and he wondered if she'd had any luck with the job-hunting. Judging by the tan she was sporting, he guessed she had been more focused on sunbathing than interviews. He didn't know whether to feel exasperated or amused but he certainly wasn't surprised.

She really was a bit of a lost cause, Finn thought to himself with a frown. He wondered at how different Jules and Cassia were. Still, he and Dom were poles apart, despite being siblings, so it wasn't that unusual. He knew he should be cross that Jules had wasted his time that day but it was Louisa who had set the whole thing up. Besides, Jules had made him laugh and she had distracted him briefly from missing Cassia and from feeling put upon at work.

Wearing a slinky yellow dress that showed off her golden thighs, with nude heels that threatened to topple her forwards, Jules shimmied on to the banquette and fluffed her blond hair out.

'Champagne?' Dom offered extravagantly. 'Or one of these Purple Heart things?'

Jules smiled. 'Oh, I'm a champagne kinda gal, for my sins, Dom. Thank you. Wow, is that who I think it is over there?'

Dom winked at her. 'Oh yes. That's the real deal.' He caught the eye of the prettiest girl behind the bar and ordered Dom Pérignon without even moving from his seat.

Finn turned to Jules. 'You look as though you've been on holiday,' he said, gesturing to her honey-hued skin.

Jules hoped the purple lighting hid her blushes. Not knowing Finn terribly well, despite his long relationship with Cassia, she wasn't sure if he was being nasty or not. Looking quickly into his blue eyes and detecting only faint amusement, Jules decided Finn probably wasn't capable of being nasty if he tried.

'Oh, just a spot of sunbathing between interviews. It's amazing the colour you can get in this country when the sun actually comes out.'

Dom stroked her arm with a lazy finger. 'And very gorgeous you look too.' He put a hand next to hers on the table and compared tans. 'That's not fair!' he protested. 'I had to sweat it out on a European tennis court to achieve this colour and you roll up with a back-garden tan that outdoes mine.' He pouted, knowing few women could resist him when he looked this adorable.

Finn, having seen Dom on a charm offensive many a time before, gave him a frown of warning. He wasn't sure he liked the idea of Dom seducing Cassia's little sister but he knew he didn't really have a hope of deterring him. Dom and Jules were similar ages and they might even possess similar morals, but for some reason it felt too close to home. He turned to Jules and changed the subject.

'How's Louisa? She started to tell me about something exciting happening to her at work, but we got interrupted.' Finn flushed, remembering that it was Jules who had brought that conversation to an end.

Jules looked baffled. 'No idea,' she said. 'She hasn't said anything to me.' She frowned, remembering that Louisa had been waxing lyrical about something work-related the night before but she had been too busy badgering her about Dom to listen.

'So . . . have you heard from Cassia at all?' Instantly, Finn regretted the question as Jules's mouth tightened.

'No, I haven't. She didn't even say goodbye.' Jules omitted to mention that it was she who had missed Cassia's departure, ignoring several calls and text messages from her sister and not bothering to pop over to her apartment to wish her bon voyage. Jules's eyes narrowed with spite. 'You might be interested to see this, though.' Tugging a magazine out of her bag, she flipped open the pages and pushed it across the table.

Finn found himself staring at a photograph of a beaming Cassia against a ravishing backdrop of gorgeous Sorrento countryside. A devilishly handsome man had his arm thrown carelessly round her, as if they'd known each other for years.

Finn's stomach tightened. Rocco Disanti was extremely good-looking, one of those smooth, sophisticated Italians who carried off designer suits with ease. He looked as though he could juggle sharp knives and beautiful women without even breaking a sweat and seeing him in such close proximity to Cassia was difficult to take. Finn couldn't help thinking they complemented each other's dark looks; they looked like an exotic celebrity couple.

He fought a sudden urge to tell his bosses at Lovetts & Rose to screw their job so he could hop on a plane and get Cassia back here where she would be safe from smarmy Italians. He berated himself, knowing he wouldn't do such a reckless thing in a million years. His job meant everything to him; besides, what on earth would Cassia think if he jetted off to Sorrento to protect her, when she had always been able to take care of herself? Remembering her tales of her rather wild youth, Finn felt a moment of disquiet.

'Sorrento looks stunning,' he said lightly, handing the magazine back. 'I might just pop over for a visit when I'm not as busy.'

Jules looked disappointed and she shoved the magazine back into her bag, brightening only when the champagne arrived.

'Dom Pérignon?' Dom offered, filling a flute to the brim.

'Don't mind if I do.' Jules smiled, cosying up to him. 'Wow, this place is really something. Do all your hunky tennis-playing friends hang out in clubs like this, then?'

'Only the good-looking ones,' Dom purred, sliding his arm round her.

Leaving them to it, Finn headed back to his apartment to chill out and leaf through some paperwork until sleep threatened to overtake him. Nursing a glass of Scotch, he fell asleep dreaming of Sabatier knife fights with a darkly handsome Italian chef.

*

Already regretting agreeing to meet Diana in a trendy coffee bar in Soho, Grace tightened her grip on her wedding file. It had been difficult enough to track Diana down so they could get together and discuss Finn and Cassia's wedding – let alone in dirty, busy London – but the fact that she was having to mingle with tourists and young girls in exceptionally skimpy skirts simply added insult to injury. But she had felt obliged to go along with Diana's plans when they talked on the phone, mainly because Diana, claiming in her rather vague way to be 'snowed under considering work offers', had insisted that the meeting should take place in Soho, just in case she needed to dash off to an audition nearby. Unfamiliar with this area of London, Grace checked her *A-Z* again, wondering if she was even on the right road. She had only agreed to this meeting because Henry had gently suggested that it would be 'correct form in these circumstances', something he knew she would feel obliged to respond to. Whatever her opinions of Cassia and her family, Grace always wanted to do what good breeding dictated was appropriate.

Why couldn't they have met somewhere more upmarket, like Knightsbridge? Grace thought crossly. Feeling rather sweaty in the early May sunshine, she flapped a hand in front of her face and wondered how she and Diana would get on. They were so different; Diana resembled a glamorous, brightly coloured butterfly, flitting from one social event to another without a care in the world, whereas she, Grace, tried to live life in a more meaningful way, focusing on simple things such as family and charity.

She found the coffee shop and pursed her lips, realising how out of place she was going to look here wearing a subdued grey linen dress with a lightweight cashmere cardigan. She immediately spotted Diana, who was sporting a raspberry-pink silk dress and matching heels that would have been more at home at a summer wedding. Grace headed towards her, thinking the short length of Diana's dress revealed rather too much tanned thigh. However old she claimed to be in the media and however smooth her forehead, Grace was certain Diana had to be over fifty these days. Far too old to be showing her knees, in other words.

'Grace!' Diana leapt up and made a show of kissing Grace's cheeks with far more enthusiasm than was necessary. Grace, with her steely-blue eyes and perfect housewife status, always made her feel nervous. 'How lovely to see you again! And thank you so much for coming into London to meet me; it's really kind of you.' Diana looked rueful. 'What can one do? Work is always so demanding.'

'It's no problem at all,' Grace said insincerely, eyeing the nearby stool with some apprehension.

'Oh, we should sit in one of the booths at the back,' Diana asserted, taking pity on Grace and noting her conservative linen dress in discreet horror. Grace really didn't make the best of herself; was it necessary to have such hideously weather-beaten hands with all the lovely anti-ageing hand creams on sale everywhere?

'I only sat at the front here to watch the world go by,' she added, knowing Grace disliked the venue.

Refusing to consider any of the outlandishly named coffees on offer, Grace ordered a milky coffee with plenty of sugar and opened her file. 'Right, on to business. Let's discuss bridesmaids.'

'How wonderfully efficient you are,' Diana commented blithely, sucking her skinny, low-carb, berry frappuccino through a pink straw. 'A file, no less. I do hope it's alphabetised.'

Grace shot her a glance, aware Diana was mocking her. 'I feel it's the best way to organise something, especially when the person who should be in charge is in another country.'

Diana stiffened. Cassia was right, Grace clearly disapproved of her and her career. Diana believed both of her daughters to be good catches, in their own ways, for any man – even touchy

Jules. She felt both defensive and offended by Grace's tone but she wasn't sure how to wage war on someone whose hair looked like a brittle, blond helmet.

'I'm . . . er . . . not sure Cassia wanted bridesmaids,' Diana offered, doing her best to put some of Cassia's views forward. 'That is, I know for sure that she doesn't want bridesmaids. Maybe just Jules but only if she were allowed to choose her own outfit?'

Grace shot her a withering glance.

'Cassia prefers simple, non-fussy things,' Diana added weakly. 'Classy is her thing.'

Grace drew herself up. 'I'm sure, but this is also a Sunderland family wedding.' Her words seemed to suggest a chasm between Finn and Cassia, as though she wanted to make the point that they were an unsuitable match. 'And the Sunderlands prefer to do things properly, observing tradition and good form.'

Diana was so affronted, she chewed her raspberry lipstick off without realising. Grace really was objectionable! Grinding her teeth as she listened to Grace bossily outlining her plans for Cassia and Finn's wedding right down to the fold of the napkin and the type of fruit in the tiered cake, Diana finally cut in.

'Cassia detests those tiered fruit cakes,' she said, almost quailing when Grace's cold blue eyes turned towards her. She was glad she was already drinking an iced drink; she wouldn't have held out much hope for a hot one lasting under such a frigid stare. 'They're very old-fashioned. What about one of those dark chocolate affairs with sculpted cream roses, or perhaps cupcakes covered with gold sparkles?'

Grace snapped her file shut. 'Absolutely not. Finn and Cassia will be having a four-tiered cake, with three fruit layers and one vanilla sponge, like Henry and I had at our wedding.'

Thinking about the hastily bought chocolate roulade from Fortnum's she and Marco had bought to celebrate their nuptials with a bottle of Krug, Diana guessed she was going to have to let that one go. Feeling as though she'd let Cassia down, she tried to claw back some control. 'Cassia and Finn have so much in common, don't they?' she said, seeing a message from Fliss flashing up on her phone. 'They're both so dedicated to their careers . . . both so hard-working.'

Grace's mouth puckered. 'Cassia's certainly focused on her career.' She made it sound like the worst crime in the world. 'Perhaps she gets that from you. Maybe you'd both benefit from doing some charity work or some gardening. I find both pastimes incredibly grounding.'

'But *so* tough on the hands,' Diana returned sweetly, her patience with Grace finally running out. Grace might think she was from the top drawer in her crease-proof linen but she wasn't above bitchiness. Well, two could play at that game. 'I feel I must remind you that Cassia is also in Italy to find out more about her father, whom she adored, not just to boost her career,' she said pointedly. Then she offered Grace the name of a miracle hand cream recommended for those who did manual work and swept out into the sunshine.

As she strode down the street, Diana opened the message from Fliss. Her heart sank. She hadn't got the incredible part in the TV show she'd auditioned for, after all. She was too old, by all accounts. Ouch. The harsh blow of the text message hit her just as poignantly as a physical slap to the face would have done. Too old? Why did they have to pick the one thing she couldn't do anything about? she thought to herself glumly. The afternoon had been one of the most terrible she had suffered of late. She called Angelo and told him to leave his recording session and join her. Then she headed into a nearby bar and ordered herself a huge bloody mary with a double vodka chaser.

'I'm doing all right,' Cassia said to Finn, her phone crackling annoyingly as she tried to get a good reception in the restaurant. 'Missing you horribly, obviously.'

'Me too,' Finn said, instantly feeling better at hearing her voice. 'The flat feels really empty, which is silly, isn't it? I mean, you're often at yours and I'm often at my flat but for some reason it feels all lonely now you're over there.'

Cassia smiled. 'My room here is incredible, but I know what you mean. It's all a bit strange, but it's not for ever. How's work?'

'Very busy.' Finn sounded tense. 'I'm working silly hours at the moment. What have you been up to since you got there? Has Rocco been regaling you with cooking tales?'

'Not yet; he's been tied up with business stuff.' Cassia checked her watch. She was due to meet Rocco in the kitchen for the first time and she didn't want to be late, but she also didn't want to cut her call to Finn short. 'I've been into Sorrento a few times, I've eaten far more than I should have done in cafés and also here. Sofia makes all these pastries . . .' Cassia groaned. 'Jules will have a field day when she sees me. Oh, and I've been trying to start up the whole investigation into my father's family.'

'Any joy?'

'None,' she said glumly. 'I don't know where to begin, really. I can hardly knock on people's doors asking them if they remember a little boy called Marco, can I? He might not have even been called Marco, for all I know; the adoption people might have changed his name.'

Finn frowned. 'You need someone specialist in tracing people. You're not going to find out much by just asking around, your father did all that and he didn't get anywhere.'

'True.' Cassia wondered if Sofia might know of someone in the area who might be able to help. 'Listen, I must go but I'll call again soon.'

'Great. Love you, Cass,' Finn said as cheerfully as he could. 'Come back soon and save me from my mother calling me every two seconds about the wedding.'

Cassia felt panicked for a moment and hoped her own mother was fulfilling her promise to put her wedding preferences across. 'Don't. I'll be back as soon as I can.' She rang off and hurried to the kitchen. According to Sofia, Rocco had been shut away in his office for the past few days wading through red tape and paperwork pertaining to the Vegas restaurant and Cassia hoped Sofia was being truthful. She was beginning to think Rocco seriously resented her presence and was avoiding her. She still hadn't met Aurelia or Raffaelo either. Sofia assured her that Aurelia was expected back soon to film a bikini shoot on the estate, but she was rather vague as to Raffaelo's whereabouts.

The weather had turned noticeably warmer now that it was May, almost as if a switch had been flipped to tell everyone summer was on its way. A refreshing sea breeze, wafting up from the Amalfi coast, kept the stickiness at bay and, in the distance, Mount Vesuvius looked hazily grand.

Arriving in the kitchen just as Rocco was giving his team a rousing talk before lunchtime service, Cassia waited in the doorway, not wanting to announce her late arrival.

Watching Rocco commanding his team with understated eloquence, Cassia noticed that every single member was paying close attention. His eyes flashed when he spoke, revealing the depth of his commitment, but he barely moved, there was no clichéd, flamboyant hand-waving, he simply delivered his words efficiently and with utter conviction.

This was a man who knew he would be obeyed, Cassia thought, mentally taking notes instead of using the notepad in her hand. He presided over his team calmly; his stillness was hypnotic and his words were infused with passion. Cassia was certain he rarely needed to raise his voice to be obeyed.

As his staff scurried away to do his bidding, Rocco turned to Cassia and motioned for her to come into the kitchen. 'Sorry about that. I speak to my staff now and again, just to ensure they remember how important high standards are. How are you settling in?'

'Oh, very well, thank you,' she said, hastily closing her empty notepad, lest he think she hadn't been listening. She noted his polite tones and wondered if she would ever be able to chip beneath the surface to the real Rocco Disanti.

'I've met your grandmother. She's a lovely lady.'

'Lovely unless you cross her,' Rocco agreed. His unexpected grin threw Cassia off track. 'But you're right, she's fantastic, a real treasure. I have a lot of time for her, and she really helps me out in the restaurant. Thank goodness someone does.' Realising he sounded disloyal, Rocco quickly continued, his expression more sombre, 'Sorry, that's not fair. Raffaelo works in the restaurant but more in a handyman capacity. My grandmother takes care of bookings and we work on the menus together. She's a fantastic cook herself, of course. She and my grandfather Nico taught me everything I know.'

'I'm sure.' Cassia thought about Sofia's moment of melancholy and spoke without thinking. 'I got the impression she misses your grandfather terribly.'

Rocco frowned. 'After all this time? I don't know about that. Of course they were devoted to one another but I'm sure she must have moved on by now. It's been five years or more.'

Cassia disagreed but she kept her thoughts to herself. She was fairly certain she had read Sofia's expression correctly when she'd sat with her at the breakfast table the other day. Cassia wondered if Rocco simply disliked the idea of his grandmother with another man, a concept she had some sympathy with. After her father's death, she had found her mother's launch on to the dating scene uncomfortable to say the least, but she understood that her mother needed male attention. Angelo was the sweetest by far.

'By the way, I asked one of my staff to put the best language system I could find in your bedroom,' Rocco said. 'You mentioned you wanted to brush up on your Italian.'

Cassia turned pink. 'That's so kind of you . . . gosh, I must be making all sorts of mistakes as I'm talking to you. I do apologise.'

Rocco turned to face her, the sunshine streaming through the restaurant windows turning his hair a shade lighter. 'There is no need. It wasn't a criticism.' The refracted light threw his face into shadow, playing across his tanned cheekbones and sensual mouth.

'Shall I talk you through the kitchen set-up?' Rocco made the offer reluctantly and with a heavy air of obligation.

Wishing she could say no, Cassia nodded, following him as he started to laboriously talk her through the process. Rocco reminded her of the men she used to date in her teens. Granted, they hadn't been quite as handsome as he was, but they had been exciting, sexy types with passion and ambition bubbling just beneath the surface. Not the total bastards her sister Jules had a yen for, but potentially dangerous in their own way, all the same.

Cassia frowned. She couldn't quite remember when she had stopped dating men like that and choosing men who were more reliable – men like Finn – but she supposed it must have been around the time Jules had gone off the rails. Listening to Rocco discussing how the orders were dealt with, she remembered an occasion years ago when she had been unsure Finn was the man for her and she had confided in her father. He had grimly pointed out that Jules hadn't found happiness with any of the 'players' she had dated and that sometimes, being loyal and reliable wasn't a bad thing. Cassia, still unsure, had taken that to mean that her father approved of Finn and she had stayed with him. Further down the line, she had realised she really did love him, so she supposed her father must have been right. Cassia felt a pang. She missed her father so much; being in Italy made her feel close to him but also somehow made his absence more acute.

She mentally shook herself and gave Rocco her full attention. He told her how his ideas were translated into dishes by his team, and showed her high-quality cured meats hanging in the pantry and delicious-smelling plates of *fior di latte*, a local cheese characterised by a hazelnut crust and a creamy centre. Rocco talked her through the evening menu, showing her trays of fresh pasta dusted with flour, lobster shells bubbling away in pans for stock and piles of shredded dark chocolate, ready to be made into rich puddings. Being an avid foodie, Cassia was practically in gastronomic heaven.

'The service is prepped in advance for efficiency, but I also pride myself on the food being as fresh as possible.' Rocco leant against the counter, pushing his hands into his pockets. 'It's something my grandfather insisted upon.' He checked his watch with slight impatience. 'I'm afraid I have some calls to make now. Do you have enough to be going on with?'

Cassia nodded, once again aggravated by his obvious dismissal. She knew she was probably going to sound cool in response but she couldn't help it. 'Yes. Thank you for your time. I'll get my column written immediately.'

Rocco stared at her, seemingly about to say something but he closed his mouth as if he'd thought better of it. Cassia gazed back at him, feeling the air crackle with tension. Then all at once the moment passed and without betraying any emotion whatsoever, Rocco turned away and left her standing alone.

Back in her suite, Cassia noticed the sophisticated language system Rocco had promised her on her bedside table. She wondered if Sofia had suggested the gift; she couldn't imagine Rocco being so thoughtful, he had made his irritation towards her rudely obvious. Cassia sat down at the lovely writing desk in her suite and the words she sought were soon flowing with ease, English being a far easier medium with which to express herself.

'*Rocco commands his team with an almost sexual power,*' she typed rapidly, '*and they hang – slavishly – on his every word. Rocco Disanti is an enigma, successful, passionate and intensely attractive. Watching him at work brings to mind Michelangelo painting the ceiling in the Sistine Chapel; every move is made with . . .*' Cassia continued until she had run out of steam.

Sitting back, she reviewed her piece and hesitated. Remembering her colleague Pete mocking her for her sexually charged wording, she wondered if she had allowed herself to get carried away. The kitchen experience had been a real privilege and Rocco, despite his reserve towards her personally, was charismatic in the extreme. Surely this was what the readers wanted to know about him? Rereading the column, she decided to send it off anyway; her boss was scarily honest and Gena would soon let her know if she had moved beyond sensuality into soft porn.

Cassia sent the email and decided to go for a quick swim to clear her head. Quickly changing into a simple but well-cut black bikini, she added some leather flip-flops and a black-and-white striped sundress and headed downstairs. Searching out the vast, oval-shaped pool at the back of the house, she found it drenched in sunlight, apart from a shady corner overhung with wisteria, beneath which sat an astonishingly pretty girl.

Not more than nineteen or twenty, she was stretched out on a lounger wearing an electric-blue halter-neck bikini with a pair of wedge-heeled sandals. With flowing dark curls and the same compelling green eyes as Rocco, Cassia didn't need an introduction. Aside from recognising her from the front cover of many a glossy magazine, including the much-lauded Italian *Vogue*, this could only be Aurelia Disanti, Rocco's sister.

No wonder she was a model, Cassia thought enviously, taking in the lean lines of her body and the beautiful face. Close up, Aurelia resembled one of those heartbreakingly gorgeous girls in a Botticelli painting, all flowing hair and exquisite colouring.

God, but this family were glamorous, Cassia thought to herself, wondering if Raffaelo could possibly be as devastatingly good-looking as the rest of the Disanti clan.

'You must be Aurelia,' she said in Italian, offering her hand to the girl.

Aurelia sat up, putting her wedding magazine to one side with bad grace. Fixing Cassia with a chilly stare, she said, 'And you are Cassia Marini.'

Cassia faltered. 'Sorry, am I interrupting you? I can easily have a swim another time.'

Aurelia waved a careless hand, her mouth twisting petulantly. 'No need. I am trying to sort out my wedding, something which seems to be proving rather difficult.' She eyed Cassia's sensible outfit with an unsubtle eye roll. Did the woman possess any clothes in colours outside of the beige and black spectrum? Aurelia wondered cattily.

Cassia was shocked to be reminded of her own wedding, realising she hadn't thought about it once in the past week, not even to fret about Grace taking over.

'I'm trying to do the same thing at the moment,' she said. 'I'm getting married at the end of September.' She sat down on a lounger suddenly, stunned that her nuptials hadn't crossed her mind for the past couple of days.

'September? And you're arranging it from here?' Aurelia was incredulous. 'Impossible! It's taken me two years to finalise the details of my wedding and there is still so much to do. Especially without a wedding co-ordinator. I fired her,' she added with some remorse. 'An annoying girl, but she did have her uses.'

'Yes, well, my mother and mother-in-law are taking on quite a bit of responsibility,' Cassia said, Aurelia's words making her

117

feel distinctly panicky. More likely Grace was taking over the entire wedding, if her mother's apologetic texts were anything to go by. She'd phoned the day before to give Cassia a blow-by-blow account of her recent meeting with Grace in Soho and Cassia now knew she hadn't a hope in hell of retaining any level of control when it came to her nuptials.

Aurelia's full mouth curled. 'I wouldn't let my mother decide upon any aspect of my wedding, and as for my mother-in-law . . .' She shuddered comically. 'Dino's mother is very nice and she was a model in her day, but she's also very . . . Australian,' she finished, as if that explained everything.

Cassia said nothing. Aurelia reminded her of Jules in some ways. Jules was slightly older but they both seemed sulky and child-like, pouting regularly and looking disgruntled when things weren't going their way. Cassia thought Aurelia and Jules would probably get on like a house on fire if they ever met.

'We are getting married in August,' Aurelia said, turning back to Cassia. 'Traditionally, a very unlucky month in Italy, did you know that? Dino chose it, said it was the only time we could marry due to our work schedules, but I don't know . . .'

Cassia wondered if Aurelia was as superstitious as Sofia. She looked up as a shadow of a man blocked the sunlight.

'Raffaelo Disanti,' the man said, leaning over her hand to kiss it gallantly.

Rocco's younger brother, Cassia realised, taken aback by his appearance.

'I do hope you are enjoying your stay,' Raffaelo added, giving her a genial smile.

'Yes . . . thank you.' Cassia gazed up at him. He was exceptionally tall and his shoulders were even broader than Rocco's, but he had missed out on the good looks the rest of the family shared. He was dressed in a dark suit, dark shirt and white tie. He should be sweltering in this heat, but if he was, he didn't show it.

'Have you had a chance to sample Rocco's food yet?' Raffaelo asked, removing his sunglasses and revealing friendly brown eyes.

Cassia shook her head. 'Not yet. I can't wait. I've been lucky enough to have a few meals with your grandmother, though, and she's a wonderful cook.' She squinted up at Raffaelo. 'You work in the restaurant too, I understand.'

Raffaelo nodded. 'I do.' He smiled. 'Not such an important role as my brother, of course.'

Cassia wasn't sure if she could detect a glimmer of resentment in his eyes. Surely the man wouldn't be human if he didn't begrudge his older brother his devastating looks and his much-lauded cooking talent? Still, he looked affable enough and if he was jealous of his brother, he hid it well.

'I will leave you to your sunbathing,' Raffaelo said with a pleasant bow. 'It is very nice to meet you, Cassia, if I may call you that? A lovely name, which suits you perfectly.' He shot his cuffs and strode away.

'He's very charming,' Cassia commented.

Aurelia shrugged. 'I suppose so. Raffaelo is very sociable, he's much better at the front-of-house work than any of us. I've often wondered why Rocco hasn't put him in charge of that side of things rather than keeping him behind the scenes. Mind you, Raff doesn't seem bothered either way.' Abruptly, she snatched up her phone and let out a torrent of expletives.

'What's wrong?'

'The team for the model shoot, they're planning to arrive early. That's all I need. Rocco will go mad!' She leapt off her lounger.

Cassia thought Aurelia was probably right; Rocco didn't look as though he could cope with any more stress. 'Er . . . is there anything I can do?'

Aurelia threw her hands in the air, nearly tossing her phone in the pool. 'No, there is nothing anyone can do. It's a mess and I'm going to get the blame.' Jutting her bottom lip out and seemingly not acknowledging that the 'mess' was entirely of her own making, Aurelia tossed her wedding magazine aside and stomped away from the pool like a spoilt child being told 'no' for the first time.

Cassia glanced at the magazine, thinking that she really needed to devote herself to some of her own wedding details. She hadn't even started to look for a dress yet.

She picked up the magazine and began to leaf through the glossy pages. A feeling of terror began to set in. Aurelia had been planning her wedding for two years and she, Cassia, had a matter of weeks to put it all together from a different country. She stared at the array of wedding dresses, feeling intimidated. Where did she even start?

Chapter Six

'Are you sure it's a good idea for you and Dom to get together? The last thing I want is for you to get hurt again.'

Louisa felt deeply worried. Her brother was nearly an hour late, but that wasn't the only thing that was making Louisa feel apprehensive. Dom had arranged to meet Jules in a trendy sushi bar in the West End and Louisa, not trusting him one bit, had decided to keep Jules company until Dom put in an appearance.

Jules repositioned her low-cut pink dress and glanced round the loud, buzzy restaurant. It had open sides which allowed people to spill out on to the warm, sociable street outside and she had already spotted a few well-known faces. Trying not to stare, she'd recognised a soap star, two glamour girls and an up-and-coming TV presenter. Jules realised she wasn't entirely comfortable in her surroundings. She enjoyed the glitz and glamour but she didn't enjoy the thought that most of the pretty girls in the restaurant were probably there for the sole purpose of meeting famous sportsmen and celebrities.

Glancing at Louisa, she realised her friend looked anxious. 'Why wouldn't it be a good idea if we got together, Lou?' She frowned. 'He's dreamy and I'm really into him. And from the way he was all over me the other day at that club he asked me to check out, I'm pretty sure it's mutual. Thanks for suggesting that I take your place, by the way; it was a stroke of genius.'

Toying with her cocktail, Louisa bit her lip. 'It's just . . . Dom isn't Finn, Jules. He's unreliable, he doesn't treat girls very well. I mean, he does in the beginning, but then he gets bored and someone else comes along.' She stopped, seeing Jules's pained expression. Louisa wasn't even sure Dom was that keen; she knew her brother and when he was really into someone, he didn't risk being late, especially when he barely had a day off at the moment. When Dom was out to impress, he was punctual, attentive and utterly focused – usually on getting his wicked way. The only reason he was in the country at all was because he'd suffered a slight ligament strain – a real one this time – and his coach wanted him to save himself for the pre-Wimbledon matches and some others in England and Europe.

Louisa discreetly checked her phone, wondering how on earth she was going to manage damage limitation if Dom stood Jules up. In her thigh-skimming dress and heels, Jules looked the epitome of youthful confidence but the sleek appearance hid a deceptively vulnerable nature.

'There he is!'

Brimming with excitement, Jules leapt up as Dom's head appeared above the crowds. He's so handsome, she thought to herself breathlessly. She watched several girls flicking their hair and eyeing him as he made his way through the crowds. She felt mixed emotions. Dom was drop-dead gorgeous, as well as being a hotshot on the tennis court, but did she really want to date someone who was in such demand from an adoring public? She felt a flicker of doubt, but she knew she couldn't resist him. He wanted to meet her tonight, didn't he? He had taken the initiative and set up the meeting, not the other way round. That had to count for something.

Louisa gave Dom a sour look as she caught him pocketing a few girls' numbers on the way over. Not only did he look tanked up, as though he'd already been out to several bars before ending up at the sushi restaurant, but he also had a telltale pink lipstick smear on his cheek.

'Jules.' Dom kissed both of her cheeks, missing her mouth by millimetres. 'Wow. You look absolutely gorgeous.' Catching sight of the candy-pink stain on his cheek in the mirror behind Jules's head, he smoothly wiped it away as he removed his suit jacket. Noticing Louisa's disapproving expression, he shot her a cold stare.

'I wasn't aware we were double-dating,' he commented, loosening his tie.

'We're not.' Gathering up her wrap and purse, Louisa got to her feet. Face to face with Dom she could smell the whisky on his breath. She couldn't stand it when he drank; he turned into a prize dickhead. 'I just wanted to make sure Jules wasn't left sitting by herself all night. Silly of me, I know.'

Dom's eyes darkened. He resented his sister; she reminded him of his judgemental mother and one family member acting as though he was a failure was more than enough. Sliding into the booth next to Jules, Dom defiantly slung his arm round her.

'Thanks for babysitting, Lou, but I think I can take over now. Shouldn't you be out finding yourself a man?'

'How do you know I don't have one?' she threw back at him. 'You're too self-absorbed to have the first idea about my life.' Tight-lipped and uneasy, Louisa left them to it.

'She's just concerned about me,' Jules informed Dom, sliding Louisa's barely touched cocktail across the table towards him. 'Not because she needs to be, but because she's my friend. Don't take it the wrong way.'

Dom drained the cocktail in one, catching the eye of a passing waitress and ordering another round. He knew exactly why his sister was giving him a hard time but she wasn't his keeper and he did what he liked, when he liked. Showering

Jules with attention and compliments, he kept the cocktails flowing as they dined on sashimi salmon roses and Jules's favourite spider rolls, which contained mouth-wateringly delicious fried soft-shell crabs.

At the end of the night, dazzled by Dom's charm and easy patter, Jules found herself back at a modern penthouse apartment in Knightsbridge. She was impressed, unaware that Dom had borrowed it from a fellow player. Feeling smug and wishing Cassia could see her now so she knew she wasn't the only sister capable of landing herself a decent man, Jules stood on the balcony and stared out at the view.

She shivered as she felt Dom's warm hands on her back, noticing how rough and calloused his palms and fingers were, no doubt from all the years he'd spent wielding a tennis racket.

'I can't believe we haven't got together before,' Dom murmured as he caressed her shoulders.

Jules leant against him. 'Me neither.' Feeling him slowly sliding down the zipper on her dress, she eased it off her shoulders so it slithered to the floor. Still standing with her back towards him in the shell-pink silk underwear and high heels she'd selected just in case this very moment came to pass, Jules shivered again as the cool evening air caressed her bare skin.

'You're so beautiful,' Dom whispered, lifting her hair and dropping hot kisses on her neck. With one practised movement, he unhooked her bra and discarded it, placing his hands on her breasts. 'No tan marks,' he said, admiringly.

Jules sucked her breath in. 'Topless is the only way to sunbathe,' she managed, willing him to touch her more.

Dom obliged. Squeezing her tanned breasts, he thumbed her nipples until they throbbed and, unable to bear it any longer, Jules spun round and kissed him, sinking her hands into his blond hair. Dom kissed her back ardently, picking her up and wrapping her tanned thighs round his waist.

'I think I've found a perfect fit,' he mumbled against her mouth. As he lowered his head to her breasts and flicked them with his tongue, Jules arched her back in ecstasy, her stomach fizzing with anticipation. Noticing an enormous bulge in Dom's trousers, she reached for it excitedly, squeaking as she felt his fingers tugging her knickers to one side.

Feeling happy for the first time in months, she gave in to Dom's expert touch and hazily wondered what professional tennis players ate for breakfast.

Standing outside Rocco's office for a meeting they had scheduled, Cassia frowned as she heard his voice coming from the restaurant. Switching direction, she walked into the well-polished silver kitchen area and came face to face with Rocco icily firing his head chef, Antonio. The rest of the staff were making a show of looking after their stations but it was obvious each one was straining to hear the conversation between Rocco and one of his most valuable members of staff. Silvana, Antonio's plain but earnest sous-chef, stood by fearfully.

'Do you think this is good enough?' Rocco asked in a soft but deadly tone. Picking up a nearby fork, he prodded the contents of a dish as though inspecting a dead jellyfish. 'Seriously, Antonio, you would serve this . . . this overcooked monstrosity?'

Cassia swallowed, feeling sorry for Antonio. Monkfish in saffron sauce was one of Rocco's signature dishes and, already familiar with his exacting standards, Cassia imagined that in Rocco's eyes Antonio had committed a crime worthy of death, let alone unemployment. She stole a glance at Rocco, thinking she would personally detest being on the receiving end of his glacial disapproval. His wintry demeanour was somehow far more intimidating than an over-the-top display of hot-headed gesticulation.

'No, I wouldn't serve it,' Antonio agreed. 'This dish wasn't intended for the restaurant, it was a practice dish for—'

'I don't care.' Rocco placed the fork on the dish with calculated precision, the gesture speaking volumes in a way that hurling the dish and fork out of the window couldn't. 'It's substandard and I can't imagine why you even bothered to take it out of the pan.' He shook his head. 'No, Antonio, it's not good enough. You must leave. If I can't trust you to recreate my dishes, you don't deserve to be here.'

Silvana gasped and shook her head. Antonio bit his lip. Torn between ripping off his chef's whites and hurling them in Rocco's face, and standing his ground because he knew it was all a storm in a teacup, Antonio stood motionless in front of his boss. Loath to drop his trainee sous-chef in it, he refused to let on that it was she who had attempted the dish, admittedly on his instruction as he felt she was becoming too cocky and needed taking down a peg or two, and he shot Silvana a warning glance, forbidding her from speaking up.

Not giving herself time to think, Cassia stepped forward. 'Can I make a suggestion?' she said, almost quailing as Rocco's intimidating gaze swung her way. Realising belatedly she was taking her life in her hands by daring to challenge him in what was his environment, even if he didn't cook in it these days, Cassia swallowed.

'Sorry, it's just that . . . I wonder if you could, you know, run through the recipe and demonstrate exactly what's required to create the perfect dish.' Feeling Rocco's eyes boring into her, she shrugged. 'I just thought the team might benefit from your expertise.'

Coldly furious, Rocco stared at Cassia. Who the hell did she think she was, barging into his kitchen and challenging his decisions? If he wanted to fire his head chef, it had nothing whatsoever to do with her. No, Antonio was out of order and he deserved to be punished. As for Cassia Marini, she was an aggravating, interfering journalist who should keep her nose out of his goddamned business . . .

About to coldly tell Cassia to pack her things and go home to England, Rocco paused. As always with him, his icy anger rapidly subsided. Like an unwatched pan of spaghetti, he could boil over at any second, but once diffused and removed from the heat, he soon calmed down.

Aware of his staff watching and waiting to see how he was going to respond, it occurred to Rocco that he might have overreacted. And that his stress levels might be behind the knee-jerk reaction of firing Antonio who, he had to admit, was the best chef he'd ever had the pleasure of working with.

Noticing Antonio's proud, defensive stance, he wondered if it had been young Silvana who had cooked the dish. Knowing how fiercely loyal his head chef was, Rocco immediately backed down. Abruptly, he found himself laughing and his staff looked stunned at the astonishing about-turn.

'That's not such a bad idea,' he said, eyeing Cassia with a twitching mouth. 'If you can find me some whites, I'll do just that.'

A white jacket was thrust into her hands by a staff member, and Cassia handed it over wordlessly, hoping Rocco couldn't hear her frantically beating heart. What on earth had possessed her to butt in like that? She was usually so reserved. Finn would have been horrified if he'd witnessed the scene; he abhorred any kind of confrontation.

Flushing at her daring, Cassia watched as Rocco threw on the chef's whites with the casual familiarity associated with a professional at work.

Antonio provided a fresh tray of ingredients, standing back respectfully as Rocco picked up a bowl of mussels and a small crowd gathered to watch.

'So we boil the water with some of the garlic cloves,' Rocco said, tossing three in, followed by the mussels. 'Once the mussels have been cleaned and debearded, they can cook until they open.' Watching the pan closely, at just the right moment he swiftly hooked the mussels out, discarding any that hadn't opened. 'Strain the liquid through a sieve and add the saffron powder – a quarter of a teaspoon, no more.'

Stirring it quickly, Rocco set it aside and cut the monkfish into chunks. Cooking some tomatoes on a low heat, he sautéed some garlic with onions and butter. An aromatic smell drifted up from the frying pan. Adding the monkfish, Rocco didn't take his eyes off it for a second, stirring it occasionally before pouring in white wine.

Cassia stole a glance at Rocco's staff. They were completely focused on each word and every flick of Rocco's fingers. They were watching a true master at work, and Cassia couldn't help but be deeply impressed by Rocco. There was something so thrilling about watching him work, something so skilful about the way he handled the ingredients and talked through the process calmly but with passion.

'When the monkfish is cooked – and you can tell when it's perfectly cooked by testing like this . . .' he pushed his finger gently against the meaty flesh and nodded in satisfaction. 'When it's cooked, you add the mussels and the herbs.' Flamboyantly adding the final ingredients, including a few secret ingredients that made the dish a Disanti classic, he cooked the sauce down and tasted it, then seasoned it until he felt sure he had the balance just right.

Plating it up with an understated flourish, Rocco pushed the dish towards Antonio. 'Taste it,' he said modestly. 'I think you'll find that's how it should be made.'

Antonio helped himself to a mouthful. Saying nothing but putting his fingers to his mouth appreciatively, he pushed the dish towards Silvana. With trembling fingers, she forked up some monkfish and tasted it.

'It's perfection,' she mumbled.

Noticing Cassia inhaling the aroma with pleasure, Rocco nudged the dish in her direction. 'Please, be my guest.'

Helping herself, Cassia savoured the mouthful. It was exquisite. The sauce was rich but light and the monkfish was meaty yet succulent. It was such a simple recipe, but the combination of Rocco's skilful fingers and the subtle, secretive touches he had added made for a superb dish.

'It's divine,' she said out loud, noticing Rocco's staff melting away and returning to their stations. Antonio nodded curtly at Silvana and took a discreet step back, obviously unsure if Rocco's unexpected change of heart meant he still had a job.

'That sauce is absolutely wonderful,' Cassia continued, hoping Antonio wouldn't be kicked out. 'It is so aromatic with the saffron but delicate too. I wish I could cook like that, but I'm hopeless.' She put her fork down with an admiring expression. 'What a shame you don't have time to cook more. Your . . . your passion is infectious, I've never seen anything like the reaction you just invoked in all your staff.'

Rocco shrugged elegantly. 'I am far too busy to cook these days.' He gazed at the dish with something resembling regret. He hadn't realised how much he missed being in the kitchen until now. Recreating one of his favourite dishes had reminded him of his true passion; some years ago, it had been his zealous appetite for crafting dishes, along with his obsessive desire to be considered one of the best chefs of his time, that had driven him forward to succeed and achieve greatness.

'I enjoyed that,' he commented, his tone surprised. 'Cooking, I mean. I really enjoyed it.' He frowned, as if mystified by the revelation.

Cassia was puzzled. Didn't Rocco realise how much he still loved cooking? Had he really been away from the kitchen for so long that he didn't even remember how much it made his heart race?

'Look, I'm sorry for butting in like that,' she said, thinking it might be pertinent to explain her reckless behaviour. 'I am honestly not normally so rude.'

'Rude?' Rocco gave her a half-smile. 'It wasn't rude. Someone needed to calm me down. I can get a little carried away if my carefully built-up empire crumbles even a little.'

Remembering how close he had been to sending Cassia back in a taxi without so much as a goodbye, Rocco felt rather guilty. He still resented her presence and the way her requirements encroached on his time, but it wasn't her fault.

Cassia began to feel rather flustered by Rocco's scrutiny of her. Still, it was awfully hot in the kitchen, she thought, resisting the urge to fan herself.

Rocco admired Cassia for standing up to him; hell, even his own staff baulked at doing that, but sometimes he needed someone to rein him in. And she had watched him recreating his famous dish with absolute commitment, as if she intended to commit the details to memory, and what's more she had tucked into the finished product with gusto.

Cassia was passionate about food, that was for sure, Rocco thought, pleased to find another female aside from the ones on his staff who appreciated food. His grandmother aside, the women in his life tended to see food as a necessity rather than a God-given pleasure. Stefania never really talked about his talents as a chef, and knowing extra weight would mean avoiding the latest fashions, she ate like a bird. Aurelia was just as bad, always stressing about calories and fat, Rocco thought impatiently.

He ran his eyes appreciatively over Cassia, noting the professional-looking biscuit-brown dress that stopped at the knee. It was demure but clingy, hugging her curves. He wondered if Cassia's rather reserved manner, like her deceptively modest dress, hid a more flamboyant personality. She appeared to be shy, prim even, in some ways, yet the spark in her eyes and the odd flash of impulsiveness suggested otherwise.

Rocco frowned. He liked thin, leggy blondes, not curvaceous brunettes, and he only ever dated Italian women; not through conscious choice, he was simply drawn to them.

He turned to Antonio, who was still hovering. 'You are, of course, reinstated, my friend. Please forgive my loss of control earlier. I'm afraid I am rather busy at the moment and it seems to be making me rather unreasonable at times. Forgive me.'

Antonio beamed. 'No matter,' he said, clearly beside himself that he had held on to his prestigious job. He shot Cassia a grateful grin, certain that without her intervention, he would have found himself in a very different situation. 'I'll get back to work,' he added, watching Cassia and Rocco curiously.

Trying to ignore a sexy waft of aftershave as Rocco leant across her to check a sauce, Cassia gestured to the dish. 'I've never cooked monkfish before. I should give it a go when I get home.'

'Do it here,' Rocco found himself saying. 'My kitchen is at your disposal when it's not in use.' He paused. What was he doing, offering his kitchen to this woman he barely knew?

'Really?' Her eyes lit up. 'My father . . . Marco Marini, used to cook all the time. I dabble when I can but I'm honestly not that great.'

Starting, Rocco realised he hadn't even picked up on her surname. Marco Marini was a renowned food writer in Italy; his books were on the shelves of most self-respecting chefs and food lovers, including his own. About to tell her how much he admired her father, he was interrupted by the sound of her mobile phone.

Annoyed at being contacted at such an inopportune moment, Cassia was even more put out when she saw that the caller was Grace.

'Your fiancé?' Rocco asked politely. He hadn't heard much about Cassia's husband-to-be, but he assumed he must be making constant contact.

Cassia shook her head. 'It's my future mother-in-law, actually.'

Noticing that several text messages had also been left, she realised she would have to take the call, otherwise Grace would hound her relentlessly. Cassia felt faintly embarrassed. She hardly ever allowed her private life to filter through to her professional one, but she was trying to organise a wedding and with Grace apparently in sole charge now that her mother had given up, Cassia knew she needed to keep her sweet for the time being.

Glancing at Rocco, who motioned for her to take the call, she answered her phone.

'Hello, Grace. Lovely to hear from you . . . The flowers, you say?' She sighed. Noting a hint of contempt in Rocco's eyes, she felt her blood boil. Who the hell did he think he was? She'd just saved him from making a terrible business decision – as well as earning him increased adoration from his army of already devoted fans – and yet he was looking at her as though she was a silly little girl with nothing better to do than discuss details of her wedding when she should be working.

Oh, the irony! thought Cassia. Back home, she had to endure taunts from Grace about how ambitious she was, how much emphasis she placed on her career rather than her personal life, whereas now she felt she had to defend herself against an unspoken insinuation of doing the reverse.

Throwing Rocco a look of fury, Cassia turned her back on him, fuming inwardly. She respected his skills as a chef, but as a human being he was sorely bloody lacking, the arrogant bastard.

Rocco tore off his jacket and stalked out of the kitchen. He was glad Cassia had received the personal call; up until that point, he'd been dangerously close to thinking she was something special. As it was, she was no better than Aurelia, wedding-obsessed when she should be focusing on doing her job. Telling himself his brief fascination with her had been a passing fancy, Rocco shut himself in his office and groaned at the pile of paperwork on his desk. Not sure why he felt so unsettled by the way the morning had panned out, he put the kitchen incident – and Cassia – firmly out of his head and dialled Las Vegas to get an update on his new restaurant.

Flicking through wedding magazines as his mother prattled on endlessly about buttonholes and table settings, Finn realised he was bored rigid. Home for the weekend to catch up with his family in Kent and lonely beyond belief at his London apartment, he had accepted an invitation to Sunday lunch.

Sitting in the conservatory with a gin and tonic with ice and a slice, Finn wished Cassia was here. Not so much because he wanted to discuss wedding details (frankly, he couldn't care less what colour the napkins were or how tall the centrepieces), but because he missed chatting to her, whatever the topic. She had been gone for over three weeks now but it felt like an eternity. Finn was glad they'd managed to chat the other day; he'd been so busy, he'd ignored several calls, but it had been great to talk to her. He wasn't sure why he hadn't talked to her about what was happening at work, but for some reason he hadn't wanted to. Did he feel like a failure when her career seemed to be going so well?

'I managed to grab a few, precious seconds with Cassia on the phone the other day,' Grace was saying, making it obvious she felt fobbed off, 'and she was happy to let me go ahead with my flower choices. Do you approve?' Thrusting some photographs under Finn's nose, she wondered fleetingly, hopefully, if Finn's apathy towards fine-tuning the details of his nuptials meant his feelings for Cassia might not be as fervent as before.

Ensconced in a wicker chair filled with plump, fern-green cushions, Henry shot his son a look of sympathy. He couldn't think of anything more inane than discussing floral arrangements and he was sure Finn felt the same way. Henry really wished Grace would stop bullying Finn. It was clear he was missing

Cassia and if Henry wasn't mistaken, things weren't going so well for him at work.

'Whatever you think,' Finn answered tiredly, meeting his father's eyes. 'Seriously, I couldn't care less about any of these details, Mother.' Pinching the bridge of his nose as he felt the past few manic weeks at work catching up with him, he glanced at his mother, wondering why her blue eyes looked so hopeful.

'I just mean that none of these things matter, do they? I'd marry Cassia at the local register office if I could.'

Distractedly, Finn wondered if he should mention that he had been passed over for promotion at Lovetts & Rose yet again. It had been the dismal end to an exhausting week and he despaired of climbing further up the somewhat slippery ladder at the law firm. He earned good money and, comparatively speaking, he was doing well for himself, but he wanted to make sure he had everything in place for his marriage to Cassia. After all, he planned to be the main – make that the *sole* – breadwinner once things had settled down and Cassia had taken more of a back seat on the career front. He assumed she might want to do a bit of freelance work, but apart from that, he really needed her to support him at home. He hoped that didn't make him sexist but he supposed it was how he had been brought up.

Suddenly noticing how dismayed his mother looked, Finn realised she was having a seizure at his mention of a register office. 'Oh, Mother, relax! I wouldn't do such a thing, of course, because I know how much you're enjoying putting together this extravaganza. But marrying Cassia is really all that matters to me.'

Grace's stomach plummeted. So much for Finn's ardour fading; if anything, he seemed all the more determined to marry Cassia.

Perhaps the old adage about absence making the heart grow fonder was true after all, she thought to herself with some frustration. Cassia was a nice enough girl but Grace knew in her heart that she wouldn't be happy fulfilling the role that she herself enjoyed so much. Cassia would see being a stay-at-home wife and mother as a comedown, Grace thought with pursed lips.

She could tell Finn was preoccupied; the furrow between his eyes and the restless way he kept drumming his hands on his glass were a dead giveaway. Oblivious to Finn's work concerns, Grace cursed Cassia's decision to go to Italy, blaming her for his disquiet.

'Oh good, Dom's here,' Finn said, brightening at the sight of his brother. At least they could present a united front against their mother, he thought, relieved. His eyes narrowed as he realised Dom wasn't alone. 'Who's that with him? Dom never brings girls to Sunday lunch.'

'Jules,' Grace said, looking smug. 'I was hoping he'd bring her along. They've been seeing each other quite a lot recently.'

Finn watched Dom helping Jules out of the boxy white jacket she wore over her pretty floral tea dress and noted the way she blushed as Dom dropped a deliberately suggestive kiss on her bare neck. She clutched Dom's hand as they made their way into the conservatory.

Finn watched them in astonishment. He'd known nothing about the relationship. The last time he had seen Jules had been at the nightclub Dom was thinking of investing in; he had no idea things had gone any further. Finn wondered why Dom hadn't mentioned anything. Surely he would know it was news-worthy to mention the fact that he was dating Cassia's sister.

For some reason, the situation made Finn feel nervous. He wasn't sure if he was worried about Cassia's reaction or if, knowing Dom's fearful reputation with women, he was simply concerned for Jules's welfare. Dom had a habit of promising women the world and treating them like princesses, right before he tossed them aside like an unwanted toy. Many a time in the past Finn had felt compelled to step in and console yet another girl Dom had misled, but this time felt more personal, Jules was practically family. But she was hardly a shrinking little flower, Finn reminded himself.

'Nice to see you, Jules,' he said, getting to his feet. 'I didn't know you were coming today.'

'Me neither,' Jules replied, thinking how different Finn looked in casual clothes. Less uptight. 'It was a last-minute decision.'

Dom smiled broadly. 'It seemed silly not to bring Jules along. After all, we've been inseparable for the past couple of weeks, haven't we? Well, when I've been in the country, anyway. I'm flying out to France later today for some training and prep for the French Open, so I thought it would be nice to spend the rest of the day together.'

Looking blissful, Jules accepted a gin and tonic from Henry, even though she abhorred gin. Eager to please, she took a seat next to Henry and tried, unsuccessfully, to help him with his crossword.

Taking Dom to one side, Finn fixed his eyes on his brother. 'What are you playing at? Jules is Cassia's sister, it could be very awkward at the wedding if you've dumped her.'

'Don't stress, bro,' Dom said, flicking his blond hair out of his eyes. Conscious of Jules's infatuated gaze, he kept his expression impassive. Fresh from an energetic session in bed together, followed by a hot shower and a repeat performance, Dom was feeling rather loved up himself. Or was it lust? he wondered lazily. 'Jules is lovely, and I have absolutely no intention of dumping her, so you have nothing to worry about.'

Finn couldn't help feeling out of sorts, what with Dom acting completely out of character and his mother banging on obsessively about buttonholes.

Helping himself to another drink, Finn couldn't help thinking things wouldn't be the same until Cassia was back where she belonged.

*

'What's that?' murmured Angelo, kissing Diana's bare back as she lay in bed reading.

Diana held up a script. 'It's a character part my agent is trying to convince me to play. On stage. God knows why I even agreed to read it.' Her tone was derisive as she flipped another page but Diana knew why she had agreed to read the script – desperation. She wasn't getting any of the TV parts she'd gone for, so she'd relented and allowed Fliss to send her the script for the play.

Entitled simply *Jealousy*, it had been written by a distinguished playwright and the quality of the writing was undeniably superb. However, the play required the female lead to appear make-up-free in at least two scenes, as well as half-naked in several others. Diana was less intimidated by the nude scenes than she was by the ones where the character was required to deliver soulful soliloquies without wearing a scrap of make-up. Nude scenes she was familiar with but when had she last appeared in public without mascara and lipstick?

'Why don't you want to play the part?' Angelo asked, leaving a trail of suggestive kisses along Diana's spine. 'You are a wonderful actress.'

Diana absent-mindedly turned and kissed his muscled bicep. 'Thank you, darling. It's not that I can't play the part, I just don't *want* to play it. There's a big difference.'

She wasn't about to explain to Angelo that appearing without make-up was the deal-breaker; she knew how vain and silly that would make her sound. However, she couldn't deny that the part itself was intriguing – challenging in a way that Diana hadn't come across before. The character was fifty-two – this fact alone was enough to cause palpitations, but it wasn't the issue of age that had Diana turning the pages to find out what happened next. It was the subtlety of the piece, the raw emotion displayed by all the characters, that made the play one of the most powerful things Diane had read in a long time.

The premise was that Clarissa, an older woman, was having an affair with a much younger man called Kyle, a painter. The affair is very sexual and the scenes depicting this side of the story were explicit and energetic. Clarissa, a vain woman already struggling to come to terms with her age and rapidly disappearing looks, finds her self-esteem boosted from indulging in secret, passionate sex with Kyle behind closed doors. He also paints her time and time again, the paintings absurdly flattering and depicting Clarissa as youthful and blooming, rather than the more truthful version of herself, sagging slightly and losing her sparkle.

Falling deeply in love with him, Clarissa becomes obsessed with Kyle, jealously questioning his movements and repeatedly accusing him of losing interest in her. When Clarissa's vicious taunts finally drive the young painter away and into the arms of Clarissa's fresh-faced and much younger daughter, Clarissa becomes unhinged. In an ugly scene, she kills both her daughter and Kyle, a crime of passion which goes unsolved but which ultimately destroys Clarissa as she retreats from society and descends into madness. Not having told any of her friends about her lover, no one believes Clarissa when she tries to confide in them about her passionate relationship. Even when she confesses to the authorities, they laugh at her, unable to believe the virile young painter would contemplate an affair with such a faded, desperate old woman.

Diana pushed her blond hair out of her eyes and slowly turned another page. She wanted to discuss it with someone but she wasn't sure who she could call. Not Fliss; she was biased. Cassia, perhaps? Her daughter was always searingly honest and Diana knew she could rely on her to at least listen without judging.

Jules wouldn't be much use, Diana thought drily. She would wet her pants laughing at the thought of her mother having to appear naked and free of make-up on stage in front of hundreds of people. And what she would make of the issue of gaining weight didn't bear thinking about.

Diana wasn't sure what disturbed her most about the play. The similarity to her own life, naturally; she would be stupid if she didn't make reference to that. She was the same age as Clarissa. She had lied for years about her true age but, in reality, she and Clarissa shared much in common. Their age, their vanity, even their constant desire for attention. Diana was many things but she refused to live in denial about who she was and she knew she was seeing Angelo because he made her feel good about herself. He made her feel younger, of course, but unlike Clarissa, Diana didn't hide Angelo away like a dirty secret; the opposite, in fact. But still, she couldn't help seeing much of herself in Clarissa, a fact that was both captivating and troubling.

Reading over her shoulder, Angelo laughed. 'I promise I will not run off with either of your daughters. Not if you plan to kill me because of it.'

'Don't be so ridiculous,' Diana snapped, sitting up and yanking the sheet round her naked body. 'It's a play, it's not real life.'

Angelo lay back and grinned. 'That is true. For a start, I paint like a four year old.' He wiggled his long, tanned fingers. 'These are good for the guitar but terrible with a paintbrush.'

Diana was unamused. She got up and walked to the window with the script in her hand, catching sight of herself in the mirror of her Venetian-glass dressing table. She still had last night's make-up on – she wouldn't dream of going to bed with Angelo without it because he'd never seen her without her foundation artfully applied.

Diana studied herself critically, lifting her chin this way and that. Her skin was fairly taut still and her arms were slender, without a hint of the dreaded bingo wing. But it was an uphill battle and she knew it. Diana watched Angelo as he picked up the guitar he always left by the bed and began softly strumming it. His inky-black eyes were cast downwards, his mouth twisted in pleasurable concentration as he played a riff over and over to perfect it. His lips moved as he murmured the words of some Spanish song to himself. Then he lifted his dark head, flicked his long hair out of his eyes and smiled at her.

As he returned to his guitar, Diana faltered, wondering what Angelo saw in her. Was he like Kyle in the play – did he see her as some sort of muse from a bygone era, one he would lose interest in soon? Would he run off with a younger woman? Maybe not one of her daughters, but a girl in the first flush of youth with everything on her side, including her age?

Suddenly, Diana felt overwhelmed by sharp little daggers of insecurity. The horrible, gut-wrenching feeling was swiftly followed by an overwhelming blow of grief. Marco, Marco, she thought to herself despairingly. So charismatic, so intellectual . . . he had always been able to make her feel desirable and beautiful, whatever she looked like. It should have been enough. She had hungrily absorbed Marco's loving, heartfelt compliments, but even when he was spent from reassuring her, she had demanded more. More than anyone was capable of giving.

Feeling Angelo moving up behind her as her legs began to buckle, Diana turned to him, imploringly. She needed him to make the pain go away, now, before it took hold. Whether he understood how desperate her need, Angelo obliged, sinking his mouth to hers as her arms wound round his neck. The fingers that had been sensitively plucking his guitar only seconds before began to work their magic on her body, rhythmically stroking her skin, caressing her into submission.

Feeling him peeling away her silk nightgown until she was naked and vulnerable, Diana allowed Angelo to lift her to the bed, hoping her body wasn't as heavy as her heart. As Angelo leant over her, slowly kissing every inch of her bare skin, his hair tickling her stomach as he swept from one graceful arch to another, Diana caught her breath.

'Help me,' she mumbled into his shoulder.

Angelo looked up in confusion, not sure he had understood correctly. After living in England for some years now, his English was of a good standard, but he had always thought 'help me' was an expression used by someone in distress.

Diana pulled him closer. 'I need you,' she managed.

'My darling,' Angelo said, sinking inside her with a joyful groan.

As his swarthy young body moved against hers, Diana turned her head to one side as a single tear trickled out. Seeing the script she had abandoned on the floor, she made a decision. She would never play Clarissa, not in a million years. It was too close to home . . . way too close to home.

As Angelo pleasured her with exquisite, heartbreaking tenderness, a sad thought occurred to Diana. Why, when Angelo's desire for her was so palpable, did she suddenly miss Marco more than ever?

'Did you get all of that?'

Cassia checked her notes and nodded. 'I think so.' She was more than satisfied with all the details Rocco had given her so far; she really felt she was getting to know him at last. He'd been short-tempered and moody while discussing the Vegas restaurant, brightening briefly to talk about one of his signature dishes, a rich chocolate *semifreddo* flavoured with rum and muscovado sugar. Carried away with the story of Nico showing Rocco how to make the dessert as a small boy, Cassia was already planning her column in her head.

'*Made with Love* – semifreddo *with a twist . . . Whisk the cream until soft, luscious peaks appear, folding in glossy, melted chocolate and rum. Add egg white peaks and scoop dollops of the mixture into chilled dessert glasses, topping with crunchy meringue pieces and rich, dark muscovado sugar. Scatter fresh, edible flowers on the glistening surface and devour . . . preferably in the company of a loved one . . .*'

Forcing herself back to the present, Cassia realised Rocco was staring at her curiously.

'Sorry,' she mumbled, going red. 'I just get so engrossed in your recipes. I feel as if I can practically taste these desserts.' She shuffled her notes together.

Rocco linked tanned fingers and leant on his desk. 'Don't apologise; I'm glad you enjoy food so much. I . . . enjoy talking about it with you.'

He surprised himself with his honesty, but it was true. He did enjoy chatting to Cassia. Even though their daily sessions were impacting on his already stupidly busy schedule and making him late for meetings, he couldn't help looking forward to them. Rocco told himself it was simply because he had the opportunity to talk about the things he was passionate about, but the fact that Cassia was enthusiastic certainly made things easier.

And she was disturbingly attractive, Rocco thought to himself. It was as if every day they spent together underlined that fact more and more. He glanced at the photograph of Stefania on his desk, semi-clad and gorgeous. Perhaps he missed her; maybe it was time they saw one another again.

Rocco was cross with himself. Cassia was no more attractive than any other woman he knew; he must be suffering from cabin fever, that was all. Being stuck away in his office working all hours, surrounded by his staff and his family was clearly getting to him.

Cassia felt uncomfortable as Rocco scrutinised her. Even now, after four weeks had passed, he unnerved her. At first, she had been a little in awe of him, and he had aggravated her with his arrogant detachment. But she was finding her sessions with him increasingly enjoyable. Rocco was so interesting, his stories about Nico were fascinating and the way he talked about food was akin to someone quoting exquisite poetry.

'I have a conference call with my team in Vegas,' Rocco said abruptly. 'There are a few problems, I think . . . the

142

opening may well be delayed. So I'm afraid our session is over.'

Noting the curt tone, Cassia felt her warm feelings towards him evaporating once more. Whenever she started to feel as if they were forming some sort of uneasy friendship, Rocco managed to revert back to the conceited idiot he had been when she first arrived. And what was that about the opening of the Vegas restaurant possibly being delayed? She felt alarmed. That would mean her spending more time in Sorrento and even though she was enjoying every minute of it, she had a wedding to sort out back in England. And what on earth would Finn say if she had to phone him and tell him she was going to be away for even longer?

Still cross that Rocco had been so dismissive, Cassia picked up her notes. 'No problem,' she replied carelessly. 'Just let me know when you might be free again.'

Rocco checked his watch, the gesture insolent. 'Not today. I have too much to do.' He started pulling paperwork together. 'Take the day off,' he suggested, not looking at her. 'Do some sightseeing or whatever you want to do. You might as well. I won't have any free time later on.'

Her jaw set, Cassia nodded and left his office. God, he was a pain in the backside! Still wound up by his rudeness, she gave Gena a quick call to update her and then she decided to take Rocco up on his offer. An hour later, she was happily strolling around the streets of Sorrento with her language headphones on. Idly, remembering Rocco's talk of *semifreddo*, she wondered whether to treat herself to a gelato. There were many shops displaying colourful tubs of sumptuous-looking ice cream in a whole variety of mouth-watering flavours and Cassia felt her resolve disintegrating.

Putting the thought of wearing a tight wedding dress out of her head for the time being, she pondered the choice of flavours. Eventually settling on a scoop of lemon because the fruit was so good in Sorrento and a scoop of *stracciatella* in honour of her father as it had been his favourite, Cassia savoured the heavenly vanilla ice with chocolate shavings first.

Pausing for a moment, the ice cream transporting her back to holidays spent throughout Italy, Cassia thought about her father. He would love it here, she thought, her heart swelling with happy memories. He'd be so pleased she had taken the trip. Even though he had always instilled in her a sense that her life should be stable, Cassia had a feeling he would heartily approve of her decision to work with Rocco Disanti. He had always been keen for her to live her life without drama, perhaps as her childhood had been so full of it with her mother's chaotic schedule and her sister's erratic moods, but Cassia knew he had always wanted her to be happy, no matter what. And right now, she felt absurdly happy.

Cassia made a mental note to ask Sofia if she had any advice on how to track down her father's family. Finn was right; asking around wasn't going to do the trick, she needed someone to look into it properly. The trouble was, all she knew about her father was that he had been told he was from Sorrento. He was an orphan who had been brought to England when he was about five years old because his Italian parents had died, but that, aside from some obsure memories he had noted down, was all Cassia knew. Her father hadn't had much success tracking down his family; he had tried to do it on and off over the years but every time he found a clue, the trail would turn cold. Cassia finished her ice cream with a contented sigh and took in her surroundings. Her mind went into travel mode and in her head she started writing a piece, luxuriating in finally being able to explore the 'travel' part of her food-travel title, which was something Gena had tasked her with.

'The area's ancient roots are apparent in the Roman remains at Punta del Capo and the original Greek town plan. Fishing boats head in and out of the colourful harbour at Marina Grande, punctuated by shabby but charming houses on the waterfront and

in the distance. There are small, pebbled beaches and rows of pretty fishermen's cottages and as you walk along the streets, you will happen upon the statue of Torquato Tasso, the sixteenth-century poet who was born in the town . . .'

Removing her headphones from inside her ears, her head full of Italian from her language system, as well as from the chatter around her, Cassia realised she had stopped outside a tiny but expensive-looking wedding-dress shop. Each dress in the window was like a work of art. Made of the most luxurious fabrics – silk, chiffon, organza – the gowns appeared to be hand-embroidered with elaborate beading and wonderfully long trains and veils.

Cassia sighed. She couldn't see Grace approving of any of these dresses but she couldn't help thinking she would love to walk down the aisle in one of them. She was fairly certain Finn wouldn't care either way, he'd be happy for her to wear whatever she chose but Grace was another kettle of fish.

Noticing that Aurelia was inside the shop twirling round in one of the gorgeous gowns, Cassia hesitated. Aurelia hadn't exactly been welcoming the last time she'd spoken to her, but Cassia couldn't resist going into the shop. If she couldn't wear a dress like one of these Italian creations, she'd at least like to see Aurelia in one of them close up. Heading inside, she caught her breath as Aurelia turned round.

Wearing a slinky, oyster-coloured column of silk with a halter neck and a plunging back, she looked stunning. The hue of the silk made the most of Aurelia's creamy-gold Mediterranean colouring, highlighting her youthfully toned shoulders and the cascade of dark curls that hung down her lightly tanned back. The bodice was covered with embroidery and tiny pearl beading and the skirt hung in soft folds around her thighs.

Cassia knew that Italian wedding dresses were traditionally lightweight due to the hot weather and that they tended to be slinky and slim-fitting, rather than the large, meringue-type concoctions often worn back in England. They were also rarely strapless, tending to make a feature of the neckline with ornate beading or unusual shapes. The owner of the shop cooed and fussed over Aurelia, tweaking the material and dusting imaginary specks from the bodice.

'What do you think?' Aurelia asked, swatting the owner's hands away. She stamped her foot as the owner attempted to tweak the skirt and with some edginess she asked Cassia again.

'I think it's wonderful,' Cassia assured her warmly. 'Really, Aurelia, it's one of the most beautiful dresses I've ever seen. You look incredible in it . . . it truly has the wow factor.' She said the last part in English, not having a clue how to translate it. Her language system was superb, but it didn't run to 'wow factor'.

Obviously understanding, Aurelia broke into a delighted smile and she swung back to check out her reflection in the full-length mirror in front of her. 'I wasn't sure . . . it's very daring.' She glanced over her shoulder at her bare back. 'They may faint in church but I thought I could wear a really long, thick veil around my shoulders like a cape and no one would notice until afterwards.' Her mouth twitched mischievously.

Cassia smiled. 'Perfect. You must wear this dress though, it was made for you.' She caught sight of the seamstress hovering. 'That probably sounded really stupid. I expect it *was* made for you, literally.'

'It was, but it has taken many designs and refits.' Aurelia tried a bejewelled tiara on and grimaced. 'I know you love these in England, but I'm not a fan.'

Cassia shrugged. She hadn't given tiaras much thought herself – but then she hadn't really had time to focus on any of these details. 'Don't you have designers clamouring for you to wear their dresses?' she asked.

Aurelia nodded. 'Yes, and I have agreed to wear one for the reception. But this shop,' she gestured to her surroundings, 'they

146

gave me my first modelling job years ago. Loyalty is important, yes?'

Cassia nodded. 'Totally. And that gown is so gorgeous, it's not that much of a hardship, I should imagine.'

Aurelia smiled. 'True. But I would still wear something from this shop, regardless.' She stared at her reflection. 'I don't have a clue what to do with my hair.' She frowned, pulling it up to test out a style.

'Just wear the front up,' Cassia suggested, stepping forward. 'May I? Look . . . this would highlight your face but still show off the length of your hair.' She showed Aurelia what she meant by holding some dark curls back from her face. 'It would also draw attention to your back even more once you reveal the whole dress.'

'I like it,' Aurelia said, her tone surprised. She shot Cassia a glance. Wearing yet another one of her very professional but tediously modest dresses, Cassia hardly looked able to give fashion advice.

Her Italian was much improved though; she must have been practising, Aurelia thought approvingly. 'How are the arrangements for your wedding going?' she asked, feeling she should show an interest. Truthfully, the only wedding Aurelia cared a jot about was her own but she supposed she should make conversation. She disappeared into a cubicle to get changed, swiftly followed by the owner of the shop who seemed irritatingly over-attentive.

Cassia reached out and felt the fabric of one of the dresses with her fingertips. 'I wouldn't know,' she called to Aurelia behind the curtain. Seeing how much Aurelia had already completed in terms of her arrangements not only made her own wedding seem very real, it highlighted how little she had actually achieved. Obviously Grace was hard at work on the wedding back in England but that didn't mean the arrangements were to her taste. Her mood plummeted.

Aurelia poked her head out. 'You need to take control of the situation,' she said bossily. 'No one would dare tell *me* what to do with my wedding. Well, my planner did and look what happened to her.' She disappeared behind the curtain again.

Cassia pulled a face. Aurelia's wedding planner was obviously very silly if she thought she could tell a spoilt princess what to do on the biggest day of her life. But Cassia didn't have much choice; besides, she could just imagine what Grace would do if she stamped her foot and pouted to get her own way.

Seeing a divine, coffee-coloured silk dress hanging amongst the others, Cassia tugged it out and held it up against her. The cut was flawless, the detail delicate. The dress came with spaghetti-thin straps that crisscrossed over a scooped back. The silk had an overlay of pale, cappuccino lace that gave it a Grace Kelly feel.

Aurelia emerged from the changing room wearing a pair of chic black shorts with a loose, emerald-green top. Her tanned legs looked endless and even though she had dressed the outfit down with a pair of flip-flops and a long, silk cardigan, she still looked camera-ready. She glanced at the dress Cassia was clutching to her.

'You like that dress?' The owner leapt forward, hopeful for another sale. 'You can try it on,' she offered, already peeling the dress from the hanger.

'No, no. Grace, my future mother-in-law, would think I'd lost my mind if I wore something like this.' Regretfully, Cassia tucked the dress back in with the others. 'Aurelia, you're surprised at my choice.' A little hurt, she was once again reminded of Jules. 'You think I'm boring and conservative.'

Twirling her sunglasses between her fingers, Aurelia shrugged. 'What can I say? You dress like a teacher,' she remarked honestly. 'Surely this is not news to you?'

Looking down at herself, Cassia was puzzled. She supposed her dress was a little conventional, especially to someone as

148

dazzling as Aurelia. But a teacher? Cassia rubbed her chin, appalled at the comparison. Not wanting to disrespect teachers, she was fairly certain she didn't look that conservative.

Upset, she glanced round the shop. She hadn't always dressed this way; there had been a time when she had worn daringly short dresses, low necks and bright colours. She couldn't even blame it on her job, because she had been dressing this way for years. Not quite sure she could pinpoint the exact moment it happened, Cassia had to acknowledge nonetheless that it had.

Catching sight of a glorious, dark red dress hanging up on a nearby rail, Cassia fingered the lace and silk concoction longingly. 'I used to wear red all the time,' she said out loud, rather surprised at the admission.

Aurelia looked stunned. 'You? Red?'

'Occasion dresses,' the shop owner interjected with hopeful eyes. 'Suitable for parties, weddings and—'

'Oh, do stop it!' Aurelia told her crossly. 'You're on enough commission. I have eight bridesmaids. Leave us alone.' She flapped her hands until the woman backed off. 'She is not the original owner of the shop,' Aurelia confided in Cassia. 'She only comes in now and again. This one always overdoes the sales pitch.'

Cassia laughed, wishing she could be as forthright with people who annoyed her. She held the red dress up against herself and glanced in the mirror. 'God, I love this colour but my fiancé hates it; I do know that for a fact.'

'Really? Rocco adores red.' Aurelia thought the wonderful colour brought out Cassia's dark features beautifully. 'Buy it. Treat yourself.'

Cassia shook her head. 'Where on earth would I wear such a thing?' She hung it up on the rail.

Aurelia threw her hands in the air. 'What does that matter? Dresses like that are for fun, and invariably an opportunity to wear them presents itself. Oh, look, there is Dino, come and meet him.' Her face lit up as she caught sight of her fiancé sipping a beer outside a nearby café. Reading something intently, his blond hair sticking up over the top of his magazine, he didn't even notice them.

Cassia followed Aurelia out into the sunshine, thinking she had never seen a man reading Italian *Vogue* before. Still, she was interested to meet Aurelia's fiancé; she couldn't imagine who had managed to woo a fluttering butterfly like Aurelia at such a young age.

'Cassia . . . Dino.' Aurelia did the introductions. Ordering two glasses of Prosecco for them, she caught sight of one of her bridesmaids and she ducked inside the café for an excitable chat.

Dino kissed Cassia warmly on the cheeks. 'So you're the famous Cassia Marini.'

'Hardly famous.' She smiled, enjoying his lazy grin.

Dino slyly held up the magazine he'd been reading. Behind his copy of Italian *Vogue* was a copy of *Scrumptious* magazine. 'You didn't think I really got off on looking at dresses and shoes, did you?' he remarked, breaking into a wide grin as he tossed the copy of *Vogue* across the table.

Left alone with Dino, Cassia was certain she recognised him from aftershave and beach ads. He had the most infectious grin and he really was very handsome in a 'surfer dude' kind of way. She liked his Aussie twang too. If she hadn't seen him in an Italian magazine recently, with slicked-back hair, an arrogant stare and a suit by a very well-known designer, Cassia wouldn't have believed Dino would ever secure work in image-conscious Italy. But she supposed his chameleon-like ability to change his appearance so drastically was why he was such a successful model.

Dino sipped his beer, unruffled by her stare. 'I've been reading something far more interesting. You are rather naughty, aren't you?'

Cassia groaned. 'Oh God, you've been reading my column, haven't you?'

Dino turned a page and read aloud. '*Enjoying the sensual delights Sorrento had to offer, I found myself drowning in an orgy of sun-drenched terraces, chocolate truffles with dreamy, ganache centres and chefs with mesmerising eyes and talented hands . . .*' He paused and laughed at Cassia's reaction. 'Hey, don't be embarrassed, I think it's brilliant. I couldn't write like that in a million years. I'm lucky I've got my looks; words aren't my thing.' He leant in closer. 'Has Rocco read it?'

Cassia cringed and put her face in her hands. 'It sounded all right when I typed it on my laptop and I'll have you know I toned that article down.' She emerged from behind her hands sheepishly. 'My colleague Pete is always telling me I sound like a soft porn channel. I guess he's right. And no, I don't think Rocco has read it.' She gave him a self-deprecating grin. 'At least, I hope he hasn't otherwise I'll have to explain that I get a bit carried away when I start writing about things I enjoy.'

Dino realised Cassia had no idea how beautiful she was, a quality that made her all the more appealing. He was glad he was so in love with Aurelia because Cassia was rather gorgeous, now that he'd had a chance to look at her close up. Dino idly wondered if Rocco had noticed.

'So, how are you enjoying Sorrento?'

'I love it. I came here with my father many years ago so I feel a bit emotional about being back.' Cassia filled Dino in about her father.

Dino patted her hand. 'My father's Italian too.'

'I didn't know that.'

'Oh yes. You don't think the Disanti family would have welcomed me with open arms if I didn't have even the teeniest bit of Italian in me, do you?' Dino's grin couldn't be any wider. 'I'm adorable, as you can see, but being half-Italian helps, trust me.'

'Does your father live in Italy?'

'No.' Dino looked stricken for a moment. 'No, he doesn't. I miss him, actually.'

'Is he . . . ?'

'Dead?' He shook his head. 'No, he and my mum are divorced. Very acrimonious; I hardly ever see him because me and my mum are so close. I don't even think he's coming to the wedding, which is such a shame. I really wanted him to come back to Italy and fall in love with it again. But hey, some things aren't meant to be, are they?' He sat back. 'I hear you're getting married too.'

Cassia nodded, an image of Finn behind his office desk slipping into her mind. 'I really miss my fiancé,' she admitted. 'I reckon I should pop home to see him but I keep hearing how few seats there are because of the holiday season and how expensive they are.'

Dino slipped a pair of Ferragamo sunglasses on as Aurelia returned. A waiter followed her out, carrying their drinks on a tray. 'Ask Rocco if he'll fly you back in his helicopter.'

Cassia laughed. 'Yeah, right.'

Aurelia glanced at her. 'He really does have a helicopter,' she said, sipping her chilled Prosecco. 'He flies it himself. I'm sure he wouldn't mind taking you back to England for a weekend.'

Drinking more than half her glass of Prosecco as she digested this information, Cassia was speechless. Rocco had his own helicopter? And he was actually able to fly it? Was there anything this man couldn't do? He wasn't perfect, far from it, especially with his irrational, icy temper, it was just that each time she thought she had him sussed as a talented but shallow rich kid, she discovered something new about him that changed her view again. Helicopter licences took time and effort to earn, they didn't just hand them out to playboys with money to burn.

Dino noticed Cassia's expression. 'Sickening, isn't it? Rocco's like a textbook romantic lead, isn't he? A talented chef, drop-dead gorgeous to anyone with a pulse, and if that wasn't enough, he loves danger and he chases it at every opportunity. Disgustingly glamorous and a great guy to boot.' Dino ticked the last few words off on his fingers as though he was reciting a singleton's romantic wish list and grinned. 'Bastard.'

Fearful of sounding like the conservative prude Aurelia clearly thought she was, Cassia didn't mention that the thought of travelling across the Mediterranean in a helicopter terrified the life out of her. She also didn't agree with Dino's list of Rocco's attributes. Hadn't he left out 'rude workaholic' and 'annoyingly private playboy'?

'Does Rocco need to fly the helicopter himself? I mean, don't you have people who could do that?' She directed her question at Aurelia.

Aurelia looked amused. 'Of course! We have "people" who can do most things but just as my grandmother likes to take care of the menus and the bookings in the restaurant, Rocco prefers to fly himself.' She fanned her face with Italian *Vogue*, oblivious to the fact that her golden face was splashed all over the perfume advert on the back of it.

'Rocco is ambitious and very driven, and he believes life is there to be lived and that we should all take every opportunity to taste danger. Hence the helicopters and the motorbikes. It's just the way Rocco unwinds and enjoys himself.'

Bemused, Cassia drained her glass. Helicopters and motorbikes . . . how Finn would frown on such boyish pastimes. He was far too steady and composed to feel the need to fly things or do wheelies. Which was a good thing – wasn't it? Cassia realised she desperately needed to see Finn again. It was a bit like when someone died; she couldn't quite remember what his face looked like. She knew she missed him like crazy, but for some odd reason, she felt she could do with a top-up to reassure herself why he was the man she had loved for nearly a decade.

'You should ask Rocco,' Aurelia insisted. 'It has to be worth asking the question and you must check up on that mother-in-law of yours. She's organising Cassia's wedding,' she told Dino in appalled tones.

Dino pulled a face of mock horror. 'Your worst nightmare, babe. Not to worry, my mother's millions of miles away, not much chance of her telling you what shoes to wear.'

Aurelia spluttered into her Prosecco at the very idea.

Having no intention of asking Rocco about helicopter lifts, Cassia got to her feet. 'I must go. I want to have a proper look around.'

'If you have time, you must check out the Cimbrone gardens,' Dino said, pointing his glass of beer at her. 'And the cove at Furore – too romantic for words, if your fiancé is thinking of coming out here to visit.'

'Thanks. See you later, Aurelia, and it was lovely to meet you, Dino.'

Drawing out her tourist guide, she left them to it, breaking into a smile as she heard Aurelia demanding to know if Dino thought bejewelled clutch bags were passé for someone of her status. They were so well-matched; even Grace wouldn't be able to find fault with that union, Cassia thought wryly.

Strolling away, she caught sight of Raffaelo. Dressed like a Mafia don as usual, he looked around furtively, as if checking he wasn't being watched before ducking inside a dodgy-looking doorway on the square. Seconds later, he reappeared, his expression nonchalant. Catching sight of her, he faltered for a moment before waving at her and grinning widely.

'*Bellissimo!*' he called to her, kissing his fingers.

Not quite sure how to react to such a public compliment, Cassia blushed and gestured to her tourist book. Heading off in the other direction, she wondered briefly what someone as rich and privileged as Raffaelo was doing in such a shady-looking alleyway. She soon lost herself in the sun-dappled streets of picturesque Sorrento and forgot about the entire Disanti family as she indulged in some serious sightseeing and reminiscing about her father.

Chapter Seven

Having promised Dom he would attend a local charity match he was playing against one of the top seeds, Finn arrived late and only managed to see the last thirty minutes or so. Having been given a special pass by his brother, he watched the match in a box, rubbing shoulders with a blandly pretty Norwegian model who was the celebrity wife of the German player on court with Dom. Also in the box was Carlton Budford, Dom's coach. A stern-looking American with mahogany forearms and Ray-Bans permanently propped on his nose, Carlton snapped gum throughout and watched like a hawk.

Finn felt quite nervous watching his baby brother playing a match. Until recently he hadn't shown much interest in Dom's career and guiltily he realised that, like his mother, he hadn't really taken Dom's tennis career seriously until now. Deep down, Finn wasn't sure it was really surprising given Dom's uninspiring track record before this year, but he was beyond pleased that his brother had finally found some form.

Watching him dart all over the court with his blond hair flopping into his eyes and his muscles covered in sweat, Finn was impressed. Wearing baggy white shorts with a loose navy top and pristine white trainers, Dom's eyes were focused and his shoulders were tense.

'He's playing well,' commented Carlton, Dom's coach, as

he chewed rhythmically on a fresh piece of gum. 'I was worried he'd been burning the candle at both ends recently, but he's putting on the performance of a lifetime here.'

Finn nodded and glanced at the scores. It was two sets all and the final set, but Dom was six-four down. One more game might just put paid to his chances of winning and Finn willed him to pull something out of the bag. Watching the ball thwack backwards and forwards smartly across the net, he realised Dom had improved enormously over the past year or so.

'What are Dom's chances at Wimbledon, do you think?' Finn asked.

Carlton shrugged non-committally. 'Depends.' Watching a nail-biting rally closely, he spoke when Dom had won the point. 'You know your brother pretty well, and you know what his weaknesses are.' He glanced at Finn, his eyes hidden by his sunglasses. 'Women and booze, and those things don't mix well with tennis. I'm surprised he's as fit as he is, actually, but he does put the training hours in. And of course he's magnificent on grass.'

Finn smiled. 'Dom's always been the same. At school they said that he worked hard but that he was easily distracted. Different distractions these days, obviously,' he added. He remembered how bored Dom would get during their childhood tennis matches; despite loving the game with a passion, he could easily be enticed away with the promise of something less arduous and more fun.

Carlton grunted. 'Don't I know it. I've had to bail him out of trouble more times than I care to remember, but he has to realise that a pro tennis player lives and breathes the life, there's barely any time for anything but practising and playing. Bloody good shot!' he shouted, jumping out of his seat. 'Jesus, he might actually beat this guy. Amazing publicity . . . What?' he said belligerently to the increasingly stony-faced Norwegian wife.

Finn refocused his attention on the match, feeling inordinately proud of his brother's flair. At the same time, he couldn't help wondering if Dom was still dating Jules. He hadn't mentioned anything to Cassia, mainly because he hadn't had time to talk about it during their recent phone call, but also because he was secretly hoping the fling would peter out soon. Watching Dom smack an ace down the baseline, Finn contemplated the relationship. Jules and Dom had seemed totally wrapped up in one another at Sunday lunch the week before and an apparently besotted Dom had been unusually attentive, topping her wine glass up and feeding her strawberries. His hand had seldom strayed from Jules's neck, hand or thigh during the visit and he had seemed utterly enthralled by her. Regardless of any of this, Finn couldn't shake off the feeling that Cassia's sister was about to get hurt.

Jumping up and cheering hoarsely as Dom scored an incredible point, Finn was almost deafened by Carlton bellowing next to him and he found himself in a clumsy hug with the burly coach. Seconds later, however, the top seed showed the spectators exactly why he held such a prestigious position. Sending Dom all over the court as he found a surge of energy from somewhere, the young German managed to claw back the points needed to clinch the match. The Norwegian wife made a big show of screaming at the top of her voice, sourly glaring at Carlton before she teetered out of the box.

'Silly broad,' Carlton commented blithely. 'It's only a charity match.' Showing brilliant white teeth as he gave a wolfish grin, he motioned Finn to follow him out. 'I would have preferred a win, but Dom will have really set himself up nicely for Wimbledon with that. Nice to meet you,' he said, shaking Finn's hand as he headed down to the changing rooms.

Waiting in the bar and enjoying a glass of good claret, Finn was soon joined by a freshly showered, ecstatic-looking Dom. Dressed in a sharp suit with an open-necked shirt, he radiated good health and triumphant satisfaction.

'Did you see me, bro? Did you see the ace?' Dom whooped. 'I couldn't believe it when I managed to get that one in. Of course, Karl is too hard to beat these days, he's practically a machine, but I think I held my own, don't you?' He mimicked the swoop of his ace in delight, almost colliding with a beautiful Sloaney type with blond hair reaching to her buttocks. 'Oops, sorry, angel.' Dom gave her a heartbreaking grin. 'Just reliving the moment.'

'And so you should,' she purred, tucking her number into his top pocket as she shimmied past with much boob-jiggling. 'Call me later,' she added.

Dom said nothing but his eyes met hers suggestively. Ordering some expensive champagne, he caught Finn's disapproving frown and protested roundly. 'What's the matter, Finn? It's only a bit of harmless flirting.'

Finn leant against the bar. 'It's not, though, is it? You'll call that girl later and take her home – and where does that leave Jules?'

'Oh, don't you start,' Dom grumbled, swallowing down half a glass of champagne. 'You sound like Mother. She's been on the phone, going on about how thrilled she is that I'm dating Jules. She even told me to take the relationship seriously – can you believe that? And some journalist called me the other day to ask who Jules was.'

Finn couldn't help laughing. It made a change for a relationship of Dom's to be under the spotlight; aside from the gossip magazines who swooned over Dom's glamorous looks and roguish charm, his relationships were usually too short-lived to warrant comment.

'But you're not taking the relationship seriously. Are you?'

Dom smoothed his freshly washed, golden hair into place. 'Not everyone meets their perfect woman straight away, bro.'

'I didn't meet Cassia straight away,' Finn reminded him firmly. 'I dated a few girls before her, remember? The difference is, I didn't promise any of them anything I couldn't deliver.' He saw a familiar look of boredom clouding Dom's eyes, a look he had often adopted when their mother had berated him for his lack of application at school or on the tennis court.

Finn sighed. 'Look, Dom, it's nothing to do with me. And I'm sure Jules can look after herself. It's just that she's Cassia's sister, so it makes things more complicated.'

'I know.' Dom realised he sounded snappy. 'It's very nice of you to worry about my love life, Finn, but it's all under control, I promise.'

Finn had no idea what that meant, but he knew when there was no point in pursuing the issue with Dom.

Seeing Carlton beckoning him over with a flick of his mahogany-hued hand, Dom handed Finn a glass of champagne. 'Look, thanks for coming today; I appreciate it. I invested in that nightclub, by the way, so one way or another, I'll be making big money soon. Speaking of which, Carlton wants me to meet a new sponsor. Catch you later, Finn.'

Finn watched Dom suavely greeting the new sponsor, turning on the charm like a pro. Finn smiled, realising he was probably worrying unnecessarily about his baby brother. Dom looked as though his life was finally coming together and whether or not Jules was a part of that was none of Finn's business.

As the evening sun slid down behind Mount Vesuvius with a warm, orange glow, Sofia wandered into the kitchen with a book containing the reservations for the following week. She wanted to warn Antonio that several celebrities were due in, as well as a well-known, acid-tongued food critic, but she was sure most of the staff must have left by now. She was right; the kitchen was in near darkness because the restaurant had closed down after lunch for some repairs to take place.

About to head back to her quarters, Sofia was taken aback to find a spotlight on, with Cassia beneath it, peering into a bubbling pot. She was wearing her language headphones and an over-sized white chef's jacket over her clothes. She caught sight of Sofia and tore the headphones off.

'Hi. Sorry, I can't hear a thing with these on. I get so engrossed.' Cassia was flushed from the heat. 'I was just trying out this monkfish dish Rocco cooked the other day. He said I could use the kitchen when it was empty. Oh, please don't taste it, it's a very amateurish first attempt . . .' She held her breath as an intrigued Sofia grabbed a spoon and tasted the liquor.

'It's not so bad.' Sofia shrugged, her green eyes shrewdly inspecting the sauce. 'The trick is to balance the saffron perfectly with the seasoning. A beginner rarely gets this right. You were too heavy-handed with the saffron, an easy mistake to make.' Helping herself to some monkfish, she noticed Cassia worriedly awaiting her verdict. 'The fish is superb; well done.'

'Really?' Cassia leant over and speared a piece of monkfish. 'Mmmm, it's quite tasty. This is the best thing I've ever made. My sister is a far better cook than me. But still, it's nowhere near as good as Rocco's.' She pretended to look vexed. 'Damn. He made it look so easy.'

'He's had plenty of practice.' Sofia eyed Cassia with interest. 'Did you cook with Marco, your father?'

Cassia nodded. 'Every weekend, from a very young age. He taught me and my sister everything he knew about cooking but I'm afraid I'm better at writing about food than I am making it.'

Sofia leant against the counter. 'Rocco was glued to Nico's hip as a child. Like Michel Roux Junior learning at the feet of his famous father, I don't think Rocco was destined to be anything other than a chef.'

'Is it true that whatever Nonna says goes?' Cassia asked, giving Sofia a smile. 'I've heard that each family has its own set of rules when it comes to certain products and ways of doing things in the kitchen.'

'It is.' Sofia nodded, her eyes twinkling. 'Luckily, Nico's grandmother and my own shared some of the same ways. Otherwise, I'm sure me and Nico might have come to blows.'

Cassia decided that she liked Sofia immensely. She was so warm and friendly and it was obvious she adored her family. 'What about Raffaelo? Hasn't he ever shown an interest in cooking?'

Sofia laughed. 'Raffaelo was always far too busy out social-ising and enjoying the high life to be interested in learning a real craft. He's wonderful with his hands; not creative, as such, but very practical. As for Aurelia, well, I'm sure you can see that she is far too spoilt to knuckle down and pay attention to any-thing for too long. She's far too much like my daughter, Flavia – more's the pity.' Sofia's twinkling eyes softened the critical comparison.

'I can't see you spoiling anyone.' Cassia grinned, tugging off the white jacket she was wearing. 'And I mean that in a good way.'

'It was Nico,' Sofia said, but her tone was indulgent. 'He couldn't say no to his little angel and he was just as bad when Aurelia came along. Nico was so soft-hearted, so thoughtful. Rocco reminds me of him, you know.'

Cassia refrained from comment. She hadn't seen much in Rocco that redeemed him in any way; she certainly wouldn't have imagined he was thoughtful or soft-hearted. 'You must miss your husband terribly,' she blurted out instead. 'I miss my fiancé like mad and I've only been away from him for a few weeks.' She blushed, realising how trite that sounded. 'Which is nothing compared to losing your soulmate for ever.'

Unexpectedly, Sofia's eyes filled with tears. 'My soulmate . . . that's exactly what Nico was.' She gave Cassia a watery smile. 'And you are quite right, I miss him more than I can say.' Sofia turned away, her usually rosy cheeks turning pallid. Why, after all this time, was Nico's death hitting her so hard? She had cried, she had mourned . . . in fact, Sofia was pretty sure she had run the gauntlet of clichéd grief steps right through from shocked anger to hopeful acceptance.

Clutching the edge of the kitchen counter, she wondered if it wasn't so much that she was missing Nico any more but that she was missing *someone*. She hadn't met a man yet who could compare to Nico, but even so, she knew it was probably inappropriate to say she missed the feel of strong, male arms round her at night. Watching Sofia's slightly shaking shoulders, Cassia was mortified. Clearly, she had put her foot in it. She was caught off guard when Sofia turned back to face her, her cheeks pink-hued again.

'Enough of this morbid talk,' she said in a firm voice. 'Now, you mentioned your Italian heritage and it occurred to me the other day that I might be able to help you out with that. A family friend, Luca, who lives in Rome specialises in family trees. He'd look into your Italian background for you. You said your father had made some notes about his family over the years?'

Cassia accepted gratefully. 'That would be wonderful. I haven't had any luck with my search so far.' She frowned. 'It's like a jigsaw puzzle . . . I have some names and some dates and a few memories scribbled down, but I think it needs an expert to piece them together. Thank you, Sofia.'

'Leave it with me,' Sofia said briskly, gathering up her paper-work. She paused. 'Incidentally, Rocco can fly you back to England at the weekend. Aurelia mentioned your predicament, so I made arrangements.'

Cassia didn't know what to say. She missed Finn, but Rocco was so incredibly busy, she was sure he had far better things to do than fly her back home on a whim. Nor did she fancy risking her life flying back to England in a small metal ball with a couple of spinning metal blades to keep it off the ground.

Cassia could only imagine what Grace would say if she knew the trip back had been made via private helicopter.

'That's very kind of you, but I really wouldn't want to—'

'It's all arranged,' Sofia interrupted, almost as if she had anticipated Cassia's protests. 'Rocco needs to go to London to check on his restaurant, so the timing is perfect.' She beamed at Cassia. 'Everybody is happy, yes?'

'Er . . . yes.' Cassia looked up as several beams of light played through the kitchen windows. 'What's that?'

Sofia peered outside. '*Non puòessere!*' she muttered under her breath. 'It can't be, Rocco is going to go mad.' She gestured at the cars pulling up outside the restaurant, people spilling out of them as soon as they screeched to a halt. 'It's the team who are due to shoot Aurelia's new advert here. I'm sure they're early,' Sofia told Cassia with a grimace. Watching the throngs of people milling around outside with piles of luggage and loud voices, Cassia couldn't imagine Rocco being too pleased. 'Your Italian is much improved, by the way,' Sofia commented as she gathered up her reservations book. 'Even Aurelia wouldn't be able to laugh at your grammar now.'

Cassia flushed. Had Aurelia been laughing at her behind her back? Not realising Sofia had been having a dig at Aurelia for being bitchy, Cassia felt affronted, especially after their bonding session in the wedding-dress shop.

'I'm glad I'm making more sense. I assume you were behind the language system?'

'Oh no, that wasn't me,' Sofia informed her. 'All Rocco's idea. He looked into it and ordered the best one.' She sighed. 'I suppose I'd better get all these people settled into their rooms. Aurelia's bound to be out having a romantic dinner with Dino.'

Cassia slowly packed up her cooking things. She wasn't looking forward to the helicopter flight with Rocco but she supposed it wouldn't last long. Besides, it had to be worth it to see Finn again. Sending him a text to let him know her plans, she grinned when he immediately sent one back saying, 'YAY!' followed by, 'Sorry, in meeting.'

As she headed back to her room, getting caught up in the bustling crowd of glamorous photographers, make-up artists and hair stylists, Cassia decided to treat herself to something new before she headed home that weekend, her mind fixed on the gorgeous red dress she'd seen in the wedding-dress shop. Finn wasn't keen on red but surely even he would be bowled over by the exquisite dress?

Her phone rang and seeing that it was her mother, Cassia answered it. 'I was just about to call you. I'm coming home this weekend.'

'Oh darling, what brilliant timing.' Diana sounded distressed. 'I'm having the most awful crisis of confidence about this shocking play Fliss wants me to consider. I can't ask Jules because she'd laugh at me, but I know you'll be honest.'

'What's the problem?'

'Aside from it being a play instead of TV?' Diana sighed extravagantly. 'There isn't just one problem, Cassia, there are three. Weight gain – dire. In addition, nudity and absolutely no make-up.'

'Wow.' Cassia abandoned her packing and climbed on to her bed. 'No make-up. Nightmare.'

'See, I knew you'd understand.' Diana sounded self-righteous. 'I mean, how on earth am I going to manage that? No one's seen me without foundation, eyeliner and lipstick for two decades, darling . . .'

Cassia grinned and settled back against a plump pile of pillows. This wasn't going to be a short phone call.

'Any joy with getting another job?'

Louisa glanced at Jules as they flicked through the rails of a pre-summer sale in a one-off boutique on the Kings Road. Louisa had no idea what they were doing in there because unless Jules had secured herself more work, she could scarcely scrape her rent money together. But Dom was off at some tournament or other and for the first time in ages, Jules had suggested a shopping trip and Louisa thought it would be a chance to have a proper chat.

'Hmmm? Oh, jobs. No, nothing doing at the moment,' Jules replied airily, seemingly unruffled by the reality of living on the breadline. 'I'm sure something will come up, it always does, doesn't it?'

Louisa eyed her warily. Jules seemed far too upbeat in the circumstances. Being fired normally depressed the hell out of her and not getting another job for nearly a month tended to send her spiralling into a pit of despair. She was certain Jules's good mood was down to Dom, but how long would it last? Casually, she asked after her brother.

Standing at a mirror holding a non-sale, bodycon dress against her, Jules looked dreamy. 'He's fantastic, Lou. I don't think I've ever been so well-treated. Late-night suppers, flowers, champagne . . .'

Louisa stood by the mirror, her stomach sinking. Jules had it bad; she'd never seen her best friend so happy. Her skin glowed as if it had been buffed from the inside and her messy blond hair had been recently cut and now fell sexily over one eye. Jules looked as though she'd gone on holiday to the Bahamas and had come back relaxed, rejuvenated and thoroughly loved up. And Louisa couldn't help feeling uneasy.

'You sound as though you've fallen head over heels as usual,' Louisa commented.

Jules frowned. 'So what if I have? Dom feels the same way. He told me.'

'He told you he loved you?'

Jules looked stung as she slung the bodycon dress on to the counter. 'There's no need to look so shocked, Lou. I told you we were serious about one another.'

Louisa bit back the negative response that sprang to mind. Jules was in so deep, there was no way she would be deterred and Louisa knew that if she said any more, Jules would think she was putting a deliberate downer on things. About to apologise, Louisa was taken aback when Jules turned on her.

'You're spoiling everything,' Jules spat, hurt by Louisa's lack of conviction. 'Can't you just be happy for me?'

Louisa recoiled. 'Hey, I'm only trying to look out for you. And for your information, I'm not . . .' She stopped as she watched Jules hand a credit card over to pay for the three hundred-pound dress. 'Can you afford that?'

'That's none of your business!' Jules glared at her. 'What's the matter? Are you worried about the rent or something? Well, don't be because Dom's lending me the money. See how much he loves me?' She punched her pin number into the machine with jerky movements. 'I think he's about to propose too. Go on, tell me what you think about that!'

Louisa shook her head, stunned that Jules was being so touchy. The only time she'd seen her behave this way before was when she was having an unnecessary dig at her sister Cassia.

'You're taking this all the wrong way,' Louisa started, keen to smooth the waters. She was nonplussed to hear about a possible proposal from her commitment-phobe of a brother, but she wasn't about to pass comment on it. 'I'm saying this stuff because I care about you.'

'Really?' Jules snatched the bag from the counter, close to tears. 'I don't think you care at all, Lou. I think you're jealous.'

'Jealous? Me?'

'Yes. Because you can't believe your brother has fallen for me and because you're single and nothing's going right for you.' Jules stormed out of the shop, closely followed by Louisa, who grabbed her arm.

'For your information, Jules, things are going very well for me right now. I've been promoted at work and I've been given a huge pay rise.'

Jules whipped her arm away, still smarting. 'Well, good for you. At least one of us is earning some money.'

'Why do you think I didn't tell you about it? I know how depressed you've been about your work situation.'

Jules stared at her friend, feeling guilty. Normally, she and Louisa would have celebrated such a thing together, no matter who had enjoyed a bit of good luck. She could see how hurt and angry Louisa was; her cheeks were flushed and she looked suspiciously close to tears. Jules felt awful. They had been friends for years and they had never rowed like this before.

Louisa wasn't done. 'And just to set the record straight, I'm not single. I met an amazing man weeks ago and I've been dying to tell you about him ever since.' Louisa folded her arms, her lip quivering. 'But you've been so wrapped up in yourself and with this relationship with Dom, you haven't even noticed. You're just as bad as my bloody mother.' A tear trickled down her cheek. 'But she's not my best friend, so I don't care when she doesn't remember I exist, Jules. I'm glad you're happy with Dom, but I can tell you one thing, this relationship has turned you into a really shit friend.' Turning on her heel, Louisa stalked off, her shoulders shaking.

Horrified at what had just happened, Jules burst into tears.

Standing beneath a blue-and-white spotted umbrella in the grounds of the venue, Grace decided she liked it immensely. Cassia's sister Jules had recommended Parkland Heights Manor and Grace had to commend her on her taste. The stately home was lavish and it would certainly accommodate the long guest list that seemed to grow by the day.

Grace glanced at the notes she had made in her neat hand-writing when Cassia had first outlined her thoughts for her wedding. 'Small, but stylish . . . a beautiful building . . . nothing stuffy or old-fashioned – somewhere with a real sense of romance and style.' Without a shred of remorse, Grace glanced out across the looping driveway that led to the Georgian-fronted stately home. Even drenched with rain it looked superb with its splendid pillars and magnificent British racing-green double doorway. Inside, the house was a mass of showy staircases with richly painted walls in peach, moss green and Wedgwood-blue, sweeping balustrades and vast hallways boasting marble columns and heavy, velvet drapes. Small but stylish, however, it was not.

Grace sniffed. She didn't care. It was grand and traditional and it reeked of the 'good form' she was so fond of. She was aware that it was the height of high-handedness for her to book the venue without either Finn or Cassia clapping eyes on it but in the circumstances, beggars really couldn't be choosers, she told herself snippily.

'Bit on the dated side,' Henry commented, his freckled nose wrinkling as he peered through the rain. 'It smelt musty inside too . . . must be all those ugly old curtains and rugs.' He straightened up and rubbed his rounded belly, already looking forward to afternoon tea. Rain always made him hungry. 'Young Cassia would detest it, it doesn't exactly have the romantic charm she was after, does it?'

'We'll take it.' Grace turned to the rather regal-looking wedding co-ordinator trailing behind them, a rigid-backed old lady called Henrietta who was dwarfed by a white golf umbrella. 'And we'll need exclusive use, including all of the bedrooms, so we intend to book the entire place out.'

Henry looked aghast but Grace ignored him.

'Marvellous,' Henrietta said, her beady eyes lighting up at the thought of the exclusive-use fee. 'I'll get all the paperwork prepared right away.' She hurried away to print it all out before they could change their minds.

'Grace!' Henry admonished his wife, taking her arm. 'What on earth are you doing?'

'Now isn't the time to go all frugal on me, Henry,' Grace returned, twirling her umbrella rather defiantly. 'I know it's expensive but it's Finn's wedding, he deserves the best.'

'It's not about the money and you know it.' Henry stared at her through the rain. 'I don't care how much the wedding costs, you can have a blank cheque as far as I'm concerned.'

His normally jovial expression had vanished and his slightly bushy brows knotted together. 'But I do care about Finn and Cassia, and with all due respect, I want them to have the wedding *they* would like, not the wedding you think they should have.'

Grace flushed. 'Henry, how can you say that? I might not agree with Cassia jetting off to Italy just before her wedding, but Finn's needs have always been uppermost in my mind.'

Henry turned away, knowing Grace was being truthful about that, at least. A superb housewife who had supported him throughout his career with aplomb, Grace's desire for perfection had reached a whole new level when Finn had arrived. Treating him like a little prince, she had indulged her firstborn's every whim, spoiling him relentlessly. It was a mystery to Henry that Finn was so grounded; by rights he should have turned out to be a vile and petulant adult in view of his cosseted upbringing. It was the other children who had suffered at the hands of Grace's obsessive adoration of Finn. When Louisa had arrived, Grace had shrugged off her daughter's girlish demands, rigidly teaching her to fend for herself with the minimum of female bonding. As a result, Louisa was highly capable but somewhat emotionally stunted and Henry hoped to God she met a man who could chip away at his daughter's rather brusque outer core.

By the time Dom made an appearance, it seemed that Grace had all but run out of love and attention. A good-looking child with an abundance of charisma, Dom had barely seemed to notice his mother's lack of interest and had simply turned elsewhere for reassurance, beguiling female relatives and friends until they were eating out of his hand without even realising they had been manipulated. Such a strange childhood had, however, given Dom a brittle, slightly unkind edge.

Henry rubbed his nose as he glanced up at the Georgian monstrosity he knew Cassia would be horrified by. The wedding arrangements were getting out of hand and Henry couldn't help thinking it was perfect timing that Cassia was due back from Sorrento at the weekend. She would no doubt be flabbergasted at some of the things Grace had arranged and Finn would most likely get an ear-bashing. It was unfortunate but Henry hoped his son stepped in and stopped Grace in her tracks, because he didn't seem to be doing a very good job of it.

'Come on, Henry. Let's go and sign the paperwork.' Grace glanced at Henry, wondering why he looked so preoccupied and decided he was probably hungry. 'She might even give us tea and cake,' she added, attempting to cheer him up.

Henry, following her inside, didn't hold out much hope. Parkland Heights Manor was so up its own backside, it probably thought a good slice of cake was for the lower classes.

Hearing the loud, rhythmic drone of the helicopter blades whirling outside, Cassia hurriedly threw some toiletries into the smallest of her cases with a vintage bottle of Chianti that Rocco had given her from his personal cellar for Finn. She glanced at the wine, touched that Rocco had thought of such a thing. Finn would love it too. Cassia headed out to the balcony to take in the view, excited to be going home. As much as she loved Sorrento, she couldn't wait to get back to England and see Finn again. Grace she could do without, but with some regret Cassia had accepted long ago that they came as a package.

Leaning out and catching a waft of the purple wisteria hanging over the balcony, she saw the helicopter in the distance, planted squarely on a landing pad at the edge of one of the lush, green fields. Spotting Rocco's conker-brown head as he strode towards it, Cassia realised she needed to get a move on. Aurelia's rowdy photo shoot crew were outside on the grass, pointing and exclaiming at the helicopter, and she could see Rocco and Raffaelo exchanging words on the landing pad.

Tugging her new purchase out of the cupboard, Cassia wondered if she had made a mistake buying it. Unsettled the other day after her chat with Sofia, she had popped into the centre of Sorrento the following afternoon and bought the exquisite red dress she had seen with Aurelia. It had been uncharacteristically rash of her and she wasn't sure she'd done the right thing. Cassia hesitated, before folding it carefully and adding it to the rest of the clothes inside her case. She took a quick glance around her room, realising she'd grown attached to the fresco of cherubs who chubbily presided over her while she slept, as well as the ornate writing desk she had spent hours at, savouring every delicious word of her column.

Wearing a cream, halter-necked sundress she rarely wore because it showed off her bare (now golden) arms and shoulders, Cassia realised that she probably should have checked the weather reports for England, but it was too late now. Dashing outside and hurrying past Aurelia's gossipy photo shoot crew, the deafening noise of the helicopter took Cassia's breath away. Rocco was inside, talking to what must be the co-pilot, and she waved at him as the wind from the helicopter blades tore at her loose hair. Cassia slid into a seat, snapping the belt across her lap. Rocco, wearing loose but expensive-looking grey trousers with a white linen shirt and sunglasses, was impeccably dressed, but he looked slightly more approachable than usual.

Gesturing for Cassia to put a set of headphones on, Rocco removed his shades.

'Ready?' he asked with a disarming grin. 'I'm going to get us off the ground and then I'll join you back there.'

Cassia didn't know whether to be more unnerved by the realisation that she was about to travel from Italy to England in little more than a whirring metal bubble or by the fact that Rocco was so different from the moody man she had spent so many hours with since she arrived in Sorrento. She could hear him chatting to his co-pilot in her earphones, and guessed he was fired up about flying.

The Disanti estate disappeared beneath her as the helicopter rose, and Cassia's knuckles turned white as she clutched the arms of her chair. She was sure she could see Sofia in one of her black dresses in the restaurant and Raffaelo mending the fence at the front but they soon looked like toy figures. Hyperventilating, Cassia watched Rocco expertly flicking switches on the small dashboard in front of him and she let out a yelp as the helicopter soared smoothly upwards. Cassia forgot everything and concentrated on not dying. She watched the Disanti residence become smaller and smaller, the fruit and olive groves becoming comically tiny as the helicopter climbed into the sky and started its journey towards England. Rocco slipped his headphones off and, leaving his co-pilot in charge, joined her.

'Can't say I'm disappointed to leave Aurelia's film crew behind. I could kill her for organising that.' Rocco caught sight of Cassia's green face. 'What's wrong? Are you . . . ah, right. Why didn't you say you were scared of flying?'

'I'm not,' she retorted through clenched teeth. Seeing his raised eyebrows, she relented. 'All right. I'm scared. Petrified, in fact.'

Rocco laughed but not unsympathetically. 'Well, I wish you'd told me. I feel terrible now.'

Cassia shook her head. 'No, no . . . it's my fault.' She tried to stop shivering. 'I'm embarrassed to admit this, but I didn't want to look stupid in front of Aurelia when she suggested it. She . . . she's been laughing about my awful Italian and she thinks I'm a boring prude.'

'Aurelia thinks everyone is a boring prude,' Rocco informed her wryly. 'And if she did laugh about your Italian, it could only have been in the first few days when she didn't know you, I'm sure. Your Italian is excellent now; your brain obviously just needed a kick-start. Anyway, talking about Aurelia, I have to say that however she might seem on the outside, she has a very soft centre.'

Focused on keeping her breakfast down, Cassia said nothing, but she hoped Rocco was right. Aurelia had been quite sweet to her in the wedding-dress shop, and when they were with Dino she had been lovely. Dino obviously brought out the best in her – not surprisingly, since they were so devoted to one another.

Rocco glanced at her. 'Besides, I completely understand your fear. I have a phobia of water. All to do with an accident years ago, but I'm still terrified.'

Cassia remembered Sofia talking about the near-drowning incident. 'Your grandmother mentioned it. In the swimming pool, I think she said.'

Rocco nodded. 'I haven't swum since, not to this day.' He shuddered. 'I can still remember the horrible feeling of being under the water, under the pool cover, and feeling utterly helpless.'

Cassia leant back in her seat. That was kind of how she felt now.

'Anyway, it's natural to feel more vulnerable in a helicopter,' Rocco commented. 'It doesn't feel as robust, for one thing. And of course you are far closer to the engine and the blades than you would be in a plane . . .' He stopped, seeing Cassia's eyes widen with panic. 'Sorry. That's not helping, is it?'

Her teeth chattering, she closed her eyes. 'Not as such.' Feeling him take her hand and squeeze it tightly, Cassia's eyes snapped open. 'You don't need to . . . I can easily . . .'

'Sssh.' Rocco held on to her hand firmly. 'If you can bear to, check out the view. It's stunning.'

Her heart pounding in her chest, Cassia forced herself to peer out of the helicopter. They were directly above the glittering azure sea of the Mediterranean and it looked incredible. Forgetting about her nerves for a moment, Cassia suddenly felt swept up by the glamour of it all. She was in a helicopter, flying above tanned sunbathers and rippling waves. It was scary but it was also absolutely thrilling. Feeling Rocco's warm fingers curled around her own, Cassia wondered if he'd ever taken Stefania for helicopter rides, but of course he must have done.

Rocco discreetly took in Cassia's appearance. She was wearing a new dress, something that revealed more skin than usual and it suited her. She'd caught the sun across her shoulders, cheek-bones and nose and the golden glow complemented her dark eyes and hair.

She really was astonishingly beautiful, Rocco thought, startled. He had noticed this before, of course, more than once, but still. He couldn't even put his finger on what had him so spellbound, but perhaps it was simply down to chemistry. He couldn't help wondering if the attraction was one-sided but he guessed it must be. Cassia was about to be married; she probably didn't pay much attention to any other man.

'Does Stefania enjoy flying?' Cassia asked, blinking as she found herself almost nose to nose with him. He was practically in her seat, for heaven's sake. Was he being flirtatious or was it accidental that they were almost kissing distance apart?

Cassia felt her heart thumping dangerously and her eyes dropped to his mouth. She could easily . . . it would only take a matter of seconds to just dive right in and . . . She brought herself up short. What on earth was she thinking? She was shocked at herself. Years ago, she might have done something reckless like that, but she was a changed woman these days. And she was engaged to be married.

'Sorry.' Rocco shifted back a few inches deliberately but his eyes lingered on hers. 'Stefania? I have no idea, she refuses to fly with me.' A brief look of irritation crossed his face. 'Actually, she finds all of my hobbies puerile – this, the motorbikes.' Rocco felt disloyal for a moment, even though he was speaking truthfully. 'But she understands that I need an outlet for my stress, at least, even if she doesn't join me when I feel the need to get away and indulge myself.'

Cassia felt herself relaxing into her seat as the conversation became more general, but she resolved not to get that close to Rocco again. It felt faintly dangerous. She breathed in and out slowly to calm herself, allowing the overhead thrumming of the blades to reassure her that she was safe.

'Do you . . . do that often? Cassia asked. 'De-stress, I mean?'

Wondering if she'd switched to journalist mode or if she was actually interested, Rocco considered the question. 'I suppose so, although not as often as I'd like to. I'm so busy these days, there's little time left for anything much.'

'That's a shame,' Cassia said, thinking Rocco would benefit from some downtime. He seemed more human when he wasn't caught up in business, approachable, more charismatic and, dare she say it, sexier. 'Everyone needs space to do the things they enjoy, don't you think?'

Rocco waved a tanned hand expansively. 'I enjoy work too, it's what drives me. When I was old enough to appreciate what my grandfather had created, all I wanted to do was take over his legacy and make sure the family wanted for nothing.'

Cassia could understand that. Her father Marco had been poor once, living in England with various foster families, but he was determined to make something of himself. She said as much to Rocco.

'My father, he taught me so much. My work ethic, for one thing. My future mother-in-law probably wishes he hadn't instilled that one into me.' Cassia felt Rocco's eyes on her and even though she wasn't sure how much to reveal about her personal life in view of his scornful reactions to her impending wedding in the past, she grudgingly explained. 'Let's just say she's not my biggest fan. She doesn't exactly approve to me, or of my decision to come to Italy.'

Still holding her hand, he squeezed it involuntarily. 'Why does she disapprove of you? What's not to like?'

His voice was teasing, but feeling the familiar hurt at Grace's lack of appreciation for her come flooding back, Cassia looked away. 'I have no idea. I've never understood it and Finn's oblivious. But you know, don't you, when someone doesn't think you're good enough. It's unspoken, it's subtle, but it's there.'

Seeing her clouded eyes when she turned back to face him, Rocco sensed the raw vulnerability beneath her normal composure. He wanted to say something to make the bright spark return to her eyes but words failed him. He couldn't for the life of him think why Finn's mother-in-law didn't think Cassia was good enough. It seemed pretty unreasonable to him, unless Cassia was hiding some dark secret he wasn't aware of.

Suddenly realising he had been holding her hand for a long time, Rocco relinquished it. He couldn't imagine Stefania being too impressed if she knew he'd been doing something so intimate, even if it was because Cassia was scared of the helicopter. Rocco glanced down at his hand, feeling oddly bereft.

Cassia thought about her father, wishing she could speak to him all of a sudden. She missed him constantly but at times the grief was momentarily suffocating. He wouldn't even be walking her down the aisle, she thought, tears pricking at her eyelids.

'Something wrong?' Rocco's eyes were full of concern.

'Oh, it's silly, really, but I'm devastated that my father won't be walking me down the aisle.'

Rocco stared at her. 'Yes, that must be incredibly hard for you. You were obviously very close to him.'

'I was. I probably hero-worshipped him a bit, to be honest.' Cassia stole a glance out of the window and realised she wasn't

177

nearly as scared as she had been. 'My sister felt the total opposite for my father, which is a shame. I have no idea why either.'

'Really? Haven't you ever asked her about it?'

'We're not close, sadly. We used to be, but . . . but now we're not. It's something that has always troubled me.' Cassia realised her comment was inadequate but it was true; she had no idea why Jules and her father hadn't got on and she had always been bewildered by Jules's rejection of her in their teens.

'Sofia mentioned some curse,' she said, changing the subject. Talking about her relationship with Jules always saddened her. 'From a rival family. It gave me the shivers, if I'm honest, but she says you don't believe in such things.'

Rocco looked amused. 'I'm afraid not. My grandmother gets carried away with such things but I'm a realist, I deal with problems and staff and money, not fanciful curses. And talking specifics, I'm not sure that anyone could have survived that landslide. And if they did, where are they now? The young boy people talk about must have been whisked away to another part of Italy or to another country, because he was never seen again.'

Cassia sat up. Rocco's comment had reminded her of something. Was it that first conversation with Sofia? Or was it the possibility that her father might be the rumoured boy who'd escaped from the landslide? Cassia felt apprehensive. She relaxed again, deciding to wait and see what Luca, Sofia's historian friend, came up with.

Rocco scratched his head, his thoughts already moving on to other things. He was tempted to open up about one of the issues that was bothering him and because Cassia was so easy to talk to, he decided to go for it. 'One of the main things I'm dealing with at the moment is Stefania . . . or rather, her desire for me to move to Rome with her and open another Disanti's.'

'Do you want to open another one?'

He shrugged non-committally. 'I don't know. It would take me away from my family and I really don't know if I have the appetite for it. Excuse the pun.'

Cassia noticed the sky darkening outside and gloomily realised they must be over England. She was used to English weather, but having enjoyed glorious Italian sunshine for a few weeks now, it was a bit much to come back to rain. Still, it matched her mood for seeing Grace again. She noticed that Rocco looked absurdly good-looking in the shadowy light, his profile pensive, his mouth twisted.

Rocco was thinking about Rome. And about Stefania. From a business perspective, he could see the sense in opening another Disanti's in the beautiful city of Rome. It was frequented by tourists from all over the world and its famous landmarks made the most of Italian history and architecture. It was just . . . well, that was the problem. Rocco didn't know exactly what was stopping him from making the move. Was it because he knew Stefania would take it as meaning that he was serious about their relationship if he left his family behind? That she would expect formalities he wasn't prepared to offer right now?

Rocco sometimes felt as though he was trying to be something he wasn't when he was with Stefania. It was as if he had to turn off a part of himself, the most passionate part, because she loathed talking about food. The restaurant, the business, these were topics of conversation she thrived on, but food, recipes, any of the more creative and sensual aspects were strictly off limits.

'Maybe once you have Vegas out of the way you'll be more open to the idea,' Cassia commented, wondering why Rocco looked so preoccupied.

He turned back to her. 'Yes. The Vegas project is proving to be extremely time-consuming. It's pretty hard to deal with staff you haven't come face to face with yet and builders who aren't feeling the pressure of someone breathing down their necks.'

Rocco frowned. 'I'm fairly certain the opening is going to be delayed, the way things are going. I guess that might cause issues for you.'

Cassia gave a short laugh. 'It would cause issues for Finn's mother, that's for sure. Let's just see what happens. Maybe you should go out to Vegas and see if you can hurry everything along.'

Rocco considered the idea. 'If I can squeeze it in, that would probably be for the best. Perhaps you could join me. You could have a good look at the restaurant and make a start publicising it in your column.'

'Sounds good. And if it means I'm not delayed here, risking the wrath of my future mother-in-law, I suppose that can only be a good thing.' Cassia wasn't altogether sure she was bothered about having to stay in Sorrento for longer, but she knew Grace would go crazy. And she would miss Finn even more, Cassia reminded herself. 'I've arranged a lovely meal out for myself and Finn tomorrow night to make up for being away.'

'We'll organise that Vegas trip when we get back. Actually, I was going to talk to you about some ideas for the Vegas restaurant, the desserts, in fact, as I know you're a big fan. I thought the readers of *Scrumptious* magazine might like to hear the details . . .'

Transfixed, she watched his sexy mouth as he outlined his thoughts, talking about traditional Italian desserts with a twist – a deconstructed tiramisu, a Sicilian nut and chocolate cake with a frozen element, and a simple dish involving figs, honey and an incredible wine from the Tuscan hills.

'That all sounds amazing,' she said when he'd finished. 'My mouth is watering. Thank you for that wine, by the way. Finn will love it.'

Rocco shrugged away her thanks. It was an exceptionally good bottle of wine, but he was happy for her to have it because he knew how much she appreciated such things.

Before either of them realised it, the blurred lights of London swam into view through the rain. Cassia tensed her fingers on the arm of her seat and without being asked, Rocco's fingers moved imperceptibly into hers.

'About to land,' Sergio announced into their headphones. He skilfully lowered the helicopter and Cassia turned to Rocco. Still holding her hand, he stared at her as if he was about to say something else. She waited, feeling anticipation curling through her stomach. They held the moment tensely, then as they heard Sergio shutting everything down, broke away from one another.

Rocco held out his suit jacket. 'You're probably going to need this,' he commented smoothly. 'The rain is terrible. Give it back to me another time.'

'Thank you,' Cassia murmured, as he lifted his hand from hers. What the hell was the matter with her? She was about to meet up with Finn again and her heart was thumping in her chest as though she was a silly adolescent with a crush. Standing up, Cassia came to the conclusion that it might be best to avoid Rocco for a while, especially while they were in England. She clearly needed a break from him if she was going to behave in such a ridiculous manner after a bit of harmless hand-holding.

'I hope to catch up with you while we're in England,' Rocco said, even though he was sure it wouldn't be a good idea at all. He welcomed the idea of getting to know Cassia better, but it occurred to him that he might feel even more drawn to her afterwards. Nodding but privately and firmly forbidding any such notion, Cassia dashed away to the shelter of a nearby hangar.

Chapter Eight

Several hours after Rocco and Cassia had set off for London, Aurelia morosely struck a pose. She had tried to steer the director of the shoot towards the lush green fields and picturesque lemon and olive groves on the Disanti estate, but for some reason the photographer seemed to think posing amongst the rubbish bins behind the restaurant was the best option.

Wearing a two thousand euro lace bra and thong teamed with gold, spike-heeled sandals and a long gold chain round her throat, Aurelia was sweltering in the heat and about to storm off set.

'It's irony, darling,' Matteo informed her, the sleeves of his scarlet shirt rolled up and a cigarette hanging out of his mouth. 'Everyone expects to see Aurelia Disanti against a backdrop of wealth and privilege. This,' he gestured to the steel rubbish bins and bags of deliberately half-spilled food remains, 'brings you down to earth. Like I said, it's irony.'

Aurelia smiled sweetly at him, wondering if she should tell him she could see his tiny meat and two veg in his absurdly tight trousers. Matteo wasn't a photographer she worked with often, but she couldn't bear him. He wielded his camera like a porn star might brandish the most vital part of his body, but he was outrageously talented and he had photographed some of the most beautiful women in the world. He was also such an

182

obnoxious moron Aurelia could barely stand to seduce his camera lens.

Matteo knelt down and took some more shots, shouting out commands and flapping his arms to get the attention of his lighting man. 'More light here, please!' he yelled, looking as though he might explode. 'And Teressa, sort that make-up out, will you? Aurelia looks like she's melting, her face is practically falling off.'

Teressa, sensing Aurelia was about to have a fit, rushed forward to touch up the young girl's foundation. It was flawless, as she expected, but she made a show of blending and applying more powder.

'I think what Matteo means is that this setting makes you look even more gorgeous, the debris makes you stand out like a glittering jewel, do you see?' Hired for her tact as well as her incredible skills with her colourful palette, Teressa had saved many a photo shoot from collapse. She was also being truthful; Aurelia, with her lush, golden skin and dark mane, looked like an exotic show pony. The underwear looked as expensive as she did and her body was in the best shape possible.

Wishing she had something remotely resembling Aurelia's toned buttocks, Teressa applied a touch more nude gloss to Aurelia's pouty mouth and tried not to choke as the hair stylist swirled spray on the oversized sixties mane she'd created.

'The lingerie looks fabulous on you and you look sensational.' Teressa coughed. The smell emanating from the rubbish bins was almost unbearable; the strong May sunshine was making the already pungent aromas even more pronounced. 'Just . . . try not to inhale the terrible stench from all this filth, all right?'

Throwing her a grateful smile, Aurelia held her breath, sucked her stomach in and allowed her body to assume the 'broken doll' position. She had learnt long ago that editorial photography was all about looking awkward and gauche and even though she tended to do more commercial modelling, she prided herself on being adaptable. She also knew this lingerie shoot was worth a stupid amount of money, as well as raising her profile several notches, so she did her best to keep her mouth shut. Her mind was swirling with troublesome wedding details and she was finding it hard to concentrate.

Raffaelo appeared with a tray of espressos, the tantalising aroma making even Matteo lower his camera and tear his eyes from Aurelia.

'Help yourselves!' Raffaelo called, ever the gregarious host. He set the tray down and ran a finger around the tight-looking collar of his black shirt, clearly suffering in the heat.

'Another new suit?' Aurelia frowned, giving his latest pin-striped effort a disparaging glance. 'You don't always have to dress like Don Corleone, you know. It's such a cliché when you're Italian.' Raffaelo irked her; she might be lazy when it came to the restaurant, but he really didn't lift a finger and he had a proper role in the business. Yet he always seemed to dress impeccably – and was that a new Rolex he was sporting on his tanned wrist?

Aurelia shrugged to herself. Raffaelo had always been flashy.

Raffaelo looked unruffled by her taunts. 'It's glamorous being a model, isn't it?' he asked.

'Oh, shut up, Raff,' Aurelia retorted, stomping off behind a screen to get changed into a cream silk camisole and some tiny knickers. Shimmying into them, she was glad for the severe bikini wax that had brought tears to her eyes a few days before. It was professional suicide to turn up for a lingerie shoot with so much as a stray hair showing. Aurelia knew she had to look like a prepubescent schoolgirl before she paraded around in knickers. She scowled at Raffaelo as she picked her way through the chicken carcasses, knowing he was entertained by her discomfort.

'What the hell do you know about modelling, anyway?'

Raffaelo smiled good-naturedly. 'Not much,' he agreed. 'I just hadn't realised that frolicking in rubbish was fashionable.'

'It's ironic, apparently,' Aurelia snapped.

Raffaelo shook his head and headed back inside the restaurant.

Aurelia was beginning to feel thoroughly fed up. Dino had been away for days now, posing on some glorious beach back in Australia, and Aurelia hated it when he was gone. Jealously, she kept envisaging him surrounded by bronzed Amazonian beauties with wandering hands and she couldn't bear the thought of it. She wished she had someone to talk to about it and for a second she missed having Cassia around. They didn't have much in common but at least Cassia understood how hard it was to be away from loved ones.

'Let's take a break,' Matteo said, swaggering to a standstill with his camera thrust in front of his groin. 'Good work, Aurelia.'

'Thanks,' she returned, tight-lipped. Wishing she'd never invited the lingerie crew to the house in the first place, she hoped they'd all jet off back to wherever they'd come from sooner rather than later. Throwing a rose-pink dressing gown on over the lingerie, Aurelia stormed into the restaurant.

'Finished posing amongst the food scraps?' Raffaelo mocked, making a half-hearted attempt to put up a ravishing Canaletto print Rocco had recently purchased.

Stressed to breaking point, Aurelia burst into noisy tears.

'Now, now,' Raffaelo said, feeling guilty for baiting her. He led her to a nearby table and sat her down. 'What's all this about?' Reading between the lines of Aurelia's tearful explanation and gulping sobs, he realised his baby sister was struggling to juggle her wedding and her busy modelling schedule, and she was missing her fiancé badly. Without the laid-back Dino by her side to calm her tempestuous nature, Aurelia was flailing about like a painter without her muse.

'I just can't do it all on my own!' Aurelia spluttered into her hands. 'I'm organising the wedding of the century and no one's helping me, no one!'

Discreetly pushing back the gleaming cutlery and exquisite white and gold dinner plates Rocco had had handmade in Florence, Raffaelo sighed. He really wasn't equipped to deal with Aurelia's moods. Rocco had always been far better at defusing her emotional outbursts. He also didn't want to remind Aurelia that she had created this problem for herself by firing her wedding co-ordinator.

'I want . . . Amnesia roses,' Aurelia was saying in a jerky voice. 'And people keep telling me I can't have them. It's too much!'

Raffaelo was baffled. He didn't have a clue about flowers, in season or otherwise. All he knew about weddings was that lilac was considered to be unlucky in his country and he didn't even know the reason behind the tradition. He was surprised that Aurelia had booked her wedding in August, again notoriously unlucky in Italy, but he didn't dare question her about that in her current mood.

Raffaelo had a feeling he had led Aurelia to the best table in the restaurant, one due to be enjoyed by Italy's most famous politician. He started straightening cutlery, knowing Rocco would go insane if standards slipped in his absence.

'Er, I think we'd better vacate this table . . .'

'Well, I can see you don't care!' she cried, flouncing back outside to get her make-up redone.

Taking an important call he'd been waiting for and forgetting all about the Italian politician, Raffaelo accidentally left the best table in the restaurant askew and covered in mascara splashes.

Watching Aurelia strutting her stuff between the rubbish bins from one of the restaurant windows, Sofia rolled her eyes. She'd never understand the world of modelling; why on earth would people want to see a beautiful girl in lingerie cavorting amongst piles of rancid potato peelings and globs of chicken skin? Sofia could only imagine how awful it must smell out there in the heat; she didn't know how Aurelia could stand it. She was such a spoilt girl in many ways but she was coping with this latest situation with admirable stoicism.

Crossly, Sofia noticed Raffaelo playing the genial host, handing out coffees and pastries. He still hadn't mended a chipped door frame and there was still some storm damage to attend to. Sofia sighed. How could one grandson be so focused and ambitious while the other one seemed happy to take a back seat and not fulfil his potential? Sofia felt guilty thinking badly of Raffaelo; he was such a lovely man underneath all the self-consciously sharp suits and amiable manner – just like his father, Gino. Neither the brilliant first child nor the over-indulged baby of the family, Raff seemed to flounder, never really establishing his identity.

As a teenager, Raffaelo had always walked a fine line between right and wrong, never involving himself in anything too serious, but sometimes veering towards it without a thought about the consequences. Minor drinking offences, smoking and causing fires, the odd bout of gambling . . . Raff had always been one of those sociable types who found it impossible to stick to rules and to say no when his life threatened to implode. Still, he had sorted himself out by the time he'd hit twenty, Sofia mused, and he seemed happy enough working in the restaurant. Rocco had tried countless times to involve Raff more or to encourage him to learn a specific trade of some kind, but Raff had always resisted.

Sofia forgot about Raffaelo as she watched Aurelia slump her exquisite body over one of the rubbish bins in a painful-looking basque. Her expression almost – but not quite – gave away how disgusted she was, but she was doing a sterling job of looking at home in the debris.

Sofia realised it was the first time she'd ever seen Aurelia in action and she didn't blame her granddaughter for throwing the greasy-looking photographer the odd hostile look. Catching sight of the very clear outline of the photographer's crotch in the too-tight trousers he was wearing, Sofia suppressed a laugh and headed out of the restaurant at the front to check on a delivery. She didn't normally look after such things but in Rocco's absence she knew he preferred it if she double-checked everything was running smoothly. Belatedly remembering that the delivery wasn't due for another half-hour, Sofia was about to go back inside the restaurant when she came face to face with a tall man in a dark suit.

'I am so sorry to trouble you,' the man said politely, ducking his head slightly. 'I wondered if I could speak to Rocco Disanti.'

Sofia gazed up at the man, her cheeks colouring a little. He was tall and rather good-looking. His suit was both expensive and tasteful, designer but made to measure, Sofia decided, trusting herself when it came to the cut and quality of exceptional tailoring. Realising he was waiting for her to answer, she hurried to do so.

'I'm afraid Rocco is away at the moment, on business. He'll be back in a few days' time.' She gave a short nod and made to move past him.

'What a shame,' the man murmured, stopping her politely. 'Although perhaps not, as I have been lucky enough to meet you instead.' He held his hand out. 'Allesandro Raldini,' he added.

Sofia allowed him to take her hand, cross that she felt a frisson of chemistry between them as he bent to kiss it. 'Sofia Disanti,' she said primly, snatching her hand back. How old was he? she wondered. She guessed he must be in his late fifties judging by the lines creasing his eyes and cheeks, but his healthy tan and confidence gave him a much younger, rather dashing air.

Allesandro raised his eyebrows as he registered her name. 'But . . . that means you are Rocco's grandmother,' he said in surprise. Seeing her start, he waved a hand in the air with panache. 'I am here to do business with Rocco, so I researched the family. I hope you don't mind, but you look far younger than I expected.'

Sofia shook her head, annoyed to find herself wishing she was wearing something more dazzling than her usual black shift dress. 'Of course not. You are free to do whatever you choose.' She realised she sounded snippy but she couldn't help it; the man made her nervous. Or perhaps excited, she thought with a frown. How strange.

'Have you eaten here before?' she asked, keen to keep the conversation casual.

'No, but I hope to very soon,' Allesandro said with a wide smile, his manner suggesting he either hadn't noticed her abruptness or that he didn't mind it. 'Incidentally, I am in the wine business. I own a vineyard in Tuscany, producing some wonderful wines, which I am confident would be perfect for your restaurant.'

'We already have a wine merchant.'

Allesandro shrugged. 'I'm sure you have. But there is always room for manoeuvre, yes? Especially if a product is good enough.' He pressed a business card into her hand, his fingers closing over hers momentarily. 'If you could ask Rocco to call me when he returns, I would be very grateful. Alternatively, *you* could call me?' Allesandro grinned suddenly, his dark eyes lighting up.

Sofia blushed. Was he flirting with her? She couldn't be sure; she was so out of practice these days. She and Nico had spent a lifetime together and she hadn't once looked at another man, let alone flirted with him. Deciding she must be mistaken and berating herself for being so conceited, Sofia pocketed the business card.

'I'll let Rocco know you were looking for him,' she said, in an offhand tone.

Allesandro gave a small bow. 'Thank you. I hope to see you again . . . very soon.' With that, he turned and walked away without a backward glance. Climbing into a cherry-red vintage Alfa Romeo that reeked of style, he waved a hand out of the window before shooting off in a swirl of dust.

Feeling flustered for the first time since she and her late husband Nico had first met, Sofia told herself to stop being so ridiculous. Touching the card in her pocket thoughtfully, she wondered why she, a woman who was not prone to fanciful behaviour, felt so bowled over by a stranger she would probably never see again.

Finally back in her flat in Pimlico and surrounded by mess from her unpacking, Cassia was going through her unopened post and doing her best to figure out why she felt so unsettled. Rocco had been so different to the man she had been spending time with over the past month; he had been attentive, interesting, and disturbingly attractive. Loath to dwell on the matter too much, Cassia welcomed a call from her boss Gena to take her mind off things.

'Good trip home, Cass?'

Glad to be speaking English again after almost exclusively speaking Italian since she'd been in Italy, Cassia considered.

'If you like flying in helicopters, yes, it was lovely.'

Remembering Rocco's warm hand enclosing hers briefly, she felt herself flushing. Gena gasped. 'He flew you back in his helicopter?' Her voice rose to a squeak. 'How thrilling! No, wait, you're scared of flying . . . Was it awful?'

'It was . . . better than I thought it would be.' It was true; Rocco had made the trip much more bearable. In fact, looking back, Cassia realised she had been far too engrossed in conversation with him to worry too much about being up in the air.

'So, are you getting on well with him? It certainly seems that way from your column.'

Detecting a slight provocativeness to Gena's tone, Cassia was quick to dispel any suggestion that her relationship with Rocco was anything but professional. 'There isn't even a hint of romance between us, honestly,' Cassia laughingly chided her boss. 'I know you, Gena, you're going off at a tangent because you see romance everywhere, but you're very much mistaken.'

Gena tutted in disappointment. 'Shame. Still, you have the lovely Finn to drool over, so I'm sure you'll cope. Anyway, Rocco has some on-off girlfriend, hasn't he? Gianfranco's met her a few times. Stefania, is it? He says she's pretty but very demanding. I was calling to let you know how well your column is doing.' There was a scuffling noise at the end of the phone. 'Seriously, Cassia, we've been inundated with responses since your first column went out. The online stuff has had people going crazy. Seems they love your connection with Rocco and the descriptions of the restaurant, the area and the food – everything, really. I'm so pleased!'

Cassia grinned. She could just imagine Gena's blond curls jiggling with excitement at the other end of the phone. 'That's amazing, I had no idea the column was going to do so well.'

Gena sounded as though she was slurping coffee. 'I know, I know, it's even better than we could have hoped for. I'm just waiting to get the figures through for the website hits, as well as the latest copy of *Scrumptious*, but I know they're going to be fabulous.'

Cassia felt a surge of pride. Ever since she'd left England, she'd spent most of her time feeling guilty about putting her career in front of her personal life and her failure to discover anything about her father's family had made her feel even worse. She hoped Sofia's friend in Rome would be able to point her in the right direction, but for now she was painfully aware that she had nothing to show for her efforts so far.

'Actually, I did have a favour to ask you,' Gena said, sounding cautious. 'I know you and Rocco have been living in each other's pockets for the past few weeks but while you're in England, it would be good if we could get some shots of you together.'

Cassia hesitated. She was certain she should stay away from Rocco for a while, but how on earth could she explain such a thing to Gena? It would sound strange and she had no desire to discuss the fleeting, inappropriate things she had thought and felt on the helicopter ride, especially not to someone who could see romance in the most innocuous situations.

'I don't know if I'll have time, Gena,' she said eventually. 'Besides, I was planning to spend all of my time with Finn. We've only spoken a few times over the past month as he's been so busy with work.'

'I can understand that, obviously, but I'm only talking about a few photographs. We could always take them at the . . . er, well, I don't know; we can think of something.' Sounding evasive, Gena abruptly cut her comment short.

Cassia frowned. Gena had sounded as though she had put her foot in it somehow. About to ask her about it, Gena suddenly seemed keen to get off the phone.

'Must dash, Cass. I'll be in touch about the photographs. *Ciao!*'

Puzzled, Cassia forgot about Gena when she heard a knock at her door.

Finding Finn standing in front of her with a broad smile on his face, Cassia threw her arms round his neck. She breathed in his scent, revelling in how solid and reassuringly familiar it was.

'Finn! I missed you so much.' She pulled back and took a good look at him. Clearly he had come straight from the office; he was wearing a suit and carrying a briefcase. His red-blond hair was ruffled and his eyes were bloodshot but Cassia was so happy to see him, she barely noticed.

'Same here,' Finn said, squeezing her. 'It feels like you've been away for ages, much longer than a month.' He kissed her, a long, sweet kiss that made Cassia remember exactly why she loved him.

Smoothing her dark hair away from her face, Finn took a proper look at her. She looked different somehow. She was wearing a slightly crumpled, cream halter-neck sundress that complemented the golden glow of her shoulders perfectly but it was a bit more daring than her usual style. In addition, unusually, her dark hair hung in loose waves down her back. The whole effect was unnerving; it was as though a sun-kissed, more sensual version of his fiancée had turned up, rather than the person he knew like the back of his hand.

Finn felt nonplussed by this new Cassia; she seemed so self-assured and stylish. He felt a flicker of apprehension curl around his stomach. If Cassia had changed this much after just a few weeks of being away, how unrecognisable might she be after her stay in Sorrento was over?

Catching sight of her battered Prada shoes on the floor where she'd kicked them off, as well as her trusty laptop open on the coffee table, Finn told himself to stop being silly. Cassia was back and he wasn't going to worry about her wearing a more daring dress or leaving her hair down.

'Come on, sit down and tell me all your news,' Cassia said, dragging Finn to the sofa. 'Obviously we've spoken since I left for Italy but it's not the same as being face to face, is it?'

Truthfully, Cassia couldn't help feeling disappointed with the lack of contact she'd had with Finn over the past few weeks. He was always so busy, more caught up with work than usual, but she knew his job sometimes became intense if there was a big case going on.

'Well, I've been stupidly busy,' Finn admitted, removing his suit jacket wearily. 'The law firm has taken on so many big cases recently. I thought I should get some brownie points in, you know, especially since going home isn't so much fun any more.' He smiled but it was half-hearted.

'You look absolutely shattered.' Cassia poured him a glass of the wine Rocco had given her. Good wine always cheered him up. 'This is a 2001 Chianti, not quite as impressive as the '97, by all accounts, but a good year. Rocco gave it to me as a present . . . for you, I mean.'

Finn took the glass but didn't enthuse. 'Thanks. It's been manic since you left,' he said, tugging on a strand of her hair fondly. 'I suppose it's been a blessing in some ways, because otherwise I think I'd have spent far too much time thinking about you over there in Sorrento. As it is, I've been dashing around like a crazy person, barely speaking to anyone.'

Cassia tried not to feel hurt that 'anyone' obviously included her. Finn looked away. 'I didn't get that promotion,' he blurted out. 'But I really don't want to talk about it, if you don't mind. I made the mistake of telling my mother the other day and she hasn't stopped going on about it since.'

Cassia wasn't surprised as the signs hadn't been positive before she'd left for Italy but she instantly forgave Finn for his lack of contact over the past month. She knew how much the promotion had meant to him and she could only imagine how gutted he must feel. A tiny part of her resented him for confiding in his mother rather than calling her about it, but she squashed it down. Hadn't she just said herself that speaking on the phone wasn't the same as face-to-face contact?

'Have you seen much of Dom?' Cassia said, deciding a subject change would be prudent. 'I saw something in a magazine about his tremendous form. I can't wait to see how he gets on at Wimbledon this year.'

Finn looked sheepish. 'Yes. Look, there's something I've been meaning to tell you about Dom, actually. He's dating Jules and he has been since you left for Italy, more or less.'

'What?' Shocked, Cassia nearly splashed wine all over her

sofa. 'You're kidding me. Is it serious? Ha, what am I saying? Dom is never serious about anyone.'

'Well, quite. And having seen Dom flirting with anything that moved after a match recently, I can't say that he's changed at all.' Finn lay back against the sofa, his head flopping tiredly to one side. 'But Jules told Louisa that she thinks Dom is about to propose. I think my mother's already planning wedding number two even though she probably hasn't heard that bit of news.'

Cassia raked her hair out of her eyes. Grace had always had a soft spot for Jules but it was probably because she was so good at domestic things, like cooking. Cassia had always felt envious of Jules's easy relationship with Grace and the way that Grace seemed to accept her so readily, but she had always supposed it might be different if Jules had been dating one of her sons. Obviously not, and this heightened Cassia's paranoia that her future mother-in-law truly had it in for her.

Remembering something, Finn reached for his briefcase. 'Incidentally, my mother has booked our wedding venue.' He removed a batch of photocopies from his case. 'It's called, er, Parkland Heights Manor and . . . well, I'm pretty sure you're not going to be happy when you see it.'

Not going to be happy? Cassia's heart literally plummeted with dismay when she saw the photographs. The grotesquely named Parkland Heights Manor was a vast stately home with pillars and a double doorway. Inside, the building was just as vulgar with showy, sweeping staircases and old-fashioned hangings. In short, it was stuffy, old-fashioned and everything she detested. Cassia wasn't sure if Grace could have searched out something more opposite to the small, romantic venue she had requested if she'd tried.

'Oh no. Finn, this isn't what I – what we – wanted at all! Why would your mother book this place after everything we discussed? And Parkland Heights Manor? That's not even a real name, surely?'

'I know. Look, it's obviously her taste rather than ours. I'm so sorry, Cass. I know you must be really disappointed.' He covered Cassia's hand with his own. 'I know you'll think I should have put my foot down, but she was so excited about it, she couldn't wait to talk me through all these photos. And unfortunately, she put down an enormous, non-refundable deposit, so we're a bit screwed really.'

Cassia felt anger crawling up inside her. How could Grace have gone ahead and booked the wedding venue without consulting either of them? And why on earth hadn't Finn challenged her? Cassia couldn't believe he had let his mother get away with disregarding their wishes so arrogantly. Rightly or wrongly, and she knew she was being irrational, she couldn't help thinking that someone like Rocco wouldn't have allowed such a thing to happen.

Finn squeezed her hand. 'If it's any consolation, I think my father gave her a huge rollicking over it because he knew it wasn't your cup of tea. Or mine, for that matter.' He leant back against the sofa again. 'But you know my mother, once she gets an idea in her head . . .'

Barely listening, Cassia fumed. She knew that if confronted, Grace would defend herself by claiming that with Finn so busy and herself out of the country, she had had no choice but to book the hideous Georgian monstrosity.

Was this to be her penance for daring to take the trip? Was she going to have to suffer Grace systematically destroying every aspect of her big day, just because she'd dared to focus on her career and find out about her father's Italian family? And some use her mother was, Cassia huffed. Where was she when this stuffy manor house was being viewed? She knew her mother wasn't the most assertive of people but at the very least she could have viewed the venue and told Grace how horrific it was. Her wedding was going to be a total disaster, with only kindly Henry gently sticking up for her every time Grace ignored her wishes.

'Whilst I'm dropping bombshells, I'm afraid I have another one.'

Finn's apologetic expression made Cassia feel quite alarmed. She swigged her wine. 'Hit me with it.'

'My mother's arranged an engagement party for tomorrow night.'

Cassia's face fell. She had been so looking forward to spending some time with Finn alone.

'We were supposed to be going out. I've booked a table at your favourite restaurant.' She felt exasperated. Grace must have done this on purpose.

Finn was contrite. 'I know, and that was so thoughtful of you. But I only found out about it today, when I told my mother we were planning to go out for a meal. It was meant to be a surprise, so she wasn't best pleased when I told her about our plans.' He put down his untouched glass of wine. 'But she's gone to a lot of trouble, invited the whole family, apparently. She wanted us to formally mark our engagement before we get married. And it's in London, a friend who runs one of her charities has lent her some fancy venue.'

Consumed with impotent rage, Cassia bit her lip. So far, her visit home had yielded nothing but disappointment and bad news. It was great to see Finn again, but she could do without any more bombshells and changes of plan. Remembering Gena's gaff earlier, Cassia guessed her friend was invited to the big engagement bash.

'Fine. I guess we can't really get out of it if she's invited everyone,' she said, knowing she sounded sour. 'And while we're both dishing out bad news, Gena wants to get some shots of me and Rocco this weekend. Reckons it's good publicity for the magazine or something.'

Finn yawned. 'Invite him to the party tomorrow night. Mother's asked an official photographer to come along – I know, I know, it's way over the top. Either he can take some shots of you and Rocco, or maybe Gena can bring someone along.'

'You don't mind?'

'Why should I mind?' Finn kicked his shoes off, put his feet up on the table and closed his eyes. 'Is he an idiot or something?'

Cassia shook her head. 'No . . . it's not that.'

Finn blearily opened one eye and squinted at her. 'Well, what then?'

'Er . . . nothing.' Cassia knew she couldn't tell Finn why she wanted to avoid Rocco for a while. 'Right, I'll invite him.'

Cassia put all thoughts of Rocco out of her head. 'Let's take this delicious Chianti into the bedroom,' she suggested. 'I'll run us a lovely, hot bath and we can sink into the tub together, before drifting into the bedroom so we can remember exactly why we're getting married . . .'

Finn was fast asleep and within seconds he was snoring steadily. Cassia let out a frustrated sigh. Somehow she had expected him to make the effort to stay awake, if only to maybe let her know how much he'd missed her.

She covered him with a blanket and tucked a cushion beneath his head, gazing down into his craggy, handsome face. She had hoped he would whisk her off into the bedroom and make mad, passionate love to her, but that obviously wasn't going to happen tonight. Oh well, there was always tomorrow after the party, she thought wryly, helping herself to Finn's wine. She toyed with her phone, thinking she should text Rocco about the party before he was invited elsewhere, but her mind kept wandering. She had nothing concrete to base it on but she couldn't help thinking that if it had been Rocco waiting for her to come home after a few weeks' absence, he'd probably have torn her clothes off and tumbled her into bed before the Chianti had even been opened.

Scooping up her wine, she headed for the bedroom, and to prove she felt no attraction towards Rocco whatsoever,

Cassia sent him a casual text inviting him to the engagement party.

Rocco glanced at his watch, wondering how Cassia's romantic reunion with her fiancé was going. She had mentioned meeting up with him, so he guessed they were probably catching up over the wine he had given Cassia – that, and a whole lot more, no doubt.

Sitting at one of the few empty tables in Disanti's London, Rocco sipped the superb Dolcetto d'Alba his head chef, Ben, had poured him and put Cassia out of his mind. He knew he'd be far better thinking about Stefania, but it always gave him a headache. Rocco drummed his fingers on the base of his wine glass. They barely saw each other these days, but he knew that shouldn't matter. If their bond was deep enough and their feelings strong, what should a few miles matter? Rocco was acutely aware that he needed to either end the relationship with Stefania or propose. The latter idea scared the hell out of him, but equally he couldn't be sure he was ready to let her go. He gazed out at his restaurant, knowing his grandfather, Nico, would feel immensely proud if he had been around to see it. Rocco sat back and enjoyed watching the team of staff efficiently clearing away after a busy evening's service. The restaurant had been packed when he'd first arrived and it had been a pleasure to see his hand-picked staff smoothly tending to the needs of the customers. Exquisite meals he was more than satisfied to stake his reputation on had appeared seamlessly, the appetising aromas wafting through the air, exciting the waiting customers just as much as the extravagant presentation. Good, traditional Italian food with a twist, with an emphasis on quality and luxury, was served time after time.

Which didn't mean the restaurant was without issues. Rocco knew for a fact that his head chef Ben was tearing his hair out over some of his staff, but none of the clientele would have noticed anything remiss.

'Can I get you anything, Mr Disanti?' asked an extremely pretty waitress who had downed an entire glass of leftover dessert wine in order to pluck up the courage to approach him.

Rocco smiled at her as his fingers lazily played with the stem of his wine glass. 'No, thank you. I'm waiting to speak to Ben, but I appreciate you taking the time to check on me.'

The waitress swooned and backed away, eagerly reporting back to her colleagues about Rocco's delicious accent and sexy eyes. Rocco turned back to survey his restaurant. It didn't have the breathtaking views of its Sorrento sister but it featured some fairly impressive fresco reproductions on the ceiling and it had a prime spot in Mayfair.

'Here are the menus,' said Ben, depositing them on Rocco's table. 'Are you sure you want to work on them?' He looked uncomfortable as he took a seat. 'I usually have this sewn up midweek, but as you know, I've been left in the lurch a bit recently on the staff front and I've been interviewing every day after lunchtime service.'

Rocco nodded. 'I heard that Noah on the dessert station walked out.'

Ben looked stressed. 'He said he found the menu too demanding. Obviously some of the desserts are pretty fiddly and difficult to master but Noah was trained by the best so I don't see why he couldn't cope. You had reservations about him when we hired him; I should have listened to you.'

'Everyone deserves a chance.' Seeing that his head chef was almost at breaking point, Rocco grasped Ben's shoulder. 'Listen, why don't you head off home now? I can sort this out.' He knew how easy it was to get caught up working late into the night in the restaurant business and although he rarely took his own advice, Rocco could see that Ben needed a breather.

Clearly tempted, Ben faltered. 'I shouldn't . . . I have things to do and you're only here for the weekend.'

'We'll catch up tomorrow,' Rocco assured him. 'And I'll do some interviewing with you or in your place, if you want. Seriously, go home and see your wife – she must miss you.' He gestured to the menus. 'I want to do this, honestly.'

Gratefully, Ben stood up. 'Well, if you're sure. It would be good to see Sarah. How's Stefania, by the way?'

Rocco pulled a face. 'Demanding, as always.' He flapped his hands. 'Go, before I change my mind.'

Watching Ben removing his chef's jacket with a spring in his undoubtedly tired step, Rocco picked up the menus. Taking on the review hadn't been a purely benevolent gesture on his part. He wanted to put some new ideas together; it was something he enjoyed and for once he had the time. Just for a few hours, he wanted to focus on food. Not paperwork or business meetings or staff with grievances, just food.

Working his way quickly through the starters, Rocco became more animated. Puntarelle with anchovies, he decided. Delicious. Maybe a baked tagliolini with veal ragu . . . a beef carpaccio, or perhaps one of swordfish? Fois gras in balsamic or wild boar with truffles?

Rocco scribbled all over the page. There was a recipe his grandmother, Sofia, used to cook for his grandfather all the time. What was it now? Milk-roasted veal served with minute, stuffed peppers. Rocco smiled. It was enough to make his mouth water. Adding a linguine with sea urchins and garlic he randomly thought Cassia might like, he finalised the desserts and added a list of accompanying wine suggestions.

Sitting back and sipping his wine, Rocco wondered at how fulfilling he had just found the exercise. He really missed being involved in the creation of recipes and the food side of the restaurant business. Glass of wine in hand, he strolled over to the window, enjoying the romantic sight of Mayfair dappled by moonlight. Stefania had visited London with him a few times, but she hadn't been taken with it and she could rarely be lured away from the glamorous streets of Rome.

Was Cassia still awake? Rocco leant against the window, thinking about how vulnerable she had looked in the helicopter. Holding her hand had felt like the natural thing to do at the time, but looking back, he wasn't sure he could make sense of that. There was something wild and untamed about Cassia, Rocco thought, something in her eyes that hinted of a simmering passion bubbling just beneath the surface. Yet on the outside, she often seemed cool and reserved, as though she was holding herself in check, and that fascinated Rocco. He wanted to get to know her, to work out what made her tick. Most of all, he wanted to know if he was right about the glimmer of sensuality he had glimpsed on the trip to London.

Rocco realised his phone was whirring in his pocket. Thinking it must be a text from Stefania, he was taken aback when he saw that it was an invitation to Cassia's engagement party. The message was concise and not overly friendly and for some reason it made him smile. The party would also no doubt put paid to the plans she had mentioned about spending quality time with her fiancé.

Thoughtfully, Rocco sent back a text accepting the invite. It would be interesting to meet her friends and family, not to mention Finn, and he had been hoping to see Cassia again while he was in London. Noticing how late it was, he tapped his phone against his chin. What was Cassia doing texting him at this hour? Shouldn't she be catching up with Finn in one form or another?

Turning back to the window with his wine, Rocco watched young, glamorous debutantes and their dinner-suited beaus tripping tipsily by as Mayfair slowly closed down for the night, all the while trying his hardest not to think about Cassia possibly lying alone in bed.

Chapter Nine

Moodily, Diana checked her hair in one of the Venetian mirrors. The swanky venue in Kensington was certainly impressive; the restrooms were decked out in glossy grey and ivory, with a buttermilk-coloured marble floor, and upstairs, the banquet room was ostentatious to say the least, with large chandeliers, vast ceilings and a loud, plush carpet.

Diana grimaced. She really wasn't in the mood for a party, and watching Grace lording it over everyone as she played Lady Bountiful was grating on her nerves. Diane could only imagine how tiresome Cassia would find it once she arrived; anyone would think it was Grace who was getting married, not her son.

Raking her flirty blond fringe into place with jerky movements, Diana stared back at her reflection. On the outside, she looked fairly together; the crepe Donna Karan dress she'd picked up in Harvey Nics draped around her slender figure to perfection, the exotic teal shade bringing out the blue of her eyes. And after being buffed and spray-tanned, her skin glowed as though she'd spent the past fortnight in the Seychelles.

On the inside, however, she was falling apart. Snatching up her glass of champagne – her fifth, if memory served – Diana drained it, hoping the bubbles would pep up her flat mood. Work, or rather the lack of it, was playing heavily on her mind and she couldn't seem to pull herself out of the doldrums.

Another, recent, crushing rejection for a TV show she was sure would have put her back on the map had left her floundering around without a purpose and she had no idea what to do next. Angelo kept bugging her to take Fliss up on the play, but what did he know? Cassia had enthused just as much on the phone the other day, at pains to persuade her that such a challenging part would prove to everyone what a superb actress she was, but Diana still wasn't convinced. It was too risky, too exposing – and not just because of the general nakedness.

She spritzed on a generous slug of Visa, the peachy, oriental Piguet fragrance Marco had always adored, and told herself to stop being such a sourpuss. She couldn't wait to catch up with Cassia now that she was back for the weekend, but Diana felt apprehensive about Jules. The two sisters hadn't been in the same room together for weeks and Diana couldn't help thinking that the atmosphere would be tense with prickly resentment, on Jules's side, at any rate, especially since the party was being held in Finn and Cassia's honour. Still, Jules was in a fantastic mood at the moment, courtesy of her fling with Finn's younger brother, Dom, so perhaps the evening would pass uneventfully. Overcome by a wave of regret, Diana wished she could change the past. She knew why Jules felt so antagonistic towards Cassia and she wished things were different. The hostility was misplaced, of course, but Cassia didn't know that; she was the one person in the family who knew nothing about the terrible secret. Diana gripped the edge of the sink with white knuckles, intensely aware that she was the only person who knew exactly what had happened all those years ago. Well, Fliss knew – but there was one other, someone Diana would never speak to again.

Thinking about everything brought Marco to the fore, as it always did. God, how she missed him! How she wished he was here so they could have indulged in a harmless but enjoyably bitchy chat about which party guest was the dullest and which hapless designer had been responsible for the vulgar décor. Marco had complemented her flamboyant personality so wonderfully; the handsome intellectual and the frothy actress. Not quite Arthur Miller and Marilyn Monroe, but in the same ball park.

Diana stared at her reflection with haunted eyes.

'Are you all right in there, my darling?'

Angelo. Diana frowned. His heavily accented voice sounded silky-smooth from the other side of the door and she could almost see the warmth in his dark eyes from his murmuring tone.

'I'm fine,' she snapped. 'I'll be out in a minute.'

'I'll be waiting,' he returned huskily.

Delaying emerging from the restrooms, Diana examined the toe of her leopard-print D&G stiletto. What was she doing messing around with a boy in his early twenties? They hardly had anything in common. He was immature, Spanish, and a musician, for heaven's sake. She was the proverbial older woman, messing around with a young man who played his guitar in smoky clubs – just like Clarissa in Fliss's wretched play, in fact.

Diana opened the door.

'My darling,' Angelo said, jumping up from the ugly, wooden chair with claw feet he'd been lounging in. 'I was worried about you.'

Diana accepted his kiss ungraciously. 'No need to worry about me,' she responded tightly. 'I can always look after myself.' Gazing at Angelo, she was struck again by how absurdly young he was. Christ, she was making such a fool of herself, she thought, shocked. They must look ridiculous together. Women like Grace must be tittering behind their hands and waiting for Angelo to run off with someone younger and fresher.

Diana felt panicked. She hated looking stupid more than anything and the thought that people might be laughing behind her back was excruciating.

'Go and have fun,' she said out of the blue.

His dark eyes clouding over, Angelo looked thoroughly perplexed. 'Fun? I have fun with you. Why would I need to "go" and have fun?'

Diana looked round for a drinks waiter. 'I mean it, Angelo. You shouldn't be hanging round with an old crow like me. Go and play with someone your own age.'

Hurt, Angelo did as he was told. Diana watched him slouch off like a rejected puppy, but she knew she was doing the right thing. She wasn't sending him away; she was simply urging him to chat to some young girls so he realised how inappropriate their relationship was. Diana knew it would be a darn sight easier if Angelo realised how absurd it all was, rather than her having to take the initiative and finish it.

She caught sight of Grace and headed in the other direction, bumping into Cassia. Diana caught her breath. Not only did Cassia look absolutely stunning, her dark looks were so reminiscent of Marco, it was quite astonishing.

'Mother,' Cassia said, giving her a hug.

'You look wonderful in that dress, darling,' Diana told her, admiring it. A tight-fitting gown in a gorgeous shade of garnet, it suited Cassia's colouring to perfection. Her dark hair was loose and her skin glowed from the light tan she'd acquired in Sorrento.

Cassia was pleased. She hoped Finn would like the dress too. Where was he? Putting aside the disappointing night with him, she'd spent the day catching up on her post and her emails, as well as writing a quick column about her trip back to England with Rocco. Leaving out the embarrassing details of her fear of flying and the intimate hand-holding, she had focused on Rocco's recipe discussions and childhood memories, enjoying a blissful few hours at her laptop.

'*Rocco has plans to create a delicious, deconstructed tiramisu,*' she had typed, her senses stirring pleasurably, '*with a luscious*

mixture of mascarpone, rum and eggs, with savoiardi, finger-sized
sponge cakes, and a thick layer of bitter cocoa powder to balance
the sweetness . . . plus a rustic but mouth-watering dish of softly
warmed figs, rich dark honey and a dash of Tuscan wine . . .'

Cassia waved to a few of her friends, promising she would
catch up with them properly later. She couldn't help noticing
that not many of her friends and family were in evidence;
typical Grace, she had made the party all about her.

'Where's Angelo?' Cassia asked, trying not to think about
wanting to throttle Grace for the moment.

Diana's eyes flickered. 'I sent him on his way, told him to
find someone his own age to play with.'

'Ouch.' Cassia flinched, knowing her mother's sensitive
young boyfriend would probably have found such a comment
offensive. Angelo was an absolute sweetheart; she did hope her
mother wasn't about to screw things up. As odd as it was to see
her with someone other than her father, Cassia had nothing but
good things to say about Angelo. 'Are you sure you want him
to do that?'

Diana shrugged, not sure what she wanted any more. A
heady mixture of career indecision and booze had thrown her
mind all over the place.

'So where were you when Grace was booking the most
hideous venue in the whole of England for my wedding?' Cassia
asked. At the thought of Parkland Heights Manor, her stomach
tightened, threatening to spoil her good mood.

Diana looked rueful. 'Oh, darling, I'm so sorry about that.
I was hoping to go and view it but I had to dash off to an
audition.' Her expression darkened. 'I shouldn't have bothered; I missed out on the part anyway. Again.' Snatching
up two glasses of champagne from a hunky young waiter she
would normally have flirted with, Diana reluctantly handed
one of the glasses to Cassia, almost draining the other with
one gulp.

'I just can't believe Grace booked that horrible place,' Cassia commented. 'I really want to have it out with her, but I don't know if Finn would like it.' She threw her mother a caustic glance. 'And so much for saying you'll fight my corner for me while I'm in Italy, eh?'

About to defend herself, Diane realised she was on the brink of tears. 'I-I'm desperately sorry, Cass. You're right, I should have gone with Grace. It's your wedding, your big day, and I should have made more of an effort to be your voice in your absence.'

Astonished by her emotional reaction, Cassia guessed her mother must be feeling fragile about something. Perennially buoyant as well as a consummate actress, she rarely let her guard down in public. Cassia placed a hand on her mother's arm. 'What's wrong?' she asked softly. 'Are you upset about not getting the part? Or are you worrying about doing that play? You mustn't, you'd be fabulous.'

Not strong enough to handle Cassia's sympathetic tone, Diana almost came undone. 'It's not just the part,' she admitted. 'It's . . . it's . . .' Realising she couldn't exactly tell Cassia why she couldn't stop thinking about Marco, Diana faltered. Marco was Cassia's hero and her eldest daughter was the last person she should confide in . . . for so many reasons.

'Must go, darling,' she managed, tearing away.

Cassia felt helpless as she watched her stumble away. Then she saw Jules arriving. Clinging possessively to Dom, she looked like the proverbial cat with a very much sought-after saucer of cream. Dom, sporting a healthy tan and a confident smile, looked as though he'd come straight from the tennis courts. Wearing snug shorts teamed with an ivory blazer with purple piping that his hero Roger Federer had given him, he was greeting various guests who were fawning all over him. He even had his tennis racket slung over his shoulder for good measure, clearly playing up his role as Britain's latest sporting heartthrob with aplomb.

Keen to outshine the young Sloanes Jules knew would be in attendance, she had taken time over her appearance and she was glowing in a ravishing, pale pink strapless gown that left her golden shoulders bare and exposed a length of toned thigh through a daring split, à la Liz Hurley. Spotting Cassia, Jules broke free from Dom.

'So, what do you think about me and Dom?' she asked, watching him shake hands with an old school friend of Grace's.

'I'm really happy for you,' Cassia replied. She had reservations, but she knew better than to voice them aloud to Jules, especially when she was looking so wistfully hopeful.

Jules gave Cassia a critical once-over. Her sister looked rather beautiful for once; the unusual red dress, no doubt something she had picked up in Sorrento, suited her. Jules wanted to say something complimentary but for some reason she didn't.

'Finn says you and Dom have been together since I went to Sorrento.'

Jules shrugged. 'More or less. It feels like longer because it's been so intense. Dom's been away a lot, but when he's back, we spend every minute together.' She smirked. 'He's romantic and sweet, and between you and me,' Jules leant in, 'he's hung like a donkey.'

'Er . . . well, that's great,' Cassia said, her eyes widening at the graphic details. 'I hope he appreciates you, you deserve to meet a great guy.'

Jules bit her lip. Cassia was so nice, it made disliking her very difficult at times. In fact, Jules wasn't sure she disliked Cassia at all at the moment, but that was probably because she was so loved up with Dom. Her eyes darted around the room, trying to locate Dom, and she felt jealous when he greeted an exceptionally lovely girl with enthusiastic kisses on both cheeks.

'Finn tells me it's serious between the two of you,' Cassia said, hoping to God Dom felt as strongly about Jules as she very obviously did about him. If not, Jules was going to suffer a terrible blow at some point in the future.

Jules nodded confidently. 'Oh yes. He's told me I'm the only girl he's ever had real feelings for. Isn't that amazing?' She could barely contain her excitement. 'I'm just so happy, Cass.'

'That's brilliant, good for you,' Cassia replied warmly, feeling her heart sinking with every word. Watching Dom flirt his way round the room, she wished she could stop feeling so cynical about her sister's relationship.

Jules didn't notice. She was too busy wondering if Dom might propose that night. It would be perfect, a double celebration. 'Excuse me, I'm missing him already,' she said, sashaying away.

Putting Jules out of her mind, Cassia decided to go in search of Finn. She hadn't seen him all day and she wanted to make things right between them. They needed to connect and she couldn't wait to spend some time with him, even if it was in a room that was mostly full of Grace's stuffy relatives.

Strolling into the party wearing a dinner suit with a spotless white shirt and bow tie, Rocco realised he didn't know a single soul apart from Cassia, who was nowhere to be seen. He accepted a glass of chilled champagne and decided that the venue – one of the few remaining buildings in South Kensington that hadn't been sold off and turned into modern flats – was beautiful but showy.

Unaware that his devilish good looks were causing the female contingent to stare at him in hushed awe, Rocco swung round and found himself face to face with a pink-cheeked lady with a strange, blond helmet of hair that looked as if it wouldn't move in a gale force wind.

'You must be Rocco Disanti,' the woman said, clasping his hand in her own, rather cold one. 'I'm Grace Sunderland. Cassia told me she'd invited you tonight and we're all delighted that you're here.'

210

Truthfully, Grace had been furious at Cassia's high-handedness; after all, she had arranged this engagement party as a surprise and *she* was in control of the guest list, not Cassia. Still, now that Rocco was here, Grace couldn't quite find it in herself to be impolite towards him. He was so dashing, for one thing, the epitome of European elegance and heart-stoppingly gorgeous, to say the least. Not prone to feeling girlish in any circumstance, Grace felt uncharacteristically flustered.

'Mrs Sunderland.' Bowing respectfully over her hand, Rocco gave it a polite squeeze. 'It is so kind of you to allow me to join you at the last minute like this. And what a wonderful party you have arranged. Truly, I am honoured to be here. I would have been lost for something to do tonight otherwise.'

'Oh, I'm sure you wouldn't,' Grace gushed. She turned to her friends, who had sidled up during the exchange, forming a breathy huddle.

'This is the famous chef, Rocco Disanti,' Grace announced, taking full credit for his unexpected presence. 'He owns a wonderful restaurant in Mayfair as well as the most beautiful place in Sorrento. Cassia is working with Rocco at the moment, you know. A fantastic opportunity for her,' she added blithely, smoothing over the fact that she had been dead set against the idea until a few moments ago.

Sipping his champagne, Rocco greeted the crowd of women modestly. Had he done the right thing, accepting Cassia's invitation? In spite of his self-deprecating claim of an empty diary for the night, he had actually been invited to three other parties that day, as well as two more intimate dinners, courtesy of women he had dated during some of the 'off' phases of his on-off relationship with Stefania. Yet here he was, making courteous chit-chat with sweet middle-aged ladies.

Rocco tuned Grace's prattle out and watched her discreetly. She was an imposing woman and despite the overly feminine yellow prom dress, her cool blue eyes hinted at her steely core.

Remembering what Cassia had said about her, Rocco knew Grace to be one of those ferociously protective mothers, one for whom no woman could ever be good enough for her son. There were many such women in Italy, Rocco mused. They went under an alternative guise, fiery scorn tending to be the weapon of choice towards unsuitable or unworthy women, and Rocco was thankful that his own mother wasn't this way inclined. If anything, she had always encouraged him to have lots of relationships, believing he would choose a wife more wisely when he was ready to settle down, as well as being less likely to stray. Because one thing his mother was dead set against, despite many of her Italian friends thinking she was a naïve fool, was infidelity.

'Ah, Cassia.' The warmth dropped out of Grace's voice. 'There you are. I was just introducing Rocco to everyone in your absence.'

Cassia's dark eyes flashed. 'Sorry I wasn't here when you arrived,' she told Rocco apologetically, somehow feeling better now that he was here. She didn't know if he was her ally or not, but he certainly bore the friendliest expression in the current crowd. 'I was catching up with my mother and sister.'

'No matter,' Rocco replied, staring at Cassia appreciatively.

Cassia noticed Grace gazing at Rocco with something close to hero worship and she was amused – no, impressed – that he had managed to melt the ice maiden. Cassia's opinion of Rocco went up another notch.

'Great dress,' he commented in an aside. 'I love red. The colour of passion, yes?'

Cassia flushed slightly. She felt good in the dress; it had been years since she'd worn such a vibrant colour and the bold statement had boosted her. Sensing Grace's disapproval, Cassia felt exasperated. Anyone would think she'd turned up in a basque and suspenders with her backside hanging out. It was utterly ridiculous.

Observing the change in Cassia's expression, Rocco felt compelled to intervene. 'Mrs Sunderland . . . Grace, if I may? You must be so proud of Cassia, and so happy that your son is marrying such an intelligent, beautiful woman. My family love her, as I'm sure yours do.'

'Er . . . er . . . yes, absolutely,' Grace stuttered, lost for words.

Cassia shot Rocco a look of surprised gratitude. What was he playing at? Catching sight of a mischievous smile tugging at the corners of his mouth, she realised he was deliberately winding Grace up. Cassia almost laughed, but she managed to restrain herself. She wasn't sure Rocco was telling the truth about his family loving her, but she appreciated the gesture all the same.

'Have you been to Sorrento, Grace?' Rocco asked, continuing the charm offensive. 'I would love to have you dine at my restaurant.'

Grace simpered.

'In fact, why not join us for my sister Aurelia's wedding?' Rocco added, getting carried away and not noticing Cassia's look of horror. 'It's supposed to be *the* event of the summer in Sorrento.' He rolled his eyes in a comic manner, causing the surrounding women to titter coyly.

Cassia gaped. Without wishing to be a killjoy, she didn't think Rocco needed to be quite so generous and she caught his eye pointedly.

'Oh, really, Rocco, there's no need, I'm sure Grace has far too many social functions lined up over the summer . . .'

Grace ignored her and beamed. 'I do, but I'm sure I could make time for such an event. Thank you, Rocco. How thoughtful. Don't you agree, ladies?' She preened at her friends. 'An invitation to an Italian wedding, how exotic. Aurelia, you say? Not . . . not the famous model?' She called Henry over.

Cassia was amazed. How on earth did someone like Grace know who Aurelia Disanti was? She must have done some homework on Rocco's family.

'Come and meet Rocco, immediately.' Grace grabbed Henry's arm and yanked him to her side. 'We must co-ordinate diaries, Rocco, but we'd love to attend if we're free.'

Overjoyed to see Cassia again, Henry grinned at her. 'Darling Cassia, you look divine.' He gave her an effusive hug. 'And you must be the infamous Mr Disanti,' he said, shaking Rocco's hand. 'Friend of mine dined at your Mayfair place yesterday, said it was absolutely top notch.'

Rocco inclined his head. 'How kind. I was just inviting you all over to Sorrento for my sister's wedding. You will stay at the house, naturally; there is plenty of room.'

Henry pumped Rocco's hand heartily again. 'Of course, Cassia's wedding isn't too far away either,' he stated. 'In fact, we just booked the venue.' His smile faded as he noticed Cassia's pained expression. 'Ah. Thought so. Not really your taste?'

Feeling Grace's ice-blue eyes on her, Cassia gave an uncomfortable shrug. 'Er, not really. I'm indebted to you for all your help while I'm in Italy, of course, but . . .'

Grace bridled and proceeded to publicly reprimand her future daughter-in-law.

'Well, really! I feel very let down by your reaction, Cassia.' She pursed her lips. 'I think it's a superb venue and without you here to take care of all these details, someone has to make a decision.' Grace glowered at her. 'I would have thought you'd have been thanking me, not disagreeing with my choices.'

Cassia could feel her cheeks colouring. 'I'm not disagreeing, Grace, it's just . . . the venue isn't exactly what we discussed before I went to Italy, is it?'

Grace visibly prickled. 'I don't know what you mean.' She sniffed. 'Parkland Heights Manor is a marvellous estate, perfect for a Sunderland wedding.' How the girl had the audacity to challenge her future mother-in-law was beyond her. *She* wasn't the one who'd jetted off to Italy, putting her career before her wedding and her fiancé.

214

'But it's my wedding too', Cassia exclaimed in frustration, 'and I know I'm away but I didn't expect you to completely disregard my wishes. Mine *and* Finn's.' She knew Finn wouldn't be happy about her confronting Grace, but enough was enough. Cassia knew if she didn't put her foot down now, her wedding would turn into a fiasco. Besides, shouldn't Finn have stuck up for her and defended her right to detest the wedding venue?

Henry threw Grace an accusatory glance. 'See, Gracie, I said we should have waited to check with Cassia about the—'

'Oh, do shut up, Henry,' Grace snapped. Forgetting her desire to appear genteel in front of Rocco, Grace let rip. 'I think you need to remember who's doing you a favour right now,' she ranted. 'A little appreciation wouldn't go amiss, for starters. And I know you say your trip to Italy is about looking into your father's heritage, but let's be honest, you've put your career before Finn and that's not acceptable.'

Too late, Rocco regretted the impulsive invite to Aurelia's wedding. Grace was a spiteful piece of work and she was making mincemeat out of Cassia.

Grace continued nastily, 'I've made huge sacrifices to take on your wedding, I've even given up work on my charity committees. I've let my housewifely duties go and . . . and my dahlias are positively wilting without my attention.'

Cassia stared at her. Good God, now she was being blamed for Grace's droopy flower arrangements as well as everything else. Embarrassed that Rocco was witnessing the whole sorry confrontation, Cassia was deeply upset by Grace's attack. Everything she had suspected about her future mother-in-law had been proved right in the past few minutes and her thoughts were all over the place. She wanted to defend herself but she couldn't find the words.

'I do hope it's not impertinent of me to step in,' Rocco said softly, taking Grace's hand. Feeling slightly repulsed as her chilly blue eyes met his, he gave her a gentle smile. 'I am sure you are doing your very best with the wedding arrangements, Grace, but you must be patient with Cassia. She is finding it very difficult, being in Italy when really she would prefer to be at home, arranging things herself.' Rocco held on to Grace's hand and patted it reassuringly. 'If anyone is to blame here, it's me. I work her too hard, I'm sure.'

Cassia stared at him. For a minute, she felt so overwhelmed, she thought she might cry. Rocco was fighting her corner the way she had hoped Finn would – if he'd been here. She wasn't sure she could cope with this version of Rocco; irrationally, she found him easier to handle when he was being obnoxious. She was moved by his loyalty, even if it was because he was a consummate gentleman rather than anything else.

'And to set the record straight,' Rocco continued firmly, 'it certainly is of the utmost importance to Cassia to track down her father's family. She has been searching for clues relentlessly since her arrival in Sorrento and she will now be assisted by a historian friend of ours in Rome so that she can finally end her search.'

Grace looked utterly flummoxed and gazed at Rocco speechlessly.

Rocco stared back at her, hoping he was managing to hide his dislike. What a disagreeable woman. The way she had launched her diatribe at Cassia in front of her friends was verging on bullying and Rocco could see that Cassia was too shaken by the public confrontation to stand up for herself with any determination. And where was Finn? Shouldn't he be performing the role of Cassia's knight in shining armour?

Cassia was mortified. 'Thank you, Rocco. I'm so sorry you feel so strongly about this, Grace, and I can assure you, I had no intention of upsetting you.' She swallowed. 'Do excuse me . . . and apologies, Rocco . . . I'm sure you have better things to do than listen to these embarrassing family squabbles.'

Ducking her head, she moved past Rocco and hurried off to find out where Finn had got to. Rocco had no desire to spend any more time with Grace; he smiled at Henry before backing away. Poor Cassia; marrying Finn would mean inheriting the mother-in-law from hell. She must think an awful lot of her fiancé to put up with this. Either that, or she was just exceptionally nice. Rocco hoped Finn had a good reason for leaving his fiancée to be criticised and publicly humiliated by his mother because it was pretty unforgivable.

An hour later, having been tied up at yet another meeting, Finn finally arrived. He glanced around for Cassia but he couldn't see her anywhere. Bumping into a rather anxious looking Jules carrying a vodka-laden Bloody Mary, Finn couldn't resist canvassing her opinion. Coaxing her to share a window seat with him, he drew a small box out of his pocket.

'What do you think?' he asked. The box contained diamond earrings; small, tasteful and very Finn, they glittered prettily against the royal blue velvet of the box.

Jules glanced at Finn's earnest, freckled face. Putting her Bloody Mary down to take a closer look, Jules decided the diamond earrings were exquisite.

'What has my sister done to deserve those?' Jules asked, wishing Dom made gestures like this. He favoured lavish bouquets of exotic blooms but he hadn't yet bought her jewellery, which Jules saw as a more meaningful present. She felt a stab of insecurity, wondering where Dom was. She had been trying to track him down for ages and she was beginning to feel paranoid that he was trying to avoid her.

'I've just been missing her, I suppose,' Finn said. He didn't know Jules well enough to admit that the earrings were a guilt gift – for all he knew, Jules would run off and tell Cassia just to spoil the moment. He sighed. The night before had been a disaster and he hadn't even been able to make it up to her today because he

217

had shot off in the early hours of the morning to finish some work that had ended up taking him all day. He just hoped Cassia would forgive him, not least because he was late again.

Finn knew he needed to give Cassia some proper attention and he intended to do just that tonight. He had bought the earrings on the advice of a work colleague and he hoped they would distract Cassia from the disastrous night before, as well as her romantic dinner plans being cancelled because of the engagement party.

'God, I bet you've booked the Bentley Hotel or something equally fabulous for the night to totally spoil her,' Jules commented, looking put out. The stylishly elegant hotel surrounded by couture shops and designer boutiques was one of the places she'd loved to stay in and she'd been dropping endless hints to Dom about taking her there.

Finn hadn't, but it occurred to him that a night in a hotel would be the perfect end to the evening. He took out his phone, planning to call them and book a last-minute room.

Jules felt edgy. Finn always did the right thing; he could be relied upon to come up with the goods. Dom was rather more unpredictable, but she was sure she had guessed correctly about his proposal plans. She held her left hand up and visualised a ring on it. Would Dom have bought a classic diamond, like Finn? If so, would it be larger? Jules wondered hopefully. Or perhaps he would have gone for something more unusual – a sapphire to match her eyes, or a pear-shaped diamond, the only time such a shape was acceptable.

'How are things going with Dom?' Finn asked. Jules looked quite pretty in the pink dress. She suited pastels, he thought vaguely. Truthfully, he was only making conversation until he spotted Cassia, but he supposed he should make an effort if Dom was Jules's boyfriend.

'Very well,' she said with a bright smile. 'I'm so happy, I can't tell you, and he told me he feels exactly the same way.'

Finn felt relieved; whatever he had seen at Dom's charity match had obviously been a one-off.

Jules looked over her shoulder, searching for Dom's face in the throng of party-goers. She felt oddly disillusioned; being with someone like Dom was more stressful than she'd imagined. Sure she would make a wonderful WAG, Jules's eyes had been opened to the more unsavoury side to dating a celebrity. She lived her life on a knife edge wondering where Dom was when he wasn't with her, tormenting herself with thoughts of girls who turned up at sporting events and parties with the sole ambition of bedding a star. No matter that he might be married, have children or simply not be interested, these days bagging a famous name was all the rage. Jules wasn't proud of her actions but, aware of Dom's colourful past, she followed him frenziedly on social networks, searching for clues that he might be cheating on her. So far, there hadn't been a hint of a misdemeanour, but Jules couldn't relax.

'Are you . . . all right?' Finn asked tentatively, putting his hand on her bare arm.

Jules nodded but her outwardly serene exterior melted in the face of his obvious sympathy. Burying her head in Finn's shoulder, she gave in to her anxiety. 'I'm sorry,' she mumbled into his suit jacket. It smelt reassuringly of aftershave and she clung to his solid shoulder. 'Dom's just so . . . I don't really know where I am with him,' she managed.

Lifting her chin with his finger, Finn shook his head. 'Women rarely know where they are with my brother,' he confided. 'But hey, you're with him for the excitement, I'm guessing. Unfortunately this is the downside.'

Wiping some mascara away with his thumb, Finn wondered where Dom was – and what he was up to. Still, Jules wasn't his problem; it was Cassia he needed to focus on. 'Look, I'm sure everything is fine. Go and find Dom and he'll tell you the same. I need to make amends with Cassia for disappearing all day.'

Watching him stride away, his strapping shoulders filling the doorway as he headed out into the garden, Jules stirred her Bloody Mary with a stick of celery. Finn was right; she just needed some reassurance. If only she could track Dom down . . .

Having drunk far too much champagne, Diana was having second thoughts about sending Angelo off to find someone else to play with. Staggering off to find him, her eyes crossing slightly, she gasped when she saw he was chatting to Finn's sister Louisa, who looked fabulous in a long, bias-cut frock that only the truly slender could get away with. Louisa looked blissfully happy and Diana felt a crazy urge to hurl a drink into her pretty, pixie-like face. Henry was standing by a magnificent yellow and white cake that Grace had paid a fortune for, summoning everyone to the front for some speeches about the engagement as Diana teetered over to Angelo.

'Well, you didn't waste any time,' she slurred loudly.

The crowd gathered for the speeches turned round, looking for the drunken voice. Grace was appalled but Henry did his best to clear his throat and draw attention away from Diana. Angelo looked up, his liquid-black eyes wide. 'My darling Diana,' he said, clearly pleased to see her. 'I was wondering where you were.'

Diana snorted, feeling sour champagne bubbles fizzing in her throat. 'Oh, I can see that!' she returned. She glared at Louisa.

Louisa gave her a bemused stare. 'We were only chatting,' she said, wondering what all the fuss was about. 'About you, as it happens.'

'How sweet,' Diana snapped, resenting Louisa her youth and prettiness. Seeing everyone staring, Angelo said quietly, 'Shall we go home, my angel?' Diana had consumed far too much champagne and he knew she might cause a scene. He adored Diana and all he could think was that he needed to get her home.

Throwing Angelo's arm off dramatically, Diana was barely in control of herself. 'Home? What, to my house, do you mean?' Seeing him flinch at the veiled criticism that he did not own his own place, Diana carried on. 'No! Enough's enough, you need to collect your things and go elsewhere. You're a child, not a man. I need a man.' As Marco's absent face swam in front of her, Diana nearly keeled over. A white-faced Cassia grabbed her mother and spun her away from the crowd.

'Don't do this,' she begged, feeling everyone's eyes on them. 'You love Angelo and he loves you. Don't ruin things just because you've had too much to drink tonight.'

Angelo took Diana's hand. 'Diana, please. Let's go.'

'No!' Diana yanked her hand out of Angelo's. 'Leave me alone. Juss . . . juss leave . . . me . . . alone.'

Crushed, Angelo left. Cassia sighed and ushered her mother into a quiet corner of the room.

'I miss him so much,' Diana told Cassia in a drunken whisper.

Cassia frowned. 'What? You miss Angelo? Then why on earth did you tell him to go?'

Diana's eyes crossed as she tried to focus on Cassia. 'Not Angelo,' she muttered in confusion. 'Marco . . . I miss Marco . . .' She burst into noisy tears. 'I loved him so much but I ruined that too. How could I do that? Why was I so . . .'

She pulled away from Cassia suddenly, momentum causing her to totter into the centre of the room. Unable to stop herself, Diana hurtled headlong towards the five-tier engagement cake next to Henry. Tripping on her high heels, she crashed into the table, sending the cake flying comically into the air. Everyone watched as it separated into layers, pirouetting twice before exploding all over the floor, sending sponge and icing in every direction. Henry, his suit pebble-dashed, tried desperately to catch Diana as she toppled after the cake, but to no avail. She slid over and sat up immediately, brandishing a handful of cake.

'Whoops,' she said, dazed.

Cassia gasped in horror. Catching sight of Grace's appalled face, Cassia rushed over to Diana, helping her to her feet.

'Get up,' she hissed.

'Oh God.' Realising what she had done, Diana flushed. 'Get me out of here, Cass.'

Cassia didn't waste a second. 'Will do, Mother. Sorry, do excuse us . . . thank you so much . . .' Not even daring to imagine what Grace was saying about the incident, she headed outside with a staggering Diana and hailed a taxi. After a few minutes, one pulled up next to them and Cassia deposited her mother inside it and told the driver her address.

Unable to face speeches right now, Cassia slipped away from the main hall and escaped up a nearby staircase. The evening couldn't get any worse, and Finn was still nowhere in sight. Finding herself on a rooftop terrace, Cassia breathed in the cool night air and wondered if it was inappropriate to leave one's own engagement party early. Mind you, appropriateness had gone out of the window, hadn't it? Cassia surveyed the twinkling lights of London below and wished she could hop on a plane back to Sorrento.

Upstairs on one of the carpeted landings, Jules was totally oblivious to the drama unfolding beneath her because she was busy coping with her own. Having searched for Dom for nearly an hour in total, she had finally discovered him in one of the upstairs rooms, but as soon as she'd flung the door open, she would have done anything to retrace her steps and go back to the safe, ignorant place she'd been in before.

For Dom wasn't alone. With Roger Federer's preppy blazer – his most prized possession – flung carelessly on the floor,

Dom was enjoyed a private but very debauched party of his own.

Confronted by the sight of Dom's bum cheeks pumping away enthusiastically as a blonde girl shrieked like a banshee beneath him, Jules gasped. As if it wasn't bad enough to find Dom doing the dirty with one girl, there was also a brunette on the bed, balanced on all fours, with bare and very pink buttocks in the air. Keeping perfect time with his thrusting hips, Dom was thwacking the brunette on the bottom with his tennis racket as if he was swatting aces down the baseline, cheering as the girl let out muffled yelps of pleasure from the pillow she had her head buried in.

Rooted to the spot, Jules didn't know whether to run for her life or snatch the tennis racket off Dom and beat him soundly round the head with it. Whatever she had been expecting to find, this wasn't it. Feelings of utter betrayal washed over her – God, she had thought Dom was about to propose. How stupid she had been!

Jules clutched her Bloody Mary shakily, cursing herself for her naivety. Louisa's explicit warnings about Dom and Finn's rather more veiled ones rang in her ears and she cringed as she thought about the way she had gushed about Dom to anyone who'd listen. She had been so desperate to believe it was a fairytale romance, just like Cassia's with Finn, that she'd allowed herself to believe Dom's declarations of love.

Sensing someone behind him, Dom turned his head. 'Jules!' he cried, his eyes crossing crazily as he continued to plough in and out of the blonde like a randy horse covering a mare.

Grinning broadly, he jerked his head towards the bed. 'Don't be shy, join us!'

Jules gaped. Had he really just asked her if she wanted to join in his filthy threesome? The glazed look in his eyes made her wonder if he was off his head on something illegal.

Wanting to hurt him as much as he had hurt her, Jules did

the only decent thing she could think of in the circumstances and hurled her Bloody Mary all over his precious blazer.

'You bitch, Jules,' Dom growled, seeming to sober up at the sight of his tomato-spattered jacket. Yanking his shorts back up, he stabbed the air with his tennis racket. 'What the fuck did you do that for?'

'I don't know, Dom. What the fuck did you do *that* for?' Jules cried hysterically, gesturing to the two girls on the bed.

Dom gave her a withering stare. 'Christ, Jules, you didn't really think we had a future, did you?' His handsome face twisted contemptuously. 'It was just a bit of fun, you, them . . . it's all just *fun*.'

'Why . . . why did you say you loved me? I thought you bloody loved me.' Jules hated herself for sounding so needy.

'Oh, Jules.' Dom shook his head pityingly. 'It's just something people say. Hardly anyone means it, do they? Even my mother says it on my birthday, but it's all just bullshit, isn't it?'

Jules backed out of the room. The bastard. The utter, utter bastard. Tears streamed down her face and she wiped them away, appalled at herself for caring so much. She staggered down the corridor and she headed into a bathroom where she splashed cold water on her face, willing herself to stop hurting inside. Staring at her reflection in the mirror, Jules knew she had to leave. She couldn't stay here, not after this. She had boasted to Cassia that Dom was about to propose, when all he was actually doing was indulging in his favourite pastime: dropping his trousers and playing with balls.

'Are you all right?'

Cassia turned to find Rocco standing behind her. His accent was rather charming when he was speaking English, she thought as she gave him a watery smile.

'Er . . . yes. It's just . . . I don't think this party could get any worse for me.'

Rocco looked sympathetic. He didn't like to say that he had witnessed the incident with her mother and the cake, but he could see that Cassia was deeply upset. 'You were right about Grace, not your biggest fan, I think you would say in English?'

Cassia looked away. 'Yes, that's what you would say. Not my biggest fan.' Her voice was flat.

Rocco shrugged elegantly. 'She has the wrong impression of you. It happens.' He gazed out at the view of London which twinkled with multi-coloured lights. 'Women like that, they can be difficult to impress, especially when it comes to their own flesh and blood.'

Seeing her giving him an inquisitive look, he laughed. 'Oh no, I'm not speaking from experience! My mother thinks the world of me but she doesn't put me up on a pedestal. She's not a very typical Italian mama in that way, but my grandmother is protective enough for two, as you've probably seen.'

Cassia nodded. Sofia was fiercely protective of her family but she was also warm and welcoming – everything Grace was not, in fact.

'You're lucky, Rocco. I don't think it does anyone any good to be seen through rose-tinted glasses.'

She frowned, suddenly thinking of her father. He had always supported her in every way possible, delighting in her achievements with as much passion and joy as he had celebrated his own. Had he done the same for Jules? Cassia wasn't sure. Her memories of her childhood seemed so confused since her father had died.

'Sorry I invited Grace to Aurelia's wedding,' Rocco said, looking contrite. 'I realise now that she is the last person you'd want there.'

Cassia shook her head. 'That's all right. I know you were just trying to be nice to her.' She laughed. 'Grace will be living off that invitation for months, all her charity cronies will be so impressed.' She turned to Rocco, her expression sombre. 'Do you ever get tired of it? Of people wanting you to be something you're not?'

Rocco looked startled. 'I don't know, I haven't really thought of it like that.'

'I just mean that your parents . . . the public, even, want you to be this figurehead for the Disanti empire. They wish you weren't so private and that you'd grant them more access.' Cassia rubbed her bare arms as a breeze ruffled the silk of her dress. 'On a much smaller scale, I wish people would accept me for who I am. Grace, for starters. She behaves as though wanting to have a career and a husband is a cardinal sin.'

He nodded thoughtfully, wondering whether to offer her his jacket again. 'I see what you mean. My parents are definitely a little guilty of that; they'd prefer me to be more like them, more into the whole celebrity thing.'

And what about Stefania? Rocco stared out at the view. Wasn't she just as bad? She wanted him to open more and more restaurants and to move away from his family home, which had to mean she didn't understand what mattered to him in his life. It wasn't something he had given much thought to, until now, but yes, on reflection, he supposed he was rather fed up of being judged and found wanting sometimes.

He glanced at Cassia. He couldn't help thinking she looked absolutely beautiful in spite of her distress. The dark red dress suited her exotic colouring. He wanted to tell her to wear rich colours more often but he knew it was none of his business. What did he care about Cassia's clothes?

Looking into her liquid brown eyes, Rocco found himself lost for a moment. There was such depth there, such passion. As she looked away abruptly, he studied her features. Her nose was a little too wide, her mouth an unapologetically soft curve that seemed to have a mind of its own, expressing her inner thoughts without her being aware she was giving herself away.

Rocco's eyes dropped to Cassia's mouth again and, randomly, he wondered what it would be like to kiss her. As a breeze lifted her long, dark hair from her shoulders, Rocco almost acted on the thought. He wanted to kiss her thoroughly until both of them were breathless and gasping for air, until she had forgotten about her drunken mother and that some dried-up old lady had made her feel less than good enough – also that her fiancé hadn't seen fit to arrive on time for his own engagement party.

Rocco was perturbed. Cassia was a colleague, a guest in his house. Furthermore, she was about to be married. And he wasn't prone to losing control of himself as far as women were concerned; his wild side came out in safer ways, like flying helicopters and riding motorbikes. Yet he'd been thinking about her non-stop since they'd arrived in London.

Aware of his scrutiny, Cassia felt her heart thumping in her chest. Up on the terrace alone, it felt as if they were the only two people in the world. It was a romantic spot the terrace was covered with pots of flowers, with chairs and tables dotted about. There was muted lighting from discreet bulbs in the corners and under the inky blanket of sky stars winked and added to the ambience.

Anyone would feel like this, Cassia told herself. In these surroundings, anyone would be hoping someone would come along, sweep them into their arms and kiss all their lipstick off. Turning towards Rocco, she found him staring back at her intently. His hand was on the edge of the balcony, his fingers centimetres from hers.

'Cassia,' he started, his voice thick. 'You're so . . .'

Cassia's breath caught in her throat and she found that she couldn't tear her eyes from his. She sensed his fingertips almost touching hers and she fought an urge to slide her fingers through his.

Rocco moved closer.

A flash of light made them both blink.

'A lovely shot!' Gena said, emerging from the darkness with a photographer in tow. 'We've been trying to find you, and here you both are.'

Cassia plastered a smile on to her face. 'Gena! I . . . er . . . I forgot about the photographs.'

'Photographs?' Rocco looked annoyed. He withdrew his hand from the balcony, his eyes turning wintry. 'Was that why you invited me here?'

Cassia shook her head. 'No, no . . .'

Gena stepped forward. 'The photographs were my idea, Rocco. Lovely to see you again, darling. Gianfranco is downstairs somewhere; he's dying to catch up with you.'

Ever the gentleman, Rocco kissed Gena's cheeks, trying to catch Cassia's eye as he did so.

Cassia couldn't meet his gaze. The photographs had been Gena's idea but she couldn't honestly say she would have invited Rocco to the engagement party if it hadn't been for Gena pushing her to do it. It had been an act of defiance, if anything, a way to prove to herself that she felt nothing for him. Which was pretty ridiculous in the circumstances.

Gena made a swift exit, throwing Cassia a curious glance as she did so. Remembering the spark of tension between herself and Rocco and the deliciously hot sensations that had flooded through her, Cassia flushed. She had wanted him to kiss her, she had been willing him to take her roughly in his arms. But judging by Rocco's chilly expression, he regretted making any sort of overture towards her – if indeed that was what had happened. Cassia now thought she must have misread the entire situation.

She was about to attempt to smooth the waters with him when Finn arrived.

'Cass!'

Seemingly delighted to see her, Finn strode towards her, his arms outstretched. Going into them awkwardly, acutely aware

228

of Rocco watching them, Cassia hugged Finn. Immediately, she remembered how cross she was with him.

'Where have you been?' she asked, knowing she sounded snippy. 'You're over two hours late.'

Finn looked slightly annoyed. 'I know, I'm sorry. Work stuff, you know. Look, my father told me about the row over the wedding venue. I'm sorry I wasn't here to back you up.'

Cassia shrugged. 'Not to worry, Rocco stepped in for you.' Turning to Rocco, she introduced him. 'Rocco, Finn . . . Finn, Rocco.'

Finn held his hand out and shook Rocco's hand, somewhat taken aback by his appearance. Rocco had looked attractive in his photograph in *Scrumptious* magazine, but Finn hadn't quite been prepared for how brooding and charismatic he would be in person. And what a very good-looking couple he and Cassia made. How perfectly matched with their dark colouring and sensual features. The thought came out of nowhere and Finn swallowed.

Rocco was also discreetly regarding Finn. With his tufty, red-gold hair and bright blue eyes, he was ruggedly attractive and his face was open and friendly. Rocco wouldn't have picked him out as Cassia's fiancé in a million years, but he couldn't quite say why. Was it because Finn seemed rather sensible-looking? But on reflection, seeing Cassia in her home environment, with her fiancé's family, made her seem a more withdrawn and unassuming woman than the one he had been working with in Sorrento.

'Good to meet you, Rocco,' Finn was saying pleasantly. 'I do hope Cassia's not taking you away from your work too much?'

Rocco thrust his hands into the pockets of his trousers. 'Not at all,' he responded suavely. 'It is a pleasure to have her staying with us.'

About to comment, Finn did a double-take at Cassia. 'You're wearing red,' he commented.

Cassia raised her eyebrows. What did that mean? Was he pleased about it or not?

Finn didn't know the answer to that himself. Seconds later, he did and he knew he wasn't pleased. The bold colour made her look wanton . . . available. And not like his Cassia at all.

She felt his faint disapproval and it irked her. But what had she expected? Finn – and his mother – had always preferred her in safe, neutral colours. Cassia suddenly felt suffocated. Why did she always have to conform to be accepted? What was wrong with her wearing a bright colour, for heaven's sake?

'Anyway, I have a lovely gift for you,' Finn said, smiling warmly at her. 'Would you like it now or later? Later, maybe. There are speeches soon, I think, and then I plan to whisk you away to a hotel for the night. The Bentley, in fact. How does that sound?'

'Er . . . lovely.' Cassia shot a glance at Rocco, wondering what he was thinking. His face was impossible to read; the shutters had come down.

Finn slipped his arm through hers and Cassia smiled up at him, knowing he was making an effort to appease her for what had turned out to be a disappointing couple of days.

'The hotel sounds lovely. How thoughtful of you.'

Finn thought it best not to mention that it had been Jules's idea.

Cassia turned to Rocco. 'Will you join us for the speeches?'

Rocco inclined his head. 'Yes, of course. I will just enjoy this stunning view for a few moments more, if you don't mind.'

Watching them leave, Rocco tried to figure out why he felt so unsettled by what had happened on the roof terrace. The near-kiss – for that was what it had been, surely? The urge to kiss her, and the emotions that had accompanied it, had taken him by surprise.

Rocco watched the twinkling lights below, thinking that London could be one of the most romantic cities in the world – with the right woman at his side. He didn't relish the thought of a night alone in his hotel, especially not since Finn had mentioned taking Cassia to the Bentley later on. For some reason, the thought of them together in a room near his made him feel slightly off-kilter.

The sooner I get back to Italy and to my job, the better, Rocco decided. London – and Cassia – seemed to be bewitching him.

Chapter Ten

Dom's betrayal hit Jules hard. For days after the party she kept telling herself she didn't care and that at least she wasn't going to have to compete with all the hair-flipping, cleavage-showing public school girls at Wimbledon, but inside, she felt crushed.

She leafed through her post and found a handful of job rejection letters. No job and no man – what a familiar state of affairs.

When the phone rang, she answered it listlessly, sitting up when she realised it was Grace at the other end. She accepted the unexpected invitation to lunch straight away. She had no idea why Grace wanted to talk to her, but whatever the reason, she felt it was important to appear appropriately demure. Grace dressed like a born-again virgin; therefore, she should do the same.

Jules tugged on a spotless white dress that skimmed her knees and left only a few inches of décolletage on show. She tied her hair back with a pink ribbon and added a mint-green cashmere cardigan she'd swiped from Cassia's wardrobe years ago. Glancing at her reflection, she decided she looked like the goody two shoes version of Sandra Dee – which was ironic since she better suited the leather-jacketed version with the spray-on leggings. Jules retied her hair and wondered what the lunch was about. She had always had the impression that Grace preferred her to Cassia, which was rather baffling in some ways, but Jules could only assume that Grace admired her more homely qualities. The fact that she could bake and keep a house clean presumably meant that she passed muster, whilst Cassia, barely having time to flick a duster around, let alone bake a perfect Victoria sponge, was sadly lacking. Jules shrugged at her reflection. She supposed it was all swings and roundabouts; Cassia was blessed in so many ways that having a future mother-in-law who thought she wasn't quite good enough for her favourite son was just deserts.

Jules met Grace thirty minutes later in a traditional brasserie famous for its basic but good-quality fare. She was amused to see that Grace was dressed in a similar fashion to herself, sporting a pastel-coloured frock with a Peter Pan collar and a pair of sensible white flats. With a beige handbag on her lap and her pale hair set in rigid waves, Grace looked rather like the queen as she stiffly waited for her lunch guest.

Greeting her with the reverence Jules knew Grace expected, she slid into the seat opposite and kept her expression neutral. Not sure if Grace would pay or ask her to go Dutch, Jules chose a small duck breast salad with a white wine spritzer – modest enough not to offend Grace and appropriate for someone suffering from a broken heart and no appetite. Jules had in fact been gorging on biscuits since Dom's betrayal, but it didn't hurt to keep up appearances.

'I was so sorry to hear the news,' Grace told her, giving Jules an approving once-over. Why couldn't Cassia dress like that? Grace sniffed to herself. The red dress she had worn to the party had been far too sexy and if that was the effect Italy was having on her, there was trouble ahead, in Grace's opinion. She focused her attention on Jules. 'I don't know exactly what happened with Dom and, frankly, I'm not sure I want to.' She shuddered, imagining all sorts of depraved acts. 'The silly boy shot off to the French Open after the party so I didn't get a chance to talk to him but I hope you know how cross I was that he treated you badly.'

'It was very . . . painful,' Jules allowed as her minuscule salad arrived. She rather thought the brunette with the bruised buttocks at the party had taken the brunt of the pain, but she was sure she was suffering the most emotionally. She assumed a suitably injured expression.

Grace tutted. 'You poor thing, you must be devastated.'

Jules picked at her salad and said nothing. She did feel pretty awful but in all honesty she wasn't sure if that was simply the result of yet another crushing relationship failure rather than anything to do with Dom specifically.

'I can only apologise,' Grace sighed as she tucked into a whole baked sea bass stuffed with fresh herbs. 'Dom is a terrible reprobate, always has been. The total opposite to his brother, more's the pity.'

Jules wondered if Grace knew how unsubtle her favouritism was – or how wounding.

'So, did you get a chance to speak to Cassia much while she was back?' Grace changed the subject adroitly.

Jules shook her head carefully. Was this the reason behind Grace's lunch invite? 'No. But we're . . . we're not that close, as you know. We don't have much in common.' She paused. 'Cassia's always so busy with work, whereas I'm more of a homebody. I love to party, but deep down I like the idea of getting married and being . . . settled, I suppose.'

Grace dabbed daintily at her mouth with a napkin. 'The thing is, I was planning to ask Cassia if she would like to wear my wedding dress, but at the party she was more concerned with blasting me for booking the wedding venue you recommended.'

Jules felt guilty. She had only suggested Parkland Heights Manor to Grace out of mischief; she really hadn't envisaged her booking it, especially without consulting Cassia. As for Cassia 'blasting' Grace over the wedding venue, well, Jules couldn't imagine that. Cassia was extremely mild-mannered most of the time, even if she did have a feisty streak. As for Grace's idea that Cassia might wear her wedding dress, Jules gulped.

'Oh, don't tell me; Cassia wouldn't think my dress was good enough,' Grace snapped, misreading Jules's expression. 'Well, I wouldn't have expected anything less. She's a strident young lady, rather disrespectful, if you ask me, but I would still like to offer.' She sighed. 'What a shame Cassia isn't more like you, Jules.'

Jules frowned. 'I didn't say she wouldn't wear—'

'You didn't need to,' Grace interrupted her. 'I am well aware that your sister doesn't think much of me. I just wish we had a better relationship – more like ours, really.' She studied the dessert list. 'Ooh, they have chocolate torte. That's Finn's favourite, and I'm a bit partial myself. I mustn't though; one must think of one's hips.'

'You don't need to,' Jules told Grace, sucking up shamelessly. Even though she felt badly about Cassia, it was a bit of an ego boost being made to feel as if Grace preferred her over her sister. 'You're lovely and slim.'

Grace preened and smoothed her skirt down over her narrow hips.

After coffee, she paid the bill, leaving a mean tip, and collected up her handbag. 'Well, it's been delightful to catch up with you, Jules, and thank you for listening to me about my woes with your sister. At least I have you to confide in.'

'Not at all,' Jules replied warmly, giving Grace a kiss on her soft, powdered cheek. 'Thank you for lunch.'

On the way home, she sent Cassia a text message about the wedding dress, thinking she should at least give her a heads up about it. Back home, she couldn't help thinking it had gone exceptionally well and, oddly, Grace's support made Dom's betrayal drift away a little. At a loose end, Jules wandered into the kitchen, her place of sanctuary when things were going badly. She picked up one of her favourite cookery books and flipped through the pages without interest, until her eyes alighted on a recipe for a luscious chocolate truffle torte.

Finn's favourite, Grace had said. Well, Jules thought, she wouldn't mind a piece herself, especially of this version which contained coffee and cinnamon. Opening the fridge, she decided she had just about enough double cream left over in a pot to make it.

'What are you up to?' Louisa asked, strolling into the kitchen. Dressed in a yellow tracksuit with a healthy glow to her face, she looked like the perfect advert for the gym she worked at.

'Making chocolate torte,' Jules replied, her head still in the fridge. They had barely spoken since their heated exchange a few weeks ago and Jules was dreading Louisa saying 'I told you so' about Dom.

'Look, I'm so sorry about Dom,' Louisa said, her eyes full of concern. 'I honestly can't believe what he did to you.'

Grabbing some dark chocolate and golden syrup, Jules put them on the worktop and looked away. 'Go on, say it. You knew he was going to do something like this.' She put a saucepan of water on the hob to boil.

Louisa pulled her into a hug. 'No, I didn't know that, Jules. I just hoped he wouldn't.' She squeezed her. 'What can I say? He's an idiot and you can do so much better.'

'Really?' Jules looked doleful as she started to break up chunks of dark chocolate. 'I'm beginning to wonder.'

'Don't be daft.' Louisa leant against the counter. 'Of course you can.'

Jules glanced at her. 'I'm sorry about . . . you know, not listening when you were trying to tell me about your job and stuff. I can't believe I didn't know you'd met someone.'

Louisa smiled. 'It's all right. We all get a bit self-absorbed now and again.' She glanced at Jules's outfit. 'Have you been out somewhere?'

'To lunch with your mother, actually.' Jules efficiently added syrup and some cream to the melted chocolate and stirred it. Whipping up the rest of the cream with some coffee and cinnamon, she checked that it was wobbling like a milkshake and folded the chocolate mixture in.

'My mother asked you to lunch?' Louisa looked incredulous. 'She doesn't even ask me to lunch. You're very privileged.' She looked miffed.

Jules concentrated on her torte mixture, cutting a figure of eight through it with a metal spoon. 'I think she wanted to pick my brains about Cassia more than anything else. We do get on, though.' Sure that the mixture was pillowy and soft, she tipped it into a tin and smoothed the top over. Glancing at Louisa, Jules realised she was upset.

'Sorry, that was insensitive of me. We only get on because we're not related. She doesn't want to be my best friend or anything.'

Louisa folded her arms. 'I wouldn't be too sure,' she answered lightly. 'Still, Finn's the only one who's ever been good enough for my mother, so you've got a lot to measure up to.' She nodded at the torte. 'You should take that to Finn, it would cheer him up now that Cassia's gone back to Italy. I got the impression that they rowed after the engagement party, but he's not talking about it.'

Still looking hurt over Jules's lunch with her mother, Louisa left.

Jules stared at the torte. Maybe she should take it to Finn's office. Either that, or she would devour the whole thing in one sitting, which wasn't going to help her chances of meeting someone else.

Some hours later, Jules changed into skinny jeans, some heels and a silky camisole, and with the torte safely tucked away in a large biscuit tin, she took a bus to Finn's office. In the reception area, Jules faltered. She felt a bit strange just turning up like this; she hadn't been to Finn's office since the day they had chatted about her CV, but she was here now.

Finn greeted her at the lifts, looking faintly bemused, and Jules guessed he probably thought she was here to talk about Dom. He took her to his office, looking distracted and preoccupied, so she decided to be quick and she thrust the tin into his hands. 'Sorry, this is odd, I know, but I was having lunch with your mother and she mentioned that you love chocolate torte. I had nothing better to do so I made one and, well, here I am.' Jules stopped, feeling her cheeks flushing with embarrassment.

Finn looked dumbfounded. 'You made a chocolate torte for me?'

'Well, not for you, as such, but I thought you might like it – better than me eating the whole thing in some fit of misery.'

Finn opened the tin and inhaled. 'Oh my God, that smells delicious. Everyone will want a slice. Thanks, Jules.' Touched, he leant over and kissed her, thinking that she still looked very pretty, considering what she'd been through. He wondered slightly about his mother inviting Jules out for lunch, but resolved to ask her about it later. 'And I know you might not want to talk about it, but I am truly sorry about my brother.'

Jules flicked her hair out of her face casually. 'Thank you. Yes, I've had better evenings.'

'Me too,' Finn agreed, without thinking. Seeing Jules's surprised expression, he supposed he should explain. 'Oh, nothing serious, but me and Cassia had a bit of a row after the party. She was upset about the confrontation with my mother, and annoyed that I was so late.'

'But you'd bought her those earrings and everything.' Jules was indignant on his behalf. If someone could only treat her half as well as Finn treated Cassia, she thought crossly.

Finn held a hand up. 'And she loved them. I think she just felt a bit let down, that's all.'

Truthfully, Finn wasn't sure how he felt about the row with Cassia. On the one hand, he saw her point and he should have been there to defend her and fight her corner, but on the other hand, he couldn't help thinking she was being a bit dramatic about the wedding arrangements. After all, with both of them so busy, shouldn't they just be grateful that someone was stepping in and sorting it all out for them?

As for the night in the Bentley Hotel, Finn sighed inwardly. What a disaster. The expensive, lavish room had been wasted as neither of them were in the mood for romance. They were up half the night arguing and, feeling insecure about Rocco, Finn knew he'd been unreasonable and accusatory. Cassia had been uptight and standoffish and even though they had eventually slept together, it hadn't left them feeling particularly connected. Cassia had flown back to Italy with Rocco the following morning and Finn had felt bereft but wound up ever since.

He knew he needed to make a concerted effort to get things back on track with Cassia but he was so busy at work, he wasn't sure what he could do about it. He stared down at the chocolate torte. What a lovely gift. Not just his favourite cake, but a homemade one. Feeling disloyal, he wondered when Cassia had ever made a gesture like that before. Granted, she wasn't the world's best cook, despite her in-depth knowledge about food, but still.

'This really was very thoughtful of you. Thank you,' he said to Jules, feeling thoroughly confused about everything. He resolved to call Cassia and make things right between them. He couldn't stand feeling so antagonistic towards her; it was like falling out with a best friend.

'Oh, it was nothing.' Jules backed out of his office, looking uncomfortable. 'I'm so glad you're pleased. I'll leave you to get on.' As some of his colleagues came over to see what smelt so tantalising, Jules left, feeling inexplicably warm and fuzzy inside. Waiting for her bus, she caught sight of a girl in front of her reading *Heat* magazine. Salivating over a photograph of Dom with his top off on the 'Torso of the Week' page, Jules let out an angry squeak. Could she ever get away from his irritatingly handsome face?

'Something wrong?' the girl asked, turning round.

'Oh, it's just him. Everywhere I go, I see his bloody face and I'd much rather forget it.' Jules smiled apologetically. 'Sorry, he's not my favourite person at the moment.'

'You know him?' Missing the fact that Jules was upset, the girl looked excited. 'Wow, does he look like this in person?'

Jules let out a short laugh. 'Better, actually. He's absurdly good-looking.' Naughtily, she pasted a disappointed frown on to her face. 'Tiny penis, though. Really minute,' she added, wiggling her little finger for emphasis. '*Such* a shame.' Deciding to forgo the bus and splash out on a taxi, Jules jauntily headed off to hail one.

All in all it hadn't been a bad day, after all, she decided with a grin.

Cassia couldn't lie; she felt relieved to be back in Italy. It wasn't so much that Sorrento felt like home – she hadn't been there long enough for that – it was more that the Disanti family seemed a damned sight more welcoming than Finn's. Well, Grace, at any rate. Cassia knew Henry was always supportive of her but there was only so much he could do with a bulldozer like Grace. Remembering the way she had laid into her about the wedding venue, Cassia felt a rush of resentment.

Set up on her veranda with her table and laptop in front of her, Cassia pushed Grace out of her head and enjoyed the prime view she had over the Disanti estate and the rest of Sorrento. The southern arm of the Bay of Naples, with its limestone rocks and villages clinging to the cliffs and hills, was spectacular. Ever present was the shadow of Mount Vesuvius, but even the occasional soft feather of smoke couldn't mar the unparalleled beauty of the sweeping draperies of vines and the lush green grass and wild flowers that looped across the cliff face.

She sighed happily, feeling the tension of the past few days seeping out of her. She hoped she'd get to visit Capri before Aurelia's wedding; she couldn't wait to catch a glimpse of the atmospheric streets with their smart little shops and the tiny sandy beaches favoured by the glitterati.

Cassia's fingers paused above her laptop. The Mediterranean was indescribably blue today with dapples of violet dancing across it, its brilliant surface reflecting the rays of the sun lovingly. Cassia could imagine how busy the elegant town must be with tourists lapping up the sunshine amidst the rows of colourful cafés and bars but back here on the estate, it felt tranquil and relaxed. Downstairs the Disanti restaurant was enjoying an exceptionally busy lunch period but the noise from the terrace was muted, as though the chattering and laughter was further away than it really was.

Frowning, Cassia thought about Finn. So used to enjoying an easy, laid-back relationship with him, she found the sour tension between them unbearable. Guiltily, Cassia wondered if she was taking her negativity towards Grace out on Finn, but she genuinely didn't think that was the case. As aggravating as Grace was, it was Finn's lateness and general lack of support about the wedding that had really upset her. She bit her lip, hoping things would get back to normal between them soon. Everything had been fine before she had left for Italy and knowing Grace would crow if she knew, Cassia was beginning to wonder if she had done the right thing by coming. It was so desperately important to her to feel close to her father and to find out about his family, but it seemed to be causing her relationship to splinter.

And what about Rocco? Cassia had no idea if she was imagining things, but they had barely spoken during the helicopter flight home and it almost felt as though Rocco was avoiding her. Cassia had no idea if he had found the altercations at the party distasteful but she couldn't help feeling more disheartened by Rocco's cold-shouldering than she was about the chasm between herself and Finn – something she was sure would be remedied once she was back on English soil again. She and Finn were always all right; they rarely rowed and if they did, things were invariably back on track before the dust had even settled. But Rocco was a different kettle of fish altogether. Cassia didn't know him well enough to read his mind the way she could Finn's, so for all she knew, the spark she had felt between them in England had been well and truly extinguished. Not that it should matter in the slightest.

Cassia cheered herself up by focusing on her column. Having spent a day in the kitchens with Antonio learning about traditional Sicilian desserts, she was soon lost in an erotic description about *cassata*, a cake featuring marzipan, ricotta and candied fruit.

'Pan di spagna, *a basic, sweet sponge cake made with potato flour and lemon zest, is sprinkled with Marsala before being layered with ricotta cheese, candied peel and a chocolate filling similar to cannoli cream. The delicious cake is then covered with a shell of rich marzipan, pastel-coloured icing and more candied fruits.'* Cassia paused, remembering how tasty the cake had been when she'd sampled the one Antonio had made. She knew she had to capture the very essence of it in her words. '*Biting into a slice of* cassata Siciliana *is reminiscent of tasting one's first truffle,*' she typed eventually. '*Incredibly sweet, wickedly enjoyable and the absolute height of decadence.*'

Sending the column off to Gena, Cassia stood up and stretched. Hearing a knock at the door, she was about to open it when Aurelia flounced in. 'I am having a nightmare!' she announced, flinging herself on Cassia's bed. With her dark hair loose around her tanned shoulders and her mouth fixed in a pout, she looked the absolute personification of a spoilt brat.

'What's the problem?' Cassia asked, suppressing a smile. Now that she had seen Jules again, she realised that she and Aurelia really were similar. They both appeared bitchy and selfish, but underneath it all they both had redeeming qualities. Cassia had to admit that she hadn't seen much of Jules's for a while, but she knew for a fact that they were there. Poor Jules, too, Cassia thought. Dom's threesome was now more or less public news and Cassia knew her younger sister would be utterly humiliated by Dom's betrayal, especially since she had been all set to accept what now appeared to be an entirely imaginary proposal. Cassis hoped Jules would meet the right man soon; she had been hurt so many times now, it wasn't surprising she was so cynical and moody.

Aurelia frowned, not sure Cassia was listening to her.

'Dino is still away and I have so much to do with the wedding,' she wailed. With her golden shoulders exposed by her strapless sundress and her long legs sprawled out carelessly, she looked as though she was posing for a sexy photo shoot. Not quite editorial enough for Italian *Vogue* but a pretty vision, nonetheless. 'I have more invitations to send out, dress fittings to attend, jewellery to source. It's too much! My girlfriends are off modelling so they can't help me and I can't do it all myself. Even my bridesmaids are off on holiday. Oh, I wish I hadn't fired my wedding co-ordinator.' She punched a pillow childishly and sat up, suddenly remembering Cassia's wedding.

'Did you speak to your fiancé's mother about your wedding?'

Cassia's jaw tightened. 'Look at this place she has booked for the reception.'

Tossing the brochure on to the bed, she watched as Aurelia's eyes widened in distaste.

'What an ugly building! Are you really going to let her get away with this?'

'What can I do? She's there and I'm here.' Cassia's chin took on a spirited tilt. 'The one thing I'm not letting Grace get involved with is my dress, though. I thought I might buy one here, maybe from that shop in town.' She faltered, thinking she didn't have any real idea what would suit her as a wedding gown, although she did remember one spectacular dress catching her eye before.

Aurelia scrambled off the bed. 'Let's go to the dress shop now. I am due for another fitting.' She still wasn't sure she cared too much for Cassia; they were too different to become very close friends, surely. But in the absence of anyone more suitable, Aurelia was rather enjoying her company and she was definitely pleased she was back from her trip to England.

Cassia pointed to her laptop on the veranda. 'I shouldn't, I'm supposed to be researching traditional food and wine from Sorrento for my column.'

'We can do both,' Aurelia said, waving an airy hand. 'I know a wonderful store we can go to.'

Not entirely sure visiting a 'wonderful store' was what Gena had in mind, Cassia couldn't resist taking Aurelia up on her offer. Soon, they were wandering around the cobbled streets of Sorrento, taking in the sights of the local markets, Aurelia stopping every so often as she was recognised, graciously signing autographs for aspiring models and fans.

'Does it annoy you?' Cassia asked.

Aurelia shook her head ruefully. 'No, I enjoy it, to be honest. When it gets too much, I hide a bit.'

Cassia glanced around at the pretty square they were in. 'It feels so safe here. Is there much crime?'

'Not here,' Aurelia replied. 'But don't wander around Naples at night, if you can help it. Mind you, they have a code there, that no crime should be committed in front of women and children, can you believe that? I have heard a story about a woman who was ushered into a shop by a gunman, just so she wouldn't witness a shooting.'

'What a gentleman.'

Aurelia laughed. 'I know.'

Aside from her little anecdotes about the area, Aurelia proved to be a very useful guide, demonstrating that she had picked up more than her fair share of expert knowledge from her famous, food-focused family, despite her claims of ignorance about all things culinary. Discussing various wines and pointing out a couple of reds that were always served chilled, she moved on to liqueurs.

'This is Nocillo, also known as Nocello,' Aurelia told Cassia, passing her a bottle from a market stall. 'It's made from green unripened walnuts which are picked on the twenty-fourth of June. It's made mostly in Florence and Naples and it's very alcoholic. It's sweet and aromatic and made with lemon zest, cinnamon and cloves, usually.'

Cassia sniffed the bottle; it was certainly potent. It reminded her of a strong-smelling liqueur her father had enjoyed over vanilla ice cream but she couldn't be sure it was the same one. 'Could you drizzle it over gelato?'

Aurelia nodded. 'Definitely, many Italians enjoy it that way.' She picked up another bottle with frosted glass and a colourful label. 'And of course there is Limoncello, produced here in Sorrento as we have the best lemons, and in the region around the Gulf of Naples. It's served chilled as a digestif after a meal.' The market owner handed them small, ceramic cups containing a slug each and they sipped it. 'We'll be drinking this at my wedding, it's a tradition.'

'Wonderful,' Cassia murmured, savouring the taste. 'It has such a strong tang of lemon but it's not remotely bitter.' She purchased a bottle of Limoncello and a small one of the walnut liqueur, as it was probably the one her father had liked so much.

'Have you spoken to Luca yet?' Aurelia asked. 'Our historian friend,' she added. 'Grandmother said she'd spoken to him about your father.'

Cassia shook her head. 'Not yet. I'm dying to meet him, though. It's the main reason I'm here.' She flushed. 'Sorry, I wanted to work with Rocco, of course, but my father . . .'

'Exactly.' Aurelia shrugged off her apology. 'Family is more important than anything else. I can understand you wanting to find out more; I can't imagine life without my father around.'

Following Aurelia into the store she had mentioned and liking her even more after the conversation, Cassia learnt about *gnocchi alla Sorrentina*, a potato dumpling recipe that was covered in sauce, parmigiano and diced mozzarella before being baked in the oven and topped with fresh basil. She also sampled a minute piece of *Delizia al Limone*, which translated as 'Lemon Delight' and comprised a domed cake covered with thick, whipped lemon cream.

'Very calorific,' Aurelia warned, refusing a piece. 'Again, this is a traditional cake to have at a wedding in this area. We're having one of these and another, more elaborate creation. It was created by the famous pastry chef, Carmine Marzuillo, in . . . oh, I can't remember when. There is also a gelato based on the same flavours.' She glanced at her watch. She'd had enough of all the food talk; only Rocco could match Cassia for being such a food bore, she thought, feeling restless. 'We should go to the dress shop now, before it closes.'

'All right,' Cassia said reluctantly, wishing she could just stay and meander around the markets and food shops. Knowing she could easily do that another time, she honoured her agreement with Aurelia to visit the wedding-dress shop. After signing another three autographs, Aurelia slipped on a sun hat and a pair of dark glasses for some peace and no one bothered them after that.

'So, how was the trip to England?'

'Not what I expected.' Cassia told Aurelia a bit more about her run-in with Grace and about her mother's hideous meltdown at the party.

'She really fell into the cake?'

'More or less. It was terrible.'

Aurelia thought for a minute. 'Maybe she misses acting,' she commented, pausing to look in the window of a jewellery store. 'I mean, when something is a passion, it's hard to stop doing it, isn't it?'

Cassia was taken aback. 'Well, yes, I suppose so. But honestly, my mother always seems more focused on being famous than she does on the craft of acting, as it were.'

Aurelia shrugged elegantly. 'Ah, well, fame is a very addictive thing – look at my parents. But anything like acting and modelling, or in fact anything that really gets you hyped up, it's like a drug. When you're not doing it, you crave it. I miss modelling when I'm not doing it, it's my life.' She glanced at Cassia. 'Wouldn't you feel the same if you couldn't do your food writing?'

Cassia raised her eyebrows. 'Yes, yes, of course I would.' Surprised that Aurelia had given her an insight into her mother's psyche, she wondered if she had been too hard on her mother. Maybe she really was missing her job; maybe she felt terribly insecure about it too.

'And how was Rocco?' Aurelia asked, pulling a face. 'He can be so serious at times, especially when he's working. It's easy to forget how much fun he can be when he's not worrying about the business.'

Cassia paused. Rocco had been so different on the trip to London, so approachable and, yes, he had been fun to be around. She realised she had probably been different too. Something about Rocco made her feel more reckless, for some reason. During the helicopter ride out, she had felt a thrilling sense of exhilaration, a dizzy feeling that had made her feel wildly impulsive and out of control. She had conquered her fear of flying, which was incredible, but maybe it was more than that. That said, she felt rather foolish about it all. Rocco hadn't been leaning in to kiss her on the rooftop at all; Cassia was sure of that now. He had simply been concerned about her, as a friend. Whatever she had thought she had seen in his sensual green eyes had all been of her own creation.

'Rocco was . . . he was fine,' Cassia offered lamely, not sure what else to say.

'What's your fiancé like?' Aurelia asked curiously. She took the photo Cassia tugged out of her wallet.

'Umm, Finn's lovely. Very sweet and loyal . . . funny too.'

Thinking Finn was nice-looking in a rather forgettable way, Aurelia handed the photograph back and led the way into the wedding-dress shop. She immediately fell on a gorgeous dress made of Italian lace.

'What do you think? I think this would look sensational on your figure. Trust me, I have a good eye for shape.'

Allowing herself to be talked into trying it on by both Aurelia and the overly keen seamstress shop owner, Cassia found herself standing in front of the mirror wearing the fitted dress. It had cross-over straps at the front which laced across the back. It was a dream, with exquisite lace the colour of clotted cream, a frothy kick-flare at the bottom and minute pearl buttons all the way down the spine, each one outlined by a delicate scallop of lace.

'It looks amazing,' Aurelia said, surprised at how stunning Cassia looked in the gown. It suited her colouring perfectly, bringing out the nut-brown hue of her eyes and her ripples of chocolate-coloured hair, as well as highlighting the curve of her slender neck. The boned corset made the most of Cassia's full hips and bust, whilst drawing attention to her narrow waist.

'Sophia Loren!' the seamstress said excitedly, kissing her fingers. 'Beautiful,' she added in English. 'Almost as if it were made for you.'

Knowing the shop owner probably said the same thing to every woman who tried a wedding dress on and refusing to get too carried away, Cassia couldn't help thinking the dress did something for her. She would have been too self-conscious to even pick up such a dress but now that it was on, she realised it was exactly what her hourglass curves needed.

Glancing at the price tag, Cassia baulked. It might be stunning but it was also outrageously expensive. Finn would have a seizure if he knew she was even contemplating spending such a sum of money on a dress she'd wear once. He wasn't tight, by any means, but he had always been contemptuous of women who wasted money on what he called 'frivolous things'.

'Buy it,' urged Aurelia, kicking her shoes off in readiness for her fitting. Having grown up with more money than most people could even visualise, as well as now supplementing it with her own substantial income, it wouldn't even occur to Aurelia to look at a price tag.

About to point out that she was a food writer, not J.K. Rowling, Cassia heard her phone beeping in her handbag. Taking it out, she saw that she had a message from Jules and, reading it, she turned pale.

'Who's it from?' Aurelia asked, ducking behind a curtain as she slipped out of her dress, accidentally flashing her small, tanned breasts.

'It's from my sister,' Cassia said slowly. 'She says my mother-in-law is planning to ask me to wear her old wedding dress.'

Aurelia poked her dark head out. 'Don't tell me, it's as ugly as that building.'

Distractedly, Cassia nodded. She remembered Grace's wedding dress from all the photographs on the walls at the house. It was some dull, sixties-style number that only the truly thin could get away with. Jules would look fabulous in it but on Cassia it would resemble a shapeless smock.

'So tell her no.' Aurelia offered the comment with the complete naivety of someone not at odds with their in-laws.

Cassia wasn't about to be outmanoeuvred by Grace for a second time.

'I'll . . . I'll take it,' she told the shop owner spontaneously. 'I'll take the dress. At least, I'll put a deposit down on it.'

The seamstress clapped her hands with delight and Aurelia was clearly impressed. Cassia waited for Aurelia to try her dress on, feeling oddly elated. It was a small thing, but she felt back in control again. Even if Grace – and Finn, for that matter – thought her wedding dress was over the top and expensive, she had chosen it and that was all that mattered. She just hoped the rest of the wedding arrangements were as easy to sort out, but gloomily she thought they probably wouldn't be.

Feeling thoroughly dejected, Diana checked into the exclusive spa she'd booked. It was housed in a beautiful former stately home with plush furnishings and discreet service, but best of all it was set in leafy grounds in the middle of nowhere. After her mortifying behaviour at the engagement party, Diana wanted nothing more than to fade into the background and not be recognised – at least for a few days.

After selecting a number of exotic-sounding treatments aimed at rejuvenating her looks and, more importantly, pampering her soul, Diana allowed herself to be shown to her room. Slipping into a luxurious white robe with a maroon monogram on the breast pocket, she let out a shaky sigh. The break at the spa was just what she needed – a chance to lick her wounds in private and claw back some dignity. She barely remembered all the sordid details but she recalled ending her relationship with Angelo in front of all and sundry and rambling on about Marco to Cassia, a terrible blunder. And then, of course, there was the dreadful incident with Grace's cake . . .

I feel old, Diana thought, heading down to the indoor pool with her head down. Without Angelo to pander to her ego and tell her how vibrant and gorgeous she was, Diana felt like a neglected orchid, wilting sadly without the nourishment she needed to flourish. She hadn't heard a single word from Angelo, but she couldn't blame him; why on earth would he want to come back after the way she'd treated him?

Diana settled herself on a lounger next to the vast oblong swimming pool and ordered an iced tea. Lying back, she let out a long, shuddering sigh. It was time to stop thinking about Marco and, without question, it was about time she stopped feeling so damned sorry for herself.

'Diana? Diana, is that you?'

Her eyes snapping open, Diana's heart sank as she recognised an old actress friend who'd known herself and Marco back in their heyday. Dripping wet from the water and wearing a violet, boned one-piece that made the most of her long legs, Evelyn Winters was showing her age more than Diana but she was glamorous in her own way.

'How lovely to see you again,' Diana said weakly, wondering how she was going to avoid her old friend for the next few days. Evelyn was sweet but she was bound to talk about the 'good old days' and Diana really couldn't bear dwelling on memories of Marco at the moment.

'Oh, darling, what a wonderful coincidence!' Evelyn wrapped herself in a monogrammed towel and sat down on the lounger next to Diana. 'I was only talking about you the other day to a friend and saying how much I missed you and here you are.' Her eyes became sober. 'So sorry to hear about Marco, darling. You must miss him horribly.'

Diana nodded, not trusting herself to speak. Why on earth did it still hurt so much?

Evelyn squeezed Diana's hand. 'Poor you. But you have so many fantastic memories. I mean, weren't you the most dazzling couple? The intellectual and the actress . . . so romantic.' She smiled fondly. 'Do you remember the time when . . .'

Nearly two hours later, Diana realised she'd been reminiscing so enthusiastically with Evelyn, she'd missed a chocolate and shea butter body polish and a paraffin wax pedicure. However, instead of feeling suicidal talking about her past, Diana felt invigorated. It was the first time in ages she'd allowed herself to feel really happy about Marco and to remember all the good times.

'Any acting projects on the go, Di?' Evelyn asked, preparing for another dip. 'You're such an incredible actress, far better than me. It would be a shame if you didn't carry on.' She stabbed her finger in the air. 'Do you know what you need? A really *meaty* part, a . . . what do they call it? A character part, something that really showcases your talent. I mean, everyone knows you're still fabulous-looking, so perhaps it's time you reminded them that you can actually act your socks off too.'

As Evelyn dived cleanly into the water, Diana lay back thoughtfully. Was her old friend right? Maybe she'd been too busy chasing parts that would stroke her ego and make her feel glamorous again, when in reality she needed something to challenge her emotionally and remind everyone why she had been such a good actress.

Remembering the gritty part of Clarissa, the wronged older woman Fliss had tried to tempt her with, Diana felt a rush of adrenalin. And for the first time in years, it had nothing to do with a man.

Holed up in his office, Rocco was drowning under a mountain of paperwork. The few days spent in England had left him with a huge backlog and he felt exasperated that everything seemed to grind to a halt in his absence. Couldn't anyone step in and take up some of the slack? he griped to himself. He was certain his grandmother had been running the restaurant proficiently; it was more his siblings he felt disappointed by. Obviously Aurelia was busy with her modelling and her wedding, but wasn't there anything she could do to ease his burden? And what about Raffaelo? Rocco frowned. His brother might be a gregarious host, but he was useless when it came to doing his actual job. The restaurant looked incredible, as always, but there were details . . . tiny details that no one else would notice, but nonetheless, Rocco preferred them to be dealt with as soon as they occurred.

He glanced out of the window as something caught his eye. He looked more closely, not sure what he had registered in his peripheral vision. No, there it was again, a shadowy figure was lurking by the back of the restaurant wearing loose, casual clothes and a dark fedora pulled down over his eyes. Rocco stared at him. What was he doing? Who was he? There was something about the man's body language that suggested he was up to no good but Rocco decided he was probably being paranoid.

Was it Raffaelo? Rocco got up to take a closer look. The man was dressed nothing like his brother, but still, the height and the broad shoulders . . . Rocco shook himself. What on earth would Raffaelo be doing, lurking at the back of the restaurant? He had no need to slink about in the darkness; he lived here.

'Ah, there you are,' Sofia said, poking her head round the door. She did a double-take at the pile of paperwork teetering on Rocco's desk. 'Oh, I'm so sorry I didn't get time to look at any of that. One of the waitresses left, she was six months' pregnant and hiding it very well, and that apprentice girl of Antonio's burnt her hand on the grill so she was out of action all weekend.'

Swinging his head back to the window, Rocco realised the shadowy figure had gone. He hadn't imagined seeing the man, he was sure of that. And it couldn't be Raffaelo because Rocco remembered him excusing himself from the restaurant that morning because he had some business to attend to in town.

Welcoming the sight of his grandmother's twinkling eyes

and dimpled cheeks, Rocco beckoned Sofia in with a smile. 'Don't worry, it's not your problem,' he said, gesturing to the paperwork. He would be up all night dealing with it but he wasn't prone to voicing his irritation out loud.

'Listen, have you seen Raffaelo? He said he would be in town this morning but I need him to sort out some of the problems in the restaurant later on. God only knows how so many things can have gone wrong; I've only been away a few days.' He rubbed his eyes tiredly, baffled by the goings-on. He could have sworn the window at the back of the restaurant had been intact before he left on Friday, and that none of the light bulbs needed replacing, yet all of a sudden, several things seemed to need attention. If he didn't know better, he would have begun to think someone had it in for them, but he refused to think the issues in the restaurant were anything other than bad timing and laziness on Raffaelo's part.

Sofia sat down and shook her head. 'I haven't seen him today but he was in very good spirits yesterday. While I remember, Rocco, someone came to see you.' She drew a card out of her pocket and handed it over. 'He said something about doing some business with you.'

Rocco glanced briefly at the card. 'Allesandro Raldini,' he read. 'Never heard of him. A wine merchant . . . what was he like?' He trusted her judgement on such things.

Sofia's cheeks went a little pink. 'Late fifties, tall, quite charming. Well-dressed, I suppose.'

'I meant, did he seem professional, legitimate? I'm not too bothered about his appearance.' Rocco looked amused as he tossed the business card on to his pile of paperwork, not sure when he'd last seen his grandmother blush. 'I'll call him if I have time.'

Sofia nodded and stood up. 'Stefania's been calling non-stop,' she informed him. 'I don't think it's anything urgent; I think she just wanted to know where you were.'

Rocco smacked his hand against his head. Had he really forgotten to call his girlfriend and tell her he was heading off to England for a few days? Rocco couldn't believe he'd been so forgetful. An image of Cassia in the dark red dress, her hair blowing in the breeze on the roof terrace slid into his mind. He recalled the edges of her mouth lifting into a smile as she laughed at something he had said. Then he frowned. Gena's husband, Gianfranco, had been at pains to tell Rocco that Cassia's invite hadn't just been about getting some photographs taken of them together but Rocco wasn't so sure. He was also irked that it bothered him either way. As a result, he had barely exchanged a single word with her on the helicopter flight home, even though he hadn't been able to resist checking on her constantly to make sure she wasn't as terrified as she had been on the way out. As soon as they had arrived back at the Disanti estate, Rocco had locked himself in his office to focus on work and, yes, he could admit it, to put Cassia out of his head. Whatever he had felt for her had been fleeting . . . ridiculous . . . and now he was back in control.

'What was Cassia's fiancé like?' Sofia asked, pausing at the door.

'Finn?' Rocco's eyes slid away from hers. 'Nice enough. Dependable, trustworthy, I should imagine.'

Sofia raised her eyebrows. 'Really? That's strange. I see Cassia with someone exciting, someone a little wild and unpredictable.' Giving him a pertinent stare, Sofia withdrew.

Rocco shook his head crossly and drew his pile of paperwork towards him. Thinking about Cassia was pointless and he had far too much to do.

It was only thirty minutes later, when Antonio came in asking him to check the food order, that Rocco realised he hadn't touched a single piece of work.

Chapter Eleven

Finn drummed his fingers on his desk as he waited for some legal files to be delivered. He was working long hours again but with Cassia absent, it didn't matter so much.

He was still trying to think of a way to make things up to Cassia after their recent disastrous weekend, but so far, he had drawn a blank. He supposed he should fly over to Sorrento, something he knew would please her greatly. She had always wanted him to see her father's birthplace and Finn knew he should probably have made the effort to do this in the past. He thought about Rocco Disanti, knowing he had no reason to dislike him, but all the same, the Italian made him feel uneasy. Rocco was good-looking, suave and apparently also generous; his mother hadn't stopped talking about his impromptu invite to his sister Aurelia's flashy Capri wedding.

Finn felt a renewed interest in visiting Sorrento. But as he scrolled through some flight details, he couldn't stop thinking about a big case he had coming up, a case he knew would be on his boss's radar when it came to looking at appraisals. Checking his phone absent-mindedly when a message arrived, he was surprised to see that it was a jokey text from Jules. Laughing out loud at it, he sent a quick line back to say how funny it was. Since she had dropped into the office with the chocolate torte, they had exchanged the odd message here and there, nothing serious, just jokes or a quick hello. Finn hadn't mentioned it to Cassia because she and Jules had such a strained relationship, it would probably hurt Cassia's feelings.

Looking up, he saw his mother approaching his office and his heart sank. The only reason she could possibly be here would be to discuss wedding details and Finn didn't think he had the energy. Grace barged into his office wielding a bulging file.

'No, don't get up,' she told him bossily. 'I'm just here to drop off an updated guest list because I've added a couple of names here and there.'

Finn skim-read the list, spotting at least another twenty-five new names, most of them double-barrelled and unrecognisable.

'Mother, who *are* all these people? I don't even know them and I'm pretty certain they're not Cassia's relatives. Who on earth is Hortensia Pensonby-Jones when she's at home?'

Grace looked vague. 'She's someone I recently met through my charity and the others are distant-ish relatives of ours I didn't want to offend. Did you hear about Dom, by the way?' She changed the subject expertly. 'He did very well at the French Open, almost made the quarter-final, which is thrilling, but knowing him, he'll do something to mess things up.'

Finn noted the criticism, wishing his mother could praise Dom without adding something negative immediately afterwards. 'I assume that means his recent bad behaviour hasn't put him off his stroke, as it were?'

Grace missed the joke. 'He's a disgrace, Finn. Treating poor Jules that way. Honestly, how that boy has turned out this way is beyond me.'

Finn stared at his mother. Was it possible she genuinely didn't realise how her gross neglect of Dom had left him wildly out of control and headed for disaster in every aspect of his life? Finn had always thought being left to his own devices suited Dom down to the ground, but having witnessed his recent freefall, he was beginning to realise how his mother's disregard had damaged Dom irreparably. It was on the tip of his tongue to say something but he knew his mother would either curtly dismiss the comment or fake tears to make him regret daring to say such a thing. Looking up, he saw a clerk arriving with several boxes of files for his latest case. About to tell his mother she would have to leave shortly, she cut him off.

'I must go, Finn. I've managed to secure a cancellation with a firm who said they can provide us with a fleet of bullet-grey Bentleys for the big day.'

Bentleys? Finn felt utterly panic-stricken. Cassia had explicitly requested one cream vintage MG, so what on earth was his mother doing ordering fleets of Bentleys? Finn eyed her suspiciously. The wedding venue was one thing, but she had to know she was in the wrong here, surely. He told himself that perhaps Bentleys were the only cars available, but he knew that was most likely rubbish.

Was Cassia right? Did his mother detest her, after all? She certainly seemed to be going out of her way to annoy her when it came to the wedding. Finn was so caught up in his thoughts, he forgot to protest and demand that the Bentleys were cancelled.

'Speak soon,' Grace trilled as she left Finn's office. 'And don't forget Sunday lunch!'

Sunday lunch? Finn didn't even recall being invited. He picked up the first box of files and with a groan started to unload it. As he became immersed in another taxing case, all thoughts of a trip to Sorrento were totally forgotten.

Rocco threw himself into a seat at one of the larger tables in the restaurant. He was fuming that his grandmother had called a meeting to discuss them all pulling together as a family, but he guessed she had a point. There had been all manner of calamities recently – broken windows, messed-up bookings, toilets flooding. The list was endless.

Rocco was baffled. Could it really all just be down to bad luck? Or was someone trying to sabotage them? Remembering the shadowy figure he had seen a couple of days ago, Rocco wondered if it was significant, but he impatiently told himself to stop being stupid. He'd be banging on about rival families and curses like his grandmother if he didn't get a grip.

He glanced at his watch, not sure he could spare the time for a meeting. He was expecting a delivery of rare truffles any minute, Stefania had decided to visit unexpectedly and he was due to hold a conference call with his Vegas team, one he knew with a sinking heart would probably confirm a delay to the Vegas opening. Looking up, Rocco saw Cassia slipping into one of the chairs at the far end of the table.

'I hope you don't mind me being here,' she said, seeing his face darken. 'Sofia asked me to come and I thought it might be rude to say no. I realise I'm not part of the family or anything.'

'It's fine,' he snapped curtly. 'I just wish she'd get on with it. She seems to have invited anyone she pleases, so the least she could do is be on time.'

Cassia bristled. It was the first time she and Rocco had come face to face since they had returned to Sorrento four days ago and she could see that the sensitive, funny guy she had glimpsed in England had once more been replaced by the truculent businessman she had been dealing with before the trip.

Seeing her stiffen at his sharp tone, Rocco regretted being so touchy. It wasn't Cassia's fault she'd been invited to the meeting. Nor was it appropriate to take out his bad mood regarding his grandmother and Stefania on her, just because she was the only person in the room. He stared at her, thinking she looked different somehow. She was dressed in one of her professional beige outfits, with her dark hair piled up on top of her head. She looked like the woman who had first arrived here all those weeks ago, rather than the one he had spent the weekend with, and Rocco couldn't help feeling disappointed.

The excitable, passionate side of her personality was almost undetectable now.

Sofia bustled in clutching a list and Raffaelo and Aurelia trailed in behind her. Aurelia, wearing a pristine white kimono over a purple bikini which made her golden limbs look endless, reclined elegantly in the chair next to Cassia, her dark curls hanging loosely down her back. Raffaelo, dressed as incongruously as ever, gave them all a genial smile as he sat opposite Rocco. About to greet Cassia, he was cut short by an exasperated Rocco.

'Grandmother, what is this all in aid of?'

Sofia fixed her eyes on him patiently. 'I wanted us all to get together to discuss some of the issues the restaurant has been facing,' she said. 'And to see what we could do about running things more effectively.'

Aurelia pulled a face. 'What does this have to do with me?' she said. 'I'm not even involved in Disanti's.'

'That's exactly my point.' Sofia looked aggravated. 'You've never been involved, Aurelia, but perhaps you should be.'

Aurelia scowled. 'Yes, Grandmother, perhaps I should tell Italian *Vogue* to put my editorial shoot on hold so I can take coffee orders. Or maybe you think I should abandon my wedding, just so I can mop the toilet floors?'

Seeing that Rocco was about to explode, Sofia intervened. 'No, Aurelia. I just mean that you could support your brothers as much as possible. Don't bother them with details about your wedding – I am here for that.' She turned to Raffaelo. 'But you, Raffaelo, you really do need to pull your weight. The restaurant has suffered a run of bad luck over the past few weeks. You must get on top of everything.'

Raffaelo had the grace to look embarrassed. 'Apologies, I've been a little . . . tied up recently.' He didn't elaborate but he flashed his laid-back smile again. 'Don't worry, I'll get it all sorted out.'

Rocco looked visibly relieved. 'Thank you, Raff. That's a weight off my mind.'

Sofia, however, was annoyed. She couldn't fathom what Raffaelo was up to, but he had been seriously lax of late and Aurelia was becoming increasingly demanding as her wedding approached. Sofia linked her fingers together. She had arranged this meeting in an attempt to bring the family closer together, even going as far as inviting Flavia and Gino to join them and show Rocco he had their support, but predictably, they had both claimed to be too busy on their European book-signing tour to return to Sorrento any time soon. Sofia seethed but she moved on with her agenda. 'I'm planning a party. It's something I've been thinking about for a while and it will involve inviting local businesses to join us to see if we can work together.' She glanced at Rocco. 'I thought I might invite that wine merchant we talked about. Allesandro Raldini, do you remember?'

Rocco frowned. 'Vaguely. Grandmother, is it the right time for a party? There would be so much to do.'

Sofia stood up. 'I'll take care of everything,' she assured him. 'All you need to do is turn up and drink fine Chianti.' She smiled and patted his cheek. 'Trust me, Rocco. It's all in hand.' She glanced at Raffaelo and Aurelia with less affection. 'And anything you can do to assist your brother would be much appreciated.'

'Er . . . I can help out too,' Cassia said, hoping she wasn't speaking out of turn. 'I don't know what with, exactly, but apart from researching and writing my column, I'm available.'

About to refuse, Rocco realised it might help to have another pair of hands. 'Thank you and I'm sorry if I was curt earlier. I'll have a think about what you can do.'

'Taking coffee orders . . . mopping toilet floors.' Throwing Aurelia a smile, Cassia shrugged. 'There must be something.'

Out of the blue, Rocco grinned at her. Just as swiftly the grin disappeared as his thoughts returned to work and he left.

'At least he smiled at you,' Aurelia commented gloomily.

Cassia laughed. 'Oh, but it was only a brief one.'

'Well, that's better than nothing.' Aurelia looked put out. 'Rocco always used to be supportive of my modelling but now he doesn't seem to care.'

'I'm sure he's very proud of you.' Remembering the indulgent way Rocco had talked about her in the helicopter, Cassia was sure she was speaking the truth. She didn't know why she felt duty-bound to defend him, however. 'He's just . . . I think he's really stressed at the moment, that's all. Things haven't been running very smoothly around here, have they?'

Aurelia looked bored. She couldn't be less interested in the restaurant. Cassia couldn't help thinking Aurelia was expecting too much from her brother. He was ridiculously busy and even though Aurelia was used to being cosseted by her family, she had to cut Rocco some slack, surely?

'You should invest in some new bikinis,' Aurelia said out of the blue.

'Some what?' Cassia was wrong-footed. Hadn't they just been talking about Rocco?

Aurelia nodded. 'Yes. Yours are boring. You should make the most of yourself and stop being so conservative.' She handed Cassia a card. 'This friend of mine does gorgeous ones and she has a concession in one of the best stores in Sorrento.' She named a chi-chi shop Cassia had seen in an alley full of expensive boutiques. 'She'll give you a huge discount if you mention me – my ad campaign for her bikinis made her a millionaire.' She stated this matter-of-factly.

'Right.' Cassia took the card. Maybe she should re-vamp her wardrobe while she was here.

'See if you can get Rocco cooking again,' Aurelia said over her shoulder as she made for the swimming pool. 'Maybe you can succeed where everyone else has failed.'

Cassia wasn't sure anything could drag Rocco away from his paperwork, least of all her. She glanced at her phone, frustrated to see that she hadn't heard from Finn. She left him a message on his voicemail, worried that they couldn't seem to reconnect. Thinking about the Disanti family meeting, however fruitless, made her feel sentimental about her own family. She thought about calling Jules, then called her mother instead. Within seconds, she was swept up in a full-on chat about the pros and cons of stripping on stage and Cassia immediately brightened.

Delighted she'd been included in the Sunderlands' Sunday lunch plans in spite of her messy break-up with Dom, Jules took time with her appearance. Slipping into a peach-coloured shift dress that was modest but required her to go bra-less due to a low back, Jules added a pair of wedge-heeled sandals. Arriving at the house in Kent, she was surprised to find Henry wearing an apron and a chef's hat as he busied himself with something in the garden. Grace, chopping celery and spring onions in the kitchen, was sporting casual white trousers and a peach-coloured shirt with the collar turned up. Jules wasn't sure what she thought about them being so matchy-matchy, but she guessed Grace would at the very least approve of her outfit.

'It's perfect barbecue weather,' Grace explained, her hands full of spring onions. 'You must excuse Henry; he'll think he's Rocco Disanti for the next few hours.'

Jules smiled. 'All men do when they're in charge of a barbecue, don't they? Rocco Disanti . . . I didn't get to meet him at the party, but then . . . I was dealing with other things.'

'Of course you were,' Grace soothed. 'Well, I have to say that you missed out, not meeting Rocco. He was absolutely charming. Such a gentleman and handsome too.'

Lucky Cassia, Jules thought to herself enviously. 'Now, what can I do to help? I'm sure I'm not in your league, but I can cook a bit, you know.'

Grace handed her a small chopping board and a knife. 'How helpful you are, Jules. I don't think Cassia has ever helped with one of our Sunday barbecues before.' She laughed, but there was an edge to it. 'Could you chop some garlic, do you think?'

Jules gingerly picked up the knife. Chopping garlic wasn't exactly what she had in mind; it would make her fingers stink, but it was easy, at least. She peeled the cloves and holding the knife expertly, she quickly chopped up the garlic, scraping it into a neat pile at the side of the board.

Grace looked impressed. 'You certainly know your way around food,' she commented, rather patronisingly. 'I had no idea you were that competent.'

Jules shrugged. 'Cassia inherited our father's way with words and I managed to pick up his cooking abilities. There's nothing more I like doing than pottering around in the kitchen and baking.'

'That's marvellous,' Grace trilled. 'Who inherited your mother's acting skills, I wonder?' Her tone suggested that Diana's talent was thin on the ground.

Jules looked sour. 'God knows. Besides, being in a few TV shows hardly makes her worthy of an Oscar, does it?'

'Well, quite.' Grace looked up as Finn arrived. 'You look exhausted, darling. And that shirt . . . no one is looking after you, are they?'

Finn rolled his eyes and handed over a bottle of Rioja. 'If you're making a dig at Cassia, she doesn't iron my shirts even when she's here, Mother, nor would I want her to.' He peered tiredly out of the window. 'Is Father doing a barbecue? Lordy. That means we'll have to pretend he's turned into a professional chef for the afternoon.'

Grace caught sight of Henry listening to the cricket on the radio outside. 'Let's hope he's lit the coals otherwise we won't be eating for hours.' She went off to chastise him.

Jules turned to Finn and held up her garlicky fingers. 'I would come over and greet you properly, but I'm afraid I'm rather fragrant at the moment.'

Finn ran a hand through his hair, making it stick up even more. 'How are you, Jules? I do hope you're feeling better now. That torte was spectacular, by the way. My colleagues have requested another when you have time.'

'How sweet of them. I'm sure that can be arranged. And I'm feeling much better, thank you,' she added. 'You've all been so kind to me.'

'The least we could do.' Finn noticed that she was wearing a rather nice little dress that showed off an expanse of back as well as her toned calves. 'Didn't you come with Louisa?'

Jules shook her head as she washed her hands with Grace's Crabtree & Evelyn gardener's handwash. 'She's coming soon, I think, but she's been out with that new boyfriend of hers.'

'Oh yes, she mentioned him a while ago. She seems happy, for once.' Finn pinched the skin between his eyebrows to alleviate a bad headache. 'God, I've been so ridiculously busy, I haven't even charged my phone up recently. I have this nasty feeling I accidentally deleted a ton of messages from Cassia too. My mother said some of hers about the wedding went astray, but I wasn't sure if she was making it up to get away with something.' He smiled to soften his words. 'Or maybe my phone's about to give up the ghost. I'm due a new one soon, but I might have to change my number if I get the one I want.'

Jules decided Grace was right; Finn looked shattered. 'Can I fix you a drink or something?'

'I'll open this if you fancy a glass.' Finn held up the Rioja. He poured out two glasses, grabbing a third as Louisa arrived. He wandered into the sitting room carrying the wine bottle and they followed him in. Not wearing a tracksuit for once, Louisa was in jeans and a floaty top. She looked relaxed.

'How are things?' Finn asked her. 'Still with this new boy-friend?'

She nodded. 'I was going to tell Mother about him the other day, but she can't seem to stop ranting about Dom or . . .' She stopped. She couldn't exactly tell Finn that the other thing her mother had been complaining about had been Cassia.

Finn sipped his wine. 'Yes, she is a bit of a broken record at the moment.'

Jules picked up a photograph of Dom and pursed her lips. Around ten years of age wearing tennis whites and a cocky grin, he looked supremely confident even then. 'God, he looks like butter wouldn't melt, doesn't he? No indication that he'd grow up with a tendency towards S and M and threesomes, but still.'

'He's an idiot,' Louisa told her, giving her arm a supportive squeeze.

'Absolutely,' Finn said, nodding. 'Don't take any of this personally, Jules. Dom has had his finger hovering over the self-destruct button since . . . well, since he was a child, really. He can't help it, I don't think. And it's not all his fault either.'

Louisa swigged her wine moodily. 'I'm hearing that.'

'Lamb, please, ladies!' Henry roared from the garden.

Finn led them outside, suppressing a laugh as his father was told off for waving a huge pair of tongs in the air.

Henry repositioned his chef's hat. 'Sorry, Gracie. I need to get the meat on the go.' He shot Jules a curious look as she wandered out into the garden with Louisa. He had no idea why she was dressed like a nun when she usually flashed her knickers willy-nilly, but he supposed she looked rather nice with her blond hair all fluffy around her tanned shoulder blades.

'That lamb is going to be lovely,' Jules called to Henry. 'It smells divine.'

'It is rather,' Henry called back. 'Garlic, some seasoning and cooked nice and pink.'

Jules smiled. 'I do mine Moroccan-style,' she said to Finn. 'It's to-die-for.'

'I love Moroccan lamb,' Finn said, looking wistful.

About to say she could cook it for him, Jules reined herself in. It would be an inappropriate thing to suggest, especially with Cassia away.

Studying Jules and wondering why he had never really noticed how pretty she was before, an idea occurred to Finn. If he couldn't make it out to Sorrento because of the mess he was in with his company, perhaps Jules could. Even though he knew Jules and Cassia weren't exactly bosom buddies, surely Cassia would welcome a familiar face? Maybe it would help her relationship with Jules, Finn thought hopefully, deciding his plan was flawless.

'Hear me out with this,' he said, catching Jules's eye. 'But how do you feel about an all-expenses-paid trip to Sorrento?'

'Me? Go to Sorrento?' Jules looked taken aback. 'Er, why would I want to do that, Finn?'

Finn waved a hand. 'Look, I'll be honest with you. I should go myself, especially bearing in mind the way things are between us right now, but I simply can't spare the time off work. Not right now. So I thought if you went, you could smooth the waters with Cassia a bit for me . . . maybe even mend some bridges of your own.'

Jules winced. Finn, like Cassia, had no idea why there was a chasm between them, but she wasn't about to open up about it. It was private and she had never discussed it, not even with Louisa.

Finn looked at Jules pleadingly. 'I'll come over as soon as I can, but in the meantime, you'd be doing me a big favour. You can't say no to a desperate man, surely?'

Jules didn't know what to say. Was it really as straightforward as that or was there another reason for Finn wanting her to head over to Sorrento? 'You're not worried about Rocco, are you?' she asked curiously, trying to figure out what was behind Finn's offer. 'I mean, he's a handsome guy, but really, Cassia isn't the sort to cheat.' Her sister was many things – most of them dull – but Jules didn't think she'd do the dirty on Finn.

Deciding Jules had come up with the perfect excuse, Finn seized upon it.

'Jules, you've absolutely hit the nail on the head. I trust Cassia with my life, but Rocco? I don't even know him, and he's a handsome devil. It would make me feel so much better if I knew you were there looking out for your sister. And I do genuinely have a lot on at work right now,' he added, not feeling entirely comfortable with the lie about Rocco.

'I think you should go,' Louisa said. She couldn't help thinking Finn's offer had come at just the right time for Jules. With no job on the horizon and Dom's disgrace very much in the news still, it was the perfect get-out clause. 'It's a free holiday for you and maybe Finn's right, maybe spending a bit of quality time with Cassia would be a good thing.'

Jules mulled it over. She didn't especially relish the thought of spending time with Cassia, but she supposed she could do her own thing. Remembering that Rocco's sister, the very glamorous Aurelia Disanti, would be milling around planning her Capri wedding was a plus, though, and Sorrento was supposed to be beautiful. Jules had no attachment to it the way Cassia did – anything that reminded so acutely of her father was to be avoided, not embraced – but she could get past that. 'I'd love to,' she said finally, giving Finn a warm smile. 'Thank you so much, Finn.'

Grace frowned, not sure how she felt about the news. She had rather enjoyed the thought of having Jules around to talk about weddings and moan about Cassia, but she supposed it would be a nice break for Jules after everything that had happened with Dom.

Finn was feeling mightily relieved. He hoped Cassia would

see the gesture for what it was, an attempt to make amends (albeit in a rather strange way), and it would certainly take the heat off him needing to jet off to Sorrento for a while. He sat back and drank some wine, feeling the tensions of the week slipping away from him. His mother and father were gently bickering over whether or not the lamb was cooked yet and Louisa was chatting on her mobile, presumably to her boyfriend because she was beaming from ear to ear. Finn turned his attention to Jules, who was ducking in and out of the kitchen bringing salad and potatoes to the table. As she leant across to put a bowl of homemade coleslaw in front of him, her dress gaped and Finn received a rather alluring view of Jules's bra-less breast. It was small but perky with a rose-pink nipple and no visible tan lines.

Finn blushed, confused to find himself rather turned on by the accidental flashing. He had never viewed Jules sexually before now, she had always been Cassia's younger, rather shallow sister, but all of a sudden, he was confronted with an image of her that he found disturbing.

Unaware that she had just thrown Finn into a state of disarray, Jules took a deep breath in the kitchen. The trip to Sorrento was just what she needed. She could get away from England, away from Dom and all the bad memories, and she could think about how to get her life back on track at the same time.

Literally, the only fly in the ointment was being away from Finn, Jules thought. Well, Finn's family, she corrected herself with a frown. She felt as though she fitted in around here, as if she didn't have to try too hard to be something she wasn't.

Perturbed, Jules rejoined the Sunderland family and chatted brightly about Sorrento.

Thinking about the wording for a piece she was writing for Gena about Italian wedding traditions, Cassia watched Rocco striding up and down outside Disanti's on his mobile phone, looking as if he could spontaneously combust. Clearly, something was bothering him, but Cassia was loath to interrupt him when he was in such a foul mood. The trouble was, according to Gena, the readers of her online column for *Scrumptious* magazine were craving more of an insight into 'Rocco Disanti, the chef'. As much as readers were enjoying tales of 'Rocco, the glamorous and successful businessman', they wanted to hear more about him working his magic in the kitchen, about him creating mouth-wateringly delicious new recipes. But that was the problem; Rocco was so busy and so successful when it came to running the Disanti empire, that cooking – and creating exciting new dishes – was the very thing he rarely had time to do.

Inhaling the heady aroma emanating from the tangle of purple and lavender wisteria hanging over her balcony, Cassia wondered if she was capable of luring Rocco back into his beloved kitchen. Thinking she was most likely taking her life in her hands by even daring to think she could do such a thing, she shut her laptop and headed back into her room. Rocco looked badly in need of a break but she was fairly certain he wouldn't take one, not unless he could be convinced it was business-related.

As Sofia scurried around getting everything ready for the party which was due to take place the following weekend and Aurelia joyfully greeted a very tanned Dino with a piercing shriek, Cassia strolled outside. Rocco was still on the phone with his back to her, his black linen shirt crumpled and his tanned neck exposed. With one hand shoved in the pocket of his well-cut, beige trousers, he looked elegantly furious. Waiting patiently until he had finished his call, Cassia faltered. The worst he could do was say no, right?

'I have this idea . . . I know you're busy but I wondered if you could show me how to make pasta.'

Rocco stared at her as if she was mental. 'Make pasta? Now?' He shook his head in bewilderment. 'Do you know how busy I am? I've just been on the phone to the company who deliver our fresh vegetables. Apparently someone called and cancelled the order.' His eyes turned frosty, as they always did when he was angry. 'Whoever did that better have a good explanation because as far as I'm concerned, they're dead after a mistake like that.'

Cassia bit her lip. An awful lot of things were going wrong in the restaurant and she couldn't help thinking someone was deliberately sabotaging them. Disanti's Sorrento had an incredible reputation for providing five-star service and cuisine but if news of some of the recent cock-ups started to get out, Cassia knew Rocco would be battling to maintain his family's superb reputation. A shiver went down Cassia's spine as she remembered Sofia talking about the rival family and the curse they had put on the Disantis. Surely it couldn't be anything to do with that.

Rocco felt aggravated but he had to admit that the idea of making pasta was oddly appealing. When had he last done it? He used to do it on a daily basis when Nico, his grandfather, was still alive, and before Disanti's London had opened two years ago, he had still been diving into the kitchen whenever he had the chance, just to enjoy the therapeutic process.

'I could show you how to make crab ravioli,' Rocco offered, surprising himself. He wasn't sure what on earth had possessed him to make such an offer, but he couldn't deny that spending a bit of down time wouldn't be a bad thing.

Cassia's face lit up. 'Oh, would you? Crab ravioli is my favourite dish of yours, I adore it. All that scrumptious, succulent crab meat with the unctuous tomato sauce, it's just . . .' Stopping, she smiled. 'You get it; I adore your crab ravioli. And . . . and since it's going to be on the Vegas menu, it would be wonderful publicity for you.'

Rocco's face darkened slightly. 'Of course. We wouldn't want to forget that, would we?' He stood aside to let her past. 'After you.'

Cassia regretted her comment. She had intended to make herself sound more professional after all the gushing, but she seemed to have offended him. Rocco followed her into the kitchen, his eyes travelling over her curvaceous figure. She was wearing a white sundress that exposed her shoulders and neck, and a crimson bikini underneath it, the ties of the halter neck trailing down her back. Briefly distracted and aware that his grandmother, who had just emerged from the kitchen with a coffee, was watching him in some amusement, Rocco pulled himself together and glanced at his watch.

'Lunch service is over so we have an hour before they start prepping for the evening. That's ample time.' He threw on a crisp, white chef's jacket, reaching for another one.

Cassia put on the proffered coat. 'I must warn you that I'm hopeless in the kitchen,' she said, feeling it best to mention it. 'My sister is the expert and I'm such a novice, it's untrue.'

Rocco gave her a brief smile. 'I'm sure you're not. Now, you must only use the freshest eggs,' he stated authoritatively. 'If you don't, you are not doing the pasta justice. But first, we must prepare the crab.' With infinite care, he dissected a crab he told her had been caught that morning. Easing the flesh out and mixing it with other ingredients, talking softly as he did so, Cassia was utterly mesmerised. As he disappeared to find something from the store cupboard, an impressed Antonio joined Cassia.

'How did you convince him to do this?' Antonio whispered in delight. 'It makes him so happy to cook.'

Cassia really had no idea how she'd managed to do it; no one had been more astonished than her when Rocco had made his offer. 'I haven't a clue. But I think it will do him good.'

Antonio nodded. 'It will, it will. It's great . . . you've done a wonderful thing.' Ducking out of sight, Antonio carried on tidying up and getting things ready for the squid appetiser on the menu later, but he kept one eye on Rocco as he returned with some eggs.

'By the way, I have some bad news about the Vegas opening.' Rocco felt duty-bound to tell Cassia about the recent update he'd had.

'What's that?'

'The opening will definitely be delayed.' Rocco eyed her, concerned about her reaction. 'Only by a few weeks, from what I can gather, but still. You can go home and come back again, of course. Although I was hoping we could go to Rome soon to see Luca about your family tree.'

Cassia felt oddly comforted by the news. She knew Finn would probably be annoyed when he heard that she might have to stay in Italy for a bit longer and Grace would probably have a seizure. But she wasn't ready to go home any time soon, she felt far too happy here for the time being. And hearing that the trip to Rome to see the Disantis' historian friend was music to her ears. She couldn't possibly go home when she had the chance to finally get to the bottom of her father's family background.

'Well, let me know some dates and we'll take it from there. Now, pasta. Do you make yours on the worktop? My father always said it was the best way.'

Filled with an unexpected sense of relief at her response about the Vegas opening, Rocco gestured to the marble surface they were about to use. 'Your father was right. And marble is the very best surface for pasta, it's cool and smooth, which is perfect. Here, you make some too.' Rocco raised a dark eyebrow. 'You didn't think I was just going to perform, did you? Let's see what you can do as well.'

Copying him as she made a Mount Vesuvius-shaped mound with a well in the centre, Cassia picked up some large eggs.

'Crack them into the well,' Rocco murmured, totally focused on his own volcano. 'Use your hands to mix the eggs into the flour until it makes a coarse paste. Feel the dough . . . it will start to come together and you will sense when it's ready. Although . . . yours is too sticky,' he commented, frowning at the sight of the gooey mess in front of her. 'You've added one too many eggs perhaps.'

'I told you I was useless at cooking . . .'

Shaking a little more flour into the mound with an expert eye, Rocco positioned himself behind her and instructed her to draw the mixture together.

Cassia sucked her breath in, jolted by his proximity.

'Like this,' he said, covering her hands with his own. Their hands moved together in the mixture and Cassia held her breath, feeling Rocco's hard body pressed against hers. She felt flustered, sure she was imagining the tinge of erotic promise in the air.

'That's it,' Rocco murmured, his breath hot against her ear. 'Pull the dough together . . . good . . . that's perfect. See, it feels right, doesn't it?'

Cassia gulped and nodded. She could feel the heat of his body against her back and without even thinking, she leant back against him. Absurdly, it felt like the most natural thing in the world and her body moulded to his easily, slotting against the most disturbing places as if it belonged there.

Rocco paused, his fingers still linked through hers in the dough. Inhaling the scent of her hair, he savoured the soft contours of her body against his. He could so easily loosen the ties at her neck and allow them to fall away; it would require a mere flick of his fingers. Rocco wondered what her body would feel like . . . the flare of her hip, the curve of her breast. Fighting the urge to bury his face in her neck and leave a trail of hot kisses alongside the crimson ties of her bikini, he abruptly moved away.

Cassia felt a thud of disappointment. Just for a moment, she had been allowed another glimpse of the other side Rocco possessed, the one she'd shared a helicopter with . . . the one she'd been close to on the roof terrace. It was as though all the awkward tension between them since the trip to England had evaporated and they had found themselves back in sync again. These thoughts were swiftly followed by a surge of guilt. What on earth was happening to her? She was acting like her teenage self again, the one that was more than capable of throwing caution to the wind and doing something recklessly dangerous.

Finn, you're marrying Finn, she told herself repeatedly.

As she washed her hands in the sink, Rocco joined her and their fingers connected again. Cassia looked up, surprised to see Rocco's eyes fixed firmly on hers.

Rocco was startled. Standing behind her, his fingers linked through hers as they made pasta together had been stupidly, headily sensual and his head was all over the place. Fighting a sudden urge to shove the half-made pasta aside and make passionate, frenzied love to Cassia on the marble worktop, Rocco struggled to restrain himself. He was stressed, that was all, stressed out and in need of a release. He probably just needed a ride across the countryside on his motorbike to get this pent-up tension out of his system.

Well, that and a cold shower, he told himself wryly. Drying his hands slowly, he focused his mind on his recipe.

'We need to leave this dough for thirty minutes or so . . .'

'Here, use some I made earlier,' Antonio said, appearing seamlessly with a fresh batch. 'I'll deal with this.' He scooped their dough up and left them to it.

'What do you think is causing the problems in the restaurant?' Cassia asked, grappling with the pasta machine Rocco had prepped for her. 'I found myself wondering if Sofia was right about a family curse. Silly, I know.'

'Ha! Me too.' Rocco adroitly flipped a lever on the side of the machine and fed some rolled-out pasta through it. 'It can't be, though; all the family members are dead, for a start. If they

275

weren't, I might be more worried, but like I say, no one survived the landslide as far as we know.'

Cassia nodded, clumsily fumbling with the machine. She dropped a piece of pasta on the floor and laughed raucously as Rocco rolled his eyes and joined in.

Unbeknownst to either of them, Stefania arrived. Told that Rocco was in the kitchen by Sofia, Stefania stood at the doorway. Not only was she stunned that Rocco was back in the kitchen – something he claimed to never have time for any more – she was furious to find that the person who had apparently convinced him to do the thing he talked about constantly was Cassia Marini, the one person Stefania would rather it hadn't been.

Unaware he was being spied on by his girlfriend, Rocco showed Cassia how to roll the pasta dough, before spooning crab mixture into it. When some of the crab mixture ended up on the work surface, Rocco jokingly pushed her hands away as she attempted to clean it up.

As they worked alongside each other, murmuring the odd word, Stefania looked on jealously. It was perceptible, the electric chemistry between them. There was something about the intense eye contact, the way their bodies leaned in towards each other that made alarm bells go off in her head. There was a taut but somehow oddly informal vibe between them, as if they were relaxed in one another's company but sexually attracted too.

Stefania was fairly certain neither of them even realised they were so deeply attracted to each other, but that didn't matter. The attraction was tangible and dangerous. She seethed. She wanted to pin Rocco down to a commitment, to a proposal, preferably, yet here he was, cooking and laughing with another woman in a way he never did with her.

As Rocco whipped up a batch of the creamy tomato sauce that accompanied his famous *ravioli al granchio*, he let out one of his unexpected belly laughs over something Cassia said.

Clenching her fists, Stefania was almost suffocated by envy. When had she last made Rocco laugh like that? When had she ever been able to make his olive-green eyes light up with such obvious passion and fire? She watched, stunned, as Rocco fed Cassia a bite of the hot ravioli. He actually speared a succulent ravioli with his fork and fed it gently into her mouth and Stefania's stomach tightened as she watched the intimate, erotic gesture.

'Perfection,' she heard Cassia stammer in awe.

Rocco tasted a piece. 'It's not bad,' he commented critically. 'My crab filling could do with tweaking. What do you think? Perhaps a touch of—'

'Am I interrupting something?' Stefania snapped, stalking towards them.

'Stefania.' Rocco's smile died. 'I . . . wasn't expecting you until later.'

'I can see that.'

Letting out a jerky breath, Stefania composed herself. Wearing eau-de-nil cotton shorts and a loose, white silk shirt, she looked almost as polished as Aurelia. With one hand on her hip, she managed to convey both supreme self-confidence as well as an icy hostility that no one in the room could miss. Even Antonio, lurking behind a cluster of cured wild boar salami, looked alarmed.

'Well, I guess I should thank you for looking after Rocco in my absence,' Stefania drawled, glancing at Cassia. 'You've certainly made him laugh more than I do.'

Rocco's jaw tightened and Cassia felt the temperature drop to glacial levels. Tearing off her chef's jacket, she backed away. 'I'm . . . I'm sure I haven't,' she managed.

Wow, if looks could kill, she thought, feeling a tremor of apprehension. Stefania's eyes were channelling pure hatred. How long had she been standing in the doorway? Cassia felt extremely uncomfortable, knowing how she would feel if the

277

boot was on the other foot. With a shock, she realised she had been flirting with Rocco. Or had he been flirting with her? Cassia wasn't sure which way round it was, but either way, it was inappropriate. Rocco and Stefania were serious about one another and Finn, however distant and allergic to communication he seemed to be, was her fiancé.

Cassia looked contrite. 'I'm so sorry,' she told Stefania. 'I'm afraid I got a little carried away. A pasta-making lesson with the great Rocco Disanti – who wouldn't? Er . . . do excuse me.'

Handing her chef's jacket to a stony-faced Rocco, Cassia left the kitchen. Her thoughts and her senses were in complete disarray and she had to get away from Rocco. About to slink off to her room, she decided a dip in the pool would be far better. She guessed Stefania would be doing the complete opposite and would be dragging him off to bed immediately – either that or she would hear the crash of breaking china as Stefania vented her fury.

Having had the opportunity to ponder her choices, Stefania decided the best path would be to treat Rocco to a sexual marathon that would make any first flickerings of lust he might feel towards Cassia fade into insignificance. She was delighted when Rocco threw her on to his bed unceremoniously, before satisfying her in ways she couldn't possibly have imagined. She would have been less smug if she'd realised that Rocco's mind was totally elsewhere at the time.

Standing on his balcony later, Rocco was in turmoil. Swigging red wine, he tried to make sense of the thoughts swirling in his head, but it was impossible. He felt like two people; one half of him was a consummate professional, the slick businessman he believed Stefania to be in love with, the other half was a chef, a zealous, creative force with an untamed passion for food and cooking.

Rocco couldn't help thinking that the chef side of him had been sorely neglected for a long time. Back there in the kitchen with Cassia, he had felt alive, truly alive for the first time in ages. It was like flying his helicopter, or racing through the Italian countryside on his motorbike, only much, much better.

How much of it had been to do with getting his hands in the flour and the eggs? he wondered. How much of it had been to do with Cassia? One thing was for sure, none of it had been to do with Stefania, who seemed to prefer him in his office rather than dipping his hands into delicious ingredients. Knowing that meant something important, Rocco couldn't face lingering on it right now.

Turning as he heard a splash, he caught sight of Cassia's sleek, dark head emerging from the depths of the swimming pool. Watching as she climbed out of the pool, her sopping wet crimson bikini clinging lovingly to her Botticelli curves, Rocco knocked back his wine savagely.

Too complicated, he told himself firmly. Complicated, messy and totally foolhardy. Tearing his eyes from Cassia's luscious body, he went inside and firmly set his shower temperature to sub-zero.

Chapter Twelve

'All right, I admit it.' Diana met Fliss's eyes in utter terror. 'I want to play Clarissa. I want to do *Jealousy*.' She let out a throaty gasp. It had been a difficult decision but now that she had made it with Cassia's help, Diana was absolutely petrified she might fail.

Her hands clasped tensely on her desk, Fliss did her best to hide her elation. For weeks she had been putting subtle pressure on Diana to at least think about the wonderful character part, and she could barely believe what she was hearing.

Deep down, Fliss hadn't been holding out much hope that Diana would actually find the courage to express an interest in the part, not with her fragile ego. Playing Clarissa involved taking herself out of every single comfort zone. The actress who took this part on would be confronting her own insecurities, not least the trial of ageing. Yet here was Diana, not only registering her interest, but unreservedly stating that she wanted the part – a part which could be the absolute making of her as an actress, Fliss thought, with rising excitement. Still, however euphoric she felt about the situation, Fliss also knew she was going to have to tread carefully. The abject fear in her client's wide blue eyes suggested Diana was one heartbeat away from changing her mind and fleeing from the office. She looked composed enough overall, with her blond hair in a neat up-do and her make-up flawless, but Fliss knew her old friend like the back of her hand.

'Well, that's wonderful news,' Fliss said smoothly. 'I'm so pleased.'

Diana nodded, her eyes darting about the room. 'It's the right decision, isn't it? I mean, I don't want to make a fool of myself. I can't bear the thought of taking on something I can't cope with . . .'

Fliss leant forward. 'You can cope,' she said firmly. 'This part was made for you, Di.' She smiled, unable to hide her pride at her friend's courage.

Diana wrung her hands in her lap. After her time out at the spa, she had thought about nothing else but the play and she had spent days reading and rereading the part, acting little sections out and trying the lines in different voices. Diana felt a thrill inside at the thought of playing Clarissa – someone she now felt she knew intimately, as she would a best friend – but a part of her was still horrified at the thought that she might not be up to it.

'It's a brave move.' Fliss cursed herself for being crass as Diana trembled. 'I mean that it's a brave move because it's an intense piece, and because it's such a beautifully written part.'

Diana nodded. 'So, what's next? I assume I have to audition?' The very thought of having to try out for the part had almost been enough to send her scuttling back home to safety, but she had forced herself to accept that it was part and parcel of the process these days.

'Er, no.' Fliss looked sheepish. 'I didn't want to put too much pressure on you to accept the part, but you were always the production company's first choice.'

'I-I was?' Diana didn't know whether she should feel hugely flattered or doubly panicked.

Fliss nodded. 'That's why they've held off for so long,' she explained. 'They were holding out for you because they thought you were the best person to play Clarissa. They were shaking in their boots about losing the theatre in the West End, but they particularly wanted you to do it.'

Diana gulped, fighting back tears. It meant so much to be seen as a serious actress.

'They had one condition,' Fliss added hesitantly. 'They wanted me to send them a photo of you without make-up on . . . you know, stripped down to nothing. I suppose they need to know you're capable of doing it for real.'

Diana swallowed. Telling herself this was the first step towards playing Clarissa, she opened her handbag and took out a packet of wipes. Slowly removing every trace of make-up, she raked her fingers through her blond hair to remove the pins and the hairspray. Standing up, she moved to a bare wall at the end of Fliss's office and leant against the wall, feeling her heart thumping in her chest. Edging the jersey dress she was wearing down her shoulders to give the impression she was naked, Diana held her chin up bravely towards Fliss, mentally channelling Clarissa's fragility.

Mesmerised as she watched Diana get into character, Fliss almost forgot to take the picture. Then she lifted her camera and fired off a dozen shots, knowing she was witnessing something special.

'You know this means no more botox,' Fliss said gently, touching on a subject she and Diana had never discussed.

About to deny she had ever had such a thing, Diana decided it was time to start telling the truth about herself. She nodded slowly. And as tears slid down her bare cheeks, she wished Marco was here to see her doing something he would be proud of her for.

Heading through the kitchen to finish writing her column outside, Cassia winced as Sofia shouted out instructions to the restaurant team. Used to Sofia being rather more warm and cuddly, the team were finding this new, bossy person unsettling and not altogether likeable. Ruling the team with a rod of iron, Sofia was swiftly ticking items off her checklist but putting everyone's backs up in the process and her eyes were anything but twinkling today.

Setting her laptop up under an umbrella by the pool and almost changing her mind when she saw Stefania stretched out on the opposite side, Cassia felt a stab of sympathy for Sofia. She was under enormous pressure juggling the restaurant bookings in the height of season as well as frantically trying to arrange the party for the local trades people single-handedly. The party was Sofia's idea and the rest of the Disanti family had pretty much left her to the arrangements without lifting a finger, mostly due to previous commitments. Rocco was holed up in his office and Aurelia had barely left her bedroom since Dino had returned to the villa from his modelling shoot. Raffaelo was actually doing his job for once, the sleeves of his black shirt rolled up as he wielded a hammer and paintbrush almost simultaneously. He had proved himself to be rather talented and speedy when it came to the repairs and Cassia could understand why Rocco had been so frustrated with Raff leaving them unattended to for so long.

Doing her best to ignore Stefania who was wearing a tiny white bikini with her blond hair tucked up into a fetching Stetson, Cassia nibbled her fingernails as she sat in front of her laptop. She was trying to recapture the time she'd spent in the kitchen with Rocco for her column, but somehow it kept ending up like an erotic scene from a bonkbuster.

'*Concentrating intently, his olive-green eyes focused on the task ahead, Rocco leant over me, guiding me with his hands . . .*' she read. She felt a delicious throb between her thighs at the memory it conjured up and guiltily ignored it. '*With his expert fingers caressing mine in a luscious, eggy mixture the colour of a melting Sorrento sunset, I had the sense something magical was being created, something sensual that once eaten, would be climactic . . .'*

Blushing, Cassia quickly erased the words, knowing she couldn't possibly send this to Gena. Her boss would be on the phone in seconds asking what was going on in Cassia's head. Cassia felt uncomfortable. She glanced at Stefania, feeling awful for thinking anything untoward about Rocco when his girlfriend was sitting a few feet away. But Stefania hadn't even acknowledged her presence. Wearing dark glasses and reading a magazine, Stefania was resolutely ignoring her and making it very obvious that she had no intention of speaking to her.

Cassia looked away. Glancing at her phone, she felt concerned that she hadn't heard from Finn. She had sent him several texts over the weekend and thinking he might have been too busy to charge his phone, something Finn had been guilty of before, Cassia had given him the benefit of the doubt. However, having not heard from him for a few days now, she was beginning to think he was giving her the cold shoulder.

They were getting married in a couple of months' time. It was now June and the wedding was in September. Admittedly, the wedding felt rather surreal, as if it wasn't really taking place at all, Cassia mused, but still. Neither of them had been actively involved in the plans since she had arrived in Italy and it almost felt as though it was happening to someone else, not them. She and Finn were due to walk up the aisle shortly, but she felt so anxious every time her thoughts drifted in that direction, she always tried to think about something else when that happened.

Tetchily, she returned to her column, noticing that Stefania hadn't turned a single page of her magazine for over half an hour now. Cassia stared at her laptop screen, drumming her fingers on the edge of her chair. She should focus on the dish that she and Rocco had created, not the electric chemistry between them.

'Ravioli al granchio *when cooked by an expert such as Rocco Disanti is an unparalleled, melt-in-the-mouth indulgence,*' she typed diffidently. '*Biting into the perfectly al dente pasta, the unctuous, silken crab mixture oozes out providing a rich, satisfying burst of flavour that's akin to an explosive orgasm . . .*'

Cassia exclaimed in frustration and deleted the final words. She really had to get a grip; her mind was obviously set on an erotic track at the moment. Wondering if this was all shamefully down to a simple case of sexual frustration, she looked up and caught sight of Sofia heading towards her with a pile of cards and two espressos.

'Thought you might need this,' Sofia said, setting one of the tiny coffee cups down. 'I certainly do.'

'Thank you.' Cassia snapped her laptop shut and moved it out of the way. She'd tackle her troublesome column later on when she'd managed to pull her mind out of the gutter.

'Are you all right?' Cassia realised Sofia looked preoccupied.

Sofia nodded. She wasn't one for complaining but Cassia's kindly expression was too sympathetic to resist. 'I'm just tired, I think. There's so much to do for this party.' She gestured to the pile of invitations in front of her. 'It was my idea, of course, but I hadn't realised the preparation would be so time-consuming.'

'I guess that's because you're doing it alone.' Cassia picked an invitation from the top of the pile. 'Allesandro Raldini,' she read, pushing her dark hair out of her eyes. 'Where have I heard that name before?'

Sofia shuffled the pile of invitations into a neat stack. 'I mentioned him in the meeting the other day,' she replied casually. 'He's a wine merchant.'

'Handsome?' Cassia inquired, with equal nonchalance. She met Sofia's eyes. 'It's just that you're blushing and I've only ever seen you do that twice. Once in that meeting and . . . well, now.'

About to blame the hot sunshine, Sofia fanned her face. Then she smiled. 'All right, Cassia. Yes, he is rather handsome. But I know nothing about him. He came here while you and Rocco were in England and he asked about doing some business with Rocco.' She looked troubled. 'I'm not even sure I should ask him to the party.'

Cassia shrugged. 'Why not? It's just a party for local tradespeople, and that's what he is.'

Sofia let out a jerky breath. 'I suppose. I heard you managed to convince Rocco to cook the other day.'

It was Cassia's turn to look evasive. 'Yes, I thought he could do with getting away from his paperwork for a while. We made *ravioli al granchio*, which was delicious, and we chatted a bit, laughed, and then . . .' She lowered her voice. 'Stefania turned up.'

Sofia arched a brow. She could just imagine what Stefania must have thought, arriving in the middle of a cooking lesson and witnessing Rocco laughing for the first time in ages. On a personal level, Sofia couldn't help being delighted that Cassia was having such a positive effect on Rocco – unlike Stefania, who seemed to have her own agenda. Sofia was sure Cassia's motives were far less self-indulgent, but she wondered where it was all leading. Cassia was due to be married in a few months' time and Rocco's life was so complicated with work and with Stefania hinting heavily at a proposal.

The trouble was, Sofia mused, sparks were flying between Cassia and Rocco and such strong feelings of physical attraction were hard to ignore longer term. Sooner or later they made themselves felt and if any kind of emotional attachment were to be thrown into the mix, something explosive usually occurred.

Sofia glanced at Stefania's stiff frame, wondering if she had spotted the electric chemistry between Cassia and Rocco. She'd have to be blind not to, which probably explained why she was still here and why she had been glued to Rocco's side since she arrived, in spite of having commitments back in Rome. Sofia sighed inwardly; she knew Stefania was wrong for Rocco but she didn't dare confront him about it. She had such a good relationship with her grandson, the last thing she wanted was to cause him to coldly tell her to keep her nose out of his business.

'You're privileged, anyway,' Sofia commented, as she checked her long 'to do' list with panic-stricken eyes. 'None of us can get Rocco in the kitchen these days.'

Cassia made a non-committal noise. She had no idea what had lured Rocco into the kitchen the other day. Perhaps he had simply been in the mood to cook. And whatever had gone on between them in the kitchen was irrelevant now as Rocco was working away in his office and making no attempt to communicate with her.

'Rocco mentioned that he'd asked your fiancé's family to Aurelia's wedding,' Sofia said, sipping her espresso.

Cassia nodded unenthusiastically. 'I don't know if they'll come or not. Grace, Finn's mother, is rather . . . reserved.' She let out a laugh. 'I don't know why I'm being so polite. What I should say is that Grace detests me. With a passion. She thinks I should forget about my career and become a good little wife.'

Sofia looked shocked. 'But you are so talented!' she said, gesturing to the laptop. 'You write beautifully. What a shame your fiancé's family don't appreciate you.'

Cassia was touched. 'I . . . I feel so much more at home here in Italy,' she confessed, out of the blue. 'It's strange, my father was Italian, of course, but for some reason I just feel as though I fit. Not into the Disanti family, as such, although you have been very welcoming. I just mean that I feel as though I'm at home in Italy.'

Privately, Sofia felt Cassia had been able to slot into the Disanti family far more naturally than Stefania, but she refrained from commenting. 'Did you mean what you said about helping out with the party the other day?'

Cassia nodded; her column could wait. She was writing tripe, anyway. 'Just tell me what you need me to do.'

'You're probably going to regret that offer,' Sofia warned, drawing her checklist towards her with a wide smile. 'You know we only have a week to sort everything out?'

Feeling Stefania's eyes on her as the girl stood up and advanced upon them, Cassia knew she'd be glad to have something to occupy her time and she took the list from Sofia.

Sofia bridled as Stefania paused at their table.

'Hard at work?' Stefania asked.

Cassia looked up, smiling easily at her. 'We're just organising the party the family are hosting next weekend.'

Stefania looked bored. 'Fascinating,' she drawled, tipping her Stetson back slightly. 'I'm going to see if Rocco fancies a big, long . . . *sleep* in our bedroom.' Her words were loaded with innuendo.

Sofia shook her head disapprovingly as she watched Stefania sashay back to the house, giving them a prime view of her long tanned legs. 'Silly girl, how unsubtle.'

Cassia tore her eyes from Stefania's perfect pins. 'Unsubtle?'

Sofia waved her hand. 'Take no notice of me. Or of Stefania, for that matter. Now, about this party, how do you fancy helping me with some of the promotional flyers?'

A week later, Jules was busy piling pastel-coloured sundresses into her suitcase with Wimbledon on in the background. Impassively, she watched Dom serve up yet another flawless ace that had his opponent flummoxed and the crowd cheered and whooped. A gang of giggling groupies flicked their long manes of hair madly as they jiggled their bosoms in tight T-shirts with Dom's name emblazoned across them. Wearing pristine white shorts and a loose top, as the Wimbledon dress code dictated, Dom looked athletic, tanned and handsome – in his prime, in fact.

Jules rolled her eyes. She had to admit Dom looked dashing on the court; his blond hair and tanned thighs were the perfect foil for the almost garishly green grass and the brilliant, overhead sunshine that was beating down relentlessly on the players, but Jules couldn't care less. Seeing him wielding his tennis racket with such panache brought back unwelcome memories.

Heading into the bathroom to grab her toiletries, Jules was horrified when tears came into her eyes. What on earth was wrong with her? She was over Dom and she had Sorrento to look forward to. Hearing the doorbell, she called out that the door was open, knowing it was probably Louisa arriving to take her to the airport.

'Are you still packing?' Louisa frowned. 'Jules, you're so disorganised! We don't have long before your flight, you know.' Glancing at the television, she watched Dom convincingly winning a rally.

'Goodness, he's on top form, isn't he?' Louisa caught sight of Jules's expression. 'Sorry. I know he was horrible to you but he's my brother and I'm just saying he's playing some incredible tennis right now.'

Jules waved a hand, hoping Louisa couldn't spot any evidence of her earlier tears. 'I couldn't care less about Dom.' Catching sight of her reflection, she decided to change her outfit, despite Louisa's protests. She wanted to look her best when she arrived, so she shimmied into a strapless dress in a flattering shade of apricot. Adding some slingbacks and a sheer scarf around her throat, she snapped her suitcase shut and heaved it off the bed.

'Let's go,' she said, flicking the television off and pushing Dom out of her mind for good.

Louisa followed her out, somewhat relieved that Jules was going through with the visit. 'Have you told Cassia you're coming?' Louisa asked as she unlocked her car.

'Nope.' Jules looked unconcerned. 'And as far as I know, Finn hasn't either.' She settled herself into the passenger seat. 'It'll be a surprise for her, I guess. Maybe not a great one from her point of view, but I didn't want to give her a chance to tell me not to come.'

Louisa said nothing, deciding to stay out of it. Jules's relationship with Cassia was complex and unfathomable. Who knew what was behind Jules's resentment of her sister? She didn't, and neither did Cassia.

Jules stared straight ahead. She wasn't worried about Cassia's reaction to her arrival, she was more concerned with getting herself back on track emotionally and sorting her life out. And this trip to Sorrento was going to do just that.

Wearing grey trousers with a tailored silver and white striped shirt that was a gift from a well-known Italian designer who frequented the restaurant almost weekly, Rocco looked deceptively relaxed.

Strolling outside into the humid night air, he glanced back at his beloved restaurant. The creamy terracotta exterior looked sensational lit up against the aromatic citrus groves stretching out behind and the twinkling lights of the Bay of Naples to the right simply added to the stunning view. In the distance, Mount Vesuvius rose majestically into the skyline, and next to the restaurant, the sprawling Disanti estate with its imposing villa and land looked enviably beautiful.

Outside, the air was thick with the scent of oranges and lemons from the grove and the humid air was buzzing with insects that clustered around the pretty lights studding the lawns. Champagne cocktails and canapés were doing the rounds, giving off their own, mouth-wateringly delicious aromas, and inside the restaurant an impressive buffet had been laid out. Large wedges of cheese from the surrounding area, glistening vegetable salads and good cuts of cured meat were displayed in local pottery, complemented by lavish floral displays in whites, purples and greens, and the aroma of lobster, garlic and prawns coming from the kitchens promised some delicious hot food later on.

Rocco also knew his grandmother was planning to present a dish she was famous for, a wonderful stew made with veal tail. Simmered for hours with onions, pancetta and garlic until the meat came away from the bone, herbs and spices were added, alongside bittersweet chocolate and a garnish of pine nuts. A dish of Roman origin, it was rustic, flavoursome and very Italian.

Rocco caught sight of Raffaelo, talking loudly to a group of local food providers. Holding court with plenty of gesticulation and guffawing, he looked to be in his element. Rocco was taken aback. Raffaelo had always been a people person, but Rocco hadn't really observed him liaising with people before, not like this. He reminded Rocco of his father, they had the same genial, open way of engaging people and making them feel important.

Was Raff wasted on maintenance and security? Rocco wasn't sure. His brother had never shown the slightest interest in developing his role at the restaurant.

'Rocco!'

Looking loved-up with a mahogany-hued Dino on her arm, Aurelia shone in a golden shift that was cut short across the thighs and high at the neck. Wearing a long silver chain Dino had brought her from Australia down the length of her tanned back, with her dark curls piled on top of her head for maximum effect, Aurelia looked every inch the top model she was.

Realising that expecting her to work in the restaurant was ridiculous, Rocco felt contrite about his impatience with her lack of involvement. What did he think she was going to do, serve tables or something? None of his male clients would be able to concentrate, for a start, Rocco thought with a rueful smile. He turned to greet Dino, who amiably hugged him, speaking in English as usual.

'Sorry I haven't been around much since I've come back from Oz. Aurelia's been keeping me busy . . . with wedding arrangements, ha ha.'

'Wedding arrangements? Is that what you call it these days?' Rocco pretended to roll his eyes. He liked Dino immensely and he enjoyed his strong Australian twang. 'Thank God Aurelia's room is miles away from my apartment.'

Aurelia nudged Rocco. 'I actually have been making him pull his weight on the wedding front.'

Dino's brown eyes crinkled mischievously. 'Yeah, that too. Great party, by the way. You've got some decent beer in for once.'

'Nothing to do with me, it's all down to my grandmother.' Rocco fixed Aurelia with an amused glance. 'Unless you've been helping out with the party preparations, that is?'

Aurelia's soft, pink mouth curled into a pout. 'I haven't had time for such things,' she returned. 'I've been far too busy calling in favours from shoe designers and florists in between modelling contracts.' She sighed dramatically. 'There's still so much to do.'

Rocco gave her an indulgent nod. 'I can imagine. It is going to be the wedding of the century, after all.'

Aurelia gave him a sweetly innocent smile. 'Any idea where Cassia is?'

He regarded her. 'I haven't the faintest idea. Should I know all her movements?'

'I don't know, Rocco. That depends.'

Rocco frowned. What was that supposed to mean? Catching sight of Stefania wearing a daring white dress that was almost cut to the navel, she threw him a hot glance, trailing a finger between her breasts suggestively. She had obviously made an enormous effort with her appearance but somehow it looked as though she was trying too hard. Her blond hair was coiffed to perfection and her make-up was flawless but she looked rather brittle.

Rocco silently groaned. Ever since she'd arrived, Stefania had been commanding his time and attention like never before, rampantly dragging him to bed every five minutes as well as putting some serious pressure on him about moving to Rome. Stefania rarely stayed with him for prolonged periods and he could only assume her decision had something to do with Cassia. Rocco was sure her demands in the bedroom were fuelled by her jealousy over their relationship. Stefania had always been a tease, sexually available but intriguingly out of reach, but suddenly she had become all too accessible.

Was it just that, though? Rocco asked himself. It wasn't in his nature to complain about having too much sex so he knew it wasn't that. No, it was more about his lack of focus where Stefania was concerned, his tendency to drift off and think about someone else, even at the most untimely of moments.

Rocco grimaced as he accepted a glass of champagne from one of his waitresses. He knew he should feel remorseful about that but he didn't. Not because he didn't care about Stefania but because he couldn't help the way he felt. Feeling her beady eyes on him, he glanced at her again. Their lack of common ground was revealing itself daily and Rocco wondered if she felt it too.

Aurelia giggled at something Dino whispered in her ear as he pulled her closer by the waist. Watching the lovebirds drift off together, two beautifully glossy halves of one perfect whole, Rocco felt a pang. He was so incredibly tired at the moment. So tired, he couldn't get his head around the latest set of accounts he'd received that week, something that had never happened before. He had a good head for figures and it wasn't often that he was flummoxed by neat columns of numbers. It was just that something didn't add up – literally.

Gulping down a melt-in-the-mouth scallop smothered in hazelnut butter and fresh lemon zest shavings, Rocco pondered the situation. Disanti's London had been doing exceptionally well since his recent visit, with head chef Ben taking full control of his team of staff. He was more than capable of running the restaurant and he could also be relied upon to deliver the impeccable standards demanded by the Disanti family. The projected forecast for the next quarter looked good and there had been several excellent reviews in some significant publications.

Disanti's Paris, a restaurant located in one of the best arrondissements of the stunning capital, sat next to some of their most well-respected competitors. It practically ran itself, thankfully, and Rocco was relieved he rarely had to get involved in it, knowing he could trust the staff implicitly. With the young son of one of France's most revered but now retired chefs in charge of the kitchen, the Paris restaurant was in safe hands, with every tradition of Disanti's being honoured, plus the bonus of extraordinary creativity and flair from the head chef who, like Rocco, had spent most of his childhood next to an oven.

However, the same couldn't be said of the Vegas development, which appeared to be lagging hideously behind schedule, with no signs of gathering momentum again. Rocco knew he needed to go out there to check what was happening – and also to be fair to Cassia, who needed to head home as soon as the Vegas restaurant had opened. And as for the restaurant here in Sorrento, well, aside from the odd calamities that kept happening without warning or explanation, it was doing well. So, all in all, Rocco couldn't make any sense of the bizarre discrepancies in the accounts he'd just been sent.

'What do you think of the party?' Sofia asked, slipping her arm through his. 'A success, if I say so myself.'

'It's wonderful.' Rocco squeezed her arm with his hand. Wearing an emerald-green dress with high heels instead of her usual low-heeled courts, she cut a colourful figure. 'As I knew it would be.'

'Cassia helped me out and came up with several lovely ideas,' Sofia said, patting the loose bun Cassia had helped her with. Unusually, she was wearing a little more make-up, shimmering creams and greys making her green eyes stand out more.

'Did she?' Rocco sipped his champagne.

'Yes, she's been an absolute godsend, I couldn't have done it without her. She even helped with the cooking – some of the pasta you'll be sampling later was cooked by her.' Sofia looked approving. 'She did well, especially considering she isn't the best cook. She did, of course, say that your expert training helped.'

Rocco contemplated his grandmother. He was probably mistaken but he couldn't help thinking that certain members of his family kept mentioning Cassia to him.

Sofia's eyes lost warmth as she changed the subject. 'Did Stefania find you? She was searching for you earlier.'

Rocco shrugged. 'I've seen her, but not to talk to. She . . . er . . . she looks beautiful.'

It was Sofia's turn to remain silent. Stefania might be beautiful but she was also disgustingly lazy. She had done nothing but swan around the estate in a bikini for the past few days, most likely, Sofia thought, to make Cassia acutely aware of her presence. She hoped Stefania hadn't been pressurising Rocco about moving to Rome and opening yet another restaurant again; she didn't think he could take any more stress.

About to talk to his grandmother about her opinion of Stefania, Rocco closed his mouth as he caught sight of Cassia. Emerging from the restaurant shyly, her appearance had literally taken his breath away. Wearing a tight-fitting cream dress with a knee-length skirt and a sweetheart neckline teamed with nude heels, she was the epitome of sophistication. She was showing hardly any flesh, but the dress was such a fantastic fit, she could have been naked. Stefania stepped out behind her, and the contrast was marked. Stefania looked cheap in comparison to Cassia.

Watching the emotions flicker across Rocco's face, Sofia was fascinated. About to comment, she noticed who Cassia was speaking to. 'That's Allesandro,' she said, her throat feeling dry all of a sudden. 'The wine merchant. Don't you think you should introduce yourself?'

Rocco tore his eyes away from Cassia. 'Sorry, what?'

'Allesandro,' Sofia repeated. She tugged at his arm but Allesandro was already on his way over, drawing a reluctant-looking Cassia with him.

'Rocco Disanti,' Allesandro said, holding his hand out. Wearing a dashing suit with a bright blue tie only a man supremely confident in his own skin would risk, he was brimming with enthusiasm. 'What an honour to meet you. I'm such a fan, I can't tell you.' He turned to Sofia and kissed her cheeks, clasping her hands in his in a rather familiar fashion.

After a few seconds, Sofia snatched her hands away, turning pink.

'Thank you, how kind,' Rocco murmured. He met Cassia's eyes then made an effort to focus on Allesandro. He noted that he was in his late fifties, with dark hair and sallow, almost swarthy skin. He had an air of sophistication about him, a worldly charisma that suggested he had lived life successfully. 'I'm so sorry I haven't been able to get back to you. I've been incredibly busy in the restaurant recently but my grandmother did pass on your business card.'

Allesandro let out an affable laugh and clapped Rocco on the arm. 'No matter. There is plenty of time for us to talk business.' He gestured to Cassia. 'I understand this beautiful woman is staying with you?' he said, staring at her with obvious appreciation. 'I don't know how you concentrate on work, Rocco.' Flirtatiously, Allesandro touched Cassia's shoulder with his deeply tanned fingers. 'I don't understand how anyone can accuse the English of being anything less than stunning.'

'Indeed,' Rocco agreed lightly. 'Although Cassia is half-Italian, so she has the best of both worlds.' He met her gaze, his eyes giving nothing away.

'Ah.' Allesandro's eyes crinkled at the corners. 'What a perfect combination. And it explains your wonderful Italian accent.' He removed his hand and replaced it with his business card. 'My details, in case you wish to contact me.' His eyes flirted lightly with hers and then he turned to Rocco. 'I hope we can talk business another time, but for now, I thank you for your kind invitation to this party.'

Rocco was equally gracious, even though he thought Allesandro was forward for giving his card to Cassia. 'Please, have a look around, sample the food. My grandmother will show you where everything is.'

'That would be wonderful,' Allesandro said, holding his arm out to Sofia with a wolfish grin.

As a flustered Sofia led Allesandro away, Cassia sucked her breath in and stuffed Allesandro's card into her handbag distractedly. She had been hyped up about seeing Rocco all day but she felt like an idiot now she was standing in front of him. He looked absurdly sexy, even with dark shadows under his eyes; he looked so tired, she wanted to ask him if he was all right. But before she could find the right words after they had avoided one another for an entire week, her mouth fell open in shock.

'Are you . . . what's wrong?' Rocco asked, alarmed.

'It's . . . it's my sister,' Cassia said, jolted. She couldn't quite believe her eyes but there was Jules, larger than life and dressed up to the nines in a peach-coloured sundress and strappy sandals, almost as if she'd known she was about to gatecrash a party.

'Your sister? What's she doing here?'

Cassia felt a rush of panic. Seeing Jules brought back all the issues she had been ignoring – Grace, the wedding, Finn. She felt happy here in Sorrento, she felt at home. The fact that she was so far removed from everything else going on in her life had been a blessed relief.

'There you are,' Jules cried, spotting Cassia. She hurried over, dragging her suitcase behind her. 'Now, I know this is a bit strange, but Finn sent me over here to see you.'

'Finn?' Cassia blinked in bewilderment. 'Are you sure?'

'Of course I'm sure.' Jules looked petulant.

Wondering why Cassia looked so unnerved, Rocco welcomed Jules by kissing her on both cheeks. 'Well, it will be lovely to have you here. Naturally you will stay with us at the villa?'

Jules looked up at it in awe. 'Oh no, I think Finn has booked a hotel for me in—'

'I insist,' Rocco said politely. He could do without any more complications but he wouldn't hear of Cassia's sister staying in a hotel.

Jules thanked Rocco, staggered at how darkly sexy he was in the flesh. Briefly, she wondered if it was worth making a play for him, just for the hell of it, but she got the distinct impression he hadn't even noticed she was female.

Rocco glanced at Cassia, puzzled by the strength of her reaction to her sister's arrival. She had talked about her troubled relationship with Jules on the helicopter, so maybe she was feeling uneasy about spending time with her. He wondered what was behind Finn's seemingly generous gesture; surely it would have been better for Finn to visit Cassia himself, rather than sending Jules over in his place. Still, he couldn't help feeling secretly pleased that Finn had remained in England, even though he knew he shouldn't be thinking such a thing.

'I'll get your room sorted out,' he told Jules. 'Please help yourself to champagne and enjoy the party.'

Cassia turned to Jules. 'Sorry, I have to ask. Why on earth has Finn sent you over here?'

Jules hesitated, but she was put out by Cassia's question. Talk about making her feel unwelcome! She was loath to drop Finn in it about being too busy at work and, remembering his comment about Rocco, she latched on to that instead, her tone snippy. 'Well, to be honest, I think he's a bit concerned about Rocco. Or rather, you and Rocco.'

'Me and Rocco?' Cassia felt a surge of resentment towards Finn. He hadn't contacted her for days and now he had sent Jules – Jules! – to Sorrento instead of making the effort himself, using Rocco as some sort of excuse.

Jules shrugged, her attention already drifting. There were some exceptionally handsome men at the party and she couldn't wait to sample the food she could see on a heaving table nearby.

'It's not you he doesn't trust, it's Rocco,' she murmured, handing her suitcase to a member of the Disanti staff. 'Wow, this place is something else, isn't it? No wonder you're having such a great time.'

Cassia still felt affronted. What had Rocco done to make Finn suspicious of him? Feeling edgy, she wondered if Finn had seen how close they had been on the rooftop terrace in London. Perhaps he had seen more than he had let on, perhaps he had mistakenly assumed they had been about to kiss? But if Finn genuinely had concerns about her working with Rocco in Sorrento, why hadn't he spoken to her about them? Why had he sent Jules over to do his dirty work for him?

'By the way,' Jules said, turning back to Cassia for a second. 'You might not be able to get hold of Finn for a while because he said he's going to be tied up with some big case. He's also having problems with his phone.'

'Oh, really?' Cassia felt relieved that Finn was having problems with his phone; it explained the lack of contact. But the fact that he had mentioned to Jules that he was going to be too busy to talk was irritating to say the least.

Watching her sister's face, Jules was intrigued. 'Is there something going on with Rocco?' she asked slyly. 'Does Finn have reason to worry?'

'Absolutely not!' Cassia flushed. 'I'm marrying Finn in a few months' time; how can you even ask me that?'

'Keep your hair on, sis,' Jules snapped. 'I couldn't care less what you're up to.' Turning on her heel, she left Cassia gaping after her.

Cassia was shocked. First Finn was doubting her and now Jules. Accepting another glass of champagne, she realised she felt deeply uncomfortable about everything. Was it guilt because she'd had a few improper feelings about Rocco lately? Or was it simply frustration at Finn for not coming to Sorrento himself? As for sending Jules in his place . . .

Cassia watched her sister flirting outrageously with an attractive friend of Rocco's, laughing and clutching his arm. She was obviously over Dom, but Cassia knew what that meant. It meant that Jules would be on the lookout for someone to replace him because she wasn't a girl who enjoyed being single. Jules fell in love frequently, tending to think each relationship was more serious than the last, and even though Cassia knew Jules craved stability and loyalty rather than excitement, it also meant she tended to flit from one relationship to another. Knowing she would have to pick up the pieces if Jules fell for a hunky Italian and got rejected once more, as well as probably fielding sly questions about her friendship with Rocco, Cassia cursed Finn for not even consulting her about the visit. If he wasn't careful, he was going to turn into his mother, she thought uncharitably.

Deciding to do something totally out of character, something she knew Finn would heartily disapprove of, Cassia drained her glass of champagne and grabbed another one. Finn detested her drinking too much – he had told her so once when she had been tipsy at a party – so, childishly, she was going to indulge.

Glancing at Jules, Cassia wavered. Had Jules been sent to spy on her in more ways than one?

Wishing that Stefania wasn't stapled to Rocco's side so she could tell him everything Jules had said, Cassia threw caution to the wind and proceeded to get deliciously drunk. Unaware that Rocco was watching her intently, she chatted, she laughed and she danced delightedly when a band struck up at the end of the night. Throwing Rocco a lingering glance as she headed off to bed, Cassia fleetingly, drunkenly, thought about what it would feel like to tumble into bed with him.

Chapter Thirteen

Flashing the special pass that had been couriered over to him by Dom's coach, Finn headed inside an extremely busy Wimbledon and asked for directions to the players' lounge. Pausing to take in his surroundings for a moment, Finn soaked up the amazing atmosphere of Wimbledon in its second, rainless week – a rarity indeed. The pomp and ceremony it was famous for was very much in evidence; players were decked out in the all-white outfits that the All England Lawn Tennis Championships required and excitable ball boys and girls zipped past officials in blazers. Crowds were still gathered beneath the TV screens rigged up over Murray Mount, or whatever nickname the hill now bore.

Running a hand through his hair tiredly, Finn wondered what Jules was up to in Sorrento. Well, what Jules and Cassia were up to in Sorrento, he corrected himself. He had hoped to hear from Cassia after Jules's arrival but so far she hadn't sent so much as a one-line text. Was she pleased? Angry? He had no idea. He realised that Cassia was probably busy but he couldn't understand why she hadn't been in touch. He supposed he should have warned Cassia about Jules's visit before she set foot in Sorrento, and looking back he wasn't really sure why he hadn't done so. Cowardice, perhaps? Guilt at not making the effort to go to Italy himself? Finn sighed. Until he spoke to

Cassia, he wouldn't be able to figure out why she was treating him to a deafening silence. Jules, by contrast, had been in contact constantly, sending chatty texts about her stay at the Disanti villa, about the glamorous family and about how beautiful Sorrento was.

Finn showed his pass to several distinguished-looking officials in blazers and sharply pressed trousers, briefly wondering what would happen if someone caused a commotion at Wimbledon. They would probably just quietly eject the offender – with impeccable manners and dignity, naturally – before swiftly changing into another pristine blazer.

'Finn!' His suntanned face splitting into a grin, Dom appeared from the changing-room area. 'Well, what do you think?' He swept an arm extravagantly to encompass everything that was wonderful about Wimbledon.

'Really impressive.' Finn smiled, clapping his brother on the shoulder as they headed towards the lounge, which turned out to be as 'proper' as the rest of the venue. Trying not to gawp at the number one seed as he strolled past with an absolutely ravishing girl on his arm, Finn turned back to Dom. 'You've done exceptionally well. We're all really proud of you, even Mother.'

Dom's grin faded slightly. 'Goodness, even Mother. I really have made it.' He looked pensive. 'Mind you, if she finds out about that nightclub investment . . .'

Finn frowned. 'Don't tell me you've lost all your money?'

'There was a bit of an incident with a fire and also some dodgy money-laundering thing, apparently.' Dom rolled his shoulders carelessly. 'Hey, don't worry about it. Easy come, easy go. I'm making plenty of money right now, so I'll soon get it all sorted.' He glanced at Finn, wondering why his brother seemed so preoccupied. 'Everything all right, bro? Missing Cassia or something?'

Finn nodded vaguely. He did miss Cassia, but he was more concerned about how tense things were between them. The wedding wasn't too far off and they were barely speaking. He told Dom about sending Jules out to Sorrento, asking him what he thought of the idea.

Dom raised his eyebrows and ordered some drinks. 'What do I think? I think Cassia might be a bit pissed off, if I'm honest. She and Jules are hardly best pals, are they? When we were together, I got the impression Jules was really jealous of Cassia for some reason.'

Finn looked contrite. 'I didn't really take that into account too much. I suppose I was just trying to make things right with Cassia and I thought sending Jules might be better than nothing since I'm too busy at work.' He tried to appear unfazed as the famous pop star girlfriend of one of the players shimmied past him in leather shorts. 'Have you spoken to Jules since you split up?'

Dom turned away evasively. 'No. I know I should have called her after that thing at the party, but I just couldn't face all the accusations.'

'She didn't deserve that, Dom. I'm convinced she's not as bolshy as she appears.' A memory of Jules leaning across the table at the recent family barbecue shot into Finn's head and feeling hot under the collar, he pushed it away again.

'True. I think I misjudged her a bit, actually.' Dom sipped his mineral water. 'I did lead her on in the beginning, but I honestly didn't think she was going to take me so seriously. She's a paradox, or whatever the word is. She comes across as this party girl who's just out for fun, but she's the total opposite.'

Finn nodded, seemingly deep in thought. 'I hadn't realised she was that way inclined either. She's actually very sweet.'

Dom eyed him curiously. His brother seemed uncharacteristically concerned about Jules; he had only ever treated her as Cassia's superficial little sister before now. 'Well, thanks for coming, bro. Looks like I'm needed for some promotional stuff, so I'll shoot off now. I'm not sure when I'll be in touch again as it's all getting a bit crazy, but I'll definitely be there for the wedding, all right?'

'The wedding. Right, yes, of course.' Finn clapped him on the shoulder. 'Good luck, Dom. Keep playing the way you are and you'll do great. Centre court tickets if you make the finals, please.'

Dom laughed. 'Sure thing.' Leaving his mineral water practically untouched, he disappeared into the throng of players, commentators and breathlessly good-looking girls.

Finn sipped his beer. Dom's comment about being there for the wedding underlined how important it was to mend bridges with Cassia. Once things had calmed down at work and Cassia was back from Italy, he was sure everything would slot into place again.

Stretched out on a lounger by the Disanti pool in her bikini, enjoying the view of gorgeous Sorrento in the distance, Jules was feeling rather blissed out. The party she'd gatecrashed a few nights ago had been the most glamorous event she'd attended in a long time. The wine and champagne had flowed, the canapés and buffet had been exquisite – five-star cuisine at its best – and the dancing had gone on into the early hours. Even Cassia had been dancing, something she rarely did these days.

Jules sighed happily. She was deeply grateful to Finn for sending her here because the trip had come at just the right time. She had escaped from England and she was away from Dom, and she could hardly complain about her surroundings. Jules wasn't overly sure Cassia was pleased about her being here, but there wasn't much she could do about that.

Her sister had certainly landed on her feet with this secondment. It seemed more like a holiday than a work assignment; Rocco was so busy running his empire, Cassia was left to her own devices a lot of the time. Jules supposed she was looking into their father's family history whenever she could and the mere thought of it made her stomach tighten with rage.

Cassia certainly seemed different here in Italy, though, Jules mused, squashing down thoughts about her father. She seemed less uptight and happier, somehow; even her clothes were less conservative. In fact, Jules thought, nonplussed, she seemed more like her old self, the fun-loving girl without a care in the world, sparkling and upbeat. The total opposite to the terribly boring girl she had become of late, Jules thought bitchily, instantly regretting the thought. Still, the secondment wasn't meant to last much longer. Once the Vegas restaurant was opened, Cassia would go back to England and finalise all her wedding arrangements and presumably revert back to the more sensible girl she was at home.

'Ah, you've nicked the best spot. Never mind, I'll take this one.'

With a grin that revealed straight white teeth, Dino rolled up beside Jules. She guessed it was him from the Australian accent and she was glad of a chance to chat to him because he seemed so friendly. Throwing a towel on to the lounger next to her, Dino tore off his crumpled white T-shirt and hurled himself into the pool. For several seconds, he remained under the water, before bursting out and slicking his blond hair back, mirroring a number of ad campaigns he was famous for.

Jules sucked her breath in. Dino was very pretty and she could understand what Rocco's sister Aurelia saw in him. She giggled as he shook his hair out and showered her back with water, but she rearranged her features when she caught sight of Aurelia approaching. Looking fabulous in one of those cut-out swimsuits only the perfectly proportioned could get away with, Aurelia's expression was somewhat hostile. Jules, getting the idea that Aurelia was fearfully jealous and that it would be madness to get on the wrong side of her, gave the young girl a sunny smile to reassure her that she hadn't even noticed how gorgeous Dino was.

'Enjoying the weather?' Aurelia asked in English.

Jules nodded. 'It's glorious. Apparently it's lovely at home too, but it won't last.' She stretched her arms out, enjoying the warmth on her skin. 'I'm such a sun worshipper, I can't get enough of it.'

Aurelia didn't respond. She sat down on a lounger, hoisting a large folder on to her lap.

'Aurelia's stressing about the wedding again,' Dino commented, tugging a best-selling novel out of Aurelia's wicker bag. 'This looks saucy – right up my street.' He glanced at Aurelia as he flipped it open. 'Babe, I'm sure it will all be fine.'

Aurelia sulked. 'There is so much to do still.' She gave Jules a withering look. 'Don't you speak Italian?'

Jules shook her head. 'I leave that sort of thing to Cassia,' she said defensively. 'She was such a daddy's girl she didn't even need to take lessons.'

Aurelia and Dino exchanged a glance. Clearly there was bad blood between the two sisters – she remembered Cassia once mentioning that they weren't close – but Aurelia wasn't about to dig deeper and stir up trouble. She had too many of her own problems to get involved in Cassia and Jules's childhood squabbles. She leafed through her folder, feeling stressed. 'Anyway. I just wish everything was arranged for my wedding. It's in August.' She looked vexed. 'I'm so busy with my modelling contracts I can't cope with all these things. I'm due in Croatia at the weekend for some sports clothes shoot.'

Feeling a spark of excitement, Jules spotted a golden opportunity. What was the best way to suggest herself as wedding co-ordinator? The Disanti family were like Italian royalty, with Aurelia the reigning society princess. What a coup it would be to organise such a wedding, even if most of it had been finalised already; if she pulled it off, she could add it to her CV and

307

she'd be sure to get a job back in England afterwards. She had no idea if she would be able to stay in Italy until the end of August, but hopefully the Disanti family wouldn't mind putting her up at the villa for a bit longer if she was actually doing something other than sunbathing.

Would Finn mind? Jules hoped he wouldn't. Perhaps she should call him and ask first, but her gut told her that he would most likely support her anyway. He had been lovely to her since she'd split up with Dom, she thought affectionately. She really hadn't given Finn credit for being such a great guy; he'd always just been Cassia's nauseatingly perfect boy-friend and she hadn't bothered to get to know him too well on principle.

Putting aside her previous failures at event organising, Jules prepared to dazzle Aurelia with her qualifications and experience, loath to miss the window of opportunity she'd been presented with.

'I could help out with your wedding,' she offered in a casual tone. 'I don't know if my sister, Cassia, mentioned it but I worked as an events co-ordinator in England. I've organised many weddings in the past. Not as grand as yours, of course,' she added hurriedly.

'Really?' Aurelia looked surprised. 'I had no idea.'

Thanks, sis, Jules thought crossly, conveniently forgetting that Cassia had had no real reason to extol her virtues as an events co-ordinator.

'Oh yes, and weddings are my speciality,' she explained with airy indifference. 'Especially large, celebrity-style ones.' Omitting to flag her recent sackings or that the biggest wedding she had overseen had totalled sixty guests and had been an unmitigated disaster, Jules smiled blithely.

Aurelia hesitated. It would be a godsend if an experienced co-ordinator could step in and take away the headache that was her enormous wedding. As long as Jules didn't impose her opinions or tell her she couldn't have something she wanted, Aurelia couldn't see a problem. In fact, even though she didn't know Jules very well, she was sorely tempted.

'How many weddings have you co-ordinated?' Aurelia asked, feeling the need to check Jules's credentials. After all, her wedding promised to be one of the best in Italy; her co-ordinator needed to be an expert at diplomacy and persuasion and possess the organisational skills of a prime minister's PA.

'Oh, hundreds,' Jules assured her, sitting up and clutching her bikini top to her chest. 'Seriously, this is what I'm good at; well, what I'm *great* at,' she corrected herself.

Aurelia's eyes flitted to Dino, who shrugged his agreement. As far as he was concerned, anything that would calm Aurelia down had to be a good thing and if Cassia's sister was as efficient as she made out, what could go wrong?

With great ceremony, Aurelia handed over her prized folder to Jules. 'Don't let me down,' she stated with the utmost seriousness. 'This has to be the wedding of the century and nothing, and I mean *nothing*, can go wrong.'

Jules felt apprehensive but she was confident she could pull this off. The mishaps that had occurred at work before had been bad luck, nothing more. 'It will be spectacular,' she assured Aurelia.

Aurelia beamed. 'I feel more relaxed already.' She sighed, leaning back on her lounger.

'Hooray to that,' Dino said, leaning over to kiss her. 'Come here; that novel has made me horny . . .' Aurelia shrieked and slapped his hand away unconvincingly.

Jules flicked through Aurelia's folder. It was scarily detailed and the 'to do' list was far larger than she had expected, especially since the wedding was so close. Final payments needed to be made on the venue, guest lists needed to be finalised and there were countless small but no doubt highly significant details to tie up.

Jules knew she was going to have to work harder than she ever had in her life before to make sure she could tick off all the items on the list before the wedding day. But this was the career opportunity of a lifetime and she was going to make damned sure she didn't mess it up.

Wondering what Cassia would make of the latest turn of events, Jules sent Finn a breezy text to update him. She was taken aback to receive one back from him almost immediately, telling her he was delighted for her and asking her if she wouldn't mind reminding Cassia to call him.

Jules agreed to do so, but as soon as she delved into Aurelia's wedding folder again, she forgot all about it as acute panic set in.

'I think this cucumber salad will be most suitable as a starter, don't you, Henry?' Delicately laying down her fork, Grace turned to Henry, tutting at his pained expression. 'It's so light and refreshing, the champagne dressing is the ideal accompaniment.'

The wedding co-ordinator preened. 'I'm so glad you approve. I'll bring you some other options to try.'

Waiting until the wedding co-ordinator had left the room, Henry grimaced.

'Style over substance,' he observed, picking at the long slivers of pale green cucumber which were covered in a froth of bubbles. 'I can't imagine Finn and Cassia wanting something as pretentious as this, Gracie.' He let out a disgruntled burp. 'And cucumber always gives me wind.'

Grace shuddered. 'Henry, it's haute cuisine. And very appropriate for my guest list.'

Henry wrinkled his freckled nose worriedly. 'The thing is, Gracie, it's not your wedding, is it? It's Finn and Cassia's and who cares what the Honourable Lady Whatsit might fancy?'

Grace flushed. She really wished Henry could be more supportive. He'd always had a soft spot for Cassia, but whilst she was swanning around in Italy, Grace expected him to take her side. 'Someone has to make some decisions. Poor Finn is so busy at work, but Cassia really should pay more attention to my text messages. And to Finn, while we're on the subject.'

Henry sighed. 'Not everyone can be the perfect housewife, Gracie. Cassia has her career and she loves it. Besides, you know how she feels about her father. She's so excited about that historian fellow Rocco's family know. And just because neither of them are here doesn't mean we should pick a starter they wouldn't choose in a million years, darling. That's all I'm saying.'

Grace sniffed. 'Perhaps they should postpone the wedding.'

Henry looked appalled. About to disagree, he looked up to see Finn arriving hot on the tails of another starter option.

A newly acquired phone in one hand and a briefcase in the other, Finn sat down, tearing off his tie. He'd obviously come from a late meeting and he looked gaunt.

'Bad morning,' he explained. 'Spent it trying to unpick a case we lost at Lovetts and Rose two years ago. Not my doing, but it doesn't look good for the firm.'

'Sounds stressful, my boy. Here, taste some of this.' Henry grabbed a plate of chicken livers that were oozing with butter and accompanied by crisp bacon slices and slivers of prune.

'Mmm, delicious. This is a winner for me.' Finn munched on the livers, distracted. He'd heard some disturbing news about Dom on the grapevine that morning, a whisper of scandal he didn't dare mention to his parents until it had been confirmed. Carlton, Dom's coach, was refusing to take his calls, which didn't bode well, but knowing his parents would be devastated if the gossip was true, Finn was praying it was all a storm in a teacup.

Henry winked at him. 'Your mother has her eye on a cucumber thingy with a fizzy dressing.'

Finn rubbed his eyes. He sensed a fight on his hands if he didn't agree and he honestly didn't have the energy. 'Look, whatever you think best. I know Cassia would prefer the livers, but I don't think she'll mind too much.' He sighed, knowing she probably would, but frankly, he was a bit fed up with all the wedding stress. And Finn wished Cassia would just hurry up and come home; the longer she stayed away, the more resentful he felt.

Grace smirked and made a note on her page. Henry grumbled to himself. Finn must be seriously under pressure at work to agree so readily to such a snobby starter; he was one of life's easy-going types but normally he would be far more opinionated.

'How is Jules getting on?' Grace asked, more interested in hearing about that than anything Cassia might be up to.

Finn brightened. 'She's having a wonderful time. She's offered to co-ordinate Aurelia Disanti's wedding and she's throwing herself into everything.'

Henry gaped. 'Aurelia Disanti's wedding? That's not advisable, is it?'

Finn laughed. 'I know. I didn't have the heart to put her off because she sounded so thrilled about the whole thing.' He looked sombre for a moment. 'I haven't really heard from Cassia too much. I can only imagine she's exceptionally busy with the Vegas opening. It's supposed to be happening soon, I think, and then she'll be back where she belongs.'

Grace plastered an expression of kindly concern on her face. 'Well, that's as maybe, but I had a thought I wanted to discuss with you.' Ignoring Henry's warning glance, she pushed ahead. 'It's just an idea, but I wondered if you might consider cancelling the wedding. Or just postponing it perhaps.'

About to sample a vegetarian terrine, just because he was famished, Finn faltered, aghast. 'Why on earth would we do that?'

'Just to . . . well, to buy yourselves a little more time. To . . . to make sure you're doing the right thing.' Grace was shaken by the vehemence of Finn's tone. She hadn't expected him to overreact.

'Of course we're doing the right thing!' Finn was stunned that his mother would dare to suggest postponing the wedding, but he couldn't help feeling a flicker of doubt curling in his stomach about Cassia. Did she still want to go ahead with the wedding? After the awful weekend they'd shared a couple of weeks back, he was at a loss as to how things had fallen apart so badly afterwards. He felt as strongly about her as he always had – at least, he thought he did. It was so difficult when she was miles away and when they had barely exchanged a text since she'd returned to Italy.

Finn turned to his mother defiantly. 'We're going ahead with the wedding and that's the end of it,' he told her, despite his own misgivings. He was concerned he had missed something in a major case at work and he couldn't bring himself to think about anything more complicated, especially not when it involved emotions and feelings. 'Now, let's get on with the main courses. What do you fancy, Father?'

Henry grunted. 'Some sort of stuffed meat, but who's going to listen to me?'

'No one, if you're going to make silly suggestions,' Grace said dismissively. She turned to Finn, proffering a menu with neat pencil marks scribbled all over it. 'I was thinking along the lines of this wonderful poached salmon with a caviar dressing . . .'

Henry regarded Finn across the table. He could see his dessert plans for a chocolate fondant with hot cherry sauce going out of the window, but more importantly, he was beginning to think his son had given up on his wedding completely.

*

A few days later, almost suffocating under the strain of his workload, Rocco gazed outside at the sweltering sunshine. He was longing to cut loose and relieve his tension, but he wasn't sure he could spare the time. Stefania had headed back to Rome in a sulk, unhappy about returning to work but having no choice in the matter. She had used up most of her holiday entitlement already and although she was clearly loath to leave him, her PR company back in Rome would begin to suffer.

It seemed that both of them had been thinking about Cassia, Rocco thought with a frown. Stefania out of jealousy and him, well, why exactly did he keep thinking about her? He was fascinated by her, attracted – definitely – but it was more than that and he knew it. Rocco thought back to the party at the villa a few days ago. Cassia had looked so desirable in her dress and having loosened up after a couple of glasses of champagne, she had sparkled and charmed everyone. Later, she had danced with such freedom and wildness it had been all he could do to stand by watching, rather than scooping her up in his arms, regardless of Stefania looking on with hawk-like intensity.

Rocco looked up to find his grandmother watching him anxiously.

'Take some time off,' she urged. 'And yes, I know you can't spare even a second, but you're going to crash and burn if you don't step away from this place.'

'Where would I go?' Rocco studied a spreadsheet, still baffled by the financial deficit he had spotted. He simply could not figure out where the huge withdrawal had gone to, or who had taken the money.

'To Rome.'

'Rome?' Rocco looked up incredulously. 'I've spent quite enough time with Stefania, thank you.'

Sofia took a seat. 'Not to see Stefania, to take Cassia to see Luca. You know how desperate she is to look into her family background and she should be off home shortly.' She shrugged, as if it had only just occurred to her. 'And you could have a look at that restaurant Stefania wants you to open – make a decision about it. Whatever you decide, it would be one more thing off your list.'

Rocco looked up from his spreadsheet. 'I could kill for a ride on my bike,' he confessed. Should he really be spending even more time with Cassia? Aside from the fact that being around her seemed to mess with his head, what would Stefania say if she found out?

'Think about it,' Sofia said, seeing that Rocco was grappling with himself. 'By the way, did Allesandro send over those wines you requested?'

Rocco nodded, gesturing to some crates behind his desk. 'I tasted one of them. It's superb. I think we can do business with him.'

Sofia looked pleased. 'That's wonderful. For the restaurant, I mean. I can contact him, if you like.' She looked faintly embarrassed. 'To take it off your hands.'

'Thank you, that would be very helpful.' Rocco sat back and glanced thoughtfully after his grandmother. She was acting strangely at the moment, but maybe he was just being fanciful. After all, he also thought that Raff was behaving weirdly. He kept disappearing without explanation and he could never be reached on the phone. It was almost as if he had ducked out of the family, as if he was involved in something else. Rocco fleetingly wondered if the recent spate of bad luck at the restaurant had anything to do with Raffaelo, before dismissing it out of hand. That was absurd.

Rocco thought about Rome and made a decision. Chucking the mismatched spreadsheets into his desk drawer to be looked at when he had a clearer head, Rocco headed out to the vast garages behind the villa to dust off his motorbike.

*

Feeling very virtuous after sending two columns off to Gena as a result of purposefully avoiding both Rocco and Jules over the past few days, Cassia headed down to the kitchen in search of a cold drink. It was six o'clock in the evening and roughly forty degrees in the shade outside, but as much as she would love to dive into the cool, clear water of the Disanti swimming pool, she knew Jules had staked her claim on a lounger hours ago. Not only that, it appeared that she was now best pals with Aurelia and Dino, if them all laughing together and mucking about in the pool was any indication.

Feeling out of sorts, Cassia pushed her hair out of her eyes. Since Jules had arrived, she had felt like a prisoner on the Disanti estate, as though she was the one who needed to tiptoe around on eggshells rather than the other way round. Cassia wished things weren't so strained between herself and Jules, especially now that they were at the Disanti villa together, because it was making things extremely awkward. Jules wasn't being anti-social as such, but she wasn't exactly making an effort to make friends either. Cassia checked her phone again. She couldn't understand why she hadn't heard from Finn for days now and she vaguely remembered Jules saying something about him getting a new number. Her annoyance towards Finn over Jules's visit had abated – she knew he had meant well – but she would feel much better if he got in touch so they could talk about it.

In fact, why on earth hadn't he called her before Jules arrived? Who did he think he was? Cassia felt frustrated all over again, particularly when she remembered the reason. He was concerned about Rocco, he thought something was going on. How ridiculous. She had talked it over with her mother who, uncharacteristically calm, had suggested reasonably that Finn was simply feeling insecure with her being so far away and that Cassia should give him the benefit of the doubt.

'Any of that lovely Vermentino around, Antonio?' she asked.

He nodded and went off to find some from the chiller cabinet.

Cassia turned to find Aurelia at her side, looking fabulous in very short shorts and a khaki-coloured halter-neck top.

'Wonderful wine,' Aurelia informed Cassia, shaking her dark curls out. 'It's from that wine merchant, Allesandro . . . whatever his name is.' She gave Cassia a sly glance. 'Or do you only drink champagne?'

Cassia blushed. 'Oh dear. Was I terribly badly behaved at the party? I don't usually drink that much.' She recalled the crashing hangover she'd experienced the following morning. 'I'm very out of practice these days.'

Aurelia grinned. 'So I noticed. But no, you were great fun. Less . . . reserved.' She silently tutted at Cassia's drab dress. Since her sensational party outfit, she appeared to have reverted back to her usual unadventurous clothes.

By 'reserved', Cassia knew Aurelia meant 'boring' and she flinched. She and Jules had far more in common than they realised, she thought defensively. She knew Finn would probably have disapproved if he had witnessed her behaviour at the party; she had well and truly let her hair down and she hadn't done that in a long time.

Aurelia looked puzzled. 'Why are you looking like that? I wasn't being rude; I was saying that I think you should do that more often. You know, let go a bit.'

'That's all right. I'm a bit touchy about everything at the moment. I . . . I seem to have become a bit of a stick-in-the-mud and I'm not quite sure when it happened.'

'Is it your fiancé, do you think?' Aurelia helped herself to a glass of the fantastic Vermentino and splashed some into a glass for Cassia.

Cassia accepted the glass. 'I haven't a clue. I don't think so . . . I think it's just something that happened when I was younger and then when I met Finn, I calmed down completely.' She bit her lip, not wanting to talk about her issues with Jules.

Aurelia was reading Alessandro's surname on the bottle. 'Raldini. Is that a really old name or something? It reminds me of something . . . no, it's gone. I think he might fancy my grandmother.' She shuddered. 'Isn't it gross? My grandmother is far too old for another relationship.'

'Too old?' Cassia echoed. 'That's so sad. Isn't she allowed to be happy again?'

Aurelia stared at her, not sure how to respond. 'Changing the subject, I've hired your sister. To organise my wedding.'

Alarmed, Cassia's mouth fell open. Jules, organising Aurelia's high-profile, celebrity-studded nuptials in Capri? She couldn't think of anything more inappropriate, not with Jules's track record. What on earth was Jules playing at? Guessing she was desperate to curry favour with Aurelia and perhaps add the glamorous wedding to her CV, Cassia wasn't sure she should intervene. But Aurelia would be devastated if her wedding was ruined, so she had to do something. The trouble was, what? If she told the truth about Jules, she would drop her sister in it completely and scare the hell out of Aurelia in the process. Cassia decided to tactfully put Aurelia on her guard.

'Jules is . . . well, she's . . . weddings aren't really her speciality.' She thought it best not to draw attention to the fact that the last wedding Jules had organised had resulted in a punch-up between two girls who had both been exes of the groom.

Aurelia looked worried. 'Really? She gave me to understand something of this size was very straightforward. Should I be concerned?' She bit her fingernails, the gesture childish. 'I'm about to fly her over to Capri to see my venue. I won't bother if she's lied to me.'

Cassia shook her head. 'Please don't be anxious. Just . . . just make sure Jules knows how critical all the tiny details are.'

Aurelia looked visibly relieved. 'I will.' She gave Cassia a sideways glance. 'You and Jules . . . there is some jealousy there, yes?'

Cassia stiffened. What had Jules been saying? 'No, I'm not remotely jealous of Jules,' she told Aurelia evenly. 'She's my sister and we're like . . . chalk and cheese.' Cassia said this last bit in English, her Italian failing her at that point. 'But I love her and no one defends her more than I do. So, no, I don't envy her, even though I'm sure you think I should.' Her dark eyes flashing, she put down her glass of wine and left the kitchen.

Aurelia was flummoxed. She realised Cassia had got the wrong end of the stick; she meant that she had the distinct impression the other day that Jules was envious of Cassia, not the other way round.

Cassia stalked past the villa and out towards the edge of the estate. She found herself in the middle of the lush lemon groves behind the restaurant and she paused, taking in the view. She had seen many a terrace in central Sorrento covered with decorative lemon trees but here, the fragrance was strong and distinctive, even though only a few small lemons remained. The *verdelli*, the green variety, had just been harvested so the terraced grove was fairly empty and covered with matting. It was reminiscent of many a painting of the local region, where an abundance of yellow, oval-shaped fruits, dazzlingly bright against the deep green foliage, hung over pretty walled gardens.

'Beautiful, aren't they?' Rocco said, emerging from a cluster of trees.

Cassia started. 'Er, yes. They're amazing.' What on earth was Rocco doing, loitering in a lemon grove?

He plucked a small lemon from a branch, the stalk and leaves still attached. He tore the lemon open, releasing its citrusy aroma. 'The bright yellow ones are at their best in March. They are known as Femminello.' He offered her a hunk of skin. 'The skins are soaked in alcohol and sugar to make Limoncello and they're packed with essential oils. They're not too tart, which makes them perfect for cooking.'

'What are those funny mats?' Cassia asked, nibbling on the lemon skin and feeling more relaxed than she had in days.

'They're to protect the lemons against the saltiness in the air,' he explained. 'It delays the ripening.'

Wearing a pale grey shirt with the sleeves rolled back and casual trousers, Rocco looked immaculate, apart from his hands, which were stained with oil.

'I was just tinkering with my motorbike,' he provided. 'I haven't touched it for months but I've been thinking of taking it out for a spin.'

'Anywhere nice?' Cassia tried to get a glimpse of the bike but it was obviously tucked away behind the garage doors.

'Rome, actually.' Rocco turned to her. 'Fancy joining me? I'm thinking of checking out the venue Stefania has located for a restaurant and we could visit Luca too.'

Cassia paused. She wasn't sure she should spend time with Rocco – at least, not in a non-professional capacity – and she didn't imagine Finn would be pleased if he was concerned about their relationship in some way. But she couldn't pass up the chance to meet up with this Luca they had told her so much about.

'Count me in. When shall we go?'

'Can you be ready at eight a.m. tomorrow?'

Cassia blinked at him.

'No time like the present and if we don't do it immediately, I'll change my mind and remember how much work is sitting on my desk.' Rocco glanced at his watch. 'Speaking of which, I'd better get back.' He wanted to look at the account discrepancy one more time before they left.

Feeling excited about the thought of meeting Luca and finally getting to the bottom of her father's background, Cassia headed back towards the villa. Stopping, she caught sight of a shadowy figure standing at the edge of the Disanti estate. The man seemed to have found the only spot of shade at the edge of the driveway and he was staring up at the house as if fixated.

Cassia felt a shiver down her spine. Who was he? And what was he looking at so intently? Almost as if he had felt her scrutiny, the man disappeared, melting out of view like an apparition. Wondering if she should mention it to Rocco in the morning, Cassia realised she'd better get hold of Finn before she left for Rome otherwise Jules might tell him about the trip and it would sound far worse.

Chapter Fourteen

Diana stared back at her lover, agony in her eyes. Cowering as she covered her half-naked body with her hands, she pleaded with him not to leave but he wouldn't listen. Pushing her away roughly, he turned away from her as if she disgusted him. Grabbing his hand, Diana fell to her knees, tears sliding down her face.

'Please don't leave me,' she whispered, terror imbued in every shaky word.

Spinning back to face her, he shook her hand off. 'I don't love you any more. There's nothing else to say.'

Diana's head whipped from side to side. 'Don't,' she choked. 'It hurts . . . I can't bear it . . .' She cradled his hand to her face, kissing it all over. With a deliberately cruel gesture, he used his thumb to smear her red lipstick across her face.

Humiliated, Diana flinched and let out a strangled gasp.

'Kyle . . . please . . . don't do this to me,' she managed, before collapsing in a heap on the floor.

'Forget about me, Clarissa,' he hissed. 'Forget about me the way I've forgotten about you.'

Looking utterly crucified, Diana lifted her head from the floor as she watched him leave. Letting out a bloodcurdling howl, her face contorted with pain, she curled her hands into fists.

There was a moment's silence, before the rest of the cast

burst into appreciative applause. 'Wonderful, Diana, just . . . wonderful.' The director helped her to her feet, covering her modesty with his arm. Nodding at an assistant, he made sure a robe was thrown around her shoulders within seconds.

'Thank you.' Diana shrugged her arms into the robe and knotted the cord around her waist, secure once more. 'Are you sure it was all right?'

Ross smiled. 'It was more than all right, it was magical.' He squeezed her shoulder. 'I know that must have been hard for you . . . very exposing.'

She nodded. She had never felt more vulnerable in her life.

'But the desperation in your eyes was simply heartbreaking. You've captured Clarissa's unhinged frailty to a T.' He checked the script. 'I can't wait to rehearse the scenes where Clarissa completely loses it tomorrow. I know you're going to be incredible, Diana. I might just do a brief lighting check in a few minutes, if that's all right?'

A make-up artist handed Diana a wipe for her face. 'That scene was mesmerising,' she said admiringly. 'And so brave.'

Doing her best not to show how dazed she felt inside, Diana rubbed her face gratefully, removing the greasy smear of lipstick. 'That's very kind of you.'

'She's not being kind,' Ross insisted, gesturing for the lights to be dimmed. 'You're going to show everyone what a great actress you are. Just you wait and see.' He buried his head in the script while the lighting crew set everything up.

The actor playing the part of Kyle, a tall, chiselled guy called Robson, came over and kissed her cheek. 'I wasn't too rough, was I? With the lipstick thing? I just wanted to make sure it looked realistic.'

Diana shook her head. 'It was perfect, Rob. Really. Absolutely mortifying, but you must do it that way every night.' Retreating, she took a seat in the theatre, hiding her shaking hands in her lap.

She was doing the right thing, she was sure of it. Taking on *Jealousy* had been a bold move, a risk for any actress her age. She had been instructed to put on weight and she had done so, gorging on chocolate and fattening pastries for the first time in her life. Diana wasn't sure how she felt about her new, softly rounded body. She wouldn't describe it as plump, exactly, but she was fleshier all over, with more shapely thighs and hips and a waist that made her sleek clothes strain at the seams.

Diana wasn't used to having curves; she had spent her entire life on a diet which allowed her to wear practically anything she liked, especially when it came to designer clothes that were often made for size zeros. She supposed this was a more natural figure for her. It resembled Cassia's in many ways and Diana realised her strict eating regime had probably stopped her from having the figure she had been born to.

She had breasts, something that was taking a lot of getting used to – and by God, they were difficult to squeeze into some of her dresses! Diana supposed it was rather fun in some ways to have a cleavage; it reminded her of when she'd been pregnant with Cassia. And Jules, she added, her face twisting at the memory. What a terrible time that had been, full of recrimination and pain. Diana felt nauseous, but she pushed the horrible thoughts away, knowing she had spent far too long blaming herself for her stupidity. She noticed a good luck text from Angelo on her mobile phone and her heart melted a fraction. He was adorable, she thought, sending him a gracious thank you. They weren't back together; Diana needed to focus on her career. But they had maintained a rather sweet friendship, something Diana had been touched by. Expecting the break-up to be messy and bitter, she had been impressed by Angelo's maturity – the one thing she had accused him of lacking. She missed him greatly, but she couldn't be with him. This play was taking up all of her energy and Diana knew she owed it to herself to immerse herself fully in Clarissa.

Diana wondered how Jules and Cassia were getting on in Sorrento. She knew from her recent phone calls with Cassia that her eldest daughter had been dismayed to see her sister arriving out of the blue. And as much as Diana thought the world of Finn, she couldn't help wondering if he'd lost his mind. Sending Jules to Sorrento had been an act of madness, probably the one thing that was guaranteed to unnerve Cassia and make her feel even crosser with him than she already did.

'Shall we do that lighting check?' Diana asked brightly, stepping back into the throng of people. Her hands rested on the knotted cord of her robe. 'I guess I can cope with stripping off again.' She was going to have to; soon she would be baring all in front of a theatre full of people each night, some of them most likely baying for her blood and poised to criticise.

Be proud of me, Marco, she pleaded silently, slipping off her robe. Be proud and maybe then I can finally be free.

Stuffing clothes haphazardly into a holdall at the crack of dawn in preparation for the trip to Rome, Cassia hoped jeans, a white T-shirt and a beige linen jacket were appropriate attire. She knew the jacket would be hopelessly crumpled by the time she arrived in Rome, but she wanted to look smart and professional on this trip.

It was a work thing, after all, Cassia reminded herself. Gena had suggested writing her column from Rome, plus a feature about typical Roman food. Besides which, Rocco would surely be meeting up with Stefania as soon as he'd introduced her to Luca, his historian friend. She jumped when her mobile started whirling on her bedside table. Snatching it up, Cassia frowned when she saw a number she didn't recognise, but she answered it anyway. Seconds later, she was glad she had.

'Finn? Finn, is that you?' Forgetting how cross she was with him, Cassia broke into a smile. 'I can't believe it's finally you!'

'Finally me?'

Cassia was mystified by his edgy tone. 'Yes, I've been trying to . . . oh, look, it doesn't matter. How are you?'

'I'm fine . . . busy, but fine. You?'

He sounded distant. Cassia sat down on the edge of her bed. 'I'm all right. Just off to Rome, actually. With Rocco. A business trip, obviously.'

'Right. Sounds more like a jolly to me.'

Cassia recoiled. What on earth was the matter with him? 'Have you changed your number?' she asked, loath to question him about his mood.

Finn let out an impatient sound. 'Yes, didn't Jules tell you? I sent my number on to her and asked her to get you to call me.' Cassia was confused. Jules hadn't told her any such thing. Knowing her sister, Cassia guessed she was caught up in Aurelia's wedding arrangements and Finn's messages had fallen by the wayside.

'There seems to have been some sort of mix-up. Never mind, it's great to hear your voice.'

'Thanks. You too.' Finn was aware that he sounded rather formal, but they hadn't spoken for weeks now and he felt rather disconnected from her. 'Listen, about sending Jules over in my place, I've been so busy at work, I thought you might welcome a familiar face.'

Cassia sat down on her bed. 'I would have preferred yours,' she said softly, wishing she could tell him everything face to face. 'It's just that . . . I have told you that me and Jules aren't close. She's not my biggest fan, to put it mildly.'

Finn cleared his throat. 'Yes, well. I'm afraid I'm drowning in work at the moment so I can't join you just yet. Actually, I thought you were due back any day soon.'

'I'm just waiting to hear what's happening with the Vegas restaurant,' she said, feeling her hackles rising. Finn's tone was so accusatory, she couldn't help but feel defensive. 'As soon as I know, I'll call you with a firm date.'

'Good. The wedding isn't that far away, you know.' Finn knew he must sound moody, but he hadn't expected Cassia to be annoyed with him about the Jules thing.

'I'm well aware of that, Finn,' she snapped. Cassia couldn't understand why Finn hadn't apologised more and why he seemed so crabby. He didn't even seem to realise it would be hard for her to have Jules around. Hadn't he ever listened to her when she'd told him how resentful Jules had always been? Snatching the beautiful red dress she'd worn to her engagement party out of her wardrobe mindlessly, Cassia stuffed it into her bag. Was he changing in her absence? He wasn't usually so high-handed or so insensitive – at least, she didn't think he was. She was truly beginning to doubt that she even knew him right now.

'I've sorted the food for the wedding breakfast,' Finn said, more to fill the silence than anything else. He didn't elaborate, assuming that Cassia would fume if she knew he'd been talked into a pretentious menu by his mother.

Cassia sighed. 'Do I even want to know what's on the menu, Finn?'

'Er, probably not. I was kind of railroaded . . . Look, it will be fine.' He let out a short laugh. 'We're lucky we haven't postponed the whole thing. Mother suggested it, but of course I told her not to be absurd.'

'Your mother suggested what?' Cassia's tone was shrill and Finn could have bitten his tongue off. Why on earth had he said that?

'I'm sure she was only joking,' he said quickly. 'And there's absolutely no question of it. Unless you want to?'

'No!' Cassia was in shock. Was he saying he agreed with his mother?

At that point, Finn saw a colleague approaching him with a finger on his watch to indicate that their ridiculously early meeting was about to start. Relieved, he nodded and collected up some paperwork.

'I have to go, Cass. Talk later, maybe.'

'Er, all right, but I think there are things we need to . . .' Cassia stared at the phone dumbfounded. He'd hung up on her. Finn had actually hung up on her. In the whole eight years they'd been together, he'd never put the phone down during a conversation. She had never felt more sidelined and unappreciated in her life.

'Ready?' Rocco stuck his head round her open door. Wearing jeans and a soft, brown leather jacket that matched his hair, Rocco looked rather more dashing than he should do at seven o'clock in the morning.

Glancing at her badly packed luggage, she stuffed a few remaining items in, zipped up the bag and nodded, trying to forget about the call with Finn. 'Yes, I'm ready.' Sweeping past him moodily, Cassia faltered, realising she didn't know where he had parked his motorbike.

'Shall I lead the way?' he asked with a smile. Once they were downstairs, he headed out to the front of the villa where his bike was waiting on the driveway. His luggage was already strapped to the back and he added her bag to his and secured it with leather straps.

'We're taking the motorway,' he explained as he put his sunglasses on. 'The road from Sorrento to Amalfi is terrible, it's far quicker to take the north coast road towards Pompeii. Rome is about one hundred and seventy miles away as it is.'

Cassia eyed the motorbike, feeling fearful and excited at the same time. She had no idea about bikes, but Rocco's was a large, stylish contraption. A Ducati Diavel, according to the name discreetly emblazoned on the side, a sleek, black machine with a touch of glossy ruby-red here and there.

'Won't you be hot in that?' She gestured to Rocco's jacket.

He shook his head. 'No. It can be chilly once we pick up some speed. You might be cold in that. Let me know if you are, although it's very sunny today.'

Handing her a helmet, Rocco jammed his on and climbed on to the bike. Nodding for her to join him, he pulled her arms around his waist and set off. About to indignantly tell him she had no need to wrap herself around him in such a familiar fashion, Cassia shut her mouth and concentrated on not falling off the bike. It zipped in and out of the traffic at an alarming but invigorating rate and as much as she wanted to be independent and not cling to him like some girly limpet, it was impossible to safely let go. His aftershave tickled her nostrils and her face was crushed against the soft leather of his jacket. Cassia experienced a thrilling rush of adrenalin as Rocco leant the bike this way and that on the high-speed motorway and she wondered how she had gone through life without ever going on a motorbike before. Due to the speed the bike was travelling and the wind rushing past their helmets, there was no chance to talk, but Cassia had no wish to bore Rocco with tedious tales of Finn and Grace, even though she could happily vent about the situation for hours. Inside, she felt nervous. How could she and Finn survive a marriage if a few months apart were driving such an enormous wedge between them? Just for a second, it had sounded as though he was having second thoughts about the wedding, that his mother's suggestion of postponing hadn't been such a hideous idea.

Conscious of Rocco's hard, flat stomach beneath her fingertips as the bike undulated and wove around cars and other bikes, Cassia wondered what Finn would think if he could see her sitting astride a throbbing bike, groin to buttock, with her arms wrapped round the taut torso of a man she barely knew.

Before she knew it, they were leaving the motorway and Rocco was heading confidently into the city centre. It was incredibly warm; the air was deliciously hazy and there wasn't a cloud in the sky. Rome was busy, its streets full of locals and tourists alike, and it oozed style with its glamorous boutiques, upmarket ice-cream parlours and grand restaurants.

Pulling up outside a glamorous-looking café in the Tridente area, not far from the Spanish Steps, Rocco parked the bike and let her off, swinging his leg over the bike to dismount. Cassia's legs felt wobbly when she stood up and her hands still felt warm from clasping Rocco's body. She turned away as he tore off his helmet and ran a hand over his dark hair.

Cassia studied the café they were about to enter. The front window was filled with pastries and bread, and the interior – glossy red walls and banquettes – looked like something from a bygone era. Tables were dotted around outside on the cobbled streets, arranged in artistic lines, with chattering Italians in sunglasses watching the world go by and looking fabulously stylish as they did so. She glanced at Rocco, noting that in his slightly battered leather jacket and jeans, he was the epitome of sexy Italian elegance. He grinned like a schoolboy who'd been let out of lessons early.

'Wasn't that incredible?' he said, taking off his sunglasses. He fixed his eyes on hers as if gauging her reaction. 'You can't beat the buzz of a motorbike, can you? I always say it's like . . . falling in love. That first, stomach-dropping feeling of lust and anticipation.'

Disturbed by his analogy, Cassia removed her helmet, assuming her hair probably looked hopelessly dishevelled. She raked her fingers through it then gave up. 'Er . . . yes. It was pretty . . . exhilarating.'

'Exhilarating. Exactly.' Rocco straightened. 'I could do with a coffee. Shall we?'

Cassia followed him to a table outside the café. The owner, a rotund man with a fine head of dark, wavy hair, approached, about to tell them the table was reserved for special customers only. Recognising Rocco, he kissed him effusively on the cheeks.

'Rocco! It's been a long time. Sit down, sit down. I'll bring your usual. And for the lady?' He eyed Cassia appreciatively and nodded when she asked for a caffè Americano with plenty of extra hot water.

'Friend of yours?' Cassia took a seat opposite the tourist-swamped Spanish Steps.

'I did some of my cooking training here,' Rocco explained. 'The place is teeming with chefs. My grandfather had many friends here too.' When his *cafferisetto* arrived, he inhaled it with intense pleasure. 'Aaah, I've missed this. No one makes it the way they do here.'

'Isn't that just coffee essence and not much else?'

Rocco laughed. 'I guess so. An acquired taste, but if you love coffee as much as I do, it's like elixir.' He relaxed in his seat, his eyes running over her. 'So, why the bad mood earlier?'

Cassia stirred her coffee. 'A row with Finn. Very boring, actually.' She waved a hand uncomfortably. 'You don't want to know.'

'Try me. What happened?'

Rocco studied Cassia as she fiddled with her coffee cup. Her dark hair was sexily tousled from the helmet but apart from quickly combing it away from her face with her fingers, she seemed unconcerned. Rocco liked that; he was so used to Stefania's high maintenance and her obsession with how perfect her make-up was or what state her hair was in, he found Cassia's laid-back nature and natural beauty refreshing.

Cassia was unnerved by Rocco's intent gaze but she did her best to appear unruffled. 'Just . . . the wedding seems to be veering off in a direction I'm not happy with. And Finn's mother suggested postponing the whole thing.'

Rocco raised his eyebrows. 'She really does seem to want to drive a wedge between you, doesn't she? But Finn, he doesn't agree, I'm sure.'

'Doesn't he?' Cassia's mouth twisted wryly. 'I haven't a clue what he thinks, to be honest.' It was true; suddenly, Finn seemed like a stranger.

Guessing she didn't want to talk about Finn any more, Rocco changed the subject. 'So, have you spoken to your sister much since she arrived in Italy?' He sat back in his chair, loath to admit to himself how much he was enjoying her company.

Cassia sipped her coffee. 'Sadly not. As I said, we're not close. Not any more. It's . . . complicated.'

'How so?'

Cassia's dark eyes clouded over. 'That's the thing. I haven't a clue. We were great friends when we were younger but something happened to Jules when she was in her teens and she changed completely.' Cassia caught sight of a magazine outside a nearby newsagents and squinted to see what it said. She thought it said 'Wimbledon Scandal!' but she wasn't sure.

Realising Rocco was watching her curiously, she turned away from the newsagents. 'My relationship with Jules has always tormented me, but what can I do? I've asked her, many times, but she won't talk about it.'

Rocco nodded. 'I know how frustrating that is. Raff can be very secretive. There is something going on with him, I'm certain. But I can't get him to open up, to confide in me. Even my grandmother . . .'

'Sofia? You think she's hiding something too? Surely not.'

Sofia seemed to be the most straightforward member of the Disanti family and Cassia couldn't imagine her keeping anything from Rocco, they seemed so devoted to one another.

Rocco's mouth twitched. He wasn't so sure. He wasn't prone to voicing his inner thoughts about his family aloud, especially not when they weren't based on anything specific. It was just that his grandmother had seemed reticent of late, awkward even. And as for Raff . . . he had never been the most open of men, despite his gregarious nature with friends and customers, but Rocco was sure something was afoot.

He glanced at Cassia, realising she was talking, attempting to reassure him about Sofia. Saying nothing, Rocco watched her, noticing the way she moved her small, expressive hands as she spoke, the way her full mouth pouted unconsciously when something was troubling her. Rocco frowned. He felt like a sick man in need of a fix when he was around Cassia; a very unsatisfactory state of affairs. He wasn't entirely sure he had made the best decision by inviting Cassia to Rome but his grandmother's suggestion had stuck in his mind and once it had taken hold, it was almost too tempting to resist.

What did she think of him? he wondered. He couldn't read her – another thing he found both captivating and irksome. Stefania, on the other hand, was an open book, her inner emotions were plain for all to see, punctuated by sulking, beaming or furious displays of temper. She also hated his motorbike, complaining of the noise, the effect the wind had on her hair and clothes, and how uncool she looked with a helmet on.

Stefania! Rocco sat up straight in his chair. He hadn't even told her he was coming to Rome, hadn't even thought of her once since he had decided to visit. Feeling guilty, he wondered if he could claim he had intended to surprise her, although part of him couldn't be bothered with the subterfuge.

Deciding he would worry about it later, Rocco quickly drained his coffee, almost scorching his throat. 'Shall we go and meet Luca?' he suggested, coughing slightly. 'I said we'd join him at his place for lunch.'

Not bothering to finish her coffee as it was still too hot, Cassia joined him on the back of the motorbike again, conscious of the lingering stares of several Italian women as they prepared to set off. Even if they didn't recognise Rocco, they obviously thought he was attractive. Cassia swallowed as she pulled her helmet back on, detesting herself for what must be a cringesome schoolgirl crush. She had feelings for him, feelings she could ignore when he wasn't around, but when she spent time with him, she felt so close to him, drawn to him in a way she never had been with Finn.

She turned her mind to the historian she was about to meet, someone who might finally unearth the past. She had thought about her father often since she had been in Sorrento, but it had been frustrating not being able to find out anything about his background. She felt as though she had somehow let him down. Hopefully, that was about to change. They pulled up outside a smart townhouse in the depths of the Via Veneto, which Cassia privately thought looked faintly musty from the outside.

'Rocco!'

An elderly gentleman dressed in a crisply pressed lilac shirt and dark trousers opened the door and kissed Rocco's cheeks effusively. Blessed with waves of snowy-white hair and a surprisingly youthful face, this was clearly Luca. He had to be in his sixties, possibly even older, but he seemed sprightly and full of vitality.

Rocco hugged him, patting him on the back. 'Great to see you! My grandmother sends her love. And this is Cassia,' he said, stepping back to introduce her. He put an arm loosely round her shoulders to usher her forward but as their eyes met briefly, powerfully, his arm fell away.

Luca, watching the exchange with interest, welcomed Cassia. 'Don't be shy, child. I'm eccentric but very friendly, and I'm Italian. We kiss in this country, both cheeks, if you please.' He grinned engagingly before throwing an appreciative wink at Rocco, to show he approved of Cassia.

'You don't need to speak English, Luca; Cassia's Italian is excellent.'

'Really?' Luca looked even more captivated. 'How wonderful.'

Flustered by the compliment, Cassia went into Luca's arms. His hug was surprisingly firm; he might be old, but he clearly looked after himself and he smelt of some unusual citrusy cologne. All Cassia knew about Luca was that he was a historian of some kind, but he must be a very successful one because his clothes were discreetly expensive and his house was full of historical artefacts, marble statues and exquisite paintings carefully positioned away from direct sunlight.

'I wrote a very well-received book some years back,' Luca informed her, with a twinkle in his eye, accurately guessing what she was thinking. He handed her a copy of a heavy book, covered with a terracotta-hued jacket. 'Keep it. It's a very dull tome, but it's allowed me to indulge my love of historical memorabilia, so why should I complain?'

Cassia took the book with a smile. It looked terribly highbrow and, as Luca said, dull, but she tucked it in her bag nonetheless. Glancing out of the window, she saw that Luca had a distant view of the park once belonging to the wealthy and noble Borghese family. The formal gardens were flanked by exotic plants and trees and her father had told her that the park now housed the National Zoo.

'I have prepared cold meats and cheeses,' Luca said, gesturing to a table laden with plates of delicious-looking produce, some still in their greaseproof wrappers. 'I also have bread. Will this do, Rocco?'

Rocco looked unimpressed. 'Let me whip up something extra,' he suggested, tossing his leather jacket on to the back of a chair.

Luca smiled, looking impish. 'I thought if I kept things sparse, you wouldn't be able to help yourself. There's wild boar in the fridge, spicy sausage, whatever you like.' He raised his eyebrows at Cassia expressively. 'It's good for him,' he added in an undertone. 'To cook, you know. He doesn't do it nearly enough these days.'

She nodded and watched Rocco turn his cuffs back before expertly whipping up a perfect ball of pasta and searching through the fridge for ingredients. As ever, Cassia found watching Rocco in action utterly enthralling; she could literally watch him cooking all day. It was something about the firm, rhythmic movements of his tanned hands, the intensity in his green eyes, maybe even the sensual twist of his mouth as he focused on whatever minuscule aspect of the process he was involved in. When he was cooking, Rocco appeared so single-minded and in control, it was like watching an artist create a magnificent, awe-inspiring fresco.

What on earth was going on between these two? Luca wondered, enthralled by their chemistry. A good friend of Nico Disanti and with no children of his own, Luca had taken on the role of benevolent uncle as Rocco, Aurelia and Raffaelo had grown up. Fondly bestowing them with lavish gifts when he visited and showing a great interest in everything they did, he had always had the most in common with Rocco. Although he knew Rocco would never retire from the restaurant business – or, God forbid, cooking itself – Luca had always hoped the handsome chef would fall in love and settle down.

And it would take a hell of a woman to make that happen, he thought, watching Cassia. Was she the one? She was certainly gorgeous enough, with those luscious curves and exotic looks. It remained to be seen if she was bright and passionate enough to steal Rocco's complicated, romantic heart.

Realising she probably looked idiotic for staring, Cassia tore her eyes away from Rocco. She noticed several photographs of Luca with a much younger girl and assumed she was his daughter, until she caught sight of a candid shot of them kissing.

'So, your family tree,' Luca said, his mouth twitching with amusement as he grabbed a large roll of paper that was coiled up on a nearby dresser. 'Talk me through your family,' he instructed. 'I work from present day backwards, obviously, so throw some names at me.' He called out to Rocco. 'Pour us some wine, Rocco. I have a fabulous Barbaresco I've been waiting to enjoy.'

'A Barbaresco?' Cassia grinned. 'Isn't that considered to be one of Italy's most sought-after wines?'

Luca kissed his fingertips. 'Indeed it is. Exquisite, simply exquisite.'

Rocco brought over glasses of brick-orange wine, which Luca held to the light.

'This is one of the heaviest of the Nebbiolo grape variety,' he said. 'It needs to age to give the best flavour but it's worth the wait. A decade or more, at least. So, what can you smell? Inhale, child, and tell me what you pick up.'

Nervously, Cassia buried her nose in it. 'I'm afraid I'm a complete novice at this . . . ummm . . . maybe roses?'

'Always roses.' Luca nodded approvingly, glancing at Rocco and raising his eyebrows. 'And tar. But also cherries. Can you smell that cheeky, fruity aroma? Damsons, leather, mulberry – it's like a good perfume on a young woman's hot skin.' He sat back and exhaled pleasurably. 'This wine is beyond superb.'

'It's amazing,' Cassia agreed, her mind already turning over the literary possibilities of such an indulgence. 'Why the orange colour?'

'The tannins.' Luca sat up, remembering he was supposed to be helping Cassia with her family tree. He grabbed his pen again. 'Apologies. I get so excited by wine. Tell me names.'

Enjoying the wine, Cassia recounted as many full names as she could remember from her father's side of the family, not easy given his orphan status, but she had her father's notes to help. Watching as Luca scrawled all over the curling sheet of paper, filling it with names and rough dates, Cassia stole a glance at Rocco again. He was in his element, concentrating on constructing some pasta dish, which she had no doubt would be scrumptious. The air was soon filled with aromas of meat cooking in the pan, as well as garlic and white wine.

Cassia felt a shiver. Once again, she was gripped with fear that her father could be the long-lost son rumoured to have survived the landslide. Was that what she was going to discover, after all these years – that her father was, in fact, a member of the Giorelli family, the family who had placed a curse on the Disantis? Cassia swallowed. It would be awful, but she guessed she might as well find out the truth now that she was here.

Luca glanced at Cassia, wondering why she looked so shell-shocked. He guessed it might be because she knew he would get to the truth of her father's history, whatever it took. He had seen this expression before on many a client's face; the thudding realisation that they might finally get to piece together a jigsaw puzzle that had evaded them for so long.

He wondered if Rocco would be meeting up with Stefania while he was in Rome. If so, he sincerely hoped Rocco didn't take Cassia along. Having met Stefania several times, Luca felt sure she might scratch Cassia's eyes out because unless she was blind, the chemistry between Rocco and the lovely Cassia was so tangible, he could almost taste it.

A tiresome girl, Stefania, Luca mused. Stunning, but emotionally empty. He had always wondered why Rocco had stayed with her for so long but aside from the obvious sexual attraction, he guessed convenience had an awful lot to do with it.

Cassia scribbled her mobile number on the back of a business card she found in her handbag. 'Please call me if you find any-thing . . . exciting,' she said. She turned to Rocco, suddenly feeling as though their relationship – whatever it turned out to be – was hanging by a thread. Would he still want to know her if it transpired that she was related to the Giorelli family?

Luca glanced at the business card she'd given him and carefully placed it on his dresser.

'Let's eat,' called Rocco, putting a huge dish of mouth-watering pasta in the centre of the table.

Luca rolled his scroll up. 'Leave it with me, Cassia. And I'll be in touch about your family tree shortly.' He ushered her to the table, knowing he was going to enjoy watching the pair of them pretending they weren't absurdly attracted to each other for the next few hours.

'This is incredible,' Jules commented enviously.

She shielded her eyes as she took in the breathtaking view of Capri in the glittering, early morning sunshine. Having flown over in Rocco's helicopter, courtesy of Rocco's part-time pilot friend, she and Aurelia had headed along one of Capri's prettiest pathways until they reached the Hotel Capri Presidentiale. Overlooking the spectacular Bay of Marina Piccola, the five-star hotel was covered in brightly coloured Mediterranean flowers which cascaded down the pastel-hued walls like clusters of exotically vivid butterflies.

'It is perfect, yes?'

Aurelia pointed out the Santo Stefano Church, where many a bride exchanged their vows. It was located at the top of the flight of steps in the famous Piazzetta. Once the cathedral of Capri, the church had been designed by a royal architect in the flamboyant, baroque style Capri was famous for, with cupolettas, vaulted ceilings and moulded chapels.

'Of course, we are getting married at the Cloister of Sorrento,' Aurelia commented. 'It's a family thing, everyone gets married there, you see – my parents, my grandparents.'

'It all sounds divine.'

Jules leant over the balcony and stared out at the Faraglioni rocks – three immense stacks of rock that rose majestically out of the azure sea. Their sheer size was head-spinning and made all the more pronounced by the tiny boats that scudded through the water, looking like brightly coloured wooden toys next to the vast rocks. The enchanting, cobbled Marina Piccola sat nearby, showing off shamelessly and letting the world know why it was one of Capri's most fashionable suntraps. With fabulous sea-edge restaurants and bars studded with glitterati, reclining like film stars, it was glamorous in the extreme.

'I'd love to get married here,' Jules said, envying Aurelia all over again. She realised for the first time just how rich the Disanti family must be to be able to host a wedding of the size Aurelia had discussed. She felt a glimmer of trepidation in her stomach at what she had taken on, but she pushed it aside. Aurelia's mind wandered. She missed Dino. Away on another photo shoot in Milan for a few days, he had just sent her a very camp photo of himself modelling the exceptionally tight pants Italian men favoured. Shortly afterwards, she had burst into tears because she missed him so much and Jules had been at a loss as to how to comfort her. Aurelia couldn't help thinking that at least Cassia would have given her a hug and some reassuring words, but Jules didn't seem the emotional type. Aurelia returned to her wedding details.

'The most important thing to do is ensure that all the payments to the venue go through on time,' she instructed. 'We have left deposits, naturally, but the venue requires full payment by the middle of the month – they like to keep these payments close to the wedding date in case of cancellations. They've had a few recently,' she confided. 'They also require an email confirmation a week before the final sum is paid.' She frowned at Jules pointedly until Jules realised she was expecting her to take notes. Tugging out a pen, she started scribbling on the back of a notepad she'd fished out of her handbag.

'Absolutely, consider it done. Don't worry, I have the most marvellous memory,' she informed Aurelia untruthfully. Jules had the grace to blush as she realised belatedly that she hadn't passed on any of Finn's messages to Cassia – not deliberately, but because she had been so caught up in herself and, more recently, Aurelia's wedding.

Aurelia threw her a doubtful glance. Cassia's warnings about her sister, accurate or not, had stuck in her mind, but she was doing her best to give Jules the benefit of the doubt. After all, how hard could it be to email details through and move money on time? Aurelia wasn't the most organised of people but she knew she was more than capable of dealing with such things; she simply didn't have the time.

'I hope so,' she told Jules imperiously, hoping she hadn't made a mistake by affording her the privilege of organising the final stages of her wedding. 'Because this venue has two back-up options if we fail to pay on time. One of them is Mia, a horrible bitch I know from the modelling circuit.' Aurelia's green eyes darkened. 'I would rather die than let her take this place from me.'

Jules nodded rapidly. 'Leave it with me,' she said in a confident voice. As Aurelia turned away, she grimaced. Had she said the middle of the month or the end? Never mind; she would check with the hotel once she was back at the Disanti estate.

'Let us have a drink here,' Aurelia said, feeling the sun beating down on her head. She noticed a few people staring at her and realised she might need to tone her look down a bit. The last thing she wanted to do was spend the afternoon signing autographs or being photographed.

Incapable of doing 'understated', Aurelia popped some fabulous pink Valentino sunglasses she'd swiped from a recent fashion shot on to her nose and tied a lilac scarf around her hair. The silk scarf matched her sundress perfectly and turning on the high heel of her designer slingbacks, she swanned off into the hotel looking like a gorgeous Italian film star from the sixties.

Jules hurried after her, suffering from a thumping great girl crush for the first time in her life. Everything about Aurelia was glamorous, her looks, her background, her career. If she hadn't made what she hoped was a lifelong connection with Aurelia, Jules knew she'd despise her wholeheartedly. She didn't usually enjoy being friends with girls who were so much prettier than her, but Aurelia came with so many bonuses. She was dazzling and although clearly spoilt, she was fun to be around. And her clothes . . . Jules wished she could raid Aurelia's wardrobe with gay abandon but she wasn't sure they were quite on those terms yet.

'So, do you have a boyfriend back in England?' Aurelia asked as they sipped appletinis by the hotel's vast swimming pool.

Jules pulled a face. 'I was dating a tennis player, he's playing at Wimbledon this year.' An unwanted image of Dom wielding his tennis racket in rather less noble circumstances popped into her head. 'Let's just say he wasn't the most faithful of men.'

Aurelia crossed her long legs. 'How boring. If Dino behaved like that, I would have his – how do you say it – his testicles? Yes, I would have those cut off. For jewellery, you know.' She made a slicing motion and gestured to her ears.

Jules laughed at the comical image of Dino's balls as dangly earrings, but she could tell by the glint in Aurelia's eyes that she was, at least, semi-serious. 'Well, I did have a fleeting moment when I wanted to do Dom some serious harm, but then I realised I wasn't really that bothered about him. I mean, I liked the idea of him, but he wasn't the man I thought he was, so I got over him pretty quickly. And I didn't like the fact that he was famous. Girls followed us everywhere and it was so intense.'

Jules sipped her appletini. What had been perplexing her most since her arrival in Sorrento was not how much she hadn't thought about Dom, but how much she had found her thoughts drifting to Finn. He had been so kind to her, but Jules knew she shouldn't confuse her feelings and turn them into something they weren't. Finn was besotted with Cassia and if he was being nice to her with all his amusing texts and constant contact, it was only because she was Cassia's sister.

'And what is Cassia's fiancé like?' Aurelia asked curiously, toying with her cocktail glass. 'I imagine him to be a little dull . . . you know, conservative.' She felt disloyal as she said these words; she might have thought Cassia was reserved when she first met her, but Aurelia knew she wasn't remotely dull.

Jules frowned. She supposed some people might think Finn was conservative, but that was a negative way of looking at him. Steady, loyal, reliable – they were all lovely qualities and certainly ones that Jules valued these days. 'He's actually lovely,' she said sharply. 'Fun, sweet and totally honest. And ruggedly handsome too,' she added consideringly, almost surprising herself with the admission.

Aurelia eyed Jules behind her pink sunglasses. Was Jules protesting too much? Finn was Cassia's fiancé, all after, not Jules's.

Jules stared out at the magnificent view. 'Actually, Cassia used to date guys who were the total opposite of Finn,' she said, more to steer the conversation away from her views of Finn than anything else. 'When Cassia was younger, she used to hook up with absolute heartbreakers – you know, drop-dead gorgeous, sexy men. The ones who are usually great in bed but allergic to commitment.'

Aurelia was intrigued. She was beginning to think there was far more to Cassia than first met the eye. 'Really? What happened? Why did she stop dating men like that?' She glanced over her shoulder and noting that people had stopped staring, removed her headscarf.

Jules regretted talking about the way Cassia used to be and she chided herself silently for bringing up Cassia's trans-formation into the sensible sister all those years ago. It didn't pay to open a can of worms, especially, she decided, with someone like Aurelia. Aside from the fact that she barely knew Aurelia, she was loath to discuss events from the past in too much detail because she suspected Aurelia might be a terrible gossip if she thought there might be scandal to unearth.

'Oh, who knows?' she responded airily. 'Perhaps Cassia just made the decision to settle for someone more reliable.' Knowing this wasn't remotely the case, Jules hoped her statement would put an end to Aurelia's interest. She realised immediately afterwards that she was wrong.

'It sounds as though my brother, Rocco, would have been Cassia's type back then,' Aurelia remarked, ordering more appletinis. She smiled mischievously, aware that she was making Jules uncomfortable, even if she wasn't sure why, exactly. 'He's not so much a heartbreaker – well, not intentionally, I'm sure, but he's into dangerous sports, that kind of thing. Rocco's a bit wild on the inside, and he's also allergic to commitment.'

She lifted her sunglasses and propped them up on her head, her dark curls falling perfectly into place around her heart-shaped face. 'He's been with Stefania for over a year now but he can't seem to make his mind up when it comes to making a more serious commitment.'

About to attempt another subject change, Jules paused.

'Do you think there's something going on between Rocco and Cassia?' she asked casually.

Guessing there was far more intent behind Jules's question than her nonchalant tone suggested, Aurelia thought carefully before answering. 'I doubt it. Rocco's with Stefania and . . .' Not caring to comment on Rocco's rather complicated relationship with Stefania, she glossed over this part. She was also reluctant to comment on Rocco's feelings for Cassia; she knew her brother incredibly well and she sensed he might be deeply attracted to Cassia and not just on a physical level, even if he wasn't acting upon it.

Aurelia changed tack. 'The thing is, Cassia's besotted with her fiancé, isn't she? She's always trying to get in touch with him. Between you and me, Cassia's been very upset that she hasn't heard from him for so long.'

Jules chewed her lip, knowing that was mostly her fault. But Finn and Cassia knew each other inside out; they would figure out that it was all a simple misunderstanding and hopefully she, Jules, would emerge from it all unscathed.

Aurelia abruptly stood up. 'We need to leave,' she said, tying her scarf around her hair again. 'That party of people over there have recognised me, I'm about to get asked for photos and autographs. Let's go.'

Grabbing Jules's hand, she paid the bill hurriedly and they left the hotel, giggling like schoolgirls.

'Oooh, clothes,' Aurelia breathed, spotting a row of pretty, expensive-looking boutiques. 'Shall we? My treat,' she added persuasively, mostly because she hated shopping alone.

Jules wasn't about to turn down such a generous offer and she willingly accepted, allowing Aurelia to drag her into the kind of boutique she would normally have avoided for fear of being ejected like Julia Roberts's character in *Pretty Woman*.

After a few hours trying on wonderful outfits and being treated to two to-die-for new dresses, a designer handbag and some over-sized sunglasses Victoria Beckham would have killed her for, Jules headed back to the Disanti estate in the family helicopter in an exceptionally good mood.

Chattering away to Aurelia as if they were the sisters she and Cassia had once been, Jules also promptly forgot all about phoning the hotel in Capri to check the payment schedule.

Chapter Fifteen

Finn stood outside his parents' house, his heart sinking. Family meetings were a rare occasion in the Sunderland household but he guessed he could understand why this one had been called and he also knew he'd be expected to act as family mediator. It was the role he had unconsciously assumed as a child, partly because he was his mother's favourite and partly because his logical, calm nature was the perfect antidote to the squawking and yelling that everyone else bar his father did.

This time, however, Finn was at a loss. What did one say to one's parents when their youngest child had disgraced himself so spectacularly? At Wimbledon, of all places. Being caught in a compromising position on centre court late at night was bad enough, but the discovery that Dom's partners in crime were the ravishing young daughters of one of the most established and well-respected umpires was, in the eyes of the All England Tennis Club, categorically unforgivable.

The incident, initially kept under wraps by the Herculean efforts of Dom's coach Carlton, had inadvertently leaked out two weeks after it happened. Now, nothing could prevent it from being splashed across every newspaper and magazine in the UK and Finn was sure most of Europe and America had probably heard about it by now. Tennis was, by and large, a very 'clean' sport, untouched by the kind of scandal other sports had suffered from, but Dom had managed to drag it through the gutter. Worst of all, having made such a name for himself over the past year, he was all the more newsworthy now that he had fallen from grace.

Many a witty headline had been thought up and emblazoned across the front pages of gleeful red-top newspapers and even some of the more sedate ones had jumped on the story ravenously, using close-ups of Dom's handsome face to sell more copies.

Finn had provided Dom with legal representation, sending over a bolshy hot-shot of a lawyer who specialised in digging celebrities and sports personalities out of whatever pile of scandalous shit they had buried themselves in. However, Finn had a feeling his parents – his mother in particular – were going to be far harder to placate. He let himself in with his key and made his way through the house to the conservatory.

'Finn.' Henry looked up, his usually genial face troubled. 'Good of you to come over.'

Finn caught sight of his mother in the corner of the conservatory, her defeated shoulders in her mint-green sundress and downcast eyes a sign that all was not well in her world. Louisa, sitting upright in one of the wicker armchairs, was glued to her phone, presumably flicking through gossip pages about Dom.

Dom himself was noticeable by his absence, but Finn guessed he would rock up sooner or later; he might be defiant but even Dom must know he had to come home and face the music sometime.

'How could he, Finn?' Grace said, holding a lace-edged handkerchief to her eyes. 'I can't understand why he would do this to us. Haven't we given Dom everything he ever wanted? I can't believe he would repay us in this way.'

Louisa looked scornful. 'Oh God, Mother. It's not about *you*, all right? This is about Dom. He didn't shag those girls on centre court to get back at you, he did it because he wanted to.'

Henry nodded his agreement.

'I'm sure Dom feels terrible about it,' Finn soothed, holding a clean handkerchief out. 'But Louisa is right; this is just what Dom does, unfortunately.'

Grace angrily dabbed her eyes. 'But why, Finn? Why does he have to ruin everything like this? He was doing so well . . . all those years of paying for expensive tennis lessons were finally paying off and now this.' She gestured to the open pages of a local newspaper that had jumped on the bandwagon by dedicating the centre pages to Dom, with photographs of him as a baby, a few of him as a cheeky-faced schoolboy and larger ones depicting a promising teenager wielding a tennis racket.

Grace, tearfully distraught at Dom's outrageous behaviour, was also livid. If she found out which of her friends – and it could only be someone in her close circle – had betrayed her by stealing the photographs of Dom, she would cut them out of her life without compunction.

'Cut him some slack, Gracie,' Henry ventured, taking his life in his hands by attempting to defuse the situation. 'Dom must have been under enormous pressure at Wimbledon and he—'

'Don't defend him!' Grace snapped. Her cheeks were flushed with anger. 'And I won't be cutting him any slack whatsoever. How he can let us all down like this is anyone's—'

'Singing my praises as usual, Mother? What a surprise,' Dom drawled, pausing in the doorway. Wearing smart beige trousers with a white linen shirt that emphasised his tan, he looked unruffled by his predicament and rather as if he had returned from a relaxing vacation.

Grace shot him a poisonous glance, furious that he seemed so together when she was falling apart and humiliated beyond recognition. 'What do you expect me to do, Dominic? Congratulate you?'

'As if.' Dom sauntered in and threw himself into a wicker chair. 'God, these are uncomfortable. Would it hurt to get something a bit more welcoming?'

Henry shook his head. 'Not the time to make jokes, son. Your mother is very upset about everything.'

'I'm sure.' Dom yawned and checked the expensive-looking watch on his tanned wrist.

'You look pleased with yourself,' Louisa commented, disappointed that Dom wasn't slinking in with his tail between his legs. The exact opposite in fact; he looked nauseatingly chilled out.

Finn assessed him, wondering what had brought about the change. The last time he'd spoken to Dom, which had been a few days earlier, he had sounded scared and desperate for help. Now he looked rather as if he'd spent a few days on holiday in Cannes unwinding with a crowd of friends.

'Was the lawyer I recommended any good?' Finn said.

Dom nodded. 'Superb. Apart from committing a cardinal sin at Wimbledon, I haven't actually done anything too terrible.' He gave his mother a mocking glance. 'The girls weren't underage so it's all above board, really.'

Grace let out a shuddering breath. At least she wouldn't have to suffer the shame of Dom going to prison, but she wanted to slap him for being so frivolous about what had happened.

'Not only that, Finn,' Dom went on smoothly, 'but your lawyer buddy has put me in touch with one of the execs on that gossip show in the States.' He dropped the name with glee and carried on. 'They want me to do a primetime interview. Kind of a Hugh Grant "Ooops, I messed up big time, but I'm quite self-deprecating and endearing with it" sort of a thing.'

Finn's mouth fell open. He instantly regretted recommending the cocksure lawyer to Dom. He had only done it to make sure Dom had appropriate legal representation if Wimbledon

349

Tennis Club had decided to press charges, not so that Dom could become a celebrity off the back of his mistakes.

Dom grinned. 'I'll probably have to say I'm suffering from a sex addiction, but hey, that's not so bad, is it?'

Louisa couldn't help laughing. 'God, only you could come up smelling of roses from something like this! Most people would disappear from sight, mortified by their actions, but you, you're going to turn it to your advantage completely and become a major bloody celebrity.'

'That's the general idea. I might not be playing tennis but my agent – yes, I have an agent now – reckons he's got several guest spots lined up for me on comedy shows and sitcoms. I've even got a screen test for a movie next week.' Dom sat up and gave his mother a pointed look. 'And just as you were about to totally write me off too, eh, Mother? The black sheep of the family plays to type then manages to turn it all around. Hardly fits with your plans for us all, does it?'

She stared back at him coldly. 'What is that supposed to mean?'

Finn felt his stomach tightening. Over the years, his mother's obsession with him and her brutal sidelining of both Louisa and Dom had always been an unspoken truth, something they had all been aware of but had never voiced aloud. Seemingly, Dom's recent brush with danger had given him the daring to finally confront their mother's favouritism out loud and Finn wanted to stop him before he did the family some serious damage.

'Look, I'm really pleased you've managed to come out of this situation in a positive way,' Finn started. 'But I really don't think this is the time or the place for—'

'It never is!' Dom stood up angrily, his fists clenched. 'We've all skirted round this issue for years and I'm sick of it, Finn. Louisa must be too, except she's too much of a wimp to even admit it.'

Louisa looked affronted. About to comment, she changed her mind. She had plenty to say and now that her life had taken a turn for the better, she was definitely prepared to take the plunge, but not when Dom was taking centre stage on that front.

Dom's eyes narrowed contemptuously. 'Thought so.' He turned to Grace. 'Mother, you shouldn't always expect the worst of people. Of me and Louisa, anyway. It makes us feel as though we might as well fuck everything up because that's what you've already decided is going to happen.' He shoved his hands into the pockets of his trousers, the gesture oddly aggressive. 'Finn's your favourite; we get it. But we're not so bad either, you know, me and Louisa. We're not perfect, but we don't deserve to be ignored and criticised constantly.'

Grace recoiled.

'Oh, don't deny it,' Dom mocked. 'Everyone knows it's the truth, even you.'

Louisa looked away. 'Why do you have to say all this stuff, Dom? Why can't you just leave it alone?' She burst into tears before jumping up and dashing out of the room.

Dom stopped in his tracks. He was all set to lay into his mother, but not if Louisa was going to get so upset. He went after her.

Grace put her hand to her mouth. She had been intending to tear a strip off Dom and tell him exactly what she thought of his deplorable behaviour; instead, he'd turned the tables and blamed her for everything.

Was she responsible? In her mind, Grace stumbled over the question. Had she really made Louisa and Dom feel as though whatever they did, it would never be as good as anything Finn achieved? Grace felt guilt slowly creeping up on her. She fought it, but it kept on coming.

Henry gravely rubbed his chin, knowing the fallout from the family meeting was going to be immense. He also knew he should be the one to deal with it all. Finn, having assumed the role of peacemaker for so many years, had done enough. And Henry had let him do it, which had probably widened the chasm between Grace and her other children as well as increasing her bond with Finn. But it wasn't Finn's job to glue the family back together, not this time.

'I'll take it from here,' he told Finn.

Finn got to his feet. 'Really? I can always—'

'No.' Henry met his eyes firmly. 'It's about time I sorted this family out. You've done more than enough.' He shook his head at Finn. 'You look terrible. You're working too hard, I should imagine. Ever thought of taking a holiday?'

'A holiday?' Finn looked dazed. Work had died down in the past week and he was finally getting home at a decent hour. In fact, he suspected that he had been taken off the major cases because of the recent cock-up he'd made. He'd missed a vital detail in one of the files. But a holiday? It was a novel thought, even if his bosses would probably encourage it right now. The thing was, where would he go?

Henry pulled an exasperated face. 'I hear Sorrento is lovely at this time of the year, son.'

Finn started. Sorrento. Of course. He should go and see how Jules was getting on. And Cassia, of course.

'I've heard that too,' he said, patting his father's shoulder. He glanced at his mother, who looked quite stricken. 'Is she going to be all right?'

Henry nodded. 'I think so. But that's my problem, not yours. Go and see Cassia, Finn, and get things back on track. That's what's important for you right now.'

Finn nodded. His father was right. The wedding was just weeks away and they were barely talking. Feeling shattered as he left his parents' house, he hoped he had the energy to deal with whatever had made him and Cassia fall apart in the first place.

*

Diana sat at her tiny mirrored table in her cramped dressing room, preparing herself for the next rehearsal. Acting in the play had been cathartic, surprisingly so, and she felt as she had in the early days of her acting career; eager and motivated. She even felt energised by her nudity. It was a powerful thing being naked in front of so many people. Diana pulled her unwashed hair back from her face. It looked lank and greasy, just as the script demanded, and she had achieved the look naturally. Rejecting the offer of assistance from the on-set hairdresser and offers of talcum powder and Vaseline to make her usually glamorous blond hair unkempt, Diana had chosen to go 'au naturel', which meant not washing her hair for two weeks, hitherto unheard of.

She thought about Robson, the chiselled actor who was playing Kyle. He was such a sweet boy, an absolute gentleman and very charming too. Diana smiled to herself. She had an idea that handsome Robson might have a crush on her and she found the thought rather thrilling.

She headed out on to the stage. They were using a smaller theatre in London for some of the scenes, but it still gave her a buzz every time she set foot on stage.

Robson, dressed as Kyle, Clarissa's painter lover, strode across the room and kissed Diana's cheek. They had a particularly harrowing scene to act out, one where the character of Kyle, knowing Clarissa is watching, purposefully has explicit sex with Clarissa's young, beautiful daughter. Clarissa, her self-esteem destroyed, then begins a slow descent into madness, becoming a faded, saggy has-been of a woman whose murderous thoughts are the only things keeping her going.

Robson was feeling nervous and it showed.

'It's a big scene,' he commented.

Diana patted his cheek. 'You'll be fine.'

She caught sight of the ravishing young actress playing her daughter Rosalind and baulked slightly. Wearing a wine-coloured dress that hugged her ripe body and Louboutins that made her slender legs look endless, the girl was all pre-Raphaelite curls and plump, bouncing bosoms. She was going to look fabulous writhing around naked on all fours with Robson faking a climax on top of her.

'Ouch.' Diana winced. 'I actually feel rather wounded and jealous like Clarissa.'

Robson grinned. 'You have no need. But you're such a method actress; this probably will feel distressing to you, all this shagging the younger daughter stuff.'

'Method actress, me?' Diana laughed but stopped when she realised Robson was being serious. 'You actually think I get so into my acting parts that I feel my character's pain?'

Robson held his chin out as a trainee make-up girl touched up his foundation. She and a couple of friends were being allowed in on rehearsals because they were part of a charity Rob was involved in. 'Definitely. But it's a compliment, Di. Me, I just learn my lines and hope I'm convincing enough in a part, but you, you're the real deal.' He gestured to her hair. 'Look what you're willing to go through, and I know you were upset after that scene where Kyle had to reject you when you offered yourself to him like some vulnerable animal. It was amazing, truly.'

'Thank you,' Diana replied slowly.

'You probably even think you're a bit in love with me,' Robson joked. 'Or that I am with you. I mean, I think the world of you, but you know I live with Giles.' He strode over to the actress playing Rosalind, greeting her in the same warm and friendly manner with which he had Diana.

Diana went rigid. Robson was gay; of course he was. She knew that and she had heard the crew making comments about how straight he looked and how convincing he was in his sex scenes with women. She had just blocked the thought out because she hadn't wanted to think her young lover wasn't interested in her sexually.

Diana blinked. Was Robson right when he said she was a method actress? Perhaps she did get overly involved in the characters she played; she did feel very exposed right now, just as Clarissa would. She was vain, she knew that – she had lied about her age for years and she was struggling to come to terms with ageing. And just as she was feeling useless and at the end of her life, her daughters were blooming and starting theirs with marriages, new careers and trips abroad.

Diana caught her breath. What part had she been playing back then, back when it had all gone so horribly wrong? Beatrice . . . Beatrice in Shakespeare's *Much Ado About Nothing*. Benedick and Beatrice, both sarcastic and witty, both scathing of marriage and love – tricked into falling in love with one another.

Diana sank down on to a chair. She wouldn't use that as an excuse, she mustn't. She was responsible for her reprehensible behaviour and she refused to clutch at straws, however convenient it might be. She felt hot tears pricking at her eyelids. Robson was right; she did live the parts she played. Sometimes, far too much. To her cost, she thought with bitter regret.

'Flowers for you, Mrs Marini-Blake,' said one of the girls who worked on the production crew, proffering a bouquet of pale pink roses. 'Beautiful, aren't they? So romantic.'

Diana took them, choking down her tears. Reading the card, she realised they were from Angelo. 'Take them,' she said, thrusting them back at the girl.

'W-what? But they're yours.'

'I don't deserve them . . . I don't deserve him.'

Wiping away a few tears as she dashed back to the tiny room she was occupying during rehearsals, Diana thought about Angelo. She missed him, so much. For a while she had been consumed with thoughts about Marco, reliving their marriage, blaming herself for all that had destroyed it, but now she couldn't help being hit by waves of sadness and loss over

Angelo. She didn't deserve him; she was a silly, vain woman who couldn't separate reality from the stage. With nothing left to prove but her talent as an actress, Diana steeled herself for the scene she knew she was going to find heartbreaking to act out. An idea occurred to her about exorcising her ghosts from the past, but she would think about that later.

'So, what do you fancy doing today?'

Cassia glanced at Rocco over the froth of her cappuccino, thinking he looked irritatingly handsome in a tight, black T-shirt and jeans. After the meal at Luca's the day before, they had strolled around Rome for a few hours, visiting some of the haunts Cassia's father had taken her to as a child. They had enjoyed the very sociable and theatrical Piazza Navona with its palaces and pavement cafés and Cassia had exclaimed over the three flamboyant Baroque fountains she hadn't appreciated when she was younger.

Rocco had then given her a whistle-stop tour of the Pantheon, the temple to 'all the gods', a beautiful, ancient building that was one of the best-preserved in Rome and another sight Cassia had found rather yawnsome as a child. They had even managed to squeeze in a visit to the Colosseum, which had been Cassia's favourite place when she had last visited with her father. The great amphitheatre, witness to many a gladiatorial combat and wild animal fight, had been every bit as breathtaking as Cassia remembered, disappointing only because members of the public still weren't able to investigate the remains of the underground passages or get closer to the stone seating.

They had shared a meal that night in a lovely, family-run restaurant, enjoying a wonderful antipasti of deep-fried artichoke hearts and courgette flowers, followed by *gnocchi alla Romana* with a fragrant, tomato sauce, and ending with a slice of the popular Roman dessert of *torta di ricotta*. After the meal and all their sightseeing, they had returned to Luca's house, to stay in the rooms he had provided them with in the apartment block he owned next to his house. They were simple but surprisingly luxurious, with vast windows and splendid views.

Settling down with her laptop, Cassia had fired off a column to Gena, filled with passionate descriptions of Rome, the amazing food and Rocco's off-the-cuff pasta dish.

'Torta di ricotta,' she had typed, *'an indulgent cheesecake filled with ricotta, Marsala and lemon, coats the roof of the mouth with each delicate bite, filling the senses with sharp tastes cut through with a creamy, fluffy cake with just the right amount of wobble . . . homemade pasta, filled with a mixture of wild boar, onions and fresh herbs . . . a superb dish to accompany the perfection of the fruity, rose-scented Barbaresco . . .'*

She had assumed Rocco had headed off to see Stefania after leaving her at the apartment, so she had been surprised to hear him chatting outside her window with Luca. Hearing her name mentioned once or twice, she had strained her ears to listen but the Italian was too fast and she had been far too tired to concentrate. So she was taken aback when Rocco asked her what she fancied doing the following day.

'Aren't you seeing Stefania?' Cassia inquired, not answering his question directly.

He shook his head, his eyes meeting hers contemplatively. 'No. She's . . . Stefania's not in Rome this weekend. She had . . . business to attend to elsewhere.' He was telling the truth. He had phoned her very late last night and had heard the message on her answerphone.

Rocco finished his coffee and popped his sunglasses on, not so much because of the glorious July sunshine overhead but to hide his eyes. He didn't want Cassia to see the relief in his eyes – relief that he hadn't had to spend time with Stefania, exhaustively explaining his presence in Rome and why Cassia had accompanied him.

Rocco stared at Cassia, wondering what she was thinking. His stomach lurched as she met his gaze, the look so imbued with . . . something . . . he could feel his insides catching fire and melting simultaneously. Today, Cassia wore a cream shirt tucked into khaki shorts which showed off her shapely legs, and her sunglasses, propped up on her head, held her dark hair away from her face.

'So, if you fancy doing something today, I'm all yours. As it were,' he added.

Cassia berated herself for feeling so upbeat about spending more time with Rocco. It's good for the column, she told herself.

'Sounds great,' she said casually. 'Any suggestions?'

Chucking some euros on the table, Rocco stood up. 'I was going to quickly show you the site of the restaurant Stefania is keen for me to open. After that, I thought we could take a tour of gastronomy, sample the local cuisine and soak up the atmosphere.' He paused. 'Let me know if you need to take any notes for your column.'

'Right. Absolutely.'

Cassia strolled alongside him, feeling a slight stab of disappointment. The tour sounded more professional than friendly, but why shouldn't it? However close they had become during the visit to England and over many food-related discussions, they weren't friends; they were effectively colleagues.

Rocco resisted the urge to sling his arm round her shoulders and pull her in closer. She was engaged and he was in a serious relationship – of sorts. It was just that it was difficult not to touch her when she was so close, but he knew it would be crazy to overstep the mark. He led her to the site of the restaurant, which was just around the corner. Positioned in the centre of a busy street and encompassing three buildings boasting spectacu-larly bombastic architecture, the site was stunning.

Cassia peered into the restaurant through one of the huge

windows. Inside, it was dusty and messy but its potential was obvious. It was grand and statuesque and some of the features inside were lovely.

'It's beautiful,' Cassia observed. 'I could really see this as a Disanti restaurant.'

Rocco shot her a glance. 'You think I should go ahead with it?'

'I didn't say that.' Cassia met his eyes. 'As a site, it looks pretty perfect to me – not that I'm an expert. But whether or not you go ahead with it is your decision.' She touched the heavy door speculatively. 'What do you think?'

Rocco ran a hand over his short hair. 'I haven't a clue. From a business point of view, it makes sense. And I can't help thinking my grandfather would be immensely proud, because it was always his dream to own a restaurant in Rome.'

'But?'

'But on a personal level, it just makes me think of all the additional stress.'

Cassia nodded. 'And surely your grandfather wouldn't want you to be unhappy? It's one thing wanting to carry on Nico's amazing legacy, but I can't imagine he would have wanted you to spend this much time away from the kitchen.'

'I suppose not. But it's like me arranging with Gena for you to come to Sorrento.'

Cassia looked at him inquiringly.

He struggled to explain. 'You know I don't do interviews or any of that stuff, this is all new to me. My parents love it, but I've always been more about the food. But this bond I have with my grandfather, it's so important to me. And he wanted me to carry on this legacy of his. He impressed upon me how the family needed to be looked after so they never returned to their humble roots.'

'I understand but I truly don't think Nico would have wanted you to become so involved in developing new restaurants all over the world that you no longer had time to enjoy cooking.' Her voice was earnest. 'Look how much you enjoyed cooking at Luca's.'

Rocco stared inside the restaurant moodily. She was right. His grandfather wouldn't have wanted him to spend this much time away from the kitchen and he certainly wouldn't want him to be killing himself with all the pressure. Nico had been an astute businessman but he had always been focused on his passion for cooking.

Recently, Rocco knew he'd been obsessed with issues such as the figures. He had an inkling what might be behind the discrepancies, but he couldn't bring himself to fully face up to it yet. And he could be totally wrong, of course.

He straightened up. He couldn't cope with thinking any more about the possibility of a restaurant in Rome. 'Fancy tasting the best meringue and hazelnut ice cream in Rome? In Italy, even?'

Realising he wanted to steer the conversation away from business, Cassia gave a delighted shudder. 'Oh dear, there go my hips. My sister is always telling me I owe my hips to chocolate.'

'Your sister is very rude,' Rocco told her, eyeing her body with a glint in his eye. 'And she clearly doesn't know what she's talking about. Come on, you're going to thank me for this.'

Sofia checked her reflection in the mirror for the umpteenth time. Her black dress was demure and stylish and her hair was neat and tidy in a chignon. The only concession she'd made was to add a pair of low-heeled shoes to her outfit, plus a slick of pink lipstick. Which she'd immediately wiped off, thinking it made her look obvious.

Was she doing the right thing? Feeling Nico's eyes on her from a photograph by the side of the bed, Sofia turned to face him.

'Am I really doing something so terrible?' she asked his photograph, her words heavy with guilt. 'You know I haven't done anything like this since you died.' Her eyes filled with tears. 'I miss you so much, you see. I can't bear being alone.'

Sofia's shoulders shook a little as she sank down on to the bed. Was that a good enough excuse for what she was about to do? If she had been the one to go, leaving Nico behind, she knew that she would have wanted Nico to pine for her for ever. Nico had felt the opposite, he had always told her that he loved her so much, he didn't like the thought of her being left behind if he went first. If anything, he had encouraged her to think it was all right to be with someone else if he died. Of course, neither of them had really contemplated the reality of it happening, so Sofia had no idea if Nico really wanted her to be happy with someone else in his absence.

She pulled herself together. It was lunch, nothing more. It wasn't a commitment, it wasn't a relationship. It was small talk over some nice food somewhere, probably focused on business mostly, Sofia told herself firmly.

Grabbing her handbag, she headed downstairs to wait. Finding Allesandro sitting in the restaurant lobby wearing a smart suit and shiny shoes, Sofia's heart skipped a beat. Just a tiny, insignificant one.

'You look wonderful,' Allesandro said, leaping out of his chair to kiss her hand. 'Are you ready?'

Sofia hesitated. She didn't know the answer to that question but she had come this far, so she might as well do it. 'I am,' she said, hoping her voice didn't give away how nervous she felt. 'Have you chosen somewhere good for us to have lunch?'

It was Allesandro's turn to look apprehensive. 'I hope so. Obviously the quality won't match that of Disanti's, but I think it's a rather nice little place.'

Sofia let out a shaky breath. 'Then let's go.' Taking his arm, she headed out into the sunshine and pushed down her anxiety.

Enjoying himself immensely, Rocco proceeded to take Cassia on a gastronomical tour of Rome, which was enjoying a busy, hot summer. Reaching some places by foot and others, later, on his motorbike, they sampled some incredible slices of *pizza bianca*, with olive oil and salt, and a couple of *filetti di baccalà*, Jewish cod fillets that were now a feature of Roman cuisine. Before lunch, in picture-postcard Piazza San Lorenzo under broad market umbrellas, they enjoyed some gelato made with fresh fruit and cream, the best Cassia had ever tasted.

'Their other location, between the top of the Spanish Steps and the entrance to the Villa Borghese, has some of the best views over Rome,' Rocco explained, 'but this one has more charm, in my opinion. Some people say it's over-priced and only for tourists, but I love it.'

'The gelato is gorgeous,' sighed Cassia, worrying about the amount of calories she was consuming. Food-tasting was part of her job to a degree, but still, with her curves, she couldn't afford to go mad. The trouble was, she was finding pretty much everything in Rome hard to resist. Including Rocco. Cassia turned away from the sight of him licking ice cream off his tanned fingers.

'I do love the Spanish Steps,' Rocco said, aching to kiss a dollop of pistachio ice cream from the edge of Cassia's mouth.

'Me too.' Cassia nodded, declining to mention she had always felt it to be the most romantic area of Rome.

Rocco finished his ice cream. 'We'll go there later . . . for some dinner? I know a wonderful place. You'd need a smart dress but we could always—'

'I have one with me,' Cassia interrupted, remembering her haphazard packing. 'The red one I wore to the party in England. Is it suitable?'

'Very,' Rocco responded. Removing the ice cream splodge

would be far too intimate a gesture, even with his fingers, so he discreetly let her know she needed to dab her mouth.

Turning crimson, Cassia wiped it away. Why did she always seem to act like such an idiot around him? She couldn't even eat a gelato without making a fool of herself. Somehow managing to cram in a lunch of Roman-style roast suckling lamb with a selection of herbs, Parmesan and anchovies, Cassia was in awe of the unique, tender flavour and the golden-brown crust that was achieved through cooking over an open fire.

Later, back at her apartment, she had a shower before dressing for their night out. With a towel wrapped round her, she sat at the mirror of her dressing table and wondered why her heart was thumping in her chest like a jackhammer.

Get a bloody grip, she told herself sternly. You're going out to dinner, that's all. Nothing more than that, and he's only doing this so you can write a good column. Sending Finn a message to try and make amends, Cassia was crushed that her inbox was empty. Nothing from Finn by way of apology or even an attempt to make things up, which didn't bode well.

Feeling confused and deeply unsettled by recent events, Cassia added a defiant slick of red lipstick and a generous spritz of the spicy Habanita perfume she knew Finn detested. He wasn't here, so he couldn't disapprove. Wriggling into the exquisite red dress, Cassia half-wished she was wearing something Rocco hadn't seen her in before, even though she knew that was silly. Downstairs, she found him waiting by a car he'd arranged for them.

'You look . . . lovely,' he told her, his eyes running over her in the most disturbing manner. 'That dress, it suits you. Red is your colour.' Try as he might, Rocco could barely drag his eyes away from her slender waist and her smooth shoulders in the sumptuous scarlet gown.

'Er . . . you too,' Cassia said, thinking Italian men had a knack of carrying off a dinner suit. She flushed, realising she had just told Rocco he looked lovely, hardly the most macho of compliments.

At the top of the Spanish Steps, he led her to a restaurant that was accessed by a private entrance, with tables overlooking the whole area. It was breathtakingly romantic and Cassia realised the discreet team of staff knew Rocco well. She wondered if it was because he'd been here with Stefania.

'I did a summer apprenticeship with the chef who runs this place,' Rocco told her, over the top of his menu. 'Please try the taglioni with truffles, it's his speciality.' He put his menu down. 'I brought Stefania here once and she refused to eat anything because she said it was all too fattening and over-seasoned.' Rocco pulled a face. 'She can be so ignorant sometimes.'

He was shocked to realise how true it was. Stefania really didn't have a clue when it came to food. He didn't mind her eating healthily, that was her choice, but now he came to think about it, she always criticised the seasoning and flavour combinations when they ate out, even in the most revered of restaurants.

Following Rocco's advice, Cassia chose the taglioni, followed by a duck breast. They were good choices; the pasta was rich but the delicate portion was just enough to enjoy the earthiness of the truffles, and the duck breast, thankfully on the small side, came with a deliciously zingy raspberry sauce and baked artichokes. Unable to say no, Cassia weakly accepted a complimentary sliver of what she now knew to be Rocco's favourite dessert, tiramisu. She closed her eyes as he spooned a mouthful of moist sponge and soft, magnolia-coloured mascarpone topped with a thick layer of cocoa into her mouth.

'Unbelievable,' she mumbled, breaking into laughter as Rocco helped himself to the rest. 'Ha! You're worse than me.'

'Sorry,' he mumbled. 'It's just too good.'

Not even noticing the admiring glances of the staff as Rocco placed a hand in the small of her back and guided her back out on to the busy street above the Spanish Steps, Cassia couldn't remember when she'd enjoyed herself so much. She was startled to find she couldn't recall the last time she and Finn had done anything fun – or truly romantic, for that matter. Their last weekend away was over a year ago and their holidays tended to be short due to work commitments. Cassia suddenly realised their relationship was more like a friendship than anything else – they were like best friends rather than romantic lovers. Shouldn't that sort of thing only happen after years and years of marriage, or perhaps once children were on the scene? They had to get back on track; they simply had to. They were about to be married and Cassia was desperate to get the spark back into their relationship, but she just didn't know how to. If only it all felt as easy as it did with Rocco, she sighed to herself.

Rocco, his warm hand still positioned on the most delectable curve of her spine, pointed out the stunning and well-known Hotel de Russie, where countless film crews and celebrities had stayed over the years. 'Down there is Babington's Tea Rooms, set up by two English spinsters in 1896, I believe,' he informed her. 'They serve English teas still, surprisingly popular, even with Italians. And further along is the Caffè Greco, which is the eighteenth-century café frequented by writers and musicians.'

Cassia let out a pleasurable sigh. 'It's great being here with someone who knows the area so well,' she said. 'When I visited with my father, he was just as much of a tourist as the next person, despite loving the city with a passion.' She looked sombre for a moment. 'He said Rome had a special place in his heart because it was the only place you could turn a nondescript corner and find a breathtakingly gorgeous fountain.'

'I think he was describing the Trevi Fountain,' Rocco murmured, pulling her in closer and heading down the steps. 'Let's be tourists and visit it.'

Unable to even respond when Rocco had his arm wrapped around her waist so proprietorially, Cassia allowed herself to be led. His touch felt incredibly intimate, but she told herself she mustn't get carried away. There was Stefania to think about, and Finn . . . As they turned the corner into the Piazza di Trevi, Cassia gasped. The fountain was magnificent and so much bigger than she remembered it. The Baroque-style fountain, the most famous in Rome, glowed creamy gold in the balmy summer light, its grand statues, so pale and marble-esque by day, shimmering with golden, artificial lights. Not caring that she looked like one of the many tourists milling around with their mouths hanging open in awe, Cassia drew closer, staring into the surface of the aquamarine water, which was also lit up with tiny lights. Coins glittered up from the bottom of the fountain and she tried to remember the legend.

'Toss a coin over your shoulder with your back to the fountain to make sure you come back to Rome,' Rocco provided, 'although the current interpretation is that two coins leads to a new romance and three will bring about either a marriage or a divorce.' He threw her a sideways glance, still holding on to her. 'I personally think it's just about creating a moment . . . undeniably romantic, of course. And I won't spoil it by saying how many of those coins are fished out by tramps.'

Cassia swallowed down the flash of excitement that had just shuddered through her, knowing she was getting swept away by the moment. She tried hard to stay grounded, but the day had been so unbelievably perfect, she was finding it difficult. Remembering that the fountain had been used in scenes in one of her favourite Audrey Hepburn films, *Roman Holiday*, wasn't helping either.

'That's . . . that's Neptune, right?' She gestured to the central figure, a spectacular specimen of manhood with angelic curls and strapping thighs. Riding a chariot in the shape of a shell, pulled by two sea horses, the sculpture was unashamedly dramatic and sensual.

Rocco nodded, not taking his eyes from hers. 'God of the sea. The scene is supposed to symbolise the contrasting moods of the sea, with one Triton trying to master an unruly sea horse, the other leading a calmer, more manageable version.' Rather like the contrast between Stefania and Cassia, Rocco thought, shaken by the notion. Stefania was the wild, out of control horse that needed constant and rather tedious constraint, whereas Cassia resembled the calmer sea horse, serene and beautiful with an incredible strength and passion shimmering just beneath the surface.

Not even taking a second to think, Rocco slowly turned her to face him. Her dark, liquid eyes were wide with shock but her full mouth quivered expectantly. Rocco caught his breath. What was it about her? Why did he sense this wild, untameable quality within, and why did it have such a magnetic pull, an irresistible, head-spinning sensation that made him feel as though he could be himself with her, that he could lose himself with her . . . in her, even?

Forgetting everything else, Rocco went with his gut feeling. Pulling Cassia's face towards him, he sank his mouth against hers, savouring the soft feel of it. Kissing her softly at first, but with more intensity as he felt her hands sliding beneath his dinner jacket, Rocco parted her lips with his, plunging his tongue inside her mouth. His head spun as lust shot through his body.

Cassia clutched Rocco desperately, willing him to carry on. The kiss felt so, so right; romantic, full of promise and lust. As erotic sparks charged through her stomach and headed south, Cassia pulled his head down harder, cupping her hand round his neck. Their bodies entwined, they kissed and kissed.

Pausing to take a breath, Rocco drew back, wanting to look into her eyes. Seeing them glazed with desire, the way he knew his own must be, he reached for her again, needing to feel her soft body crushed against his. Rocco breathed in the spicy fragrance she was wearing, adoring the way it drifted off the warmth of her skin. Whatever it was, it suited her.

I shouldn't be doing this, Cassia told herself urgently. Stop this, stop him . . . Feeling Rocco's mouth searching out hers again, she melted, unable to resist. His hands caressed her waist as though it was the most exquisite curve he had ever encountered and Cassia felt a sensual throb course through her. No one had ever made her feel like this, Finn had never made her feel like this . . .

Finn. Cassia's head snapped up. What the hell was she thinking?

At the same time, Rocco noticed his phone buzzing in his inside pocket, reverberating against his thumping heart. Fully prepared to ignore it, he realised it was the ring tone he had set for his grandmother and felt a moment of disquiet. Why on earth would his grandmother be phoning him now?

Cassia drew back as the realisation that for the first time in eight years, she had cheated on Finn – albeit with a kiss – hit her. Looking up at Rocco nervously, she noticed his worried expression.

'God, I'm sorry. This is all my . . . I should never have . . .' Cassia didn't know what to say but she knew she had to stop Rocco from looking so distraught.

'It's my grandmother,' he said, noticing several messages. 'She wouldn't call unless it's an emergency.'

'Take it,' Cassia urged. 'You must.'

Still holding on to her waist with one firm hand, Rocco checked his messages. Turning pale beneath his tan, his mouth tightened. 'We need to get back to Sorrento,' he told her in clipped tones. 'Tonight.' He dropped his hand and started to walk away.

Cassia hurried after him, her heels almost sending her sprawling across the pavements of the piazza. 'Slow down,

Rocco. What's happened?' She grabbed his arm, pulling him round to face her.

'There's been an accident,' Rocco said, visibly choked. 'My grandmother . . . something happened at the restaurant and she's in hospital. That was a doctor who left all those messages.'

Cassia turned white. 'Is she all right?'

Looking grim-faced, Rocco shook his head and called the car to collect them. He knew he needed to think about the ridiculously erotic kiss they'd just shared and what it meant but he couldn't. Right now, he had to get back to his family.

'I'll call my pilot,' Rocco said, looking dazed. 'It'll be much faster if we take the helicopter back. Luca can send on my bike. I just can't understand it; there has to be an explanation.' His voice trailed away.

Cassia squeezed Rocco's arm. 'Rocco, what happened?'

He lifted his eyes to hers. 'The surgeon . . . he said my grandmother was rambling when she was bought in, but she was adamant.' Rocco bit his lip. 'She was adamant that what happened to her wasn't an accident.'

Cassia frowned. What did he mean?

He held his hand up as the hire car pulled up at the end of Via Di San Vincenzo. 'This is going to sound crazy but my grandmother thinks someone tried to kill her.'

Gasping with shock, Cassia grabbed the hand Rocco was holding out and hurried towards the hire car.

Chapter Sixteen

Arriving at the elaborately named Santa Maria Della Misericordia hospital on the outskirts of Sorrento after landing at a nearby helipad, Rocco and Cassia dashed inside. The journey hadn't taken long and Rocco had spent most of it trying to find out what had happened. But he hadn't been able to make head or tail of what a clearly hysterical Aurelia was gabbling on about so he had given up.

Cassia allowed Rocco to take her hand again as they tore round the corridors. Her head was spinning with everything that had happened in the past few hours, but she pushed everything out of her mind so she could focus on Sofia. Her heart pounded as they eventually found the room Sofia was in and Cassia was taken aback at how much she had come to care about Rocco's grandmother. She had been the most welcoming member of the Disanti family, but Cassia knew it was more than that. Sofia was so motherly and caring, it was horrible to think something terrible had happened to her. Even worse to think that someone might have intended to do it. Cassia couldn't get her head around that idea.

'Rocco!'

For once, Aurelia looked less than perfect, her dark curls twisted up in a messy ponytail and her face devoid of make-up. She looked young and scared and she was sobbing uncontrollably. She fell into Rocco's arms as soon as he opened the door.

'Thank God you're here. Raff's being totally useless and it's been so awful . . .' Catching sight of Rocco's tanned hand grasping Cassia's, Aurelia looked startled.

Cassia immediately let go. It had seemed the most natural thing in the world when Rocco had taken her hand in Rome, in the helicopter . . . even outside the hospital, but she suddenly felt awkward. She bit down on her lip, remembering the kiss by the fountain and the erotic shockwaves it had sent shooting down her spine and she knew she should feel ashamed. She did, but a part of her felt so utterly intoxicated by the whole experience, it was difficult to see it as a terrible thing.

Anxiety for Sofia took over her thoughts and she glanced at Dino who was standing by her bed. He looked pale beneath his tan and his blond hair was in disarray. Raffaelo sat by Sofia's bed in a black shirt and trousers, his huge frame slumped as he held his dark head in his hands.

Cassia gasped as she caught sight of Sofia. Lying in the sterile-looking bed, connected up to various beeping machines, she looked frail and small, not like herself at all. Normally robust and vital, it was shocking to see Sofia in such a delicate state. Cassia followed Rocco to the bed, holding back slightly. She wasn't family so she had no right to even be here really, but she was dreadfully worried about Sofia.

'Tell me everything,' Rocco fired at Raffaelo. Aurelia might think his brother wasn't much use at the moment, but Rocco knew Aurelia would be even less coherent. He kept his arm round her as she needed the support, but he directed his gaze at Raffaelo.

Raffaelo lifted his head. His eyes were bloodshot from worry and his genial smile was nowhere to be seen. He looked awful, in fact.

'She was walking up to the villa after a meeting with . . . oh,

I don't know what she was doing, and anyway, this car came out of nowhere and hit her.' He rubbed his face as if to extinguish the thought of it. 'She's been going on about that rival family again, that curse, Rocco. Which is stupid, but I think she might just be trying to make sense of what's happened. Because it's appalling, isn't it?' Raffaelo was rambling. 'I mean, I can't make sense of it, I can't even believe she's lying there like that strapped to all these machines . . .'

Cassia hoped her intake of breath was inaudible. It was entirely possible her own father was the long lost descendant of the rival family the Disantis were so opposed to. She couldn't bear the thought that Sofia had been hurt by the horrible curse in some way.

Rocco cut Raffaelo off impatiently. 'Why on earth would this accident be anything to do with that stupid curse?' He couldn't imagine why Raffaelo had verbal diarrhoea; that usually only happened when his brother had done something wrong.

'Why wouldn't it?' Hysterically, Aurelia spun away from Rocco and grabbed at Dino. 'When that car had hit our grandmother, it just drove off. It drove off, Rocco! It didn't stop to check she was all right. The driver just left her bleeding on the ground like an animal. Who does that? No one innocent, that's for sure. So if Grandmother thinks it's something to do with this curse, well, I believe her.'

'Don't, babe . . . shhh . . . it's all right. She's going to be fine; the docs have said so.' Dino squeezed Aurelia as she buried her head in his shoulder. 'Sofia . . . your grandmother has concussion,' he informed Rocco, repeating what the doctors had told him earlier. 'And a broken arm. Bruised ribs but no internal bleeding. Her leg and hip were knocked hard, as was her back . . . we really should be grateful it's not more serious.'

Rocco nodded. 'She'll have to rest, which she'll hate, but she won't have any choice.' He tenderly took Sofia's hand. When the doctor had left messages saying his grandmother thought someone had tried to kill her, he had taken it with a pinch of salt. He had assumed Sofia was mistaken, that she had suffered an accident and that she had ended up confused as a result. Now, he didn't know what to think, but he refused to believe it was anything to do with this ludicrous curse his grandmother was always talking about. Whatever was behind the accident, Rocco couldn't help feeling responsible. He had promised his grandfather, Nico, that he would take care of his grandmother and here she was, lying in a bed like a broken bird, all the energy and twinkle knocked out of her. Rocco felt sick at what she had been through and about how much pain she must be in.

'Mother has been on the phone,' Aurelia said jerkily, still not in control of herself. 'They want to come home but I told them not to. What good will that do?' She dabbed her wet face with a tissue. 'The press will get wind of what happened if they come home early and they'll only cause a drama.'

Rocco nodded. 'I agree. Dino, can you call them and make sure they continue the tour? I'll speak to the doctors here and make sure everything is all right, but I really think it would be best if our parents stayed away so we can keep things as normal and as calm as possible. I'll give them regular updates.'

Glad to make himself useful, Dino took his phone out and left the room.

'Should I cancel the wedding?' Aurelia asked tearfully. 'What if Grandmother isn't up to it, what if whoever tried to hurt her comes back and . . . and . . .'

'Aurelia!' Rocco's voice was stern. 'You need to control yourself. And no, I do not think you should cancel the wedding. I think we all need to stop being so melodramatic and focus on getting Grandmother better.'

Aurelia looked upset. 'You're right, Rocco . . . I'm sorry. I'm just so worried about her.'

Rocco brushed her hair out of her eyes and kissed her forehead gently. 'Of course you are. We all are. Look, whatever we think happened, I refuse to think this is anything more than an unfortunate accident. These . . . hit and run incidents,' he paused, the phrase distasteful, 'are more common than you think. It doesn't mean anything sinister is behind it, it means that there are some uncaring bastards out there.'

'And some very bad drivers,' Cassia said, not meaning it as a joke. Curse or not, there was one thing that made her think Sofia might have a point when it came to the accident being suspicious in some way. Were hit-and-run drivers really that common, especially in the back lanes that ran around Sorrento? Wasn't it a little unusual not to check a person was all right after ploughing into them, especially someone of Sofia's age?

'Go and find Dino,' Rocco suggested to Aurelia kindly, sensing that she needed a break. 'And maybe get everyone some coffees?'

Sniffing, she nodded and left.

Rocco turned to Raffaelo. 'Was Grandmother really saying this accident was to do with the curse?'

Raffaelo stood up and nodded quickly. He looked smaller somehow, as if he'd had all the stuffing knocked out of him, and he shoved his hands into his pockets defensively. 'Maybe she's right,' he said, not meeting Rocco's eyes. 'Things have happened whilst you've been in Rome, orders messed up, bookings cancelled. There's even been a case of food poisoning . . .'

'Impossible!' Rocco looked furious. 'All of my staff are highly trained. That sort of thing never happens in our restaurant.'

'I know. But it has.' Raffaelo rubbed his chin with trembling fingers. Noticing them, he hastily put his hand back in his pocket. 'And Mike from the Vegas building team has been on

374

the phone to say they've been having problems over there; he says that's why the opening will be delayed.'

Rocco glanced down at Sofia again. 'This is serious. I need to know everything, Raff.' He glanced at Cassia, his eyes softening for a moment. 'Could you keep my grandmother company? And call us if anything changes?'

Cassia took the seat Raffaelo had vacated immediately. 'I won't leave her side.' Meeting Rocco's eyes, she swallowed, not sure what emotions she could detect in the olive-green depths. Did he regret the kiss? She couldn't tell. Nor should she even be thinking about it in the circumstances.

Seemingly about to say something, Rocco thought better of it and ushered Raffaelo out of the room.

Cassia took Sofia's hand in hers, dismayed to find it so limp. The machines beeped reassuringly next to her, so she tried not to feel too troubled, but it was unnerving all the same. Out of the blue, Sofia's eyes jerked open.

'The curse . . . it was the curse.' She licked her dry lips and groaned in pain. 'Need to talk to him . . . he was there . . . he knows . . .'

'Who? Who was there?' Cassia bent her head and strained to hear.

'Al . . . Al . . .' Sofia's eyes began to droop.

Cassia squeezed her hand. Al? Who was Al? 'Allesandro?' she said, with a flash of inspiration. 'Do you mean Allesandro Raldini? The wine merchant?'

Had Sofia been on a date? For some reason, Cassia was caught off guard by the news, but she didn't blame Sofia one bit. She was lonely and she deserved to be happy. Cassia was a little surprised that Sofia had chosen Allesandro to accompany her on her first date, but that was a personal thing. It was irrational, but Cassia wasn't sure she liked Allesandro very much. He was a little too charming for her taste; he reminded her of an older version of Finn's brother, Dom.

Sofia let out a fluttering sigh. 'It's a secret,' she whispered, her eyes wide open. All at once, they were full of terror. 'We went to lunch and then for a walk. The boys will think . . . but it wasn't anything . . .' Her eyes fluttered closed and her breathing became laboured.

Panicking, Cassia jumped up and ran to the door. 'Doctor!' she called, forgetting to speak Italian. 'Rocco, Raff, she just woke up!'

Cassia stood back as Rocco, Raffaelo and a stream of doctors dashed into the room. Breathlessly, she watched as they checked Sofia over, with Rocco barking out questions and Raffaelo looked fraught with tension. The next minute, she was knocked sideways by someone wearing a khaki trouser suit and pungent perfume.

'Rocco!' Stefania cried, her blond hair almost taking Cassia's eye out as she flipped it. 'I've just heard about Sofia. Is she all right?' She threw herself at Rocco, clinging to him with quivering hands.

Rocco looked taken aback to see Stefania and he found himself forced to grip her so she didn't collapse. 'She's fine, the doctors are checking her out now.' He frowned, wondering why Stefania was being so dramatic. 'Where have you been? I was in Rome for a few days and you weren't there.'

Stefania didn't meet his eye. 'I've been doing some business – just down the road, in fact. Anyway, that doesn't matter, I'm just worried about Sofia.'

Cassia faced Rocco and they stared at one another for a long, searing moment. In the back of her mind, Cassia also couldn't help wondering why Stefania seemed so poleaxed by Sofia's accident – she had never seemed to care too much for her before.

Not sure what Stefania was playing at, Cassia nonetheless felt mortified at finding herself face to face with Rocco's girlfriend. She mumbled an excuse and fled.

Waking up from one of the best sleeps she'd had in years, Diana stretched pleasurably. The rehearsal schedule for the play was demanding, but thankfully Robson had a one-day commitment out in Ireland at some charity thing he'd arranged to do, so they had all been allowed time off.

Diana was relieved. Playing Clarissa was intense and even though she enjoyed the challenge of acting out the agony her character was going through, a day to get her head together was much needed. When she was engrossed in work, she became so focused on her acting, there was barely time for anything else. Her housekeeper had left a stack of unread newspapers in the kitchen next to a teetering pile of unopened post and Diana knew she needed to get her life in order.

She glanced briefly at the other side of the bed. It was empty, achingly so. The pillow was plump and missing the indentation normally left by Angelo's dark head and the sheet was pristine and unruffled. Feeling a pang, Diana swallowed. She mustn't keep thinking about him. She'd hurt Angelo badly and the best thing she could do for him was to stay away and get on with her job, despite his caring texts and messages.

Throwing on a dressing gown, she was wryly amused to find that the cord was even tighter than normal, probably due to all the cheese toasties she grabbed during rehearsals. She was also astounded to find that she didn't care. Wow, Diana thought, tickled. I've grown . . . in more ways than one.

Inhaling the aroma from her coffee mug, she took a seat at the sunlit breakfast table in her kitchen and pulled her stack of unopened post towards her. As she ripped envelopes open, she listened to a message from Cassia, breathlessly recounting a wonderful day in Rome with Rocco. Diana paused, certain she could detect a level of excitement in Cassia's voice that she hadn't heard for a long time. She frowned as she heard about Sofia's accident, hoping it wasn't too serious. Glancing down,

Diana realised she'd just opened an invitation to Aurelia Disanti's wedding. Checking the date, she saw that it was just after her two-week run in the West End, so it would be the perfect distraction after all the hard work. It would also be a great way to escape if the critics savaged her, Diana thought ruefully.

Feeling saddened that Jules hadn't been in touch once since she'd gone to Sorrento, Diana caught sight of a face she recognised on the front of a newspaper on the top of the pile. Drawing it towards her, she was horrified to find a close-up of Dom Sunderland on the front, with a promise of the inside scoop on his apparent sex addiction. Gaping, Diana raced through to the relevant pages and skim-read the article. God, she really had dropped off the planet if she'd missed this scandal. Sordid details of a myriad of threesomes Dom had indulged in over the past year (pastimes he allegedly credited his recent 'top sporting form' with), plus lurid accounts of his sexual exploits on centre court were there for all to read about in detail. The last part of the interview detailed how Dom was now 'doing the rounds' in LA, seeing film executives with his agent and being touted around Hollywood as a potential hot new thing, as if tennis players on the brink of the big time and caught in a salacious threesome were the latest 'must have' accessory.

With wide eyes, Diana perused the accompanying photographs of the two girls he had been caught with, two nubile and mouth-wateringly sexy girls aged seventeen and twenty-one respectively, whose father was the most senior and well-respected umpire in tennis. Speechless, Diana laid the paper down. Her first, uncharitable thought was one of wicked wonder at what Grace's face must have looked like when she heard what Dom had been up to. Her second, more sobering, thought was how she, Diana, would feel if this was the face of one of her children splattered across one of the UK's most popular newspapers.

Abandoning her unopened post, she raced upstairs and threw on a wraparound dress in a summery shade of cerise pink and phoned the driver she always used when she was working. Grabbing her handbag on the way out of the door, Diana phoned Grace and Henry's house to see if they were in. Hearing from Louisa that they were at the wedding venue 'supervising arrangements', Diana instructed her driver to take her to Parkland Heights Manor.

What a hideous monstrosity, she shuddered to herself. Poor Cassia was going to have a seizure when she saw it in person. Diana instantly felt dreadful about not taking more of an interest in Cassia's wedding. If she had stood up to Grace when they first started talking about the details, perhaps she would have been able to stop her from taking over and creating the wedding she thought Finn and Cassia should have, rather than the one they'd asked for. Finding the venue a hive of activity due to a wedding that was due to take place the following day, it took Diana some time to find Grace. Asking various members of staff, she finally got lucky with one who pointed her in the direction of a side room.

'There you are, Grace,' Diana said, pausing in the doorway. Sitting out of the dazzling sunlight in a gloomy corner, Grace was surrounded by swatches of pink in a variety of shades and the table in front of her was piled high with boxes of ribbons and pearls. 'This isn't . . . this isn't for Cassia's wedding, is it?'

Grace looked thunderous. 'Who else's wedding would it be for, Diana?' she snapped. 'I'm not in the habit of offering my services for any passing stranger who might be getting married, you know. They're just letting me use this room to sort some things out because we're using the same company for all the finishing touches,' she added tersely.

Instructing her hackles to back down, Diana reminded herself that Grace was most likely being extra vile because of what had happened. 'I was so sorry to hear about Dom,' she started.

'Really?' Grace shot her a scathing glance. 'I would have thought someone like you would have found it hilarious.'

Diana bit her tongue, deciding it was best not to admit that her first reaction had indeed been mirth. 'Not at all. All I could think was how terrible I'd feel if I picked up a paper and saw Jules's face all over it with those horrible headlines.'

Grace's hands, delving into a box of seed pearls, faltered.

'And I can't apologise enough for my behaviour at the engagement party,' Diana continued, realising she might as well go the whole hog now that she was face to face with Grace. 'It was inexcusable. I was in a rather bad place at the time and I'm afraid I let my emotions get the better of me. And alcohol. Your beautiful cake . . . I can't apologise enough.' Diana picked up a piece of dusky-pink ribbon and toyed with it. 'But I'm working on it. And I promise I won't fall over and make a show of myself at the wedding. Or, God forbid, send whatever cake you've organised flying.'

Grace looked jolted by Diana's heartfelt apology.

'How are you coping?' Diana asked sympathetically. She noticed that Grace was looking rather ashen beneath her powdery-pink blusher and she felt a rush of compassion. Wasn't Grace just like her, in her own way? Wasn't she just another woman struggling to come to terms with the mistakes she'd made as a mother?

'Oh, one has to get on with things,' Grace said in a strangely flat tone. She waved a hand to encompass the table full of ribbons and vases. 'I have plenty to keep me busy here.' She looked away. 'It's horrifically embarrassing, of course. All my friends have been terribly nice about it but I know they're all gossiping about it behind my back. One of them even stole photographs and sold them to the papers.'

Diana put down the ribbon. 'It's one of those times you find out who your true friends are, isn't it?' She thought about Marco and wondered if some of her friends would stick around if they knew the hideous truth. Diane refocused her thoughts. 'Is it . . . is it true that Dom's out in Hollywood now? I read it in a newspaper but you never know if you can believe such things.'

Grace stood up abruptly. 'Yes, he is. It seems they forgive such behaviour over there far more easily than they do here.' Her mouth tightened. 'I expect you're delighted Jules isn't seeing Dom now. Hardly husband material.'

'Not yet, perhaps,' Diana agreed, keeping her expression neutral. There was no way she could answer that question without being derogatory about Dom and she hadn't come to see Grace for that. Diana was fairly certain Grace didn't appreciate her sympathy over Dom's antics or her apology, but oddly, she was still glad she'd made the effort.

'Put on bit of weight, haven't you?' Grace commented maliciously, giving Diana's curvaceous figure a critical once-over.

Diana gave a faint smile. 'It's for a part I'm playing. Good job too, otherwise I'd probably feel quite offended by your frankness.' Noting Grace's flushed cheeks with some satisfaction, she stood up. Not meaning it in a nasty way, Diana did feel that it was about time Grace realised how utterly crushing she could be at times.

'This acting job has saved my life, I think. And it's made me realise that I need to think about other people, not just myself.'

Grace looked baffled.

Diana walked to the door. Hesitating, she looked over her shoulder and decided it was time to be bold. 'Grace. Forgive me for speaking out of turn, but I think Cassia wanted cream and old-gold for her colour scheme.'

Grace slowly turned to face her, reams of pink ribbon clutched in her hands.

'Cassia hates pink,' Diana added gently. 'I'm so sorry if she forgot to tell you that because I just know you wouldn't choose it if you knew. That would be . . . well, it would be terribly bad form, wouldn't it?'

Passing a glum-looking Henry on her way out and giving his weathered cheek a kiss, Diana stepped out of the grotesque building and into the sunlight, deciding she would spend her day off chilling out with a good book in her garden. She knew she had more work to do on herself – her own family needed sorting, for starters – but she felt braver for taking the first few tentative steps towards honesty.

Henry, heading into the room to see what Grace was up to, found her slumped over a box of pink ribbons, her shoulders shaking. When he attempted to offer some words of comfort in his usual conciliatory manner, he was taken aback when Grace shrugged him off and refused to say what the matter was. He was even more flabbergasted to see that Grace – the wife he always described with the utmost fondness as being 'constructed from stone, like a nurse in the Second World War' – actually looked guilt-stricken. More disturbingly, she had what looked like tears in her eyes.

What on earth had Diana said to her? Frowning, Henry wondered if Parkland Heights Manor might be able to rustle him up some tea and coffee cake. He needed something to get him back on an even keel. With Grace bursting into tears every five minutes, Henry felt most off balance.

Spotting Jules from her terrace window, Cassia watched her for a second before deciding that it was about time she and her sister talked. After all the drama with Sofia, Cassia was conscious that family ties were important and that however distant she and Jules were, one of them should make an effort to break the ice.

Cassia put her scarlet bikini on and threw on a floaty red kaftan Aurelia had talked her into buying. Sofia was back from the hospital, but she was still being monitored by nurses, so

Cassia wasn't sure of her progress. She had spent the past week trying to speak to Rocco about the words Sofia had murmured when she had woken up in the hospital, but he had been tied up with restaurant business since the accident.

Cassia felt her stomach lurch with pleasurable memories. She hadn't been able to stop thinking about that kiss by the Trevi Fountain. It had kept her awake at night and it was burnt into her memory like a forbidden fantasy – except that it was real. It had happened and Cassia had to get her head round it. Why on earth had she done it? She was engaged to be married. In fact, she was getting married in . . . Cassia gasped inwardly. Less than two months, she realised, counting the weeks on her fingers. It was almost August.

Poor Finn; he didn't deserve this. Cassia was consumed with remorse; she had never cheated on Finn before and she couldn't understand why she had done such a reckless, stupid thing. Lust was one thing . . . but still. And that was all it was, Cassia told herself emphatically. She pushed aside any notion that Rome had been heart-stoppingly romantic, or that there might be more to her feelings for Rocco than basic attraction. Sizzling, head-spinning attraction, as it turned out, but she was an adult, not a teenager. And whatever it was, she shouldn't have acted upon it.

Stefania hadn't left Rocco's side for the first few days after Sofia's accident, but work duties had called and she was now back in Rome. Cassia felt uneasy about Stefania and more than a little guilty.

'Oh, it's you,' Jules said, shading her eyes with her hand and peering up at Cassia with slightly hostile eyes. 'What do you want?'

'Just a chat.'

'Shoot.'

'I just thought we should . . . you know . . . clear the air a bit.' Cassia sat down on a nearby lounger. 'I'm sorry if I didn't make you feel more welcome when you turned up here. Things have been rather strained between me and Finn recently and I guess if anyone was going to visit, I was hoping it would be him.'

'Fair enough.' Jules scrutinised Cassia, thinking she looked decidedly on edge. Had something happened on the recent trip to Rome with Rocco? If so, Finn was right to worry about them, obviously, but she wasn't sure she really believed Cassia capable of such a thing. And from a personal point of view, she didn't get the hooha about Rocco Disanti. He was handsome, there was no two ways about it, and as hot as hell too, but he was so tediously deep and brooding. The helicopter-flying and motorbikes were sexy, but Jules knew she wouldn't have the staying power to chip away at the complex layers of intensity to see what was underneath. She preferred her men more straightforward and less intense. Men more like . . . well, more like Finn, in fact.

Surprised at herself, Jules stole a glance at Cassia again. Grudgingly, she decided that her sister looked rather good in her bikini. The bright colour suited her dark colouring and the flattering cut suited her curves, as did the tan she'd acquired since she'd been in Sorrento.

Who'd have thought it? Jules thought to herself, put out. Put Cassia in a different country and she suddenly resembles Monica bloody Bellucci or whatever that gorgeous Italian actress was called.

'Did you hear about Dom?' Cassia asked cautiously.

Jules rolled her eyes. 'Well, we all know he likes a threesome, don't we? But with the daughters of an umpire? That's taking it to a new low.' Her expression became scornful. 'I knew he was an arrogant bastard, but this is bad, even for him. I mean, that's his tennis career up in smoke, isn't it?

Cassia nodded. 'Grace must be devastated.' She assumed that must be the case and probably more out of embarrassment than anything else, knowing how Grace felt about public indignity.

'She is,' Jules said, picking up her phone. 'Especially now that Dom has some new agent and he's about to make it big in the States.'

Cassia was puzzled. 'I didn't know he had an agent. Was that in the papers?'

Jules twirled her blond ponytail between her fingers. 'No, Finn told me. We . . . text each other now and again. Dom turned up at that family meeting and told them all he was off to LA.'

Cassia felt peeved. What family meeting? Finn hadn't told her about any of this. 'I thought he was too busy with that case to text anyone.'

'The Angel Preston thing?' Jules was impressed with herself for remembering the name of Finn's case, but it was because it reminded her of the name of a shop in Notting Hill she loved. 'He is, but these are only short little texts, nothing serious.' She held her phone out. 'See for yourself.' She felt antagonistic towards Cassia. Finn might be a friend now and he might be sending her jokey texts, but Cassia was the one lucky enough to be marrying the guy.

Cassia drummed her fingers on the lounger, vexed. Finn might only be sending short little texts to Jules, but that was a damned sight more than he was sending her. Annoyed with herself, she took Jules's phone, hoping to reassure herself. Seeing the number of text messages from Finn in her inbox, however, Cassia couldn't help but feel totally paranoid. She didn't bother to read any of them. They might be short but they were frequent. How was it that Finn was unable to contact her, his fiancée, when he seemed to find communicating with Jules an absolute breeze?

'Are you saying things aren't as perfect in paradise as I'd assumed?' Jules mocked, sitting up. She couldn't help baiting

Cassia a little more. 'I thought you and Finn were quite the nauseating couple.'

'Thanks,' Cassia said, recoiling. 'I didn't realise we were "nauseating". And when have I ever said things were perfect between us? I told you earlier that we were having issues.'

Jules raised her eyebrows disbelievingly. 'Really? The huge diamond ring on your finger begs to differ.'

Cassia threw her hands up in exasperation. 'It's a ring, Jules! It doesn't mean anything – at least, it does, but it doesn't mean that everything is all right between us. Because it really isn't. You have no idea.'

Jules stared at her curiously. She had never heard Cassia talking about Finn this way.

Just then, she received another text from Finn. This time it wasn't a jokey message, it was more informative. Finn was coming to Sorrento. He had decided to take some holiday because he had worked himself stupid and he would be there in a few days. Jules smiled broadly. What lovely news. She was looking forward to seeing him again.

About to update Cassia in case she didn't know, Jules looked up to see her sister storming away from the pool in a major strop.

Oh well, she thought, picking up Aurelia's wedding folder. She really should make some calls. And Finn was sure to tell Cassia about his visit anyway.

Prickling with irritation, Cassia wished she hadn't bothered to try and smooth the waters with Jules. Once more she was reminded that her sister really didn't have her best interests at heart and it hurt – quite a bit, actually. Not only that, Cassia now felt even more infuriated with Finn for his lack of contact. It had been irksome in the first place, but now that she knew he was sending text messages to Jules every hour, Cassia almost felt betrayed. It was all going on behind her back and, as innocent as it most likely was, it felt as though she was being sidelined in some way.

She stopped dead, feeling tears threatening to spill over. How had things got to this stage with Finn? And how could they possibly fix everything before the wedding?

'What are you going to do?'

Rocco glanced at Raffaelo, his mind racing. 'I'm going to have to go out there, aren't I?'

'To Vegas?'

Rocco nodded. 'What choice do I have? The opening is almost definitely going to be delayed and I have to find out what's going on. Cassia needs to get back to England . . .' He hesitated, finding the thought deeply unwelcome. 'Aside from that, I need to see if there's any link between the issues we're facing here and the ones that are happening over there.'

Raffaelo clasped his large hands together. 'So you agree that it might not be a coincidence, then?'

Rocco looked impatient. 'Don't tell me you're buying into this family curse business, Raff! Honestly, just because Grandmother suffered an unfortunate accident and a few things have been going wrong in the restaurant, we don't have to start turning into superstitious idiots.'

'No, of course not.' Raffaelo fiddled with his cufflinks. 'Sorry, Rocco. It's just all been rather stressful recently.'

'Tell me about it,' Rocco said grimly. He had done nothing but deal with issues since Sofia's accident; he had been so busy fighting fires and trying to figure out why they were suffering such bad luck, he hadn't even had time to get his head around what had happened in Rome. He hoped Cassia didn't think he was avoiding her, because he wasn't, but there had been no time to even collect his thoughts, let alone talk to her about it.

Rocco stared past Raff, trying to clear his head. What did the kiss mean? Was it simply a drunken moment between them? Just a natural progression from an intimate dinner to the absurdly romantic setting of the Trevi Fountain? Rocco dismissed the thought. He knew the kiss wouldn't have even been on the cards if he'd been in Rome with, say, Jules. Or even Stefania, Rocco admitted to himself. He had been shocked to see her at the hospital and of course he felt badly about what had happened with Cassia, but he knew his feelings of guilt were based on principle, not on regret.

I have to finish with Stefania, he thought, the realisation not a huge revelation. He wasn't being fair to her and he knew it; Stefania wanted something he couldn't give her. It wasn't just some sort of commitment issue; his reluctance was down to his feelings not being as deep as they should be for Stefania.

'When will you leave for Vegas?' Raffaelo asked, his brow furrowed with worry.

'As soon as I can,' Rocco said, getting to his feet. He looked at Raffaelo, concerned. Clothes aside, his brother had never been too fussed about his personal appearance. Lately, however, he had begun to look rather dishevelled, as if brushing his hair was the last thing on his mind.

'It will all work out,' Rocco said, jiggling Raffaelo's immense shoulder reassuringly. 'Just leave it to me. I promise I'll get everything back on track.'

Raffaelo nodded his dark head but his eyes remained apprehensive.

'Raff, is there something on your mind?' Rocco couldn't help feeling alarmed by his brother's strange manner. 'You know you can talk to me. About anything – anything at all.' Rocco willed his brother to confide in him, to confirm the suspicions that had been swirling around in his mind for the past week or so.

Raffaelo looked up, meeting Rocco's eyes, seemingly indecisive. Then he shook his head finally. 'No, no. I'm fine.' He heaved his large frame out of the chair. 'I'll go and check on Grandmother.'

Rocco watched him, then set about organising the trip to Vegas, booking hotel rooms and flights. He was sure Cassia would want to come – she needed to visit the restaurant even if the opening was going to be delayed; she could get the information she wanted and head home after the trip. He sincerely hoped she wouldn't do that, but he couldn't force her to stay.

What would happen in Vegas? Rocco mused, feeling exhilarated at the thought of spending time with Cassia again. Lost in memories of the heady kiss in Rome, he totally forgot to find her and tell her about the trip.

Chapter Seventeen

Finn threw some T-shirts into a small suitcase and wondered where the hell his tailored shorts had got to. Perhaps he could buy some at the airport, along with all the other things he couldn't seem to lay his hands on. He was already feeling stressed out about his visit to Sorrento. His bosses at Lovetts & Rose had encouraged it, assuring him that whilst his role at the company was watertight, a holiday was just what the doctor ordered. Finn had a nasty suspicion the firm might be carrying out an investigation into the error he'd felt obliged to own up to, but he had no proof. Besides which, he had other things to worry about, namely his relationship with Cassia.

Finn sat down on his bed and took a ring box out of his bedside drawer. He stared at the contents. The rings were unpretentious, classic bands in white-gold, without diamonds and bearing a simple set of numbers inside to mark the date of their wedding. No coded messages, no flowery prose and absolutely no soppy nicknames. Which was as it should be, right? Finn frowned. Should he and Cassia share secret information that no one else knew about? Should there be something more exciting etched inside these rings?

Finn snapped the box shut. Recently, he had found himself doubting everything about their relationship, but he was sure that much of it was down to their lack of communication. After returning from Rome, Cassia had sent him a short text informing him that she was back. No details, no chit-chit and a cold tone to the message that hadn't been present before. He was shocked that after a strong, eight-year partnership, being apart for a few months seemed to have destroyed their bond.

How would Cassia react to his arrival? At this point, he wasn't sure she would be remotely pleased to see him, but he had to make the trip, he had to salvage their relationship before it was too late. He had booked himself a room at a nice hotel in Sorrento, even though Jules had assured him that the Disanti family wouldn't hear of it. He was open-minded about staying at the villa, but he didn't like to assume.

Pausing on his way to the door, he glanced at a text from his mother. She was wishing him 'bon voyage', as well as instructing him to say hello to Jules. Finn smiled wryly. He was aware that Jules and his mother had been in regular contact since she split up with Dom. Having witnessed the way his mother had welcomed Jules into the family fold made him realise that Cassia had perhaps been right to feel that Grace had never really warmed to her. Jules seemed more part of the family than Cassia ever had, and certainly more now than when she'd been seeing Dom. And it wasn't just his mother. He felt the same way himself. They had only recently struck up a friendship, but he felt closer to Jules right now than he did to Cassia. They certainly exchanged far more texts and they had even spoken on the phone on the odd occasion. He was aware that he was more comfortable speaking to Jules than he was to Cassia, but that was why he was headed to Sorrento now; he had some serious bridges to mend.

Finn scooped up his luggage and prepared to make the trip to Sorrento, painfully aware that he wasn't so much embarking on a holiday as he was making a complicated journey towards make or break.

*

'Fittingly described as the world's biggest open-air museum, Rome is achingly romantic. Stunningly beautiful, it simply bubbles with history; lost empires, dynamic leaders and a vibrantly colourful past have been well documented, but nothing compares to seeing the gloriously extravagant architecture in person.'

Cassia paused, her fingers poised over her laptop. She could almost be back there, right now, standing by the Trevi Fountain with Rocco. His body hip to hip with hers as he kissed her, sending shock waves through her body . . . Cassia shook herself. The last thing she should be doing is thinking about Rocco. He'd left a message asking her to come and see him in his apartment that morning; he had some news, apparently, but Cassia was putting it off. They hadn't come face to face since they had come back from the hospital and she had no idea how to behave around him. Would he act as if nothing had happened? Would he be awkward around her to make sure she didn't read anything into it?

She sighed and returned to her laptop.

'Decadence oozes out of this breathtaking city, from its well-dressed priests cloaked in red and purple silks to its designer shops and espresso drinkers ensconced outside the bustling street cafés. Devour a heavenly slice of crostata di ricotta *(ricotta cheesecake) or a* crema di miele gelato *and prepare to be seduced . . .'*

Seduced. She latched on to the word. Was that what had happened to her? Had she simply been seduced by the romance of Rome . . . or by the heady chemistry she had felt between herself and Rocco? Even if she had, chemistry didn't necessarily mean anything, it didn't equal eight years of a relationship with Finn.

Should she tell him about the kiss? Cassia was undecided. Her father had once bitterly told her that confessing all to someone relieved the guilty of the burden and heaved heartache on to the innocent. She had never understood what he meant by that and she couldn't see how keeping something like a kiss with another man to herself could be right – morally, at least. Cassia knew she would hurt Finn if she told him what had happened in Rome, but she also couldn't see how she could go ahead with their wedding when she was hiding something like that from him. With a heavy heart, Cassia realised she probably had no choice but to admit to the kiss and hope to God Finn forgave her. As soon as she saw him face to face, she would pluck up the courage and tell him what had happened.

Pulling on what she hoped was one of her more conservative and professional-looking dresses, Cassia set off towards Rocco's apartment. I'm indifferent to him, she told herself with renewed determination. Or rather, I owe it to Finn to be.

Knocking tentatively on the door, she heard him calling her in, but when she slipped inside, he was nowhere to be seen. Cassia wandered around edgily, taking in every aspect of his personal space. He liked fine art, judging by a couple of prints on the walls and the odd ink print propped up against the wall on dressers. He was also a fan of sculptures and a few carved from wood and marble were dotted around his living area.

'Sorry to keep you waiting, I was in the shower.'

Cassia spun round. Standing in the doorway of his bedroom wearing a pair of unbuttoned beige trousers and nothing else, Rocco was rubbing his dark, wet hair vigorously with a towel. Cassia, conscious that appearing unmoved was absolutely vital, wasn't sure whether to look away and casually comment on the gorgeous prints on the walls or stare back coolly and feign disinterest.

Because it would be feigning, Cassia thought, swallowing. Stylish in a dinner suit and dynamic in a chef's coat, Rocco was as hot as hell with his top off. Muscular without seeming overly macho, he was broad-shouldered and tanned. Around his neck he wore a platinum chain with a cross on it and after tossing his towel on to the back of a chair, he slipped on a heavy silver watch.

'It was my grandfather's,' he explained, mistaking the focus of her stare. 'Vintage and Italian-made. Not that I care; it's just because it's his, really.'

Cassia tore her eyes away from Rocco's torso. Pull yourself together, she muttered to herself firmly.

Rocco watched her. Was she, like him, unable to get that sexy, heart-stopping kiss in Rome out of her mind? Or was she simply regretting it with every fibre and hoping he wouldn't mention it ever again? Rocco couldn't tell, at least not without being able to look properly into her eyes. 'I asked you here as I wanted to know if you would still be interested in coming to Vegas?' He reached for a duck-egg blue polo shirt.

Cassia turned to look at him. She had agreed to go to Vegas even before she had arrived in Sorrento, when Gena had first discussed the trip with her. But faced with going with Rocco now, after everything that had happened in Rome, was a different thing entirely.

Rocco tugged the polo shirt over his head and padded into the kitchen in his bare feet. 'I know it's a bit inconvenient, especially since the opening has been delayed, but I still think it will be good for publicity – for your column, I mean.'

Cassia wasn't sure how she felt about him saying that. She knew he was trying to keep things professional between them, but for some reason it made her heart thud with disappointment. 'Er, yes. You're right. I suppose it's better than nothing.'

'Coffee?' he asked, pointing to a gleaming espresso machine. He glanced at her, wishing he didn't find her so desirable. Even in her work clothes, she looked delectable and it was all he could do not to reach out and tug her into his arms.

He thrust his hands into the pockets of his expensive-looking trousers, feeling the need to keep temptation at arm's length. He could see that Cassia felt uncomfortable and he knew he had to tread carefully. He also knew he couldn't contemplate going to Vegas without her; spending even a few days from her, that far away, seemed unthinkable. He had no idea what that meant for him longer term, but that was how he felt right now.

'I'm concerned about the things that have been going wrong over in Vegas,' he said, filling the awkward silence between them. 'I'm beginning to wonder if someone has it in for the Disanti chain.'

Cassia accepted a cup of espresso, frowning. 'Really? You're not . . . you're not thinking it has something to do with this curse?' Thoughts of her father sprang to mind and she couldn't help wondering how Luca was getting on with his investigations. It was horrible to be so excited at the thought of finding out more about her father while at the same time being poleaxed by the terrible thought that he might be a member of the rival family that had caused the Disantis so much pain over the years.

What would they all say if that was the case? Would they immediately turf her out? Would Sofia, who had always been so warm and friendly, suddenly reject her and see her in a different light? Cassia couldn't see how she could do anything else and she was petrified that her presence at the Disanti villa was under threat. Which was ridiculous; she was due home as soon as her secondment had reached its natural end and it wouldn't matter then who her father was.

'Of course I'll come to Vegas,' she found herself saying. 'It'll be fun. Even though it's business,' she added hurriedly.

Rocco let out a breath of relief.

'I have to fly out early – today, in fact, but I know you need to pack, so I'll leave a ticket at the airport desk for you, all right?' Rocco felt a moment of panic. Would she duck out of the trip if he wasn't around to persuade her to come? It was a risk he was going to have to take.

'Thanks. I guess I'll see you there.' Cassia met his eyes, certain she saw a flicker of longing in them before he nodded impassively. Her heart hammering in her chest, she left Rocco's apartment. Leaning against the door, she let out a shaky breath. What was going to happen in Vegas? Could she resist Rocco if she spent even more time with him? Cassia knew she should pack her case, head straight home to Finn and never speak to Rocco again. But like a junky in desperate need of a fix, she knew she couldn't. Forcing herself to think about Finn, Cassia headed off to pack.

'What do you think?' Aurelia held her coral-painted nails up for inspection.

'I love it,' Jules responded, relinquishing herself to the touch of the beauty therapist as she massaged her instep.

'I don't know,' Aurelia said, scrutinising her nails critically. They were the stumpy-chic nails most models sported; short, perfectly shaped and nonchalantly stylish. 'I don't want to be totally on-trend, but this looks a bit too predictably bridal for my taste. Remove it, please,' she instructed the girl who had painstakingly painted the colour on. 'Let's try something else.'

Jules smiled to herself. She was becoming used to Aurelia's fickle nature and, frankly, she found herself rather envious of Aurelia's ability to change her mind on a whim and be granted whatever wish her butterfly mind alighted upon. Being a top model and Italy's socialite darling obviously helped, Jules thought, glancing admiringly at Aurelia's naturally golden complexion. And being her wedding co-ordinator – no, make that friend, Jules corrected herself confidently – came with wonderful bonuses. Trips to Capri, rides in helicopters and now this, an afternoon of indulgence in one of Naples' most exclusive beauty salons.

While Aurelia tried out nail colours, Jules had been treated to a facial, a full body massage and a pedicure to die for. A soak in a rose-scented food bath had been followed by cascading drizzle of warm almond oil and a massage that had Jules arching her back in ecstasy.

The trip to Naples had been a last-minute thing, a recommendation by one of Aurelia's model friends, and Jules barely had time to take in the historical, breathtaking sights of Vesuvius, the swanky shops in the main city area and the aromatic restaurants before being whisked inside the select salon that looked and smelt intimidatingly expensive. The air was scented with exotic wafts of the rose that seemed to be present in most of the treatments and the atmosphere was discreet, tranquil and focused on luxury.

'I wonder how my grandmother is doing,' Aurelia fretted as the nail technician laboriously removed the coral polish and applied yet another layer of base coat.

'I'm sure she's on the mend,' Jules replied reassuringly, picking out a candy-pink shade for her toenails. She wondered what it felt like to be so family-focused, she found it all a bit alien. She didn't have grandparents; the Italian side of her own family was non-existent of course and her mother's parents were long gone. Jules had a vague recollection of them from when she was very young but she hadn't felt any particular bond with them.

Aurelia looked worried. 'I just can't stop thinking about that car knocking her down like that and driving off. Who does such a disgusting thing?' She held a hand up and chewed her lips as she assessed the new shade. 'Or maybe it's the famous family curse. What do you think?'

Jules shrugged non-committally. She wasn't sure she bought into the whole family curse business, but she knew Aurelia was deeply superstitious. Surely such things didn't exist in modern society? Years ago, Jules could believe feisty Italians with a grudge threw flamboyant curses out to all and sundry when they wanted to cause a drama, but she couldn't get to grips with the idea that something as outlandish as that went on nowadays, or that one from so many years back could have an effect today.

Jules briefly thought about her family. Her relationship with her father had been difficult, to say the least, and if she was honest, she supposed she had some regrets about the way it had panned out. Since her father's death, she had had a chance to review the situation and she could admit to herself that she had reacted violently to the truth when it had accidentally emerged. But didn't her father need to take some responsibility too? Shouldn't he have been able to bury his feelings of resentment, as far as she was concerned, at any rate?

Jules's lip curled. Her mother had a lot to answer for, especially since her father wasn't around to explain himself. These days, most of her resentment and bitterness was directed at her mother, purely out of necessity, but the more Jules thought about it, the more she felt that was where it should have been directed in the first place. Her mother had been in touch a few times, wittering on about some play she was involved with, but Jules couldn't be bothered to answer her. Why should she care about her mother's tedious career? It was the least of her worries.

She wiggled her candy-pink toenails to dry them, feeling a squirm of excitement about Finn's imminent arrival. She wondered what Cassia thought about the visit, but she had barely spoken to her sister recently so she didn't have a clue. Jules knew that Finn was apprehensive about his trip because he'd said as much in a call to her the night before. He was anxious about seeing Cassia, seemingly under the impression his fiancée was annoyed with him and being distant. Jules was sure he was over-reacting; Cassia was busy, nothing more, and it wasn't in her nature to bear grudges, she was far too nice.

Jules pulled a face. Her sister was boringly predictable; if anything, Cassia was simply caught up with work and too busy to give Finn more than a modicum of her time. Grace was right about her sister, Jules decided, snuggling down into the luxurious robe she was wearing. Finn deserved better, he was a man any normal woman would want to pay attention to.

'Hey, has Cassia mentioned that her fiancé Finn is on his way over?' Jules asked Aurelia.

Aurelia shook her head.

Jules tutted. 'Cassia should have told you.' She paused, wondering if Finn was keeping his visit from Cassia, but maybe Cassia had just forgotten to make arrangements. Too busy most likely, Jules thought critically. 'I think he has plans to stay in a hotel in town, but I thought it would be great if he could stay at the villa, if you don't object?'

Aurelia shrugged. 'Sure, why not? I'm assuming he'll stay with Cassia in her room.'

Jules bit her lip. For some reason, the thought bothered her. 'Well, maybe it would be nice for him to have his own room, if you have the space. I mean, just so he has somewhere to chill out.' She faltered, aware that her reasoning was flimsy, but she couldn't backtrack now. She looked up as Dino bounded into the salon like an exuberant puppy. The girls in the salon looked annoyed at the noisy interruption, but soon brightened when they caught sight of Dino's sun-bleached hair and visible pecs. Clearly recognising him from one of his ad campaigns, the young owner of the salon rushed forward and ushered Dino to a nearby leather chair. Grinning, he took a seat and allowed himself to be tended to.

'Nice place, very relaxing,' he said in perfect Italian, causing hearts to flutter even more.

'Stop it,' Aurelia admonished him, wriggling with pleasure as he leant over and kissed her juicily. 'He knows the girls go all silly when he speaks Italian, he has the best accent. His father's Italian,' she added, seeing Jules's look of surprise.

'Oh yes, I did know that, actually. Still, so was mine and it hasn't helped me.'

'Really? I thought you were the most fabulous cook? Cassia said you were.' Dino held his hand out with a charming smile as a therapist offered to file his nails.

Jules started. She wasn't aware Cassia had talked about her being a good cook, but she couldn't help feeling pleased. And she supposed she did rather owe that particular skill to her father.

'By the way, the hotel in Capri phoned,' Dino said in an aside. He lowered his voice, not wanting Aurelia to hear and spoke rapidly in English. 'They said something about an urgent payment. I told them it must be a mistake and that you'd call them as soon as we got back to the villa.'

Jules went pale underneath her tan. She had forgotten to pay the wedding venue balance! Despite all of Aurelia's reminders and cautions not to mess up, it had somehow slipped Jules's mind to settle the bill and secure the hotel. She felt panic rising at the thought of Aurelia's fury if she didn't manage to sort it out in super-quick time.

'Er, leave it with me,' she told Dino hastily. 'They're wrong, but I'll sort it all out immediately.'

'Glad to hear it.' Dino nodded. For once, he didn't look laid-back. 'Because this wedding means everything to Aurelia, and I really do mean that. We've been planning this for a long time and that venue is so important to her; it's where we first met.'

Jules felt her stomach plummet just a little more.

'What are you both chatting about?' Aurelia asked crossly, annoyed that she'd been left out.

Dino squeezed her hand. 'Nothing, babe. I was just asking Jules if she thought I was too metrosexual.'

Aurelia relaxed and laughed. 'You? Perish the thought!'

Jules laughed with them, hoping to God she could sort out Aurelia's wedding venue without incident.

Cassia tentatively knocked on Sofia's door. She had been meaning to visit her for a few days now, but with the almost Mafia-like nurses in attendance, gaining entry to Sofia's quarters was rather like being granted a viewing with the pope. Shown in by a stern, matronly-looking type who practically asked Cassia for proof of identity and a fingerprint before she was allowed inside, Cassia approached Sofia's bed with caution.

However, instead of the fragile scene Cassia had been imagining, Sofia was propped up in bed flipping through a magazine, her cheeks restored to their usual rosiness and her green eyes as keen as ever.

'Cassia!' She patted the bed in delight. 'Join me. I've read this magazine so many times now. I asked for some more magazines yesterday but that shrew won't let me read more than a few lines an hour. I'm not sure if they're army cadets in disguise.'

Cassia laughed then stopped when the nurse shot her a warning glance. 'Gosh, they're pretty scary, aren't they?' She wondered if Sofia's comment had been more accurate than she realised. Were the nurses actually there to oversee Sofia's security? After all, the accident had been rather shocking and with all the talk of curses . . .

Sofia sighed and sank back against a pile of plump pillows. 'Rocco organised them. They're wonderful, actually, but they do take themselves, and their jobs, very seriously.'

If Rocco had organised the nurses, Cassia had no doubt they weren't bouncers in disguise and were simply dedicated to making sure Sofia didn't overdo it. Rocco didn't believe in rival curses and Cassia was sure he was right. She couldn't shake off the feeling that the accident had been a little on the sinister side, however. She glanced at Sofia, noticing her troubled expression. 'What's wrong? Do you feel unwell? Shall I get one of the—'

'Absolutely not!' Sofia looked alarmed. 'I just can't stop thinking about the accident.' She shuddered. 'Every time I close my eyes, I can see the red car hurtling towards me. And not stopping.' She let out a jerky breath. 'It was terrifying, Cassia. I'll never forget it.'

'I don't blame you.' Cassia thought about the red car, racking her brains for some sort of clue about the driver. Didn't Stefania drive a sporty red thing that went from nought to sixty in a few seconds? No, that was silly. Why on earth would Stefania be behind Sofia's accident? She and Sofia didn't get on, but Stefania wasn't evil. 'Has Allesandro visited you yet?' Cassia asked, hoping she wasn't speaking out of turn.

Sofia blushed slightly. 'A few times. I detest appearing so weak and feeble in front of him. I'm an invalid, it's hardly a glamorous look.'

Cassia smiled. Sofia couldn't really look like an invalid if she tried. It had only been in hospital that she had seemed truly frail and sick. 'I'm sure he doesn't think of you that way.'

'Yes, well.' Sofia was offhand. Hesitating, she started to say something.

'Go on,' Cassia said. 'Say whatever you want. I'm not going to judge you.'

Sofia swallowed. 'It's just . . . Allesandro . . . he made it clear he wants more. A relationship, I think.'

'And how do you feel about that?'

'Guilty,' Sofia confessed in a rush. 'I can't stop thinking about Nico. Which is stupid, isn't it? He's been dead for four years.' She paused. 'Did your mother wait long before she started dating? You know, after your father passed away?'

Cassia waved a dismissive hand. 'My mother is probably not the best person to compare yourself with, Sofia. She started dating . . . well, within about a year, I would say. Although, honestly, I don't think it meant that she wasn't torn apart by my father's death because she was, totally.' She shrugged. 'It's just the way she is. My mother loves male attention; always has done.'

Sofia shifted in the bed with some discomfort, still obviously undecided about her feelings for Allesandro. 'So. You are off to Vegas with Rocco.' She nodded. 'A good idea from your perspective, I think, because after that, your visit will be over. You must be keen to get back to England to your fiancé.' She raised her eyebrows at Cassia, her mouth twisting mischievously.

Cassia looked away. 'Er, yes. I really must get home and get myself organised.'

'A shame,' Sofia said lightly. 'You are staying for Aurelia's wedding, I take it? Your fiancé's family are all coming, aside from the younger boy – Dominic, is it?'

Cassia grinned. 'Oh yes. He probably has . . . better things to do.'

'Well, quite. And your mother has accepted too, she says her West End play will be finished by then. I'm excited to meet her,' Sofia added. 'She was in one of my favourite sitcoms years ago, but don't tell Rocco. He doesn't even know I watch some of these shows, he says they're all trash.'

Cassia could well imagine and she smiled to herself. 'But as soon as it's over, I must get back. I've stayed far longer than I said I would as it is and I can't see my fiancé or his family being pleased unless I head straight home at the earliest opportunity.'

Sofia eyed her shrewdly. 'I don't think they view anything you do favourably, do they? It seems that you are desperate for their approval, yet whatever you do, it's not enough.'

'True, but I suppose they're right in this case.' Cassia's expression became rueful. She was touched by Sofia's sympathy, but she knew she couldn't blame Grace this time. 'I'm getting married in just over a month and I'm still in Italy, dashing around after Rocco when I should be sorting my wedding out.' She coloured slightly, realising how her comment sounded.

Sofia pretended not to notice, but she couldn't help twinkling a little more. She patted Cassia's hand. 'Well, I think your fiancé's family are totally missing the point. We all find you delightful and you know you are welcome to stay for as long as you like.' She changed the subject. 'You will enjoy Vegas, I'm sure. The gambling is second to none.'

Cassia couldn't help laughing. 'I can just see you playing poker all night long.'

'Roulette,' Sofia corrected, her eyes twinkling. 'So addictive. And I do love poker too, now that you come to mention it. I taught the children how to play every card game under the sun when they were little, which was probably very irresponsible of me, but they loved it, especially Raff. Go, pack your case.' Sofia flapped her hands. 'I don't think any of us are as impulsive as we should be, do you?'

Cassia rather thought she'd been nothing but impulsive since she'd arrived in Sorrento, but she nodded as she got to her feet and kissed Sofia's soft cheek. She hoped she and Sofia would always be friends, even when she'd returned to England. As long as she wasn't related to the Giorelli family, Cassia thought desolately.

Outside, she started as she bumped into Allesandro.

'Ah, Cassia.' He inclined his head slightly and squeezed her hand. 'How is the patient?'

She relaxed, wondering why she had felt that she didn't trust him. Now that she had come face to face with him again, she realised Allesandro was harmless. He was charming and pleasant to talk to and if Sofia liked him, then that was good enough for her.

'Sofia's much better, I think. She's desperate to get up and walk about but those nurses won't let her so much as lift a finger.'

Allesandro nodded. 'Ah yes, the frightening nurses. A little unnecessary, but I do believe they have her best interests at heart.'

Cassia agreed. 'Listen, Allesandro. Do you think there was anything sinister about the car accident? Anything... untoward?'

He shrugged. 'I don't think so. I know you are talking of this curse . . . Sofia has informed me about it, but I honestly think it was just one of those wrong place, wrong time occurrences.'

'Fair enough. Nice to see you, Allesandro.' Cassia left and before she could change her mind, she packed a suitcase and set off for the airport. She missed Finn as he arrived in Sorrento by roughly half an hour.

Chapter Eighteen

Swept up in the moment, Diana felt his strong arms around her naked body and she shivered as his fingers lazily trailed down her spine. She clung to his shoulders, pulling him closer, breathing in his scent. At last, he had come back to her.

As helpless tears slid out, Diana frantically wiped them away, lest he notice her distress. Allowing him to roll her on to her back, Diana arched to meet him, her eyes meeting his as she lost herself once again, the way she had done when they had first met. She felt jolted as, out of the blue, a vision of Angelo swam into her mind. Darling Angelo . . . how she missed him.

'Brilliant!' the director called, jumping out of his chair. He checked his sheet and gave a jubilant nod. 'Well done, everyone, rehearsals are officially over. Here's to putting this play on in the West End at the weekend!'

To a ripple of applause, Diana sat up and wriggled into her robe. She thanked the director formally, overcome when he pulled her into a hug. She kissed Robson affectionately, smiling as he was met by his boyfriend Giles. How silly she had been to imagine that Robson was in love with her, Diana thought. It just showed that method acting or not, it was always best to keep one eye on reality. If only she'd done that all those years ago, she thought to herself unhappily.

Turning down cake and champagne, Diana slipped to her dressing room. It was bare and empty because she had already packed her personal effects, but it was only the rehearsal theatre. Throwing off her dressing gown, Diana quickly dressed in a flattering black and white dress. Slipping on a pair of bright red heels, she couldn't be bothered to remove her make-up and she added a slick of scarlet lipstick and an extra layer of blush to brighten her complexion. Due at a celebratory lunch with her agent, Diana gathered up her bag of personal effects and took one last look around her dressing room. She could hear the laughter and cheers of the cast and crew as they celebrated the end of rehearsals, but for the first time, she felt no urge to join in. Lunch with Felicity seemed fitting for the moment.

Not like the old days, Diana mused. Back then, she would have been the last to leave, downing champagne with gay abandon, nibbling at a slice of cake for show and clinging to her co-actors like a limpet; she had never wanted any acting experience to end. As much as she adored Marco and the girls, returning to normality and domesticity had felt too much like reality. Diana realised how much she had always enjoyed living in a bubble, swept up by the magic of the moment and keen to prolong it as much as possible. How incredibly selfish.

Diana bit her lip, full of regrets. It was too late for all that now, though, she thought to herself. Plastering a smile on to her face as she walked through the set, she blushed as the crew and cast members gave her a raucous cheer. Kissing her finger-tips and giving them a modest wave, Diana left the building and hailed a cab. Fifteen minutes later, she was sweeping down the trademark staircase of the not-so-cosy but seriously decadent Quaglino's in Mayfair.

'I'm surprised you didn't book Disanti's,' Diana said to Fliss as she did her best to slip into her seat unnoticed. 'It's far more discreet.'

Fliss kissed her cheeks, surprised by the comment. 'Actually, I tried but it was fully booked. And since when have you cared about being discreet?' She gestured to the glossy ceiling. 'I thought you loved this place. It's rock star, royalty and high society all rolled into one.'

Diana nodded grudgingly. She did love Quaglino's. It was famed for its divine crustacea bar and the crème brûlée was out of this world. But strangely, since rehearsals for the play had started, she had rather enjoyed the more low-key existence she had assumed. Gaining weight had made her all but unrecognisable and since she was deliberately playing down her normally flamboyant persona, Diana was able to slip in and out of quieter restaurants without attention.

'How is Cassia getting on with Rocco Disanti?' Fliss asked, keen for gossip. She decided Diana looked exceptionally good at the moment. She didn't know if it was the extra pounds or the new-found confidence Diana seemed to have discovered during rehearsals for the play, but she looked and seemed different. She was . . . serene and understated, Felicity realised with surprise.

'Rocco?'

Fliss's eyes widened. 'Yes, Di, Rocco Disanti. The gorgeous chef your daughter is living with at the moment. Isn't he just the most handsome man you've ever seen?'

Diana frowned at the menu. She'd met Rocco at Cassia and Finn's engagement party but she had been so drunk, she couldn't quite remember what he looked like in person. She knew about him via Cassia, of course, and she did recall that he was rather delicious to look at.

'Yes, yes, he is. Terribly handsome. And Cassia seems captivated by him.' Diana felt another stab of something indefinable in her chest. She couldn't think or talk about another man without thinking of Angelo. She felt Fliss's eyes on her and she rushed to cover her melancholy. 'Her column is doing fantastically too, which is wonderful. The online one is getting thousands of hits and the monthly one has given *Scrumptious* record sales.' She gave her order to the waiter without looking at the menu, handing it back at the same time.

'Good for Cassia,' Fliss commented, eyeing her friend with interest. Something was going on with Diana and Fliss was keen to get to the bottom of it. From what she had seen and heard, *Jealousy* was going to be big news when it started and there were already rumours of an extension. The last thing she needed was Diana going off the rails at this critical point.

'And the wedding plans?' she asked.

Diana looked up. 'Going well, I think.' She gave Fliss a quick synopsis of her chat with Grace at Parkland Heights Manor. 'It was all very uncomfortable, but I felt I had to say something. Grace is so controlling and it's easy to just let her have her way when it comes to things like this. But it's Cassia's wedding. I . . . I should have been more involved from the start.'

Fliss shrugged. 'Weddings aren't really your sort of thing, are they, Di? Besides, you've been working . . . you know how focused you get.'

'Focused?' Diana almost laughed. 'Is that what you call it?' She gulped down an excellent Semillon Sauvignon Blanc without even tasting it. 'I get so lost in the parts I play, I practically become the person I'm playing, Fliss. Much to my detriment.'

Fliss was perplexed. 'Darling, what's wrong with that? It's what you do, it's what makes you so brilliant. You've always been one of those actors who gets totally engrossed in the part and I guess that means that your personal life suffers from time to time. I'm sure Cassia will forgive you; she's used to it.'

'I'm not worried about Cassia. At least, not really.' Diana swallowed. She was sure Cassia would be fine, she always was. Of her two daughters, Jules was the one she lost sleep over. For obvious reasons. Diana felt tears pricking at her eyelids. Her past, it wouldn't leave her be. It couldn't, of course; the past was the past and there was no way of erasing it.

Could she make amends? Diana fiddled with her cutlery restlessly. Was there some way of exorcising her soul? Marco was long gone and it was far too late for that, but perhaps . . .

'Has something happened?' Fliss asked Diana gently. 'Since you've been rehearsing this play, you've seemed different, changed somehow.'

'I know.' Diana looked agonised. 'It's been such a positive experience, but it's made me think . . . about everything. About the past, and more importantly about my life now. I've made so many mistakes, hurt so many people.'

Fliss met her eyes across the table. She knew exactly what Diana was talking about. In fact, she had something to tell her but she wasn't sure now was the right moment. It had been in the papers but she knew Diana barely managed to open her post when she was working, let alone read newspapers or magazines. Fliss chose not to mention it. They were supposed to be celebrating and it could wait.

'Look, there's nothing you can do about it now, Di. It's the future that's important.' She drew a file out of her handbag. 'Look at this. This is full of offers we need to discuss. There has been such a buzz about the play, we've been inundated with scripts and interview slots.'

'Really?' Diana was flabbergasted to hear that she was in demand again. She felt the sudden urge to cry. 'I've been so worried about everything . . .'

'I know,' Fliss told her soothingly. 'But you have no need. This is the beginning, a new beginning for you, Di. It's all coming together.'

'Is it?' Diana was embarrassed to find tears sliding down her face. 'So why do I feel as if I'm falling apart?'

Fliss was astonished. This wasn't the reaction she'd been expecting. 'Darling, what on earth is the matter?'

'There are things I need to put right . . . with various people.'

'Angelo?'

Diana flinched at his name. 'If only. No, it's too late for Angelo and I don't deserve him, anyway.'

About to tell Diana that Angelo had been in touch several times over the past few weeks to ask after her, Fliss was distracted by Diana's comment. 'Make things right with whom?'

'I mean . . . other people.' Diana exhaled jerkily. 'Jules needs to know, Fliss. The proper truth, I mean. Not the one she thinks she knows. Cassia too. Cassia doesn't know anything.' She wrung her hands. 'I've wanted to tell her so many times. Can you imagine how baffled she is by Jules's resentment? All these years poor Cassia has had to bear the brunt of all of this, rather like Jules did with Marco.'

'The proper truth, Di?' Fliss shook her head, certain it was a bad idea. 'Are you sure you're up to that?'

'I have no idea.' Diana felt panic-stricken. 'But I think I have to do this. I don't think I have any choice. It's . . . it's haunted me for too long.' She leapt up and grabbed her handbag. 'I'm so sorry, Fliss. I-I have to go.'

Dumbfounded, Fliss watched Diana hurry out of the restaurant.

Rocco hadn't been entirely truthful when he'd told Cassia he was off to the airport earlier. Or rather, he had kept part of his destination secret. Unable to put it off any longer, he had taken a quick helicopter ride to Rome before taking a taxi to the empty building Stefania had secured for the new Disanti venture. As suspected, he found her inside, making copious notes and taking photographs on her phone.

'Rocco!' Her face lit up when she saw him.

He instantly felt like a bastard. He must have given something away in his face because Stefania put her notebook down.

'Is something wrong?'

'I'm afraid so.' Rocco sat on the edge of a nearby table. It was covered in dust and would probably ruin his suit, but in the scheme of things, it was hardly relevant. 'It's . . . us, Stefania. It has to end.'

Horrified, Stefania swallowed. What on earth was he talking about? Nothing was going to end if she had anything to do with it; she had far too much invested.

Rocco ran a hand over his conker-brown hair, something she knew he did when he was troubled. 'I'm under so much pressure with the business right now. I really can't cope with a complicated relationship as well.'

'Complicated?' Stefania moved towards him. 'I wasn't aware that our relationship was complicated, Rocco.'

Her smile was light but, inside, she was seething. She had always done her level best to keep her distance from Rocco when he needed to get his head down, and sensing that this was one of the times he needed space, she had stayed in Rome, even though she had been dying to visit him in Sorrento. Whenever she saw him – at his request only – she made sure she was sexually adventurous, considerate of his needs and very much behind him professionally. The perfect girlfriend, in fact. Stefania pursed her lips, knowing she had made his life difficult over Cassia, but she had every right, surely? The two of them had incredible chemistry, even if they wouldn't admit it. Any girl in her position would have done the same.

She advanced upon Rocco, certain she could change his mind. 'Now, don't you think you're being a little hasty?' She reached out a hand and massaged his shoulder. 'You're so tense, you need to relax more.'

'How can I do that, Stefania?' Rocco stood up, his eyes glinting with anger. 'I am already running three restaurants and I have another under construction in Vegas. And you think I need another one to take up my time.' He swept an arm, encompassing the building. 'It's too much, Stefania.'

Stefania narrowed her eyes. She had seen this side of Rocco before. When he was under pressure, he became increasingly stubborn and tried to cool things off between them. He had done such a thing twice before in their relationship and even though Stefania found it tiresome, she had too much at stake in the partnership not to go along with it. The Disanti name under her wing in Rome would put her PR company on a par with her competitors in no time at all. Being Rocco's girlfriend was one thing; having one of his restaurants within her control was quite another.

'I understand,' she said demurely.

Rocco stared at her, not sure he believed her.

Stefania ran a finger down his lapel, making sure the gesture was reassuring rather than provocative. 'You are stressed and you can't contemplate opening another restaurant whilst the Vegas one is still undergoing work.' She shrugged. 'This can wait . . . I can wait.'

Rocco let out an impatient sound. 'Stefania, you're not listening to me. I said it's over. It's not like the other times, this is about us and about this venture in Rome. It's not what I want any more. The relationship or the restaurant. I'm sorry to be brutal, but I need you to understand.' Couldn't she see how much pressure she'd put him under? Wasn't she aware that he was already too far from the most important thing in his business – the cooking?

Rocco was suddenly infuriated. She was supposed to have his best interests at heart, but he suspected she had her own motivations for not listening to a word he was saying. Stefania was like a brick wall, sometimes; he simply couldn't get through to her. And this was just one of the many reasons they were incompatible, Rocco thought, realising with absolute conviction that he was doing the right thing.

Stefania frowned. Rocco sounded serious. Was it Cassia? Stefania scrutinised him, but he wasn't giving anything away. Perhaps he thought he was in love with the silly English journalist, but Stefania was arrogant enough to think she could lure him back once he had Cassia out of his system. It hurt, of course, but if Rocco was in the throes of basic infatuation, she was prepared to wait it out. She refused to believe it was over and wouldn't allow it to be. They were going to open a restaurant in Rome together! It was all planned. It would add another string to Rocco's already successful bow and it would put her on the map as a serious promoter and business woman. She had put an entire year of her life into this and she wasn't about to back out now. Still, she knew Rocco well enough to see that he was at breaking point, for whatever reason. So, as much as she hated the idea, she would agree to his suggestion that they split up. For now.

'All right, Rocco,' she responded tightly. 'I can see you mean what you say.'

Rocco ran a hand over his short hair in frustration. He was certain Stefania was still playing games, but he no longer had time for it. He had toyed with the idea of being more honest with her, of telling her that he thought he had feelings for Cassia, but now he realised it was pointless. Stefania would rage and she would probably still think she could convince him that they should be together.

'Goodbye, Stefania,' he said with some regret. 'I'm so sorry things have ended this way.'

'Me too,' she said meekly, giving him a chaste kiss on the cheek. She lingered, leaning her body against his to give him a reminder of how well they fused together.

Rocco moved away with gentlemanly politeness. Stefania was beautiful, but he no longer loved her, not in that way. 'I will speak to you soon,' he said, moving towards the door. 'To see how you are. I care about you and I would like us to be friends, if we can.'

Shocked, Stefania nodded. Watching Rocco leave, she sat down abruptly and started planning in her head. She had to get him back, somehow, and whatever he said, she would do just that.

Friends? Stefania thought scornfully. Over her dead body.

Feeling weirdly excited about going to Vegas, as well as annoyingly guilty every time she thought about Finn, Cassia checked in at the airport. Flustered to find Rocco had booked her a first-class ticket, she self-consciously entered the lounge, enjoying a drink while she waited to board. When her flight was called, she found herself in a surprisingly large area in first class and did her best not to appear uncool as she gawped at the bar and massage area. She wondered who might be sitting next to her.

Expecting someone rich but terribly dull, an overweight, ageing banker perhaps, Cassia was stunned when a very well-known American reality star slid her famous bottom into the seat next to her. Averting her eyes, certain the star wouldn't want to make idle chit-chat with anybody, Cassia tried not to choke on the heady waft of perfume the girl was giving off. It smelt lovely, but it had been liberally applied.

Checking her phone for the last time before switching it off, she noticed a text message. Hopeful it might be Finn, she felt cross when she realised the message wasn't from him at all, it was from Luca, Rocco's historian friend. Her heart leapt. Was it the awful truth she'd been dreading? Cassia cursed the fact that she couldn't contact Luca immediately. Whatever he had found out, she was going to have to wait until after the flight.

Switching off her phone at the gentle insistence of a beautiful air hostess in a tight-fitting uniform who looked like a model,

Cassia sat back, trying not to stare at the reality star next to her. 'Please check your menus,' the air hostess said in an upbeat voice. 'We have a lobster special today and an extensive selection of wines. And you really must turn your phone off now, I'm afraid,' she said in a firm but pleasant tone.

'Isn't it annoying?' the reality star sighed. She switched hers off with much eye-rolling. 'I can't survive without checking my messages every five seconds.' She turned to Cassia with a friendly expression. 'I'm Carlotta Moore, by the way. I'm famous for . . . well, for being famous, really.'

Cassia held out her hand. 'I know who you are. It's lovely to meet you. Cassia Marini.'

Carlotta grinned, her dark locks rippling. 'I thought I'd probably end up sitting next to an old pervert; I seem to attract them. You look like much more fun.' She reached into her handbag, a cavernous Hermès that Cassia knew had a very long waiting list, only because Aurelia was incandescent with rage that she hadn't been able to lay her hands on one yet.

Carlotta held up a box of perfume and thrust it into Cassia's hands. It was black, with amber writing. 'My new fragrance, try it.'

Cassia accepted. 'Really? Thanks. I smelt it on you when you sat down. It's gorgeous.'

Carlotta thanked her. 'I'm drenched in it, I know. I've come direct from a campaign and I had to spray so much of it on, I thought I was gonna puke.' She settled back in her seat and snapped her belt on as the plane prepared to take off. 'Are you meeting anyone fun in Vegas?'

'Er . . . Rocco Disanti, actually.' Cassia's cheeks went pink. She felt like a dreadful name-dropper but she supposed Carlotta was used to that sort of thing.

'Rocco Disanti? No way. You're shitting me!' Carlotta's dark brows shot up. 'Oh my God, I love his restaurants! You must introduce me. He's so handsome. Is he handsome in real life? I bet he is. Wow, how do you know him? He's so private . . .'

Cassia smiled, the text from Luca forgotten. She was glad of Carlotta's non-stop chatter. It would stop the butterflies from racing round her stomach at the thought of meeting up with Rocco in the next nine or ten hours.

Unaware he had missed Cassia by mere minutes, Finn was sweltering as he put his luggage down outside the airport. Looking around for a taxi, he turned to find Jules standing next to him.

'Surprise!' she said, breaking into a smile.

'W-what are you doing here? How . . . how did you know which flight I was on?' Finn was annoyed to find himself stammering. It was only Jules, but he was really pleased to see her. Wearing a pale blue halter-neck dress that enhanced the dark golden tan she had acquired, she looked as pretty as a picture and before he could stop to think, he embraced her and accidentally landed a kiss on her fragrant neck.

Jules grabbed his hand luggage, gesturing for him to pick up his suitcase. 'I phoned your mother, of course. She told me your flight details and I wasn't sure if you'd arranged transfers so . . .' She laughed. 'Anyway, I've organised one of the cars the family use and you're staying at the Disanti villa.'

'What? But I've booked a hotel . . .'

'They won't take no for an answer and neither will I. Trust me, you're going to love it.'

Jules waved away his protests and led the way to the car. She knew Finn would probably object but she told him not to be silly. 'The Disanti family can't wait to meet you,' she told him chattily once they were ensconced in the back of the car. She craned her neck to point out a landmark, not noticing that the split in her dress had flashed her tanned legs.

'Are you sure it's all right if I stay?' Finn tore his eyes away from her legs. He had convinced himself that the incident at his parents' house had only affected him so much because he felt bad for not looking away from Jules more quickly, but the sight of her golden skin was sending his head all over the place. He turned and stared hard at the Amalfi coast.

'I'm sure. Would you like some water? You look rather hot.' Handing him a bottle from her bag, Jules hid a smile. Poor Finn. He was such a Brit abroad. He looked thoroughly uncomfortable, probably because he was dressed for drinks at a polo match, not a hot, muggy summer's day on the Amalfi coast.

'Are your legal firm all right about you having some time off?' Finn was relieved when Jules flipped her skirt back into place. 'They're positively encouraging it. I told you about that mistake I made with that file? Well, I reckon they're looking into it in more detail while I'm away.' He took a swig of water. 'I can't believe it; I've never done anything like this before. I can only imagine it's because I have so much on my mind, but still.'

Jules looked sympathetic. 'Poor you. I'm sure everything will be fine. You've been so loyal to the company and you said they've been very reassuring about your position there.'

Finn nodded, not wanting to talk about it any more. 'How's Cassia?'

Jules shrugged. 'Well, I think. To be honest, I really haven't spent much time with her. She's been really busy with all the Rocco stuff.' She looked contrite. 'I've been feeling a bit guilty about Cassia, actually.'

You and me both, Finn thought to himself. 'Why?'

'Well, we're not close, as you know.' Jules looked thoughtful. 'But it's not her fault, it's just something that happened years ago.' She glanced at him curiously. 'Do you know anything about it?'

He shook his head. 'Not really. Cassia mentioned that you two used to be great friends and that everything changed one day. But that's all she knows. Or is there something she hasn't told me?'

Jules bit her lip. 'No. It's something I haven't told her.' She folded her hands in her lap. 'And I should have done, I just haven't been able to bring myself to do it. I feel so ashamed, you see, even though I shouldn't. But I shouldn't have taken it out on Cassia in the first place.'

Finn leant back tiredly, closing his eyes to the searing sunshine. His brain was fuddled enough as it was without Jules talking in riddles. He was trying to think about what to say when he met up with Cassia, but for now, words were failing him. It was going to be almost like greeting a stranger, really. The last time he had seen her was the engagement party and that felt like a lifetime ago. So much had happened, but none of it related to Cassia, when Finn came to think about it.

'How's Dom?' Jules asked, interrupting his reverie.

Finn opened his eyes and stole a glance at her. Did she still care for Dom? Surely not, not after the way he'd treated her. For some reason, the thought of it irked Finn. 'Oh, he's fine, I think,' he said, watching her reaction.

'He reckons he's going to be the next Brad Pitt. He's on E Entertainment this week, for goodness sake.' Jules laughed, but there was no edge of bitterness in it. 'Idiot,' she said, knowing Dom would be thoroughly excited about such a development. He had always wanted to be famous, after all, and Jules was fairly sure he didn't mind it being for something other than tennis. His rejection still stung whenever she thought of it, but since she had been in Sorrento, she had come to accept that it was largely her own fault. Dom was still wrong for misleading her, but she had been all too ready to believe his lies and accept his false promises of a future together.

'I still feel stupid about the whole thing,' she said, looking shamefaced. 'Dom was feeding me lines and I was lapping them up.'

'He's a fool to have lost you,' Finn said without thinking. They stared at each other, not speaking for a moment.

'Um . . . we're here,' Jules said, tearing her eyes away. Had she imagined what she had just seen there? Her heart was thumping, but she told herself to calm down. Finn was Cassia's fiancé, not hers, and hadn't she just been berating herself for reading too much into the way Dom had behaved around her?

'Wow.' Finn got out of the car, glad to stretch his legs. He wanted to get into his room and have a shower, preferably a cold one. 'I wasn't expecting a palace. What a breathtaking place. No wonder Cassia has enjoyed being here so much.'

'Impressive, isn't it?' Jules gazed up at the villa, still dazzled by it, even now. 'And I know what you mean about Cassia, but she has plenty to enjoy back in England, doesn't she? I mean, there's you, for starters . . .' She stopped, her cheeks flushing. What on earth was she saying? 'Sorry. Anyway, shall we go and find her?'

Finn nodded, not looking forward to coming face to face with his fiancée one bit. But he knew he had to get that first awkward meeting out of the way. 'Good idea. Lead the way.' Feeling unnerved, Finn followed Jules up to the villa, doing his best not to enjoy the view of her bare back and her sun-bleached ponytail.

Chapter Nineteen

Standing in the window of her penthouse suite in the Bellagio Hotel overlooking the vast fountains, Cassia couldn't quite believe she was in Vegas. The flight had been absurdly luxurious due to Rocco's first-class generosity and Carlotta's company had made the hours shoot by.

The plane had landed and Cassia had been agog at the sight of the glossy black pyramid which was the Luxor Hotel rising majestically out of the desert opposite the airport, as well as the rest of the hotels on the strip. They stretched out like a row of gaudy gems, mirrored surfaces shimmering in the sunlight, their bright colours dazzling the eye. Accompanied by firm friend Carlotta who had told Cassia her entire life story on the flight over, they had headed through customs arm in arm, not realising they were being chased by paparazzi. As soon as Carlotta had spotted them, she had clutched at Cassia, giggling as they ducked their way through the tourists to find Carlotta's agent. Outside, they had taken refuge in a private car her agent had furtively led them to, with Carlotta insisting on giving Cassia a ride to her hotel.

'Don't take a cab, honey,' she had said dismissively. 'Not when we can drop you off. The Bellagio, you say? Your friend Rocco certainly likes to do things in style. Hey, I'm just next door in the Cosmopolitan, so I'll probably be able to wave at you from my suite.'

Cassia had tried hard not to gasp as shiny, metallic towers, medieval castles and the regal lions of the MGM zipped past her air-conditioned window. She caught sight of a mock-up of the New York skyline, complete with a hair-raising rollercoaster looping round it, and further down, she found herself staring at a miniature Eiffel Tower set against a sweeping example of opulent, mock-French architecture. The Bellagio, on the other side of the road, looked discreetly expensive, as did the Romanesque façade of Caesar's Palace. The Mirage with its mock volcano, the Venetian, complete with its Rialto Bridge replica and the brash funhouse that was the Treasure Island caught her eye in a flash and just as the stylish curve of the Wynn came into view, Carlotta's driver had doubled back on himself to park outside the Bellagio entrance.

Barely able to articulate how amazing it all was, Cassia had waved goodbye to Carlotta and checked in, finding herself treated like a VIP as she was sent up in a soundless lift to the thirty-sixth floor. Before she had time to appreciate the stunning view over the Vegas strip or the immaculate coffee-and-cream-coloured penthouse suite, she discovered a note from Rocco asking her to meet him at the restaurant.

Quickly changing into an aubergine-coloured sundress Aurelia had assured her made the most of her dark colouring, Cassia added some black suede slingbacks and went in search of a taxi. Not having a clue how near the hotel Rocco's restaurant was, she was embarrassed when it dropped her a few hotels down. It had a super-shiny exterior and a grand driveway and even though it wasn't a themed hotel as such, it was classy and the attention to detail inside was incredible. Asking some-one the way, she was shown to a glittering gold doorway with 'Disanti's Vegas' emblazoned across it in rhinestones. It was too kitsch for words.

Inside, the building work was in full flow. Cassia gaped as she took in the dark purple drapes on the walls and the discreet tables and booths. Despite the glitzy image of the restaurant from the outside, the interior looked exclusive and very Disanti's. There were crowds of people working on the project, either perfecting work inside the restaurant or standing in small groups with clipboards, discussing issues.

Spotting Rocco in one of them, Cassia headed towards him. Expecting him to look harassed, she was taken aback when he caught sight of her and grinned. Wearing tight beige chinos only an Italian could get away with and a black linen shirt with the sleeves rolled up, Rocco looked surprisingly relaxed.

'Cassia,' he said in English, taking her hand and leaning in to kiss her cheeks. 'I'm so glad you came.'

Flustered by the gesture, Cassia almost bumped heads with him.

'Good flight? Feel free to speak English, by the way.' Rocco jerked his head in the direction of his team in amusement. 'They refuse to speak one word of Italian to me, so let's go with English while we're here.'

'All right.' Cassia rather wished they could stick to Italian. Rocco's English accent was absurdly sexy. 'The flight was lovely, thank you. First class . . . I wasn't expecting that.'

Rocco waved her gratitude away, his olive-green eyes sweeping over her in the most disturbing manner.

'I was sitting next to Carlotta Moore on the way over. The reality TV star. She's so down to earth and a big fan of yours.' Cassia smiled. 'She wants to meet you whilst she's in Vegas if you can fit it in.'

Rocco laughed, still holding her hand. 'All right. If you like her, we can do that.' He hoped he didn't look too happy that Cassia had arrived. Having done his best to convince himself in her absence that he was merely having a moment of madness when it came to his feelings for her, Rocco now knew that was rubbish. Standing in front of him, with her creamy-golden shoulders exposed by the sundress and her dark hair hanging loosely down her back, Cassia looked utterly ravishing. And rather than thinking his feelings had been exaggerated, Rocco realised with some force that they actually ran far deeper than he had thought. And that he wasn't scared about it any longer either.

Cassia wondered why Rocco seemed so laid-back. His eyes were as intense as ever, but his body language was resolutely chilled out.

'Is everything all right with the restaurant?'

'Totally.' Rocco pulled a face. 'Just a few glitches that needed sorting out but as soon as I was able to have a proper talk with my project manager, we were able to resolve everything in a few hours.' He looked vexed. 'I'm annoyed with myself, to be honest. I was so sure something was going badly wrong here, but I think I allowed myself to get caught up because of all the issues back in Sorrento. The opening will still be delayed, but only by a few weeks. It should go ahead just after Aurelia's wedding.'

'I see.' Conscious that Rocco was still holding her hand, Cassia withdrew it and thrust it into a pocket in her sundress. It still felt warm from his grasp and she was struggling to concentrate. 'I-I don't know if I'll still be around for that. I'll be in Sorrento for Aurelia's wedding, of course, but after that . . .'

Rocco's good mood plummeted slightly, but he pushed it away. He refused to think about Cassia going back to England, particularly when she had just got here. 'Well, we can talk about that another time.' He gestured to the glitzy doorway. 'Ludicrous, isn't it? It looks like something out of Liberace's mansion, doesn't it? I was annoyed at first, but I suppose it has a certain something.'

'It has rhinestones in it . . . rhinestones, Rocco.' She burst out laughing.

Rocco joined in. 'Don't.' He shuddered. 'I almost hopped back on the plane when I saw it.' He glanced at his watch and frowned. 'A friend of mine, Bobby, runs a restaurant in the hotel opposite and he asked me to do a food demo with him. It's for his TV show, I think. I said no, obviously.'

'Not . . . Bobby Swan?' Bobby was a very well-known American chef with several restaurants under his belt. He was also a TV pro with a fine line in non-stop, cheeky banter. He had achieved the God-like status that meant that women adored him and men couldn't help but admire him, but he wasn't as handsome as Rocco.

Which was a shame, Cassia thought. He kept himself to himself and didn't often like to put himself out there, but she personally thought it would do Rocco the world of good to have some fun with something not so business-focused.

'It's not really my cup of tea, Cass,' Rocco said warningly, seeing her eyes lighting up at the thought of it.

Barely noticing the easy familiarity they seemed to have slipped into again, Cassia joined him as they strolled through the swanky lobby. The plink-plonk sound of fruit machines was muted but constant, and occasionally, there was a cheer as random symbols matched up and churned out a payment. Nearby, a crowd of people wearing tuxedos and cocktail dresses stood whooping by a craps table, clearly not caring that they had been gambling round the clock. There were no clocks anywhere to be seen, in fact, which Cassia guessed was deliberate on the part of hotel owners; it meant that ardent gamblers had no idea whether it was night or day and would be more likely to continue ploughing tokens into machines and betting their house on red or black.

Kept cool by the brute-force air con in the hotel, they were hit by what felt like a heat wave as soon as they went outside.

'Wow, I love this heat, don't you?' Cassia held her face up to the sun. 'It really puts a smile on my face.' She turned to Rocco. 'Hey, why don't you do this food demo? I know you're Mr Private and all that and I'm not saying you should do it for the publicity, but you could just do it for the sheer hell of it.'

Strolling alongside her, Rocco considered the idea. Just for the sheer hell of it. He hadn't done something like that since . . . well, he couldn't even remember when he had done it last.

'I'll do it if you come with me,' he said, his eyes flirting with hers. 'Come on, do the demo with me. Just for the sheer hell of it,' he added, tongue in cheek.

Cassia hesitated. She was a food writer, not a presenter. She had never done anything like this before. And she was a nobody. Who would want to watch her? She met Rocco's eyes. His enthusiasm was infectious. She had seen glimpses of it in Rome and the odd time in Sorrento, but here in Vegas, it was as if he had totally let go of everything stressful in his life.

'What would I do?' She laughed, protesting as he egged her on.

Rocco thought for a second. 'Give us a running commentary? You know, describe what we're doing at each step?' He smiled, his eyes twinkling. 'Just check if there are any geriatrics in there, you might cause a few heart attacks here and there with your sexy descriptions.'

Cassia blushed. 'All right. I'll give it a go.' She felt her stomach shift nervously as soon as she'd agreed to do it. What was she thinking? It was Rocco who would benefit from more exposure, not her.

Rocco looked pleased and he checked his watch again. 'We'd better go then. We're on in half an hour and they'll probably want to do make-up and all that stuff.' Grabbing her hand, he took charge and led the way through the crowds of tourists bustling along the pavements. Bobby Swan's team efficiently swept Rocco and Cassia up into proceedings, barely batting an eyelid at the introduction of two last-minute attendees who needed hair, make-up and scripts.

In a whirlwind of make-up, hairspray and stylists who added hooped earrings, a slim patent belt and an armful of bangles to Cassia's outfit, they were escorted to an auditorium.

'Lovely to meet you,' Bobby said, his booming voice instantly recognisable. He kissed her cheeks and gave her an appraising look. 'Phew, you're going to blow the socks off our viewers, seriously. Sexy, sexy. Wow.'

'Wait until you hear her describe food,' Rocco said, watching Cassia's cheeks turn pink.

Bobby guffawed. 'I can't wait. Right, these are the dishes we're going to be creating,' he said, showing them both some photographs and a list of ingredients. 'I was hoping you'd join me, Rocco, so I designed an Italian-inspired menu, but the crowd are gonna go crazy, they were only expecting lil' old me. Hey, Rocco, I'll get them to send a copy of the show back to Italy, shall I? I bet Sofia would love to see it.'

Rocco agreed. He knew his grandmother wouldn't believe it until she saw it, anyway. He had always shunned such events in the past. Not listening to their banter, Cassia read the recipes frantically as Rocco checked them over her shoulder. She didn't know what was freaking her out more, the thought of live TV or Rocco's proximity. She could feel the warmth of his breath on her neck and his aftershave was tickling her nostrils. She forced herself to focus on the menus. There was shrimp and octopus ceviche to start, which troubled her; how on earth could she make raw fish sound attractive?

Panic set in. A pasta dish with pancetta and cream sounded delicious and there was a *torta di miele* – a moist honey cake – to finish. Cassia thought she could probably handle the last two dishes, if only she could pull off the starter.

'H-how many people come to these sorts of events?' she asked, slapping away the hand of a make-up artist as he attempted to put even more bronzer on her cleavage.

'Oh, a few hundred,' Bobby replied airly, voluntarily holding his face up for more concealer and a mist of fake tan. 'Chill, honey; you're gonna be fine.'

Rocco raised an eyebrow, knowing Bobby was playing the numbers down. He was nervous himself but he was also oddly elated. It felt good to be doing something outside of his comfort zone. Especially something so closely related to food. Rocco couldn't wait to pick up a razor-sharp Global knife and get stuck in.

Gulping, Cassia allowed herself to be led into the auditorium. Realising the 'few hundred' people Bobby had mentioned were actually more like a few thousand, she almost darted out of the room. Especially when she saw the banks of cameras lined up to catch every second of the demo.

'Relax,' Rocco whispered, squeezing her hand. 'This is supposed to be fun, remember?'

'It might be for you,' she retorted, hoping she didn't have sweaty palms. 'This is all new to me. And actually, how come you're so chilled out? I thought you hated this sort of thing.'

Rocco shrugged. 'I do, usually. It must be because of you.' He met her gaze, his eyes intense. 'You make me feel so . . .'

His words were lost as the floor manager started whipping the crowd into a frenzy. Introducing Bobby, who received a riotous round of applause and plenty of cheers, Rocco was next.

'And we have a surprise for you all today. Notoriously private chef, Rocco Disanti, is joining us.' There was a pause, before the crowd starting yelling like mad. A few women even screamed like groupies.

Meeting his eyes, Cassia couldn't help giggling. Rocco, realising how ridiculous it was that women were acting as if he was a rock star, fell about laughing.

'And Rocco brings with him British food writer Cassia

Marini, daughter of Marco Marini!' the floor manager cried, as if it was the most exciting thing in the world. 'Let's hear it for Rocco and Cassia!'

The cameras swung round, capturing them holding hands and laughing. Immediately, they pulled themselves together and leapt apart. They looked pained as Bobby pointed at them and made kissy noises and Rocco rudely pulled a face. Waving to the crowd and walking to the white counter with all the ingredients lined up on in next to two hobs, he took his position next to Bobby, while Cassia hung back and smiled as they mucked about together for a bit, talking about the menu. The crowd were in raptures, hanging on every word.

Rocco's a natural, Cassia thought, impressed. Matching Bobby's easy banter flawlessly, Rocco was soon causing the audience of Bobby fans to switch allegiance, not least because his Italian good looks trounced Bobby's rotund cheekiness. Seeing the floor manager motion for her to join in, Cassia cleared her throat nervously.

'So, as you can see, the ceviche is nearly ready, a deliciously light starter with plump pink shrimp and mouth-watering slices of octopus.' Cassia gulped, wondering if she was on the right track, but seeing the floor manager giving her a thumbs-up, she carried on, trawling her memory for facts about the dish. 'Traditionally marinated in citrus juices that almost "cook" the seafood, the origin of the dish is disputed. But with the addition of chilli and avocado, you're left with a starter that will tickle your taste buds and leave you breathless with anticipation for what's to follow . . .'

Looking up, Cassia caught Rocco's eye. Seeing his smile of approval, she grinned back, feeling absurdly happy. Bobby jerked his head in their direction, making a show of shaking Rocco's hand as if to congratulate him on Cassia.

Moving on to the pasta course and oblivious to the cameras catching every glance and blush, Rocco and Cassia roared with the crowd as Bobby flamboyantly juggled nests of dried pasta in the air.

Feeling uptight, Aurelia stalked past the swimming pool. Catching sight of Jules stretched out on a lounger wearing a black, strapless beach dress, she glowered slightly. The wedding was a few weeks away and Jules didn't exactly look as though she was buckling under the pressure. Unless she was more efficient than Cassia had given her credit for, Aurelia felt cross that Jules didn't look remotely stressed out.

'What's the matter?' Jules asked, quickly picking her phone up again. She had been desperately trying to get through to the reception venue in Capri since Dino had told her about the money issue, but they kept gabbling at her in Italian and she couldn't understand a word. She couldn't remember how much the balance was because she'd lost the letter Aurelia had given her and she couldn't get anyone to speak to the hotel in Italian because that would mean admitting her mistake.

Jules had toyed with the idea of getting a staff member to help her, but she didn't trust anyone enough to do it. She had even thought about going over to Capri herself, but aside from Aurelia giving her daily 'to do' lists that meant she was unable to tear herself away from the villa, Jules was loath to leave Finn on his own now that he had arrived. Since he'd heard about Cassia jetting off to Vegas with Rocco, he had been horribly down in the dumps.

Aurelia frowned, flicking her long, dark ponytail over her shoulder. Wearing a white maxidress with gold gladiators and accessories, she looked flawless. 'I'm due on a shoot and I'm late,' she said in English. 'But I've left my phone somewhere and I can't . . . ah!' She spotted her mobile on one of the ornate, wrought-iron tables and snatched it up.

'Ooh, there's Finn, Cassia's fiancé. You must meet him.' Jules sprang off the lounger as Finn approached. She had a brainwave and she swiftly ran it past Aurelia to get permission. 'I thought I might ask him to come to Capri with me so that I can finalise some of the wedding details.' She was sure she could find someone who spoke English once she got there and then the whole worrying mess of the venue bill could be sorted out without any fuss.

'Great,' Aurelia said, pleased that Jules's mind was still on her wedding. 'Feel free to use the helicopter. It's the quickest way to travel to the island by far.'

'How generous. Thank you.'

Dressed in tailored shorts, a pale blue, short-sleeved shirt and deck shoes, Finn had already caught the sun on his nose. Looking slightly pink under his freckles, his red-gold hair was dishevelled and sticky with sweat.

'Finn, Aurelia.' Jules smiled at him.

Finn held his hand out, looking gauche. He felt like a spare part at the villa with Cassia in Vegas, as if he shouldn't really be there.

Aurelia shook Finn's hand. 'It is very nice to meet you,' she said in English, suspecting Finn's Italian wouldn't be as good as Cassia's. She had seen a photograph of him, so she wasn't that startled by his appearance, but Aurelia certainly wouldn't have picked him out as Cassia's fiancé. Finn was nice-looking, good-looking even, in a freckled, sandy kind of way. Lovely blue eyes too, Aurelia mused. But he was so . . . British, so proper. Aurelia realised she wasn't an authority on Cassia, far from it, but from what she knew about her, Finn just didn't seem like her type. She was aware, however, that she had been mistaken about Cassia when she first met her, assuming her to be uptight and dull when she was anything but. Perhaps she was having the same preconceptions about Finn.

'It's terribly nice to meet you,' Finn said, clearly intimidated by Aurelia's beauty. 'And so kind of you to allow me to stay with you at the villa.' He glanced at it. 'If you can call it that.

My mother will pass out when she sees it, I can assure you. I do hope you've received her RSVP to the wedding?'

Aurelia's expression became vague and she turned to Jules. 'Er, I think so . . . have we, Jules?'

Jules nodded. 'Oh yes, definitely. I've ticked the Sunderland family off the list. Except for Dom, of course. He's far too busy working his way through Hollywood.' She and Finn exchanged a glance and he looked amused by her comment.

'He wouldn't dare show his face here,' Finn assured her. 'I think he knows he's burnt his bridges on the home front.'

Jules leant against him briefly. 'How did he turn out to be such a bastard? You two aren't remotely similar.'

'Ah, but I had my mother's adoration to keep me on the straight and narrow,' he said, seeming at ease with her proximity.

Jules moved away with some reluctance. 'Hmmm, true. Still, I can't get over how different you and your brother are.' I chose the wrong one, she thought, shocked at the admission.

Aurelia watched their body language in bewilderment. If she didn't know better, she would have assumed Jules and Finn were the ones getting married. They even looked similar, their blond colouring perfectly in sync and their blue eyes almost matching. They certainly seemed far closer than a sister and a prospective brother-in-law should be. Aurelia couldn't imagine being anywhere near as intimate with Dino's older brother and that wasn't only because he looked a bit like a monkey.

'I do hope your room is comfortable?' Aurelia asked Finn. 'Jules thought it would be nice for you to have your own suite, but of course you must feel free to move in with Cassia when she is back, if you would like to?'

'Er, yes. Quite possibly.' Finn looked evasive. When he had heard about Cassia's trip to Vegas, he had felt guilty for feeling so grateful for the breathing space. He knew that was absurd; they had had nothing but breathing space, for heaven's sake, but nonetheless, Finn couldn't help feeling thankful that he had some time to think about what he needed to say to her. Spending time with Jules was no hardship either, he thought, finding himself smiling at her like a fool.

What on earth was going on? Aurelia thought, watching Jules and Finn in wonderment. She had half a mind to call Dino and ask him to keep an eye on the pair of them while she was away on her shoot. 'I'm afraid I have a plane to catch,' she said apologetically. She gave Finn a polite smile as she left, watching as Jules told him about the Capri trip. Aurelia caught sight of Raffaelo hanging around the restaurant entrance and even though she was late, she called him over for a chat.

Raffaelo looked up moodily. With obvious unwillingness and much looking over his shoulder, he came over and joined her.

'Grandmother is up and about now, Raff. Have you been to see her?'

Raffaelo shook his head, his eyes unreadable. 'Not yet. I'm sure she's fine.'

'She is, but still. I think she'd like to see you, Raff.'

'I'll try and see her later.' He didn't smile and his words were said with a total lack of conviction.

Aurelia crossly watched Raffaelo check his watch for the third time since she'd called him over. What on earth was the matter with him? Ever since their grandmother's car accident, he had been acting like a total idiot. He was doing his job for once, but he seemed on edge and he would frequently disappear without explanation.

'Look, I have to go,' Aurelia said, ducking into her car. 'Rocco should be back in a few days' time, so you're in charge, all right?'

'Of course. Whatever.' Raffaelo was already walking away and she wasn't even sure he was listening to her. For someone normally so gregarious and amiable, Raff could be incredibly

433

morose at times. What did he have to worry about? He had the most laid-back job in the entire family!

Arriving at the airport with minutes to spare, Aurelia dashed through the first-class check-in and ignored the paparazzi shoving cameras in her face.

'Aurelia, darling,' a voice purred. 'Are you shooting the Butterdine clothes line too? How nice.'

Finding herself face to face with a vampy German model she detested, Aurelia gritted her teeth and air-kissed. The last thing she needed was a four-hour flight with Mia Hausen; they were rivals on the model circuit and often vied for the same contracts.

'I do hope there are no bad feelings?' Mia asked sweetly as she took a seat next to the window.

Aurelia checked her ticket and grimaced, noting that Mia had taken her seat. 'Bad feelings? About what?' She slipped into the other seat tetchily. Mia crossed her long legs which were encased in black leather, despite the heat.

'I was talking about the wedding venue.' She flashed her vulgar, oval-shaped diamond ring at Aurelia for emphasis.

Aurelia went cold. 'What do you mean?'

'Capri, darling,' Mia said smugly. 'Your cancellation meant that I was able to have the booking, after all. I assume you found something better.' She looked doubtful. 'Although what could be better than Capri, I have no idea!'

Aurelia felt sick. Cancellation? What was Mia on about? She wouldn't joke about such a thing, though; Aurelia knew that. So either there had been a mistake or . . . or Jules had messed up and not paid the final balance, Aurelia realised with a sinking feeling. How could she? How could she do such a thing when she knew how important it was? Aurelia frantically tried to dial Jules's number, but she couldn't get through and, seconds later, she was told to turn her phone off.

Impotent with rage, Aurelia thrust some huge sunglasses on

her nose to hide her tears. Cassia had been right about Jules, she wasn't up to co-ordinating a wedding as large as hers. Aurelia cursed herself for trusting Jules and for not listening to Cassia. At the time, she had been charmed by Jules and she had been so grateful to hand her wedding over to someone she thought could cope with it, she hadn't really wanted to listen when Cassia had warned her that Jules was inexperienced. Aurelia gripped the arms of her plush seat, wondering how she was going to get through the modelling shoot with Mia nastily rubbing her nose in it about Capri every five minutes. One thing was for sure: Jules had better have a good explanation for screwing up the most important day of her life.

Diana looked up at the building and swallowed. It looked just the way she remembered it and the sight sent shivers down her spine. Knowing there was no turning back now that she had finally plucked up the courage to do this, she pushed the door open and entered the lobby. Dating back to the art deco era, the building, located in the eastern end of Pimlico, had retained some of its original features, but it no longer seemed grand or glamorous. These days, the paint on the walls was peeling off and the staircase looked grubby and uninviting.

Diana picked her way through the debris on the stairs and made for the second floor. The corridor had the same pale blue wallpaper on it, embossed with white swans, and she trailed a finger along the faded paper, choked by memories. Finding the door she was looking for, Diana stood outside, taking a deep breath. She had come a long way since she had last been here, and she felt as though she had lived through a great deal since that last visit. Yet she felt as if she had only just emerged from the guilt of the whole situation. Playing Clarissa had unleashed something within her, something that had allowed her to open up and face the past. It had been painful, and it still hurt now, but Diana knew it was inevitable.

She put her chin in the air and knocked on the door. She was strong, far stronger than she had been back then. She could cope with this. It was just something that had to be done. There was no answer, even when she knocked again. The knock had a hollow sound too, as though there was nothing on the other side of the door.

A young woman emerged from the apartment next door, juggling a large parcel wrapped in pink paper with teddy bears on it, a holdall and a keyring full of keys.

'Hello there,' she said, looking harassed. 'You couldn't just hold this for me? I have to lock my door and I know I'm going to drop something.'

'Of course.' Diana took the pink parcel from her. 'Who's the lucky girl?'

The woman locked her door. 'My sister had a baby girl yesterday. I bought a gigantic teddy bear, not thinking about all the wrapping paper it would need! Thank you so much.' She took the parcel from Diana and frowned at her, not sure if she recognised her. 'Were you knocking at Joseph's door?'

Diana hesitated then nodded. Hearing his name made her shiver. 'Er, yes. Does he still live here? I don't expect he does . . . he probably moved ages ago.'

'No, he did live here, but he died a few weeks ago. It was in all the papers. Joseph Dane was some really famous actor back in the day, apparently. Popular with the ladies.' The woman looked doubtful as though the thought of her neighbour, ancient in her youthful eyes, could have ever been a heartthrob.

Dead? Diana was speechless. She hadn't been expecting that. And why hadn't she known about his death? Remembering the stack of newspapers she still hadn't had a chance to go through in her flat, Diana guessed she had missed the news because she'd been so engrossed in the play rehearsals. She cursed herself for not making more of an effort to keep up with current events; if she had, she wouldn't be standing here now, feeling so cheated.

'Was he someone special to you?'

Diana shook her head quickly, wishing the young woman wasn't looked at her so kindly. 'No. No, not at all. He was just . . . just someone I knew a lifetime ago. Listen, I must go, but congratulations. You know, on becoming an auntie.'

'Thanks. Bye then.' The woman hoisted her parcel up again and walked away.

Diana stared after her. Letting out a slow breath, she leant against the wall. She felt deflated. It had taken enormous courage to come here today and now she felt as though she had put herself through hell for nothing. Drawing her wallet out of her handbag with trembling fingers, she rubbed the photograph of Marco's handsome face.'

'I'm so sorry, my darling,' she whispered, wishing she could go back and change everything. But she knew she couldn't. Time resolutely refused to go backwards, however much anyone wanted it to at times and one had to live with the decisions made during a lifetime. Diana tucked the photograph away again and straightened up, changing her thought process.

So, the confrontation she had finally felt brave enough for wasn't going to happen. So what? It didn't matter. Not about Joseph. Now that she was here, Diana wasn't even sure she knew what she would have said to him. There were far bigger conversations she had to have and she was going to have to be even braver to cope with those. She only wished she had some support, someone to talk to. There was always Fliss, of course, but it wasn't her sympathy and support Diana craved. Taking one last look at Joseph's door, she walked away from the past, her heart feeling just that little bit lighter.

Having made the impulsive decision to drop everything in Rome in order to get back with Rocco, Stefania stormed into his office in Sorrento, determined to convince him that a reconciliation was the best course of action. Finding him absent, she cursed out loud and flicked her blond ponytail over her shoulder. Where the hell was he? He hadn't told her he was going anywhere, so she had expected him to be here, ready to talk things over.

Stefania frowned. She knew Rocco hadn't meant it when he said they should split up; he was stressed, that was all. Stefania had no idea why Rocco felt their relationship was complex in any way; if he could only step away from his family and from Sorrento, he'd be much happier. It was being responsible for all of them that made his life such a major headache. If only his silly parents would stop chasing fame and look after Disanti's Sorrento the way they were supposed to, Stefania was convinced Rocco would suddenly find himself itching to open another restaurant – in Rome. Stefania tossed her designer handbag on to Rocco's desk. Together, they would create a magnificent restaurant they could work in together, he as the accomplished entrepreneur and she as the promoter and organiser. He no longer needed to cook, Stefania thought contemptuously. There were any number of chefs who could do what he did – well, who could do it *almost* as well as he did it. And who cooked in their own restaurants these days? No chef who wanted to be seen as a public figure got their hands dirty and there was no reason why Rocco should either.

Having a nose around his desk, Stefania touched a key on his laptop. It was warm and it sprang to life. Not pausing to wonder who might have been going through his personal information in his absence, Stefania had a good look herself. Noticing a file in Rocco's email entitled 'Cooking Demo – Las Vegas', Stefania narrowed her eyes. Las Vegas? Was that where Rocco was? Taking a quick look outside the office and finding the restaurant to be relatively quiet, she opened the file and waited. Watching Bobby Swan come out in front of a large crowd, Stefania relaxed. She knew Bobby and Rocco were friends; this was just one of Bobby's shows, that was all. About to turn it off, she heard someone announce Rocco's name. Stiffening, she watched as the crowd went crazy and then she heard the commentator announcing someone else, but it was drowned out by cheers. As the cameras swung round, Stefania saw Rocco and Cassia laughing together, their hands entwined. Noticing the cameras on them, they immediately pulled apart.

Stefania caught her breath. So Rocco was in Las Vegas, and he was there with Cassia. With a jolt, she realised Rocco had meant what he said when he ended their relationship. Worst of all, she knew exactly why he had done it. It had nothing to do with work at all or with their relationship being 'complicated'. Whether he had admitted it to himself or not, Rocco was in love with Cassia Marini and that was why he had flown to Rome before the trip to finish things with her, so he could be free. Instead of being devastated, Stefania was livid. No one treated her like this, no one.

Grabbing her handbag, she stalked out of his office. This wasn't over by a long shot.

'What do you think?' Jules asked Finn, enjoying the look on his face as they strolled through the pretty streets of Capri.

'It's very pretty,' Finn answered, gaping as a famous actor walked past wearing a straw hat. 'Was that . . . ?'

Jules giggled. 'I think so. Incredible, isn't it? I love it here.'

'It's . . . it's . . . lovely,' Finn agreed unenthusiastically. Catching Jules's eye, he looked contrite. 'I guess I'm a little more English than I realised. Don't get me wrong, I can appreciate the glitz and glamour and it's great for a holiday, but I'm just very happy at home. This place isn't really me.'

Jules smiled. She knew what Finn meant, funnily enough. She had enjoyed every moment of her time in Sorrento and she had lapped up all the luxury being around Aurelia afforded her, but she was very aware that she would be going home at some point. And the thought didn't fill her with gloom at all, far from it.

Spotting the hotel Aurelia's reception was being held at, she motioned for Finn to follow her inside.

'I need to go in and sort out a payment here. Do you want to get a drink and wait for me? There's a wonderful bar over there.'

Noticing the dazzling clientele in the hotel bar area, Finn looked uneasy. 'Ummm, I'll just come with you, if that's all right? I'm not sure I'm going to fit in very well with the glitterati, drinking . . . whatever they're drinking.'

'Apple martinis,' Jules provided, giving Finn a fond glance. He looked thoroughly uncomfortable in his surroundings but she couldn't help finding it rather endearing. He had gaped at the sight of the family helicopter and had held on to her for dear life when it had taken off. She had laughed, not realising he shared Cassia's fear of flying, and she had rather enjoyed the feel of his warm hand clutching hers.

Jules gave the people enjoying cocktails a lingering glance, wishing she could be so carefree. With Aurelia's wedding approaching and with a list of things still to sort out, she felt stressed out and under pressure. She had so badly wanted to impress everyone with her organisational skills and she had been hell-bent on pleasing Aurelia and making sure her CV back in England benefited from one successful attempt at wedding co-ordination, but yet again she seemed to have messed things up.

'Apple martinis indeed,' Finn said mockingly. 'Would they serve me a pint of Stella if I asked for one?'

Jules rolled her eyes. 'Finn! You can't ask for a pint of *Stella*!'

At reception, she put her serious hat back on and asked to speak to the wedding co-ordinator, who emerged a few minutes later. Wearing a Bluetooth and clutching a mini iPad that was clearly her version of a clipboard, she looked impatient.

'Fiorina Rosatti. Can I help you?' she barked out in Italian.

'Oh hi, yes, I hope so. Sorry, do you speak English? A little? That's great.' Jules drew out the company chequebook that Aurelia had pre-signed for her to use for the wedding. 'I'm in charge of Aurelia Disanti's wedding and I'm here to make a final—'

Fiorina cut her off in excellent English. 'Aurelia Disanti is no longer holding her reception here. Mia Hausen has taken her slot because payment wasn't made on time. I did send several letters,' she added accusingly. 'And I called three times as well and left messages for you. Didn't you get them?'

Jules stared at her hopelessly. 'Well, I had a problem with my phone . . . I accidentally deleted a few messages. I did call, but I couldn't understand anyone.' She hadn't got round to opening the letters until yesterday. 'But look, there has to be something you can do. Aurelia has to have her wedding here, it's her dream, this is the wedding of the year . . .' Her voice trailed away.

Fiorina shrugged. 'We would have liked to host the Disanti wedding here, but we couldn't hold the venue without payment. Miss Hausen was desperate to have her reception here, so we happily accepted and she paid in full at her last visit.'

Jules shook her head, gibbering. Aurelia detested Mia Hausen; she had said as much when they were last here. Jules clutched her hair in agitation, wondering what the hell to do. She was going to be in so much trouble when Aurelia found out. She had to make things right; she simply had to.

'Listen, can we come to some sort of arrangement?' Jules had no idea where she was going with this, but she had to try to salvage things. 'I mean, there has to be something we can . . .'

Fiorina gave her a cold stare. 'I do not know what you are suggesting, but there is absolutely nothing that can be done. We have taken payment from Miss Hausen and her reception

441

has been finalised. Have a good day.' She turned back to her office.

Jules almost threw herself over the reception desk. 'But . . . but . . . you have to help me . . . please . . .' Watching Fiorina's retreating back, she gave up and joined Finn. 'Oh God, Finn. I'm in serious trouble now. I mean really deep shit. The kind you can't get out of.'

Finn steered her away from the reception desk and into the bar area by the pool. Ordering two of the horrible-looking apple martinis, he found them a table.

'What's happened?'

Ashen-faced, Jules filled him in. 'I'm a moron, truly. I knew I had to sort the payment out and it just kept slipping my mind. There's no excuse and Aurelia will never forgive me. Rightly so.'

Staring at Jules, Finn toyed with his phone, not realising he'd accidentally dialled Cassia's number. 'Jules, darling, when are you going to realise you're simply not cut out to be a wedding co-ordinator or an events co-ordinator? This isn't the right line of work for you, you must know that.'

Jules wasn't even aware that tears were trickling down her cheeks. 'But what am I good at?' she wailed, knowing she sounded bratty. 'Everything I do, I mess up. I-I try so hard, but I can't seem to . . . to find my niche, or whatever they call it.' She shuddered. 'Aurelia's been so good to me,' she added, feeling wretched. 'How can I ever make things right?'

Finn sipped his apple martini and winced, but good manners prevented him from commenting on it. 'You're just going to have to be honest with Aurelia. There must be a way to fix this, we're just going to have to put our thinking caps on.' Truthfully, he didn't have a clue how to get Jules out of this fearful mess, but he felt protective of her and keen to help.

Jules wiped the tears from her face, grateful for Finn's support. 'I'm just so furious at myself, Finn! If I'm honest, there are times when I really wish I could be more like Cassia. She's so bloody well-organised, so infuriatingly capable. She'd never make a mistake like this in a million years. God! It's been like this all my life. Cassia's always been so lucky, so bloody blessed. My father . . . Oh, it doesn't matter.'

Finn raised his eyebrows, waiting for Jules to elaborate. She didn't. 'No,' he agreed with a sigh, 'she probably wouldn't make a mistake like this.'

Jules put her head on one side, intrigued. The comment had sounded almost like a criticism. 'Does that bother you?' she asked, surprised by his reaction.

'A little,' he admitted reluctantly. 'Cassia's amazing, she's a powerhouse. So focused and efficient. It's just . . .'

Jules said nothing, stunned that Finn was opening up the way he was. They had become good friends but apart from the odd comment here and there, he rarely talked about Cassia.

Finn stared out at the colourful view of Capri soaked in sunshine and teeming with tourists. 'I hate myself for even saying this, but she sometimes makes me feel rather . . . useless.' He met Jules's eyes, troubled but oddly relieved to be voicing his thoughts out loud. He was aware that he had been feeling this way for a while, but he hadn't trusted anyone with the information before now. 'If Cassia made a mistake, it would make her more human, if that doesn't sound awful.' Finn frowned, not sure that was what he meant to say. 'Not that she's like a machine, she's not. I'm really not explaining myself very well.'

'Try. I'm listening, honestly.' She was. In all honesty, she was glad of the distraction. And a tiny part of her couldn't help feeling hopeful that Finn wasn't as in love with Cassia as she'd thought. She hated herself for feeling that way, but it was the truth.

Finn groped for the right words. 'All right, well, this will sound stupid, Jules, but I'm old-fashioned. I was brought up that way and I can't help it. I want to look after Cassia, I want us to have a family and for her to be at home when I get in so we can spend the evening together.' Finn ran a hand through his red-gold hair, clearly feeling guilty. 'Which would mean her giving her career up. And call me selfish, but I want her to, I really do. I . . . I want to be enough for her. I want to feel as though I'm the man in the relationship, the one looking after everyone.'

Jules nodded. She could understand that. In fact, Finn had probably just described her yearning for the future perfectly. Wasn't that what she craved? She'd had the excitement and the money and the bad boys and look how that had turned out. She felt weary from it all. She would love to be looked after, she would adore being taken care of and to take care of someone else in return. Dazed, Jules stared at Finn. She was developing feelings for him, she thought in astonishment. Real feelings, deep, romantic ones that she shouldn't be feeling for her sister's fiancé. Dismayed, Jules turned away.

Noticing her troubled face, Finn realised he'd been wittering on about Cassia when all Jules needed right now was support. 'Jules, I'm so sorry. Here you are wondering what to do about Aurelia and all I'm doing is banging on about Cassia.' Wiping her tears away with his thumb, he was overcome with a need to protect Jules and make her feel better. 'You poor darling. You look as though you could do with a hug. Come here . . . it's all right . . . everything will be all right . . .'

Jules swallowed and even though she knew she shouldn't, she went into Finn's arms. Closing her eyes, she breathed in his now-familiar scent, feeling safe. Putting his arm round her clumsily, Finn broke the accidental call to Cassia's answerphone without even realising the conversation had been recorded. 'You're much braver than you think,' he said softly. 'You've been through such a lot.' Finn realised he was being incredibly disloyal to Cassia, but he couldn't help holding on to Jules.

'God, I don't know why I was saying all that stuff about Cassia anyway, or where it came from.' He frowned into Jules's hair. 'Although I have been feeling . . . look, it doesn't matter. What matters is what we can do to help you.' He pulled back and smoothed the hair out of her eyes. 'What else can I do while I'm here? I'm totally at your disposal and even though I seem to be rather crap at legal things back home, I'm actually quite the organiser when I put my mind to it.'

Unable to stop herself, Jules burst into a fresh bout of tears. She felt awful. Cassia was her sister and whatever had happened in the past, none of that was her fault, and she didn't deserve this. A part of Jules wondered briefly if Cassia would be overly devastated if Finn left her but she knew it was just wishful thinking, a way to ease her own guilt over the situation. Of course Cassia would be upset; she and Finn had been together for years.

Appalled that he didn't appear to be able to reassure her, Finn hugged Jules again. 'God, I'm not helping one little bit, am I?'

'You are, you are.' She pulled back, jolted by his tenderness. 'You're unbelievably lovely. Do you . . . do you really think we can make things right with Aurelia?' She had a million un-answered questions in her head about Finn, but she knew she had to put Aurelia's wedding first.

Finn stared at Jules, biting his lip. Despite her tears, she looked ravishing, and endearingly vulnerable as she nervously pleated her skirt between trembling fingers. Finn felt an irrational urge to make her feel better . . . to kiss her. Which was terrible – wasn't it? Cassia's sister, of all people. Finn tried to get his head together but it was spinning.

'Thank God I wasn't in charge of your wedding,' Jules joked, desperate to break the tension between them.

The wedding. Looking as though he'd been slapped in the face, Finn blinked and the spell was broken. Withdrawing his hand from Jules's hair, he stood up and cleared his throat.

'Well, quite. Er, do you think we'd better go now?'

Jules nodded dumbly. Why had she said that? Although perhaps it was for the best. She shouldn't be thinking about Finn the way she had been and she certainly shouldn't be hugging him and thinking about what it would be like to kiss him. Because she had been thinking that, hadn't she?

'Right.' Finn went into business mode. 'Plan of action. We stay here in Capri and we work out what to do about Aurelia's wedding. We . . . we make a million phone calls and we sort out everything that's left on your list. You've got the list, haven't you? Good. How does that sound?'

'It sounds . . . it sounds great.' Jules hesitated. She wasn't sure it was a good idea to spend even more time with Finn on his own, but what choice did she have? Aurelia would have time to calm down and they could return to Sorrento with everything done and something else in place for the reception – although God knew what.

'What would I do without you?' Jules said, staring at Finn.

Finn stared back. He had just been thinking the very same thing about her.

Chapter Twenty

Sofia poked her head out of her suite tentatively. She half-expected one of her domineering nurses to be lurking in the corner, ready to jump out and wrestle her back to her sickbed. Relieved to find that her worries were groundless and that the medical team had indeed left the building, Sofia headed downstairs, desperate to familiarise herself with the restaurant again.

She steadied herself on the banister. She wasn't totally back to normal, she knew that. Her back was still bruised and aching from the blow caused by the wheel of the car and she had been told that her leg and hip would probably always suffer stiffness in the future. At least her arm had knitted itself properly, she thought, flexing her fingers inside the loose sling she was wearing. She hadn't realised how much she used her arm and hand until she had been incapacitated and she knew she would never take such a thing for granted again. But the most acute and lasting damage from the accident was the panic attacks she occasionally suffered. Not that she had mentioned these to anyone except Allesandro. She knew her family would be anxious and Rocco would probably have her cornered by militant nurses indefinitely if she confessed to suffering even the tiniest palpitation.

Sofia shivered. There had been something so sinister about the way the red car had coldly rammed her, such menace to the thrust of the wheel as it had connected with her bones. Sofia supposed all car accidents felt the same, particularly when an unsuspecting pedestrian was struck, but she couldn't shake off the feeling that there was more to it than just a random hit-and-run. She knew she should listen to Rocco when he said that there was no such thing as a curse, but she couldn't stop thinking about the sneering face of the Giorelli grandmother who had babbled out the terrifying chant, cursing the Disanti family all those years ago.

Sofia closed her eyes and gathered herself together. Rocco was right about one thing: there was nothing to be gained by obsessing on what had happened. The most important thing was that she had survived and that she was on the mend.

She entered the sun-dappled restaurant with a rush of joy and took a deep breath, breathing in the familiar ambience and smell. Disanti's was in the throes of a busy lunchtime service and Sofia revelled in the muted chatter and the whirling stream of waiting staff discreetly going about their business. Nothing had changed; the sprawling frescos looked as fresh and as breathtaking as ever, the tables were laid immaculately with gleaming cutlery and spotless china, and the staff glided through the restaurant carrying exquisite dishes like dancers in a well-rehearsed waltz.

Sofia enjoyed working in the restaurant and she had missed it enormously. She felt that in some small way she was assisting Rocco from having the entire burden of the family's income sitting on his shoulders. She derived great pleasure from organising the staff and taking control of some of the finer detail that went into the smooth running of Disanti's Sorrento and a tiny bit of Sofia had to admit that she felt closer to Nico when she worked there.

Stiffly nodding to a couple of regular customers so as not to jar her neck too much, Sofia moved through the tables slowly, lingering to make small talk here and there, straightening the odd piece of cutlery even though it was already perfectly placed and generally getting a feel for the place again. Slipping past the kitchen which was as loud and frantic as the restaurant was quiet and calm – all just as it should be – Sofia decided to pop into Rocco's office. He was still in Vegas and now that she was back on her feet again, she thought it would be a good idea to check that everything was running well behind the scenes.

She opened the door and started. Raffaelo was sitting behind Rocco's desk, rifling through some paperwork. Unaware of her presence, he leafed quickly through some pages, letting out a growl of frustration. Sensing someone watching him suddenly, he looked up.

'Why are you creeping around like that?' he cried, jumping to his feet. His cheeks were stained with an ugly flush. 'You gave me a fright.' He gathered up the papers he'd been looking at and stuffed them into a drawer.

'Creeping around?' Sofia frowned. 'I am hardly creeping around, Raffaelo. It's a bit difficult for me to move, actually, when my hip is so stiff.'

Raffaelo winced. 'Yes, of course, Grandmother. I'm sorry; I didn't mean to be rude.'

Sofia was perplexed. What had he been up to, going through Rocco's paperwork? What could he possibly be looking for?

'And . . . how are you feeling? Better, I hope.' Looking genuinely concerned, Raffaelo took her hand and squeezed it.

There was something in his eyes, thought Sofia. It was only a glimmer and he was smiling affably at her, but it was true that since the accident Raffaelo hadn't been himself. He had barely visited whilst she'd been laid up and had seemed desperate to get away when he had actually made an appearance. Aurelia was busy with her wedding and her photo shoots and Rocco had been working furiously on the business before his trip to Vegas, but both of them had come to see her several times, spending as long with her as their schedules would allow.

Raffaelo had been conspicuous by his absence and it wasn't in his nature to be thoughtless or crass.

'Is there anything I can help you with?' Sofia asked him, troubled by his odd behaviour.

Raffaelo frowned. 'Er, no.' Assuming she was asking about the paperwork he'd been rifling through, he straightened defensively. 'I was just . . . seeing if there was anything I could do to help Rocco. I've been thinking about the way he always asks me to get more involved with the business.'

Sofia believed him, but she still didn't understand why he had looked so guilty when she came in. 'Is that something you'd be interested in now?'

Raffaelo shrugged. 'Maybe. Perhaps it's time I focused more on the family.'

'Well, I'm glad to hear it,' Sofia said warmly. 'But . . . is everything all right, Raff? You know you can talk to me about anything, anything at all.'

Raffaelo let out a short laugh. 'No, Grandmother, I can't. Not about this.'

'About what, exactly?'

He became evasive. Realising he had let his guard down, Raffaelo plastered a genial smile back on to his face and looked her directly in the eye. 'Everything is fine, honestly. You mustn't worry about me.'

Sofia didn't want to doubt him but she didn't believe a word he was saying. Raffaelo had never been able to lie; as a child he had been terrible at concealing his wrongdoings. She knew he was up to something, his shifty body language was a giveaway, but she also knew by the firm set of his chin that he wasn't going to confess to anything unless he was forced to. Thoughtfully, she watched him leave and decided to speak to Rocco about it when he returned from Vegas.

She dug out the paperwork he'd been nosing through and ran her eyes over it. Nothing important, by the looks of things, just some accounts. About to leave, Sofia noticed Rocco's desk phone flashing. Running quickly through the messages, she made notes on a pad and sent him a couple of texts about the more urgent issues. Hearing the last one, however, Sofia's pen hovered over the notepad. It was from their good friend Luca, in Rome. It was a short message and it didn't say much, but the inference behind it made Sofia extremely uneasy. She listened to it again, hoping she was mistaken.

'Found something astonishing about the rival family after your visit with Cassia,' Luca said. His voice sounded guarded. 'It's . . . let's just say that story about a surviving member might not be such rubbish after all. You need to call me when you get back, Rocco. Immediately.'

Staring at the phone, Sofia's blood ran cold. Had she been right all along? Did her accident have something to do with the rival family and the curse, after all? She wondered what Luca meant about Cassia. Surely he wasn't . . . was he saying that Marco Marini, Cassia's father, was the surviving son of the Giorelli family? She put a hand to her chest in alarm, starting to hyperventilate.

It could all fit together, Sofia thought. Cassia said she thought her father was from the area, that he had arrived in England as an orphan. How old would he have been now, if he'd still been alive? Sofia wasn't sure but she guessed the timing could fit. She felt a shiver down her spine. It couldn't be . . . could it?

Sofia supposed Cassia must be having the same concerns. She was intelligent enough to have spotted the possibilities with the timing and with what little she knew of her father's background. Grabbing the phone, Sofia dialled Luca. The phone rang and rang at the other end without an answerphone kicking in to take a message.

Frustrated, Sofia threw the phone down again. She had to find out what was going on, she had to know if Cassia was related to the Giorellis. Should she warn Rocco? Sofia swallowed. Only a few days ago, she had been urging Cassia and Rocco to spend more time together, certain that both of them were unhappy in their relationships and convinced that they were perfect for one another.

But this . . . this changed everything. Rocco couldn't be with a descendant of the Giorellis. It was unthinkable. As much as she adored Cassia – and they had grown close since she had been here – Sofia knew she wouldn't feel the same about her if Marco was that long-lost boy she had heard about. Nico would turn in his grave, Sofia thought, worriedly. He would feel the same way she did. Of course, it wouldn't be Cassia's fault if it was revealed that she was inadvertently related to the family that had been rivals of the Disantis since any of them could remember, but it wouldn't be right for Rocco to fall in love with a Giorelli. Sofia fervently hoped it wasn't already too late on that front.

Quickly finding the number for the Bellagio Hotel, she dialled and left a message for Rocco in his room. She felt badly about Cassia, but until they knew for sure, Sofia had to err on the side of caution. Family was too important – family was everything. She looked up.

'Allesandro.' She smiled, delighted to see him. 'To what do I owe this pleasure?'

'I thought you might enjoy a spot of lunch,' he suggested with a charming smile. 'Now that the scary nurses have let you out.'

Sofia's mind was swirling with thoughts of Cassia and curses and she knew she needed a distraction. 'That sounds wonderful. Just one thing. Shall we avoid going for a walk afterwards?'

Allesandro's smile faded. 'I couldn't agree more, Sofia. We shall take my car and we will avoid all the country lanes. I promised young Cassia I would take care of you and that's exactly what I intend to do.'

Sofia's heart lifted. How nice to be taken care of for a change. She just hoped Nico, if he was watching over her, felt the same way.

'*The scallops, sautéed to perfection in butter, were accompanied by a scattering of salty, crisp pancetta. Complimented by a flavoursome slick of pureed artichoke and truffle oil, the scallops were a stunning entrée to what turned out to be an incredible meal . . . Bobby and Rocco played the fool all night long and it was a chance to see the man behind the mask as Rocco opened up and talked openly about his restaurant and his passion for food . . .*'

Cassia looked wistful as she finished typing. It really had been an incredible evening. After the food demo, Bobby had shown them round Angelfish, his Michelin-starred restaurant, before treating them to a sumptuous fourteen-course taster menu on the house. Cassia had sampled some of the best food of her life and her mind had been racing with descriptions during each delectable course. Linguine with truffle oil and crayfish was followed by succulent beef medallions in a Chianti jus with tiny cubes of redcurrant jelly. A shot of confit tomato was the perfect balance of sweet and acidic, a square of halibut delicious with a hazelnut foam and a pile of salty samphire. Finishing with a mouthful of Caribbean cake which came with a butterscotch sauce that stuck to the roof of her mouth and one of the thickest chocolate mousses she had ever tasted (complete with a popping candy/gold leaf mix), Cassia was quite literally in food heaven.

The exquisite meal aside, Rocco had also been great company; he had been relaxed but charismatic and he and Bobby had talked non-stop about food when Bobby had joined them later on. Cassia had enjoyed watching their easy friendship and the way Bobby teased Rocco mercilessly about his good looks.

Cassia gazed out at the Paris Hotel on the opposite side of the strip, wondering what people were lunching on in the romantic eleventh-floor restaurant in the miniature Eiffel Tower. Vegas was unlike any other place she'd visited in the world – flashing lights, pool parties and casinos crossed with the sophisticated glamour of upmarket restaurants, high-end shops and dazzling shows you might not see anywhere else on the planet. It was a grown-up playground where anything was possible: watching lion cubs frolic, gliding down the Grand Canal in an authentic Venetian gondola, dining in a booth with a star-studded ceiling, or being shot into the air from the top of the Stratosphere at forty-five miles an hour.

Or was it just magical because she was here with Rocco? Cassia drummed her fingers on the table. She had seen a different side of him here, a side she had glimpsed before now and again, away from Sorrento, but it often disappeared as quickly as it appeared, usually when Rocco immersed himself in work. But here, in Vegas, he was light-hearted, fun – flirtatious. There had been something in his eyes every time they connected with hers across the table, something that had made her stomach lurch with excitement. She didn't want to feel the way she did and she was fighting it all the way. It was rather like hurtling down a water chute without any way of clawing her way back up again, and the trouble was, she wasn't sure she wanted to.

She thought about Finn and her heart clenched. They had to talk soon, they simply had to. They were getting married in only a few weeks – Cassia felt a jolt of unadulterated panic at the mere thought of it. She barely knew the details of her own wedding. Which wasn't right, any more than her relationship with Finn was. She had kissed Rocco, passionately and with far more on her mind than mere kissing, and she wanted to do it again. She was resisting and she was holding Rocco at arm's length for all she was worth, but she knew her resolve was weakening. She wanted Rocco, she wanted him so badly, it hurt.

Cassia sighed and strolled to the window to take in the view. She knew, without hesitation, that Finn would detest Las Vegas. He'd hate the glitzy lights, the noise and the crowds. He'd find the Americans overpowering and brash and the heat unbearable. And he would view the sheer, hedonistic joy of the place with utter mystification, probably citing the Grand Canyon as the only viable reason to visit the area. But then, he'd probably find Sorrento a step outside of his comfort zone, Cassia mused. Oddly, she didn't know whether this thought irritated her or made her think of him with affection. It wasn't so much that she didn't like this aspect of him – it was who he was – but it did underline how different they were. Perhaps how incompatible they were. She looked up as her mobile rang and wondered if it was Finn experiencing some weird sixth sense, she raced to answer it.

'Cass!' It was Gena. 'I've just received your column. Wow, this meal sounds fantastic, readers are going to love hearing about it.'

'It was amazing, I wish you could have been here, Gena.' Brimming with enthusiasm, Cassia talked about the food in more detail. 'There was so much I could say but I wanted to keep it as brief as possible. And Rocco, he was such great company, but again, I didn't want to sound as though I was . . .'

'Gushing?' Gena provided. The smile was evident in her voice. 'I wouldn't say that. You sounded . . . effervescent.'

Cassia smiled. Maybe she had sounded rather frothy. Gena chuckled down the phone. 'You wear your heart on your sleeve, darling, and it shows. That's all I meant. And it's a good thing,' she added. 'Reading your column is like reading a story. I'm utterly gripped and I know the readers are too. It's a shame about the opening being delayed in Vegas, but I'm not sure it matters, really. Not with all this great stuff you're sending through, it's better than I could have hoped for.'

Cassia felt slightly confused by Gena's effusive comments. What did she mean about wearing her heart on her sleeve? She was distracted from asking about it by a discussion about the next column Gena had planned for her, the one that would go into the magazine the following month.

'. . . so if you could talk about Aurelia's wedding breakfast? I think the readers would love to hear about it because it's going to be such a grand affair. Did you say it was at a hotel in Capri?'

'Yes. A stunning place, by all accounts. Jules said she would rip her right arm off to host her own wedding there.'

'So, is everything all right with Finn?' Gena's tone was casual.

'I have no idea.' Cassia sounded glum. 'We haven't spoken in ages and it all feels really weird. I hate to say it, but this trip to Sorrento has really torn us apart. It's highlighted quite a few issues in our relationship,' she added, realising it was true. 'Issues I'm not sure we would have noticed if we'd been in England blithely organising the wedding.'

'Oh, I'm sorry to hear that, Cass.' Gena was sympathetic. 'But you and Finn are so solid, surely this trip to Sorrento shouldn't have caused something as serious as that?' She paused. 'Forgive me, but it makes me wonder if perhaps there were issues there in the first place? I mean, I can't see why a few months apart should matter, even with a wedding on the horizon. Gianfranco and I often spend a few months apart when he's travelling. It's hard, but it's not a deal-breaker. I'm sure it will all turn out as it should do. Must go, Cass . . .'

Gena's words hit home. She was right, a few months apart should not be causing a rift of this kind between herself and Finn. Couples survived far worse than this, so what did that say about their relationship? Vaguely aware that someone had knocked at her door, she answered it.

'Hey.' Rocco grinned. 'Am I interrupting anything?'

She shook her head, trying not to notice how great he looked in a pair of bright blue sports shorts that showed off his tanned legs and a blue-and-white polo shirt. No tailored, buttoned-up shorts for Rocco, Cassia noted. Instantly, she felt badly for comparing Rocco's suave style to Finn's more uptight version.

'No, come on in. I just wrote my column and then Gena phoned.' She gestured to his shorts. 'You look as though you're about to go for a swim.'

Rocco recoiled. 'No way. You know I never even dip my toe in a pool. Not after . . .'

'The near-drowning thing, of course.' Cassia nodded. 'I'm not surprised it's put you off. Would you ever learn to swim now, do you think?'

'Can't see the point.' Rocco threw himself into a nearby armchair, hoisting his tanned legs over the side. 'It's not a skill I've needed so far in life.'

Cassia heard her phone beeping again. 'That's probably Gena again, hang on.' She put the phone to her ear.

Rocco watched from the safety of his armchair, glad to have a moment to observe her without interruption. Dressed in a simple black maxi dress that showed off her tanned shoulders, her dark hair trailing down her back, she looked beautiful. Rocco found himself struggling to remain in his seat. He had an overwhelming desire to leap up and cover her shoulders in kisses, to bury his head in her perfume-scented neck, inhaling the distinctive, oriental scent she had been wearing of late. When she first arrived, Cassia had worn some nondescript floral fragrance, but he was sure she had started wearing something different in Rome. He glanced at Cassia's dressing table, his eyes alighting on a dark bottle. Habinata by Molinard, he read.

Rocco stretched pleasurably. The visit to Vegas had been an enormous success. He was now sure that everything was running as it should do and that he had been wrong to worry that there was anything suspicious about the issues the restaurant had been suffering. In reality, they were the usual stumbling blocks that any new business could encounter. It was a shame that the opening had been delayed – especially from Cassia's point of view – but hopefully she had enough to keep Gena happy with for her column.

Of course, what was happening back in Sorrento was another matter altogether, Rocco thought, his mouth tightening. He didn't believe in curses now any more than he had ever done, but he had to admit that the restaurant had experienced some very strange setbacks. And then there was the issue of the missing money. As it had done back in Rome, an awful idea occurred to Rocco. It was an unpleasant thought, but he knew he had to investigate fully once he was back. If he was right, it would hurt the family more than any of them could imagine.

Glancing back at Cassia, he was jolted to find her staring at her phone as if she had seen a ghost.

'What's happened?' he asked, jumping up. 'Have you had bad news from home?'

Cassia held her phone up dumbly. 'I have a message from Finn. Except . . . I don't think he meant it to be a message at all.'

'What do you mean?'

'Finn's in Sorrento.' Cassia trembled. 'He has to be. I didn't even know – how can that be? He's my fiancé.'

Rocco didn't know what to say. He and Stefania had had an unconventional relationship when it came to their movements but he had the impression that Finn was supremely organised and anally retentive when it came to such things, so why he hadn't mentioned his impending visit was anyone's guess.

'Finn must have accidentally knocked his phone or something and it recorded him talking.' She hesitated and held her phone out. 'Will you listen to it? Tell me what you think?'

He nodded. 'Of course. If it's not too private.'

Cassia swallowed. 'It's . . . This is my fiancé and my sister. Discussing me.'

'. . . there are times when I really wish I could be more like Cassia. She's so bloody well-organised, so infuriatingly capable. She'd never make a mistake like this in a million years.' Jules's voice sounded tinny on the phone but the contempt was evident. 'God! It's been like this all my life. Cassia's always been so lucky, so bloody blessed. My father . . . Oh, it doesn't matter.'

There was a pause. 'No, she probably wouldn't make a mistake like this.'

Cassia stiffened at Finn's weary tone. She found she couldn't meet Rocco's eyes.

Rocco listened without saying a word, but he was livid on Cassia's behalf. It was such a betrayal. Finn was being disloyal, to the one person guaranteed to join in and agree with him. Hearing Finn saying that making a mistake would make Cassia seem 'more human', Rocco made an angry sound. Finn clearly didn't appreciate Cassia, he obviously didn't get her if he thought she was too focused and needed 'looking after'. Rocco had thought Finn was uptight and old-fashioned when he'd met him and now he realised he had been right. Didn't he realise how incredible Cassia was? How lucky he was to have her? Rocco was brimming over with the injustice of it and he felt a fierce urge to gather Cassia up and prove to her how special she was. If Finn didn't appreciate how beautiful, sensual, opinionated and independent . . . how *passionate* Cassia was, then Finn didn't deserve her.

Cassia couldn't look at Rocco, she only knew how destroyed she felt. Listening to the accidental message being played all over again, she saw Finn in a different light. Did he really assume she would give her career up? The one she had worked so hard for – to be a housewife? If so, he didn't know her, he really didn't. She didn't know whether it was crushing disappointment threatening to suffocate her or white-hot fury that the man she had dedicated eight years of her life to could so casually dismiss her. To her sister, of all people.

'Poor darling,' said Finn from the phone. Even Rocco could hear the tenderness in his voice. It was a murmur, a caress. 'You look as though you could do with a hug,' Finn finished. The final nail in the coffin, Rocco thought. But no, there was more. 'Come here,' Finn said soothingly to Jules, sounding all over-protective. 'It's all right . . . everything will be all right . . .' The message finished abruptly. Silence filled the hotel suite. Rocco couldn't help wondering what had happened next and he knew Cassia must be thinking the same.

She fiddled with the phone, her fingers quivering. 'Well? What do you make of that? What would you think if . . . if Aurelia had been talking about you with Stefania that way?'

Rocco wasn't sure he would care desperately, especially since he and Stefania had split up, but he knew Cassia was poleaxed by Finn's dismissive words. 'I think . . . that Finn would be horrified if he knew you'd heard him talking about you that way.' Rocco wasn't sure why he was practically defending the man, but he was more concerned about protecting Cassia's feelings. 'I think he was probably airing something that was on his mind without really thinking about how he was saying it. I don't even think he meant it.'

Cassia scoffed. 'Oh, Rocco, I think we both know that's not true. He did mean it, I know he did. I think I've been deluding myself that Finn would stop pressurising me to give up my career once we get married.' She started pacing the room. 'He's dropped hints often enough but I ignored them. I thought we had such a tight bond, we could work through it.'

Rocco put a hand on her shoulder, feeling her warm skin beneath his fingertips. 'Maybe you still can.'

He said the words with huge reluctance. He didn't want Cassia and Finn to work through anything. He didn't want them to have such a tight bond that they were able to get past this. He wanted Cassia to kick Finn out of her life for treating her this way. He wanted her . . . all of her. He couldn't get her out of his mind and he couldn't imagine his life without her in it.

Cassia felt Rocco's fingers caressing her neck. She closed her eyes, feeling her tension slipping away. She was hurt by Finn's words, but deep down, she wasn't all that surprised. She was sure she should feel something more and that spoke volumes. She leant against Rocco, feeling his breath on her shoulder.

Rocco breathed in her scent, feeling a bolt of lust shoot through him. It would be so easy to take advantage of Cassia's vulnerable state, and so blatantly, unforgivably wrong. She was hurting, she was angry and he knew she had an unpredictable, passionate streak, even if she didn't always act on it. Hoping he wasn't making the biggest error of his life, Rocco gently withdrew his fingers. If anything was ever going to happen between them, he didn't want it to be because she wanted to get revenge on Finn or because she needed reassurance. He couldn't bring himself to move away from her but he knew he had to stop caressing her silky skin before he did something they both might regret.

Cassia's turned, her dark eyes fixed on his. Her heart was pounding in her chest and she wished he would stop being such a gentleman. Right at that moment, she didn't care about Finn or about Jules. She just wanted Rocco to scoop her up and throw her on to the bed . . . she wanted him to ravish her. She needed feverishly hot kisses, clothes to be torn off, knickers to be flung on to the lampshade; she wanted to feel out of control and giddy with lust.

Fighting a serious urge to yank her into his arms and crush her mouth with his, Rocco turned away, pretending to assess the view.

'Listen, I promised my team at the new restaurant that I'd cook with them tonight as a practice run. But we could go out later on. It . . . it is our last night, after all.'

Wishing she could see inside his head to work out what he was thinking, Cassia touched her neck where his fingers had been. She couldn't even think straight. 'Maybe your new friend Carlotta Moore could join us?' Rocco turned to face her, almost undone by the glazed look in her liquid-brown eyes. 'And Bobby?'

Cassia nodded, feeling disappointment sink through her. Rocco wanted other people around them, he didn't want to spend time with her alone. Realising she had read far more into his friendly shoulder squeeze than she should have done, Cassia lifted her chin.

'I'll get in touch with Carlotta and meet you downstairs at, say, eight p.m.?'

Rocco thrust his hands into his pockets, his olive-green eyes unfathomable. 'Sounds great.' His tone was light. 'See you later and . . . I'm sorry about Finn.'

Cassia nodded tiredly. She heard the door close behind Rocco and she rubbed her eyes, tears finally threatening to fall. She couldn't think what to do next, but she had an idea she was about to end up empty-handed. If she wasn't very much mistaken, she and Finn were over and Rocco . . . Cassia sat down on her bed with a thump. Sickeningly, Rocco didn't seem to feel anything for her, after all.

Back from her photo shoot a few days later, Aurelia, uncharacteristically bare of make-up and wearing a torn T-shirt and shorts, was incandescent with rage.

The hotel in Capri had confirmed that her reception had indeed been cancelled and that Mia was hosting hers there instead. Storming through the villa with her long dark curls flying out behind her, Aurelia was like a furious bird of prey hunting her victim.

Striding past the window of the restaurant and oblivious to members of staff enjoying a breakfast espresso, Aurelia was followed by a sunburned Dino, who was hurrying to keep up. Not even his Aussie charm could mollify her in this mood; Dino had never seen Aurelia so out of control.

Once inside the private wing of the villa, Aurelia tore up the stairs two at time, streaking down to Jules's room. She flung the door open.

'Where is she, Dino?' Aurelia shrieked. The bed clearly hadn't been slept in; even the Disanti staff weren't *that* efficient.

'I don't know,' Dino chided, smoothly moving Jules away from the door and closing it. 'She went off to Capri with Finn a few days ago and she hasn't been seen since. And yes, I have tried her mobile again,' he added, before Aurelia could interrupt. 'I've been dialling her pretty much on the hour since you called me about the reception.'

Aurelia clutched at him. 'It's because we booked the wedding for August, isn't it?' she fretted irrationally. 'I knew we shouldn't do it because it's unlucky here, but you told me it would be all right . . .'

'Aurelia!' Dino squeezed her arms to stop her from losing all sense of perspective. 'This has absolutely nothing to do with us booking the wedding in August. That's just a silly tradition in Italy – no, I'm sorry, but it is. I looked into it at the time and it's thought that people avoided August because most Italians take their holidays then.' He smoothed her hair out of her face. 'Calm down, babe, please.'

Aurelia couldn't. Her dreams of the perfect wedding had just been shattered; worse still, her rival had taken her place at the hotel in Capri. How on earth could she calm down?

Dino raked a hand through his hair. Personally, he wasn't too fussed about losing the reception venue; the hotel in Capri was breathtakingly beautiful and it definitely had the classy vibe Aurelia had been looking for. But Dino would have been happy to marry Aurelia out in the olive groves at the Disanti villa. He had only gone along with the big, showy reception in Capri because he knew it was important to her. Seeing that she was about to cry, Dino pulled Aurelia into his arms. She cracked and gave in to her tears.

'Hey, it's going to be all right,' Dino told her, kissing the top of her head. He held her shuddering frame and did his best to soothe her.

'H-how, Dino?' Aurelia was sobbing so hard, she could hardly speak, especially not in English. 'The . . . the wedding is a week away and we don't have a venue. We have hundreds . . . no, thousands of people coming! We have a magazine deal and I promised them Capri. What are we going to do?'

Dino wasn't sure what to say to that. Now that Aurelia had put it like that, it did seem pretty hopeless. Invitations had gone out, people were flying over to Sorrento in the next few days and although he couldn't give a stuff about the magazine deal, he knew it would help Aurelia's modelling profile hugely. The magazine they'd managed to secure sold all over the world, not just in Italy.

'I should never have believed Jules when she said she could handle a wedding of this size,' Aurelia raged, rubbing her eyes, which were red from crying all the way home on the plane. 'Cassia warned me about her, hinted that she wasn't up to it and I didn't listen. I was charmed by Jules, she seemed like so much fun. She seemed really confident that she could manage our wedding. I could . . . kick myself?' Aurelia looked at Dino to check she'd said the right thing. 'Yes, kick myself. I've been so very stupid.'

Dino tucked a strand of dark hair behind Aurelia's ear. 'You haven't been stupid, babe. You're trusting and lovely and that's why I love you so much.' He kissed her full, pink mouth, unable to stand seeing her so distraught. 'Look, I don't know what we're going to do, but Rocco's back soon, isn't he? He'll know what to do.'

Looking child-like, Aurelia nodded and sniffed. 'I suppose

464

so. He always manages to come up with solutions to problems. But this . . . this is off the scale . . .'

'What's going on?' Sofia looked shocked when she saw how upset Aurelia was. 'Has something terrible happened?'

Aurelia quickly explained.

Not a fan of Jules since she'd joined them at the villa, Sofia was, nonetheless, horrified. 'That girl, she is so lazy,' she said to Aurelia in Italian. 'She's barely moved from the pool since she arrived. Where is she anyway?'

Switching to Italian, Dino cut in. 'I reckon she's staying in Capri with Finn, lying low, as it were. Pretty cowardly.'

'Hmmm.' Sofia pursed her lips. 'Jules and this Finn seem very close, yes? Strange, I thought he was Cassia's fiancé. Anyway, let's see what Jules has to say for herself when she comes back.' Sofia's expression was stern. 'She has to come back and face the consequences sooner or later. And when she does . . .'

Jules and Finn were, in fact, just about to pull up outside the Disanti villa. In the air-conditioned taxi, Jules's teeth were chattering, but she was fairly sure they would do the same thing when she climbed out into the stifling heat. She wasn't cold, she was just completely and utterly petrified.

'Finn, I can't do it,' she panicked, shrinking back from the door. 'They're all going to hate me. How am I going to explain myself?'

Finn suppressed a sigh. After spending a couple of days making countless phone calls to sort the wedding out whilst ignoring Aurelia's until they had something positive to tell her, he had finally forced Jules to pluck up the courage to return to Sorrento. It had been rather like talking someone down from a ledge but he had somehow managed it.

Oddly, he had found himself somewhat reluctant to do it. Trapped in their little bubble in Capri, it had felt as if no one else existed. They had both been focused on Aurelia's wedding and he hadn't even contacted work once to see what was going on. He wasn't sure when he had last done that; whenever he and Cassia went on holiday together, which was rare, they both checked up on work issues frequently.

'It's going to be all right,' he told Jules firmly as they got out of the car. 'You have to do this, you have to apologise to Aurelia. She's bound to be angry, but you're just going to have to keep saying sorry and do your best to tell her why it all went wrong.'

Jules knew Finn was right, but inside, she was quaking. She couldn't for the life of her think of a good reason to explain her actions, apart from the fact that she was hopeless when it came to organising anything. The only thing she was any good at was cooking and short of offering to host Aurelia's wedding breakfast, Jules couldn't see how that was going to help anyone. She glanced at Finn, realising she cared terribly what he thought of her. Something had changed between them in Capri. It was as if they'd been in their own little world as they did their best to sort the wedding issues out and at night they had laughed over the same things as they enjoyed simple food and wine. What had amazed Jules was that it hadn't been an effort. For once, she hadn't been trying to be something she wasn't. She had even gone out without any make-up on one day, something she wouldn't have even contemplated with the likes of Dom.

Feeling sorry for her, Finn took her chin in his hands. 'You can do this, Jules. You have to be brave and face the music, but I know you can do that.' He caressed her chin briefly. 'And when you do, I'll be incredibly proud of you.'

Jules stared at him. No one had ever said that to her before, not once. Not her father or her mother or any of her bosses. She felt overcome and she fought hard not to cry.

Finn grinned suddenly. 'It looks as though we've both found a few things out about ourselves since we've been here, doesn't it? You've worked out once and for all that event organising isn't your forte and I've . . . well, I've worked out that I'm very English and that I don't really like Italy much.' He cast his eyes away ruefully. 'Which won't please Cassia one bit.' His heart constricted at the thought of Cassia, but he pushed it aside. That was something he would deal with later on.

Jules looked earnest. 'Yes, but that's all right, Finn. We don't all have to have a nauseating love affair with Italy like my father and Cassia.'

Feeling a sudden and rather desperate need to know what was at the bottom of Jules's issue with her father, Finn touched her arm. 'Jules, what's the story with your father? Why do you feel this way about him, and about Cassia?' He saw tears spring into her eyes and he felt a rush of compassion for her. Or was it something else? Shaking the bizarre thought off, Finn tried again. 'Cassia has never known why the two of you don't get on, but now I know you better, I'm sure there's a good reason.'

'It's . . . I just resent her, that's all. She and my father were so close . . . but there's more to it than that.'

'Can you tell me about it?' Finn met her eyes searchingly. 'You can trust me. And I wouldn't tell anyone, not even Cassia, if you didn't want me to.' He shocked himself as he said the words out loud, but he knew he was speaking the truth. Jules was fragile, damaged in some way, and he wanted to protect her. Even though he knew Cassia had agonised over Jules's behaviour for years, he would respect Jules's right to privacy if she trusted him enough to confide in him.

Jules looked into Finn's eyes. She believed him. Despite his deep loyalty to Cassia, she could tell that Finn meant what he said. Jules wondered what it would feel like to unburden herself, but she had spent so many years hiding the truth, she wasn't sure she could bring herself to voice it out loud. But something about the genuine warmth in Finn's heart-meltingly blue eyes made her want to do it.

Looking down, she realised he'd taken her hand and for a moment she was distracted by the sandy-gold hairs that made his big hand look like a lion's paw. She knew she shouldn't think it, but she couldn't help wishing he was holding her hand because he was attracted to her, not because he felt sorry for her. Meeting his eyes, she was mesmerised by his gaze again. She felt so close to him, closer than she had to any man, in fact, and without warning, Jules felt the words she had held down for so many years whooshing to the surface.

'I've never told anyone this,' she started hesitantly. 'I couldn't, not with famous parents, but the thing is—'

'Oh, I'm sorry, am I interrupting something?'

Aurelia's sarcastic voice made Jules and Finn spring apart abruptly.

Flinching, Jules turned to face her. Seeing that she was flanked by Dino, who for once didn't look as friendly as usual, as well as an extremely disapproving Sofia, Jules's heart sank. She held on to Finn's hand for courage. They had been on the brink of sharing a very intimate moment, but it would have to wait. Reminding herself that Finn was going to be proud of her for owning up to her mistakes, Jules braced herself.

'I think you have some explaining to do,' Aurelia continued, her icy tones managing to bring a chill to the sweltering atmosphere. 'Maybe you would be so good as to tell me how you managed to ruin my dream wedding?'

Feeling Finn squeezing her hand supportively, Jules nodded. 'You're absolutely right, Aurelia, and I'll do my best to explain everything. And . . . and I promise you that Finn and I have been doing everything we can to make things right whilst we've been in Capri.'

Finn gave her an encouraging nod and, buoyed up by his faith in her, Jules took a deep breath and carried on.

Chapter Twenty-One

Glad she had a driver negotiating the heavy traffic on the way to Leicester Square, Diana felt her stomach shift nervously. It was the first night of *Jealousy* and she was shaking all over. It was the West End, for heaven's sake, the place where careers could be made or shattered overnight. Diana broke out into a sweat. What was she thinking? Why on earth had she agreed to this? She didn't need this kind of stress, and she could do without the publicity, especially if it was terrible.

Diana glanced down at her trembling hands, wondering how she would stop them shaking on stage. And then she realised that in a few short hours, she would be naked, stark naked on stage in front of rows and rows of strangers. She could imagine Jules saying, 'Naked, Mother, at your age?' and the thought made her chuckle. Jules was right, of course; she probably should know better than to do such a thing, especially since it was simply asking for criticism.

Well, it was too late now, she thought, squaring her shoulders. She had put in too much hard work to back out of the play now and, perversely, there was a part of her that couldn't wait to become Clarissa again. Besides which, Diana knew the play was beautifully written and she had every faith that the rest of the cast would support her through it, especially Robson. And if it all went wrong and the public hated her,

Diana had her flight to Sorrento booked and her suitcase packed in readiness for Aurelia Disanti's wedding. She would simply get through it and then escape to Italy to lick her wounds.

She had chosen to wear a silk jersey Halston number in a vibrant shade of bluebell. It was drapy and flattering on her curvier figure and she felt good in it. She glanced at her watch. She had promised Fliss that she would arrive at the theatre early for a mini celebration, but she would much rather have turned up at the last minute and just walked on stage to start acting. Arriving early was only serving to make her feel edgier and she could have done without it.

She glanced down at her more shapely thighs. She could imagine what the press – if they cared about a has-been's thighs, that is – would make of them. Obsessed with such things, the gossip mags would be full of it next week, asking if she was 'embracing' her new shape, most probably. Diana always found it such a hypocritical way of looking at weight gain; if the celebrity in question dared to be negative about it, the magazine would twist it to sound as though she was publicly reviling the curvier woman. If she said she didn't care, they would say she was in denial or that there must be something wrong with her if she was happy to be fat. Diana suddenly wished she had a man on her arm to reassure her. Marco had always been the consummate escort, gorgeous, friendly and absolutely welded to her side, regardless of the paparazzi sometimes wanting a shot of her on her own. And Angelo had been such a gentleman, kind, sweet and so handsome. The paps had loved him, even if they didn't know who he was.

As the driver turned the car towards Leicester Square, Diana gasped. There were crowds of people there. Pressed up alongside a sweeping red carpet edged with shiny gold rope stands, they stood waiting, looking thoroughly excited. Diana was bemused. Fliss had mentioned an early celebration, but this looked more like the premiere of a film.

'Is . . . is something else going on tonight?' Diana asked her driver.

The driver shook his head in amusement. 'No, it's just your play. These people are all here to see you. And . . . here we are.' Sliding to a halt, he nodded at her to get out.

Diana grabbed the door handle with clammy fingers. Blinded by the flashbulbs that suddenly went off in her face, she was relieved when a firm hand grabbed her arm.

'Thought you might need some moral support,' Felicity said with a grin. 'I was worried they might think we were lesbian lovers, but I figured you still might prefer that to walking the red carpet alone.'

Diana smiled. 'I didn't even know there was going to be a red carpet! What's going on?'

'Oh, I just told a few people you were going to be in this new play tonight.' Fliss grinned unapologetically. 'What can I say? You're acting royalty, Di, people want to see you make your comeback.'

'Don't say that word,' Diana grimaced. 'The hacks are going to crucify me.'

'Not on my watch,' Fliss said briskly, ushering Diana down the carpet.

To applause and cheers, Diana walked down the carpet, looking far more relaxed than she felt. The crowd were chanting her name – they were actually chanting her name! She signed autographs, chatted to fans and politely answered questions thrown at her by the waiting journalists. Finally, one of them asked the killer question.

'So, how do you feel about your new curves?'

Diana ran a hand over her shapely hip. 'I honestly love them. I hated it at first, because I'm used to starving myself, you know? I'm a normal woman and it's not in my nature to embrace putting on weight. But,' she paused, wanting to be honest, whatever they made of it, 'but now, I feel . . . good

471

about myself. I feel sexier and happier, I really do.'

'Wow, that's great.' The journalist waggled her recorder in Diana's face. 'And any new men on the horizon?'

Fliss gave her a sunny smile. 'That would be telling, wouldn't it? Thank you for your time.'

Catching sight of what looked like a familiar face in the crowd, Diana let out a gasp. Was it Angelo? The dark eyes had looked just like his, the hair . . . As quickly as she'd caught a glimpse of whoever it was, he ducked out of sight. Diana's heart plummeted. Of course it wasn't Angelo. He had no reason to be there.

Forcing herself to smile for the cameras once more, Diana did her best to ignore the empty pang in her heart. She still loved Angelo, but she had blown it with him. The best thing she could do was wow the crowds with her acting.

Making frantic calls to Rocco in Vegas from her upstairs suite, Sofia turned her eyes skyward and thanked the gods when he finally answered his phone.

'Rocco! Where have you been? I've been trying to call and there's so much—'

'Wow, slow down.' Rocco laughed. 'Sorry, Grandmother, I've been working and . . . having some serious fun, believe it or not.'

'Really?' Sofia's rosy cheeks dimpled. 'That's great. I take it you're enjoying yourself?'

'For the first time in ages, yes, I am.' Rocco's voice was upbeat. 'This has turned out to be more of a holiday than a work trip, but I think it's just what I needed.' He told Sofia about some of the things he and Cassia had done. 'A gondola, can you imagine? Not like the real thing, of course, and I was all set to hate it, but it was actually rather authentic. And romantic.'

Sofia felt mixed emotions. She hadn't heard Rocco sounding like this in a long time and she hated to be the one to spoil his good mood, but she really needed to run something past him.

'Cassia's sister Jules has made a terrible mess with Aurelia's wedding,' she started with a sigh. She told him the whole sorry story as quickly as she could, pausing only to let Rocco make the odd explosive comment, before swiftly moving on to her ideas to salvage the wedding.

'Obviously the church ceremony is still going ahead at the Cloister, but I wondered if we could hold the reception here? I know Aurelia has a big magazine deal, hence the Capri setting, but I thought the press might be impressed with us closing the restaurant for the night and hosting the reception. You know, play on the family angle,' Sofia added, hoping Rocco didn't think she was insane.

'It's a perfect idea,' he said at once, his mind rapidly turning over the possibilities. Under normal circumstances, he detested the idea of closing the restaurant or hosting any special events there. But for Aurelia . . . well, as far as Rocco was concerned, she could have anything she wanted, especially after the mix-up.

'I have no issue with closing the restaurant for the night. Just offer anyone booked in on that day a free meal at another time. We could allow the magazine staff to stay at the villa and we could use the rooms in that other barn behind the olive groves if it can be made ready in time.' Rocco thought for a second. 'We can organise the food . . . I'll even cook, if she'd like me to. Having done so much cooking here, I'd love to do it. And it'll give the press something to talk about.' He sounded amused.

Hiding her elation about Rocco cooking again, Sofia wrote everything down, adding some notes of her own about the food. 'I think I can make the place look really special – a candlelit procession, a marquee, perhaps?'

'I'll leave all that kind of thing to you.' Rocco said, not

hugely interested in the girlier details. 'God, that girl Jules is a pain. If she wasn't Cassia's sister, I'd send her packing.'

Sofia glanced out of the window, seeing Jules sitting under an umbrella overlooking the olive groves. Finn was there too and they both looked suspiciously cosy.

'Cassia's fiancé is here,' Sofia informed Rocco, thinking she should say something. 'I think it was supposed to be a surprise visit.'

'Cassia knows about Finn being in Sorrento,' Rocco provided, his voice tight all of a sudden. He told Sofia about the accidental message Cassia's hapless fiancé had left.

'Fool,' Sofia said, her thoughts drifting to another issue she was worrying about. 'Cassia must be very hurt.'

'Very,' agreed Rocco. 'I think she's having second thoughts about her wedding.' He paused. 'And, as awful as it sounds, I can't help feeling hopeful about that, Grandmother.'

Taken aback, Sofia bit her lip. In any other circumstance, she would have been overjoyed to think that Rocco had feelings for Cassia, but now she felt she owed it to him to speak up. 'Luca thinks Cassia's father is the surviving son from the Giorelli family,' she blurted out.

There was silence at the other end of the phone. 'I see. Has Luca confirmed that?' Rocco asked.

Sofia was wrong-footed by his seeming indifference. 'No. But . . . what if he does? It matters, doesn't it? Surely you can see that.'

Rocco was silent for a moment. 'No, I can't. It doesn't matter in the slightest. Not to me.'

'But . . . but your grandfather would turn in his grave,' Sofia spluttered. 'That curse, it almost killed you, you nearly drowned! Remember that, please. Whatever you feel for her or think you feel for her—'

'Grandmother, you adore Cassia, you told me so yourself. Can you really turn your back on her if there is an accident of birth and it turns out that she is related to the Giorelli family? Because I can't. Who cares, anyway? They are all dead now. Even if Marco Marini is that lost boy, he's no longer with us.'

'What about my car accident? Surely that is not a coincidence?' Stubbornly, Sofia clung to the idea that what had happened to her was somehow related to the curse.

Rocco hesitated. He had his own theory about her car accident but he knew better than to voice it aloud at this stage. If he was wrong, he would upset her unnecessarily and if he was right . . . well, if he was right, Rocco knew his grandmother would be devastated.

'I think you should forget about the accident and about the curse,' he told her firmly. 'None of this matters any more, all right? The only thing that's important to me, here and now, is Cassia.' Rocco stopped, the strength of his own words scaring him for a moment. He carried on. 'Do whatever you need to do to make Aurelia's wedding perfect and I . . . Cassia and I will be home very soon. And please, don't worry about anything.'

Sofia opened her mouth to beg him to think about his actions, but it was too late. Rocco had gone. She put the phone down. Rocco might be more mature these days but it didn't mean he wasn't impulsive. Hoping to God Luca was wrong, Sofia perused her notes, knowing she would have to think about the rival family issue later. And Rocco was right, she did think the world of Cassia. For now, she had a wedding reception to organise, the likes of which Sorrento had never seen before.

Sofia picked up her phone, wondering just how many fireworks were needed for a two thousand strong crowd . . .

Flipping through the dresses in her wardrobe, Cassia wished she'd brought more choices with her so she had a chance of wearing something Rocco hadn't already seen her in. Which was ridiculously girly of her, but she couldn't help it. Seconds later, a member of staff delivered a wide black box tied with an amber-coloured ribbon to her room and Cassia opened it in excitement. The colour scheme was vaguely familiar, but there was no card attached. Inside, there was layer upon layer of amber-coloured tissue paper. Nestling inside the tissue and clashing wildly was an emerald-green dress. Cassia gasped and held it up.

It was exquisite, high at the neck, low at the back, and set off by a frothy skirt that she knew would swirl around her knees beautifully. It fitted like a glove, moulding lusciously to her curves and leaving an expanse of golden-brown back bare. She wasn't sure she dared to wear it, but the thought of taking it off was impossible, the silk and taffeta felt far too sensual. Was it from Rocco? If so, was it a clichéd gift, a rip-off from the episode in *Sex and the City* where the Russian sent Carrie an Oscar de la Renta? Carlotta arrived just then and she shrieked when she saw Cassia.

'You got it! Oh, it's perfect on you! I knew it would be. It's from my new clothing line. Do you like it? I guessed your size and I was right, which is great.' She paused for breath and struck a pose. 'And what do you think of mine?' Wearing an outrageous multi-coloured dress with a fishtail and ruffles on the shoulders, her dark hair was piled on top of her head and her make-up was a riot of colour. She looked as though she was about to do the merengue, or at very least sashay through the casino like Carmen Miranda's younger sister.

Cassia realised that was why the black and amber packaging had been familiar – Carlotta used it for all her products.

'Now, shall we get going?' Carlotta said, slipping her arm through Cassia's. 'I can't wait to meet handsome Rocco. You said he was bringing Bobby Swan with him too? Now, he has a voice like molasses . . . a bit cuddly for my taste, but when I get tequila inside me, I get very, very flirty . . .'

Cassia grinned. Any nerves she'd been feeling evaporated in

light of Carlotta's infectious chatter. Whatever happened with Rocco, she knew it was going to be a fun night.

Sitting at a secluded table in the shade overlooking the Disanti olive groves, Jules edged her chair out slightly. She was sitting companionably beside Finn and the atmosphere was still and relaxed. The hustle and bustle of the restaurant was far enough away not to infringe on the peace and quiet of the little spot they'd secured, but they could hear the maids cleaning the bedrooms upstairs above them.

Jules was convinced she could hear Sofia's voice, snapping out orders in rapid Italian, and at one point, she was certain she heard her name mentioned. Finn told her she was being paranoid, but Jules knew she deserved any bad-mouthing she was receiving over the mayhem she had caused with Aurelia's wedding.

'I still feel awful about it, Finn. The look on her face . . . The only thing I'm any good at is cooking,' Jules said dolefully. 'Short of offering to lay on the entire wedding breakfast, I wasn't sure what I could say to make up for what I'd done.'

Finn leant over and squeezed her hand. 'Stop beating yourself up, Jules. You've owned up and you've apologised. It was a mistake – a big one, I grant you, but it's done now.' He held on to her hand, loath to admit that he had rather enjoyed taking care of Jules. It felt good to be useful and to be seen as someone to lean on. Finn didn't blame Cassia for not being that way inclined, and if anything he felt horribly guilty about the way he'd criticised her to Jules. He loved Cassia to pieces; it was just that he had realised they were not very well suited in some ways.

He turned back to Jules. 'Dino told me that Sofia has spoken to Rocco and they're all set to have the reception here on the estate now. Personally, I think that magazine Aurelia has a deal with will love this even more than the whole Capri thing.'

'That's great. I still wish I hadn't messed up, though. I really like Aurelia and I hate the thought of her perfect wedding being ruined.' Jules couldn't help enjoying the warmth of Finn's hand in hers. They were good friends, so she told herself it was all right to hold hands as often as they did. Every time she thought about Cassia, Jules felt stricken, but she couldn't help the growing feelings she had for Finn. She figured it didn't matter as Cassia would never know, but she was full of remorse about pretty much everything right now, Cassia included.

Finn had been the best company since he'd arrived in Italy. They had so much in common and he had supported her wholeheartedly. Not only that, Finn hadn't judged her or rejected her, even though she'd made mistakes. Jules wasn't used to that, she wasn't used to being forgiven for being less than perfect. Look at her father.

'What are you thinking about?' Finn asked, seeing how close to tears she was.

About to throw out a jokey lie, Jules swallowed. 'I was thinking about my father. About how he could never forgive me for not being perfect.'

'What do you mean?'

Jules slumped forward, her shoulders sagging. She could feel the tears coming and she couldn't stop them. She had never told anyone, not a single person – not even Cassia. 'Everyone thinks my family was so bloody perfect, Finn. You probably do because you've heard Cassia's version, and to be fair to her, life was pretty great from her perspective; she had my father's love and support and in her eyes everything was rosy. But it wasn't, not for me.' Jules wrung her hands, not even noticing the tears splashing down on to her sundress. 'My father . . . he . . . he . . .'

Finn looked appalled. 'Oh, Jules. Don't say he touched you . . .'

478

Jules's head snapped up. 'What? Oh no, nothing like that, Finn! Perish the thought. No, what I was trying to say was that he wasn't my father. Marco Marini, famous food writer, wasn't my father. He was Cassia's, but he wasn't mine.'

Finn sat up, aghast. 'But your parents were so famous, that would have been front-page news.'

'If anyone had found out.' Jules wiped her eyes. 'I found out when I was in my teens, one of those awful moments when you need your birth certificate for something. My father had refused to sign it, you see, and I confronted my parents about it because I couldn't understand what was going on.'

Finn placed his other hand on hers, squeezing them tightly. 'What did they say?'

'They didn't deny it. My father confessed that he had suspicions I wasn't his and my mother admitted it.' Jules started to sob uncontrollably. 'It was why he was so distant with me, why he lavished all of his attention on Cassia. He hated me, you see. I was a constant reminder of my mother's affair.'

Finn was nonplussed. Cassia had always said her parents loved each other to distraction. 'I can't believe it. Diana was so devoted to Marco. Well, that's what all the papers said. Why on earth did she have an affair?'

Jules couldn't answer that question. She had asked herself the same over the years, blaming her mother's selfishness, her need for male attention. But the fact remained, her mother had loved her father deeply. Jules knew it was true, however it might seem in light of the facts. It was something that had always bothered her about the situation, the fact that the affair that had brought her into the world must have been such a pointless fling.

'You do know that none of that is Cassia's fault, though?' he said gently, feeling the need to defend her. 'She's never understood why you've treated her so horribly since you were teenagers.'

'You're right, Finn. I know you are, but I couldn't help it. Every time I saw her and my father . . . Marco together, like two peas in a bloody pod, I couldn't stand it. It hurt so much and I had to blame someone. I mean, I blamed my father and I blamed my mother too, but I was so jealous, so envious of the bond Cassia had with him.'

'I understand. But why didn't you speak to her about it? I think she would have understood.'

Jules turned away. 'Because I was ashamed, Finn, don't you understand? I was ashamed and I still am. I'm the bastard child of a famous actress and God knows who. I don't have Cassia's perfect pedigree . . . my life wasn't the same as hers. I asked my mother not to tell Cassia and out of guilt, I suppose, she didn't. It's always been our dirty little secret.' She rubbed the tears from her face.

Finn felt for Jules. He didn't agree with the way she'd treated Cassia, but he could see how this awful truth had torn her apart and made her act irrationally.

'Don't cry,' Finn told her softly, wiping her tears away. 'I hate seeing you cry.' Lifting her chin, he looked into her eyes and, hesitating for only a second, he placed his mouth on her quivering lips and kissed her.

Jules stiffened, but it was momentary. Before she could help herself, she snaked her arms round his neck and kissed him back. Then Finn began to kiss her tears away tenderly, wrapping his big arms round her slender back, but Jules pulled his mouth on to hers again, unable to stop now they had started.

Finn stopped kissing her and smoothed her hair down. 'I know I shouldn't say this but this feels so right. I can't understand it. Is it just me?'

Jules shook her head. 'No. It's not. It's not just you. I don't want to feel any of these things for you because it's not fair to Cassia, but I do. I-I want you . . . more than I've wanted anyone in my life.' She started to cry again. 'You're . . . you're the person I've been waiting for . . . and it's not fair that you're not mine. I-I just want someone to take care of me . . . I want *you* to take care of me.'

Finn kissed her again, roughly. 'And that's what I'm going to do. I'll have to speak to Cassia . . . our wedding's planned for a few weeks' time, a wedding I can't go ahead with. Because I feel the same. I-I think I love you. I mean, I do. I do love you.'

'Say that again,' Jules murmured, pulling his mouth down to hers again.

'I love you,' he mumbled. Unaware they were being watched by a stunned Aurelia upstairs, Jules and Finn kissed endlessly, clinging to one other as if they were terrified the other would disappear if they let go.

'I like Carlotta,' Rocco murmured in Cassia's ear that night. 'She's mad, but very entertaining.'

'She's great, isn't she?'

Cassia could barely concentrate with Rocco's breath tickling her neck. After admiring the incredible views over cocktails at the Rio's trendy VooDoo lounge and a delicious meal in the Venetian, she, Carlotta and Rocco had been joined by Bobby, who was half-cut and on exceptionally good form. After a few rounds of tequilas, they headed back to the Bellagio to watch the fountains. At this time of night, against the backdrop of the majestic hotel and a lavender-tinted sky, the magnificent water show amazed crowds every fifteen minutes. As the fountains danced cheekily to the Pink Panther, playfully spraying the awestruck crowds with sweeping arcs and almost deafening crashes, Cassia turned to find Bobby twirling a shrieking Carlotta round on her tippytoes.

'He's very light of foot,' Cassia observed in surprise.

Rocco laughed. 'Bobby's a real smoothie, I can assure you. He can dance, sing and charm everyone in a room – a bit like Carlotta, in fact.'

'Ha! I think they've hit it off.'

'Ah yes, but Bobby is very fickle. He was head over heels in love with you the other day.'

Cassia went pink. 'Well, Carlotta is absolutely gorgeous, so I can see why he's changed his mind.'

Not even looking at Carlotta, Rocco stared at Cassia. The emerald-green dress brought out the rich brown of her eyes and the occasional glimpse of bare thigh as the material rustled and settled was positively unnerving. He knew he couldn't stay away from her, even if he tried. He frantically tried to think of something to say that wasn't too personal and remembering his phone call with his grandmother earlier, he focused on that.

Feeling his eyes on her, Cassia felt her insides melt and dip. She wanted to be strong enough to resist him. She wanted to remind herself of Finn over and over until she had built up such an impenetrable layer of armour around herself, she would be immune to Rocco's sexy green eyes and to the warmth of his fingers on her hand as he leant in to speak to her. The trouble was, nothing seemed to work. All she could think about was the kiss in Rome – and about kissing Rocco again.

Cassia realised he was talking to her but it was hard to tell with the thumping music. 'Sorry, did you say something about Jules?'

Rocco put his mouth closer to her ear. Quickly, he told her about Aurelia's wedding.

'Oh no!' Cassia looked vexed. 'I'd like to say I'm shocked, but I'm really not. Poor Aurelia – and poor Jules. I know she'll be feeling really bad about it all.'

'I'm sure.' Rocco's tone was dry. He knew Cassia was being loyal to her sister, but after the phone message with Finn, he wasn't sure she should be. 'Grandmother has it all in hand, though.' He told her about Sofia's plans to host the reception at the estate.

Cassia felt relieved. At least Aurelia's wedding wouldn't be ruined. And as stunning as the hotel in Capri sounded, it would be hard to imagine it outshining the Disanti villa and grounds.

'Your sister, is she a bit silly, do you think? Spoilt, perhaps?' Rocco asked.

'No, the opposite, actually. She wasn't exactly a daddy's girl, put it that way. If anything, that was me. I really wish I knew what had gone on back then, but none of them would ever talk about it.'

Rocco wondered what it was about, but he wasn't going to waste time trying to guess. Cassia had done that all her life and she hadn't been able to come up with the answer.

As Bobby and Carlotta staggered off together, waving as they weaved in and out of the crowds, Cassia met Rocco's eyes. They gazed at each other as Andrea Bocelli's incredible rendition of 'Time to Say Goodbye' with Sarah Brightman rippled over them like melted chocolate.

'I'm not going to be able to concentrate on the fountains if you look at me like that.' Rocco's voice was teasing but his eyes were intense.

'I'm not sure I want you to.'

Cassia's mouth was trembling and her skin was prickling all over. She knew she was heading into dangerous territory, but she couldn't help it. Rocco brought out the side of her she had buried all those years ago, the impetuous side that threw caution to the wind and sent her headlong into trouble. Her relationship with Finn had all but extinguished the fire that had once been responsible for her more passionate side, but deep down, it was who she was and she knew it.

Rocco's eyes dropped to her mouth. 'You're vulnerable,' he murmured. 'Hurt about Finn's message.'

'I'm hurt, but I'm not vulnerable,' she answered in a low voice. 'And I'm probably not nearly as upset as I should be. Stefania . . .'

'We split up, before I flew out to Vegas. I knew how I felt about you even then and I couldn't lie to her any more.'

Cassia felt her stomach lurch deliciously.

Rocco tried again. 'You're drunk. We put away the best part of a bottle of tequila between us.'

Cassia shook her head. 'Bobby and Carlotta drank most of it. I'm practically sober. Are you?'

He nodded slowly. 'What is it about us and fountains?' he joked, trying to keep things light.

She grinned but the smile faded as he moved closer.

Rocco remembered his grandmother's warning about Cassia being a possible relation of the Giorelli family, but he didn't care. He knew he should because family meant everything to him, but his feelings for Cassia were too strong. Rocco wanted to give in to them, but he had to be sure she felt the same way.

'Could this just . . . be a way to get back at Finn?'

Seeing the desire in his eyes, Cassia's stomach fizzed with expectation. 'Trust me, Finn will take a very dim view of this situation. It would be the end of us, but maybe that's what's happened anyway.'

Rocco reached out and stroked a strand of hair behind her ear, his fingers trailing down her neck. Cassia pulled him closer, until they were only a breath apart.

'We're beside one of the most amazing fountains I've ever seen,' she murmured. 'Don't let me down, will you? Not after Rome.'

Rocco didn't need telling twice. Cupping her neck, he searched out her mouth with his and kissed her. The soft kiss became harder as their tongues entwined and Rocco lost himself in her. He pushed her against the stone wall framing the Bellagio fountains, his thigh urgent against hers. His hand trailed up her bare thigh and she pulled her mouth away.

'Not here,' she whispered. 'It's illegal . . . or something.'

Laughing, they dashed inside the Bellagio and made for the

private lift area. Feeding her a gigantic chocolate-covered strawberry from the complimentary food area while they waited for the lift, Rocco licked chocolate off her lips and tasted the sweetness of the strawberry inside her mouth. In the lift, they kissed all the way up to the thirty-sixth floor without pausing for breath. Edging their way past hostess trolleys with the remains of room service orders in the corridors, they clumsily opened the door to Cassia's suite and backed into it.

Not bothering to close the curtains, they kissed all the way round the lounge area, almost falling on to the sofa, but Cassia dragged Rocco into the bedroom. As the lights of Vegas twinkled and flashed outside the window, Rocco slowly undressed Cassia, unzipping the emerald-green dress and allowing it to pool around her feet. She almost covered her bare breasts with her hands but she stopped when Rocco motioned for her to trust him.

Feasting his eyes on her luscious body, Rocco tore his shirt over his head and kicked off his loafers. Barefoot, he dispensed with his trousers until he was standing in a pristine pair of white boxer shorts. His golden skin gleamed and the cross around his neck caught the light as he snapped the curtains shut.

'I want you all to myself,' he said. 'This view is mine.'

Moving towards her, he kissed her shoulders, leaving her quivering with desire. His mouth moved over her skin with slow deliberation, his breath practically leaving scorch marks.

'You have to know something.' She placed a hand on his chest. 'Luca phoned. I haven't been able to get in touch with him yet, but he thinks I might be—'

'A descendant of the Giorelli family,' Rocco finished, kissing her bare shoulder again. 'I know. My grandmother told me.'

Cassia had no idea how Sofia knew about it, but she could guess what she must be thinking. She halted Rocco's mouth. 'What if I am? What if my father is that boy who survived the landslide?'

'I don't care,' Rocco told her simply. 'I told you I don't believe in curses. Nor do I care if your father was one of the Giorellis or a member of the Mafia, for that matter. It has nothing to do with the way I feel about you.'

Relief shuddered through her. Cassia arched her back, aching for him to touch her. It had never been this way with Finn before, not even in the early days, she thought breathlessly. Finn was an earnest lover; giving and sweet. But he hadn't ever been able to make her feel the way Rocco was now, as though nothing else mattered, apart from them. It was a giddy feeling, addictively sensual, like eating something that made your mouth tingle and come alive, something that made other food seem bland and uninteresting.

As Rocco pushed her down on to the bed, Cassia reached up and wound her arms round his neck. Pressing her breasts against his chest, she felt him groan against her and his hand slid down her thigh. Bending his head, Rocco abruptly sucked Cassia's nipple, making her gasp with pleasure. As she squirmed against him and wriggled out of her knickers, she reached down and pushed at his boxer shorts, needing him to be as naked as she was.

Meeting his eyes, she reared up against him and unable to hold back any longer, he sank himself inside her. Letting out a gasp, Cassia met his hips, urging him to move faster. He did, moving in time with her perfectly as they writhed and rolled across the bed. And then they were both lost in one another as they allowed themselves to live out everything they'd been fantasising about since Rome.

The first time was hot, fast and heady. The second was slow, delicious and sensual. And the third time, sleepily managed as dawn filtered dustily through a chink in the curtains heralding a new day in Vegas, felt rather like . . . very much like . . . love.

Chapter Twenty-Two

At Naples airport, Diana collected her luggage and waited for a taxi. She was nervous about seeing Jules and Cassia, particularly as she hadn't warned them about her early arrival. Grace and Henry were flying out in a few days' time and they had asked her if she would like to travel with them, a surprising turn of events that Diana had appreciated greatly. But she had to do this and she had to do it alone. She owed it to her daughters to speak to them directly, to get everything off her chest and to be totally honest, for once. Not because it would make her feel any better – far from it, Diana thought to herself bleakly – but because she owed it to the pair of them to confess the full truth finally.

She wasn't sure how to explain herself or what would be the right thing to say. For Cassia, the story would be a complete shock and for Jules . . . Diana faltered. Part of her felt that the truth could easily be hidden away for ever, to keep Jules from learning the full horror, but didn't she deserve to know? Diana shook all over at the thought of reliving it all, but she was going to do it; she had come this far and there was no turning back. She thought about her life and how she might have changed things, but she wasn't sure she could have done anything other than what she had done back then. Fast forward to now and she knew she owed it to her daughters to be herself, laid bare, just the way she had been when she played Clarissa in *Jealousy*. The play had been a triumphant success and it had been extended for another six months, starting as soon as she returned from Sorrento. But first she had to own up to what had happened and who she was, whatever the consequences.

Flying back from Vegas the morning after spending the night together, Rocco and Cassia were in reflective moods. Saved from too much chit-chat by a mix-up at the airport which meant their first-class seats were at the opposite ends of the cabin, Cassia couldn't stop thinking about what had happened. Images of herself and Rocco passionately rolling across the bed played over and over in her mind, tormenting her and leaving her squirming in her makeshift airline bed.

Cassia had never felt like this before. She felt dangerously out of control, heady and as though she was drunk with excitement. Maybe when she was younger, but this was different; it was addictive. She missed it already, she missed Rocco and the feel of his mouth on hers.

Looking at it from another angle, Cassia knew that she had behaved badly. Before coming to Italy, she wouldn't have dreamt of cheating on Finn. Their relationship had been watertight and she trusted him the way she knew he had always trusted her. Which was why she was so confused, because what had happened between herself and Rocco had been right. Not so much 'meant to be' or anything as cheesy as that, but just . . . right. It had been mind-blowing and sweet and passionate and sexy – everything she had always thought lust, love and anything else in between should be.

She didn't blame Finn for the fact that she had changed so much over the years. She had allowed herself to be influenced by his expectations of her, but that was her fault, not his. Unfortunately for him, her career ambitions were something he hadn't been able to dampen and Cassia also now realised that she had simply suppressed her real self to a degree, rather than burying it completely.

She stole a glance at Rocco across the cabin. Sipping a glass of champagne, his expression was unreadable and she had no idea what he was thinking.

'Hot towel, madam?'

Cassia shook her head. 'No thanks. A cold shower might be a better idea, if I'm honest.'

'We do have a shower area.' The air hostess gestured to an area to the side of the bar.

Cassia laughed. 'I was joking. Maybe later, thanks.' She stared sightlessly at the latest Jennifer Aniston romcom playing on the screen in front of her. She felt consumed with remorse about Finn. She was hurt and angry about the stupid message he'd accidentally left on her phone, about the lack of contact since she'd been in Italy and the way he had allowed Grace to dominate their wedding; nothing would change that. But he didn't deserve this; he didn't deserve to be cheated on and deceived. But she couldn't marry him, she knew that. Every time she thought about it, it was as though someone had dropped an ice cube down her spine. She had known that before anything had happened with Rocco . . . probably even before Rome, if she thought about it honestly. She and Finn were incompatible and they wanted different things out of life, and Gena was absolutely right, a few months apart shouldn't have caused their relationship to disintegrate. Whatever happened with Rocco when they touched down in Sorrento, Cassia knew she couldn't be with Finn.

And what would Rocco do when he was on home turf again? Would he shut down, the way he always did after they had stepped away from his family home and found themselves moving closer to one another? Would he become so engrossed in business once more that he would forget rolling in the sheets with her, forget the things he had murmured in her ear that had made her head reel and her heart swell until it was about to burst?

And what about her own plans? She was due back in England in a few weeks' time, not just for her wedding, but to work at *Scrumptious* magazine. Unable to cope with all the thoughts swirling in her head, she pulled an eye mask on and switched the romcom off. She would deal with everything once she was back in Sorrento.

Rocco wished he knew what was going on inside Cassia's head. Was she paralysed by misgivings and wondering why she had done something so stupid? Or was she, like him, totally blown away by what had happened, reliving every head-spinning moment? Remembering that Finn was staying at the Disanti villa, Rocco downed his champagne. Would Cassia clap eyes on him and instantly realise she had made a terrible mistake in Vegas? Or would seeing her fiancé again prove once and for all that her feelings had changed, that she couldn't possibly go ahead with their wedding?

Rocco felt trepidation wash over him. For him, what had happened in the Bellagio had changed everything. He had never felt this way about any other woman – not any of the women he had dated in the past and most emphatically not about Stefania. But everything felt so uncertain, so fragile.

Staring out of the window, Rocco wished he knew what was going to happen next. But for the next eight hours, there was nothing he could do but be tortured by flashbacks of the night before and pray that it hadn't been the last time he would be that close to Cassia.

'How does it feel?' Aurelia sauntered into Jules's suite, her hands on her hips.

Sitting at her dressing table in a daze after the kiss with Finn, Jules felt her heart sinking. She really couldn't face another confrontation with Aurelia but she knew she didn't have any choice. Aurelia had every right to hate her and to keep demanding apologies about her wedding. Jules just hoped she could muster up the fortitude to pacify Aurelia without Finn at her side. She felt bereft without him, in more ways than one.

'It feels . . . *I* feel terrible,' she said. Wearing a black, halter-neck dress with split sides and with her dark curls in a long plait down her back, Aurelia looked almost severe and her expression was scarily unforgiving. 'My actions were inexcusable. It's your wedding day and I am absolutely horrified that I've messed it all up for you.'

Aurelia stared back at her, sneering slightly. 'I didn't mean about my wedding. I meant about kissing your sister's fiancé.'

Jules turned pale beneath her tan. 'W-what?'

'Oh, don't deny it. I saw you from my window. And to think I was about to come and make amends.' Aurelia threw her a scornful glance. 'But now I realise you don't deserve my compassion. Your own sister, Jules! Doesn't family mean anything to you? I can understand you not feeling any loyalty towards me and my family, but Cassia? How could you?'

Jules sucked her breath in. Kissing Finn had felt so right at the time. But now that Aurelia was spelling it out the way she was, it felt shameful and wrong.

'Please don't,' she said, turning away. 'I can't bear it.'

'*You* can't bear it?' Aurelia couldn't believe her ears. 'What about Cassia? How do you think she will feel when she finds out?'

Jules burst into tears. 'I don't know,' she wailed, knowing she sounded childish. 'I've made such a mess of everything, but I didn't mean for any of this to happen. I didn't mean to fall for Finn, Aurelia. I didn't even think of him that way until a few weeks back. He says he feels the same way, but he's so loyal and proper, he might feel he needs to go ahead with the wedding. But I can't cope with seeing him marry someone else, and certainly not Cassia. I-I think my heart might break.'

Aurelia was dumbfounded. She had expected Jules to be brazen in the face of accusation, not emotional, and she was stunned to learn that Jules had real feelings for Finn.

'Have you come to ask me to leave?' Jules asked suddenly, her face streaked with tears.

'Leave?' Aurelia was puzzled.

'I know you must want me to go home after what happened with your wedding. I don't blame you, obviously. I'd do the same if someone spoilt the most important day of my life.' Blinded by tears, Jules rubbed her face, trying to pull herself together. She hadn't wanted to break down like this in front of Aurelia and she knew she must sound like a fool. Aurelia was hardly her biggest fan and she was probably the last person who wanted to listen to her banging on about how she'd inadvertently fallen head over heels for Finn.

Except Cassia, Jules thought dully. Her sister was going to hate her even more than Aurelia did. She swallowed, squaring her shoulders. As the saying went, she had made her bed.

'I've packed my bags already.' She gestured to a stack of bulging luggage in the corner. 'So I just need to arrange a flight. But as soon as I've done that, I'll be out of your hair. That means I'll be gone,' Jules explained, noticing Aurelia's bemused expression.

'I see.'

Glancing at the stack of luggage thoughtfully, Aurelia sat down next to Jules. She wanted to hate her and for a while she had been ready to tear her apart with her bare hands. But Dino had calmed her down and urged her to give Jules a break because he didn't think she had ruined things maliciously. Aurelia had found it difficult, but once her grandmother had set about organising the wedding reception at the villa, she found herself warming to the idea. It seemed fitting, somehow, to celebrate her nuptials at the family home. And as the idea had grown on her, her antagonistic feelings towards Jules had thawed – until she had witnessed her kissing Finn, that is, and then Aurelia had been out for her blood. But she could see that Jules felt horrendously guilty and unhappy.

'Have you really fallen in love with Finn?'

Jules miserably pleated the sumptuous silk bed sheet with shaking fingers. 'I didn't mean to, I promise. It just . . . happened.'

'If he feels the same way, he shouldn't marry Cassia,' Aurelia pointed out reasonably. 'It's probably going to cause a big drama – is that the right word? Yes, well, it will. But that's how it has to be.'

'Cassia will think I'm such a bitch,' Jules said, knowing her sister had every right.

'Well, that's something you're going to have to deal with. Actually, I think Cassia is so nice, she probably won't think you are a bitch at all.' Aurelia glanced at the pile of luggage in the corner of the room. 'And I don't want you to leave, by the way. I did, but I've calmed down now. Updates have gone out to all the guests to advise them of the change of venue and everything is in hand.' Aurelia got up and headed to the door, then turned back with a frown. 'Rocco and Cassia will be home soon, so I guess this will all have to be sorted out. Just do me one favour?'

'Anything,' Jules assured her, unable to believe she had been forgiven. She felt humbled by Aurelia's compassion and prayed that Cassia could find an ounce of it.

'Get everything dealt with by my wedding please?' Aurelia shrugged expressively. 'Call me selfish, but I'd actually like the day to be about me.'

Rocco was, in fact, already back in his office. Giving him a lingering glance that had been enigmatic to say the least, Cassia had shot off to her bedroom to unpack as soon as they had arrived back at the villa. With his head set to explode with indecision and worry about her feelings for him, Rocco did what he always did and threw himself into work. He knew he and Cassia needed to talk but he sensed that he needed to give her space to get her thoughts together. She needed to speak to Finn, for a start.

Flicking efficiently through his post, Rocco checked the accounts. He had been thinking about the discrepancies while he'd been in Vegas and something had occurred to him. He wasn't sure if he was right, and he really hoped he wasn't, but there was an angle he needed to check out. And if he was right, Rocco was pretty sure it would explain a few other mysteries too.

'You're back.'

Looking up, Rocco found Stefania leaning against the door frame. She looked beautiful; her blond hair was sleek and her make-up flawless. Dressed in a pair of skinny jeans only the truly slender could pull off, heels and a tight white T-shirt, she looked stylish and oddly dangerous.

'Stefania. What are you doing here?'

She strolled into the room, her hands balled into fists. 'I came here a few days ago, to talk. I was sure you were just being silly when you ended our relationship and I hoped you had come to your senses.'

Rocco watched her. He felt slightly alarmed. Stefania wasn't a controlled person by nature. She was more like Aurelia in personality, prone to noisy outbursts and fits of temper. Seeing her prowling around his office like a panther on a leash was making him feel on edge. He had a feeling she was building up to an almighty crescendo and he immediately went on his guard.

He was right to. Stefania felt like a tightly coiled spring; with so much anger and jealousy bubbling inside her, she thought she might spontaneously combust. She didn't take rejection well and she couldn't stand being made a fool of. And Rocco had hit her with both.

'Do you know what I found when I came all the way from Rome to see you? Do you?'

Rocco leant forward on his desk, losing patience slightly. 'That I'd gone to Vegas?'

'Yes, Rocco. That you had gone to Vegas. With her. With Cassia Marini, the woman you claim to feel nothing for.' She spat the words. 'And that was bad enough, but no, I will show you and then you can explain to me what it means.' Tugging his laptop towards her, she went into his email and clicked on the email Bobby's people had sent from Vegas. Opening the link, she stared at Rocco with her arms crossed, her eyes burning into him.

'You went through my email?' Rocco said incredulously. 'Seriously, Stefania, you had no right—'

Stefania exploded. 'No, *you* had no right, Rocco! No right to do *this*!' She stabbed the screen with her finger.

Rocco watched wordlessly as the food demo came on. Watching Bobby in action, he was about to tell Stefania she had gone mental if she thought he needed to justify doing a stupid food demo, but then he saw himself and Cassia on the screen. Holding hands and laughing helplessly, their chemistry was tangible and their attraction to one another obvious.

'Deny it,' Stefania demanded, slamming her hand on the desk. 'Go on, deny that you have feelings for this girl.'

Rocco shook his head. 'I can't, Stefania. Nor do I want to.'

Stefania stopped dead, her mouth falling open. She had been expecting him to be contrite, ashamed even. She had expected denials, remorse and embarrassment. The last thing she could have predicted was his flat admission that what she had witnessed on the video clip was very much on his radar.

'What does that mean?' she asked him, aghast.

Rocco took a deep breath. He wasn't sure what any of it meant. And the last thing he wanted to do was hurt Stefania any more than he already had. But he couldn't lie about his feelings. He couldn't speak for Cassia because he didn't have a clue what was going on in her head, but he knew for certain that he was in love. Passionately, deeply and irrevocably in love.

'You're in love with her,' Stefania whispered, staring at him. He didn't need to confirm it, the truth was written all over his face.

Rocco stood up as she backed out of his office. 'Stefania, let me explain. It was never my intention—'

'Don't bother,' she snarled. 'It's just a year of my life, Rocco. A year and you never once looked like that when you were with me.' Her face contorted. 'Well, if you thought you'd got away with not taking me seriously before, just watch what I'm capable of now.'

As the door swung shut behind her, Rocco let out a shaky breath. Christ, what an almighty mess. He had to speak to Cassia and he had to do it now. He had to know his feelings weren't one-sided.

Diana found Cassia first. Having arrived at the villa ten minutes ago, she had instructed the taxi driver to dump her luggage in the lobby of the restaurant. She knew it couldn't stay there but it was going to have to for now. Asking a few members of staff, Diana was soon directed to the private villa. She gasped as she took in her surroundings but she tried hard not to be distracted by the beauty of the place. Knocking on Cassia's door, Diana found that she was holding her breath. Nerves threatened to overcome her but she stood firm with her chin high.

'Mother!' Cassia was stunned to see her but she fell into her arms. Holding her tightly, she breathed in the familiar scent of high-quality face cream and Elnett hair spray.

'Cassia, what's wrong?' Diana frowned. She knew when something was on her daughter's mind.

'It's just . . .' Cassia stopped talking when she spotted Jules edging into the room.

Jules looked very strange. She was clearly shocked to see Diana, but when she made eye contact with Cassia, she radiated guilt.

Cassia had no idea why Jules was looking at her like that and she couldn't for the life of her work out why her mother had suddenly appeared from nowhere. With everything that had happened in Vegas, Cassia wasn't sure she could take any more drama right now.

'I . . . I have something to talk to both of you about,' Diana said, wiping her sweaty palms on her dress. 'It's important but it's private. Can we talk, please? All three of us?'

Feeling deeply apprehensive, Cassia wondered if Jules knew what was going on. She took a seat on the bed and Jules perched on the other side of it. Diana sat down at Cassia's dressing table, clasping and unclasping her hands. Swallowing it down hard because she knew that Jules, for one, would scorn her if she fell apart, Diana prepared herself.

'I need to be honest about something,' she started. 'It's something that Jules knows about in part, but Cassia, this will all be new to you. And I apologise in advance for shocking you.'

Cassia felt her stomach shift. She had never seen her mother this serious in her life before.

Feeling desperate, Jules shook her head. 'No, Mother. I asked you never to speak of this, not in front of Cassia.' She couldn't take rehashing the details from the past, not now, not after everything that had gone on with Finn. 'Why can't you just respect that?'

'I have, Jules,' Diana told her shortly. 'I haven't told Cassia anything, at your request. I'm not sure I ever agreed with that, but I felt I owed you something after you found out what happened. Part of what happened,' she corrected herself.

'Why are you saying that? I know everything there is to know about your sordid behaviour.'

497

'I'm afraid not,' Diana said apologetically. Her cheeks flushed with shame. 'And if you think badly of me now, Jules, I have no doubt you will have nothing but contempt for me in a few minutes' time.'

Jules stared at her.

Cassia looked impatient. 'God, this is killing me. What the hell is going on here?' She glanced from Jules to her mother. 'Will someone kindly fill me in?'

Diana exhaled. Horrible images leapt up like flames in her mind but she pushed them down. It wouldn't do to get too emotional; she just needed to state the facts and tell the truth. 'Cassia, when Jules was sixteen, she found out that Marco wasn't her father.'

Cassia blinked. 'What? That can't be true.'

'Oh, it is,' Jules snapped, forgetting that she shouldn't be picking on Cassia. 'There was hardly a family resemblance, was there?'

'You look like Mum. So what?' Cassia was reeling. 'That doesn't mean my father wasn't your father—'

'I'm afraid it does, in this instance,' Diana cut in. 'Jules needed something for school and she found this old birth certificate that Marco hadn't signed.' She rubbed her eyes tiredly.

'So . . . Dad knew about it, even when Jules was born,' Cassia realised slowly. 'That was why . . .'

'Go on, say it,' Jules cried. 'That's why he was always so bloody horrible to me. It's true, isn't it, Mother? He could barely look at me because of what I represented – your little bastard.' She almost spat the words out before bursting into hysterical tears. Telling Finn about it had been once thing, but hearing her mother talking about it so baldly was making her feel sick.

Cassia couldn't even speak. It all made sense. Suddenly, everything she remembered from her youth slotted together like a jigsaw. It was the reason Jules had changed from being a loving, carefree child into a truculent, aggressive teenager. It explained her resentment; she was Marco's real daughter and Jules was not. The fact that Jules had been fathered by another man was the reason Marco had been unable to connect with her; he had, as Jules put it, not been able to deal with a daily reminder of his wife's adultery.

Cassia got up and stood by the window. They had all agreed to keep this terrible secret from her. Her father, her mother and her sister had colluded to prevent her from finding out the truth, but in doing so she had felt rejected and sidelined. Glancing at Jules, Cassia realised she had no right to feel sorry for herself. Jules was the one who had been rejected, not her. She had borne the brunt of their father's disgust for her very existence and Cassia felt a wave of guilt that she had enjoyed such a connection with her father whilst Jules had not.

'Jules, I'm so sorry,' she began, moving towards her. She wanted to gather Jules up in her arms and hold her. She no longer cared about the way Jules had treated her in the past; she just knew her sister was hurting and she could empathise completely.

Jules leapt up as if she'd been burnt. 'Don't you feel sorry for me!' she choked, stumbling backwards. 'Don't you dare! That's why I didn't want you to know, because I didn't want your pity.' Tears streamed down her face.

Cassia nodded, biting her lip. 'I can understand that. It was easier for you to just cut me off, to treat me like the enemy for not living through the same complications.'

Jules stared at her. Whatever she had expected as a reaction, that wasn't it. God, Cassia was nice. How could she be so nice? Thinking about Finn, Jules felt even more crucified.

Diana cleared her throat. 'I'm so sorry, but that's not everything.'

Cassia and Jules turned to her. Neither of them were sure they could handle anything else right now, but Diana was not going to stop now.

'There was something I didn't tell you or your father about what happened,' Diana confessed, the enormity of her secret weighing down heavily on her. She rushed to get the words out. 'You see, Marco thought I'd had an affair and so did you, Jules. I didn't want to own up to how stupid I'd been and I didn't want what had happened to become public knowledge.' She stood up and began to pace the room. It felt as though she was playing a part, as if she was watching someone else act this out, but she wasn't; it was real. 'Your father was an actor called Joseph Danes,' she said to Jules, who winced at the shock of hearing her actual father's name. 'He was charming and handsome and he played Benedick to my Beatrice in the film we made, *Much Ado About Nothing*. We flirted during the film and everyone assumed that we were lovers. But we weren't. In fact, nothing happened until after the wrap party.'

Jules looked as if she might throw up on the spot. 'So what? Do we really have to hear a blow-by-blow account of your little tryst?'

Diana nodded. 'I think you do,' she said gravely. 'Because it wasn't a tryst. It was simply a situation that got out of hand.' She took a deep breath. 'I didn't cheat on Marco. Not the way you think I did. I went to Joseph's apartment for a drink after the wrap party. I admit that I was flattered by his attention because he was a good-looking man and I was totally absorbed in the character of Beatrice, giddily carried away by our chemistry.'

'That's no excuse, Mother,' Jules interjected sharply.

'Of course it's not,' Diana agreed, her expression sombre. 'And believe me, Jules, it was that way of thinking that got me into trouble. I didn't intend anything to happen, I can assure you. For me, it was just the end of the film and up until that point, Joseph had been a great friend. I didn't go to his apartment for sex.' She drifted away from them towards the window, staring out sightlessly at the view. 'We had a drink,

500

more than one – several, in fact, and the mood was upbeat between us. Then he made a move on me and I said no. He . . . he didn't listen.' Diana's voice was flat.

Cassia was dazed. 'Are you saying . . . you're not saying he —'

Diana spun round. 'Don't say the word, Cass, I can't bear it! Never say that word.' She turned to Jules who was shaking as though she was suffering from convulsions. Diana's heart contracted at the sight of her child in so much pain. She dashed to her side.

'I am so, so sorry, my darling. I was stupid and naïve and I only have myself to blame.' Tears rolled down her face. 'I was so ashamed. I couldn't believe what had happened to me, couldn't believe that Joseph had . . . done what he did. A few weeks later, I found out I was pregnant.' She sat next to Jules and gingerly touched her hand, fearing rejection.

'But I wanted you so much, darling. After Cassia, we had tried so hard to conceive but nothing had happened. You were very much wanted and for all I knew you were Marco's. Then I remembered that Marco had been away and the dates simply didn't add up.' Diana swallowed. 'I had to tell him . . . I didn't want him to work it out later on. I told Marco that I'd been unfaithful, and he couldn't forgive me. That was when he rejected you.'

Cassia blinked away her own tears, realising that was what her father had been talking about when he told her all those years ago that confessions cleared the guilty and weighed down the innocent. 'But why didn't you tell him what this Joseph had done to you? He would have understood . . . he would have forgiven you. Instead, you let him think you'd cheated on him. You . . . you broke his heart.'

Diana collapsed, overcome. 'I know, I know. But Cassia, you have to understand. It would have hurt your father more if he knew the truth. He loved me so much he wouldn't have been able to handle what had happened. I . . . I thought he might even kill Joseph or something. And I didn't want anyone to know.'

Jules managed to speak finally. 'But . . . he might have loved me more,' she said in a small voice. 'Marco, he might have been able to forgive me.'

Diana hugged her tightly. 'He did love you, darling. He just couldn't bear the thought of me being with someone else.' She pulled away and tenderly wiped the tears from Jules's cheeks. 'But trust me, if he'd known what Joseph had done, he would have found your presence just as difficult.' Diana sighed. 'Because your father – and that's what he was, Jules, whatever it says on your birth certificate – he was a flawed man in some ways. He was wonderful and clever and handsome and kind. But forgiving he was not. He couldn't help it; it was who he was and I'm sorry you had to bear the brunt of it.'

Jules wasn't sure she could accept that. She understood what her mother meant, but it didn't mean it was all right for her father to treat her the way he had. He had taken his pain out on her and, worst of all, he had lavished all the love and attention she should have had on Cassia.

Jules lifted red eyes to Cassia. 'Cass, I'm sorry. I was so jealous of the way Dad favoured you. But it wasn't your fault, I know that.' She stood up and put her arms round Cassia.

Cassia hugged her, feeling tears streaming down her cheeks. 'It doesn't matter, Jules. I just wish none of this had happened. Mother, you've been so brave. I can't believe you've held that inside for all this time.' She squeezed her hand.

Diana let out a shuddering breath. 'It was my own stupid fault. All that matters now is that we all know the truth. Joseph is dead . . . I only found out the other day. Are you . . . are you all right about that, Jules?'

Jules thought about it, but she knew she felt nothing. 'Definitely. I'm glad. It's not like I'd want some emotional father-daughter reunion, is it?'

Diana cringed at the thought. 'He never knew about you, darling, and that was the way I wanted it to stay. Listen, let's move forward, together . . . all of us.'

Jules nodded. Remembering what had happened with Finn suddenly, she gulped. How could she have done that to Cassia? Now that they had reconciled their differences, Jules felt even more of a bitch.

Shell-shocked, Cassia thought about Rocco. And about Finn. Hearing her mother's confession made her realise how important it was to be truthful and how critical it was to do the right thing.

'I have something I need to do,' she told Jules and her mother, heading for the door. 'You two should talk without me here, anyway.'

With that, Cassia left them to it and went in search of Finn. She needed a stiff drink first, or maybe a coffee, but she knew it was imperative that she spoke to Finn and told him that the wedding was well and truly off.

Chapter Twenty-Three

Feeling more nervous than he had ever felt in his life, Finn was about to knock at Cassia's door. He knew she was back from Vegas and he had waited for a while to let her unpack and settle into the villa again. But pacing across his room wasn't doing him any good, so he had given up waiting and had gone in search of her.

'Er, *scusi* . . . are you looking for Miss Marini?'

Finn turned to find one of the cleaning staff behind him. 'Yes. Cassia, not Jules, though.' He blushed slightly. 'Do you know where she is?'

The girl clutched a batch of sheets, not sure if she should say anything. All the staff were talking about Jules kissing Cassia's fiancé; they had been witnessed by around ten staff who had been smoking near the olive groves, none of whom were known for their discretion. There were also unfounded rumours that Cassia and Rocco were more than friends and the team of staff were agog with all the gossip.

Taking pity on Finn who looked utterly distraught, the maid reached a decision. 'Cassia was in her room but she said something about getting an espresso.'

'Thank you.' Gratefully, Finn gave her a brief smile, before dashing down the stairs again. Whatever happened, he had to speak to Cassia before someone else did. Finn was terrified one of the staff would let something slip in front of her, because he knew they'd been seen.

He strode through the empty restaurant, wondering why it was closed. Remembering that Rocco had shut it to prepare for Aurelia's wedding in two days' time, he headed into the kitchen, looking around for Cassia. She was nowhere to be seen. Only Rocco's head chef, Antonio, was in evidence, frantically ticking off stock against his list of requirements for the wedding, whilst keeping an eye on an appetising seafood stock he'd been nurturing for the past two days. Counting cling-filmed stacks of meat and fish, he didn't even notice Finn at first.

Finn glanced at a nearby coffee machine. It was open and there was an empty packet next to it. Guessing Cassia had gone in search of more, Finn wondered where the supplies might be.

'Who are you looking for?' Antonio asked, finally noticing Finn. Turning off his stock and giving it one last stir, he threw Finn a sideways glance. 'Cassia . . . or Jules?' His face was impassive, but it was clear he was making a jibe.

Finn guessed he deserved Antonio's mocking tone. He was out of order, whatever way he looked at it, but he was embarrassed that his recent fall from grace seemed to be common knowledge in the Disanti household. Having spent his entire life being considerate of others and upholding an unblemished image of the perfect, moral gentleman, it pained him that he had committed a relationship sin by falling for his fiancée's sister. That so many people knew about it simply added to his mortification.

Removing his chef's jacket, Antonio jerked his head in the direction of the storeroom at the back of the kitchen and smiled. 'Cassia's in there. Good luck,' he added as he left Finn to it.

Taking a deep breath, Finn headed into the storeroom. The door closed behind him and he frowned, hoping it wasn't the self-locking kind.

'It's all right, I've found it, Antonio.' Cassia emerged from behind a shelf unit, brandishing a fresh bag of coffee. 'Oh, Finn.' She looked startled. 'I was coming to find you. After this coffee, I mean.'

'Cassia.' Finn stared at her. He hadn't seen her for such a long time he had almost forgotten what she looked like, amazingly enough. And she looked different, somehow. Relaxed, beautiful, sexy. She had changed, blossomed, if that was the right word. Cassia seemed at home in this environment and she looked as if she had been here all her life.

Finn gulped. He had wondered how he would feel when he saw Cassia again after all these weeks and after what had happened with Jules. He had tormented himself that he had thrown everything away on the strength of a single kiss and that when he saw Cassia again, he might realise he was just as in love with her as he had been when he proposed back in April. But he didn't. He felt pleased to see Cassia again, but the way he might if he saw an old friend.

'I-I didn't even know you were coming,' Cassia said, wondering why Finn looked so strange. Had he heard something about her and Rocco? She bit her lip. She hoped not. That was something she should tell him face to face, not something he should hear from a third party.

She put the coffee down on a shelf, her fingers clumsy. It was all such a mess. Rocco had retreated as soon as they had returned to Sorrento, shutting himself away in his office and avoiding her like the plague. Just as she had feared he would. She had no idea where that left her and her heart ached at the thought of the incredible night in Vegas being her final, lasting memory of Rocco. And as for the bombshell her mother had just dropped, she had barely got her head round it all. The one thing she was clear about, strangely, was that she and Finn were over. She felt a stab of anguish as she scrutinised Finn properly, her eyes wandering over his features nostalgically. His dear, red-gold hair that never really lay flat, his lovely, trusting blue eyes and the wide shoulders that had always made her feel so safe. It hit Cassia that Finn had never really set her feelings alight the way Rocco did, but in spite of that, he was her oldest and most dear friend. Finn had been loyal and sweet and caring and she would always be grateful to him for that, however much they had gone off target with their relationship.

Cassia forced the tears down, feeling unexpectedly emotional. They had been through so much together and he had always been her rock. Cassia knew it was the right decision for them not to go ahead with the wedding, but it didn't mean she wasn't going to miss him terribly. She just hoped he didn't hate her for what she had done.

'My visit was meant to be a surprise.' Finn smiled, his face tinged with sadness. 'Which backfired somewhat.'

Cassia nodded. 'Finn, we have to talk.' She didn't want to waste any more time. She gulped, remembering that Grace and Henry were due in Sorrento any time.

'I know.' Finn didn't have a clue why Cassia was looking so anxious. She looked almost . . . guilty. He had never seen such an expression on her face before.

'We can't get married,' Cassia blurted out. Poor Finn looked as though he was about to keel over. 'Sorry, I really didn't mean to come out with it like that. But . . . it's . . . we really can't . . .'

Finn rubbed his chin which was uncharacteristically stubbly. 'No, no, you're absolutely right.'

'I'm . . . I'm right?'

'You are.' Finn moved closer, leaning on a shelf stacked high with cured meats. 'I was just coming to say the same thing to you.' He looked crushed. 'I can't believe I'm even saying it out loud, but we have to cancel the wedding. Don't worry, I'll speak to my mother when she gets here.'

Cassia let out a shuddering sigh. She was relieved at his reaction, but at the same time utterly bewildered. It was the last thing she'd been expecting him to say. She was about to remark that she thought Grace would be over the moon at their joint decision to abandon the wedding, in spite of all the arrangements, but she stopped herself. It was pointless bitching about Grace now.

'Look . . . has something happened, Finn? I mean, I really thought you were going to go crazy when I said we shouldn't get married.'

Finn clutched his hair with some agitation. 'Erm . . . no, yes. Yes, I suppose something has happened. Rather unexpected and totally unplanned, I can assure you.'

Cassia was stunned. She checked her heart to gauge her feelings – no, she was fine. A minor jolt, nothing more, and that was to be expected after eight years together, surely?

'I-I haven't crossed any lines,' Finn rushed on, keen to get things off his chest. 'Well . . .'

'But I have.' Cassia made the confession quietly, but she looked him in the eye. He deserved that, at least. 'I have well and truly stepped over the line, Finn. I'm . . . it's . . . unforgivable and I am so, so sorry.'

Finn looked momentarily aghast but he recovered quickly. 'Rocco?' he guessed. He had known all along that there had been an attraction there; he had seen it at the engagement party. He felt a pang; the thought of Cassia with someone else felt strange after all this time, but deep down, Finn knew it was how it should be. He and Cassia were great friends and they had been more than that for a long time, but ultimately, they were poles apart. It had taken the trip to Sorrento to fully hammer that point home for Finn and it had obviously been the same for Cassia.

'You and Rocco make a great couple,' he said, his voice cracking slightly.

'Don't,' Cassia choked. 'I don't even know if we are a couple. Which makes it even worse, I know.' She felt tears trickling down her cheeks. God, but she had cried a lot in the past twenty-four hours. 'But regardless of Rocco, I hate to hurt you like this.'

Finn shook his head. 'You haven't. I mean, I'm upset, it's weird to think of you with someone else. But you mustn't feel sorry for me, really.' If only she knew, he thought, trying to summon up the courage to own up about Jules.

Cassia's confession had shocked him but, on reflection, it wasn't entirely startling. The more Finn thought about it, the more sense it made. Cassia was passionate about Italy, she always had been, because of her father. And she was just as obsessed with food – eating it, seeing it made, writing about it. Rocco was a chef and he couldn't be any more Italian so he was pretty much the perfect man for her. And the fact that he looked like an Armani model was just one of those aggravating facts of life, Finn thought ruefully.

'I feel awful,' Cassia said, rubbing her tears away. 'You have to know that I've never done anything like this before, Finn. Not since we've been together.'

Finn reached out and grabbed her hand. 'I know. I've always trusted you, Cass. I know you would only do something like this with someone who meant something to you.'

She nodded and squeezed his hand. 'I've changed since I've been here. I'm not quite that wild girl you met all those years ago at uni, but I have sort of . . . found myself a bit since I've been in Sorrento.'

Finn pulled her into a hug. 'I made you more conservative, I know that now. I guess I need a housewife, someone to look after. And that's not you. I wanted it to be, but deep down I think I knew we weren't quite in sync. Recently, anyhow.'

Cassia put her head on his shoulder, breathing in his familiar scent. 'I think I'm just tired of trying to be something I'm not, Finn. And I'm sorry that I'm not that girl, but I really can't pretend any longer.' She felt so emotional letting him go. 'Oh, good God, Finn. I put a deposit down on a wedding dress in Sorrento. A really, really expensive one.'

In spite of himself, Finn let out a laugh.

Cassia blinked at him, failing to see the joke. 'It's not funny, Finn. It's probably three months' salary . . .'

Peering through the window in the doorway at that moment, Rocco froze. Having bumped into Antonio whilst searching for Cassia, he had known that she and Finn were having a heart-to-heart. Rocco hadn't, however, expected them to be hugging so intimately or for Cassia to look so utterly destroyed. Heavy-hearted and about to leave them to it, Rocco heard an odd, clanking sound. He frowned, wondering where it was coming from.

In the storeroom, Cassia pulled away from Finn. Something had just occurred to her. Who had Finn met? There were only a few women working at his law firm, most of who were more married to their jobs than their actual husbands, so it was unlikely to be any of those. He barely had time for hobbies with his work schedule, so it didn't seem to make sense that he would have met someone new that way, and most of the other women he knew were mutual friends. A germ of an idea took hold in Cassia's mind, but it was so out there, she couldn't quite assemble all the components together in the right order.

Fearful that she had guessed what he was about to unburden himself with, Finn rushed to get the words out.

'I said there was someone else and I really have to explain. You're not going to like it, but I'm afraid it's . . .'

A deafening crash halted Finn's words.

'What the hell was that?' Cassia cried, almost jumping out of her skin. Suddenly catching sight of Rocco on the other side of the door, her eyes widened. He was feverishly gesturing to the door and when she glanced at it, she could see the handle rattling like mad.

'Finn . . . Finn, I think we have to get out of here.'

Cassia dashed to the door and tried to open it. It was locked. Turning round, she noticed water gushing through a small vent in the top corner of the storeroom.

'Shit, Finn. Look.'

Seeing the gush of water, Finn was galvanised into action. He grabbed a nearby knife and tried ramming it down the side of the door, doing his best to wedge it open.

'There's a window up there. We need to climb on to these counters . . .' Dragging one next to the wall, Cassia started to panic. The water was coming in fast and it was swirling around their feet already. About to tell Finn they needed to hurry, the words were snatched from her mouth as, without warning, the vent widened. Within seconds, Finn and Cassia were swept off their feet, their cries lost in the deafening sound of ten tonnes of water crashing into the storeroom.

Having seen the vent burst open, Rocco tried to open the door again. It was no good; it was locked tight.

Turning, he caught a glimpse of blond hair flying out of the restaurant.

'Stefania!' he roared. Grabbing some keys, he tore after her. He caught her arm and spun her round. 'What have you done? Seriously, Stefania, this could have tragic consequences.'

She was gibbering with fear. 'I didn't know anyone was in there, I swear. I just wanted to spoil things for you . . . to ruin the restaurant.' Stefania started to shake. 'I wanted to take away the thing that you loved, Rocco . . .'

Rocco didn't know what to say. 'Get out of here,' he told her curtly. 'Seriously, get out of here. Don't let the police catch you.'

Scared stiff, Stefania did as she was told, shooting off towards her car. Rocco didn't waste any time. He dashed round to the side of the storeroom, yelling to his grandmother who was dealing with a flower delivery on the driveway. 'Get over here!'

Sofia frowned but she gestured for the flower man to take the flowers inside the villa before making her way to Rocco's side. Aurelia joined her.

'What's happening?'

'There's water in the storeroom, several tonnes of it,' he managed, leaning over to catch his breath. He pointed. 'St— the generator broke, I think. But the door is locked, I can't get in. Cassia's in there, and Finn too.'

Aurelia gasped, putting a hand to her mouth. 'But . . . but Rocco, they could drown in there.'

'I know that!' Rocco snapped, throwing her a scowl. 'That's why I'm trying to think what to do. Where's Dino?'

'He's on a modelling job in Florence . . . I can call him . . .' Aurelia started to dial.

'There's no time.' Rocco dropped to his knees to get a better look. The window at the top of the storeroom was at ground level as the room was almost a cellar. Water was swirling and it was still gushing in fast, but it hadn't reached the window yet. Rocco tried to spot Cassia and Finn, but he couldn't make them out. His stomach lurched. He refused to think they were going to die in there . . . they couldn't. Rocco thought quickly. He was running out of time and there were only a few options open to him. He was also fairly sure he knew what he was going to have to do, but he was momentarily gripped by fear.

Clutching his arm, Sofia was clearly terrified. 'It's the curse, isn't it? See, I told you, Rocco, you said I was being silly, but what are the odds of something like this happening?' Her rosy cheeks were pale.

Rocco shook his head. 'It's not the curse, Grandmother, don't be silly. It's . . . it's Stefania.'

'Stefania?' Aurelia looked shocked. 'You're not serious? Why on earth would she do this?'

Rocco started to unbutton his shirt. 'She found out about me and Cassia and she went crazy. I'm pretty certain she was behind some of the other stuff going wrong as well. Some weird attempt to make me fall out of love with Sorrento, I think.'

Sofia sucked her breath in. 'How terrible! Was she . . . was she behind my accident too?'

Rocco shook his head, catching her eye for a second. 'No. We should talk about that another time.'

'You and Cassia?' Forgetting about the storeroom for a minute, Aurelia beamed as she realised what Rocco had just said. 'Rocco, that's fantastic, you're so well-suited. Oh, what lovely news . . .'

'It won't be if I can't get them out of there,' Rocco interrupted, tearing off his loafers and socks.

'Rocco, what are you doing?' Sofia looked quite faint. 'You can't be thinking of going in there. It's too dangerous.'

'And you can't swim,' Aurelia said. 'Let me do it. I can swim, at least.'

'No way. I have to do this. Antonio has gone home, none of the staff are here and Dino's flashing his boxer shorts somewhere. I don't have any choice. Where's Raff?' Stripping off his trousers so he was standing in just a pair of white boxer shorts, he pulled the keys he'd taken from the kitchen out of one of the pockets.

Sofia shook her head. 'I have no idea. Off on one of his mysterious trips again.'

Rocco's mouth tightened grimly. 'Right. So it's down to me. Aurelia, call for an ambulance. And maybe a fire engine, just in case.' He took a few breaths, wondering if he could overcome his nerves. Water had always filled him with fear; even though the near-drowning incident had happened when he was around six or seven years old, Rocco could recall every heart-stopping second of being under the water, clawing pointlessly as it streamed into his mouth and sent him spinning to the bottom of the pool.

'Rocco.' Sofia grabbed his arm. 'Can you do this?'

'I have to.' He met her eyes. 'It's Cassia . . . she can't die, do you understand? And before you say anything, I couldn't care less if she's from that rival family, all right?'

Not daring to say a word, Sofia nodded.

Rocco crouched by the window and fiddled with the keys. He almost dropped them but finding the one he needed, he slotted it into the lock and yanked the window open. Water wasn't quite at window level yet but it wouldn't long. Sticking his head inside, all he could see was floating food and bottles.

Cassia's head burst abruptly out of the water. 'Rocco!' she yelled, catching sight of him. 'Finn's under here, he's caught on something. I've been down twice, but I can't get him free.'

Rocco stuck his legs through the window and sat on the ledge.

Cassia spat some water out and coughed. 'Rocco, don't. You can't swim!'

'Well, I'll just have to improvise.' Before he could think any more about it, Rocco hurled himself into the water. It wasn't the most stylish entrance and he wouldn't score highly for technical merit, but he was in. Swimming clumsily over to Cassia, he grabbed her hand.

She met his eyes, wishing she had time to tell him how she felt. 'You don't need to do this . . . I'll go down again . . .'

'No. I'll get him. I'm doing it for you.'

'Not for me,' she spluttered, wondering what on earth he was talking about.

Taking a huge breath, Rocco ducked underneath the water. He could see Finn's arm wildly tearing at the water and it terrified the hell out of him. The memories rushed past him but Rocco knew he didn't have time to be self-indulgent. Cleaving through the water, he quickly reached Finn. Rocco's lungs were already screaming but he wasn't giving up now.

Blue in the face, Finn pointed to his foot. His shoe was caught on the jagged edge of a shelf unit and he couldn't free himself. Rocco grabbed the unit and pushed himself downwards. He tried to yank Finn's shoe off, to no avail, so he pulled at the unit instead, rocking it hard. Nothing happened then suddenly, Finn's shoe pinged free. Shooting to the surface, he disappeared from sight.

Feeling as though his lungs were about to explode in his chest, Rocco flapped around haplessly for a few seconds. He was disorientated and his vision was blurred. He could feel himself falling, falling into the depths of the water . . .

Just as suddenly, he felt someone tugging him to the surface. Rocco's head shot out and he gulped down mouthfuls of air. As his vision cleared, Cassia's head came into view.

'Oh no you don't,' she wheezed, tears streaming down her face. She swam on her side, pulling him after her. It was difficult, but somehow she managed to climb out of the window and as the water levels rose alarmingly, she half-pulled, half-shuffled Rocco out of the window after her. There were sirens shrieking and lights flashing as ambulances and fire engines pulled up alongside them.

Checking that Finn was all right and that Sofia and two members of the ambulance crew were looking after him under a nearby tree, Cassia flopped on to the grass, panting. 'You really shouldn't try and rescue people when you can't swim,' she spluttered. 'You great, big brave idiot.'

'Thanks for saving me. I thought I wasn't going to make it for . . . for a minute.' Rocco joined her on the grass, catching his breath and shaking his ears free of water. Aurelia was running around like a headless chicken talking to the firemen who were milling around a fire engine on the edge of the grounds.

'Oh God, I thought you were all dead . . . I couldn't see you . . . it was awful . . .'

'Calm down, Aurelia.' Rocco coughed. He was beginning to feel a bit out of place in just his boxer shorts. 'No one's dead, we're all alive. And I really need to learn to swim.'

He watched Allesandro dash past towards his grandmother and when he reached her, he pulled her into a hug. Rocco felt a stab in his heart. He knew his grandmother had to move on and he wanted her to be happy, but he wasn't sure he liked seeing her with someone other than his grandfather. Not just yet, anyway.

Cassia sat up, hugging her knees. 'That was the scariest thing that ever happened to me.' She turned to Rocco. 'I can't believe you threw yourself into the water like that. I know how hard that must have been for you. Thank you . . . thank you for risking your life like that.'

Rocco sat up next to her. 'It's my fault,' he admitted, shame-faced. 'Stefania was behind it. She found out . . . about us,' he added, watching her face.

Cassia was horrified. Before she had a chance to say anything, Jules arrived.

'I just heard what happened!' She rushed up to Cassia and pulled her into a hug. 'Are you all right? Did you nearly drown?'

'I'm fine,' Cassia assured her. 'Finn got the worst of it. Rocco saved him.'

Rocco met her eyes wryly. 'And Cassia saved me.'

Jules wasn't listening. 'Finn?' she shrieked. 'Finn was in there too?' She burst into hysterical tears. 'Where is he? Why isn't anyone telling me what's happened to him?'

Cassia stood up, the thought that had occurred to her a while ago rushing to the fore again. 'He's over there with Sofia.' She took Jules's chin in her hands and made her look at her. 'Everything is all right, Jules. Pull yourself together and go to him.'

Jules's eyelashes fluttered in confusion. 'Do you . . . did he . . .'

'I worked it out.' Cassia nodded. 'Go. We'll talk later.'

Gratefully, Jules ran to Finn. Throwing herself at him, she clung to his broad shoulders, sobbing.

Rocco got to his feet. 'What the hell's that all about?'

Cassia watched them kiss before turning away. 'My sister is in love with my fiancé. And as you can see, it's mutual.'

Examining her face, Rocco couldn't tell if Cassia was devastated or not. Her dark eyes looked sad and she seemed regretful but she didn't look quite as destroyed as he might have expected, given the circumstances. Rocco's heart leapt a fraction. Was there still a chance she had feelings for him?

Cassia suddenly felt knocked for six with everything that had happened that day. Her mother's big revelation, the stress of confessing to Finn, almost drowning. And come to think of it, did Rocco's braveness prove anything? He had risked everything by hurling himself into the water like that when he couldn't swim. But was it mere obligation, rather than anything more meaningful? She couldn't tell. Feeling faint, Cassia tried to focus her eyes on the grass.

Raffaelo ran up to them, his arms outstretched. 'I just heard what happened. Are you all right?'

'We're fine, Raff,' Rocco said tightly. He wished everyone could go away so that he and Cassia could talk about everything. 'But you and me, we need to talk soon, Raff. Do you understand?'

Raffaelo jerked his head. Meeting Rocco's eyes, he realised his brother knew everything. 'Yes. Yes, I understand.'

Sofia came bustling up. 'The police are on their way. Everyone needs to make statements and we need to see what the damage is in the restaurant.' She looked frail, but she was going into organisational mode to cope. 'Rocco, I need you to come and check that it's safe to go inside.'

Throwing Cassia a lingering glance, Rocco bit his lip. 'We need to talk as well,' he said to Cassia urgently. She nodded and started to shiver. Rocco grabbed his shirt from the ground and threw it round her shoulders, leaving his arm there. 'Breathe,' he told her worriedly. 'I think you're about to faint.'

517

'I'm all right. I just felt light-headed for a second.' Cassia was about to lean into his embrace when she caught sight of two people walking towards them. There was something very familiar about the rounded head of blond hair and the rolling gait of the other person.

'Oh dear God,' Cassia murmured.

'What's wrong?' Rocco asked her urgently.

Cassia shook her head. 'Just my potential in-laws arriving.' She wondered what she had done to deserve a day like this. She watched as Grace and Henry traipsed up the grass towards them, no doubt aghast at the fire engines and sirens.

Grace took in the scene in front of her. There was Cassia, dripping wet and huddled in a man's shirt, looking wide-eyed and dazed. Rocco, standing next to her, his eyes fixed fiercely on Cassia. And he was only wearing his underpants. Which the water, wherever that had come from, had turned see-through.

Grace averted her eyes. Behind Cassia and Rocco stood a shaken-looking Finn who was being comforted by Jules. Jules, one of the only people in the vicinity who wasn't sopping wet, was nonetheless crying as if the world was about to end.

'What on earth is going on?' Grace asked disapprovingly. She was sure that whatever drama had occurred, it wasn't altogether necessary to have the police, two ambulances and a fire engine all out at the same time.

Henry, wilting in the heat, had no idea what was happening as far as the water and the emergency services were concerned. He could, however, see at a glance that there was trouble ahead. Finn and Jules didn't exactly look as if they were just friends and Cassia and Rocco could practically light a fire between them.

'Say something, Henry!' Grace squawked, giving him a nudge with her bony elbow.

Henry obliged. 'Any chance of a cup of tea?'

The following morning, having checked out the restaurant which, amazingly, was undamaged, Rocco made sure the area was made safe and that it had been cordoned off. The experts who had drained the water from the storeroom said that apart from all the food being unusable, the storeroom itself would probably just need replastering. They were now in the process of drying everything out, using industrial-sized heaters on the walls and the floor to blast hot air into every nook and cranny. The water system that Stefania had vented her fury on was being noisily replaced and, thankfully, there was a back-up system so everyone still had hot water.

Calling Antonio and his staff in, Rocco was hell-bent on getting Aurelia's wedding back on track, knowing it would be nigh on impossible to reschedule it after the late venue change. Most of the guests were already arriving, moving into rooms at the far end of the villa and into the barn that had been converted. Rocco wasn't altogether sure they had enough room for everyone, but until the barns were bursting at the seams, they were ushering guests in regardless of the cramped space. Rocco had instructed Sofia to start calling on hotels in Sorrento if need be, as well as checking with friends if they could use rooms in their houses.

The police had interviewed everyone but Rocco had made sure the event was kept as low-key as possible. He didn't let on that Stefania was behind the accident because he didn't want her charged. He wanted to brush the whole thing under the carpet, not because of the bad publicity it would undoubtedly cause – although he could do without that particular headache – but out of concern for Stefania. He didn't condone what she had done and if the outcome had been different, he wouldn't have hesitated to take things further. But he knew she would have instantly regretted her actions, especially if she'd known how close it had come to someone ending up dead. She was impetuous and what she had done had been an act of vengeance, but Rocco didn't entirely blame her. She had lashed out because she was hurt.

Strolling through the empty restaurant, Rocco was pleased when he bumped into Luca. Wearing a panama with a bright yellow shirt and beige trousers, he looked as dapper as ever, but his expression was serious.

'I wasn't expecting you until tomorrow. How are you?'

Luca shook his hand solemnly. 'I've been trying to reach you for days now. Where have you been?'

Rocco slapped his head. 'God, yes, you left messages. I was in Vegas with Cassia. Is everything all right?'

'Yes, but there is something you need to know. It's about that rival family Sofia is always going on about.'

Rocco frowned. 'Cassia's father?'

Luca thrust his hands into his pockets. 'Let's talk somewhere private.'

Rocco showed Luca into his office and shut the door. Seconds later, his mouth was hanging open in shock.

Chapter Twenty-Four

Finn prepared to knock on the door of the bedroom his parents were staying in, with Jules trembling by his side.

'Do we really have to do this?' she asked him for the tenth time.

'Yes, we do,' he told her firmly. 'My mother has spent a fortune on my wedding and she's going to have to be told that it's not taking place now.' He bent down and kissed Jules, nuzzling her nose. 'Besides, we want to get off on the right footing, don't we? I want her to love you as much as I do.'

'You do what?' she said, smiling up at him.

'Stop it,' he said, nudging her. 'I've told you enough times.'

Jules grabbed his hand as he went to knock on the door again. 'Do you really think Cassia is all right? About us, I mean?'

'I do. Obviously it helps that she and Rocco had a fling in Vegas, but yes, I think she had come to the same conclusion as me, that we're just friends, not lovers, and that we definitely shouldn't get married.'

'Is it just a fling?' Jules shook her head. 'Cassia isn't like that, Finn. You know her as well as I do, she's not the sort of person to have a casual thing with someone. Sorry if it sounds bad, but I wish Cassia and Rocco were properly getting together. They seem so right for one another.'

After feeling so antagonistic towards Cassia for so many years, Jules was unused to caring about her. But she did and not just because she was with Finn now. Unburdening herself to Finn about her father had enabled her to let go somehow; she didn't feel the resentment she had done before, not towards Cassia. And after her mother had confessed everything about the past, Jules knew she had no right to blame Cassia for anything.

Finn rubbed his chin, feeling exhausted by everything that had happened since he'd arrived in Sorrento. 'I was just about to tell Cassia about us and she had this look on her face as if she knew. I told her we hadn't crossed, you know, that line yet – and then the water came crashing in.' He shuddered. 'Anyway, I think she'd guessed about us, but if she hadn't, you gave the game away totally.'

Jules pulled a face. 'I couldn't help it, Finn. I thought you were dead! I tried to be brave but it all just came flying out of me and I couldn't stop myself. But I wanted Cassia to know, I was going to tell her, but then my mother turned up and, well, you know about that.'

Finn was glad everything was out in the open now, but he knew Jules had been through the emotional wringer. He stroked her cheek, wishing he could have protected her from all the pain.

Jules looked away shyly, not sure how to handle his tenderness.

'Let's do it,' she said. She let go of Finn's hand, thinking Grace would probably disapprove of too much physical contact early on. She could hardly bear not to touch him and she still couldn't believe they hadn't slept together. She wanted to take things slowly, do things differently. She could hardly breathe for thinking about how it was going to be when they did get together and, truthfully, she wasn't sure she'd last longer than Aurelia's wedding night before dragging Finn to bed, but she was doing her best to start afresh.

Finn knocked at the door, surprised when it opened almost immediately.

'Father.'

Henry rolled his eyes. 'We thought you were never going to come in.' He followed them into the bedroom, gesturing to the ornate dressing table. 'Look at that, worth about two thou, I reckon.' He padded over to another table, holding up a teapot. 'Shall I be mother, as it were?'

Finn grinned. He wondered whether his mother hated the room; she probably thought it ostentatious. Although catching sight of her stretched out on the bed wearing one of the ivory towelling robes Aurelia had arranged for all the guests, she looked rather comfy.

'They know how to do things well here, don't they?' she said approvingly. 'Wonderful hospitality.'

Finn wondered if his mother had been deprived of oxygen on the flight over. 'Er, yes. Very much so. Listen, I need to talk to you about the wedding. My one to Cassia, I mean. Now, I know you're aware that things have changed and that I'm now with Jules . . .'

Henry handed over two cups of hot tea. 'I can't keep up. First Jules was with Dom and Cassia was with you, now Jules is with you and her sister . . .' His eyes twinkled at a cringing Jules. 'Oh, it's all right, Jules. I'm only joking. You have to admit it's funny when you think about it.'

'I suppose it is. I'm sorry, though, Henry.' Jules accepted the cup of tea. 'I know you had a soft spot for Cassia.'

Henry grunted. It was true; he wasn't nearly as keen on Jules as he was on Cassia but he could tell that his son was besotted. He also knew that Jules was probably much better suited to Finn in a lot of ways.

'Oh, Henry can always be won over with cake,' Grace said, surprising everyone with her attempt at a joke. 'The one thing Cassia couldn't do was cook.'

Finn watched her face for signs of bitterness, but he couldn't detect a thing. 'You're right, cooking wasn't her forte. But don't tease Jules,' he chided his father. 'She has been so upset about everything.' He put his arm round her, pulling her closer. 'I want you both to know how serious I am about her. This isn't just a silly fling, it's . . . Jules is the one.'

Jules let out an excited squeak. 'Was that a proposal?'

Finn went red. 'Well, no. Oh, don't look at me like that, Jules. You know it takes me years to work up to anything like that. But I want you all to know, Jules most of all, that I'm serious. That this isn't something I plan on doing again.'

Jules kissed him, thoroughly reassured by his words. She didn't want to rush into anything either, but it felt good to know that she and Finn were on the same page.

Grace accepted a cup of tea and sipped it. She was trying to get her head around the fact that the wedding she had so carefully planned was now off, but she was so relieved that Finn and Cassia had split up, it was overriding her outrage.

'Tell me how you and Finn got together,' she said to Jules, patting the bed chummily. 'Was it very romantic?'

Still concerned about her mental health, Finn stared at his mother as Jules, delighted to be accepted into the fold so graciously, willingly climbed on to the bed and filled Grace in on the details. 'And then when we got back from Capri, we were talking about some family stuff and I found myself telling Finn things I've never told anyone.' Not willing to elaborate on the details of her past with Grace, who she really didn't trust, Jules rushed on to the good bit, blushing prettily. 'And then we kissed and it was magical and, well, you know the rest.'

'How sweet,' Grace said, realising that Jules really did love Finn. She put her teacup down, pleased. Quite frankly, she was delighted with the turn of events. She had always said that Jules was far more suited to Finn than Cassia, and Grace was certain that with a little help, Jules would make a very good housewife.

In fact, she could be the perfect daughter-in-law. Thankfully, she seemed not to have found her niche career-wise, so Grace hoped she would be happy to settle down and look after Finn. Fleetingly, Grace wondered how Cassia felt about Jules and Finn being together. She didn't wish her ill and she assumed Cassia had been shocked that her sister and her fiancé were now together. Unless she and the devilishly handsome Rocco Disanti were now an item, Grace thought, remembering the way the pair of them had stood shoulder to shoulder after the water incident. Grace shrugged inwardly. Cassia's relationships were of no interest to her now. All that mattered was Finn, how happy he was with Jules and how right it felt that the two of them had found one another.

'I'm so sorry about the wedding,' Finn offered, interrupting his mother's train of thought. 'I'll pay for everything, I promise. I can't tell you how terrible I feel about it.'

Grace wished Finn hadn't mentioned the wedding; she was trying not to think about it. The sheer scale and cost of it was enough to give her a seizure. But she knew she was going to have to let it go. Jules and Finn should take things slowly, they shouldn't rush into a wedding. Grace just hoped Finn wasn't going to take as long to get around to proposing this time round; deep down, she was certain it would be sooner rather than later. Not soon enough to salvage a wedding that was booked for a few weeks' time, but still. The good thing was, she was sure that Jules would be more amenable than Cassia when it came to wedding arrangements. In fact, she was certain she could recreate the perfect wedding she had tried to force Finn and Cassia into with a few well-placed words and suggestions.

Jules watched Grace from under her eyelashes, guessing what was going on in her future mother-in-law's mind. The thing about women like Grace was that they never expected another woman to outsmart them, Jules thought as she sipped her tea demurely, and although she wasn't above a bit of sucking up when a situation required it, she wasn't about to be manipulated when it came to the more important things in life, like her wedding. She might concede on the colour scheme, if she had to, perhaps even the flowers. But the venue? No way, no Parkland Heights Manor for her, and as for the dress . . .

Jules set her teacup down and went to slip her arm through Finn's. Even though she knew she could rock Grace's sixties shift with panache, hell would freeze over before she wore that smelly old dress on the biggest day of her life. Something terrible might happen to it when she tried it on for the first time, Jules thought. A gigantic red wine stain, an irreparable tear . . . Grace wouldn't even suspect she'd been outmanoeuvred. Jules didn't think she was a horrible person, but having been given a preview of Grace as the monster-in-law she could be when she wanted to be, she knew she didn't want to be taken advantage of.

She gazed up at Finn, feeling dizzy as she met his eyes. She wasn't sure if she could resist him for much longer, especially if he kept caressing her waist the way he was now.

'Let's go,' he whispered in her ear. 'We have things to talk about.'

'Is that what they call it now?' she teased as they said their goodbyes to his parents.

Finn laughed. 'Only when my parents are in earshot. Now come here.' Gathering her up, he kissed her until she couldn't even remember why she'd decided they should wait a while before sleeping together.

A ridiculous idea, she thought as Finn peeled her clothes off later.

Since the flood in the storeroom, Aurelia had acted like Cassia's guardian angel, following her around and making sure she was all right. Guilty that she had misjudged Cassia early on and delighted that she and Rocco had got together in Vegas, Aurelia wanted to make sure Cassia had recovered from her fright. She had forced her to take a hot shower before dressing her in one of the plush, ivory bathrobes. Now she was pointing a hairdryer at her head.

'Aurelia, no, seriously.' Cassia drew the line at having a blow-dry. 'You don't have to do this. It's your wedding day tomorrow.'

Aurelia shrugged and checked out her reflection. She too was wearing one of the wedding robes, but somehow, on her slim, modelesque figure it looked like a stylish dress. 'I am incredibly organised now,' she said, tossing her dark curls over her shoulder. 'My grandmother has taken care of all the reception details, and besides, I have a team of experts arriving at six a.m. to deal with my hair and make-up.'

Cassia smiled. Looking at Aurelia now, her green eyes sparkling and her crushed-rose mouth smiling widely, it was impossible to imagine her crying and screaming over anything the way she apparently had when she found out that Jules had messed up her Capri reception. But her wedding was back on track and all the arrangements had been taken care of by Sofia and Rocco, so perhaps Aurelia could afford to be gracious.

She was a spoilt little princess, Cassia thought affectionately, but it was hard not to fall in love with her because she was extremely kind-hearted.

'I'm sorry about Jules,' Cassia said, rubbing her long hair dry with a towel. She'd worry about how to style it in the morning. 'I know what she did with your reception was unforgivable but she doesn't mean to do these things. I've . . . I've learnt a few things about her over the past day or two and, honestly, we need to cut her some slack.'

It had been a shock for Cassia to realise that her father, the man she had worshipped for so many years, wasn't actually perfect. Hearing that he had rejected Jules when, really, he should have had an issue with their mother instead had toppled him off his pedestal somewhat and Cassia had been forced to reassess her opinion of him. She still adored him and she always would; he just wasn't the man she'd thought he was.

Aurelia raised a well-shaped brow at Cassia's suggestion that they cut Jules some slack. 'You are too nice,' she said, pointing her hairdryer at Cassia. 'Kissing your sister's fiancé is something that shouldn't happen.'

Cassia caught her eye in the mirror. 'I could hardly be annoyed with her, could I? Not in the circumstances.'

'So, what's happening with you and Rocco?' Aurelia asked excitedly. 'Are you a couple? Are you staying here? You can't go back to England, can you? Not now. You'll have to stay here and do some sort of food writing thing . . .'

'Whoa.' Cassia held her hands up to halt Aurelia's onslaught. 'I have no idea what's happening. For me, nothing has changed. I mean, everything has changed, but not my feelings for Rocco. But as far as he's concerned, who knows?' She busied herself with her wet hair. 'He's done his usual. As soon as we arrived back in Sorrento he disappeared into his office and lost himself in work again.'

Aurelia rushed to defend Rocco. 'But he had lots to do when he got back from Rome, and from Vegas. There's lots of money missing from the family account and he's been looking into it. I probably shouldn't say anything but it's true.'

This was news to Cassia but she didn't want to get her hopes up. Her thoughts drifted back to the perfect night in Vegas, to Rocco's fingers trailing up her thigh, to his mouth, kissing her all over, everywhere, whispering in her ear, making her burst with happiness and sensual pleasure . . .

Cassia snapped out of it. Aurelia was asking her if she minded Jules and Finn being together.

'Well, I'd be lying if I said it didn't hurt a bit. And it's weird to see them together. But I also think Jules and Finn are perfect for one another. She'll pep him up and he'll calm her down.

Jules needs stability, you see,' Cassia said, feeling a rush of fondness for her sister. 'She's vulnerable. All that brashness is just a front.'

'Hmmm.' Aurelia looked unconvinced. 'You're much nicer than she is, that's for sure. Hey, let's go and get a glass of something, shall we? Toast my wedding.'

Shattered to the point of collapsing, Cassia would far rather have just fallen into bed and got some sleep. But she did not want to put a dampener on Aurelia's high spirits so she followed her downstairs. She was stunned when she saw Luca talking to Rocco in the lobby. He was carrying two rolled-up scrolls of paper under his arm and, despite the hour, he was immaculately dressed in a bright shirt and tailored trousers.

'Luca!' Cassia was appalled at her rudeness. 'I meant to call you, I'm so sorry. Such a lot has happened . . .' Her voice trailed away and she suddenly felt anxious about what he might be about to tell her.

Cassia glanced at Rocco, wondering what he was thinking. He looked as serious as Luca.

Luca nodded gravely. 'I do. But it's something that affects the whole family.' He turned to Rocco. 'Shall we gather everyone together now?'

Rocco checked his watch. 'I guess we should do it tonight. Nothing must spoil Aurelia's big day, not after everything we've all been through recently.'

'Where is Grandmother?' Aurelia asked, kissing Luca's cheek with great affection.

'In the kitchen with Allesandro,' Rocco replied. 'Let's meet them there.' He beckoned to Raffaelo who was sitting at one of the restaurant tables deep in thought and looking as though he had the weight of the world on his shoulders.

The restaurant looked magical; the decorations were in place for the wedding breakfast and each table had been set up with sparkling white crockery, gleaming cutlery and handfuls of sparkling crystals. The fresco ceilings didn't need any adornment but there were lacy paper chains in caramel and vanilla draping the walls and light fittings, as well as alternate coloured swathes of material on the back of each chair. Each guest had a red horn at their place setting, a bundle of sugared almonds and a personal gift wrapped in ivory tissue paper.

The Disantis certainly knew how to put a wedding on, Cassia thought in awe.

'Coffee, anyone?' Dino offered, yawning widely. 'I need one to stay awake.'

Aurelia nodded. 'I'd love one.' She snuggled up to him, excited that she would be marrying him in the morning, especially now that everything was in place.

Sofia emerged from the now-dry storeroom, talking animatedly to Allesandro. She stopped when she saw them all crowding into the kitchen.

'Are we having a midnight coffee meeting?'

'Something like that.' Rocco sighed deeply, wishing he didn't have to do this before Aurelia's wedding. But it was probably best dealt with immediately. 'There's something we need to sort out. Family business.'

Allesandro gave them all a charming smile. 'Should I leave you all to it?'

Rocco shook his head. 'Oh no, please stay.' He turned to Luca. 'I'll hand over to you, if you don't mind, Luca.'

Luca picked up one of the scrolls of paper. 'Some weeks ago, Cassia came to me asking me to put together a family tree for her father, Marco Marini.'

Cassia closed her eyes. She hoped against hope that her father wasn't related to the Giorelli family and, on tenterhooks, she clutched her coffee cup with white knuckles.

'I checked into Marco's background,' Luca said, his face not giving anything away, 'and I discovered that he was the son of a peasant family who lived in nearby Ravello.'

Cassia felt relief coursing through her. 'So he wasn't related to the Giorellis?'

Luca shook his head. 'No. In fact, he had a rather uneventful childhood, living in poverty and remaining in Italy until both his parents died. I wasn't able to find out what happened exactly, but I think it was some kind of accident.' He glanced at Sofia. 'But nothing suspicious, I can assure you.'

Sofia stiffened defensively. She knew everyone still thought she was silly for thinking there was more to her car accident than simple bad luck.

Luca turned back to Cassia. 'Your father's mother was half-English, apparently, so the authorities sent him over to England to see if his maternal family could be traced. They couldn't and he ended up in various foster homes, as you know. It was irresponsible, really, but back in those days, they didn't have the same sort of controls in place for orphaned children.'

'Wow. It's pretty underwhelming,' Cassia commented, accepting the scroll that Luca held out. 'And I couldn't be more delighted.'

Luca smiled. 'I can imagine. What you might be interested to know is that your father did have some relatives in Italy.' He handed her some papers. 'They live in Florence and they were living elsewhere when the authorities tried to trace them.'

Cassia welled up. After discovering that her father hadn't quite been the hero that she thought he was, it was amazing to hear that he did actually have living relatives in Italy.

Luca patted her hand. 'It must have been preying on your mind, the possibility that your father was the long-lost son of the Giorelli family.'

Dino wanted to go to bed. 'So there is no curse,' he yawned. 'And there's no connection to this rival family.'

'Not for Cassia,' Luca agreed.

Rocco turned to Allesandro. 'But for you there is, perhaps, a very significant connection.'

'What?' Sofia looked confused.

Allesandro was silent for a moment before bursting out laughing. 'What? This has nothing to do with me.'

'On the contrary,' Luca said genially. 'It has everything to do with you.' He picked up the other scroll of paper. 'It was quite by accident that I found you, actually. Cassia left me her phone number, scribbled on the back of a business card. Your business card,' he told Allesandro. 'I had no real reason to look into you, I'm just naturally nosy.' Luca shrugged elegantly. 'It's what I do; names intrigue me.'

'How quaint.' Allesandro smiled back, but it didn't reach his eyes this time. 'And what does that have to do with this rival family nonsense?'

Luca flicked the scroll out and secured one end with his cup of coffee. He motioned for Dino to do the same with his cup. 'Well, it's not nonsense, is it, Allesandro? That's the point. You see, I checked out your name and it didn't exist. Well, it did, but not in a way that could be traced back to you. So I looked into it some more and I found that the name "Raldini" was a name from this area. A family name that belonged to friends of the Giorellis.'

'What?' Allesandro looked genuinely baffled. 'That's impossible. My name is just . . . my name.'

'Ah, but it's not,' Luca corrected him. 'There is always something behind a name. Even one apparently chosen at random. You see, the name Raldini was the name of a childhood friend of a young Giorelli boy. The Raldinis were local people, who worked on this very land, back in the day. Farmers, in fact.'

Rocco joined in. 'So when you chose a name for yourself, you thought you were plucking a name out of the air. But it was a memory, just not one you were aware of.'

Allesandro clasped his hands, his expression suggesting he was playing along with their silliness. 'A memory?'

'Buried in the mind of a young boy who survived a terrible accident,' Rocco provided. 'A landslide that wiped out your entire family, leaving you as the only survivor.'

Aurelia and Dino exchanged a glance. Cassia's mouth fell open.

'The long lost son of the Giorellis,' Sofia murmured, crossing herself with a shiver. She looked hard at Allesandro. 'It was you all along. Did you know?'

He stared down at the scroll. 'Oh yes, Sofia. I did know. I have known for a long time. And I know what this family did to mine. We owned all of this,' Allesandro swung his arm round to encompass the villa and its land. 'We lived here for years before the Disanti family kicked us out. And then we lived like sewer rats, poor, hungry, and just waiting for the chance to take revenge. I have been watching the house for some time.'

Rocco started – so he hadn't imagined the shadowy figure he had caught sight of in the Disanti grounds now and again.

Raffaelo leapt up and barred the way to Sofia. 'Stand back. I won't let you hurt her.'

'Very dramatic.' Allesandro shook his head jeeringly. 'But that's not my style, Raff. I wouldn't dream of physically hurting anyone. No, I had this idea . . . it was arrogant, I know, but I thought I might get you to fall in love with me, Sofia.'

'And then you would let me down spectacularly,' Sofia said, her eyes darkening. 'How very sad.'

'Isn't it?' Allesandro agreed pleasantly. 'But it would have been satisfying to bed the widow of the great Nico Disanti.'

At this, Rocco clenched his fists.

Allesandro noticed but continued anyway. 'And then all of this would have been mine again if you fell in love with me and we married.' He sneered at Sofia. 'A pipe dream, I know, but it kept me going. I don't care what those deeds said all those years ago, this family is so corrupt, I wouldn't be surprised if one of your relatives doctored the evidence.'

Rocco stepped forward. 'That's enough. You should leave now. And if you feel that strongly about the land and the villa, go through the proper channels. Investigate it, find out for definite.'

Allesandro was taken aback. 'You would risk me doing that?'

'I'm sure that you're wrong,' Rocco said simply. 'And I'd rather we put an end to this one way or another.'

'Well, maybe I'll just do that.' Allesandro headed for the door. 'You haven't seen the last of me.'

Dino shook his head. 'What a rubbish exit,' he commented, trying to lighten the mood. ' "You haven't seen the last of me" is such a cliché.'

Sofia let out a shaky breath. 'Phew. I'm so glad he's gone.' She clutched the edge of the kitchen counter. 'I can't believe I fell for his patter. We went to lunch, he was coming as my guest to the wedding tomorrow.'

Cassia squeezed her arm sympathetically. 'He was very charming. He convinced us all he was a nice guy.'

Sofia turned to her. 'I'm so sorry, Cassia. I thought it was your father and I was all set to cast you aside. Please forgive me.'

'There is nothing to forgive.'

Aurelia clutched the edges of her dressing gown together. 'So was Allesandro behind Grandmother's car accident?'

Rocco shook his head emphatically. 'No. Absolutely not. That was . . . that was just a terrible mistake.' He averted his eyes. 'Now, I think we should all get some sleep. We have a big day tomorrow. Grandmother, are you all right?'

Sofia nodded. 'I just wish I hadn't gone out with Allesandro in the first place. I felt so terrible about Nico, it proved that I'm not ready yet. And I wasn't remotely in love with Allesandro, so I'm afraid his plan backfired.'

Throwing a glance in Cassia's direction, Rocco followed Luca out of the kitchen. Aurelia and Dino weren't far behind and Raffaelo sidled out after them.

Sofia slowly turned to Cassia. 'What a terrible shock. I had no idea. Listen, don't tell anyone, but I was starting to have feelings for him. Just a little.'

'I know. I could tell.'

'What a foolish old woman,' Sofia berated herself harshly.

Cassia shook her head. 'Not at all. You just wanted someone to make you smile again.'

Sofia brightened. 'I did. And one day, someone will.' She became brisk. 'But for now, we have a wedding in the morning and we should all get some sleep.'

'*Evviva gli sposi!*'

At yet another chant of 'Hurray for the newlyweds', they all got to their feet again and raised their glasses, cheering loudly and clapping until their hands were sore.

'Seriously, does that go on all night?' Cassia asked Raffaelo.

'Pretty much,' he answered, moodily toying with his knife and fork. 'That and *Bacio, bacio!* which means kiss, kiss. It's just one of those Italian traditions.' He pointed to the red, horn-shaped charms on the table. 'Like these. They're called *corni* and they are given to all the guests to ward off the *malocchio*, the evil eye,' he explained. 'They are supposed to protect the newlyweds from harm in their marriage and bring them good luck.'

Dressed in one of his usual dark suits with a white tie, Raffaelo was in a sombre mood. Seated next to him for the meal, Cassia was struggling to make conversation because he seemed so preoccupied. Unless he was just one of those people who got depressed at weddings, Cassia thought, scraping around for something else to say. Although how he could be depressed at this one was anyone's guess. The morning had dawned with the promise of glorious sunshine, and they had been blessed with brilliant blue skies and temperatures well into the eighties. Aurelia, having arisen at the crack of dawn, had spent the morning bossing her team of stylists around and becoming slightly feverish. A calming talk with Sofia had sorted her out and she had then been seen serenely wandering around in her robe with a glass of champagne. Dino had been so over-excited he had put on his suit far too early and Rocco had forced him to change back into a T-shirt and some shorts so he didn't spill beer all over himself.

Aurelia had presided over her cocktail hour with most of her guests, while Dino was kept apart from her. Then she was suddenly cutting the long white satin bow that Rocco had strung across the Disanti gates, something she had been dying to do because it was such a lovely tradition. In rows and rows of sleek limousines, they had all made it to the famous San Francesco Cloister of Sorrento for the service, part of which had taken place in the very serious and hushed inside, the other outside in the courtyard. It was a captivating scene, with arches and pillars from the fourteenth century as the marital stage, with Mount Vesuvius and the Bay of Naples providing a colourful, authentic backdrop.

Surrounded by beautiful, richly scented flowers and ornamental trees, Aurelia, stunning in her halter-neck gown with her veil and her long, dark curls hiding the daring expanse of naked back, was beside herself with happiness. Dino, in his dark suit and looking every inch the handsome, blond groom, was so proud, he was practically bursting. He had struggled with the formal Italian in the service but he had learnt his lines admirably and he only made a few cock-ups.

After the service, confetti and rice were thrown all over Aurelia and Dino and two doves were released into the sky to symbolise love and happiness. Then they had all headed back to the Disanti residence for the reception, this time on foot. Crowds of onlookers had cheered them on, tourists and town-dwellers alike.

Cassia glanced around the restaurant. It was a vision, swamped with caramel and vanilla-coloured roses, every table heaving with food, much of it prepared by Rocco and Antonio. There were stuffed mushrooms, olives, salami and calamari for antipasto, with piles of glossy prosciutto and pickled peppers to follow. There were bowls of pasta, salads, soups and meats on each table and in the centre, there was an entire area devoted to Aurelia's cakes. As well as the *limone delize* she had promised, there was also a *millefoglie*, a sponge cake with puff pastry and vanilla pastry cream, and piles of *wanda*, which were bow-tie twists of fried dough, powdered with sugar.

Cassia could feel her hips groaning at the mere sight of it all. As there were speeches expected in a while, she took advantage of the moment of respite to speak to her mother. Leaving Raffaelo nursing a glass of red wine he'd been staring into for the past five minutes, she slipped to her mother's table. Diana tore herself away from a chat with an Italian man in his sixties who appeared to be somewhat in love with her.

'Cassia, darling! What wonderful timing. Save me, sweetie, I think this man might be proposing to me but I have no idea what he's babbling on about. I think it's these new-found curves, he keeps talking about Sophia Loren.' She laughed gaily. 'You know my Italian was never up to much.'

Cassia sat down in a free seat. She had to admit that her mother looked pretty sensational, especially after all the drama she'd been through in the last few days. Wearing a black dress with cream stripes and a big black hat perched on top of her blond hair, Diana stood out like an elegant flower amongst all the vivid colours and patterns.

'You didn't bother with the fascinator then?' Cassia asked, jerking her head out of the way as the enormous hat almost took her eye out.

Diana wrinkled her nose. 'No, darling. It looked like something frothy one would stick on top of a cake. Not flattering for a woman of my age. Besides, I think this hat is rather fetching, don't you?'

'Very. Wasn't the service beautiful? That Cloister place was gorgeous.' Cassia paused. 'You were so brave the other day. When you told us what happened with Joseph. I wish I'd known about it all before.'

Diana shook her head, clearly emotional. 'I wish I'd told you, I really do. It was Jules, she didn't want you to know. Funny really; she's always looked up to you, I think, and the thought of you knowing this terrible secret about her was just too much.' Her eyes swam with regret. 'My hands were tied, but I'm glad I told you both. As ashamed as I am about it all, it just feels better to have things out in the open. Not my finest hour, that mishap with Joseph,' she said, her voice cracking slightly.

Cassia squeezed her arm, realising her mother couldn't handle dwelling on the subject.

Diana nodded her head in Raffaelo's direction, watching him swirl his wine around. 'What's the matter with him?'

'God knows. He's in the worst mood.'

'And have you spoken to Rocco yet?'

Cassia shook her head gloomily. 'He's been so busy. He told me he wants to talk, but I have no idea what he's going to say.'

'I'm sure it will all be fine, darling. Have faith.' Diana admired Cassia's dress which was scarlet, with thin straps and a full skirt. 'Red suits you. You must wear it more often.'

'Well, I will now.' Cassia glanced over her shoulder at Finn, watching him laughing with Jules. Grace and Henry sat nearby. 'They look so right together, don't they?'

'Jules and Finn?' Diana cocked her head on one side and watched them. 'It pains me to say so, but yes, they do look oddly well-suited. I guess she will make him a bit more relaxed and he'll give her the security she's been craving.'

'A perfect match,' Cassia observed lightly.

Diana placed her hand on her arm. 'Are you sure you don't mind, darling?'

Cassia smiled. 'I'm fine, honestly. And I think that speaks volumes about how I felt about Finn.' Her eyes widened as she caught sight of someone. 'And I think it's about time I tried to cheer Raffaelo up.'

Diana frowned. 'Don't be silly, that mad Italian might come back and try to drag me off to the Cloister for a quickie. Marriage, I mean.'

'Not much chance of that,' Cassia said, getting to her feet. She nodded towards someone behind her mother. 'I think you're spoken for.'

Diana craned her neck to see who Cassia meant, her huge hat obscuring her view. She made out a dark head with liquid brown eyes and she put a hand to her mouth.

'Angelo,' she breathed.

Cassia grinned. Angelo was such a romantic. He had sent her a text to ask if she thought it was a good idea for him to gatecrash and she'd told him to get himself over to Sorrento pronto. Cassia knew how much her mother had been missing Angelo since she'd ditched him at the engagement party.

'Hello, my darling,' Angelo said to Diana in his heavily accented voice. 'I have missed you so much. Felicity told me you were here and Cassia said to come. I know you told me to stay away but I can't, all right?'

'Oh, Angelo.' Diana could have wept and, seconds later, she did. 'You have no idea how much I've been regretting sending you away like that. I was so screwed up I barely knew what I was doing.'

Angelo removed her great big silly hat and kissed her. Diana leant against him, her arms coiling up around his neck.

'Do not tell me to go and play with someone my own age again,' he murmured, his mouth against hers.

Diana pressed her forehead to his. 'Did you? I don't mind if you did . . . well, I do, horribly, but I understand . . .'

Angelo looked incredulous. 'Of course not. All I have been

doing is thinking about you.' He sat down and pulled her on to his lap, kissing her laughing mouth.

Leaving them to it, Cassia headed back to her table, feeling happy for her mother, but ever so slightly dejected about her own situation. When she sat down, she realised Raffaelo had disappeared.

Thankful for small mercies and waving Gena over for a chat, Cassia proceeded to lay into the vintage champagne.

Raffaelo was outside scuffing his feet against the wall surrounding the restaurant. Looking childlike despite his size, he waited for Rocco like a pupil outside a headmaster's office.

'Raff.' Rocco arrived, looking suave in a dark suit with a black shirt. 'We need to talk about the family accounts.'

Raffaelo nodded despondently.

'I'm sorry to do it like this at Aurelia's wedding, but we haven't had a chance before now and I certainly didn't want to do it in front of Grandmother last night.' Rocco's mouth was tight. 'She'd had enough of a shock after the news about Allesandro.'

Raffaelo shoved his hands into his pockets. 'You know, don't you?' he said, just about managing to meet Rocco's eyes.

Rocco nodded. 'I do. I know about your gambling debts and I know about you borrowing from the business account.'

Raffaelo looked distressed. 'Rocco, I am so sorry. I haven't gambled for ages but I was offered a game of poker and it spiralled from there. I could afford it at first, but then it all got out of hand.' He raked his dark hair in agitation, appalled to find his hands shaking.

'And you didn't think I would notice the discrepancies?'

'You were so busy,' Raffaelo confessed helplessly. 'What with the restaurant in Vegas and Cassia . . .' He paused, not sure he should get into that; Rocco was notoriously prickly about his love life. Raffaelo wasn't even sure his brother had admitted to himself that he was in love with Cassia. The pair of them had barely been able to stop staring at each other all day.

'Anyway, I thought I could win all the money back before you even noticed. It's unforgivable, I know.'

'Not as unforgivable as Grandmother's accident.' Rocco eyed him impassively.

Raffaelo let out a cry. 'Don't,' he pleaded, his eyes clouding over. 'I feel so guilty, so responsible . . .'

Rocco nodded. 'I can imagine. Not nice, the people you owe money to, I take it? They wanted to give you a warning?'

'Yes.' Raffaelo didn't bother to deny it. 'They were after me that day, to break my legs or something, but they couldn't find me. So they knocked Grandmother down instead.' A sob caught in his throat. 'I've wanted to confess for ages, but I've been such a coward. I can't believe what they did to her, Rocco. I've been having nightmares. I should tell her, yes? I'll go to her now and tell her everything . . .'

Rocco sat down next to him, gripping his vast shoulder. 'This is how it's going to play out, Raff. I am going to write off your gambling debts.' He held his hand up to Raffaelo's protests. 'On one condition. No, make that two.'

'Anything, Rocco.' Raffaelo hardly dared to hope his prayers were about to be answered.

'Right. One, you don't ever tell Grandmother what happened that day. As far as she is concerned, it was a freak accident. Because,' Rocco told Raffaelo firmly, 'it would absolutely break her heart if she knew you were behind what happened. So it is our secret and neither of us will ever speak of it again.' He waited for Raffaelo to nod, then continued. 'Good. Two, you come and work in the restaurant. Properly, I mean. You have formal, front-of-house training and you study to become a sommelier.'

Raffaelo lifted woeful eyes. 'You'd do all this for me?'

'You're my brother. I would do anything for you, you idiot.

I only wish you'd come to me about this sooner.' Rocco stood up. 'Now, do we have a deal?'

Raffaelo nodded, barely able to believe what had just happened. He hadn't slept for weeks worrying about everything. 'Thank you. Thank you for everything, Rocco.'

Rocco shook his head. 'Forget it. I just want everything to calm down and get back to normal. Dear God, what's that noise?'

Looking up, they both saw a helicopter circling overhead. Without even skipping a beat, Raffaelo and Rocco looked at one another and laughed.

'Mum and Dad,' they said at the same time.

'Who else would make such an entrance?' Rocco said, shaking his head.

Raffaelo laughed. 'At least they made it finally. I can't believe they got delayed and missed the ceremony, but let's face it, the pair of them would be more upset if they couldn't be here for the party.'

'Hello!'

Flavia, wearing tons of make-up and holding on to a turquoise hat that looked as though it could fly on its own, was leaning out of the helicopter, waving wildly. Gino's tanned face appeared next to Flavia's and he joined in the waving, letting out a yelp as the helicopter lurched to one side.

'Trust them to steal the show,' Rocco said drily. 'But Aurelia will be pleased they're finally here, even if they did say to carry on without them.'

'Shall we go and greet them?' Raffaelo said, starting to walk off.

'You go. I have something else to sort out.'

Raffaelo gave him a knowing glance. 'Indeed. But you have nothing to worry about. She's madly in love with you. Go . . . go and tell her you feel the same.'

Staring after him, Rocco realised enough was enough. It was

high time he and Cassia talked about their feelings; everyone else seemed happy to wade in and have an opinion. Striding off, Rocco decided that whatever Cassia felt for him, he had to tell her how he felt about her before he burst.

'Now, would you consider it?' Gena raised her eyebrows and waited.

'You want me to move to Italy,' Cassia said, speaking slowly as if to a mentally challenged person. 'And write a column from here.'

'More of a diary,' Gena corrected her, waving a hand. 'You know, food and markets, that sort of thing. Life and love in Sorrento.' Her eyes gleamed meaningfully.

Cassia looked bewildered. 'What's that supposed to mean?'

Gena fixed her with a stare. 'Oh, come on, Cass. You must know. I mean exactly what I said. Life and love in Sorrento. What your online column has been describing for the past however many weeks, in effect.'

Cassia frowned. 'I honestly don't know what you're getting at.'

'Read it back,' Gena told her, 'and you'll see what I'm talking about. But to give you a heads up, your column basically reads like . . . like an onscreen version of the film *Roman Holiday*. It's been a serialised love story, Cass. A recipe for love,' she added, warming to her theme as inspiration struck.

'Don't be ridiculous! It's been nothing of the sort. It's just been an account of what's been happening to me since I've been in Sorrento and what I've been doing with Rocco . . . oh.' Cassia stopped abruptly, feeling idiotic. Had she really been that transparent? Had her feelings for Rocco gradually found their way into her column as her attraction for him had turned to lust and then into love?

'That's right, honey,' Gena said, tapping the side of her nose. 'Like I said, it's been like a wonderful Italian love story. And our readers love it. So think about my offer. Move here, carry on working alongside Rocco and writing about it.'

'But I was only supposed to come here to publicise the Vegas restaurant,' Cassia pointed out. She was beginning to think the champagne had affected her brain; this all felt a bit like a dream.

Gena rolled her shoulders extravagantly. 'Ah, but that doesn't matter, does it? Not now that you and Rocco are a couple.'

Cassia's eyes met hers. 'Who said we're a couple?'

'Oh.' Gena clapped a hand over her mouth. 'I'm premature. I've spoken out of turn. A slight timing issue, nothing more. Why do I keep doing that? Ooh, there's Gianfranco.' She waved frantically at him and dashed away.

Cassia decided that Gena was the one who'd been guzzling the champagne.

Sitting with his arm around Jules's shoulders, Finn couldn't believe how contented he felt. Everything in his life seemed to have slotted into place finally and he felt at peace.

'So what did your boss at Lovetts and Rose say when they phoned?' Jules asked him again.

Finn smiled, knowing she just wanted him to relive the moment. 'They said they'd been thinking about my position and that perhaps I was in the wrong department, because I hadn't actually made a cock-up, after all. It was my obnoxious colleague Brian, who was happy for me to take the blame because it wasn't the first mistake he'd made.'

'And then?' Jules prompted.

'And then they offered me a better role with more money because they felt I'd been undervalued for far too long.'

Jules put her head on his shoulder. 'Amazing. I just wanted to hear it all over again. Quite right too; I'm so pleased for you.' She knew how hard Finn worked and how gutted he'd been when he thought he'd made a mistake. They had only sent him away on holiday so that they could conduct a proper investigation, but Jules was glad they had. If they hadn't, she wondered how much longer it would have taken for her and Finn to get together. She linked her fingers through his, knowing it would have been a travesty. Because they were two halves of the same whole, they matched one another perfectly. Last night had proved that. Finn had been the most considerate man she had ever been with, out to please her and an absolute gentleman. Well, perhaps not all of the time, she thought, blushing slightly.

'Louisa!' Jumping up, Jules hugged her friend, who looked slim, tanned and happy. 'You look incredible. What have you been doing to yourself?'

Louisa looked bashful. 'Thanks. Nothing. This is Greg.' She introduced her boyfriend, who was a nice-looking guy with friendly brown eyes and very short hair. 'He's the one I told you about,' she said to Jules as Finn and Greg shook hands.

'He looks lovely,' Jules told her warmly. 'Have you introduced him to your mother yet?'

Louisa shook her head. 'I'm just about to. I expect she'll be stunned. I think she thought I'd be on the shelf for ever.' She glanced at Jules. 'And what about you? Do you have a thing for my brothers, or what?'

Jules had the grace to blush. 'Oh, don't, it's terrible, isn't it?' They'd chatted about it all on the phone the day before and Jules was pleased that Louisa had seemed happy for her.

'Don't be daft. It's just the way things happen sometimes. Besides, you and Finn are much better suited.' Louisa put her hands on her hips. 'And I did tell you Dom was an idiot.'

'You did, you did. Good luck with your mother.' Jules smiled as Louisa grabbed Greg and headed over to Grace. Catching sight of Cassia looking ravishing in a slinky red dress, Rocco strolling towards her, Jules watched Finn's face. His eyes were watchful but he didn't look distraught.

'Do you mind?' she asked him, needing to know she could feel fully secure.

'Do I mind what?'

Jules pointed to Cassia. 'Seeing her with Rocco.'

Finn shook his head. 'Not in the least. It's like . . . it's like seeing your best friend finally finding happiness. I'm happy for her, Jules. But I'm not jealous.'

'Thank God.' She relaxed against him.

'I have a question for you,' Finn said, feeling anxious. 'And you must be honest.'

'Go on.'

'Will I . . . are you sure I'm going to be enough for you?'

Jules sat up indignantly. 'What sort of a question is that?'

Finn went red. 'I don't mean like that. I mean, you seem to enjoy the glitz and glamour of this place and you loved Capri. Life back home in England won't be like that. It'll be jobs and houses and . . . maybe children, one day.'

'It sounds blissful,' she assured him, meaning it. She glanced at Cassia. 'And don't worry, Finn. If this all works out as I think it will, we'll be able to holiday in this incredible villa every year. Because unless I'm very much mistaken, my sister's in love with a celebrity chef and he's absolutely madly, passionately in love with her too.'

Finn looked traumatised.

It took Jules a second to realise he was reacting to her comment about coming to Italy every year on holiday. She burst out laughing. 'Oh, all right, Finn. Not every single year. And we can always come out in the cooler months. Deal?'

He thought for a moment, but he knew he'd agree to anything she asked because he adored her.

'Deal,' Finn said decisively, sealing it with a kiss.

'Cassia. We need to talk.'

Standing by a crooked tree overlooking the Bay of Naples, Cassia turned to face Rocco. She saw everything she needed to know reflected in his olive-green eyes, but she played along. 'About what exactly?'

'Oh, about you and me and a certain night in Vegas.' Rocco leant against the tree.

'Oh, that.' Cassia nodded. 'We should definitely talk about that.'

Rocco reached out and took her hand. 'I'm thinking of stepping away from the business a bit. Going back to my roots.'

'You're going to cook again?' Cassia curled her fingers through his, his touch sending a frisson through her.

'Yes. It's one of the things that makes me happy.' Rocco reached out and tucked a strand of dark hair behind her ear, his fingers trailing down her neck. 'And the other thing that makes me happy is you. I should have told you this ages ago, perhaps in Rome, definitely in Vegas.'

Cassia swallowed and looked into his eyes.

'I love you,' Rocco said simply. 'You've made me realise how important it is for me to cook, for me to be connected to what I'm passionate about.'

She felt his fingers caressing the inside of her wrist and something in her melted. 'It's the same for me . . . this, you . . . it feels like home. I feel like this is somewhere I was always meant to be. I can be myself with you . . . my old self.'

Rocco raised his eyebrows. 'Is that a really funny, very English way of saying you love me?'

'Absolutely. Yes, I do. Love you, that is.'

Rocco pulled her closer until they were groin to groin. 'So, what are we going to do about it?'

She considered. 'Well, you can cook and maybe travel a bit? I could . . . hey, I could write a diary column thing for *Scrumptious* magazine. Just a thought. Is it a familiar one to you?'

Rocco pulled a face. 'I don't believe it. Gianfranco gossips like a girl.'

Cassia felt his hard thighs against hers. 'That's right. And Gena can't keep her mouth shut either.'

'Wow. Talk about ruining the surprise.' Rocco looked rueful. 'I didn't know if you'd say yes, of course. I just wanted to present you with as many things as I could to stop you from saying no.'

Cassia stared at his mouth, longing for him to kiss her again. 'There was no need. You had me at . . . well, *ciao*. Ha, ha.'

Rocco felt her snaking her arms around his neck and his groin flickered in response. About to kiss her, he stopped when she looked up at him quizzically.

'Wait. Where's the fountain? We always have a fountain.'

'That's right,' Rocco said, frowning comically. 'How remiss of me.'

They both jumped at a loud pop nearby. Raffaelo had opened a magnum and he was shaking it up crazily.

'He's not going to . . . oh my God, he is . . .'

Seconds later, they were showered with bubbles as Raffaelo whooped and sent the champagne flying all over them.

Rocco grinned. 'Well, there's that fountain you were after,' he said, taking Cassia's face in his hands. 'And I promise I had nothing whatsoever to do with that.'

Cassia slid her arms round his waist. 'Then there's only one thing for it.' She reached up and kissed him deeply.

As Sorrento slipped into dusk, Rocco scooped her up and kissed the champagne off her lips until the orange ball of sunshine behind them shimmered all the way down into the Mediterranean sea.

Acknowledgements

Firstly, I'd like to thank my readers. I have truly lovely fans and I'm very grateful to each and every one of you. Your messages often reduce me to tears (in a good way) and I really appreciate your support. Ditto all gorgeous EEB girls and my amazing friend Jeni (what would I do without you?). I must also applaud all the bloggers and reviewers who have supported me, some of whom have become great email buddies.

An extra, extra special thank you to my Mum this time round for her stupendous childcare services which made juggling two young children and a manuscript far easier. *Recipe for Love* honestly wouldn't have been finished without your help, so thanks, Mum; you're the best and also thanks Dad, for all your assistance.

Much love to my new pen pal, the fabulous Gemma Burgess . . . a soul sister-via-Twitter, who has amused me greatly this year with fantastically funny emails as well as introducing me to Lydia Mansi. Lydia – thanks for all the fascinating information about Italy, wedding traditions etc . . . so useful, and Gemma, Cassia's perfume is a jaunty salute to you.

Thanks to my agent, Diane Banks, for being brilliant as always, and also to Sherise Hobbs at Headline, for reading *Recipe for Love* halfway through and providing me with lots of handy tips.

And heartfelt praise for Marion Donaldson and Kate Byrne for stepping into Sherise's shoes in her absence and for making the process so seamless, along with the rest of the Headline gang.

Ant – thank you for always being there for me and for being as proud of my writing as you always are. And for confidently, publicly, taking credit for any creativity in my sex scenes, ha ha. And to Phoebe and Daisy, my gorgeous girls. Just . . . thanks. Always be kind to one another and never steal each other's boyfriends, please. x

SASHA WAGSTAFF

Heaven Scent

It all started as a holiday romance . . .

When Cat Hayes impulsively married a handsome, penniless French waiter in St Tropez, she didn't realise she'd be widowed in just a few weeks. Neither did she know that her late husband was actually Olivier Ducasse, heir to the Ducasse perfume empire.

Invited by the Ducasse family to their glamorous French mansion, Cat finds a family in chaos. What's more, she's regarded with suspicion and hostility, especially by Olivier's playboy cousin Xavier. Will she run for the hills as fast as her high heels can carry her? Or will she realise that she is exactly what this mixed-up family truly needs?

Praise for Sasha Wagstaff's mouthwateringly delicious novels:

'Glamorous characters, a gloriously dysfunctional family and plenty of "will they, won't they" intrigue' *Daily Mail*

'Brimming with sex, scandal and secrets – not to mention delectable lads' *Heat*

978 0 7553 7815 9

headline
review

SASHA WAGSTAFF

Wicked Games

TWO FIERCE RIVALS.
ONE FORBIDDEN ROMANCE . . .

Debonair and dynamic, millionaire Judd Harrington has returned from LA a glittering success. But as he stares across the valley at Lochlin Maguire's beautiful country house, all he can think of is revenge.

Meanwhile Judd's arch-rival has troubles of his own. Lochlin's record label is losing major talent to an unknown competitor, his wife Tavvy is destracted and he can't seem to see eye to eye with his son Shay.

Unbeknownst to Lochlin, his talented singer daughter Iris has fallen for irresistible racing driver Ace Harrington in LA. Ace is under orders from Judd to break Iris's heart. What he hadn't bargained for was losing his own in the process. Can he go against his father's wishes? Or will Judd's wicked games ruin love's young dream?

Praise for *Changing Grooms*:

'Glamorous girls, fabulously dishy men and all the best ingredients' Fiona Walker

'Brimming with sex, scandal and secrets – not to mention delectable lads' *Heat*

'A great plot, a gloriously dysfunctional family and plenty of "will they, won't they" intrigue to keep me engrossed till the end' *Daily Mail*

978 0 7553 4891 6

headline
review